Treat Us
Like Dogs
and
We Will Become
Wolves

Also by Carolyn Chute

Treat Us Like Dogs and We Will Become Wolves

a novel

by

Carolyn Chute

Grove Press
New York

Published simultaneously in Canada
Printed in the United States of America

FIRST EDITION

ISBN 978-0-8021-1945-2
eISBN 978-0-8021-9193-9

Grove Press
an imprint of Grove/Atlantic, Inc.
154 West 14th Street
New York, NY 10011

Distributed by Publishers Group West

www.groveatlantic.com

14 15 16 17   10 9 8 7 6 5 4 3 2 1

Greetings to all Leo's station alumni in Little Falls.
This mere book is dedicated to our hero and friend,
Leo Kimball
(in Heaven).

And also in Heaven,

Marian MacDowell of the MacDowell Colony, to her,

and to all her descendant rescuers in the wings.

And, as ever, everything is because of Beek of Beektown. ♥

Author's note:

Treat Us Like Dogs and We Will Become Wolves is one of several novels that make up the *School on Heart's Content Road* "four-ojilly," a series of overlapping or parallel books that focus on different characters and their place in the story's key events. Characters who play major roles in one or more of the books may be only walk-ons in others. Each book stands alone. No need to read them in a certain order.

Welcome

to

Treat Us Like Dogs and We Will Become Wolves

. . . as told by reporter Ivy Morelli and many other witnesses, spies, agents, friends, and foes, testimonies verifying and conflicting, some very large, others somewhat tiny.

Author's Note #2

There is a character list at the very back of this book for helping with identifying important and semi-important characters. *Don't twist your head trying to keep every character straight. Continually referring to the list is not necessary. As you read along, characters who are meant to matter a lot will become obvious. On the other hand, I, myself, love character lists because I like to refresh myself on what characters look like and their connection to others. Maybe you do, too.*

List of Icons

Home (the St. Onge Settlement)

The grays

Neighbors

The voice of Mammon

Out in the world

The screen insists, grins, cajoles

Claire and Bonnie Loo and other
women who run things at the
Settlement, usually speaking to us
from the future

The Bureau

Others speaking from the future

Progress

Ivy Morelli
(reporter for the *Record Sun*)

The forests of planet earth

Brianna Vandermast (Bree)
and Catherine Court Downey

The FCC

Jane Meserve speaks

History as it happens.

History (the past)

Waste management

History

(The old, old, old past)

An old, old, old Chinese curse: "May you live in interesting times."

(From a future time.) An excerpt from one of the hundreds of letters written by Gordon St. Onge, which remain in the custody of federal authorities (this one having been stuffed up an agent's sleeve during a Settlement public event and snuck out):

"I would smile if I heard that someone, perhaps a madman, perhaps a sane man, burned every single school building in this world to the ground."

YEAR 2000

Or was it 1999?

Well, thereabouts, one or the other.

The years do blur.

In those years,
big things
happened in America.
But you never
heard about some of
them. They were erased.

Here's

the

story.

BOOK ONE:
His Sun

JUNE

 From a future time, Claire St. Onge remembers the way it all went. She speaks.

So you've heard about us before, doubtlessly, how this tiny world, our home, our "chez nous," cradled in the lap between two mountains, got blasted straight out into the eye of America. Yes, America, what one of our adopted teenagers here calls "The Land of Panicked Mice." But really it was *us,* the family of the Settlement, who were the mice, the outside world a hale and majestic foot, the triumph of that foot set in motion by one small hand.

 At 7:33 p.m., a message left on the answering machine of the *Record Sun* columnist and feature writer, Ivy Morelli.*

"Hello. I'm not going to tell you my name. I'm sure there's the possibility of retribution by the individuals involved if you choose to proceed with this. There are several of us who are worried about what we see as very serious abuses to children at the so-called *school* located on Heart's Content Road near Promise Lake in this town . . . Egypt.

---

* Remember, there is a character list at the end of this book.

We're aware of others who have voiced concern to authorities and to one or two other newspapers. We are *furious* about the lack of even an eye blink of interest shown! Unreturned phone calls. Passing the buck. Rudeness. Treating us like we are crazy. Like *we* are crazy . . .

 ### At 7:59 p.m., on the same evening, on the same answering machine of the same Ivy Morelli.

As before, the caller doesn't introduce himself, though it is clearly a different voice. Voice tells of the "school" in Egypt. Voice is dull, weighted by a sort of weary grief. ". . . and we're talking here, ma'am, about children who are beaten, worked like animals, who have easy access to drugs, who are probably sexually abused, live in improper sanitation . . . and the parents . . . whenever anyone has seen them, seem like they are in some kind of trance, probably high . . . or, you know, could be victims of fanatical religious brainwashing. We all know these things happen. Waco, for instance. We're all grown up, aren't we? Of course, none of us would dream we'd get it right here in Maine. But here you have it . . ."

 ### Next day, a different voice. A woman, a firm-sounding woman, not one to let things slide.

". . . and we know of a woman who has a grandson in this so-called school. A thirteen-year-old who hasn't even learned to read yet! And she says that he hasn't even been pushed to do so. She doesn't want to reveal her name, either, but I'm sure there are plenty of others who will talk if you were to investigate. The place is a work camp, a prison for children. And there are *guns*. So you see what kind of people we are talking about here. *We know* about other calls you have received concerning this situation so we know you know there's something going on at that place. If you could state in writing that you would not reveal our names, we'd be more than happy to meet with you in person. One of us will call again. Thank you very much . . . CLICK."

Ivy Morelli listens to the snippet of dial tone before the next recorded message. She is picking at the rough weave of her skirt, frowning.

Claire St. Onge in recollection of that summer.

Always there were crows. Came for the cracked corn I spread on the broad sill of the big windows to my tiny sunroom, my morning room. Two chairs, some baskets, and a toadstool-shaped table, which is only big enough to hold a cup of coffee and a book. It is carved and streaky with grain and time. Looks like a relic.

One of the crows must have been a lost pet. Very chummy. And had had his tongue split or whatever cruel thing it is that is done. The first time I heard him, I thought it was the tinny voice of a small radio. I found he'd gotten in through the kitchenette door, and claimed a bedpost. The crow's voice was urgent, "Church at ten!" He cocked his head. "Church at ten!"

 Another message on Ivy Morelli's machine.

"Hello. I am calling in reference to the Home School, a sort of military compound situation on Heart's Content Road in North Egypt, on land owned and lorded over by a fellow named Gordon St. Onge. It is an *urgent* matter and I hope that one of us is able to connect with you *soon*.

I am unable to reveal my name, phone, fax, or e-mail for the reason that there are probably enough firearms in that St. Onge place . . . and explosives to eliminate fifty government buildings . . . so taking care of a few concerned citizens like us would be nothing to them . . ."

Ivy jots down a few words and slashes across the soft pink lines of her reporter pad.

This man's voice is a different voice from those who have called over the last few days. And yet equally indignant. And she knows that those who have called her editor, Brian Fitch, or reporters in other departments here, have all been indignant, even a little discomposed.

Brian tells her, "Just keep on trying to nab somebody at DHS and the supe of the SAD, which Egypt is in. You know, Ivy, nothing goes into print without the *official* lowdown first . . . 'less you can charmingly get inside that compound and tape the grunts of laboring children and the crackings of the whips." Brian flutters his eyes. "Meanwhile, good luck reaching some living breathing officials who know anything or want to spill it. There's something here. *But*. We servants of the news shan't be allowed the crumbs until we grovel a bit first." He turns away, then back. "Jesus, this whole country gets fruitier by the minute. This might be real."

 ### Claire St. Onge* speaks.

When the call came last night, a few of us were there in Gordon's kitchen. As he took the phone, we could tell by the way he held his shoulders, and how his face iced over, that the person on the other end was danger. When he hung up and said it was a *Record Sun* reporter, I felt the blood stop in my arms and jaws. He had, yes, agreed to an interview! He had always warned us of the commercial mainstream press. Now he became all gooey and helpful as he said good-bye. One of Gordon's many selves. A traitor, even to himself. And to us. He'd be taking us down with him, right?

 ### Claire St. Onge again.

And then on another morning on my white-picket gate, hopping left, then right, the crow. "Oh nooo! My floors!" and "Oh nooo! My floors!" he ranted.

This morning with the iris beds in head-spinning sweetness, he swept down, his wingspan always a little jolt to me, making the sun blank out like a missed heartbeat, and there on the sill he admired the cracked corn feast. But he didn't eat. Arranged his classy black suit of feathers, did one high-stepping turnabout, and said into my eyes, "The ending was lousy."

 ### When Ivy Morelli shows up at the St. Onge property to get her story.

Dark windshield, dark glasses, dark "modified bowl" haircut tinted with violet clipped to a hot edge at the nape of her neck. Thudding beat of the radio. Gas pedal to the floor, fixed there rather continuously

---

* Remember the character list at back of this book.

by the flabby little plastic heel of her dress sandal. The all-American driver. The race! The win! Time ticking in the blood. The engine straining to please. And Ivy Morelli wears a little stripy dress, her mouth set hard, the hard young modern woman, expression hard as nails.

Here it is up ahead. The St. Onge residence, as it has been described to her. A plain typical old farm place, gray with white trim. Cape and ell. Long screened-in piazza that was once open. There are the old lathed columns behind the haze of screening. And the dooryard, sandy with scattered plantain leaf. A nice big old tree. Everything tidy and well-kept. Seems there's even fresh paint riding on the air.

Ivy Morelli's sports car skids to a stop. Car door swings open. Nearly as fast as the speed of light she gathers her bag and camera from the passenger seat and steps out into the settling dust. She studies the bank of solar collectors across the roof of the ell. These collectors are strange. Big and boxy. She pushes her dark glasses to the top of her head, scratches a few notes on her slim reporter pad. She casts a cold eye over everything. Her eyes are, yes, a frigid blue in dark lashes. She is not tall. Her hand with pen, small.

"Hmmmm," she says to herself, gazing dreamily up into the rivu-leted limbs of the old ash. Big, dumb, old, dutiful beast. Not really much for shade. Just a ghostly gray pale shadow spread on the sand and out across the tiny front lawn of halfheartedly mowed grass, down into a ditch, then out onto the warm tar road.

Her eyes widen. "Look, Ivy!" she tells herself. She wiggles her pen. There on the great girth of the ash, a wooden sign, hand painted with letters that dribble like blood. OFICE.

Ivy Morelli snorts, then says to herself, "A school, yessir, with a misspelled sign."

There are so many doors, especially along the ell and shedways. "Where's the wacky sign that reads: 'PARKENG'?" she asks herself with narrowed eyes.

She decides on a door with a single window covered with a pink curtain. She gives it a couple of sharp raps. No cool shade here, just the ugly bare truth of sun. And silence. She knocks again. Waits. Nothing.

She knocks again. Two real *THWACKS*. She squares her shoulders. Small person, small, yes, *but*.

She speaks indignantly. "Okey-dokey, pard'ners. So what's up?" Anyone looking out at her from inside this house, seeing her here in her short striped dress and sandals, would certainly surmise she's the reporter who called last night and arranged this appointed time. The camera, for heaven's sake! The narrow lined pad and pen. She is clearly *not* a vacuum cleaner salesman!

She glances around the yard again and counsels herself, "No kiddie jungle gyms. No toys. No catcher's mitts or basketball hoops. Take note of this."

She looks at the dormer windows above, a silvery fog of brand-new screen and homey ruffled curtain. Cups her hands around her mouth. "HELLO!!!!!"

No answer.

Ivy Morelli drops her sunglasses back down onto her face and turns toward the little sandy rutted parking lot. She is so very young. On fire with the present. Her dark glasses reflect two sharp hot little suns. Her wristwatch flashes. Her small blue and pink tropical fish tattoos swim around her slim bicep. Her seven bracelets are both bright and noisy. Her earrings shriek light, spinning into lighter light. Her violet tinted inverted bowl of hair has an actual metal sheen. Her stride across the lot is filled with purpose. All that clinking-clatter. She is almost an after-image of a well-armored knight. Will she be triumphant? Will the crowds cheer: *such intrepitude!*

The field rises up. Hazy. Red clouds of devil's paintbrushes and the washed-out purples of vetch. Daisies, like a cheery galaxy of reachable stars! And all the greens, witchgrass, clovers, nettle, all on their toes celebrating heat, hell, being *their* heaven. And then the mountain, hot and close. And the other mountains humped politely behind and beside the bigger guy. Blue, spiked with hot black spruce and paler pine. Maple and beech and other leafy vegetable greens . . . trillions of individual leaves. Holy cow! And leaping lizards! It boggles the mind.

So this is the St. Onge property. Nine hundred acres in the boonies of Egypt. And how many ghosts of babies corralled within? How many Bibles? How many guns?

"What do you suppose that is?" Ivy Morelli asks herself. A peculiar thing up there along the tree line. Looks like the rusty steel roof of a pig shed, only perfectly round.

A prickly coolness (a warning?), moves up the back of Ivy's damp neck. Fear. Just a few seconds of ugly, unfettered terror.

She looks back at the house. Over at her car. Down at her sandals, her feet spread apart in the sand. She tosses her shimmering bowl of hair. "Okay, Ivy. It's okay. Easy girl. Holy horse whinnies!"

She heads for the field. The vetch and daisies grab and break at her shins. Heat shimmers in a yellowy way over the rusted roof of the faraway construction. She remembers a movie about prisoners of war in Korea kept in small corrugated steel sheds in unbearable heat. All the torture and grimness of that movie! And she was only a child. Why was she at that movie? Yeah, a goin' out movie. Popcorn? Soda in a cup? Who took her to see it? She can't remember. Because all that was gentle and loving in the real world of Ivy Morelli no longer existed as the keepers of the POW camp peeled away the steel doors to find another succumbed man or to drag a live one out to be "interviewed" once again.

She marches on with a hard soldierly expression. She considers stopping to pick a bouquet. But why? It would only wilt in this heat. Why are our hands always in some reflex to outmoded practices? Will hunting and gathering always be with us? It is a query that to Ivy feels dirty, sneaky, and fleeting, like thoughts of nudity while in midconversation in a formal place. All this nature! All this breathing, unbraiding, sexy nature! Ivy laughs. "HAW! HAW!" Shakes her shimmery metallic hair.

She hikes onward, up into the deeper brighter heat. So much silence and yet her eardrums feel assaulted and swollen. The heat buzzes louder than any insect would. Louder than a small sporty car. Her stripy tight dress, her bracelets, her shoulder bag, her camera all weigh her down . . . the weight of that other world outside this place, *her* world. The world where child abuse is considered a crime.

She turns, pushes her sunglasses up on her head. Snaps a few pictures of the St. Onge house with her solitary car in the yard as seen from this higher elevation. She says to herself in a husky way, "With this fort unmanned, all this is at my mercy." She cackles evilly.

Treks onward. Higher and higher.

Well, the rusty roof does not shelter pigs or prisoners of war. Instead it is a merry-go-round of every sort of wide mouthed, big jawed, horned monster. No pretty high-stepping stallions here. No, indeedy.

Observe "bloody" eyes and teeth made from jackknife blades and 16-penny spikes. Ivy Morelli steps *very* close. Some of these merry-go-round faces look human, as weird and anguished as faces frozen in death. Bad death. Now the epic-sized flashback of that movie returns, runs scampering cool through her hair again. What kind of merry-go-round *is* this? So many wide joyless eyes. Not many flashy tails and manes. But yes, a lot of color. Black and yellow. Red. Purple. Warrior colors. But for one creature spray-painted all over with gold, like the gold leaf on state capitol domes and other monuments to human arrogance and audacity.

Ivy's editor, Brian Fitch, has been on her back these past few months. He suggests that she get more quotes than she tends to for her feature stories, even for her columns! Readers like quotes, he says. Does he insinuate she kind of well-meaningly *invent* quotes? Maybe paraphrase, then put speech marks around these as if spoken? This, the not-so-well-guarded secret of "the press" and therefore a norm of the institution? For surely interviewees seldom actually speak in conveniently condensed newspaper-length statements. If honesty matters to you too much, the muscles of your jaws and neck will be forever knotted and your heart will crack. The wishes of business, the wishes of the clock, are all bigger than you. Bigger than humanity. Yielders are survivors. To yield is to be strong.

Funny how those things go. Honesty? Like the hunting and gathering reflex of the fingers, there is shame in these outmoded things we've evolved away from.

Down on the road (Heart's Content Road), an engine strains, that steep wriggling-like-a-viper hill making the gears hum down as with "mi re do." Can't see the road from here. Down that way, the woods are thick and tight as a green and gray weave. But indeed, there is a vehicle. A busload of manacled kids maybe. A shipment of bazookas. Replacement Bibles to replace the others worn out by wet sobs.

Through sweaty eyes Ivy studies a red merry-go-round face. Its black eyes are penetrating. Rusty teeth leering. She prints carefully on her lined reporter pad: CHILDREN ARE INHERENTLY EVIL. "I'll quote myself," she says with a low playful chuckle. Is it supposed by Ivy that kids made these in the image of their inner selves? She leans even closer through the hot blue shade of the carousel roof, her sunglasses slipping from the top of her head. Immediately a deerfly swings around her hair, a chainsaw-like buzz, and works a chunk out of her face. "ACHH!" she cries out. Feels her cheek, smearing blood.

She caresses the all-golden merry-go-round creature whose body is silky to touch, like human shoulders. But its two heads are lumpy and scarred. "Some little dear beat this with a board," she whispers into the hot stillness. They say violence is a cycle. Maniac schoolmaster beats kid, kid beats the golden watchamacallit.

She peers closer. "Yeah . . . that linty stuff in the eye sockets . . . that's glue. This thing *used* to have eyes." She gives one of the glowing bald heads another sensuous rub. Neither one of the hideous eyeless heads speaks a quotable remark.

But now the engine out on the road is making real slowing sounds, like turning, and Ivy catches her breath in anticipation. This *could* be the interviewee with an excuse and an apology for his tardiness. "Tsk. Tsk." Who is the audience for Ivy's cavalier attitude? Ivy is the audience. Ivy who wishes her sporty car were closer.

Another deerfly chips off a piece of her neck. Another grips her forehead. She whacks at them. Misses, of course. Now another. Another. They swing around her violet hair, buzzing, fast-thinking, intelligent, famished. One chisels at her arm, *yum yum*. "Ow! Jesus!" She whacks them away, and hops, her shoulder bag and camera clomping, her bracelets all aclatter. Sunglasses hit the ground. Stepped on, snatched up.

"What's this?" she asks herself. Then answers herself, "It's a lever, Ivy. A cable running to this . . . small . . . er . . . open-sided little dog-house thing . . . ah, a generator . . . gas generator with . . . yes, a pull cord. This is . . . neat." She describes this discovery in her notepad, meanwhile whacking deerflies.

A pickup truck is pulling into the dooryard below. She sees it ease in snug behind her own car, which is parked snug against the ash tree. As if to block her escape? Plenty of room in that sandy lot for it to park otherwise. A man steps from this truck, stares directly across the field at her as though he had been forewarned of her location by secret guards or hidden cameras.

She turns her back and scribbles, stout bracelets bonking together, pink and blue angelfish flexing pleasantly in the everlasting mini sea of her arm as she reads aloud some of what she writes. "Truck . . . old piece of junk . . . dark green with white cab roof." She peers around as the guy begins the long trudge up through the flowery field. "Tall . . . broad face . . . cheekbones . . . Slavic? . . . Nordic maybe . . . Viking type. No horns but would look all right with horns." She whacks at a fly. Again she misses. "His hair is dark brown. Not long. Not short. Not combed. Green work shirt. Sleeves rolled up. Unusual belt buckle. Can't tell from here what it is." She sneaks another peek as he gets closer, then scribbles, "Jeans. Ratty as hell. Filthy hands." She tsks to herself schoolteacherishly. Then, "Not going to win any Mr. Maine contests . . . a little too slope-shouldered . . . rugged . . . but . . . but slopy . . . all those guns and Bibles and teenaged wives dislocating something." She scribbles on and on, more details, more fun, keeping her head down and her back solidly to him as he comes closer and closer. She considers. Yes, this has to be Gordon St. Onge. He looks quite a lot like the guy in the clippings from the little local paper, *Your Weekly Shopping Guide*, stuff printed about him all during the time he was selectman in this town eight years ago. He was a young and popular selectman then, notable mentions paid for by the beneficiaries of some of his gracious deeds. Fair. Friendly. But not for long.

After about ten months, he quit. Just vanished. Nobody in town knew where to. Nobody saw him for quite some time. No one she's interviewed knows for sure why he quit, though speculation runs the gamut. In more paid notices in *Your Weekly Shopping Guide*, some townspeople expressed sorrow at democracy betrayed, considered his disappearance at the very least, irresponsible, at the most a sort of treason.

So at what point did he reappear? His reappearance doesn't seem as memorable. Some folks she has spoken with told her he just shamelessly eased back onto the scene, back at the bank clowning with the tellers, yakking with the state cops, the road commissioner, the game warden, and truckers at the diner . . . and in the thick of town meetings (though not as a selectman now) speechifying to the thirty or so upturned faces, engaging as ever.

"Gordie," some call him with affection and a shake of the head. Or "Gordo." Some have told Ivy he is a real comedian. Others use the word "earnest." Some say he is too "softhearted." Some have called him "loud." Some have called him "quiet." "A drunk," others have confided. "Respectable," one said. "Sad," offered another. Mostly these have been the storekeepers and town office people, the easy-to-locate types.

But yes, the first logical step for Ivy was to check with the Superintendent of Schools of the administrative district that Egypt is in. And the state's Department of Human Services. But the "supe" is never around, can never be tracked down, and all the messages she left with his secretary have dissolved. Why? Why? Why? Then she tried the Department of Education in Augusta only to be bounced back to the superintendent here. And D.H.S. Ha! What a runaround there! Agencies that behave as if *they* have something to hide. Yessir. These, the official, the authorized, the expert. The prized quotable quotes. Everything else is rumor, isn't it?

Arlene Day, the only caller so far to give Ivy her name, admits she has never laid eyes on Gordon St. Onge. But she insists there are children who may actually be buried in the woods at "that place," their cause of death being "disciplinary actions." This is the common denominator among those who describe the school with repugnance: They do not know Gordon St. Onge, have not been bewitched by him. While many of those who know him are amused by the school idea. "Probably like having your desk at Disneyland," chortled Ed Mertie at the hardware store.

And what about religious fervor? Ivy had grilled them all. And "gunzzz"? Different answers. "Oooo, there's church," one grinned. Another said, hushily, "Watch out." Another, "There's one who lives up there . . . named Glennice Hayden . . . she told my neighbor she believes St. Onge is God."

Ivy Morelli is only twenty-four years old. She is here representing a hotshot conglomerated daily. In her fledgling career, people already know her all over the state, some with a twinge of discomfort. Her column has a bit of a bite. Never predictable. Meanwhile, her people features in the paper have nearly brought trumpets and confetti from many good souls. Sometimes her photos are quite good, her wild and chancy photos. Though sometimes *too* wild and chancy. Then her editor, Brian, will shake his head and send someone from the photo lab to do the photo over. A *real* photographer.

So who is Ivy Morelli? And is this a kind of high point in her life? Yes, this is the very moment. This moment is tantalizing, tinged with the creepy. After all, Ivy Morelli is not so far removed from the day when she, a wiry scrappy little kid with a silky black ponytail would have hopped on the back of this gold two-headed monster and cried out "Giddyup!"

Behind her now, the heavy walk of Gordon St. Onge, the wild grasses whispering and gossiping around his pant legs. His keys, dangling from a belt loop, speak before he does. "There's probably gas in it." And he steps past her into the hot blue shade and stoops at the generator to check its oil and gas and then yanks on the cord hard, then harder and harder till the engine sputters to a struggling hum. Then another adjustment and the engine purrs pleasantly. Now the lever. The circle of monsters creaks into motion.

Reflections of the monsters' creepy colors swipe across Ivy's face, her small mouth even more clover-colored now and the somewhat pointed top lip showing more expression than those eyes of hers. The eyes. In their dark lashes, a diamantine blue.

She sees the man's hand on the lever. One nail smashed. The seams of his knuckles white with paint. The ordinary hand of a plain workingman. Now she is again staring into the traffic of beasts and the only one that actually rises up and down merry-go-round-like is yellow and black and glossy with hornet wings. But it moos like a cow for her calf. Now it farts. Jesus. For eyes, there are red Christmas tree twinkle lights. One eye begins to warm up. *Twink!*

Beyond the baneful circular traipse of creatures, Gordon St. Onge's face. Pure madness? His eyes squint and blink. Looks like something between doubt and befuddlement. Ivy Morelli doesn't know whether to fear this face or feel endearment. For a long moment he is caught in this distracted expression, then suddenly looks straight into her eyes. The look is so keen and unwavering that one eye actually seems to slightly cross. His beard is spotty, short, darker than his hair, and graying. Heavy brown-black mustache, untrimmed. His crowded teeth are unveiled now as he wags his head and gives her a grin. He says happily, "You have to imagine your own calliope music."

Somehow they have missed their formal handshake, formal hellos, exchange of names. This feels like a ball that's started rolling by itself.

Ivy asks, "Did the students make this masterpiece?"

He replies with a most notable fawning courtesy, "There aren't any students here." He watches her hand scribbling with the pen, down across the pad.

"You mean they are . . . off for the summer, right?"

He looks at her face, back at her hand. His right eye and most of that side of his face seem to be on short circuit, several involuntary winks, a sort of nervous tic, and such wild unreadable eyes. The carousel is creaking, moaning, mewling, farting, bellowing, sniffing, twinking. The generator hums. There are no more quotable quotes. Nothing even to dice, rephrase, and *pretend* is a quote.

She says, "Gordon St. Onge. That's your name, right?"

He says nothing. Or is it that his voice is softened so much that it is lost in the hubbub of machinery?

Ivy's really hard modern woman look goes into effect. She narrows her eyes. She is pissed. In the fuzzy heat the look of her paling forehead can be imagined as either cool or hot to touch. Her small, almost pointy clover-color mouth, which is more deeply clover-color in this light, is set in a way that makes it seem as though it must have never known smiling, kissing, sucking, or cooing, only the declarations of terrible judgments. She speaks plainly. Clearly. "Rumor has it that the students of this school of yours usually don't learn to read until they're seven or eight years old . . . or even *never* . . . that—" She looks down at her fingers as she flips a page. Now a thump makes her look up quickly.

He isn't standing on the other side of the carousel. He is now standing very near. And he is a huge guy. Like another race of people, not giants exactly, but significantly large, while Ivy is so small and now feeling even punier. His fingers, which are not only swollen and bruised and painty, are also blackened by grease or paint, or grease *and* paint, these close in around her fingers and the pen, and then slip down between, so that his fingers are now under hers. In one move he withdraws his hand with the reporter pad and Ivy is stumbling backward as she takes a swipe at him and scratches one of his forearms, not enough to draw blood, more like you scratch an itch, but she *meant* to draw blood. And she is coming to remember that size does matter. That natural laws outweigh everything.

He says, gesturing with the stolen paper pad, "Kids don't need you to do this to them."

Ivy shrieks, "I was invited here! You knew I was a reporter, Mr. St. Onge. This wasn't a trick!"

"I changed my mind," says he.

She narrows her eyes on the churning creaking horde of the steel-roofed nightmare-go-round. "Is there anything of a religious element to the St. Onge compound, Mr. St. Onge?" She looks down at her shoes. She exhales deeply through her nose, trying to retrieve her civility, her *charm* . . . which works better than anger and insults, doesn't it? She needs his trust. Charm, Ivy, charm. "Are you people deeply committed to God?"

His eyes flicker. Pale, pale eyes in dark lashes. Paler than hers. But not pretty pale. Not blue like Ivy's. More a yellowish, cooked-cabbage green, and because part of his face is in shadow, part in sun, one eye seems to glow even paler and more penetrating than the other. He makes no shrug or flinch or word of denial, just wipes across his mouth and mustache and one eye with the top of his blackened hand, like a tired kid. Ivy feels a pang of endearment.

But now he crosses his arms over his chest, a powerful threatening stance. The reporter pad is no longer in his hand.

Ivy stares at his hands, the magic of this. Again she is pissed. She snaps off some surprise shots with her camera, the holding *and* snapping done all with one hand and with her other hand she snatches her tape recorder from her shoulder bag. This is *her* magic. "I've been running this baby all along!" she tells him jubilantly. (A fib, actually, she is miffed.) She wags the thing from side to side and a wire with a black mike swings stiffly. "I plan to write this story."

He moves.

Ivy's muscles clench, ready for flight. Her anger and fear are alloyed into one solid dry-mouthed flavor. Run, Ivy, run!

But he is only turning toward the generator, squats to shut it off, gets to his feet again. And his full height, as he is standing on higher ground, fills up the sky. He suggests, "Why don't you go over to the *real* schools, the school *system*, and hear 'Polly wants a cracker'?"

Ivy smiles. "This assignment sure is turning out to be a damn dazzling sizzly scary little piece. Thank you!" She is now totally ready to run, one

thigh thickening, pulling slightly at the knee. She has had no experience with the fanatically righteous religious, only those two borderline
off-the-wall neighborhood ladies she remembers from childhood and
then the famous ones who die in newsy ways, those headline-getters,
like at Waco, but nobody Ivy has ever stood this close to.

Snap! There now. She has snapped his picture again. Snap! Another. Snap! Snap! Her grip on her camera gives her knuckles the
proverbial whiter shade of pale. The bracelets traveling up and down
her slim arms make their clonky music.

Gordon St. Onge's face is now grave and newly aged. Wretched
wet trickles of heat and worry slip through his gray and brown beard
onto his neck. He pleads softly, "Please don't."

Ivy looks up at the bald-top mountain with all those openings in
rock. Like hot mouths. And something else up there which is now
reflecting light as the sun has moved. Something metallic and moving.
She snaps a couple of frames of it.

She backs away farther and speaks searingly. "You are used to
having your own way here . . . apparently." She shivers. "Your own
little kingdom?"

He puts out his hand, pleading.

"Mr. St. Onge . . . could you comment on the fact that so many
people believe this place has a good-sized stash of firearms?"

He raises one eyebrow. The eyebrow that is over his most crazy-
looking wider eye.

Her fear and anger and lack of caution *always* get so mixed up. Ivy,
young Ivy, ruthlessly brave, stinging, prodding. "Maybe a bunch of
your people . . . the men . . . are in those trees now with guns aimed
at my head?"

He almost smiles.

Ivy presses on. "Sure . . . much can be rumor. But you know the
old saying, 'Where there's smoke, there's fire.' So what *are* you trying
to hide from the public?"

He looks at her hands, the camera, the tape recorder. And their
power.

She waits another few moments, filled with his silence. "Okey-
dokey," she says cheerily, then turns from him and starts back down
the hill, keeping to the fresh path of squashed weeds. She feels the

possibility that he *has* pulled a gun from under his shirt, squatted now in the weird carousel shade to get a solid aim at her back. A frothy hysteria claims her. She hurries now, grasses and vetch squealing, popping. Bracelets sizzling. In a moment of sheer terror, she turns to look back. He is even closer behind her than she had guessed. His hands are empty. No gun. He gives her a rather dopey smile. Gordon St. Onge, whom a whole town forgives. Well, almost a whole town.

Again she one-handedly tosses her camera up, a bit of a juggling trick, then snaps off three more frames of him as he strides heavily toward her. His big smile is getting CLOSER.

"Okay, buddy!" she hollers. "What have you been trying to tell me?!!" She is walking backward now, camera at the ready. "You see, I don't get it. You aren't clear!!! Your sign language is . . . is fuzzy! I'm sorry!"

No verbal answer from the man. Just more goofy big smile. And now, yes, he thumbs his nose at her! And then he pretends to take *her* picture, pantomiming the handling of a camera with a great long zoom lens.

"What?! What?!" she demands. "I can't hear you!"

Now he is romping toward her, keys jangling wildly, head low, shoulders hunched.

She turns and runs like hell. She remembers with horror that her sporty little car is trapped between the ash tree and his truck.

When she at last settles into the deep scorching bucket seat, she rolls both windows up, locks the doors, waits.

He has slowed down, a nice little stroll, she inside the closed-up sporty car, sweating.

He finally saunters up to her window, taps the glass, then stands with his thumbs in the pockets of his ratty jeans, arms akimbo. She can only see him from the waist down but she can tell by his stance that he is truly happy and satisfied with himself. And for the first time she gets a look at the belt buckle. A raw homemade thing made of copper. A child's rendition of that ancient face of the sun.

The volcan temperature inside the little car reminds her of something. Torrents of sweat move down her neck and ribs. Her fish tattoos have a new satin sheen, more oceany. Her eyes sting. Yes. The

Korean prisoner of war camp. A little gagging cry works around the inside of her neck.

He taps again. She gives the window crank a half twist, window opening an inch.

He asks, "Want me to move my truck?"

"Yessssss." Disgustedly.

In her rearview mirror, she watches him.

He climbs into the cab. Seems like a few weeks before he pulls the door shut. *What's he doing?* He slaps on a dark-blue billed cap, looks at himself in *his* rearview, adjusting the cap fussily, stroking his mustache, straightening the points of his shirt collar.

Time passes.

There's the clank of truck gears shifting into neutral. It rolls *slowly* without his starting the engine.

The crunch of the tires moving over gravel in the sleepy heat reminds Ivy Morelli of all the past summers of her life.

 Progress.

Flashlights with a "name brand" are on sale, a buck apiece. Sarah Ridlon in Florence, California, buys five of these. Supermarket cashier runs them over the computer, stuffs them in the bag. Little does Sarah know that none of these work except one. As each flashlight is now tossed in the trash, Sarah will say, "They just don't make things like they used to." She doesn't even jokingly threaten to blow up the flashlight company. Therefore she is a good person. She is healthy. Only insane people get mad. Sane people take it and take it and take it and take it and . . .

 Experts.

According to Dr. Roger Gould of the American Association of Mental Health Providers, "As Americans learn to adjust and deal with a faster, more high-tech, more mobile world and a less family-community-oriented society and falling dollar, cynicism and anxiety are expected to peak and level off."

The grays.

There are no mouths in our faces. Mouths unneeded, due to this, that grays are not individual but mixed and moored to one another, always whole. The moving mouths of Earthlings, wet and sticky and purveyors of fibs, are amazing to us, as is their ability to *receive* fibs without detection.

 The screen croons.

Record-breaking lovely day. Beach weather. *Everyone* is feeling hot weather joy and shopping joy! Oh, joy! Oh, joy! Soda pop, lotions, fast cars, hair blowing in the wind.

 Present Time, out in the world.

The multinational corporation Duotron Lindsey, with profits totaling 250 million last year, has laid off 11,000 people in the Midwest and 17,000 in California in its plan to restructure the two locations, primarily to part-time no-benefits positions, and at other levels, "contracting out" (or "outsourcing"), as well as relocating a section of the Chester plant to the women's prison in Pontooki. All this in order to fulfill a projected 400 million dollars for next year, and *of course*, an even more ample and sexy figure for the year after that, in order to continue tantalizing investors who, like small children with TV remote controls, are so grimly playful. Varroooom!

 History (the past), 1009 B.C.

The masters. Sometimes they are like ice or fire or beast. Honestly brutal. Sometimes they are tricksters and pose as good news.

 In the newsroom.

She is staring at the keen, ready-and-waiting screen of her computer whereupon she must ply the words of her weekly column. Something about the opening show at the Moore Gallery, by that photographer who does things like can openers and razor blades juxtaposed with wrists and ears against cardboard or wallpaper in strong flat light. But she can't get her mind off the St. Onge school story, though there really is no story. Only supposition. Only gossip. And what else? Something tough and frightening, like her own voice at the age of seven, bawling. Something beyond the scope of language, beyond all gesture.

Ivy's column is usually, well, yes, *fun* to write. And her features, if not fun, are gratifying to her, but the columns are *always* fun, opinion, *her* opinion, her humor, her scoldings, her likes and dislikes. Politics. Bad habits of other people. Terrible restaurants to avoid. "That eye steak sat on my stomach like a lonely rock." Movies and books to savor, mostly to avoid. The ways people can irk you in traffic, what Ivy calls "the mule trains" or "a mule train about to happen," which are those "partially evolved" people with their "brake lights in your face all the time." But especially politics. "Another Scary Day at Our Legislature starring Representative Deirdre Ladd and Senator B. Paul Nason." Except that Ivy makes up insulting nicknames that play up noses and slouching, stuttering, blushing, tendencies toward chapped lips. Ivy personally despises the entire legislature. And not for political reasons exactly. You can hear it in every phrase, the raffish HAW HAW head-shaking dismissal of their humanity, this, the voice of Ivy Morelli, having fun.

But as she sits now, staring not at the computer but out the window at the other windows of the six-story building beyond, Ivy isn't having any fun.

She glances around the newsroom over the waist-high "corrals" at all the firm backs there working, faces lighted by the deathly blue-gray of each screen, the executive editor and the Sunday editorial page editor in a corner talking . . . a stranger arriving, a man who limps, carrying of all things, a lawn-type campaign poster from an election previous to Ivy's birth. Everyone stops what they are doing to admire this poster and to do the anecdote exchange thing.

Two phones pulse simultaneously.

And now a siren in the street beyond the sealed-shut windows.

Ivy digs around in her bag and finds the folder with the old clippings about Gordon St. Onge, including another one she sniffed out after her trip to Egypt yesterday. This is one of him speaking to the legislative committee on "Education and Cultural Affairs" at the State House four years ago, a hearing on stricter school testing. Interesting how they show him at the batch of mikes, dressed in what looks like a light blue denim work shirt with mother-of-pearl snaps and a hunting vest with the heavy plaid wool side worn outside, the blaze orange underneath but showing at the edges, his hair, unlike yesterday, combed neatly, the beard less gray, the eyes calm with an intelligence both patient and contemplative, both hands open as one would do in showing the width or length of something, a huge trout for instance. His hands are clean.

Interesting how the photo caption reads: *Egypt resident Gordon St. Onge speaks his concerns at this morning's committee hearing on school testing.* While in the article there's no mention of him at all, let alone any reference to what he had to say even as an unnamed person. All people who are quoted are named and they are predictable and hardly worth quoting. The whole article has a sleepy jejune business-as-usual don't-bother-to-read-me feel, even though the subject matter could be seen as monumental.

How did Gordon St. Onge's quotable quote get overlooked? Certainly he had said something weird. She is sure of it.

She squints hard at the grainy newsprint face. "Speak to me!" she commands.

 She lifts the phone receiver to her ear and taps out Gordon St. Onge's number, her cold cunning eyes shining with single-minded resolve.

But nobody answers the St. Onge phone.

 An hour passes, she tries that number again.

No answer. Not even an answering machine. Just those chill suspenseful rings that are like when you watch a set of mousetraps with a mouse circling and sniffing . . . the yet-to-happen *snap*! The mouse circles and circles, sniffs and sniffs.

It can drive you nuts watching this.

Ring. Ring. Ring. Ring. "Hello."

This is a voice with the majesty of an older mother.

Ivy asks for Gordon. She does not introduce herself, but this seems not to matter because the woman with no hesitation explains, "They're all over at Berrys'. They're finally settin' the tiles for that well."

"You mean a well . . . like for water?"

Ripply, soft laugh, western Maine accent, "Yes, dear."

Ivy goes for broke. "Hey, are there any kids working on this well job?"

The woman laughs again. Tender wide ripples of hm-hm-hm's. Then silence. Then, "Who's this calling?"

Ivy is tempted to lie. To make up the name of a possible long lost friend of Gordon's. But you know, that's just not professional. Or is it? If quotation marks around paraphrases are okay these days, maybe anything goes.

But the woman is on guard now anyway and the conversation thins out into a harmless exchange about unusually hot weather for June.

 Again.

"H'lo." At last. His voice. Too deep. Too beefy.

"Mister. St. Onge." She enounces each word and letter carefully.

"Hey, Ivy." Deeply.

Ivy sighs. "Caller ID, right?"

"No. Just basic black."

She gives a nonprofessional snort. Not a pretty sound.

He grunts happily. Not a handsome sound.

The newsroom is in a hearty carpet-softened clamor this morning. She covers one ear with three fingers of her free hand. She stares at her computer, the zinc-colored glow that connects one human consciousness to the conscious*less* computerized heartless whole planet. Someday, they say, everyone will have a phone with a screen, and on that screen you will be able to see the face of your caller or callee. For instance, now it would be Gordon St. Onge's face and he could hide nothing. And, well, Ivy could hide nothing, for instance, her stark urgency, and the tapping of her trimmed nails on the desk. *Total* ID.

But if you have faith in progress, you would not see this as a threat. You would see this as a kind of superextension of the heart, you know, all peoples of the world holding hands, metaphorically, all around the wonderfully round planet, the Eskimos in fur, the Africans in brilliant orange-and-yellow wraps, Hawaiians in flowery muumuus, then those heated purple flashes of Bedouin folk, turbans and tunics and restless dark eyes, and those others out there with the little white caps, and those in dress suits, and those in sweatshirts. And all the faces would be singing, laughing, sharing secrets, passing on info about this Great Information Age, and yuh, *doing business.* Hearts to hearts. Eyes into eyes across millions of little flickering computer screens . . . and of course electronic language translators. Access! Sweet, sweet world peace!

"Mr. St. Onge, do you think you'll ever change your mind about an interview? After all, you changed your mind from yes to no before. Maybe soon, you'll go from no to yes. We could straighten out a lot of misconceptions the public might have about you." She simpers, hoping that it comes off as charming, but probably not. Why can't Ivy be charming? Control, Ivy, control.

"Hounded by the press," he says with a weary funny-ish growl.

She laughs robustly. HAW HAW. She then insists, "This isn't the *New York Times* exactly . . . or the *National Enquirer.* Just a friendly local paper . . . community stuff, you know." She realizes at once how insulting and patronizing this is, the *Record Sun* being the biggest thing around and owned by a national chain. She sighs. Her heart sinks.

He is quiet but for the rustle of moving the phone receiver around a bit.

She pictures him in some sort of drippy cave, not the grandma-grandpa gray farmhouse with its pink print door-window curtain and blowsy ash tree. She presses, "If I drive over again, it'll be at your convenience, of course . . . so you can hide everybody again." She laughs. A tight sugary laugh, which even a two-year-old would know is phony baloney.

He is quiet. Reeeeal quiet. Then speaks. "Ivy, what's the angle on this piece? If you were to write it today on what you surmise, what would you tell your readers?"

"Oh . . . adventures in education. No buses. No basketball courts. No soccer fields. No students."

Sounds like he's sucking his teeth. Or maybe drinking something. Beer or something. Rat poison. Hemlock. With his followers. Everybody on their knees. She remembers his pale eyes, that distracted crazy look, the frequent squint-blinking and nervous tic, the eye that almost turned in when he scrutinized her, the bunched bottom teeth, the awfully sloped shoulders, the heaviness of his walk *when he walked* versus his rather athletic hump-backed bull-bear routine and nose-thumbing. How does he fit the image of the striking charismatic patriarchal male who gets those three-hundred followers to drink poison for him and God? Or to hold out together behind the thin walls of their home against the murderous FBI? What would you give God's prophet? Your money? How about your wife? Ah, your teenaged girls? Your life? Indeed, his deepening voice pulls Ivy Morelli's ear harder to the phone. *His* tricky charm definitely has more honey than hers, his awkward blunders and doggy humility being creepily believable. *Could* it be real?

But what about that place *behind* his voice, so hollow and dark? Maybe there are no children anyway. Maybe he hadn't hidden them because there never were any. And maybe the older woman's voice answering the phone yesterday was really him doing an impersonation. Maybe all the calls of those men and women leaving messages to complain about Gordon were Gordon. Maybe the whole thing is a joke. His joke. Ivy sighs. "Gordon, what have you got against the press?"

"Think about this," he instructs her, his voice softening, deepening, softening, deepening. "There was a man named Harry Grommet. He was in a rush, always in a rush. So he traveled light. Small car. Small suitcase. And he found this to be less costly as well, to keep everything light. One Saturday morning, agreeing to a family outing but in a rush as always, he gave himself only five minutes to pack. And only one very small suitcase. It was a terrible and ghastly ending for all. You see, the wife and kids and golden retriever didn't fit comfortably into a small suitcase. In fact, it was grisly. You see?"

Ivy laughs, but only half a laugh. A single lonesome HAW. "I . . . ah . . . don't get it. Come again?"

"Ivy," he says softly. "I'm not trying to give you a hard time. There's just so much at stake."

"Sure, I know. So—"

"Ivy . . . I'm sorry. I can't do any interviews. I'm sorry . . . I don't like to disappoint you, but—"

"You're not disappointing me," she tells him ice-cubily, "It's just a matter of your being dishonest and sneaky. Or not being man enough to face the public. And if I go ahead and print this story without your side of it, you won't be happy."

He speaks now in a thick clay voice. "My side." Then like feet in a dirge. "There was a woman named Josephine Files. She wanted to photograph two chickens having a picnic. But being unable to find agreeable chickens, she settled on two gorillas. These were huge gorillas. And not agreeable at all. And they wouldn't fit on the tiny checkered picnic cloth that Josephine had set out for the chickens. The gorillas left. The picnic cloth was left quite wrinkled. And then she took the pictures. Showing the pictures to her kids, she said, "These are my chicken pictures." The kids, who were used to being told that certain things were other things by Josephine, smiled and everything was okay. After all, who else could they believe? And the sun smiled and the sky was blue. And the children—"

"Okay, funny man. It's your ass," Ivy snarls and hangs up.

 Ivy.

"Shit!" She hates herself. And now she even fears herself. Certainly she fears for her job. Other reporters stay cool, smooth as cream. They'd still be in Gordon St. Onge's good graces. Faces controlled, voices almost electronic. Ivy Morelli was never meant to be a reporter. Maybe a prison warden, dog trainer, a cop . . . or a school principal . . . yes. When you have people in handcuffs or you are four times their size, it doesn't really matter that you say everything wrong.

Her editor, Brian Fitch, three desks away, is playing his computer keyboard like a concerto, his expression serene. She turns her back on him. She sees her half-consumed high-fructose buttercup-colored fruit drink on the edge of her desk. She sighs. She remembers a test that was given in sixth grade.

Which would you rather be doing?
Pick one.

A. Writing a poem.
B. Doing a science experiment.
C. Watching the construction of a new bridge.
D. Debating the pros and cons of flying a kite in a thunderstorm.
E. Reading about the Battle of Waterloo.

Of course Ivy would rather be watching construction! All those half-naked bodies. All those tans. All those come-hither voices and catcalls and winks to her and her girlfriends. (Which today would be against the law; yes, illegal voices, lawsuit catcalls, and heavy-fine-to-pay winks.)

The test continued.

Which would you rather be doing?
Pick one.

A. Helping someone bandage amputated limbs.
B. Playing chess.
C. Visiting a fashion designer.
D. Reading about the rise and fall of the Roman Empire.
E. Watching a man operate a bulldozer.

Ivy had imagined the man on the bulldozer to have dark sunglasses, a hairy chest, and a tan the color of a proud lion. All the grouped choices were like this. One titillating centerpiece surrounded by the painfully deadly dull. Or fraught with tiled walls and bloody quivering goo.

A few weeks later the test results were distributed along the ruler straight rows of her class. This was not a test with a score. No ho. This test told you, in a word, what your career would . . . should be.

Other students were nurses, secretaries, history teachers, lawyers, commercial designers, artists, and so forth. But Ivy would be a heavy equipment operator.

Not a reporter.

As a heavy equipment operator, she could say stuff like, "Okay, funny man. It's your ass," and it would have no ill effects.

Ivy glances around at Brian Fitch. He looks so right and okay with himself. She considers all the others, flipping through their notebooks or gliding through *Record Sun* library info on their screens. All of them meant to be reporters.

 The grays.

Mouthless, yes. But our goals would be inconceivable to you even if we noisily explained. Our technology (fashioned and propelled by the combined mind that us grays, yes, have), we confess, has swept some Earthlings aboard temporarily, some human. We are careful to pick those seen by their society to be unreliable, in case they remember and talk of us from their wet moving concave mouths. But so far, none have remembered much, mostly confused shocking dreams of what other Earthlings often do to one another in the name of "great" systems, in the name of "reason" and "advanced" medicine or "therapy" and "national intelligence" or "national security" or "defense" or "freedom." That Earthling humans have these words with which to confuse each other causes us to mouthlessly and sadly grimace.

Again, we *rarely* invite Earthlings onto our crafts. We are committed to noninterference. Other than a few warnings and comfort beams sent through sensory perception to flush their cheeks, we keep our cool. Ah, Earth! The prickly paradoxes! Mother Nature's heartless laboratory. Mother of skulls, mother of superlatives, mother of the eensie, the roots, the blooms, the blood, dust devils and ice, milk and hungers; mother of webbed-up flies in all their forms. We ache with the wish to pluck you all from her cruel tournaments of *excellence*. Ah, here comes one now. Earthling in her craft. Red with four wheels. In our unseen dimension, we hover to watch her with our seeing hearts, our beating eyes.

The press shows up unannounced.

Ivy doesn't call to plead this time. She just shows up, her low sporty car slipping between Gordon's green-and-white Chevy pickup and one light color compact car. It is almost nine at night, but still there's a slab of soggy daylight in the higher open fields, and through the trees is the tired paleness of the west. The air is sweet and stout. The air is cake. Pie. Pudding. But no. It is a sweetness far beyond the human hand.

Ivy sings, "Oh green, the grass! Buzzy the bug! Ah paradise!" as she rushes the house, her shoulder bag slapping her hip, head bent. Whining mosquitoes whirl around her hair, ears, neck, alight on her arms, prick at her legs. She swipes them off. She says grittily, "Paradise is hell, Ivy, baby." Ivy izzz happy. Ivy the child reporter. Ivy all mean innocence. Which way will the hurt fall?

"Yerff!! Yerff!!" A dog inside the house. Smallish sounding dog.

Ivy is dressed tonight in her wholesome young-person look. Oversized off-gray US Marines T-shirt. White shorts that show her strong legs, shaved and golden and glossy. And sneakers. And thick synthetic-fiber pink socks. And a white paper painter's cap worn backward on her short bowl of lustrous dark hair. And that silent circle of pretty fish surging around her slim arm.

She sees light. She hears murmurs. Do you, the reader, ever notice how it is when a bunch of humans talk? Ivy hears that murmured kind of *rutabagarutabaga* through a set of open windows. See there the long screened porch. *Rutabagarutabagarutabaga.* Ivy has never been so ready for the SCOOP. The news, yes, but something deeper and wider, something as gritty and swarthy as the hole from a hardworking excavator. Out come the rocks! Out come the beetles and badgers. REV! REV! REV! Clang! Another big rock rolls from the shovel. *Thump!* Ah! It is ALL OF IT RIGHT HERE!

She takes the two steps to the porch in a bound. She jerks the screen door wide. Squinching her eyes for better seeing power, she peers down the porch's length. Sees many chairs, all in positions of abandonment.

The inside door to the kitchen is open and she can hear the simmering cooling down *rutabagarutabagas* beyond, due to their probably
having heard our Ivy's superhero-type landing on their door sill.

Ivy's heart is skipping all over the place, beating in her neck.

Dog squeals, a cry of pain or terror or something.

Next to Ivy's head, a set of steel-pipe wind chimes hang like the
legs of a creature freshly killed.

She hops onto the threshold, pausing now to inhale deeply that
summery old farmhouse smell. She also notes that there are *no smells of
supper*. No scorched meat. Nothing fruity or veggie. Nothing casserol-
ish or stir-fried speaks to her nose. Big kitchen. Wallpapered. A gaudy
modern print of jungle birds that you could either find gorgeous and
brave, or just tacky. Most wall space is concealed with teetering stacks
of wooden apple boxes and registered milk crates all stuffed with tools,
work gloves, jars with nails, and little doohickeys of hardware, rusty
mixed with new. Cupboard doors are shut tight. They seem clean.
She can't make out in this dim light any kiddie fingerprints.

Skyscrapers of apple boxes lean toward Ivy. They yearn toward her
pink socks, slender tattooed arm, white paper hat, welcoming her. The
rutabagas go even more hushy, then they are no more. The humans
do not welcome Ivy. No one rushes her way with tea or even just a
warm hand. There is a pause in the rotating movement of the earth.

There's only one source of light, cold and fluorescent, a fixture low
over a broad heaped workbench and desk in an impassable-looking
open pantryway that is connected to what is possibly a shedway or
second pantryway section of the ell. The door is blocked by yet another, smaller, desk, this one heaped with papers, references, manuals,
folders, a few books in a happy-go-lucky topsy-turvy stack, a roll of
postage stamps in a glass jar, a box of new envelopes, a loose calendar
page, a roll of duct tape, masking tape, every kind of tape, little towers of tape, even audio tapes, these in a big weirdly shaped glass jar,
an early model electric typewriter, a flashlight, a beer bottle, a can of
pens and markers, and very fancy postal scales. No Bibles. Not much
sign yet of heavy-duty religion. No guns.

The rest of the kitchen, including where Ivy stands, is in a kind of
desolate blue shadow. Cold to the soul.

The dog cries out again.

"Lay back, Pepper," a woman's voice commands.

Ivy can see no dog, only the backs of several women squatted down in a cluster near the lighted desks, all of them pivoting now on their haunches to glance up at Ivy who is standing there in those blue shadows, Ivy with her heavy shoulder bag and her feet wide apart in a way that looks empowered, US Marines across the chest of her T-shirt in letters that seem now about a foot tall.

Two short, square, ruddy white-haired women rise to their feet. One says, "The reporter gal," in a not-too-surprised way. The other one just smiles. Like a tightly gloved hand.

Ivy returns the smile. "Yes. I'm Ivy Morelli . . . *Record Sun*," and reaches forward for the hand of the nearest of these two little ruddy women, yes, they are shorter even than our Ivy. The nearest woman gives no name, just pats Ivy's hand and coos with one of the more dimply soft sounds of the great *rutabagarutabaga*.

Ivy asks, "What do we have here?" in her most friendly among-girls voice and stepping closer to the cluster of still-squatted women, sees that there is a woman seated in the middle of them all. It's an old-style wooden desk chair with wheels and arms. Painted gray. This seated woman is as close to the fluorescent light fixture as she can get, hunched over with a grip on a flashlight and a small muscular truly ugly, flat-faced, curly-tailed white dog who is jerking and twisting and grunting hotly like a pig.

"Trying to find a splinter," speaks a voice behind Ivy, the voice of the woman who had rubbed Ivy's hand. And Ivy is sure that voice is the same wonderfully ripply voice she spoke with on the phone a few days back.

Ivy counts five women. She burns each and every one of their faces and forms into her memory. And her cold blue eyes, accentuated by their dark lashes, glide all around.

When one of the women, a medium-aged blonde, sees Ivy doing this, Ivy hunches her shoulders and lets them drop in a guilty-little-girl way. And she sighs. She wonders what is beyond the many closed doors of this room. She wonders, wonders, wonders, wonders while the women are dealing with the job at hand, big grip on small dog.

"She'll give up the struggle after a while, but only if *we* don't give up. If *we* give up, she'll know she can win next time," insists the woman hunched over in the desk chair. She, short-legged. She, round as a bubble. And could she be age fifty? American Indian face. Metal-frame glasses. Long hair, parted in the middle, black and gray. A man's blue chambray work shirt fits taut over her truck-driver-sized arms and mighty, oh, very indeed mighty breasts. She doesn't raise her eyes to Ivy, just keeps her head bowed over the straining dog. Her dark-gold dimpled hands on both dog and flashlight wear only a simple wedding ring, nothing twinkly, nothing ornate, and yet the hands themselves are resplendent with their task.

Ivy asks, "What kind of dog is that?"

The Indian woman speaks without looking up, "Mastiff Chihuahua mix." Some of the women chortle over this.

Ivy smiles. "In other words, unknown."

The Indian woman sighs, "No one can trace Pepper to the May-flower, that's for sure." And now she raises her eyes to Ivy. Unread-able flat eyes. Through the glasses maybe something is lost. Does that dimple by her mouth mean warmth? Reflections purling and whirlpooling on the glass parts of those old-time spectacles play with our Ivy's mind.

One of the short square white-haired women speaks, not the one with the ripply warm voice and Maine accent, but a New York–type accent. "I would offer you some lemonade, Ivy . . . if you were at my house. But—"

Ivy cuts in, "This is Gordon's house, right?"

The woman seems not to have heard, but chatters on. "Nothing like lemonade on a warm evening after a hot day," and then she is saying something about little tea cakes, how she and Bev keep a lot of tea cakes for surprise visitors.

Bev. Bev. Bev. Ivy takes a mental note of this name. Bev. Who is Bev?

"Thank you anyway." Ivy tries to look friendly. She smiles. But her chilly eyes move from one short square white-haired woman to the other in a calculating way. If Ivy were an actress, she would only get the parts of killers or evil sorceresses. She twists the visor of her painter's cap to one side, "I can't stay long anyway. I just dropped in to see if Gordon was around."

"He's not around," says the Indian woman a little too quickly, without looking up from the grunting, wild-eyed dog who is locked into paralysis inside her powerful arms.

Ivy looks back to the two white-haired pinkly white women. Both seem about sixty. Both have very short straight Ringo hair cuts. No perms. One wears a men's-style shirt, sleeves rolled to the elbows. The other a T-shirt that reads GRAND CANYON. The picture beneath the words is hard to make out with the bent head of a younger blonde woman blocking Ivy's view of it, but one can assume the picture is of the Grand Canyon, all orange and purple and splendorous. Both these white-haired ruddy women look bouncy and fit and as audacious as Ivy. Marines T-shirts would not look improbable on them . . . *as the caissons go rolling along* ♫ . . . hup! hup! hup!

Ivy's pale eyes slide onto the two younger women, both blondes, and yes, indeed, all these women seem like normal average everyday women. Surprise! Surprise!

The dog ki-yi's sharply.

"It's okay, Pepper," all the women speak in unison.

Now the flashlight is in the hand of a blonde woman. The Indian woman leans in very close to the paw in question. The little bony paw now seems to be the center of a very intense spiritual universe. The yellow light of the flashlight on this paw! Everything else lit dimly blue and insignificant and filled with indescribable metaphysical pain and Ivy isn't breathing at all.

Suddenly, Ivy sees that the two blonde women must be identical twins, or at least look-alike sisters. Ivy exhales slowly, the strap of her bag slips off her shoulder, then kinda positions itself at the center of a small painted wooden table beside her, a table that is oddly bare. She explains, "I have a twin sister. Identical. Her name is Ida. You know . . . Ida and Ivy." She rolls her eyes, sighs, giggles. "What are your names?"

"Jacquie and Josee," replies one of the blondes with a big happy laugh.

Of this woman who has spoken, Ivy asks, "How are you all related to Gordon? Just friends?"

The dog screams horribly, then silence.

Ivy catches the eye of the other twin. "You live in this house?"

"Naw! Naw!" Having both hands on the dog, she kind of dips her head around to indicate the room. "Diss not co*zee* enough for me. I like knickknacks . . . dem poofy coushes, me." Her smile is sad. This sadness intrigues Ivy.

"Well there!" exclaims the Indian woman. "You see that toenail? That's it. It's her toenail. It's busted off and split up inside the quick. No wonder she hurts."

There are comforting doggie words from the group. "Poo poo poo pooo pooo" and "teeny wints is sore."

The Indian woman lifts her round face, her glasses flashing the flinty, square, bluish light. "Somehow she got it crushed or caught it in something—"

"All t'em dogs is always underfoot," complains one of the twins.

"I'll bet it's those damn plywood floors in Willie's shop. Those spaces between," surmises the ripply voiced white-haired woman.

No sounds of kids beyond the many doors. No mention of kids. No sign of kids' things. Ivy is looking and listening for all she's worth. She sees that one twin has a long thick curly ponytail, not at all a cheap blonde color, but a very handsome streaky tawny and silver. What the other twin has *is* the cheap blonde color, commercial and orangey and cut quite short. They are late thirties, perhaps forty. Both have plastic large-frame modern glasses. Their mouths look tender. Their shoulders sloped and soft. Both lively small women, dressed youthfully, one in a blazing pink cotton top, utterly pink, poundingly pink, a pink painful shaft to each eye if you look long; the other gal in a sleeveless black shell showing shapely golden shoulders and arms.

Ivy tries to imagine Gordon St. Onge in this kitchen, his height, his heavy walk, his scary unpredictable quick moves. Yes, this is his space, lair of the monster yet to be defined. Where in the hell *is* he?

"Where do you live?" Ivy asks the nearest twin who stands up and stretches and Ivy sees that upon the chest of her black shell top simmers a small bright cross. This blonde glances quickly into the bespectacled eyes of the Indian woman, then frowns.

Ivy knows now. These women have been instructed. *This is ugly indeed.* She wants to blurt out, *Where are your children?* She wants to ask, *Are you in danger? Does he insist God has chosen him to instruct you?*

Does he talk about an Apocalypse?!!!! Does he insist upon your submission? Why are you here?!!!!!!!!!!!

The Indian woman throws open her arms and the small white dog nearly flies, hits the floor at a skid, hopping three-leggedly past Ivy out onto the dark piazza, bangs itself against the screen door. Door jerks open. Dog gone.

Ivy's voice has an uncharacteristic apologetic squeak to it. "I didn't plan on stopping by. It was a spur of the moment thing. If I'd known, I'd have made my white-chip cookies, or something . . ." She falters. "On the way through town here, I checked at a store. But it was just closing. He shut the door right in my face . . . this guy did. I begged him to take pity. But he was hard-hearted."

While the white-haired women insist gifts are not necessary, the Indian woman, brushing off the wide thighs of her jeans, declares, "It's a nightie-night town."

Ivy regards the Indian woman steadily, that lap, now empty, one dimpled hand on each wide thigh. And this woman stares back, chin raised now, and her eyes behind her metal-frame glasses are lost in flat blue utility-cool reflections of refrigerator and cupboard doors and towers of cluttered shelves. Ivy says, "The kids must really love that little dog. You can tell when a dog has been given a lot of love."

One of the white-haired women touches Ivy's shoulder. The ripply wide warm familiar laugh is gone. The voice is now granular, staticky, "Don't."

The other white-haired woman, this one with the New York City accent and Grand Canyon on her chest, says in a heavy way, "Ohhhhh, I guess. Hmmmmm," then turns away and stands by the sink staring down. Prayer? Or just avoiding the big bulging not-very-nice moment where it was necessary to figuratively take a broom to the guest. SWAT!

The phone rings. The short square white-haired pinkly white woman with the Maine accent answers it, writes something on paper on the desk, slips it carefully down over a tall spike of notes. She makes no real conversation with the caller, just "Of course" and "You bet" and "I know it." Then "Yes, playing doctor to one of Willy Lancaster's little dogs." Then some listening. Then, "Bye-bye."

It has fallen into Ivy Morelli's sizzling mental notebook.
WILLY LANCASTER.

♡ ♡ **Jane Meserve speaks.**

I would run away but I don't know where I am. I would walk.

There's a phone here. It's always ringing. But it's never Mumma.
People . . . hundreds of people call Gordie. Gordie knows the whole
world. La la la la la. I hate Gordie's voice. "Hi, Bob," "Hi, Janet,"
"Hi, Mary," "Hi, Gus," "Hi, Dave," "Hi, Stan," "Hi, Art," "Hi,
Doug," "Hi, Ray," "Hi, Vic," "Hi, Pooch," "Hi, Randy," "Hi, BoBo,"
"Hi, Frank" . . . laugh laugh laugh talk talk talk. "Bye, Bob," "Bye,
Janet," "Bye, Gus," "Bye, Dave" . . . while I am right here at the
table crying and weak for food. Nobody knows how mean Gordie is.
Everybody thinks he is so nice. But if you saw me, you would see my
eyes are sinkish and I get skinnier. While Gordie is on the phone, he
eats and looks at me and is so happy to see me with nothing to eat.

 **The press calls the William D. Lancasters, after a
brief impatient search in the area directory and then a
call to Information.**

"Hello. This is Ivy Morelli with the *Record Sun*. Is this the residence
of Willie Lancaster?"

TV in the background. Into the phone a woman's voice speaks,
cigarette husky. Or husky from shouting. Or maybe a cold. Or crying? "Yes, 'tis."

"I'm interviewing people at the Home School and some of them
over there mentioned your family's name. I'm hoping you or Willie
would like to talk with me about the school."

"Mmmmh."

"Pretty nice school, huh?"

"I don't go down there. It's my daughter that goes . . . her and her
husband."

"And their children?"

"No kids . . . yet."

"Do you remember when Gordon first opened the doors of his school?"

"I dunno . . . a while back. It's not actually a school. Some people call it that . . . the Home School . . . but there's really something about that . . . something how people started calling it that . . . other people. My girl calls it the Settlement because . . . well, you know . . . it's a community."

Ivy says quickly, "Oh, I *know* . . . but, you know . . . it's *kind* of a school, because of all the kids."

"I guess you could say that."

Ivy presses on. "If you were to say the things you like best and least about the school, the Settlement, what would those things be?"

The woman's voice has no high or low tones, just throaty sluggishly paced words, strategically placed, as you might set the table with plate, knife, spoon, fork, napkin. "Oh, I dunno. Should be Dee Dee you talk to about this."

"Do you have her phone number?"

"They don't have a phone. They use ours."

Dogs bark. Several dogs. It's the voice of that small, white, curl-tailed, flat-faced dog with the hurt paw at Gordon's house last night, but multiplied five or six times.

Ivy suggests, "Your daughter must live nearby."

The woman makes no reply but now speaks to someone else, then returns to say in her deadpan voice, "Someone's here." The vivacious dither of dog voices closes in so Ivy can't hear what the woman is calling out to the someone who has arrived.

Ivy waits, squeezing her lips with her fingers and pulling them out into a long shape, then tapping her fingers on the desk, then rubs her silky hair violently.

Woman's voice returns. "You still there?"

"Yes, I am," Ivy replies so nicely, almost fondly. "I'm wondering if I can stop by soon and talk with Dee Dee?"

"You'll need to ask her that. I can't predict her comin's and goin's. I know tonight they'll be late but tomorrow she's going to be here for supper, her Dad's birthday, and you can catch her then and make your plans."

Ivy wants to ask one more thing from this lifelessly agreeable woman but the dogs seem to be knocking things over. Or maybe the visitors are knocking things over. So Ivy just says *thank you* and *bye*.

The woman's *bye* is more like "B'bye" as friends would say good-bye to each other, but oh-so calm and unruffled and toneless.

Now in boldest print, Ivy taps out the words: COMMUNITY and SETTLEMENT on the screen.

Ivy narrows her eyes.

 The following p.m. The press taps out the Lancasters' phone number. Dee Dee, the daughter, is right there.

The dogs are quiet this time but *Happy Birthday tooooo yooooooooo*, obscenities, ghoulish laughter, and screams in the background make the Lancaster daughter's soft words hard to decipher, but Ivy is *sure* that the young woman (who sounds like a little girl) has been instructed by Gordon St. Onge because the *girl* says, "Not a school. Just family. Gordon is my husband's cousin." And then quickly, "I really can't talk. I'm not feeling well." And she doesn't budge when Ivy tries to weasel another answer out of her. "I'm really sorry. I'm sick. Gotta go. B'bye," and the girl is gone, just the utterly black hollow of the hung-up phone remains. Ivy thinks this over.

The girl didn't seem sick. Nor did she seem afraid of anyone. Or drugged. If anyone is drugged, it's the Lancaster mother. The daughter's voice wasn't anything like her mother's, that methodical drone. The girl seemed *happy*. Happy and hurried. And very soft. And young! Too young to be married. How young is she? Fourteen? Ivy needs to know. The little bit she has found out so far has not disproven the prickly red-hot prophet hypothesis. The prophet and his devoted followers. Ooooo wow yes! This is the kind of story America loves.

 Ivy tails him.

On Thursday morning she packs her bag with pens, lined pads, tape recorder, spare earrings, cassettes, cell phone (which only works in parking lots of big-box stores) (and only sometimes), Kleenex, cash.

And away she goes. Her car is held tight in the grip of heavy rain, windshield wipers whacking away, radio on low. She is decked out in a black beret, jeans, sandals, and an old-fashioned white eyelet blouse. Beret and blouse and jeans now splattered and soggy from her sprint to and from the newspaper building. The earrings she wears she has kept simple. Just studs. To keep the holes from slamming shut on her. You can't turn your back on pierced flesh.

But Ivy feels so good. It is good to get out of the city. Even a small city. The wet greenness of the overhanging trees and steep fields of new corn are close and solid as surging sea. Barefoot, her soaked sandals now tossed in the bucket seat beside her, she sees, before she makes the turn onto Heart's Content Road, the dark green-and-white pickup coming downhill. She makes the split-second decision to keep going straight, speeding up, turning in a driveway a few yards after the curve, coming back fast, easily catching up with the truck as it toodles along into town.

Yep, it's him. She can make out the dark brown back of his head in the cab's steamy back window. He wears no cap. What is it that looks red? Must be his shirt.

Two other heads. One small. A *child!* Really and truly and alas.

Ivy tailgates. She hangs there right on his bumper and rides it hard. She doesn't even try to be discreet. When he brakes, she brakes. When he speeds up slightly on straightaways, she speeds up slightly on straightaways. But this is the way Ivy always drives, isn't it? Everyone knows that to drive less aggressively and more courteously is . . . well . . . part of the romantic and impractical past. A form of congealment. You'll never get anywhere if you don't progress out of those old ways. You must *go* with the *flow,* and *more.*

He must recognize her, but he never pulls off the pavement to have it out with her, either to terrorize her or to just say, "Hey, Ivy. Howzit goin'?"

He just keeps poking along as if no Ivy were there. The child's head turns. Child stands up on his knees in the seat, which means he hasn't got his seat belt fastened. No child seat, either. Hmmmm. The child rubs away some steam from the glass and stares gravely through the window at Ivy with small, squinty, deeply-lodged-looking eyes . . . not big innocent eyes. He has a small chin. Not a child who is chubby-cheeked. Nor rosy. His hair is dark. Combed like the hair of cowboys in the old forties and fifties movies. Like Ronald Reagan. Little bump of wet hair in the front. Very churchy. This is what Ivy had expected Gordon St. Onge's hair to look like before she saw newspaper clippings of him and before she met him. She had expected more "church." But here now is the first real kid Ivy has tracked down in association with "the Prophet." That's what some of those persons Ivy has interviewed had called St. Onge (jokingly, it seemed), "the Prophet." Probably due to the line of her questioning, her references to "cult," her reminders to them of the spellbinding shadow of Waco's David Koresh in flames. Okay, and here is a real live kid, finally, churchy hair, no seat belt.

The third head wears a brimmed Vietnam War–type bush hat, olive green. This head keeps turning toward Gordon. The guy is chatty. Seems to talk the whole way. Bearded chin wags, lotta hand gestures. But Ivy never sees him putting the kid back into his seat belt. The guy just talks around the kid while the kid grips the back of the seat or the empty plastic gun racks that show behind the men's heads. And the kid watches Ivy.

Yes, yes, *gun* racks. How had she missed this before?

The old truck chugs through town now, horn tooting, lights flashing in an almost celebratory way to nearly every vehicle that approaches. Left-turn signal blinks at the IGA entrance. Truck turns.

To one side of the IGA, the nearest mountain is soft and pale with fog but for its humpy, dark, hard, watchful, old, woodsy mass showing there in places where the fog is tattered.

Truck eases into a parking space while Ivy whips into a space in the next row, her sporty red car lurching to a stop.

She jams her feet into the cold squashy sandals. She hippity-hops out, swinging her loaded shoulder bag into place. There by the fender of her car, she waits in the beating-down blinding rain, kinda bouncing, ready, watching the doors of the truck but nothing happens while the long drenching seconds tick away. The bush hat guy is still talking and nodding and gesturing to Gordon with both hands. And the kid is still squinting at Ivy through the drizzling back window.

The rain thickens, big fisty close-together cold bloppy splats.

Ivy bounces. Ivy's baby blues flutter, punched by the rain, which comes even more ruthlessly now and seems to squeal, overlaid by church choir. Now the *hisssss* of tires passing through the slosh. The shoulders of Ivy's dress are as wet as if from a swim. Now the countenance of the wiggly sky roars! Ouch!! The rain is now a nail gun, grape shot, *bam, bam, bam*; she thinks of the army word: ordnance. She stands tall, taking it and taking it.

Finally both truck doors open simultaneously and s-l-o-w-l-y.

The talking man, still talking, is short and wiry and to match his Vietnam War hat, wears a loose camo shirt. The boy is small and hoppety and has lost interest in Ivy as the small wiry man grips his hand. Gordon is still stepping from the truck, alas raising up to his full Viking height and immediately turns and looks at Ivy and melodramatically covers his eyes. His chamois shirt is deep foreboding blood red.

Now he turns and walks with the man and the boy through the rain, yes, walks, not hurries. None of the three seem to mind rain. The short wiry man and Gordon chatter in pleasant tones back and forth now in a foreign language! Ivy listens for all she's worth as she slops after them, the parking lot an inch deep in water.

Under the IGA overhang, the man and boy turn a sharp right and head for the auto parts store next door while Gordon moseys through the automatic-opening door of the IGA, not looking back.

Ivy gets close enough behind to scoot in the door while it is still open for him. He doesn't acknowledge this, just strides deliberately onward while Ivy pulls off her black beret and brushes off some of the more beaded-up wetness. She takes mental note of everything about him, red damp shirt hanging over his belt on one side, not very tucked in and tidy. His cuffs flap at his wrists, unbuttoned. Hair: cowlicks galore. He stops to pick up a cellophane-wrapped lettuce that had somehow gotten dropped on the floor. He tenderly arranges it among the other lettuces. His eyes: deep and tired, the whites off-colored, the pale irises not so penetrating as the day of the merry-go-round. His beard and skin and slope-shouldered-but-brute-strength bearing seem different in supermarket light than the hot blue spotty merry-go-round shade but, yes, this *is* the same son of a bitch who grabbed Ivy Morelli's reporter pad.

He lopes on down the first aisle. No shopping carriage. No tote basket. He just ambles along straight to the deli and smacks the counter bell with his palm. Meat cutter appears in smeared apron and they talk loudly about . . . about . . . *something*. Ivy can't tell what. The fluorescent lights are buzzing. Or is it the chattering of her teeth being too loud so close to her ears? She just can't make out the exchange, though she can tell it's not in a foreign language. She lingers in the aisle nearby, "Potato Chips & Snacks" on one side, "Wine & Liquor" on the other. She is scribbling down notes and holding out her mike, which she knows won't pick up anything but various mumbles and the dusky squeak of the carriage wheels of the old woman who is shuffling past with a single can of soup in the child seat and the needs-a-nap scream of a real toddler in the next aisle. But it doesn't matter that this tape is useless, because Ivy is convinced that theatrics is the way into the Prophet's good graces, because isn't he himself a bad act? Though right now he is still ignoring her. And she is freezing TO DEATH. Wet woman juxtaposed with the supermarket's North Pole air.

She snaps off several frames of him and the meat cutter, both in profile, the meat cutter a tallish guy but Gordon towering, redwood-like, Zeus-like . . . uh . . . err, yuh, godlike, but a god that is a slob. The meat cutter points Ivy out to Gordon. Gordon whispers something to the meat cutter and then the meat cutter also seems to forget Ivy is there.

An *un*wet woman in expensive-looking tuck-waisted shorts and a nice navy-blue top and haircut of a glossy dark brown and with an adorable, dry, not-at-all-rained-upon chubby-cheeked child in the seat of a loaded carriage wheels smoothly over to the deli and studies the rows of meats and salads. It's a small deli. Little small-town-type deli. Not a massive selection. Bare spaces from understocking. The meat cutter asks the woman if he can help her. She says a brisk yes and chooses some Swiss cheese, some pastrami. She glances at Gordon who is staring at the pastrami with a wild look in his eye. She keeps glancing at his profile and she just can't help herself, she gurgles, "Weren't you here first?"

Gordon turns his head and his pale weird eyes bore right into her. "Just shooting the breeze," says he with a grin. The most amazingly beautiful grin, showing all his teeth, the jammed overcrowded bottom ones and the fine straight top ones, all framed by the wild brown and black gush of his big mustache and bearded chin and drenched hair and Ivy speaks clearly and meaningfully into her tape recorder mike, "Bewitches women."

The woman is, yes, flushing. She coaxes her child, "Elizabeth, look. See the lobsters walking around," and points to a glass tank of green, sluggishly desperate lobsters with pegged claws. The kid stares, riveted by this horror. The woman looks again at Gordon. Can't keep her eyes off him. "My daughter just had lobster for the first time this summer."

The child's eyes are getting wider on the lobsters. Her mouth trembles. Soon there may be tears.

Gordon asks the woman where she's from.

She proudly names a city, not a home state, just the name of a far, faraway city, a well-known city in another state. And maybe that city in that state is not her home exactly, just the city and state she presently resides in. Hardly an accent at all. Hard to pinpoint. A come-and-go mix. A woman from a place where it never rains, she and her hatchling just having reverse-vaporized onto the scene. This visitor and the Prophet chat a minute about weather and biting bugs as the meat cutter weighs and wraps the purchases. Gordon leans toward the woman. Close. She looks up at him with a helplessly glazed expression. He opens a hand over the child's head, then lightly touches the tip of one of the child's ears. The child does not jerk her head away from this stranger. The child is just suddenly and swimmingly serene. Her hair is a thin blonde sprawl, not scissored to perfection like her mother's.

Gordon caresses the child's ear, running a finger deeply into its curves, and tugs the little lobe. Then he opens his hand around the little foot in the little baby sandal. The child just lets her foot lay trustingly in this huge hand, her eyes into his eyes. She doesn't smile. Her expression is dreamy, like a person looking out a window at falling snow or blowing leaves.

Gordon fingers the ankle. Sweet chubby ankle. No words. No baby talk. His right eyelid and brow twitch slightly. Something Tourette's-ish there.

The mother sees all of this. There is a moment here, perhaps as this strange man had clasped the little foot, when by year 2000 standards, there would be a decision made by all who see this, that this is "unacceptable." But nobody here seems to remember this protocol of the times. Except Ivy.

Finally and reluctantly, the woman is wheeling her loaded cart away. Has she forgotten the next item on her list—Was it waxed paper or waxed beans?—while the child stares around at Gordon, or maybe at the lobsters, with solemn understanding.

Ivy follows Gordon up and down a couple of aisles, notes that he isn't buying anything or even looking for anything, just yakking with people, including the owner, who wears a short-sleeved white shirt and looks run-ragged in a composed and gentlemanly sort of way. Ivy takes pictures and notes and some audio of all this and Gordon ignores her, then, alas, he sweeps around back to "Aisle 2" and snatches up a bottle of cheap brandless aspirin and pays for it, yakking with the checkout woman. And the woman, gray-haired but with a young face and neck and hands, small-shoulders, and a single delicate gold bracelet on one wrist, points out Ivy to Gordon and laughs self-consciously as Ivy is snapping pictures of the five-dollar bill going into her hand from Gordon's hand and Ivy is really standing close for this shot, she can actually smell Gordon's damp shirt, not a wet dog smell, but not a commercial fabric softener smell, either, and Gordon puts both his hands on the counter, leaning an elbow against the lottery dispensers, and whispers to the woman and now the woman seems to forget all about Ivy. *What the hell is he telling them?* Ivy wonders.

She tugs off her so-wet-it's-flat beret and plumps it out as a young mother wearing a pale yellow T-shirt, fresh-looking if sadly soggy, and a baseball cap that reads KITTERY TRADING POST with a bull's-eye target, pushing her grocery carriage along past Ivy accidentally brushes Ivy's elbow, and Ivy sees that the carriage has three large self-satisfied-looking though rain-drenched children and a rack of diet soft drinks. And Ivy turns away and Gordon is still there close to her, tipping his bottle of aspirin from side to side as he yaks with the checkout woman, even as a guy with an armload of hotdog rolls and chips and ice cream (no wagon) comes to stand behind Ivy. He asks in a shy way if Ivy would reach him two bags of peanut M&M's and hold them for him until he has hands. He wears a rain-blasted baby-blue muscle shirt but he is more pudgy than muscley, no beard, just a kind of nondescript blond-brown-haired-type guy, looks almost too young to be out shopping alone but probably he has kids, and probably a wife, a pudgy wife. This is the story in his face and soft shoulders and Ivy agrees to hold the M&M's.

Now a woman and man are stepping through the automatic doors, the woman's face is just cream of tomato soup and crackers, not a face, though once of course it was a face, and it makes the back of Ivy's slim pretty neck go cold.

The man is perhaps late fifties. Round face. Glasses. Clean-shaven. Balding. Wears a rain-spotted green work uniform shirt and pants, a brown belt, worn, soft-looking. Sturdy thick waist.

Gordon steps away from the register and Ivy arranges the two packages of M&M's on the counter end to end like they are kissing. "These are his," she tells the checkout woman and looks back to the young guy and he is so shy he averts his eyes when he says, "Thank you."

Ivy sees Gordon reaching for the rack of free *Your Weekly Shopping Guide*s. She sees that the woman with no face wears gray sweatpants, sneakers, and a flowery top that might actually be a pajama top. Her hair is brown, touched with gray. Wet, of course. Her walk is crabbed. One eye is draped over by a satin-like wave of her red and silver skin. The other eye, her only visible eye, sits there brown and clear in the noseless stretched taffyish red mess, staring at, yes, Gordon St. Onge.

Gordon turns from the newspaper rack and goes directly to this woman and kisses her stiff terrible cheek. He says happily, "Hi, Ruth," and he looks into her single eye and smiles the same smile he used on the other woman, the expensive-looking cute one at the deli.

Ivy decides not to take pictures of this. Suddenly, she feels ridiculous. And her own good looks seem silly. Vacuous. Embarrassing. She sees that the woman's hands are also transformed, the right hand with the bone and muscle reshaped so that the hand perpetually points at the floor a few feet ahead of her.

Ivy sees that the man who accompanies her raises his hand and touches his chin as he speaks in a low voice to Gordon. Ivy sees that this man wears a wedding ring.

Gordon asks the couple, "You guys getting washed out over on the Boundary?"

And the man replies in a low voice, "Yep."

After a little chat in which the woman never speaks, just nods at everything, Gordon grips the man's upper arm in a brother-to-brother fashion, then releases, then turns for the door, newspaper under one arm, ambles out into the bellowing downpour and Ivy follows.

Gordon strides across the shining skirling pavement, in and out of violent inch-deep ponds, then turns abruptly, his loose shirt flaring. He looks at Ivy, who has dropped some distance behind him now. Their eyes don't exactly meet since the rain is smashing down harder by the second, a gray wall, a Niagara, a twinkling fortress, but there is at last his acknowledgment, which goes as follows: he pulls the bottle of aspirin from a chest pocket, struggles a while with the childproof cap and seal and fake cotton, pops a couple into his mouth, then holds out a palm, and the palm fills with rain like a cup, and he swallows his aspirin with this water, and he gives Ivy a squinched look like she is indeed giving him a headache, and then he walks away from her and the man and boy are waiting in the truck and as Gordon pulls open the door and climbs in, everything has become again too ordinary, and as the amber parking lights come alive and the truck rumbles out of the lot, the story leaves, profoundity leaves, newsworthiness leaves, and Ivy remains standing there in desolation.

Okay, so theatrics didn't win him. Or charm, of which Ivy has none. Nor has she ever perfected begging. But Gordon St. Onge *has* a weak spot. She sees it. *Weak man. Will cave in.* Ivy, the crowbar, yes! Her gift.

She runs back into the store and questions people about the Home School and Gordon St. Onge but none of them will open up to her, she just gets smiles and affectionate head shakes. No full sentences. No quotable remarks. *No weak spots.* Is the whole town sealed against her now, their loyalty to Gordon like sandbags against the storm? How far can Gordon St. Onge's brand of charisma go in protecting him? Ivy, once again, is pissed. Soggy and wet as she rides along in her sporty car, passing people on curves, tailgating, radio blaring now, drums clashing and bonking and yang yang yang, Ivy Morelli is warmed by her rage and, of course, planning her next move. The crowbar and hammer. Fuck theatrics. The fun is over.

Out in the world.

Somewhere in America, in a sunnier time zone, along a street with maple trees and parked automobiles and a helpful red light at the intersection, an SUV in a nice shade of tan whizzes along importantly. On it's back bumper, this message: MY CHILD IS A FAIRWAY REGIONAL HIGH SCHOOL HONOR STUDENT.

 The grays.

Even here in this galaxy of shadows, everything has vigor, molecules do-re-mi, protons in and out as rabbits now-you-see-them-now-you-don't wise guys. The queens of all matter are spinning and shivering, filled with the jelly of promise, little nice-guy microbes, even in backward time, pregnant with their ghosts.

Once ghosts were in everything here. Every atom bore a ghosty face, as gold will freckle certain rocks.

We grays are an advanced folk. Not much for gear, nor the "high" tech. We are as naked as . . . yes . . . ghosts. The barren interior of our craft is not impressive to the tool folk of this world. We are just sniffers, like dogs. It is our skin that reads and detects such as the turquoise deep blue symphony of Earth's nights . . . ahhh. We open the hatches of our craft and with the force of our bellies draw in the specimens to study, to test, to save in our monumental mission to document Earth's endangered ghosts.

The specimen compartments of our laboratory drip and overflow and twinkle. We select from open stretches of the buzzy fields, infant forests, and shaded brook sides the perished dragonfly, fish bone, brown leaf. Death. The ghosts treat us in a friendly manner. Hello! Hello!

But also we have stashed some *other* stuff, roadside finds: cans of the aluminum, plastic diapers from human babies' rears, concert tickets, tax bills, charge cards, canceled checks, Popsicle sticks, "floppy disks," Styrofoam cups, dental floss. We try to understand these samples, those that neither live nor die and therefore carry no ghosts.

Here now spread out on our laboratory table is a copy of the *Record Sun*. Flat as a pancake. Fresh off the press. Its mouth is very open, breathing. But no hello. Just paraphrases.

Even the trees the paper is made of, no pine ghosts remain, so raped and mortified, churned into a sulphurized turd. The rows of newsy words, the smelly ink makes our bones whir. We grays stand hunched elbow to elbow and the weariness of our findings causes vapors to grope grizzlishly up off our small, bald, newsprint-color heads as we agree that even the last page is terrible. The worst! Sports . . . yuck.

 Observe our Ivy being poisoned.

It is Friday. The end of a long hazy corrosively hot gunky funless day. Ivy returns to Egypt. Her little pseudo sports thing churns up into the St. Onge dooryard, stops next to the green-and-white pickup. No other vehicles in the lot. In the bed of the truck is a small cement mixer, gritty mucked-up plywood, and a mess of rope. Ivy takes mental note of these things but doesn't write anything down. Instead, still seated in her car, she reaches to the other bucket seat for an aluminum foil package and a bouquet of flowers she made; wallpaper petals and coat-hanger stems. She jerks her shoulder bag from the floor. She checks her light eye shadow and barely detectable lash thickener in the rearview and sees something moving, somebody in the doorway of the screen piazza, stepping down. Screen door slaps shut.

She steps like a fresh breeze from her car but pretends not to notice the sound of a heavy walk, the crunching of sand. She squares her shoulders and pretends to show a deep interest in nature. The warm sweet early evening is leaving off into warm sweet night, that never-ending twilight gray of June. Frogs are *glunk-glunk*ing nearby. Robins and wood thrushes madly tweedle from every direction.

No rest. Everything frantic and crazed and fertile. The bald rock summit of the near mountain is the last to give up the sun, glowing greenly gold. And that movement up there, slight and wavery. Another mystery contraption. The horrors of the Home School. Ivy sniffs the air.

She whirls around to face him just as he is ducking under the low limbs of the old ash and coming around the tailgate of his truck. He doesn't look pissed or wary but he's not smiling one of his various kinds of smiles, either, nor do his pale eyes have that sensuous grip on her eyes like the way he looked at all those women in the IGA, and none of his bewildered Tourette's-type blinking either. From under the visor of his billed cap he just looks at her in a direct way as if she were a tape measure stretched out along a short two-by-four. And he looks at her shoulder bag. Then back at her face, his face still expressionless.

She squares her shoulders again, stares him down, not a yearning soap opera stare, more like in a Western where this would be Main Street, and both he and she would have six guns.

His eyes lower to her feet, raising up across her dress to her beret, back down to the paper flowers. Her dress is dimpled cotton with a girlishly short full skirt. Blue and lavender check as from times when things were sturdy and well made, soft and stirring to the touch. And the beret, of course, he would remember that beret, stiff and black, squashed down low on her head, not a pretty angle. And what *are* those on her feet? Shiny black bootlets, patent leather, little buttons, heavy heels. Bought from a costume shop in some mall that sells everything? And really funny socks. Green and white candy stripes.

She insists, "There're no tools of the trade in this bag. Honest Injun." *Oops!* She squats down and dumps the contents of her shoulder bag out on the sand. "See? Just my personal beautifying equipment and these ol' addresses . . ." She flips through a little paisley notebook. "And many, many, many credit cards." She smiles a small hard smile. "I have perfect credit." As she sorts through the stuff, the homemade flowers tucked under one arm wag about.

With his arms crossed now, he stands there. His eyes sort of percolate in the shadow of his billed cap, which reads MOFFIT & SON/ PAVING & SEAL COAT. Maybe he is noticing something about our Ivy's forehead and chin and dark-lashed blue eyes. "Black Irish" and Italian? Maybe he is thinking of the long, long rivers of humanity that merge in little creeks and freshets all over the planet. Seeking more frontiers. Is this the direction of his thoughts? Or is he the punishing self-made prophet of a punishing God, his head howling with gooey illogical frettings and sheer hot disgust for Ivy Morelli, who represents all the freedoms and "disorders" of a cut-loose generation?

She gets to her feet, a mean defiant posture, small shoulders squared. "No frisking of the body. You'll just have to take my word."

He smacks a mosquito on his neck. Now a small smile. And now above one whiskered cheek, the eye gives way to several involuntary squint-blinks.

Up in the house the phone rings.

She says, "I've given up on you as a story. Honest Injun." (*Oops again!*) "I just want to . . . hear more of what the teacher has to say. I have come here to . . . oh . . . you know . . . be one of your followers . . . drink poison . . . pray . . . handle snakes . . . go to heaven." She scooches down again and stuffs the credit cards, comb, wallet, and little pouches and makeup tubes into her bag.

He sidles over to her car, places an open hand on the roof, and, in a sad voice, tells her, "I wanted to mention this before, that my mother has one just like this. Even the same color."

"Cool mother," Ivy says pleasantly.

"Yuh," he says sadly.

Ivy hefts her bag back into position, the strap in place over her shoulder, and pushes the foil package into his hands. "My offering, Allah."

He holds it up to the dying light to get a good look at it.

"Prune bread," she explains. "My sister's kids call it Junebug bread." She sighs happily. "You know." Chuckle. "If you use cranberries, it's Ladybug bread. Poppy seeds make it Black Fly bread."

He says, "I thank you."

She thrusts the boingy waggling paper flowers into his other hand.

He smells them. Deeply. "Mmmmmmmmmm."

A pair of mosquitoes claim Ivy's throat. She smooshes one. The other gets away.

He says, "Come on," and trudges along ahead of her to the house, which has only the same fluorescent light in the ell's kitchen windows as there was the last time she was here, a dim melancholy light. Up on the piazza, he holds the screen door wide for her. As she clomps up the steps in her heavy fearless goth shoes, he does a quick bow and swipes off his billed cap, paper flowers rustling, aluminum foil crinkling, and with a voice still sad says, "Enter," then stands back like a soldier, back flat against the door frame as she passes him. She glances down the long porch. No people. Just feeble rockers. Lawn chairs. Straight-back chairs. Steel folding chairs. Footstools and a couple of raggedy stuffed arm chairs.

No barking dogs or murmuring women inside.

She looks back up at her host's face. His beard and hair are darkened by wetness. He has just showered or something. And maybe a few doses of aspirin? He has a refreshed-tired-end-of-the-day look. He asks, "Coffee?"

She replies, "Decaf only . . . please."

"Okey-dokey."

Now he screws his billed cap back on purposefully and goes ahead of her into the house.

She follows. Again there's that mildewy summery rummagy old farmhouse smell. She looks around. Everything is the same as the last time, although there's another two or three layers she missed before, more tools, more paperwork, a box of kindling wood with a cardboard box of glass jars on top, and along in front of the mopboards are boots and empty plastic milk jugs, everything screaming with purpose. Yet nothing screams with scholarship, as a school ought to do.

Ivy wonders to herself, *What's that paint smell?* It mixes well with all the other smells swirling through the heat trapped in here from the long hot day.

And she asks herself, *Okay, so what is the definition of school, Ivy? Lots of plastic chrome-legged desks. Lined paper. Plain paper for math. Glossy texts updated as often as possible. American flag. Gold stars, the kind you lick. Fire extinguisher, chalk board, big clock that makes burping noises, hidden bell or buzzer that goes off when it's time for you to stand up, intercom for the principal to tell you the thought for the day and to announce assemblies and late buses, classroom smell, locker room smell, ketchuppy lunch smell. Surprise quizzes. Report cards. Computers. At least one.* She glances over at the boots. All adult-sized. None child-sized.

He finds an old empty one-gallon brown glass vinegar jug to stick the paper flowers in. The dim fluorescent light gives both his and her skin an officy papery-blue tinge, while making the flowers look real. He shakes the flowers so they wag around cheerily before he leaves them in an open window.

Right next to Ivy's dangling left hand is the small wooden table she remembers. As its centerpiece now, her Junebug bread is still wrapped in foil. Running her palm over the painted smoothness of this sturdy little table, it seems it's a different color than before. An unusual shade. Almost cerulean blue, like artists oils. And there, the chimney behind the woodstove, which she didn't even notice before. Enamel red. And there a door, crayon yellow. Yes, the storybook house where the giant lives, all the elements here for a medieval lesson, to charm, to instruct, to scare.

"Decaf. Decaf. Decaf," the giant chants, noisily ransacking his cupboards. *Clonk! Biff! Crinkle.*

So many windows. The old stiff wooden kind, painted thickly in . . . yes, three pinks . . . cotton candy, cherry, and Day-Glo, all screened. A few held up with bottles and sticks. Ivy steps over to the nearest one. Out there in the west is the last smear of creamy light behind that chirping complicated dark business of seemingly endless trees. She sighs. "I rented a place like this once. Old farmhouse." She rather speaks this to the window and the view and the tackily wallpapered and cluttered walls than to Gordon. "Only it was empty. Unfurnished. And I didn't have much stuff then. But the rent was cheap."

"What town?"

"Cornville."

He is standing with a teakettle. His bearded chin is raised. He looks confused, all that squint-blinking now in both eyes. And a drop of sweat or bath water moves out of his brown hair at one temple. Then, "Does regular coffee not set well with you?"

She spins around, crossing her arms under her small bustline, says in a husky way, "If I touch that stuff, I'll be doing bird calls and Elvis imitations till four in the morning."

No longer blinking, his pale eyes move over her funny beret, the silky even edges of her violet tinted dark hair. He gives the bill of his own cap a serious adjustment, again screwing it down tight, the printed word MOFFIT seesawing.

"Anything I can do to help, Gordon?"

He puts a blue flame under the kettle, says, "Naw. Thanks. You just relax." He comes over to the little table, pulls out a chair, and commands, "Sit."

She sits.

He squats down and feels roughly one leg of the table. "Watch out," he warns her. "It *should* be dry. But . . . it got a pretty heavy coat this time. Might be tacky." He smiles farawayishly, as though there may be some especially endearing story connected with this paint job.

He finds a place to stand, leaning back against an old corner hutch of knobbed doors and drawers next to the gas stove, pushes his cap back, crosses his arms over his chest, one leg out before the other, Viking at ease.

"The light here," Ivy says with a squint.

"Solar *heat*. Commercial *power*," he says. Then with an ugly grunt, "The electric octopus."

The what? Ivy's pointy top lip sort of vibrates, holding back.

Phone rings. The old black dial-type wall phone she has been squirming on the other end of so many times. He reaches for it, tips it to his ear with "yep"s and "uh-huh"s. Ivy watches him, his left side lighted by this osseous fluorescent light, the rest of him slipping off into warm shadow.

Okay, Ivy, she tells herself, *Check him out. Forget none of this. Details, please. Get him while he's off guard.* She stares. She memorizes his dark blue work pants, which look new. Really new, like still creased from the display rack, but his chambray work shirt is paled and frowzy from washings. And goofy. Yes, it seems rather poorly homemade. The phone looks small in his hand. Great big ol' son of a bitch with that face of a hundred expressions, who could snatch all the reporter pads he wants from little women, maybe even little men, without much effort expended. Ivy narrows her eyes and tsks. Except for these special features, he reminds her of so many you see around, hundreds of them out in the world with their dry knuckles and smashed nails, building and fixing, hefting and hawing, digging and tarring, making things float or fly, purr or roar, making things grow, cutting things down, loading them on, and always that billed plastic cap with the ads for the companies that own them, own their children, own their homes, their minds, and their hearts.

His belt buckle. A sun with a mouth that is either kissing or whistling a tune . . . or startled . . . you know, that "oh!" of surprise. Hammered-out copper. Good chance it's child-made. Like the shirt. No rings on his hands. No tattoos. No watch. Just a pair of reading glasses in the chest pocket, just the plain miracle of making it to your forties without obliteration.

Ivy frowns. She listens to the house. The antique dry-woody air isn't moving at all. She fans herself a little with the closed fingers of one hand.

He speaks one last "yep" then hangs up the phone, which immediately rings again, and he answers it and begins speaking the language of electronics, intermingled with English words like "Fred" and "Wednesday night" and "a carloada them from Monmouth."

The teakettle whistles sharply. He reaches and twists off the burner knob while still tuned in to his caller, yet when Ivy looks up the next time, he is looking right at her face with unmistakable tenderness.

She flushes deeply.

When he finally says, "Yep, bye," he goes to the drain board and makes a fuss with some mugs and spoons.

Ivy asks, "Where are the nice women who I met the other night, Gordon?"

He has his back turned to her now. He shrugs. "Damned if I know." He glances around the room. "Lotta doors here, you see. Sometimes . . . you know . . . it's like those old Charlie Chaplin movies. You'd be put to mind of them here." He turns and wags his eyebrows. He stoops and sniffs the paper flowers passionately as he passes them once, zigzagging around the kitchen in search of sugar. He doesn't know where the sugar is in his house, Ivy notes.

She fiddles with her necklace, mind brewing.

The phone rings. Hearing the person's voice, he hoots, then, "Vic! Holy shit! Watcha up to?" and then a whole long series of "yep"s. He turns and grins and wags his head apologetically at Ivy. But then his face goes slack and he's really listening ever so keenly to whatever the caller is saying, listening with a kind of hard edge, with pale and narrowed eyes fixed on Ivy. She doesn't like the feeling. It is as if they are talking about her.

When he's off the phone, he positions two beehive-shaped glazed red and green pottery cups on the table and strokes one side of his heavy mustache thoughtfully. "Do you trust me not to be wicked and give you the real stuff, dear?"

"No, I don't trust you," she says thickly. "But it'll be you who suffers if I get the caffeine gabs."

"What would that be like?" he asks. He glances at her hands as he sloshes hot water into the cups of measured coffee. He is giving her hands a careful study. And now, yes, he is looking slyly at her low-cut neckline and all the bareness of her collarbones, and the necklace, all those brightly painted wee butterflies with wings lifted nervously for takeoff and he asks, "Wood?"

And she says, "Yes."

And he asks, "Who made it?" And he draws closer.

And she says, "I don't know. I bought it. At a shop. In Vermont."

He turns away, carrying the kettle back to the stove, murmuring, "The miracle of human hands and hearts."

She dabs her sweaty top lip with an open palm.

He returns with the jar of sugar he has found, a jelly jar of cream, and a nice print saucer. Little roosters, hens, and ducks marching around the border of the saucer. Too small for the Junebug bread actually, which he is unwrapping. Upon this small dish, he bestows his most crazed, penetrating look. He jerks a knife from a leather case on his belt. "Oh, what the hell," he says good-naturedly and saws the loaf into rough quarters, stuffs one whole quarter into his mouth.

Ivy's eyes widen on the whiskery bulge of his loaded left cheek. She crosses her legs, spins her foot.

He circles the room once, chewing noisily. He tosses his billed cap onto a pile of papers on one desk. He circles the table with Ivy stirring and sipping her coffee. He seems distracted, his mind on something urgent and elsewhere. But now he is jerking out the chair opposite Ivy, then sits, looking too big for this chair, though comfortable. The sad blue light from the area of heaped desks illuminates Ivy's face and throat and the back of Gordon's head and the pale shoulders of his old soft-looking blue chambray shirt, yeah, those slopy peasant shoulders.

Ivy sips more coffee. She lifts off her beret and places it on the table. Okay, bit hot tonight for a covered head. Hot room and burning questions.

"Aren't you really going to grill me?" he asks.

"I said I wasn't."

"I'm not a trusting man."

She tsks. "Well, since I'm not a trusting woman, it's only fair that you get to be distrusting, too."

He looks down at his coffee.

She says, "Okay, if it'll make you happy. How old are you?"

"Thirty-nine."

She smiles. "I guessed pretty close."

He snorts, then says darkly, "The nines are hard."

She sips more coffee. "You make good coffee, Allah."

"What's your boss like? Hard to please? Or kinda laid back about all this?"

"He's a liberal."

Gordon grins weirdly. "Liberal? I know not what that means. Tell me."

She plays along. "He's *for* things."

"As opposed to against," Gordon offers lightheartedly, his strange eyes steady on her face.

She smiles. "He's *for* people. He's not into the great white conquering male thing."

Gordon leans back and slips his hands off the table to rest one on each thigh and says, "I am. I am for the great white conquering male thing."

"It figures," she says with disgust. "I mean, after all, God is a big white conquering male, right?" She sees a barely detectable flutter disturb one of his eyelids. It's hard to tell when he's teasing or serious. He is not consistent and so far presents only extremes. And riddles. And jokes. And weird parables. She glances at the prune bread remains. "You can have *all* of it," she tells him. "I have to watch those ol' calories." She slides the little plate toward him. Now she spies a row of six-packs of unopened beers underneath one of the desks, the curved necks shyly defined in the shadows of their hiding place. She looks back into the man's eyes. "You are a scary guy. I'll give you that. And this place . . . it must know some terrible heartache."

Gordon St. Onge looks at a closed door just to the right of the red chimney. "I'll give you that."

She says, "I've been getting a lot of calls and messages from worried people. They're saying some disturbing stuff about you and your school. They've been calling your administrative district superintendent here, even the school board, calling the police, calling child protective workers . . . calling me!"

He says evenly, "There's no school here." But she sees his face has gone drywall color and some wrath, some force is inflating his neck. Seems this news is upsetting him. He slides his hands from his thighs to his knees, rocks slowly forward and back a time or two on the back chair legs. On his jaws between the gray and brown hair of his beard, the sheen of a fearsome real sweat.

She continues, "Most don't identify themselves to me out of fear . . . of you . . . and your people. Some sound a little overexcited. But others sound like just regular nice folks who have heard and seen some things. They say they have proof . . . or at least know people who have seen bruised children, pregnant girls who you've forced yourself on through a rather self-serving definition of the Old Testament or some such. And drugged children . . . *dead* children. They claim you work kids here like slaves, make them use dangerous tools, machinery, and animals. There's mention of pagan worship, animal sacrifice . . . though it seems screwy to me how you work that into the Bible, the Jesus part anyway. And they tell me you are . . ." She closes her eyes. ". . . stockpiling weapons." She opens her eyes.

He is stroking both sides of his mustache with the spread fingers of one hand, grooming the coffee out of it, and just plain grooming.

Ivy sets her mug down with a *thwonk*. Empty. She says, "Those are serious charges."

He places his hands on the table and looks down between his spread knees at the shadowed floor. "And what luck have they in riling authorities?"

Ivy shrugs.

"What do you think? A little or a lot?" He presses her on this.

"Seems not a lot."

His expression remains frozen.

She says, "But you know, some authorities are not quick to act. They sit on paperwork until someone from above pokes 'em with a stick . . . usually for some political reasons . . . depending. You know, everything is politics. The people who call me are frustrated. That's all I know."

He is back to looking at the floor. Won't look her in the eye.

She says almost squeakily, "Why aren't you staunchly defending yourself about this stuff?"

Now he looks up at her with his searing almost-cross-eyed scrutiny. "Those accusations don't make sense. It's as though they speak from Alice in Wonderland, where big is little and little is big and rabbits and cats and playing cards talk and time goes in reverse."

The hair on the back of Ivy's neck moves spiderishly.

Gordon stands up. He stretches. Pushes his chair back into place. "More coffee?"

"No, thank you." She raises her chin high and her dark bowl of hair shimmers with a line of light across one side.

He goes to lean against the red enamel chimney, the bluish soulless infliction of fluorescent light now on his face and front, purpling the chimney. It's only Ivy's guess that it is really red.

"So," Gordon says. "What are some of Elvis's best songs? 'Hound Dog'? 'Heartbreak Hotel'?"

Heat flares along Ivy's arms. Her face. She turns and looks straight into Gordon's grin, his big blue-white evil grin, all those teeth. "You tricked me! This coffee is real! Show me the decaf jar, you worm!" She leaps from her seat, hurries to the cupboard. "Haven't you got any better light in this so-called kitchen!"

"Well, maybe that's the problem," he suggests. "I couldn't see to read the jar very well. Or maybe it's just old age." He pats the glasses in his chest pocket. "I forgot to use my specs."

She flings open the nearest cupboard door. The shelves are almost bare. No cereal. No cans of green beans or jars of applesauce. No boxes of elbow macaroni. Mostly just bare space and . . . these . . . whatever these are . . . a jar of peppercorns. A label-less jar of tan stuff . . . cinnamon sugar maybe? No, too powdery. Something ancient and metamorphed and creepy. Anything goes here in this realm. And yes, there's plain ol' coffee *with* caffeine. She slams the cupboard door. She gives her knuckles a boyish crackling. She shouts, "WHAT IF I HAD HEART TROUBLE OR SOMETHING?!!!!!!!!!!"

"You didn't mention heart trouble . . . just the Elvis and the bird thing. I wanted to see that."

She clomps along with her heavy-heeled 1800s boot-shoes back to the table. She sees through a back window a wriggling glimmer of light high up in the trees of the near mountain, light that she hadn't noticed a few minutes before. She steps closer. "You have neighbors in the woods up there?"

"A regular metropolis," he admits. "You—"

She interrupts, "So that's not your land?"

"It's the Settlement."

"Shit!"

"Some call it the Home School. I used to try to discourage that. But, oh, well. School is home. Home is school. Not to ever be separated lest one die. Like the body itself. You take a sharp knife and cut the heart from the chest of a living person. You know what happens, dear, don't you? You know what happens when the miracle of arteries and nerve endings and a happy jig and smiley face is eliminated from the heart?"

"It dies!" she answers desperately. "That's what you want me to say, right?"

"Yay, I say unto you, *my* family lives."

The biblical language, albeit old English, which Ivy has been ready to pounce on, but all she does is squinch one eye.

Something flumps onto the floor upstairs.

Phone rings.

Gordon St. Onge crosses the old floor and reaches for the receiver and speaks deeply, "H'lo. Yep. It is he." Pause. "Yeah. Sorry about that." He chuckles. Then shuffles through the curled pages of a giant desk calendar. "Yep. Thirty lambs. And some with—" He listens. "Yep." He listens. He pulls a rag from his work pants pocket and snorts something from his nose into it. "Yep, I know. Uh huh. Uhhh, could be long 'round then." Listens while pulling at his somewhat large nose some more with the rag. "I don't know where you can come by that but I'll check. Might be Aurel did that last year but I know as a rule, he doesn't lettem go for that. I'm only going by his order sheet here. Maybe . . . yuh. He's good at that." Gordon chuckles heartily.

There's the *eeeeeeerrrk* of a swollen door opening at the far end of the kitchen, the darkest end, to the right of the glossy chimney and woodstove and wood box. Now a narrow hallway shows and steep attic stairs. This draws both Gordon's and Ivy's attention, and Gordon's face changes and his expression is none of those expressions Ivy has been witness to before.

It is a girl dressed in nothing but a white sleeveless undershirt, the kind with straps and a little bitty satinesque bow. And flowerprint underpants. The girl's arms and legs are long and golden brown. Could she be ten? Eleven? Twelve? She walks straight to Gordon and leans into him. Then she turns to face Ivy. She stares at Ivy. Eyes large and sulky and black. She is clearly a mix of Africa and old Europe and probably American Indian . . . or something like that . . . the great American love-hate story. This child is breathtakingly beautiful. Dark hair floofed into a soft loose curly sphere. Long neck. Her voice is rough and deep as Ivy's own. "I thought I heard Mumma."

Gordon says, "Okay, Bryce . . . you can count on it. Thanks. Yep. Bye." Hangs up the phone. Slips one hand into the middle of the girl's back as she turns. And he pulls her to him. Ivy's eyes settle on the two of them with smoky regard.

Gordon checks the clock between two windows. He says, "Jane, I've got to go."

And Jane pleads, "WAIT!" pushing her chin into his shirt. "I want to read you a story."

"No reading now, dear. I have to go."

"Don't goooooooo," Jane pleads weakly.

"Oh . . . you mean you've changed your mind and want to come?" Jane wrinkles her nose.

"We'll read tomorrow," he tells her, guiding her along back toward the attic door.

But the girl resists, slumps weakly, gripping the front of his old worn-pale shirt. "It's lonely, Gordie!"

"Gin is staying with you. You like Gin."

"She's asleeeeep. She won't DO anything."

"That's what night is for, dear."

With narrowed eyes, she asks, "Then why do you do the stupid *thing* tonight?"

Ivy breaks in. "Is there something I can help with?"

This is ignored.

Gordon lifts the girl easily up over the front of his shirt to his shoulder, cave-man style, and she moans. "Pleeeeeeze Gordie! Just one book!" And Ivy can hear the husky-voiced piteous pleading all the way up the creaking stairs and now crying in the room above . . . and then a scream . . . and sobs . . . another scream . . . a lot of sobs . . . heart-breaking sobs . . . and something hitting the floor with a *thwonk*. A book? No, something much larger than a book.

Ivy, take note of this opportunity, she commands herself and scoots over to the fluorescent-lighted desk of piled papers and calendar pages and mail. A THICK manila folder (yes, stone-age filing folder) with CLIMATE CHANGE scrawled (as if by a bear) across its middle. An old yellowed book lies open. Old-style 1940s print. Dull-looking as all hell . . . *Calls for the Sub Treasury plan by Alliancemen were met with vituperation by both parties, sometimes murder . . .*

And what's this? She peels up one edge of a piece of scrap paper that is clipped to the page. A man's handwriting in blue ballpoint ink reads: *Waving the bloody shirt.* Then scribbled below are names, including *James Hogg* and *Charles Lamb.* Cute. And maybe there's a Pete Turkey and Bob Chicken and Madeline Cow. Oh, and here's another scribbled-on piece of scrap. *Farmer's Tribune.* But what really begs to be investigated are the three old-timey rotary files, the thousand-card-apiece kind, thick and bristling with white, yellow, pink, and blue cards. One rotary is flipped open to:

> *Nelson, Linda*
> *Turner, Maine CSA active*

Next one is:

> *Newell, Rick and Eve-Lynn*
> *CSA Egypt   pick up*

Then:

> *Norton, A.*
> *CSA Egypt   pick up*

Each of these includes a phone number. Some have mailing addresses, some with incomplete addresses. No e-mail. No fax.

And what, Ivy wonders, is a CSA?

Now:

> *Nugent, Tim and J.*
> *Peppy G. Route 113*
> *Fryeburg 4 units*
> *14-foot rotor diameter, 6kw RPM-v-current output*
> *monitor brake, √ surplus power.*

Ivy leans closer. Turns the file to face her. She flips a few cards.

> *Perkins, Don*
> *Hiram Hill Road left, right, left by burned camp*
> *one existing*
> *42 inch diameter*
> *25 watts*
> *15 mph*
> *Tip up*
> *No program.*

Ivy flips a card. But now there is a real bloodcurdling shriek upstairs. Ivy snatches her hand back fast. She heads back to the table, her heavy shoes making stealth a bit of a job. *Bloody shirt. Vituperation. Lamb. Hogg. No program. And Jane.* What to make of Jane?

In a while Gordon reappears, forcing the *errrnk*ing swollen door shut behind him, and says tiredly, "That was Jane."

Ivy nods, waiting for more, waiting for an earnest explanation of the sobs and shrieks, but he says no more.

Ivy says pleasantly, "She's a gorgeous kid."

He goes to the table and gathers up spoons and cups. He places her beret with care into her hands.

Ivy asks, "How old is she?"

"Six."

"She's tall. Really big for six, isn't she?"

He makes fast work of putting the sugar and jar of cream away. He buttons the top button of his shirt. There's something in his teeth.

Crunching. He is not interested in making conversation about Jane. And yet he looks at Ivy with such tenderness, apologetic, almost fawning, a look she's seen on his face before, even before tonight, the day of the merry-go-round.

She says, "Well, I see you're getting ready to head out. And me . . . all caffeined up and no place to go but home."

He smiles, blinking now, pushes something into his mouth. "I'll walk you to your car." Again his teeth crunch on something.

Ivy presses. "Where on earth are you going? I guess I'm not allowed to know, huh?"

He takes her arm gently, really gently, and steers her toward the door. She sees the aspirin bottle in his other hand. He is eating the things like candy. He says, "Don't be mad."

She says, "I'm mad."

He says, "How mad?"

She says, "Real mad."

He hangs his head with theatrical chagrin.

She pulls away from his hand and scoots ahead of him out onto the dark piazza, hefting her bag more securely onto her shoulder. There, only a few feet from the open door, are two men. She gasps. How long have they been there? One is standing slouchily. One is sitting still in a rocker. The one who is standing is young, maybe nineteen. Thin. Deep-set eyes. Too deep. In the near dark he looks skeletal but in a way that skeletal is appealing, sort of. If you can appreciate a wraith. Ivy can make out that he is wearing two belts, one a gun belt. Dark holster. And darker, the handle of a gun. His long mountain-man beard is black. Thin. Just a few long, long scribbles cast over the front of his dark plaid shirt. The textured dark edges of this young guy transfuse amicably with the summer night. Not in a buttery way, but slinky. He just looks at Ivy, no hello, no nod. And for once, Ivy is dumbstruck. The man in the rocker is older, forties, clean shaven. In fact, he's starkly shaved. Like the winner of a shaving contest. His jaws look hard and glassy and so white he kinda glows against the dark porch behind him. But he smiles at Ivy. And he says, "How do?" or "Hello," but so softly, it's more like a mime.

Gordon takes Ivy's hand, leads her down the steps, screen door slamming behind, now out across the twilit yard to her car, the *cheep*ing and *gloink*ing of frogs so close it is all around, over and under, a universe of ancient sound, older than music, old, timeless, but oh, no, not permanent; as we know, it *could* be eclipsed, it *could* be erased by the megahuman footprint, or so it is said. And Ivy says, "You don't trust me. I mean you *really* don't trust me."

He looks up at the sky, as if for rain. No sign of rain.

All of the field (crowned by the unseen merry-go-round) is fireflies. Sailing along and winking, smearing trails of their hiccuppy "wattage," their one-of-a-kind sex appeal, so the glowery, weedy, gray-flush dusk between them looks black.

She sighs. She squashes her beret down over her hair, right down to her eyebrows.

"It's nothing personal," says he.

"Can I . . . come here again?" She despises the snively weak little-girl way her voice is coming out.

He steps up to her car and opens the door for her.

She ducks into the seat, pulls the door shut.

He reaches down through the open window, feels along the door handle, snaps the lock in place, like tucking her in, father-like. He explains, "Everyone is welcome here. Absolutely everyone. We are not elitist here. We are not a closed society. We're just a family. I have always encouraged people to visit—"

She interrupts. "Except the press." She gives him a big tight smile. "You do not want the press."

He says firmly, "I do not want the press." He stands back away from her car now.

She starts up the engine, which is still new and obedient but has a kind of cheap toy-like buzz.

He tells her, "People out there where you live and work . . ." He gestures toward the west where the sticky summer daylight that had haloed the mountain for so long has finally died. Just that ghostly solstice gray. "They have been agreeable to a certain kind of order. A new order. Or rather an old order made more orderly, like, you know, gourmet here, garbage there. They've gottem a collection of laws that are unanswerable. Their power has no face. There are a collection of laws and a collection of sickening events that are both nature-made and man-made, but both exacted by that faceless power. That *system* that has no heartbeat but is alive. And the media are an arm of that power. You, my friend, no matter what you do, it will always turn your hand for you . . . as long as you—" He stands up straighter, grins sheepishly, wipes the top of his hand across his whiskery mouth, now makes a gesture like *forget everything I just said.* He blows up his cheeks around a wooshy sigh. He reaches in and rests his open hand on her beret, endearingly. The father. "Drive slowly, little one." He backs away, eyes into her eyes, then heads for the house.

 The grays.

Her scarlet craft buzzes away. We follow at a safe distance, *our* craft fueled not with sparks or smoke but with the circulatory currents of ourselves, the technology of our living ghosts, gray as dust, tender and rubbery as an exhale. So maybe we cause the June leaves to stir a little.

 Ivy in her car a mile away from the St. Onge place, thinking aloud.

"He really *is* a nut. Psychotic or something. Holy cow stars! I'm lucky to be alive."

 Observe our Ivy being poisoned (yes, *really* poisoned this time).

She is no longer afraid. Just mad. The cheap but earnest engine that pulls her along sings as she turns in to the driveway of a real estate agency in North Egypt, makes a wide turn, then out on the road, heads back to the hills.

When the first stone walls of Gordon St. Onge's land reappear, Ivy pulls the car off and parks on an angled sandy shoulder. She locks up, leaving her beret on the seat, hoists her bag, and starts walking. "Fuck his goddamn eyes, that arrogant son of a bitch!" she snarls.

With no flashlight, she can't see anything but a paleness of pavement, which is similar to the saggy gray solstice sky above, which shows along the thin squiggly gap between the overhead trees. The best she can do is feel her way along with one foot. When the first car comes along, headlights burning through the ferny semifoggy downhill distance, she hurtles into the foliage and waits for it to pass. She has hurtfully found out there is a deep culvert here. Rocks, roots, stumps, mooshy moss, mushy ooze, and an aluminum can. And probably a nation of wood ticks on every leaf while every leaf is sweating greenly, swallowing her legs and arms, her face and neck, creeping, crawling, ruffly exhalings as it sniffs our Ivy's ears and hair.

After about twenty-five cars and twenty-five ordeals with the culvert and that complicated sticky embrace of the woods, all in less than ten minutes, she realizes there's a suspiciously large amount of traffic tonight for Heart's Content Road, a road in the middle of nowhere, *leading to nowhere,* right?

 From among the hundreds of letters and writings of Gordon St. Onge, boxed, filed or piled around his kitchen and rooms, is this smoodgey carbon copy of a lengthy philosophical letter dated from the mid-1990s. It is addressed to Herb Butler of Berkeley, California, a professor of Victorian-era literature, and one of Gordon's ten trillion old friends. Eventually, it'll wind up in the hands of "authorities" who "attend" the Settlement's subversive public events over the months to come. Here is an excerpt:

. . . How can we explain the imaginations of children, that persistent stuff that comes from a place other than our instruction, comes from the heart of play, comes raw? We erroneously assume children know nothing. We assume we fill their emptiness with our aspirations, disciplines, experiences, laws, and mortal dreads. But maybe we only push aside rudely what they are born knowing, because surely they're born knowing the several million years of the human saga, which has been scratched like frost on their shining DNA . . .

As if the merry-go-round had come alive, and, yes, Ivy is here. It is almost dawn.

The marching army is warming up, all soldiers armed with nothing less than a good heavy stick. Some have rapiers with ornately carved handles. And guns. All fashioned out of wood, foil, cardboard, or metal tubing. Orders are shouted. The army mills about, however. And nobody listens.

The long connected porches around the Settlement's quadrangle tremble and creak. The clatter of swords and various armaments and banners are flashing in the rosy light of open doorways and the rows of citronella candles set along a vast sill. Solemn tweedling of three or four recorders. One nice flute, someone with talent. Countless merry reckless kazoos. More shouted orders. More milling. Hours pass. Soon it will be dawn. But for now the fireflies make you dizzy because, across and upward, the wide murky fields and sky seem to have reversed themselves, mad flashing stars below, murk above. But there has not been a *perfect* switch. That sticky piece of meatless bone in the bluish broth up there. That is the waning moon.

A man takes chewing gum out of his mouth and leans forward to fussily attach it to a coffee mug on the porch sill, then stands, adjusts his Vietnam War bush hat, and says, "I guess t'iss iss t'e time." (Incidentally this is the fellow Ivy had seen in the truck with Gordon and the tyke that rainy day.)

Men and women rise slowly, reluctantly, from chairs while others step out from the many lighted doors. More have assembled on the quadrangle and parking lot, those who are still arriving from elsewhere, from "out in the world," meaning mostly other parts of Egypt. Or Brownfield, maybe.

"Ready for this?!" one voice calls in a spongy, tired voice and maybe a little walk-the-plank resignation.

"Ready or not!!!!" a laughing voice calls back.

In many hands, many flashlights. But see the night isn't black, not true night, only that smelterish dun, wide-open, swollen, dizzy June, the Great Pause.

Now the low BRUOOOOOOOOOOMMMMMMMMs of a massive drum, five or six languidly-spaced beats, then nothing.

A baby makes an ugly sound, getting ready to really complain.

Motherly voice comforts, "Sweeeeeeeee."

The army clomps off the many porches onto the grass and brick pathways, churns into the parking area between the Quonset huts, between the clumps of visitors, maintaining grave soldierly expressions.

"There they go," a thin scrawl of a voice observes, an elderly voice.

The men, women, and children who have arrived in cars, trucks, jeeps, and on a few good-looking Harleys are now mixing with the Settlement folk, joining in step behind the army, adding more flashlight beams and lanterns to the undark. And now a coordinated clinking of scores of spoons. *Clinka! Chink! Chink!*

A huge form swirls past, caped and hooded in black, all but the face, which is made up in greasepaint like a skull.

The big drum BRUOOOOOOOOOOMMMMMMMMs.

See other huge shapes with faces made monsterific! The look of meanness is all around.

Several small buggy-sized cars humming like refrigerators cut slickly through the procession. The drivers of these cars have paper bag faces or papier-mâché heads or greasepaint or rubber masks in varying degrees of hideousness and splendor. One has dozens of tiny yarn braids in all colors of the rainbow. The little cars sport dim headlights that bounce over the rough ground and make a broad stagy spectacle of the backs of people's legs and their rears and the faces of toddlers turning around to stare. *Chink! Chinka! Chink!* hail the spoons.

Mosquitoes hunt for flushed salty skin.

Mosquitoes *find* flushed salty skin.

The recorders don't seem to be trying to play a real tune.

The swords are restless.

The marching feet are out of step.

Clomp! Clomp! Rattle-rustle-clink-clank! Chinka! Chink! Tromp! Tromp! Scuff. Scuff. They march east. Then upward.

And Ivy is among them, amazed.

Yes, she had stood with them for those hours before their ascent. And some of the women recognized her. Offered her goldenrod tea. *No, thanks.* Given her a tall jar of heavenly cool water. Down it went.

But now they have begun the march. They stick close to her so she can walk in the wash of their ceremonial flashlights. She has seen that the two short square white-haired women (the ones who had "welcomed" her in Gordon's kitchen a couple days ago) work their spoons deftly, practiced. One is dressed as a cowboy: chaps and a Wyatt Earp hat. The other wears that familiar Grand Canyon T-shirt but with a Minnie Pearl paper-flower hat. Close behind them, unfamiliar women ring pretty bells and back at the rear of the long river of marchers, a single cowbell has been insistently clanking.

Now a *boing*ing wish-wash of many more flashlights sunny-up this rutted lane, heading up through the woods. Actually, the humid sticky cobweb of sky is now throwing new light enough to see quite well by without all these persistent flashlights on Ivy's feet for gawdsakes. Ivy hurries way ahead. Oops! Ivy on all fours in a rutty roughy stone-strewn sort of pit trap.

Voices rain down from above.

"Oh, dear!" and "You okay?!" and "You hurt?"

There are dogs, of course. The long-tailed kind, mostly with black Lab, golden retriever, pit bull, and Rottweiler connections, tails tuned like stiff rear antennas and tongues ribbon-like and hanging from the sides of their mouths. They are interested in how Ivy is not upright. And, seeming to be everywhere at once, are countless small white dogs with pushed-in faces, curled tails, and pale-lashed pig eyes. The Willie Lancaster dogs. Ivy brushes herself off as she stands. *HAW! HAW!* "Okay, sport!" she dismisses the nearest ugly white thing slobbering on her sock. Kids offer condolences. The women worry she's broken a bone. *HAW! HAW!* Ivy's good cheer settles the air. "Leaping alligators, I'm not even going to sue you!" *HAW! HAW!*

Ivy intends to memorize. No questions. Just the sleuth with her senses flaring. She sees, marching at the head of the army now, a king. Wears a small crown with enormous jewels, a small purple robe with a realish-looking ermine border. And small sneakers. "Ho! Hey ho!" he bawls. Or maybe it's a she.

Trees close in, monsterific.

The pale solstice night gets tighter, and, yes, nighter, would seem like pitch-darkness to unadjusted eyes, the utter squares of brilliance of the Quonset hut bays sliding away behind. Now the rutted lane

rises up sharply. The true march up the mountain begins. The larger
human forms can be heard at times to be really huffing, not keeping
up with the fast-paced army. Everyone burns with rivers of sweat and
feeding mosquitoes and hardworking hearts.

From out of the leafy almost-darkness someone's watch flickers
red digits.

A tricorn hat passes.

"Who are *yooooooo*?" a small voice wonders of its companion but
there is no reply.

Two raccoon-tail hats. And a head with waggling antennae like a
fairy or an elf. These hurry past. Ivy's brain records.

"Ho! Ho! Hey ho hee!" the small king in the distance ahead is
wailing.

From the rear, pressing onward, a tall youth dressed like a biker
(maybe he *is* a biker) and another tall teen, not a good sport, wearing just jeans and a basketball-type shirt in a shameless exhibition of
plainness. The teens, much taller people than the soldiers of the army,
hang together in a tight group as if unprecedented natural disaster
might separate them. One of these teen girls is so blonde, her hair
is just tumbling watery ice. Another girl, also quite blonde, wears a
black robe like a judge. These teens go at a faster clip than Ivy and
her escorts, and soon they are merged into the elbows, shoulders, legs,
and weird heads up ahead, and then merged into coiling mashy dark
gray dawn and crisscrossing light beams.

No childly voice asks the usual question, *Are we there yet?* After
twenty-five minutes of this climb, it is a few lower voices that ask it.

Now the drum picks up. The BRUOOOOOMMMMMs closer together, quickening the sense of drama, and now a crashing of many
small drums and the perfect rhythm of at least fifty sets of spoons, but it
seems to Ivy like thousands . . . CHINK-CHINK-CHINKA-CHINK!
CHINK-CHINK-CHINKA-CHINK! BRUOOOOMMMM . . .

Meanwhile, kazoos buzz merrily with tunes that don't match. Ivy
sort of loves the kazoos.

Up ahead, the woods on either side are ready to part. Ah, yes, there
the treeless rock summit of the mountain against the whitening sky.

    . . . CHINK-CHINK-CHINKA-CHINK! CHINK-CHINK-
CHINKA-CHINK! BRUOOOOOOMMMMMM . . .

At least a hundred voices begin a chant, imperfect and layered, toddlers, kids, and teens, women and men, each layer a dark ribbon drawn through the riddle-like core of the whole. Each of Ivy's questions have become balloons, too full. The whole scene spins. The human sound is impermeable. "COMMMMME SUNNNNNNNN . . . COMMMMMME SUNNNNNNNNN . . . COMMMMMM- MMME SUNNNNNNNN . . ." Over and over and over with the BRUOOOOMMMMM and the tweedles and the CHINK- CHINK-CHINKA-CHINK! and the heavy breathing between and the yeowling of babies and now two more electric buggies come humming past, straining and jerking over the ruts and rocks, a masked youth at the wheel of each. And to each, a passenger, a crone or a geezer.

The last one is a buggy, styled like an ATV, bigger tires, less luxury, but humming quietly like the rest. Who is the lucky passenger, legs dangling? Ivy can see the bald eyeless head and patient shoulders of an ancient damaged and blinded man, his arms around the driver, the sweet thick night-dawn forced across his cheeks and skull. No mask. Just a star of dark paint on his forehead. And he smiles steadily, serenely, though the rough ride jounces and thrashes him.

Ivy has a flashback to the IGA and the woman with tomato soup and crackers for a face. What is it that makes Gordon St. Onge purr over life's lost or weird or badly damaged creatures? Kindness? Of course. Of course. Mr. St. Onge is a kindly person. Right? But those women in the kitchen the other night, stopping in a busy day to help a small dog. Eerily ordinary people.

CHINKA-CHINKA "COME SUNNN."

Everyone is itchy. Damp. Everyone trying to keep in step and keep up with the chanting. An elbow brushes Ivy's, passing by. An iridescent robe flicks against her leg, passing by. A man with a papier-mâché palomino horse's head stumbles past. The chant goes on, "COM- MMMMMMMME SUNNNNNNNN . . . COMMMMMMMME SUNNNNNNN . . ." and the sound of it is as something before memory, before calendars and computers, before plastic, before even the wheel and the flint and the knife, older than greenly lit waters, out from the first mating, before the first troubled cry. Old as June frogs. And in the distance, behind Ivy, way down below, some mashy unmoving water beyond the Settlement, frogs' voices continue, continue, continue unbroken.

The sky is growing more pale, like nervousness. Some of the soft June stars are drowning in it. A hundred yards away the first brave wood thrush tweedles and rattles out his watery soprano. The terrible masks and hats and tails and wigs all flood past, Ivy among the slower marchers, these dropping way back. A huge papier-mâché grasshopper head rides on a slim teen girl's body. A shirtless teen boy wearing a necklace of warty gourds painted silver and rusty small old-timey oil cans, his face painted primary red, keeps washing his weak flashlight over certain faces to make them complain. "Squeeze *me!* Squeeze *me!*" a phoebe pleads from distances, some woodshed or cottage eave, his castle. Now robins are warming up. Now the teacher bird, "Chee*churr!* Chee*churr!*"

Ivy itches. Ivy hurts. But whenever anyone gets a look at her face in the sloshy beam of a waved flashlight, she smiles. A preteen girl shines a flashlight directly on Ivy's striped socks and heavy 1800s button-up boot-shoes and nods fast and approvingly, thinking, of course, that this is a costume.

The sky takes on the look of pearly day.

Up ahead, filling the sky . . . what is it? A fifty-foot structure of wood and steel, its blades and turbine at rest. A windmill designed in the way of the "old countries," with a wooden door you can enter. And all around this structure are a dozen or so modern steel derrick two-blade windmills, one or two in the style of upright egg beaters. The rest can't be serious. About thirty chest-high little windmillesque sculptures. Made from old table legs, wire, broom handles, tree limbs. Mostly tipi-style. Some pink. Some zebra striped. One gold, a true brother of one of those merry-go-round beasts. And yes, some with heads meant to turn in restless air. Kiddie-tech. Could *this* be meant as school?

The armed and chanting army is the first to reach the summit . . . and dogs, of course. The army circles around on the edge of the highest drop-off of rock that overlooks the east, the narrow end of the pond that's known as Promise Lake, and the village of North Egypt.

The chanting army is sticky. It is a grave and beaten-looking army, flushed, wide-eyed, jiggling with nerved-up overtired leg willies, gummy hair, overdressed or barely dressed, bug-bitten, bleeding and itchy, bruised, swollen, ripped and torn, all smelling like hot copper pennies and the unslept night, and a cheery warm lipstick smell from several sources, which are those faces glorified with zigzags of crimson Avon. Giving the center of this army its great eminence is a single orange plume rising out of a World War II army helmet. No member of this army is over four feet tall. Ivy has been noting all of this. Indeed, the evil of militarism seems not to be discouraged here. Evil? Or ignorance? Or what? What could be worse? Ivy narrows her eyes.

More chanting painted faces arrive at the summit. And now the teens in their fraternal clump. And now the adults. Casual, mostly flop-eared dogs are everywhere, looking pleased. The electric cars hum to a stop. Slowly, slowly the light of dawn is now framed in meaty red clouds in the east and the chanting of high and deep voices intensifies. "COMMMMMMMME SUNNNNNNNN!!!! . . . COMMMMMMM-MME SUNNNNNNNN!!!!!! . . ." CHINK! BRUOOM! CHINK! BRUOOM! CHINK! BRUOOM! CHINK! BRUOOM! faster and faster and faster all the smaller drums rattle and kazoos splutter and a single flute soars, all coming to an unbearable climax like revel, like rage, like a pounding bed, like birth, like war, old and new. Not school.

So what is it? In her recent memory, Gordon St. Onge's voice: "If you were to write this story now . . ."

Now.

Now at the summit, the dawn is giving everything cool silvery and fevery pink contours and flashlights go off one at a time, two at a time. Through the climactic chanting of rough and sweet voices and the *chunk-chunk* of spoons and the soaring of the flute, Ivy sees a man-shaped creature standing with two other man-shaped figures, each with a small child riding his shoulders, each man sporting a papier-mâché head . . . and all are shirtless. Ivy's pale eyes widen. She knows one is Gordon St. Onge by his size and the way he moves. And that big copper belt buckle. He has a red bandana knotted around his neck—not in cowboy fashion but with the ends rolled up under to make it more like a dog collar, and his grimacing papier-mâché head is painted a bold enamel yellow, and out from the temples of his big weird head soar horns three feet long. Yes! The Viking!

Ivy pushes both palms hard against her eyes. All the flashlights are off now. People stand at attention. Only the dogs are circling. Ivy sees that the little towhead kid on Gordon's bare shoulders has a good grip on each of the horns like he's steering a bicycle. Ivy watches hard as Gordon absently scratches the dark hair of his chest and she edges over to the sheer rock drop-off and looks down nearly a hundred feet into the tops of trees and now the pearly and flushy sky is changing to cream and now to lemon and now to a brighter sweeter lemon all within their picture frame of hostile red gold boiling clouds. And the words to the tumultuous chant have changed now. "COMMMME SUNNNNN . . . COMMMMMMMMME SUNNNNNNNNN . . . YOOOOOOOO ARRRRRRRRE THE POWERRRRRRR . . ." CHINK-CHINK-CHINKA-CHINK! BRUOOOOOOMMMMMM . . . "WEEEEEE ARRRRRRRRRE THE POWERRRRRRRRRRRRRRRRRRRRR. WEEEEEEE ARRRRRRRRRRRRRRRRRRRRE AND YOOOOOOOOOO-OOOU ARRRRRRRE ONNNNNNNNNNNNNNNNNNE!" CHINK-CHINK-CHINKA-CHINK" . . . this for another twenty minutes . . . and another . . . and now a sturdy finger of fire in the distant treetops many towns away. Then a wriggling of that finger. Now it leaps! And now it is blinding. And the chanting and flutes have stopped cold.

That's it. A choreographed, well-planned, well-timed ceasing of their noise. But this isn't really silence because thousands of chirruping tweedling birds are still speaking from thousands of dark trees, north, south, east, and west.

The silently bellowing red-orange morning sun falls on each human face and demonic mask and glossy-eyed fake head. *Red sun in the morning, sailors take warning.* Or is it just pollution and steam from the melting poles? Is it just the end of the world?

Such a quiet army. Such dignity. Each chubby or slight hand easy on its weapon of choice. Each set of shoulders squared. Such readiness. And yet a sense of submission to the immeasurable force stationed there in the east, growing bigger. The source. Of. All. Life.

Ivy's eyes keep returning to Gordon St. Onge. And soon she realizes it's not just she who needs him in her view. She looks around at the hundred or more faces painted with blood-gold light. All these eyes seem to behold *him* as much as they do the sunrise. Oh, how humans have need for a leader. They always fall into that old-as-ice pattern. Big Man, sometimes Big Woman. Part of the elementary, top of the Needs List: The Great Figure, air , water, temperature, food, and rest. His place inexorable even if he's no more than an inelegant goofball illusion.

Okay, what's next? She expects now *the sermon* by Gordon, who else? Most surely, the moment for a self-made messiah's messages from God is ripe, and these followers are most surely primed.

But all Gordon does is monkey around like a kid, pushing at some three- and four-year-olds with the sole of his work boot while the tyke on his shoulders shrieks and hangs on to the three-foot horns for dear life. A mob of screeching little kids now comes running. A lot of towheads, with grease-painted faces and glittering eyes, grab Gordon by the legs. Some to try to wrastle him down, some just seem to enjoy hugging. And one kid sorrowfully wails, while a teenager turns to the burning sky and howls.

One of the small homely white dogs sits down and howls. And now kids of all ages are howling. Some teenagers who have a coyote's yodelly cry really perfected join in. And now a few happy delirious screams. One fine sort of Swiss-style yodeler. All this, heard from a mile away by the more civilized parts of East Egypt village would be unsettling.

 And three miles away.

In her little attic room with an octagon window to her left and tall lace-up work boots on her feet, fifteen-year-old Brianna Vandermast plunges her brush into fudgy yellow-white paint and begins today's work on a sun that will rival the real. Her genius never leaves this fumy room.

This is all she knows of the St. Onge Settlement's solstice celebration. Simply the sun. The rest is rumor.

Her attic room is hot. Her broad forehead beads and drips. She coughs. The cigs, the paint. Her serpents of risk.

She has never been to the Settlement and yet in both of her strange eyes there is a knowing and in her brain a muscular thick discord.

Her time of staying away is running out. She knows there is a plot in the works among her brothers.

 The ugly moment.

Now the people have begun to head back down the mountain to a big breakfast. The downhill trek will be, of course, easier. People will be chatting, carrying their papier-mâché heads or masks or funny hats, kids whining, a lot of tripping and falling, kids with sleepy eyes and tired blistery unreasonable demands, but no mosquitoes as the air has now gone blessedly chill. The new sun will paint the high tops of the higher-ground trees as the people step along below into blue shadow, down . . . down . . . down to the good smells of that heavy breakfast.

From across the little zigzag of stragglers, still standing at the summit, Gordon St. Onge, not yet shed of his grimacing yellow-horned head, points at Ivy, a command, like a cop singling someone out of traffic, ordering her to pull over so she can get a lecture and summons.

She stoops to pull up one of her green-and-white striped socks as the huge and ridiculous horned figure weaves its way between small Settlementers and even smaller windmills, over to her. He is no longer carrying a kid on his shoulders, just bare shoulders, muscled, and angry. People scoot aside to make way for him to reach her.

Nearby, one of the little square steadfast white-haired women, who has been occupied helping a two-foot-tall dinosaur get shed of the bottom half of his costume so he could pee, calls to Ivy, "Someone should get you some peroxide for those scratches on your face." Ivy had kinda forgotten her culvert battle scars.

The woman glances at Gordon, now standing by Ivy. His big yellow papier-mâché head is leering but his body still looks angry. She says to Ivy in a small voice, "Well, I shall go along. I see you have a friend."

Ivy watches all the women leaving in a whirl of kids and dogs, teens, men, and humming electric buggies. Just three people remain. A clean-shaven man stands with his papier-mâché toucan's head under one bare arm, smoking a cigarette in the shadow of the monstrous old European windmill. He seems to be waiting for Gordon. Ivy remembers this man from the piazza last night. He's not a small man but he seems elfin as he stands there with the windmill looming overhead.

Why are its six shingled walls all painted black with faces of ghouls and spirits and flushingly real-looking mermaids and she devils in reds, purples, and veiny taupe? Haw! Haw! Haw! These are no ladies! See the orange and fiery eyes of the largest she devil blazing with power. Why is power the obtrusive theme of everything Ivy has seen here so far? Where are the answers to the questions that Ivy must pretend not to want to ask? Haw! Haw! Haw! Haw! Ye gods! Light my *fire,* baby. Haw! Haw! Heavy equipment operator need not inquire, only to move mountains. Haw! Our Ivy gives Gordon's chest a slow seductive study, then says with her big laugh, "I know it's you."

No reply. And he doesn't pull off the head like she expects him to, and at first this seems so funny to her. She blinks happily and says, "Moo!"

But the longer he stands there, the moment turns ugly. She cannot see his eyes, only the anger in his hands and arms. Like a spider is watching her, a *big* spider. Ivy stops smiling, feels discomfort drop over her.

The sun expands larger and higher and warmer. Less red.

He says slowly, "What . . . am . . . I . . . going . . . to . . . do . . . with . . . you? I can't let you out of here with your tongue still attached to your mouth . . . you fucking little play-dirty reporter." Finally, he reaches to pull off the head. And she sees that although the body and the voice are tight with threat, his pale eyes are not dangerous, just part sullen, part jokey.

She snorts. "I thought there was about to be a human sacrifice."

He chuckles. "Wasn't the walk up here with all this stifling gear *enough* of a human sacrifice?" He turns and winks at the other man and calls, "I'm ready to eat a sacrificed hog. What about you, Edward?"

"Me? Yuh!!" the guy calls back, putting a heel to his cigarette butt.

Gordon reaches with one hand, almost brushing a knuckle over her cheek. "You've been bleeding."

"All parta the job," she says with a sniff.

And so they turn toward the road, Ivy shuffling along in her shiny black button-up bootlets between the two men. Down on the road ahead of them are some young mothers, early twenties, Ivy's age. And real small kids. The kind with fat, padded, rear ends, who stop every

three feet to squat down and admire a rock or twig. One old waddly
Labbish black dog. One circling, bouncing *young* Labbish black dog.

Ivy doesn't look at either of the men who accompany her but talks
to the rutted rocky mess of road at her feet. "You think I'm hostile.
But I'm not hostile. I'm not trying to catch you at anything, Gordon.
There was nothing here tonight anyone could call *awful*. It's no different than . . . than Halloween! Or some nice festival. Mardi Gras
or something. It's not exactly something you should be criticized for.
I . . . I think it was exciting . . . and creative . . . and . . . and great!!"

Edward, the clean-shaven man, marvels, "You liked it, huh?"

Both men look at each other and bust out in wild laughter, gone into
that stage of delirious exhaustion where everything is funny. Edward
hoists his big toucan head back on. "You call this fun?"

And Gordon makes a really stupid part chicken, part Three Stooges,
"*Bluurup! Bluurup!*" sound and both guys laugh hysterically and stagger around and Edward stumbles, goes down on one knee. "Call the
ambulance! Shoot the bird! Shoot the bird!" which makes no sense at
first until Ivy *gets it,* the bird is him, the toucan. And at this moment,
Ivy thinks, there is nothing prophet-like about Gordon St. Onge.

Is this, to our Ivy, the disappointing end, the beginning, or the
middle?

 The TV screen calls out to America.

See the November elections coming! (Yes, it's now only summer.)
Large on the horizon on smooth wheels, bubbling and popping and
tuneful. RED. WHITE. BLUE. VOTE! VOTE! It makes all the
difference. Things would be so good if everyone voted. Voting is
everything. See the big appealing faces, purple and greenly tinted
screen faces. Hear their words. A blames B. B blames A. Pick one. A
or B. VOTE! VOTE! Voting is your right. Voting is democracy. Democracy is easy. Go go go! Vote vote vote! Make your choice. A or B.

 The voice of Mammon observes.

See sheep, there you are bunched at the gate! Sheep do not see beyond
the gate. Sheep and democracy! The combination is hilarious.

Graffiti written on a wall inside one of America's "inner cities."

IF VOTING COULD REALLY CHANGE ANYTHING,
IT WOULD BE ILLEGAL.

—Emma Goldman

 The voice of Mammon (earlier in the twentieth century).

Saddlebag gas tanks will cause a few fiery deaths but are cheaper to make. We will still clear a profit, even after hard lobbying, annoying lawsuits and a number of fair settlements. You figure it in. No sweat.

 The voice of Mammon (now almost the twenty-first century).

Merchandise in towers, in piles, in giant high teetering walls, saves space. Space is money. You expect a certain number of claims. A few crushed consumers . . . boo hoo. Yeah, they sue. No problem. It still comes out that we'll look good in the next several quarters. It's like floor wax. You figure it in. No sweat. Even after you lobby the stoutly smiling safety regulators, you make millions. Yes, stoutly. America the beautiful! She's an ace!

 Concerning the aforementioned particular details, the screen—

is blank.

 The screen shows us some men being escorted to court.

Scary evil types. They are handcuffed. Here he is, Wayne Plotkowski, yet another weird and crazy man who has cut his victims into pieces. And here is John Kurtz, who took his victims from their night shifts at all-night Stop 'n Rush stores, stabbed them and stabbed them and stabbed them. And here's Jobi Allaf who, without provocation, blew away two young cops who tried to nicely arrest him in the streets of LA . . . see the faces of those young police officers here . . . they had families! And here is David Cliff James and Jon Dolly, both with known armed-militia connections, arrested in Colorado on Monday by the FBI for possession of illegal weapons. THIS IS PURE EVIL. A GROWING EVIL. WORSE AND WORSE EVERY DAY. MORE EVIL IN THE STREETS THAN EVER! We hate these evil men, don't we? Nice people HATE evil men. WE HATE THEM WE HATE THEM WE HATE THEM. We FEAR them. And prisons cost so much. And court appeals cost. SO COSTLY. Taxpayers take the burden. These EVIL WEIRDOS are draining our country. Five governors speak tonight about why the death penalty is so practical. And habeas corpus soooooo impractical. KILLLLLLLL THE EVIL SCRUNGIES!!!! Kill 'em *fast*. Save America for decent hardworking nice people who never break laws and are tired of seeing their taxes soar. Clean up the streets. Clean up the courts. Empty the garbage pails of all these inhuman terrifying types. Get practical. Get tough. Privatize prisons! Privatize police! Private is good. More efficient! Death is cheap! Bleeding hearts are expensive. Cold and mean is the way. Think of your darling little Megan and Tristam. Bleeding hearts ruin futures. KILL! KILL! KILL! Death to garbage!

 In a future time, Claire St. Onge (the age-fifty-or-thereabouts, obese, and bespectacled Indian woman Ivy met previously) remembers that day.

What was she after? Even today, looking back, I couldn't tell you what was in her head that morning. Whatever it was that caused her to impose herself on us. To move those harsh speculative blue eyes over every man, woman, and child like counting heads, tallying something. But our eyes were on her, too, maybe a few outward stares, some sidelong glances. And our arms went around her, hugs and welcomes, some unconditional welcome, some *conditional* welcome, mix and match, this is the way we had, over the years, become thus, a single big red pulsing heart. We saw that she was this stalwart little rig, beautiful and funny. With an *attitude*. With *posture*. And when those husky-voiced remarks weren't coming like barks from that mouth of hers, you noticed that mouth, how it looked so small and pink and inculpable.

She had the power to destroy us. And the vulnerability to *be* destroyed. And how do they say it? *It's in the cards*. And our little gamble with the media, which had such high stakes, had now officially begun.

 The Settlement.

Nearing the last hundred yards of the rutted road, Ivy finally asks about the thick clumsy cables that run along on stout poles to her left, twice crisscrossing overhead.

"Electricity," Gordon tells her, raising both eyebrows a few times meaningfully.

"From the wind?" Ivy offers.

"From the wind," Gordon confirms. He smiles, gazing off. And then he frowns and works his mouth around so the mustache is punctuating a kind of scramble of anguish. She is nearly breathless with questions but sounding like a reporter will be a mistake.

Edward grunts, his eyes on the lumpy road.

As they round a curve, the road is less steep, and the trees open out to rolling hilly fields of wildflowers, sheep, a lot of sheep, and a dozen or more brown and black goats with white ribbony tails like deer. And there are cattle, a lot of cattle, many dozens, mostly brown and white, some more like your western longhorn, huddled together in a chummy way, others busy at pulling grass. Mostly meat cattle. Dozens of calves. Some quite new to this world. Off in another area, brown and cream Jersey cows, ready for milking, wait and stare. No tails lift and slap. It is now, for the moment, a fresh fly-free morn.

Ivy sighs. "I heard windmills take a lot of maintenance."

Gordon: "Oooooo, indeed."

Edward: "Oooooo, indeed."

Ivy: "Thus, aren't they impractical?"

Gordon grins. "Yeah. And keeps our tinkering teens occupied. But you're probably thinking about large, corporatist schemes. Those would take place with the *purpose* of efficiency, of cutting working hands out of the equation while sucking millions from US and state treasuries. You see, it all depends on one's goals."

Ivy squints. "So windmills aren't—"

Edward giggles, says, "They're jungle gyms. They build strong bodies and light up brains and poof up pride . . . all that."

"I see." Ivy nods and nods.

Edward says, "It's all about kids." Then he *tsks* in a good-natured way.

Gordon says, "And we have wind-solar cooperatives around the state . . . very social . . . very tight. Like church. A holy spirit thing . . . almost." He yawns. Mouth like a lion's.

And across the field, in the stripy shade of young maples, a cluttered sawmill area, the three roofed-over mills unattended, a chips truck with a white blower tube at one end waits unmanned, disconnected, the red cab beaded with dew. Stacks of blond boards on a flatbed truck. No logs on the brow. Just bark and a worm-hunting robin. The robin bursts into the air, then blends into the lower limbs of the young trees.

Swallowing questions is only half the struggle. Ivy tries not to look too hard at the bare parts of these two shirtless men who walk with her, lest she be unprofessional, whorish, boorish. But the scarlet of the bandana around Gordon's neck is vivid, even from the corner of her eye, and it keeps startling her, keeps calling to her. Ye gods! Eyes ahead!

"And what you just said, Edward, about kids . . . it being really about kids. Someone said that kids painted the mermaids and devils on the big windmill and all the little windmills are—"

"Kids are in charge here," Edward says. He yawns.

Gordon grins, all those twisted bottom teeth in the dark of his beard.

Ivy sees between the sawmill and quad of buildings a giant lavender swan on a truck. And a cotton-candy pink swan on pallets. Others, lemon yellow, fresh leaf-green, sea-mist green-blue, Creamsicle-orange. Some yet to be painted. From breast to top of swan's head on arched neck, these are taller than a tall man. "Swan boats?" she wonders.

Gordon nods.

"Made by kids?"

"Well, they're in the mix." Gordon is not actually looking at the swans. He is hefting the horned head to the other arm, clenching his teeth against another yawn. Eyes spill with yawn water.

In the distances below flutter the efforts of peppy kazoos. Somebody isn't tired yet? But there is a melody that is old-fashioned, East Europeanish. Skirling in its haunting refrain. And oh, the cool air is slinky and sweet!

Edward is mumbling something. Two of his words intercept Ivy's thoughts: *SAWMILL* and *HELL*.

Now off to the left is a sunny terrace of little cottages. Really cute and spiffy. Not grim and denuded like the Mount Carmel building in Waco, Texas, which some of the nameless callers keep comparing the Home School to, as they compare Gordon St. Onge to David Koresh. Ivy flashes a look at Gordon, then back to the little cottages, some done in natural shingles, some with clapboards painted that old New England white, others done up in Easter egg colors or, yes, *swan* colors: pink, lavender, duckling yellow, buttercup yellow, and grass green, each with a set of solar collectors boxy in their, yes, *in*efficiency.

Edward kicks a rock.

Meanwhile, on the treed hillside westward, a few shady cottages and good-sized Cape Cod cottages are nestled in brotherly. Teeny yards, most with white picket fences. Some blessed with *stuff*, like yellow, blue, and white plastic industrial pails, everything saved in that shrewd old Yankee way. To each of these residences a cable runs, connected to that feeble electricity lifeline that rambles up the mountain to the intermittent generosity of wind turbines, mermaids, gremlins, devils, and the surplus energy of youth.

Fifty or more yards below is that set of connected main buildings where the solstice march had begun last night, a sort of squared U-shaped complex that reminds Ivy of the set of a Hollywood Western, with its roofed-over boardwalks and screened piazzas, much wider than the boardwalks. The whole array has a chunky look, all these porches facing each other across the too-cozy quadrangle, the quadrangle only faintly grassed, mostly toy-strewn. A few tall trees with no lower limbs.

And no surprise to Ivy, a constructed menagerie of huge, murderous-looking prehistoric reptiles, Tyrannosaurus rex, brontosaurus, and that rhino thing with the ruffled bony head, spikes at both ends and a brain in its tail. And there is a winged dragon with frowning brow and actual glass eyes. And suspended from a twenty-foot tripod, a silver space saucer with sculptured frog-like green martians standing on the roof. And there by a set of picnic tables stands a smiling purple cow . . . cow-sized. Ivy says aloud, "Yay gods."

Tyrannosaurus rex is taller than the ridgepole of a two-story barn, his leering grin way up there between the trees. Twenty-five, thirty feet? Hollow like the mythical Trojan horse. In one robust hind leg, a little doorway. Winding stairs inside take you to the head. In the face, the teeth are really bars for safely viewing the world below.

Ivy laughs one big HAW! "You've been busy."

Gordon snorts. "Not me."

Eddie says, "They weren't built. We caught 'em in the woods."

Ivy really loves these fun guys. Joking. *Plaguing,* as her grandmother used to call it.

"It's plain to see, this place is child-friendly."

To this, Gordon just grunts.

Bricked walkways go everywhere around the quadrangle, and to and from Quonset huts and parking lots and sheds. And there are handicap ramps.

Electric buggies are parked on the quad, their colors as bright as the menagerie, as the windmills, as the merry-go-round, as Gordon's weird kitchen. And color is not a stingy thing, is it? It is from generosity and joy that color comes, no? Well, yes, and pricy enamel paint.

Ivy says pleasantly, "The colors here are wonderful."

Gordon narrows his eyes. Was that a stiffening in his shoulders? At first she thought it was a proud response to her compliment. But now she's not sure. In the absence of A NICE NORMAL INTERVIEW she can only read this guy as you read a strange dog. *Will he bite or can I place my hand on his head?*

They walk on, Edward grumbling, mostly to himself, husky whispers about tiredness, heat, and again the word "hell."

Though three sides of the quad are framed by the porches and boardwalks of the big shingled U-shaped building, there is no fully open end. The large Quonset huts, sheds, pens, trucks, and equipment clutterishly stuff up that east side maw. Made of sheet metal and cement block, the Quonset huts have tall wide bays, open now. Ugly but welcoming. Sure looks nice and cool and damp inside them. Ivy, trudging now, less stumbling than on the mountain, she detects this now thickening, sweet, pollen-smelling air is heading for a full boil by noon.

Edward stops at one of the Quonset huts to join a group of men and women, all smoking, and he wastes no time lighting up. Someone calls him "Eddie."

 In another time zone.

Coming to an abrupt stop (making a bit of a rubber-on-tar *eeek* sound) at the ticket dispenser of a parking garage near New Orleans, Louisiana, a small metallic blue Japanese-make car sports this bumper sticker: MY CHILD IS AN ALFRED E. NORRIS JR. HIGH SCHOOL HONOR STUDENT.

 Back in Maine.

Solidly on cement supports at the rear left corner of the Quonset hut where Eddie smokes is a little shacky house with a communications tower rising up. Almost like at the sheriff's department and jail, but without the dishes.

Gordon sees her looking at the tower but offers no explanation. Bide your time, Ivy. Bide your time. All will reveal itself, Ivy, she tells herself. And what's the big deal? They are shortwave buffs, right? Or whatever. She shifts her heavy shoulder bag.

 Seavey Road. Three miles from the Settlement's dirt road entrance.

Brianna Vandermast of the sunset hair sniffs the open tube of Snowflake White. She is fifteen years from her birth, formed with a wretched defect. Now she begins to jiggle, her honey-colored eyes halfway closed. She can see in her mind's eye the bull's-eye of his sun, the one that rose today, that celebratory fever ball.

She touches her homemade easel with her work boot, her friend.

Only her incomplete sun lays splayed on the rag paper, but his voice, which she has never heard up close, is shouting to a frosty crowd in a canyon of cities, "Liberty!!" This also in her mind's eye, an ample moon.

She twists the cap back onto Snowflake White, the tube in her woods-scarred fingers gives as if pulsating with blood. One of her legs jiggles some more, not a dance but the madness of her heat. Now she spins, her heavy hair a fountain. The octagon window of her little room is the hole of a cannon, loaded, facing west. She unbuttons her shirt. Heat pours from breasts round enough to nourish the world. Could he be father, she mother? Of a universe. This room is not really a cage. She picks up Cadmium Red. She knows just where he is.

 The inside story.

A preteen boy with cinnamon skin and black hair, in nothing but yellow shorts, is darkly frowning. He speeds by Ivy and Gordon on a newish-looking English bike, heading away from the porches where the food is laid out.

"Hey Termite!" Gordon greets him a moment after the bike swooshes by.

"Hey," the boy calls back in a quiet, routine touching-bases sort of way.

Everywhere are chickens and the mess chickens make. Greenish splats on the brick walkways. A lost feather. The feather is black with iridescent blue.

Ivy almost picks it up.

Loudly, chickens *bok! bok! bok!* among themselves, that single chicken word worth a paragraph of good news. And roosters, who when they crow look like they are stretching their necks to be sick, but instead, out comes declarations of jubilation, pride, and possession.

Gordon St. Onge swallows drily, or is it hungrily? Then a short suppressed sigh.

On the metal roof of one of the piazzas, a white-and-black cat washes behind her ears with a licked paw.

People are heading for the porches in droves. There are so many screen doors going into the screened porches, some with steps, some with ramps.

Some young people, late teens and twenties, rush past Gordon and Ivy. These are also progressing toward the food.

One guy with an eared cap like babies wear and white and black face paint sidles up to Gordon with a wordless eye-rolling secret-code-sort-of look, then trudges hurriedly on.

Ivy squints suspiciously at this, her baby blues just narrowed cracks.

A crow cawlessly glides quite low through the openness, a fairly creepy Edgar Allan Poe *Nevermore* expression on his face, looking for small "earthly remains" to snack on. Or is he trying to *warn* Ivy?

"Well, the food must be really good," says Ivy to the side of Gordon's face. "You wouldn't see a stampede like this toward any of the restaurants I've experienced of late." She chortles. She looks to see if she's made him smile. Okay, so he's sort of smiling.

Inside the porches are dozens of doors that take you into the big side-by-side rooms of the buildings. Like a motel. And there are windows, low and many-paned, mostly uncurtained. The windows and doors, woodwork and shingling and numerous porch columns are no modern rush-rush job. These are about pride and craftsmanship. Pleasing to the soul.

Most of the inner doors are closed meaningfully. A few are wide open, emitting the sounds of kitchen work. Some areas are shadowed, some beginning to show slashes of light from the eager summer sun. The whole massive horseshoe-shaped building is stained brown, dark as creosote, while doors, windows, and trim are painted dark green. It's really handsome, even as it all seems so hard-pressed by kids and teenagers, and that mishmash of projects and tools and worktables, deep couches, homemade-looking tricycles, and slamming doors. And many long tables heaped with food.

And into this screened space Ivy and Gordon enter. As he pulls open the screen door, Gordon is still awfully quiet. Though as small kids now race past, headed out, he speaks their names in a grave low voice. Like prayer. This strikes Ivy as significant. She makes a mental note. *Erin and Tyler. Caitlin. Pria. Rozzie. Rhett. Delanie. Montana. Max. Rusty. Draygon. Katy and Karma, Andrea and Gabe. Wheatalo. Josh. Justin. Jason. Jason. (Yes, two Jasons.) Alex and Sharolta. Seth. Nick. Keya. Shawn and Kedron and Renata. Benjamin. Aleta. Zheebwaklay. Jenna. Jason. (Yes, another Jason.) Olivia. Meesha and Nora. Frank. Anna.*

In a future time, Claire St. Onge remembers.

Okay, so we welcomed her.

 Hungry?

Shifting the bright yellow papier-mâché head to his other arm, Gordon had held the screen door open for Ivy. And now here is Ivy in the heart of their world. He still says nothing, just looks into her eyes. Warmly. He dips his head in a way that means *follow me*. Her eyes flick to that oh-so-red bandana knotted around his neck, tries not to glance again to all that splendor below it. She feels around inside her shoulder bag with one hand, hoping to locate a Kleenex to wipe her sweat-gelled face.

Now Gordon steps around her and leads the way past a slumped old couch where a long-legged dark-haired toddler has needed no time at all to sail off into sleep. On this porch, Gordon St. Onge seems even taller, the slanted ceiling near the screened side barely an inch above his head. Against the inside wall between the first couch and another couch—which is heaped with cast-off costumes, papier-mâché heads, rubber hands, scarves, paper flowers, hats, gauzy veils, carved swords, spoons, and bells, and homemade kazoos—he easy-carefully parks the horned head. Ivy notes for the many-eth time that the horns are real, from some creature, utterly deceased.

The smell of smoked meat frying is thick.

Standing behind Gordon, Ivy watches a guy in his mid-to-late thirties who is just getting to his feet from retying and old woman's shoe, a woman in an expansive black rocker with carved dogs heads above its back. The guy is quite short. Ivy is taller. But he's broad-shouldered. Thick-legged in his old-timey plaid Bermuda shorts. Haw! Bright blue T-shirt that doesn't conceal his large almost hairless belly and his deep belly button. Pug-like face. Eyes big and round, blue, like his T-shirt. His face and arms are tanned, even the freckles. Carroty red beard and carroty hair are ripply, the hair stands up all over his head and there's a pink impression across his forehead. Must've just pulled off one of those papier-mâché heads. But that carroty hair, it's his *real hair!* And the beard, real. Ivy blinks. My god, he looks just like one of those adorably ugly troll dolls that were the rage before she was born.

The guy glances at Ivy, then to Gordon. His eyes widen, reading something on Gordon's face. He turns away suddenly.

Is Gordon choreographing an Ivy-boycott here as he did in the IGA?

Ivy's eyes flash to the row of elderly people, three in wheelchairs. Most are dressed winterishly, in sweaters, long pants, and heavy socks. One of these oldsters is embroidering a small pillow. Her hands are lumpy, knuckles like acorns, close-to-useless-looking but the embroidery roses she has nearly completed are satiny and perfect.

Ivy hopes one of these ancient knobby beings will smile at her. But none of these old people look up into Ivy's pretty face . . . oh, Ivy Morelli with her cold shrewd baby blues! But now she hears the whine of a fast-going wheelchair behind her and shifts around to see a white-haired guy . . . but he's young . . . a VERY blond youngish guy. White-blond dreadlocks-dense ponytail like a fanning out of lumpy grapeshot from a touched-off cannon. Very pink scalp where his hair parts. One knob of an earring. He has just whizzed from the kitchen door and is now heading out. Nods to Ivy. Winks. Ivy nods back, straining to make her cold eyes warm, less narrow, more wide open . . . the appropriate giddy look. The guy gives the screen door a hard shove with his right foot and out he goes.

Gordon whispers to a chubby young boy whose eyes flash to Ivy's face, then down to the corner of the table that he stands next to as he nods and nods, then gallops purposefully away. Ivy sees he wears a ballooning smock of black spots on white . . . a clown? A cow?

Like the piazza back at Gordon's house, here wind chimes and mobiles hang in her face. There is a mess of lawn chairs and old wooden rocking chairs, stools, and old town-hall-style folding wooden chairs as well as kitchen chairs with pretty seat cushions. But Gordon's narrow piazza was just the length of his Cape and its ell. These six vast piazzas are nearly as big as town hall meeting rooms, and even the boardwalks all swarm and thump and squeak with life and with this heavy, drizzly celebration of food. There are many long tables, many bowls and platters, all quaking and quivering with flesh and vegetables. Someone cackles, "Oh, it's the Grand and Exalted Poopah of the Physica and Mystica!" while on another porch someone groans, "It's already warm as piss out."

Oh, the details. Ivy's right hand tightens. If only she could take notes! How will she remember all of this?

Ivy says loudly, "MMMMMMM. Everything smells good. First class!" She looks to Gordon's face. Her eyes silently cry out to him. PLEASE DON'T SHUT ME OUT. DON'T MAKE THEM HATE ME. I'M YOUR FRIEND!!!! NOT A REPORTER. But now her eyes are sliding up and down the open porches, calculating. Friend? Her eyes flick toward the screen and out beyond. Eyes widen. It's the crow. Perched on the head of a midsized dinosaur. Ivy marvels at this, the crow's accusing stare. She looks away.

After the thing with the sunrise and the walk back, quite a few people leave in droves, in cars and trucks, same as Ivy had observed them coming last night. But a great horde has remained.

An overtired child on another porch whimpers, then powerfully screams. Ivy doesn't look in that direction, just hikes up her shoulder bag, which is again slipping.

The motion on these porches could give you air- and seasickness. More swinging arms pass. A couple of thick necks and falling necks, the normal stuff but also some deformities. A highly concentrated mess of deformities. Things too long, too short, too missing. Some bodies just hunched, with swinging beefy arms. Muscle fibers of the back stretched tractor-wide, probably from heavy work and too much maleness. Jeez, how they resemble our tree cousins, the orangutans, hunchy but pleasant-faced. Not totally erect. But still they're us, Ivy decides.

This is really STUPID, not to be able to ask questions. A FRIEND can ask questions. So many questions keep flying at Ivy, like a blizzard of asterisks, commas, and exclamation marks. Like how many of these kids can't read? And to start with, HOW MANY KIDS?

Though all the tables aren't filled, there is a spillover into the more comfy chairs, and while a lot of men and young boys and those Ivy thinks of as monkey men are scooched along one inner wall, some mill about, talking loud, a little bit hyped. One spit-sprays while laughing. There is exhausted edgy aimless energy everywhere. A few people are still outside, sitting on the steps or standing under the trees. The light there at the moment is sloshing from side to side. One red, bloated woman leans against the green shin of a dinosaur, drinking from a coffee mug, watching a dead-looking child sprawled in the shady grass. All are tiredly sinking.

Smoke tendrils rise above a group of women. None seem ashamed. Cigarettes down to the butts like wharf workers. One gal has a silver face. One's face is purple, her hair bleached orangey blonde. These women are smiling, laughing. Kind of lollypopping around and whispering as one lights up again, flicks an ash; her long, cold, white cig held like an old 1950s magazine ad. Inside on this porch, big casual long-tailed dogs stroll among chairs and tables, kind of smiling. White flat-faced curly-tailed little dogs are zipping around with their noses to the floor. Ivy sees one of them piss on a wall. It seems only *she* saw the wall get pissed on. She steps closer to Gordon as an army of kids with swords and guns, helmets, and feathers, charges by.

Ivy says loudly (over the murmur and roar of the humanity here), "Cute army!"

Gordon just says, "I've called you up some first aid."

Something catches Ivy's eye. She sees it is a baby being lifted from a wicker bassinet and held to a shoulder.

Meanwhile, a tiny, child-sized, pale, almost silvery old woman in a pink summer dress, socks, and sweater, is carried by an Atlas-built very Indian-looking teen boy to a deep chair with a tray set up for the old woman to eat on. The old woman is smiling all around. A closed-mouth smile. Like one of those Smiley-face buttons that, as the troll dolls, were once the rage. Ivy is more impressed by the horrors, however, slithering her blue, blue, blue eyes over all those smoking mothers and kiddies with wooden guns, the gateway to real live guns and drive-by shootings, bloodstained bank lobbies and bank tellers without heads, closed-casket funerals and *leaping lizards! Yay gods!* Front-page news.

The chubby boy with the black-and-white polka-dot smock returns with a huge bottle of peroxide and some cotton balls. He looks long into Ivy's eyes, bold and warm. He explains in a husky way, "I'm with the first aid crew." He's not more than eleven, Ivy decides. "Do I call you Doctor?" she asks.

"Yep," he replies with his eyes fixed on the scratch on her face.

"Nowadays you should wear plastic gloves," she warns him. "When dealing with blood."

He glances up at Gordon, who is turned sideways now listening to two twenty-ish-year-old guys with ball caps and no shirts talking "board feet" and "the order that was doubled." One guy has an expensive-looking watch but corduroy patches on the knees of his jeans. The other has a lot of tattoos. One entire arm a spider web, a realistic black spider on the shoulder. Chubby boy seems reluctant to interrupt this conversation, just stares a moment at the side of Gordon's face, then he turns to Ivy. "Well," he sighs. "Here." He hands Ivy the cotton and peroxide. "You do it."

And now he does a really sweet thing. He pats her, kind of rubs her arm, a comforting gesture, while she is twisting the cap off the peroxide. He nods approvingly, still patting and rubbing her arm as she touches the cotton to the open bottle. "Not much blood," he tells her as he studies her cheek.

Gordon turns now, sees this procedure, winks at Ivy, then resumes the conversation with the two young men.

"What's your name?" Ivy asks the boy.

"Alexander."

"You going to make a career out of medicine?"

He looks into her eyes warmly but with a peculiar twinkle that means Ivy's question is "cute," as if *she* were the child, he the elder.

Ivy is trying to decide if he is a healer or a patronizer, a little redneck asshole in the making. She's almost too tired to work that hard figuring it out.

 The day is growing *very* warm.

People are so hungry, many are already done eating whole hams and other smoky body parts, barely chewed stuff swallowed too speedily, stiff as fabric, bulging and biffing along down that esophagusy pathway between their lungs. Whole platters of pancakes and tender wild birds being consumed, some left with just greasy puddles or crumbs. Jam is being dumped on muffins and rolls in big globs. Cherry jam. Berry jam. Tomato jam. Maple syrup and honey and orangey farm butter. Nightmarish amounts of cholesterol-riddled eggs, jars of cream, spreadable cheeses.

The uneasy Edgar Allan Poe feeling has faded now. Ivy notices only the edge of sweetness that is all around her. And Gordon gives her a sticky too-warm one-arm hug and calls to three silk-haired teenage girls who are swinging platters of eggs and spotted muffins to a table already so obscenely loaded with food that the stuff runs together. *"Lorrie!" "Shevon!" "Dillon!"*

The three girls flash smiles at Ivy. Maybe it's the long skirts and bare feet, but they seem incapable of pouting, of sassiness, of ever knowing boredom. Or envy. Even as they reappear with more platters of heavy food, and indeed, all three girls are tall and full-breasted, they seem fairylike and light-stepping, as if the porch's wooden floor could be clouds.

Now Gordon introduces Ivy to a man around sixty who carries two plastic jugs of something watery, one in each hand. "This is Pete." "This is Ivy."

With one sharp nod, no words, Pete bears two teeth: his smile. A cut-grass smell pours out of his faded-blue T-shirt, work pants, stained straw cowboy hat, his skin, even his wedding ring, so it seems. But darn. What's in the jugs? Would the revenuers approve?

A hurried young woman with a long brown braid grasps Ivy's elbow and cries out, "Welcome Ivy!" as she sort of flies through to the next piazza.

Gordon takes Ivy's hand, leads her to a man who sits in a deep chair. He has no eyes. No teeth. Not even false teeth. And not much hair. Ivy well remembers this old guy from the march up the mountain. He had ridden in style.

And Ivy is not surprised to see Gordon bowing down to blow a kind of frisky Morse code on each of the man's badly scarred temples and the man smiles gummily and his long pale satiny fingers close around Gordon's tanned forearm and the old voice, high and scratchy, speaks a toneless, "Gorr." Seems the old man is also nearly deaf.

Gordon stands straight again, rubbing the center of his chest open-handed, staring at two men who are crossing the quadrangle. Next to his head, suspended motionless, is a mobile of pottery doves painted purple with red eyes and red beaks, which match febrificly the red bandana knotted around his neck. He squints one eye, the other eye widening, cheek twitching moth-like, and then deeply, he asks, "So, Ivy. Do you love my family? Do you feel a throb in your soul?"

Ivy laughs. A mighty HAW HAW . . . because of the melodramatic way he has spoken, and yeah, at the idea that you could LOVE a bunch of people, slightly more familiar than a swarm at any given airport. So it is teasing on his part? Or naïveté, the small-world redneck kind. Or?

His pale eyes are staring with intensity for an answer. His eyes are not icy and revealing like Ivy's eyes, but whirling with layers and junctions and those joshing interstices, as when in his gloomily lighted kitchen he said, "Yeah, I'm for the great white male thing," and that thing about cutting out her tongue back up on the mountain. This Gordon St. Onge is holding her hostage on a gravityless pitch-dark planet.

She gives her weighty shoulder bag another hike and says, "Who *wouldn't* love these folks?"

He smiles here in the heart of his great hive.

Now a teen boy, the one who had carried the old woman, comes to stand beside Gordon.

Gordon turns away from Ivy somewhat, faces the wall of screen.

The boy has a broad face with American Indian looks. Hair somewhat short. Very black. A fresh-looking green work shirt. Sleeves rolled to the elbow. No jewelry. No tattoos. His eyes are as black as possible. His hands are a bit battered-looking for so young a person. He opens one of these hands on the back of Gordon's neck as if to knead Gordon's tired muscles or pull Gordon backward by the red bandana. He is the same height and build as Gordon, almost exactly, give or take a couple of inches. And he is all manly seriousness. The two of them stare out at the quadrangle and there on the back of Gordon's neck the big boy's big hand remains. Gordon replies, "Yes," to a question that was not asked. The boy's jaws had not moved.

Now the boy speaks. "Figures."

Gordon says, "John get Webb to take his place?"

The boy shrugs. "He said he was going to."

Now appears a teen girl with short shining brown hair. Her T-shirt reads THIS BODY CLIMBED MOUNT WASHINGTON. She passes by with what looks like a scrapbook under one arm and smiles at Ivy then looks into Gordon's eyes in a warm significant way. She sneers at the Indian boy. A taunt. Then she is gone, mixed in with the mob. And now Ivy watches others pass, a slim preteen boy with plastic-frame glasses and his arm in a sling, accompanied by a man about sixty or so in work shirt and jeans and old sneakers, followed by a fat brown-and-gray dog with one blue eye, one brown. As this trio passes, the sixtyish guy with the old sneakers gives Ivy's left arm a squeeze without even looking at her or Gordon. The Indian boy is moving away now to find a chair at the table and from another table a balding man with blondish hair on his arms like two light-colored rugs gets up with his dish and comes to stand next to Gordon as he eats. He asks with a full mouth, "Danny show up? *Slisk, slisk, slurp . . .*"

Gordon says, "Yep."

"The order has doubled, huh? *Munch, munch, slisk . . .*"

"So I'm told."

There is cigar smoke tumbling through the air from the quadrangle and somewhere another kid is crying tiredly.

A skinny bare arm passes with a tattoo of a lightbulb with rays.

Ivy is thinking, there is something ABNORMAL about this. Not some broken law necessarily, not something to bring SWAT teams and DHS marauders. But a thing that is not *understandable*. It makes a NORMAL person feel EDGY. She stares at the big bare back of Gordon St. Onge, at the balding man next to him with the blond hairy arms and plate of food, and she stares at the spotty morning light flooding both men. Their talk is urgent. And all around the eyes of the many watch Gordon; the men, the children, the women, and especially the teens.

To be engulfed by nearly a hundred admiring people, to be the solid CENTER of nearly a hundred admiring people, to maintain that in a secluded place, away from the rest of America . . . well . . . it certainly would make a great feature story, Ivy. She peeks guiltily toward the crow. But he is gone.

Guy with plate of food moves away, Gordon's hot right arm crushes Ivy not painfully. But gets her attention. "We need to feed you. I'm just figuring the best way."

Ivy snorts. "Usually through the mouth."

He laughs, takes her hand. "We'll have to try that." He tugs her along, nearer to the kitchen door. Ivy sees that under one of the couches that they pass is a black cat with yellow eyes, those eyes square on Ivy. Another earnest spirit-wraith come to cleave to Ivy's conscience.

 The Voice of Mammon.

Whatever the people who work and serve believe in, whatever consumers believe in, is what we of corporatism must be the authors of. WE ARE YOUR AUNTIES AND UNKIES, YOUR PRIESTS. WE ARE WISDOM INCARNATE. WE ARE YOUR FRIENDS. YOUR ONLY FRIENDS.

 History (the old, old, old, old, old past).

I have to make him think that carrying those mastodon haunches all by himself is an honor.

 Time? Back in the present. Place? Egypt, Maine.

Now a young guy in jeans and Budweiser T-shirt and Red Sox cap blocks Gordon's way and smacks a small box into Gordon's palm. "If this doesn't fit, they say it's out."

Ivy sees the short very VERY overweight (no, *wickedly* overweight) Indian woman who had been holding the little dog that first night when Ivy arrived uninvited. The woman is not a waddler, but graceful. As a soap bubble would, she actually glides. She is wearing a cardboard crown on her graying black hair. Crown painted gold, of course. No work shirt this time. She wears a black V-neck T-shirt and a long skirt of blue-and-orange-and-red stripes. Awning stripes. Big fucking stripes. Ivy's cold blue eyes soften a notch. Our Ivy LOVES stripes. The woman's long hair is knotted up under the crown. Her nineteenth-century (or turn-of-the-century 1900) glasses are steamy. The Budweiser T-shirt guy has roamed away and Ivy speaks to Gordon, "I met her. Before." She nods toward the Indian woman's departing figure.

"My ex," says Gordon. "We go way back."

Another moment, another five degrees hotter.

Another man blocks Gordon's way and there's more talk about the "doubled order," and three small kids, all with tired silver eyes and flushy hot cheeks, stop beside Ivy and stare at her striped socks and button-up shoe-boots. Then one looks up at her and asks, "Who are you?"

"Ivy. And who are you?"

Only one replies. "Joshua Ridlon."

A kid at one of the tables quite nearby bursts into an overtired shriek.

And the short, red-haired, red-bearded troll-like guy ambles by and a woman with a green face hurrying in the opposite direction pats his shoulder and says, "Hey, Doll."

Ivy smiles at this. *Doll*. Right.

And the sun swims down through the quadrangle leaves and boughs onto the arms and backs of all these people. And on the tables of food. Spotty lovely light but the air is getting plumper with steam. Hot people. Hot coffee. Hot breads. Hot smoked meat and eggs. Hot metal screens. Hot gritty wooden floors. Hot grass and trees. Hot polleny buttery radiant sweet summer morning.

Gordon asks, "You want a beer?"

"I'm a health nut," Ivy tells him.

His pale eyes move over her a moment, over the butterfly necklace and then lower, then very quickly back to her face. "Coffee? They have the decaf kind here," he says, straight-faced but with one eye smoldering drolly.

"Fool me once, shame on you. Fool me twice, shame on me," she says huskily, and she is straight-faced, too.

He pokes her arm with a knuckle.

An eightyish woman in an old-fashioned apron over her equally old-fashioned housedress is now asking Gordon about "the reserve" and "the levels."

Ivy stands patiently, her eyes burning from no sleep, her shoulder bag weighing like a dead buffalo carried back from a hunt. She really doesn't feel that hungry. Just hot and dirty and unpresentable. She feels like *shit*. Steaming green fresh chicken shit. She stares around. So many young, middle-aged, and senior guys all mobbed together between the tables and the inner wall. Billed caps, tanned arms, wristwatches, some with glasses, some still showing those kindergarten colors of greasepaint in the lines of their faces, though they seem like such a conservative bunch. Hard to believe they'd be game for such a weird spectacle as what occurred on that mountain an hour ago. Greenwich Village, yes. San Francisco, yes. Vermont commune, yes. New Orleans, yes. But not these guys. Not these hard Yankees. Not here.

Ivy looks back at Gordon, sees that as he talks to the woman, he is turning the small box in his hands distractedly. She realizes that a couple of phrases from the woman's mouth were in what must be Maine French and that when she goes back to English, she has the accent.

Nearby, among a bunch of men in straight-backed chairs, there is a white wicker-backed rocker; deep in this chair, like a crab in sand, a woman, young but worn under the eyes, purple-frosty bags there, cavy mouth like missing teeth, but really a jaw and chin that are slight. On her lap is a floppy afghan of purples and creams to match her worn-outness. Her shirt is red plaid and oversized, giving the impression that not long ago she was heavier. Her hair is yellow growing out to brown. A carved wooden toy assault rifle lies on the floor by her foot. She is staring into nothing. Ivy wonders what the first aid crew could do for this woman.

The Indian woman glides past again, still wearing the cardboard crown. Queen, yes. Her eyes, behind the steel-rimmed glasses, cast purposefully about the big porch. In her hand are a pen and long trailing sheet of paper, some sort of list. Ivy tries to imagine marriage between this woman and Gordon. The woman appears to be older than Gordon. Ivy feels dizzy. And hotter and stickier than a moment ago. Her striped socks slide like goo down into her tall boot-shoes.

Gordon places the small box on a stack of cubbies next to a closed green door. Ivy sees that it is something automotive, electrical or plumbing-related, packaged in a utilitarian way. He turns around and faces Ivy with, again, that warm look of welcome. He actually places the toe of his work boot lightly on the toe of one of her boot-shoes. But in that instant someone grabs his arm, whispering urgently and now another oldish woman has come up to confer with him and now some little kids stop to ask Ivy, "Are you Linda?"

"I'm Ivy. Who are you?'

They laugh. All these giggles and happy smiles and big eyes. "*Yoooooooo knowwwww,*" one of them says and points at Ivy's face. This kid is as blond as a thousand-year-gone ghost.

Now Gordon's hand closes around Ivy's wrist, steers her along nearer to the kitchen, introducing her to a fiftyish woman named Celeste, whose hair is black and curly and clipped short. Her dress is a misty green-blue with delicate embroidery around the collar. Believe it or not, she is very pregnant! She is simply standing by a table, holding a glass of water, looking exhausted. How can she be fifty and pregnant? Maybe forty-five. But even *then!* Something in the water? Something in the food? Oh, ain't this otherworldly? Ye gods and hot dogs! Ivy's toes wiggle and bunch with excitement, with fear.

Gordon introduces Ivy to another woman and another and another and another, a blur of introductions, all first names. Now a man. No name mentioned. Now another and another. Ivy can't keep all these faces and partial names straight, though she will never forget the overall effect, those swimmy patches of leafy light through which they all move, the kind of oily English-Irish sound of her own name spoken in their Western Hills accent, a little different than the part of Maine where she was raised, where people mix up with outsiders more, where people *really* hurry. And different, of course, than the French, Maine's romance language, all those somersault *r*'s, the *o*'s engorged somehow, the vortex of *j*'s and *m*'s and *zhees* that pull you in deepest when you have no idea what they mean.

 She frowns.

His amazing little world. Bloated and strange, rapacious and familiar. Practical but . . . but *fun.* To give a peek of this miracle to the *Record Sun* readership would be a big present with a bow tied around it and inside it would be this richness! And inside would also be Ivy's heart. This is Ivy's story!!!! Everything else she has written about is shit compared to this.

But no, she promised not to.

But yes, the world OUT THERE needs this, needs to know!
But no.
Ummmmm . . .

 But no . . .

Now she again spies the two short and square and sun-ruddy women
she met that first night. Both gray-haired (white-haired, actually). "I
met them," Ivy tells Gordon. He nods and tells her, "Yeh-up. That's
the Bev and Barbara team." He has a nice little grip on Ivy's wrist
again, towing her now even closer to the big kitchen door. "Here's
a nice seat, Ivy. Over here. Right near the kitchen. You need food."
The really *nice seat* is heaped with hard-living grimy dolls, some
one-eyed, most nude. He pitches these on the floor. It is a fine deep
upholstered chair between two men who are both eating. Gordon
says deeply, "Sit."

"I'm afraid I'll fall asleep," she says and groaningly flumps down.

"The press never sleeps," says he.

Ivy yawns violently, her eyes watering. And then there's no Gordon.
Gordon is gone. *Poof!*

Ivy looks to the guy on her left. It's Edward again. Eddie. The
clean-shaven guy who she saw that first night outside Gordon's kitchen
and then coming down the mountain this morning. Only now there
is no sign of his toucan head. His dirty-blond hair is thinning a bit,
and appears combed brutally (and recently) with water. Looks like
he's touched up his shave in the last twenty minutes, too. He smells
strongly of soap. A weird soap. Essence of burned clover? He's not
a good-looking man. His light eyes have hardly any lashes and his
jaws are so angular. But he has such a sunny aspect, crinkles next to
those eyes; a good forty-five years of smiles? And his teeth are white
and perfect enough for television or work in sales. And that T-shirt
is as white as it gets. And those jeans are as tight as they get. And his
belt is doozied up with chrome-plated studs, pewter animals, a few
fake jewels, and coins. *Leaping Liberace!* Ivy's inner voice guffaws.
He smiles at Ivy, then returns to his conversation in progress with a
man in the chair to his left.

Meanwhile, in the chair at her right is a plain ordinary Mainer-type sixtyish man in work shirt and work pants. Bald on top. Glasses. Smiles at Ivy. But no words. His chewing mouth is full and there's more on his fork. Big scorched hunk of ham.

A teenaged boy appears before Ivy, one forearm across his front, one in back. His forearms are incandescent white and willowy. On his feet are weird slippers, pointy and curled like an elf's. Chinese-style pants. Black silky shirt with no collar. Eyes like a deer, big and sensual and brown. And a strong, bracing, cool, freshly showered smell pours out of him, too, as it does from Eddie, only less burned clover, more minty. The boy does a sweeping bow. "Ricardo," he says. "At your service, Mademoiselle Morelli. What can I get you?"

Ivy laughs. "*HAW!*"

A girl around twelve, wearing shorts, moccasins, and a cute, flowery, short-sleeved shirt, hair in short brown pigtails, also steps up. "Hi Ivy. We are *all* at your service. Your wishes are our commands." She scoots behind Ivy's big chair and stands there, hand on the back of it. She leans waaay forward to inform Ivy, "After you eat, a bunch of us'r going to give you the tour, Your Queenship."

Ivy guffaws. "If I was a true despot, I would ask you to fan me," and she sees Gordon standing on the next porch by a long crowded table, a brown beer bottle in his hand.

Ricardo says, "I can start you off with a little something . . . a glass of juice and a muffin, while you decide on the main course." He is standing with both hands behind his back now.

Ivy laughs. "I really should be helping out in some way."

"Tut tut," Ricardo scolds. "A gracious guest accepts the gift of being fussed over."

Behind Ivy's chair, the girl's voice, "Queens must relax."

Ivy laughs again, sees that the plain Mainer bald man on her right is stabbing at his eggs with his fork. She heartily tells him, "In some countries, they used to bind the feet of queens."

Then she looks over by the two kitchen doors, just a few feet away, into the glittering eyes of a really strapping young woman with thick, wild rivulets of dark hair streaked brassy orange, a really *cheap*-looking person, whorish-looking actually, dressed in a man's sleeveless undershirt, huge breasts, braless. The glitter of her eyes makes Ivy think she is wearing contact lenses. But there is something else, too, something like fury and menace, a look someone would give you just before they go to beat the piss out of you.

Ivy looks quickly back to the elegant teenaged boy's face. She can almost see her own reflection in his tender and generous eyes. "Anything," she answers gratefully. "Everything smells so nice. *You* are so nice . . . while I'm being held prisoner in this chair."

Ricardo laughs a tremulous laugh and pats her hand. "Queen, not prisoner." He turns away toward the kitchen.

The voice of the girl behind Ivy's chair says, "That's my brother."

"Nice brother," Ivy compliments.

Eddie, paying attention now, says, "High-class."

The girl leans over to Eddie and pokes him. "You are low-class, Edward."

"I know it," he admits sheepishly.

"Eddie, why don't you go find the trough," the girl advises.

He groans to his feet. "Yep, yep, yep. And I'm going to lay in it until the day is over. Don't tell the sawmill crew you heard that." He carries his dish away and Ivy closes her eyes a moment, feeling them burn against her lids. She is erasing *strict Christian discipline* on her list of preconceptions.

When she opens her eyes, the brassy-haired, angry-looking woman is still standing by the kitchen doors, *still* giving Ivy that glare. Ivy whispers to the girl behind her chair, "Who is that person by the door there, the one looking at us?"

The girl seems not to hear the question.

But the plain Maine man in the chair at Ivy's right, whose plate is clean now, says quietly, "That's Bonnie Loo. Don't get her mad. She's the world's best cook." And he laughs with meaning. And of course Ivy has no idea what the meaning is, not really.

 Claire St. Onge remembers.

They say when you drink too much, the first things to go are inhibitions and judgment. And we watched nervously as he began to drink for the first time in many months.

She watches everything, trying to answer her own questions.

Gordon steps over the outstretched legs of a young man whose arms are crossed over the chest of his camo T-shirt. This young man is snoring loudly, his head hanging off to one side of his chair as though he were freshly dead, but his snore seems to enunciate: *I'm alive! I'm alive! I'm alive!* His face is a spectacular shade of turquoise. A small, ugly, white, flat-faced dog balances on his lap. Dog has a good view of the steaming table. This is the chair just beyond the chair Eddie vacated.

Gordon has a six-pack of beer in one hand, an open beer in the other, not the beer Ivy watched him finish off a few minutes ago. This one is full. He stops in front of Ivy and asks, "Beer?"

She shakes her head. Rolls her eyes.

In a voice of sorrow, he tells her, "Nobody seems to want a nice warm beer for breakfast. It's great stuff. Made by a company. Tastes like giraffe piss."

Behind Ivy's chair, the sentry *tsks*.

Gordon squints at his open beer. Now his eyes slide to Ivy's face. Makes his voice deep, Shakespearean sort of, "President! George! Washington wazzzz a randy dandy priggy piggy ear-slicing motherfucker. And Abe Lincoln hung a lot of Indians. He was for trains. And empires. He jailed reporters."

Again Ivy rolls her eyes, smiles.

Her sentry says matter-of-factly, "Here we go."

Gordon says with a growl, "Did you know that, Ivy?" He lowers the six-pack to Eddie's empty chair. "And Eisenhower's chiefs of staff had something up their sleeve called Operation Northwoods where the CIA spooksters and that sort would do terror and death in the streets of Miami, shoot at ships and planes, and blame it on the Cubans! To get Americans to cheer over a war on Cuba. Kennedy came in and fucked that all up. He was always friggin' with the spooksters, may he rest in peace."

Ivy smiles on and on.

Gordon sneers, "This stuff would make a good story. Top of the fold. Extra! Extra! Read all about it! Better late than never." He snorts. Then tips up his beer. Two swallows. Then lowers the beer, making a disgusted face. Licks his lips. "When news *happens,* it's not available. When it's available, it's not news. It's olds."

The sentry is sighing.

Gordon stands very straight, chin up, beer held tight against his chest, eyes bore into the eyes of the sentry just beyond and above Ivy's head. "We're talking about the guy on the dollar. And the one on the *five*-dollar bill and the other one, he . . . well you know, postage stamps, tunnels, bridges . . ."

The sentry leans forward and whispers with hot bacon-smelling breath, "He is drinking."

Ivy says, "I noticed."

Gordon looks down at Ivy's face. "Did you know that only ten percent of the American population was legally human under the new constitution and the randy dandy fathers who—"

The sentry (whose name is Heather but Ivy doesn't know this) says, "Gordonnnn. Ivy is resssting."

He whispers the next part behind three fingers and the open bottle of beer. "George Wash-ing-TON and Ben Franklin and the other fathers did the ear slicing thing. To their slaves."

"History is terrible," says Heather the sentry.

"History is interesting," says Gordon.

Ivy says, "It *can* be." About as interesting as golf, she thinks. She rolls her eyes to herself yet again.

Gordon says, "But it *continues.* See under the frontispiece of dee-moc-racy . . . ahem . . . of the constitution, you were not human if you were a bonded servant, a slave, a woman, or *any* of those poor land-less types. Property is the thing. And that does not count the Indians 'cause those were just wild dogs. Had their own nation and all that, lived out there on the horizon doing unspeakable things. Oh GOD BLESS AMERICA!!!! . . . ahem . . . meanwhiles the ten percent that was human . . ." He grins. "They would cut off your ears and *other* things if you tried to escape . . . or if you tried to revolt against ears and so forth being sliced . . . this since you were *property,* not human." He grins again. Very many teeth. "Today it is different."

"I hope so," Ivy says.

"Today there is still only ten percent who are human, then a vast majority of well-trained beings who *believe* they're human until they *test* the constitution in a court of lawww. Or through so-called representative government. Saw-*ree*. Not human." Now he growls this part, "George Washington will cut off your ears, Ivy . . . if . . . yoooo tryyy toooo es-*cape*. But listen, if you're a corporation, you've been a legal person since 1886 and you will *never* die."

The sentry (Heather) says quickly, "Sometimes good stuff happened in the old days. Tell her some good stuff, Gordie."

Gordon says with his eyes shut tight, "The constitution was the first NAFTA."

The sentry places both hands ever so gently over Ivy's ears for a few moments. A glass smashes from a nearby table. The heat cranks up another notch.

Gordon scooches down in front of Ivy, moves the six-pack from the chair to the floor in a fussy way. And now also his opened beer. He finds a place on the floor for that. He doesn't face her but stares off down the length of this piazza, to the east, where the mountain behind the row of Quonset huts is a fuzzy hump of deep, heartbreaking green. Softly he says, "It would be a beautiful day if it wouldn't get so friggin' hot. Heat is hard. But Jesus, ain't those hills pretty?" He now swivels toward her, looks at her full-faced, his pale eyes in those dark lashes showing yellow-hot like the sunlight above the Quonset huts.

She agrees that it is beautiful.

"Don't hurt us," he says deeply, quietly.

She laughs, unsure how else to respond. "I promise."

She watches him stand, taking all of his beers with him to a wicker rocker a few seats away, which crackles and squeals as he sinks into it, one side of his face collapsing into twitches, both eyes rolling as if to express alarm but it's probably just his Tourette's-like affliction. In the seat next to him is a woman with a funny hat, glasses, and a jumper of navy blue with embroidery over the chest. Very pregnant. She looks to be crabby and unwelcoming but when Gordon presses his cold beer to her cheek and temple, she leans closer, gratefully. Now he slides the beer to the back of her neck. She laughs. Lowers her face. Her funny hat falls off.

Down at the end of the nearest table another something made of glass smashes on the floor and a small kid laughs hysterically.

Her thoughts.

Yeah, all of this, *here* and *now,* top of the fold.

 And then—

About seven overtired little kids start screaming simultaneously on various piazzas.

One is dragged away kicking and struggling. Spitting. Swearing.

Now Heather behind Ivy's chair yawns in a big way.

From the busiest of the kitchen doors, the one that has the fluttery light of semi-outdoors beyond, classy Ricardo, the boy with the magnanimous, goldy-brown nice-person eyes and Chinese pants and genie slippers, brings Ivy a plate. Mmmm, sausages, ham, eggs, heavy bread AND a huge muffin, dense preserves, kind of figgy-looking, a giant glass of lemonade, and a clean rag "for wiping hands," and Ivy points out that no one else but the very old and frail or mindless or new babies has had food brought to them, and Ricardo laughs at Ivy's apologetic expression as she says, "I can't eat all of this. I'm so sorry."

"You better or you'll get a spank," he says, then bends to kiss the top of her shining hair. Then he heads back out to the kitchen door, the one that looks outdoorsy. A summer kitchen?

"I love your brother," Ivy tells the girl behind her chair.

Eddie, with the belt of jewels and coins and the salesman smile, returns to his chair now with a glass of lemonade. He looks long at Ivy's plate, which she hasn't started eating from yet. "Howzit goin', Ivy? I myself would have brought you something, but Eric . . . I mean *Ricardo* . . . he always steals the show."

The sentry behind Ivy's chair clears her throat.

Eddie leans toward Ivy and whispers with cold, lemonadish breath against her ear, "Eric . . . I mean *Ricardo* is pretty Hollywoodish, huh?"

The sentry behind Ivy's chair snarls, "I can hear you, Edward."

Ivy says, "I love Ricardo. He's top-shelf."

The sentry snorts. "Unlike Eddie. He's bottom-drawer."

Eddie tee-hees. "Heather's got a one-two-three punch."

Ivy is starting to really admire this Heather, her sentry. And yes, a sentry is what she is. Ivy feels powerful and important. That she requires a guard! But she really *meant* it when she told Gordon she is no longer writing this story. Actually, as we all know, that's a lie. She *wants* this story as soon as she figures out what the hell it is. But then the job would be to convince Gordon St. Onge of the advantages of printing it. Right? The story, yes. With his blessing.

Eddie sips from his lemonade noisily.

"Slob," says Heather disdainfully.

Ivy sees that Gordon hasn't fetched a plate yet. Not only has he finished off the second or third, maybe fourth beer, but the man she saw a while ago with the jugs of *stuff* is pouring some of that stuff into a big glass for Gordon.

Ivy isn't hungry at all, but she eats. The food is hot. The air is a hot hug. Dogs are panting, staring at the floor around people's feet, watching for whatever might fly off from busy plates above them. The steam over the mountain behind the Quonset huts looks greasy and predatory. Sticky Ivy yawns vastly, covering her mouth. She watches kids accumulate around Gordon. A sedate group of preteens are playing Twenty Questions. She hears some of the questions and answers, others are muffled by the loud talk of a new group that's just arrived . . . and the army of small kids that charges past again, a small king in the lead, his crown a perfect fit.

Eddie says, "I want to die before ten-thirty."

Ivy stares a moment at a girl of about seven or eight who, with white feathers pinned in her dark auburn curls and a gorgeous embroidered white blouse, is asleep on the floor in a sprawl in front of Gordon's chair. Gordon has just raised his left boot to use this child as a foot rest, which causes the Twenty Questions crowd to scold him. Their name for him is "Gordie." Gordon looks over at Ivy and his eyes twinkle, one eyebrow raised fiendishly . . . *on purpose* . . . not his usual tic.

Ivy has *MORE* than twenty questions. Hundreds of questions. All mighty. She swallows them all.

Ivy eats. The slippery eggs and tender ham are just as hot as when they first arrived.

A kid stops to show Ivy a jar with wood ticks scuttling up the sides.

Ivy eats. She yawns. She swallows more questions. She sees that the sickly, hatchet-faced woman about eight seats away, the one with the afghan on her lap, wearing an oversized shirt, is still staring vacantly. What is that dusky purplish erotic-looking area of flesh showing there between the afghan and her midriff? It's the head of a brand-new child, which Ivy hadn't noticed until now. A child perhaps a day old. Perhaps a few *hours* old. A young girl sits next to this woman now and rubs her shoulder. Is the woman depressed?

Ivy opens her mouth and jams in a glob of scrambled egg.

She looks up and sees three young girls she has not seen before now, smiling down at her. Long hair. Long skirts. Satiated, almost dreamy eyes and the smiles of angels. And all pregnant.

"Hi, Ivy," one says in a low, too-sweet, beguiling way.

Waco, yes? The prophet who spreads his progeny like seeding the lawn? Waco, yes? Waco, no? This is different? This is nothing like self-sacrifice and puritan thrift. Here is wild celebration. The colors! Colors of jubilation! And no Bible. Not a one. Not even a quick grace before all this gobbling of food. Forget the callers, Ivy. Forget them. All of them are cranks.

"We'll take you on a tour!" one of the girls exclaims. "After you're done eating!"

Ivy smiles. "Thank you, guys. I'd love it." She sees their ankles and feet, compliant—or would the word be complementary?—with the surface of the porch floor. Feet spread to balance the body, that heft, each pregnancy rounded, pumpkin perfect under the summer fabrics, all patchworks, one dress done in variations of mints, one in yellows, one with all different prints of pink rosebuds or pinker rosebuds, and flushing rose blossoms on white and cream, blossoms large and tiny. Three girls, three fetuses, two silver wedding rings, one gold with a diamond.

The man at Ivy's right rises achingly from his chair, looks at Eddie a long moment, then says in a dark, raspy way, "Guess I'll take a nap."

Eddie says, "Shut up."

The man cackles, then walks slowly away through the hot, joyless, flabby, thick, adhesive, dizzying summer steam.

"Sawmill man," one of the girls speaks sadly, her eyes on Eddie. "In another life you were bad."

"And it was fun," says Eddie, and rocks his nearly empty lemonade glass on one knee. He yawns with great feeling, yawn-tears trickling over his cheeks.

Ivy holds back a shuddering yawn, which Eddie's yawn has inspired.

And the big hot ointmenty steam doesn't move at all, just thickens, bigger and bigger, gray-yellow in the open distances beyond the quad. It is hard to remember what a fresh breeze would feel like.

Ivy looks at Eddie, who winks. He is now no-handedly balancing his empty lemonade glass on one thigh. She knows now that she has *never* seen jeans so tight.

She peers over at Gordon. But there is no Gordon. His wicker seat is empty. Empty beer bottles around his chair.

The sentry behind Ivy yawns. She is now resting her head on her crossed arms on the back of the chair.

The sentry sighs, her too warm breath against the back of Ivy's neck, and now her fingers are touching Ivy's neck, playing with the nape hairs that have begun to lengthen again since Ivy's last clip. Ivy is starting to feel buried alive in hot hands, hot smiles, a drawstring of hospitality. Teeth are coming at her. Ears. More dog tails glide by, panting jaws. Sun dapples mixed with tendrils from hot coffee and steamy pregnancies, all of it slobbering, staggering, sticking, spraying.

Sentry says on a poof of hell-hot breath, "Before you go, you *have* to see the shops. You'll love the shops. We'll get you some guides."

Ivy has a thought. What if I just had a notion to ROAM through the shops, *what*ever these shops are, *where*ver they are . . . what if I just wanted to do it *by myself* . . . EXPLORE . . . hee ha! OBVIOUSLY, THEY DON'T WANT OL' IVY EXPLORING. Another flash of sinisterness hits our Ivy. A headline in the *Record Sun*: CHILDREN FOUND IN CAGES AS PUNISHMENT FOR READING BEFORE THE AGE OF TWENTY. SCHOLARLY ACHIEVEMENT FOUND TO BE AGAINST ST. ONGE FERTILITY LAW . . . this headline plays before Ivy's sweaty bloodshot exhausted eyes.

And the short, fat, gliding, awning-striped Indian woman, Gordon's ex, with cardboard crown and flowing hem, passes with two kettle covers, giving one teenaged boy a really mean look and he salutes her.

Voice of the sentry whispers, "I love your hair, Ivy. How'd you make it purple?"

"It's a tint," Ivy tells her.

Sentry says, "It's magical. That color. It changes as you squint."

 The French connection.

The empty seat at Ivy's left is now being filled by the man Ivy remembers from the rainy IGA day, the one who was riding along with Gordon in that old truck. Olive-drab Vietnam War bush hat. He's about fifty, her quick guess, probably a vet. His eyes are fierce and dark, close together in his small face. His beard is shapely, well-tended, dark, no gray. Shirt and pants today are khaki, light as sand. Fresh-looking. He is happily snapping gum, done with his meal. Wags a knee from side to side. Ivy remembers the rainy day well. He had spoken what seemed like a foreign language. Most likely Maine French. The patois.

Ivy says, "Hi. I'm Ivy." She puts out her hand.

As he reaches to grasp her hand, his dark eyes simmer. He doesn't offer his name, though. He snaps his gum, leans back now. Adjusts his bush hat.

Ivy says, "I'm a friend of Gordon's. It's Ivy. Like the plant."

He snaps his gum, dark eyes returning to her.

"You have a little boy. He was with you the other day in town."

He nods. Smiles. "A few, t'em. All sizes."

"What's your name?"

"Oh-RELL Soucier," he says quickly. "Good to meet you." He says this last part as he is looking away again, snapping his gum mercilessly, wagging one knee, smiling around at the busy scene. Then, "You nott mine t'iss heat, you? Fun, eh? All t'iss dribbling, t'ere?"

Ivy laughs. "Well, winter is so long. We should enjoy this while it lasts."

He squints at her, a similar wild-man expression to those that occasionally take over Gordon's face. And he says, "T'iss sucks."

Ivy laughs. One of her best HAW HAWs.

He says, "T'iss woult be okay if we coult all be up to our necks in t'Promise Lake and not some off us kept priss-norr here of t'mighty dollar." His *rs* roll like powerful sea waves toward Ivy, then recede.

Ivy is working this *kept prisoner here* confession through her head. "Your name, French?"

"Oh, yes."

"How do you spell it?"

He wags his knee from side to side on each letter as he spells out A.U.R.E.L. S.O.U.C.I.E.R. and then politely asks how she spells hers.

One of the short, square, ruddy-faced women, Bev or Barbara, passes in time to give Aurel's knee a slap. "Now don't you start teasing her!" she warns him. And then forlornly glancing into Ivy's eyes, she complains, "These men think they're clever."

Aurel says, mostly to himself, as the ruddy-faced woman is now gone into the depths of the mob, "Teassing iss naturrr'ss way of making a nice time, her." He winks at Ivy. With *both* eyes.

Gordon trudges toward them now, wiping his face with his red bandana, the one that used to be tied around his neck. He stops in front of the three chairs, Aurel and Ivy looking up, Eddie covering his face, whispering to the heavens, "It is ninety degrees, ninety-nine-percent humidity. And satan stands before me."

Gordon ignores this. He is stuffing the bandana into the rear pocket of his pants. He is squinting at the wall behind Aurel's head. No beers in his hands. And no homemade hard stuff. But he is past feeling good, isn't he? He is feeling VERY good. He crookedly grins at Aurel.

Aurel looks at Ivy. "I am nott on the sawmill crew so satan nott bot'er me a bit." He looks up again at Gordon's grinning face.

Eddie says, "I love the sawmill . . . TOMORROW. But not today."

Ivy sees the whorish-looking Bonnie Loo with the brassy orange-and-black hair who had stared at her with such venom, now out on the quadrangle with another youngish woman, both smoking. Without the knives of her eyes showing, her profile is more noticeably seared with old acne scars. She moves with thrusts of chest, wagging her hippy rear. Some could see sexy gal. Ivy sees upright bear.

Gordon's voice is gentle but gurgly, as though he needs to swallow *frogs*. "Aurel, meet the press."

"We met. But I been forbid'denn to play and be fun." He looks off sulkily in the direction that the ruddy-faced woman disappeared to.

Gordon scooches down now in front of Ivy but turns a bit toward Aurel. "Ivy," he says, clearing his throat, "This man is my cousin."

There is a long silence into which Ivy says, "Really," . . . but then more silence, and then Gordon muckles onto Aurel's ankles and then, slumping down onto his knees, kisses Aurel's boots, one smooch to each boot. "My cousin! My cousin! I love you!"

"I know it!" Aurel insists. "No need to prove it all ways, you. Get your lips off my leg, t'ere."

The ruddy-faced woman returns. She looks at the back of Gordon's head worriedly as she passes, says nothing.

Gordon swivels somewhat, now facing Ivy with his bleary eyes. "The press. Wants to write a flashy story about guns and sex."

Aurel says with a little chuckle, "She's come to the right place."

Gordon snorts. And as if on cue, the kid army with its swords and guns and clubs storms past, led by the king with a crown of jewels like the ones on Eddie's belt. Something like fifteen small kids. Painty and gritty and foody and sweaty. "Dat's him dere," Aurel tells Ivy, pointing at one of the tail end soldiers. "T'one you saw in town. Mike. He's mine."

Ivy nods.

The sentry yawns. A deep groaning booming emptying-out, almost man-sized growl.

Gordon stands. Ivy looks up at his profile as he is caressing his own bare chest in a distracted way, staring after the army, which is advancing to the kitchen doorways.

Heather the sentry touches both of Ivy's ears ever so slightly. It makes Ivy's skin feel electric and yet sleepy. She sinks a little more deeply into her chair.

 Bonnie Loo remembers.

I was cooking that day . . . as in *chef* . . . kitchen duty. Both kitchens, the summer kitchen out back, lower level, and our regular cook's kitchen inside, the whole rangy complex. And all my crew. Phew . . . pots, pans, stir, crush, and chop. Yeah, so I was cooking this banquet. And *I* was cooking, too . . . yeah, as in hot person. *And* as in pissed-off.

The sun was blazing. Everything was fuzzy and sticky and spumy and as vile to the eye as it was to the skin. The distant roofs glowed. Sand sparkled. Chickens and tweet-type tree birds were quiet. Everyone was taking their kids off to bed. For me it was another cigarette. And another. I just wanted the day to end. Be done. And the sly little bitch would be gone. Mizzz Newzy News.

 Slowing up at a sweltering road-under-construction area, just outside Abingdon, Virginia, a now-dusty two-door compact car . . .

has two serious-looking faces behind the windshield and in the back window, a bumper sticker that reads: MY CHILD IS A BOONE ELEMENTARY SCHOOL HONOR STUDENT.

 The grays.

Once, we captured an "honor student" bumper sticker. We pressed it out upon our lab bench and stared at it. It flailed under our careful study, telling us its story. Papery and stretchy, it was yet another of quadriptillions of manifestations of the tricks among all beings condemned to livingness, to time locked in the Goldilocks planet's heavy bag of gravity and succulent temperatures. It spoke in a nah-nah bray, one of humanity's bumper sticker noises we have mapped alongside the housefly larvae's bustle and the fly's own high-noon buzz. An honor student bumper sticker has no ghost. Nor kindness. A fly has a generous ghost. It calls out, "Hello! Hi! Hi! Hi!" Thus, we rate flies best.

 Meanwhile, back in the southwest mountains of Maine.

The floor shakes. Now a screech. A small boy runs. Gordon lunges around a table after him. Boy wears a man-sized black tricorn hat. Hat falls to the floor.

Both of Gordon's arms lock around the kid's middle and the kid howls, "Don't!" as Gordon mashes his hot huge bearded face into his neck and growls, "Hairy hungry swamp booger eateth the red ant . . . hee hee!"

The boy struggles free, screaming, laughing in a crazed way, runs past chairs of outstretched legs toward one of the screened doors. Gordon bounds after him, the whole broad piazza thundering with his weight and the wild jingle of the thick wob of keys on his belt. He drags the kid by a foot to the floor, warning hoarsely, "Hairy swamp monster guy says YUMMMMMMMMMMMMM . . . me eat red ant!"

Ivy looks down at her own hands. A creepiness drops over her like a fog hotter than the actual air. She peeks. Gordon's very sticky-looking body covers all but one of the kid's legs with its sneakered foot, kicking.

Gordon laughs.

Child kicks harder. And now a scream, like real terror.

Ivy stands up.

Sentry Heather edges around the chair, moves closer into Ivy's humid space.

Ivy laughs a little, still standing there, square-shouldered now, no longer in that withering sleepy undertow of the day. She doesn't meet anyone's eyes. She hears Aurel, still in his chair there, making a grave sound. No more working on his gum.

A few kids have gathered like dogs around a dog fight, waiting for signals, feeling the wildness in their own muscles and glands, ready to help the winner, or maybe the loser, depending on their respective natures.

Some of the adults are smiling. But these are vitreous smiles.

Ivy looks right at those smiles and her heart pounds hard.

Gordon rears his head back. "Swammmmmmmmmmmp man eeeeeeeeeeeat Michellllllll. YUMMMMMMMMMMMM!!!!"

The kid makes a sickening shriek. And then pretends he is going to spit straight up into Gordon's face.

So Gordon does the same, pretends he's going to spit.

Kid cries, "Stop!"

Two sweaty-looking women push through the circle of tensed kids.

"Enough, Gordon!"

"Gordon! Let him alone!"

Ivy can't believe her eyes. Gordon is now doing a really disgusting thing. A gleaming pendulant of drool is hanging from his mouth as he works up more and more serious spit to add to it, letting it out of his mouth by inches, letting it hang over the kid's screaming face. Quite a few people are laughing over this. Ivy glares at them.

Heather, seeing Ivy's face, says, "It's nothing."

Warm trickle on the back of Ivy's neck. She is going to leave now. Going home. Needs to stop the wacky scramble of her feelings. But *the story*. She needs this story. Newspaper story, maybe. But for sure, the story . . . like you wouldn't get halfway up Mount Everest and quit just because you got a mild headache on the lower slopes.

Bev is getting closer to the brawl. "Gordon, I don't believe this!"

And now another voice, *"Arrêstez-donc d'agaçer les infants!"*

Ivy turns to see several heat-pinked women coming from the kitchen, among them the blonde twins Ivy met at Gordon's farmhouse a few nights ago. *"T'es baveux! Yést trop fatigué, lui. Les enfants sont tannés de toié!"* one of them despairs.

Gordon's pendulum of spit gets longer and longer, swinging over the kid's face. Using all his earthly might, the child twists to free himself. "Uh! Uh! Inhhhhhhh!"

"He'll have terrible dreams after this," Bev laments.

The little guy seems on the verge of fainting, his gasps weakening, his face looking tranced, just as Gordon makes a horrid snorting noise and sucks the pendant back into his mouth.

"Jesus." Eddie breathes this somewhat admiringly.

"This is nothing new," one grandmotherish, bespectacled woman tells Ivy.

"No?" says Ivy. "Routine, huh?" She swallows her sarcasm, sees the bespectacled eyes of Gordon's ex staring at her in that flat measured way from a group of women and kids beyond a clump of empty chairs.

Walking backward so she won't miss any of the show, a young girl wearing a real showcase of embroidery, the whole dress splotched with creatures and flowers and suns and also small cow horns (real ones) poking out of her hair, collides with an *"oops!"* into Ivy, then speaks behind her hand. "Drinking makes men into fools."

Gordon releases the kid. Kid jumps to his feet and, violently hyped up, runs three or four paces, kicks a chair leg, grabs a one-eyed plastic doll from the floor and pitches it at Gordon, gets him square in the middle of his hairy stomach.

 And three miles away.

Fifteen-year-old Brianna Vandermast washes the pale mixed yellows from hands and brushes, the turpentine's alluring stink unfolding through all channels clear to her spine. Her human but not human eyes close tight for a moment. Though the paint is merely margarine color and other harmless tints in their travels up her arms and shirt front and now whirling in tuna cans of the cleaner, the thing she has just finished making on the easel is hurtingly sunny to dilated eyes.

But also the cheeks of her face are rosy and burn to touch. She is riled by her season for mating, so much so that this image of a sun roars through the walls to the real sun and the two suns, to her mind, are savage side-by-side ready testicles hunting for her. This causes the entire little Vandermast home to perspire.

 Yes, back there at the Settlement, the sun climbs. The hot pudding air thickens.

Shifting her shoulder bag, Ivy explains to Bev and Barbara that she really needs to go check on her car. "If I don't come back, could I have the tour another day. I'm—"

There's the feel of flypaper-tacky bare arms around her and the smell of drink. "Who is afraid of the presssssssss?" a deep voice whispers hotly against her ear. It's Gordon, locking her head against his shirtless ribs, her butterfly necklace digging her throat.

"Owwww!" she complains, puts a hand out, fingertips finding the sticky solidness of his shoulder.

His gruff whisper, "Yep! This is the press!" Now loudly, "Keep it under your hats, everybody, about our plans for mass suicide and all those stockpiled assault weapons and especially the child slavery!!!"

One or two chuckles from men sitting close by, through which Ivy can hear Eddie's coaxing. "Ivy, tell the world about the sawmill. I want to see it in the headlines. SWAT team rescues man slave from sawmill."

Many, many chuckles from all around.

Someone in the way off distance screams, "Tick!!!!"

"Gordon!" It's Barbara. "Please don't embarrass Ivy . . . and us. Stop now! Let her go!"

Gordon obeys, lifts away his long arm, and Ivy steps free.

Ivy faces him, smiling stiffly. "I'm leaving."

Very nearby, a broad-chested Scottish terrier is slurping up a cup of milky coffee someone left on the floor.

Gordon laughs. "Don't be mad. It's just playing around. We celebrate today, right?"

"No, Cannonball!" A very young-looking pregnant girl races to snatch the cup from the Scottie.

Ivy stares into Gordon's eyes. "I'm not sure if I'm mad. I'm not sure exactly what it is I feel, Mr. Teacher Man." She smoothes out her skirt.

Gordon looks at the floor. "I'm not as drunk as you think. It's just tiredness."

"All drunks have their excuses," Barbara says disgustedly, chin raised. She's as squarely shaped and sunburned as Bev, but her nose is handsome, not puggy, her eyes dark and deep and penetrating, her Brooklyn, New York–accented voice softer but even more authoritative than Bev's.

Someone is again scolding. "Stop it, Cannonball!"

A wild-haired, early-gray witchy-looking young woman places a hand on Gordon's arm but speaks to Ivy. "I have an idea, Ivy. Stay just a few more minutes. Some of the kids are going to do a beautiful solstice skit. Please don't miss it. They want with all their hearts for you to see it. And this can give Gordon some time to shape up a little, to smooth this over. Let's give him the benefit of the doubt. He's overtired. We all are. He's not always like this, not a Mr. Gorilla."

"But he is," replies Ivy, with a nasty little laugh, eyes into his eyes. "When I showed up for my promised interview last week, he was a gorilla *then*." She laughs again.

Barbara says worriedly, "Ivy, you can't know him in a day."

Gordon backs up to the rocker abandoned by Aurel, who left moments ago to take the swamp-monster-ravished little boy off to bed. (Yes, he was Aurel's son.)

Barbara makes a squinty-eyed scolding face at Gordon.

Gordon stretches his legs out. Settles in. Rubs his eyes with the heels of his hands, looks up at the trim little reporter and Barbara and the witchy-haired woman who are now conferring. Eventually catching Ivy's eye, he pats the seat of the big upholstered chair between his rocker and Eddie's. "Ivy," he says.

Ivy looks at his hand. Then a little to the right, at Eddie's bejeweled belt. Coins. Pearls. Rubies. Diamonds. Metal studs. Circles of mirror glass. And much, much more! How could a grown man want to wear a belt like that? Ivy slides her eyes back to Gordon's face.

She sinks into the big chair. She understands now, the power she has over them. Is it a good feeling? Or a shabby feeling?

 Before the solstice skit begins.

Ivy and Gordon talk. Nobody interrupts. Only small interruptions, such as his ex, Claire, stopping in front of him to drop a worn pale chambray shirt into his lap. She glides away. He stands to slip the shirt on, buttoning every button, tucking it in nice and neat, eyeing everyone, smiling crookedly at those who still flash him reproving looks. Then he sits again, one hand spread on each of the rocker's wooden arms. He answers Ivy's questions politely. His voice isn't fully free of its gooey beery hard-cider drawl. But there is an effort, at least. He tells her how it was the kids who founded the Solstice March, some of the older kids when they were younger. He tells her to ignore Eddie on the sawmill subject. "Nobody works here more than an hour without a break. Plenty of breaks. And a casual pace." Ivy replies that that is wonderful.

In the next chair, Eddie lets go with a long groaning yawn, which ends in a piteous squeak.

Ivy laughs.

Somebody brings Ivy a lemonade. She drinks it slow, *deep* and slow. It reverberates down through her soul . . . like shock.

Gordon keeps rubbing his eyes, blinking oddly, straining free of his drunkenness, it seems.

And then Jane arrives.

It's the first time Ivy has seen her since last night at the farm place, howling for Gordon not to leave, to stay and share a book.

She heads straight for Gordon's chair. She is so erect, long-legged, too graceful to be only six years old, too tall! But he had said she was six, didn't he? And she has that African stature, straight as a stab of sound. She stands in front of Gordon and says huskily, "I miss you." Her eyes are filled with shuddering tears.

He reaches for her wrist, pulls her to his lap. She climbs up and then folds her long limbs, making herself almost tiny. He takes her head into his two huge hands, her floofy dark curls boiling warmly through his fingers and he gazes into her dark, dark sultry eyes and he says, "My lamb."

 From a future time, Claire St. Onge (Gordon's ex) reflects.

So he stopped guzzling beers and cider. And she stayed awhile, but not for the tour, which we all agreed would be best on a day when we were all working the shops. For now too many people had gone home to bed. Everything was shut down. All but the sawmills, and there was no stopping that job, with so many orders coming in from Harrison. It just seemed best that she come back in a week or so when we were all fresh. And she laughed this sudden and titanic HAW HAW that seemed too robust for one so petite and pretty, and she agreed, said she'd had enough "jungle weather."

Some of our girls walked her down to her car, carrying the strawberries and peas and greens we were sending home with her. She promised she'd be back.

 Jane tells us of visiting her mother.

Beth is the one this time to drive. She has good hair, blonde curlycue's practically perfect and long. And there's the look of a scream on her face, which would go with how she'd get on her knees with the mike and have her eyes closed and growl: "Commme onnn, Comme onnn . . . give meee a little piece," and she has the right voice. Mum's favorite singer but I forget her name. But Beth'll never make it on stage cuz her nose isn't good. And her eyebrows are in the wrong place and I asked if she could sing and she said, "Nope."

When we got to the jail place she says, "This rat hole is run by noodleheads."

I said, "All of them are cop guards. You'll see."

"I've seen 'em before. I've seen this rat hole plenty," she says. She says she visited Andy here, and Mike, whoever they are. And also her sister and her other sister and her nephew.

When we finally get inside, Beth hardly says a word at first but she talks with her eyebrows, like she looks at me and wags them up and wags them down a buncha times. Secret code for noodleheads, noodlebrains, and "turds," which are her words she uses a lot.

The cop guards are standing *behind* her so they can't see the code. Good thing.

We get a special room to sit in. Mum said before that it's cuz she's so dangerous a criminal. I laughed at that.

Now here we are and it's Mum on one side of the table and me and Beth on the other side and a cop guard over by the door. He's as tall as Gordie but no hair. Maybe chemotherr-a-pee which you get like Aunt Bette for sick lungs. He might be sick. He doesn't look happyish.

Mum says, "You have a new sundress. I *love* mint green."

Beth says, "They made about forty outfits outta that bolt. We all look like moon men if we wear that green on the same day."

I frown. Usually Claire or Gordie drive here and they don't get on my nerves *this* bad.

Mum is laughing at the moon men thing but I keep my eyes squinched.

Mum's hair is blonde but not like Beth's. Mum's is called Light 'n Streak and swirls like sunny water so so pretty. And her eyes are blue jewels. But sad to say Mum's suit is orange. Nobody *really* wears *that* kind of orange on purpose. But it's the law here you have to wear orange if you live here.

I try to hold still cuz the chairs we have to sit in are the folding kind and probably could crash down under you.

Everything here is the law. Nobody can touch. So probably nobody can wiggle. It's a lot like school only at school nobody would be caught dead in orange. And no guns. Guns are evil. Cops aren't really evil, Lee Lynn, who came here once, too, told me. I guess they just want to *look* evil.

Lee Lynn is another one of the mothers at the Settlement. Those mothers all have plenty to say about everything. Beth is one of the worst cuz she butts in wicked.

I take a deep breath. I say to Mum, "*They* . . . ate . . . a . . . goat. They . . . put . . . some . . . in . . . my . . . plate . . . and—"

Beth very fast *interrupts* with saying, "Lamb, not goat!!!" and she makes her eyebrows joggle around and she is laughing like a jerk. "Goat!!!" she says again almost in a pure scream.

"Mum . . . I . . . want . . . to . . . stay . . . *here*."

Mum looks very much more pale than ever (she is of the white kind of person anyway, not the brownish kind of person like me) and she opens her mouth but Beth busts in, "The food here rots. And plastic forks. You'd hate it, Janie."

I squint very mean at Beth. I have just about *had* it.

Mum says softly, "They don't let kids stay. I wish they did."

"Kids in jail!" Beth hollers. Her voice is croaky, which I may have forgot to mention. She has a long-sleeve shirt so she's not goose bumps like me. You do *not* want to wear a sexy sundress in a cement jail that has no sun. But I wanted to look pretty for Mum.

Mum says to me with a small smile, "You ride one of Gordon's horses yet?"

I shake my head.

Beth makes a snorting noise and looks right at me. "Well, at least be glad that wasn't a roasted leg of horse on your plate." And she laughs, her voice more scratchy than it ever was. "Sometimes it is!" Her eyebrows go almost on top of her head. "Horse pie."

I look into Mum's eyes and she into mine and we are mixed together in our minds and I don't need to move my mouth for Mum to hear my misery so nobody interrupts me. My sad words just pour and pour and pour into my Mum all the details of how unbelievable it is at Gordie's and how I am starving to death cuz I cannot eat their stuff that grows *IN DIRT* or that had skin and eyes once. My brain cries into her brain: *See how I am turning into a skeleton!,* but Beth real loud says, "I don't know what it is but every time I get inside these locked-up forts I gotta pee."

I drop my face into my hands because in about fourteen seconds I am going to lose it and forget to have a heartbeat.

Ivy is not in the newsroom.

No, instead she perches woundedly (yes, like a purple, pink, blue, yellow but mostly scabby red bird after a cat attack) on the examining table and the doctor actually says, "Uh-oh," which real doctors never say, but this one might never, in all her days, have witnessed such a total, almost noisy case of poison ivy.

Ivy speaks from the crusted seam of her mouth, "I . . . was . . . in . . . a . . . ditch. It . . . was . . . night."

"Find any nightcrawlers? You can get twenty-five cents apiece."

Normally Ivy loves her funny doctor.

 From a future time, Bonnie Loo speaks.

There were several things that happened that summer that you could call bad omens . . . or turning points . . . or wrong turns. Whatever it is that puts you on that deadly course.

After the day the little newspaper cunt scoped out our solstice thing, Gordon had an old friend come visit. Skip was his name. A common occurrence. Old friends. New friends. Coming for an afternoon or evening or for a few days. But this time, it went differently.

 Claire St. Onge remembers.

Gordon had started up the beers and cider on the Solstice Day, which was a few days before Skip and Pamela's visit. Whatever came to his hand he would slobber down and this made him into his flushy, high-minded orator self, which is forever close to the surface.

 Settlement woman, Penny, tells us.

Gordon's friend Skip was married. He and his wife were staying in that nice lavender-and-white-papered room upstairs over the main part of the house down to Gordon's. The room had a table fan because the heat and humidity had come back worse than ever. Like airplane glue. The wife was a professional opera singer. A soprano.

You would not believe her voice. Like something from the sky. She sang a little piece for us, yes, opera, while our Eric played the piano. This woman was a little person and sat so straight at our big loud chaotic meals and all our girls were in love with her. As well as Eric, who was doing his showy "Ricardo" routine and charming the pants off both the guests.

 From a future time, Bonnie Loo despairs.

So they showed up at the shops the second night. Second supper. I wasn't cooking. I was a total person of leisure that night, except for the hard work of sweating. Gordon wasn't there when his friends first settled in with their plates and smiles. He had been down at his house supposedly dealing with his mail and writing out money orders, trying to squeeze it in after helping Aurel and Josee mend goat fences for the afternoon while his guests went swimming with Penny and Gail and some others who were playing host.

When Gordon finally showed up at supper, he had the most crazy look I've ever seen in his eyes. He was dirty. Streaked. Smeared. Seedy. Hadn't changed or washed up. Usually he was washed up and was a sweetie for supper. He knows it matters. Not counting the solstice and weird shit like that, supper has always been a sort of heartfelt ceremony. But he looked interrupted. His work shirt was unbuttoned and flapping. If he'd grown suddenly into a werewolf it couldn't have froze my guts any more.

 Settlementer Beth recalls.

First thing I saw of him was he was down at the far end of the piazzas, standing there by one table, eyes fixed on Shell's new baby, who was rolled up like a periwinkle in old Tante Lucienne's arms. He wasn't standing over the baby. This wasn't one of those coo at the baby routines. He was at some distance. Staring. His hair was all gummy. No cap. Wet shirt *wide* open. Like a rescue crew had just pulled him from a cove. Like a homeless man roaming in the subway tunnels of some fucking turd city. Meanwhile, his guests looked like they were going out to a ball and smelled like perfume factories.

Penny speaks again.

The visitors, at the side of one table far down into the second porch, saw Gordon, of course. Everyone saw Gordon. But the visitors just quietly murmured and munched. I guess they knew Gordon was no white-tie type anyway. And besides, the big soups were thick and heady with fresh herbs. The lamb was tender. The greens were sweet. The breads were perfect. The butter, the cheeses all shades of white and gold. Dozens of jars of preserves. We've always preserved everything. Just short of preserving rocks and beech leaves and poison toadstools! The little cukes and radishes and baby spinach and lettuce, plantain leaf, and scallions in the salad were fresh as the air. And the big pitchers of water right from the pumps were almost frosty.

 Bonnie Loo.

BANG! Gordon's fist on the table. Set off a few startled screeches and one baby started crying . . . and he bellered, "America!" He reached to spread the fingers of his right hand on the head of one of the Soucier kids. "IT EXECUTES CHILDREN!! IT BURNS CHILDREN ALIVE!!!! Pierces them with death needles! Virginia! Waco, Texas! Huntsville, Texas! You thought America only murdered kids in *other* countries? No, right here, too. Home sweet home. People fry! Armies and police! CS gas! Lethal injection! The chair and drooling mobs . . . America is a vile place! A frightening vile place! Posing. As. Para-dize."

"Pace!!" Lee Lynn's baby Hazel called out and I saw Lee Lynn hide a confused smile.

From the pocket of his dirty splotchy green work pants, Gordon tugged a folded paper, unfolded it slowly, everyone's eyes on that paper. He held it up. It showed a dark face. I couldn't make it out from where I sat but I could tell it was the face of a person who was of a dark race.

"Here's one in Texas! They're going to kill him Thursday!!! Maybe he's guilty! Regardless! Whatever. He is a poor person. They, the government, are going to kill this person because he is poor. You ever see rich folk on death row? NEVER!!!! Rich folk do killllllll. They killlll plenty. But no matter! It is the poor among us that must be washed away, the extra-useless useless poor! They *willlll* kill this moneyless captive, now rendered completely harmless, kill this person for political purposes! But this shit is supported by other lowly not very wealthy citizens for reasons of bloodlust . . . hot, fuck-hot pecker-cunt balls on the walls bloodlust droolin' in their shoes, and getting' it offfff!" He squeezed his eyes shut then opened them and they were popping out. And he was frothing at the mouth. Drooling. Spitting.

The whole piazza had become a misty gray silence with everybody embarrassed or nauseated . . . because that's what you feel . . . sick . . . when someone is screaming and sort of wet around the face.

And he railed on, "Now *that* ain't civilized! Doesn't that put America up a notch on the evolution scale! Fuck, no! Puts it down on the floor of some giant chicken house, where beings just shit and squawk and peck each other to death. I am just so proud to be American I'm about to wet myself. Wanna see me wet myself?"

My heart was skipping. I closed my eyes. When I opened them, he hadn't done it.

 Beth again. This is what she was thinking.

Fuckarooni! Thank Christ the reporter wasn't here soaking *this* up. Then the whole world would know what a coocoo looloo G was under his funzy exterior.

 Claire tells what she remembers.

After supper there was still no sign of Gordon. He had left us holding the bag as far as the guests situation. Fine. Some of us took them to the east parlor for tea, to hang out with the piano for a while. The woman, Pamela, told me that it was upsetting to see Gordon act like that in front of the children, that it would probably give them nightmares. Skip, the husband, seemed amused, and said, "He even scared *me*. I wasn't sure what he'd do next. Like next he might take all his clothes off . . . maybe wrap himself in the flag and . . . uh . . . hurt himself."

I figured he was teasing but the wife asked in her sweet, small, but penetrating and so well modulated voice, "Do you suppose he needs to see someone. A professional? A chance to talk about what might be bothering him?"

And I looked at her, eyes into her eyes, a smile and tone of voice coming to me that I didn't intend. "Now what on earth could be bothering him?" I asked.

 And now back to Bonnie Loo. From a future time, she speaks.

In the morning, Gordon was somber but pleasant with his two guests and smoothed everything over with them. They left after breakfast, all smiles, with their bright L.L.Bean packs and their bags of Settlement veggies and preserves. All our young girls moaned that their shining star, Pamela, was leaving. They promised her they'd write. And some would keep that promise. Handwritten letters were a major deal with many people here, young and old, even our dear computerphile Lily and some of the boys who thought personal computers as essential to life as iron lungs, fire trucks, and blood transfusions. So all was well.

But a few nights later, at supper, Gordon, still agitated, began another rant. Our peace man, Nathan Knapp, wasn't at supper during the last episode. A loner, he was not a regular at meals. And there were people here his wife found to be . . . well, they "ruffle her feathers" as my stepfather Reuben would say. But on nights when Nathan had a salon or committee with the kids after supper, he'd hang around on the edge of the meal, in some rocker or porch swing, or sometimes he'd sit by the table and nibble. This time, he stood in the kitchen door with Glennice and me, and I watched how he didn't take his eyes off Gordon.

Now Gordon's rant was about how America is a front for big, big megabanks and corporations, and their empire-building "intelligence" and military power. He emitted bloodcurdling screams this time. "America isn't what you think it is! It's a garbage bucket dressed up as an angel! But the flies give it away! Unless you're too dumb a fucker to know what flies are!" Then he was working up way past the screams, booming like a cannon, pacing, banging his hand on the table.

I could feel his voice in my chest muscles and tear ducts. Some of the grown-ups left the porch. The kids just lapsed into hearty chants of *"America is bad! America is bad! America is bad!"* And with their bodies, some of them struck poses of passion and militancy, smacked one palm with the other fist or thonked the table. Little revolutionaries in the making? Even toddlers. Baby rebels. Okay, it was sort of cute, *but—*

Lee Lynn and Suzelle and Lorraine and Beth and Jacquie huddled with me out in the kitchen to whisper, "What's he doing? None of this world stuff is *new!* Why's he doing this now? Why *now?*"

"He's fucking crazier than usual. But he'll land pretty soon when his hangovers get the better of him," I assured them. "He never has thought of this here as America, anyway." I laughed. "We are our own nation, by gawd."

Meanwhile, Gordon's big thick voice bellers, "EVIL GROWS!" and the children scream, "EVIL GROWS!" Quite a few adult voices chanting now, primed by the lumbering power of Gordon's theatrics. "EVIL GROWS!" Then a stomping sound. "EVIL GROWS!" *Stomp!* "EVIL GROWS!" *Stomp! . . .*

And in the doorway, committedly pacifist in every cell of his being, Nathan Knapp, still standing there, in a trim, stripy, short-sleeved sport shirt and jeans, hands behind his back, composed, terribly composed.

 Three miles away on the Seavey Road, little wallpapered room.

Supper cooking smells tumble up the stairs to meet the fumes of artist's oils. The little octagon window is open for the smell of the long weltery day to join in.

On beaverboard, she has begun another sun, this one with clots of green and a mountain-slanty horizon from which it lifts.

This artist has a spider's eye and a spider's touch, giving the ball of green fire a silken logic, none of her paintings meant to be public, not ever. There is a belief among her brothers and father that she is a painfully private person.

Another evening.

The long tables are heaped with plates of bones and bread crusts and fruit pits and grease, the piazza screens dark-streaked and glistening from a just-finished very windy electrical storm.

Gordon is conspicuously agitated, restlessly staring around at faces and feet and pools of water left on the porch floors from the rain. All through the meal he didn't sit long in any one seat, kept shifting, now mostly stands, a cup in his hand full of his favorite drink, a brew of fresh cow's milk and maple syrup. No beer or cider.

And it has come to this, as it has never been before, that the Settlement people are WITH him, inside and out. Yeah, the hale and flushy oneness of these denizens with this man, so that when he begins to rage on about a certain thing he has just heard and read, the very latest in the all-consuming earth-swallowing mess of humanity, and he throws up both fists and in a vicious, raspy, almost gurgly howl, screams, "Evil grows!!" the refrain of "EVIL GROWS!" comes back to him from the mouths of kids *and* adults, and they are all swaying from side to side as he sways from side to side, and again "EVIL GROWS!" so that back and forth, he shouts and they echo, breathing in unison. He growls, "Our system swallows us all like a ruinous pocking plague!!!" And "*Our* government, *our* Congress, the devil dollar prances among them! The dollar marches over the planet, forcing its way, followed by bombs! EVIL GROWS!"

See the batch of kids at the far end of the table, some with black brushy Passamaquoddy hair and such eyes! And those with hair of dandelion yellow. Those young mothers sitting along the inside of the longest table, the young men and older men, older women, and so forth, mixing their voices to call back, and now the foot stomping, all in sync and some people with spoons or forks striking their glasses and cups or the hollow-sounding table . . . *Stomp! Tink! Clonk!* "*EVIL GROWS!*" And, "Pencils don't vote! Money does!!!" Gordon groans. Groans echo him.

After it is finished, Gordon is walking to the kitchen and there is a sudden BANG! A chair falling? A slammed door? And he drops to the floor. Hard. Rolls onto his side. And there are all sorts of gasps and a few shrieks. "What is it!!" some people cry out.

"You okay, Gordon!!!" Helpers hurry to draw in around him.

He gets to his feet, flushing, while some hands brush off his clothes.

A few laughs now. Little nervous laughs of relief. "He said he thought it was a gunshot," someone is telling someone else.

But that is silly, isn't it?

He sits at one of the tables now, across from a Settlement man named John Lungren, who studies Gordon's face but asks nothing.

And Gordon says in a low ugly way, "I need a drink." And John Lungren knows he doesn't mean maple milk.

 In a future time, Bonnie Loo remembers.

That night after that particular *incident,* he came to my little house and of course Jetta wanted to show him how she sewed assorted buttons on her smock *all by herself.* And he admired each button, the clear plastic one made to look like glass, the maroon one, the cloth-covered one, the butterscotch one, the metal one with the eagle on it. Some of these buttons were quite old. The women had collected them over the years, enough to fill several dozen huge glass mayonnaise jars. That sewing shop had a lot of things some would call real finds.

After the kids were in bed, Gordon sat on the little sofa and rubbed and rubbed his face and beard, hard and slow. He was a bit drunk at that point, having proceeded to drink cider after his maple milk. That was his supper. Never mind food. He smelled drunk. But he also smelled good. He wore that T-shirt Lee Lynn had made, a real nice spring-meadow green, a little misshapen on one sleeve. But fresh. He had changed since supper. And his beard and hair were bathtub wet and combed, though now messy from hard rubbing.

I said, "You okay, Gordon?" I came over and sat down beside him.

"Just dandy," he said.

 The Voice of Mammon

Fulllll spec-trummmmmm dominannnnnnnce of the plannnettt, all its resources, water, energy, foooooood and human labor, technology, weapons of mass control and exterminationnnnnnn, willllll be the proppp-er-ty of meeeeee. Bend overrrrrr. Humpa-humpa. What?

What did you say little man, little lady? Obscene? Ha! You haven't seen nothinnnnnng yetttttt.

 The grays.

Meanwhile, we observe this aforementioned, most recent development, the crescendo of the spinning ages of the nongray two-leggeds and their surplus food ruckus. Interesting but no wow to us, the more sensate among this species are beginning to froth at the mouth.

 ### History as it happens (as written by Katy and Karma and Draygon with help from Margo and Oceanna and Aleta).

Some of us want to start a committee, although Whitney thinks we have too many committees. But otherwise, she's into what we suggest for a committee. A death row support project. We got Claire to help us. She got the number to call Gordie's priest buddy or minister maybe who told us the addresses. Oceanna reported to us that Claire and Bonnie Loo said okay on the postage. We have a list of names to write letters to guys the government is going to kill. Gordie's right. None of them are rich. Glennice said Jesus would approve of our committee. She said, "Pray for everybody." Maybe. So then Whitney says we have nine letters so far to Jeffrey and four to Carrie, a girl one. Samantha said this is only the start because we will change the fucking world. That was actually her word, *fucking*. What about that? Margo says do not censor. Glennice says censor.

 ### One of Gordon's weekly visits to his mother's home in Wiscasset.

She brings him coffee in a pottery mug with a textured snake wrapped around it. Her name is Marian St. Onge, her married name. She was born Mary Grace Depaolo of *the* Depaolo family . . . Big construction money, not aristocratic roots. Just Portland people. Waterfront Italian and Irish. Loud, steamy hardworking people. But sometimes, with money, vitreous (and silly) airs eventually ingrain themselves. For Marian, there have been airs, and one can never mention her name change from Catholic-sounding Mary Grace, or how Gordon's name is really Guillaume after his father Guillaume, who Marian renamed "Gary."

Marian is not a lonely old lady. She is perfectly connected to the family and to community groups and to a "better" church, one that has no kneeling. And besides, she's not an "old lady." She is tall and poised, has fashionable glasses when not wearing her contacts. Small earrings. High cheekbones and almond-shaped gray eyes. Her graying dark hair is clipped appropriately and attractively. She has a reasonable selection of conservative-dress sweater vests, which she wears over conservative blouses. Today's blouse is a soft blue-green. Vest, brown. Trousers are denim. Shoes are the slip-on kind. A wristwatch, of course, for the woman on the go, as she whizzes around in her sporty red car. One ring, a tasteful white gold with pink stones. Not gems, just pretty stones.

But today she also wears a huge plastic smiley-face button. Marian has some contradictions, yes.

What Gordon sees now is his mother's crisp blue-green sleeve, and her reaching out to place in his hand the aspirin he asked for.

She sits across from him in a white wicker chair, sunlight pouring over the deep red wall-to-wall carpet. In a moment, she will need to draw the drapes. The big TV is off. Its greenish flat glossy surface has only a reflection of the lighted kitchen through the archway. She tells him some news of the family. He nods, palms the childproof lid back onto the aspirin bottle. He is alone on this visit. He has brought no one. Sometimes he brings one of the Settlement kids along, or a friend, these who anguish Marian, these creatures he takes aboard his ship of antisocials, losers, and Aroostook Frenchies whose farms now belong to Irving (the oil company of Canada). So many relatives of Gordon's father, the Souciers, etc. She prefers to disconnect that plug. At least shake it out of her mind.

But this afternoon, it is just Gordon alone.

"You've been drinking?" Her expression now is artificially pleasant.

"Actually, I haven't. Not this week."

"I thought you always drank."

He says nothing. Sets the aspirin bottle on the white marble end table.

She fidgets with a cuff of her blouse.

He asks, "Would you like to go with me to Keene State College? I have a friend there. She's doing a lecture on charitable foundations. How they manipulate the population. How they shape minds. As in *mind control*. She's found them out. She's a socialist. *Happens* to be."

"Why do you torture me?"

"I'm not. This woman is interesting. She's an intellectual. She's . . ." He smiles teasingly. ". . . respectable. You'd approve."

"Stop."

"Maybe you'd like all my friends to be . . . harmless, mindless coward robotons with spines of Jell-O."

"Stop."

He sighs. "You should be proud of me. I have a spine. You wanna see it? I'll rip it out of my back. For you."

Her chin trembles.

He holds his face. He says into his fingers. "I'm sorry. I'm tired. Lack of sleep. It's *worse* than a hangover."

She has framed the newspaper photo of him from when a while back he spoke at the State House against what he calls "factory schooling." In the bookshelves by the hallway it presides over shadows and a small table with the phone. She is confused, sad, and yes, proud, but also angry, ashamed. Though mostly confused. Mostly worried. In fact, in the past few weeks, she has been scared. Of him? Or of the media that she has heard is investigating his private life. Oh, boy.

He looks up at her now, one eye squinting.

"Drink your coffee," she commands.

Sometimes when he visits, her sister or brother will be here, or one will call. Or one of the great uncles or cousins who Gordon used to work with, yes, the Depaolos who are funny and expressive and carry on much the same as Gordon does, with that red-hot Italian gene that Marian seems to be lacking.

But usually Marian is alone when he comes. They talk of the family. And they inevitably bicker. And they will look at each other sadly, each wishing the other were different. But he keeps coming around and once in a while, like in summer, she will drive her sporty car down to the old farm place, hoping to find him *alone*. A till-death-do-us-part loyalty. Parent and child. Old as creation.

Returning from a visit with Claire's people at one of the Passamaquoddy reservations, the long drive home.

It is nearly dark. After ten. Now coming into Egypt, they take the old back road. Six-year-old Jane is asleep, her head in Claire's rounded lap. The pickup truck they ride in is what some would describe as a rattletrap. The cab smells of tools and of the old sneezy quilted sleigh blanket that covers the seat to hold the seat stuffing in. The blanket may or may not have been washed since the days of sleighs. In daylight, you see it is made of black velvet and grizzly brown wool squares, a brisk rough weave.

As you know, Jane has no parents at the Settlement. Jane is an orphan of the "Drug War," so ordinary a thing in America, like apple pie, like Elvis, like Ford. She is a possession of the Department of Human Services. Why is she here in this truck? DHS would not approve of the Settlement. So what's up? This is a question for later. *En passant,* it will soon be told. A brief mention. Dear Reader, be alert.

Gordon St. Onge is at the wheel. His billed cap with Mertie's Hardware on the front is pushed back. Some around Egypt say he drives like an old auntie.

Ahead of them is a set of taillights that now abruptly slide over to the right shoulder. It is another truck. It stops. As Gordon steers his own truck around, he wonders aloud, "A little trouble, you think?"

"Don't stop. It's probably lovers," Claire advises.

Jane doesn't stir. The big day at Indian Township has overwhelmed her.

The stopped truck has a row of glowing amber cab lights across the top and amber parking lights on each side of the grille. But the headlights are now out.

Gordon says, "Looks like Webb's truck." Webb, a neighbor, one of the old Egypt families whose vehicles are as familiar to Gordon as their faces, some vehicles friendlier than others, lopsided and limpy as old baggy-faced dogs.

"No, it doesn't," says Claire.

Gordon downshifts to bring his Chevy to a crawl, giving the other truck a chance to signal him if help is needed.

"Lovers," insists Claire with a snort.

But now the engine of the mystery truck roars to life. Its headlights explode with brilliance on the backs of Gordon's and Claire's heads. Within seconds, the grille of the mystery truck is nearly pressed against Gordon's back bumper.

Gordon gives his billed cap a quickie adjustment. This bumper thing puts him to mind of Ivy Morelli.

The driver behind them lays on the horn. And the headlights flash off . . . on . . . off . . . on.

Gordon glances over at Claire, sees only the dark spots of her eyes behind her glasses. "Ain't lovers," she concedes. "Maybe a truckload of circus clowns." She tugs the summer-weight truck quilt (yes, a second quilt) to make it fit better over Jane's long arms, long legs.

Gordon pulls his truck off the shoulder, shifts, waits. They are only a few snuggly feet from the old stonework culvert where Mushy Meadows Brook jostles along purposefully from the swamp to the lake. Frogs on the swamp side are in thunderous session. Every kind of frog. The man-in-the-opera type. The rubber-band type. And a few of those that you would swear were really little sleigh bells. Above is the stony breast of Pike Mountain, black against the bodeful purple evening dusk of June.

Suddenly the great jangling thunderous symphony stops. The silence is stunning. Jane stirs. She can smell that old truck cab smell and the worn-outness of the old truck quilts and that smell of Gordon and Claire, the smell that all Settlement people seem to have these days since the last batch of soap was made, mushroomy, potatoey, dry rotty, peppery. Yarrow and St. John's wort? Goldenrod and turkey tail fungi? A Settlement woman named Lee Lynn is a regular magic witch when it comes to making the biggest tubs of nature-smelling soaps, Jane has overheard. And Jane, is as ever, unimpressed.

Gordon says, "It almost looks like Duey's truck."

"You'll *know* in a minute." Claire is annoyed by his chronic guessing. One of his traits that she has endured for half a lifetime.

Jane's head of poofy Africa-thick hair (part Africa, part Europe, and no doubt some 1600s or 1700s or maybe 1800s American Indian connections) this head has come up. Her husky deep-for-a-child voice asks, "So, where are we?"

Gordon says, "Almost home, dear," and squeezes one of her skinny knees.

A young man appears at Gordon's open window, a light step, no scuffing or foot dragging, probably wearing sneakers. Plain white T-shirt. His face is round. Mouth, soft-looking. A small boyish mustache with everything else shaved off. Forearms and hands look hard. He stands in a whirl of mosquitoes. Slap. Slap. Slap. Cuff. Swipe.

And now another young guy right behind him, same build of a medium kind, but taller, wearing a dark T-shirt with an illustration that Gordon can't make out. This taller guy wears glasses with metal frames. No mustache but the same soft mouth, hard-looking arms and hands. Smoking sweet tobacco in his pipe. So far they've said nothing. Just the sound of one bullfrog and two or three rubber-band frogs bravely recommencing.

And the hysterical whine of hungry mosquitoes.

It is the contentment of the man's pipe smoking that signals this encounter shall be friendly. And it is this pipe smoker who speaks, standing there a bit beyond the white-T-shirt guy's shoulder. "Gordie? You Gordie?"

"Yep."

The nearer guy asks, "Howzit goin'?"

And Gordon replies, "Good," and smiles and turns to glimpse out through the windshield. "Nice night."

"Yep," says the nearer guy and then, "Howzit we can get a kid into your school?"

Gordon says, "You gotcha some kids?"

"The sister," says this nearer guy softly. "She's fifteen. She don't like . . . you know . . . the other kind of school."

Jane squeals, "Ouch! Mosquitoes! Let's GOOO!"

Gordon tells the two guys, "Bring her over. She's welcome to check things out. Some of us will be away Monday and Tuesday. Couple little projects in Livermore. And . . . Wednesday is . . . New Hampshire. But Claire, you'll be around Monday and Tuesday, wontcha?"

Claire says, "I shall."

The mosquito whines are hale and hungry. Everyone is slapping and swiping their faces and arms. Jane moans, "My gawwwd." And covers her head with the quilt.

Gordon says, "Thursday would be real good. We'll all be around. About noon, we'll be settled in for dinner. She might like that. Pretty laid back. But a lot going on. Singing, storytelling . . . fiddle playing . . . history skits . . . karate demonstrations—"

"She's shy," interrupts the nearer brother, "of you guys."

"Ah." Gordon looks from the face of this nearer man to the other. "Well, we'll have to arrange for her visit to be quiet. If you wanna call me." He reaches for a pad on the dash and writes down his number, tears off the sheet, passes it into the near brother's open hand.

The guy looks at the sheet, folds it nice, struggles a moment with a thought, then says, "She ain't normal to look at."

Instead of getting politely softened, Gordon's eyes grow fiery, his full lunatic look, one eye big, one eye squinty. He gives the steering wheel a good squeeze.

Jane is whispering to Claire, something about the frogs being scary.

Gordon asks both brothers, "Has that been part of her school problem?"

The guy with the pipe says, "Brianna has a *lot* of problems."

"With her mind," says the other sadly, swiping at one ear, then smacking a forearm, then the top of a hand, then the back of his neck. But now he chuckles and the other joins in.

Gordon says, "You mean she's retarded?"

The two guys look at each other and the near one says, "More like she's from another planet." He chuckles again. With affection. And the guy with the pipe nods and smiles.

Everyone is slapping, smacking, swiping.

"Well," says Gordon.

Jane digs her knee into Gordon's thigh. "Let's go, Gordie. I gotta peeeee."

The nearest guy warns, "Brianna'll probably fight this."

Claire leans across with one of her stern dark looks, while reflections skitter across her 1800s-or-early-1900s glasses. "You mean to say her coming to us is *your* idea, not hers."

Both guys nod. The guy with the pipe says, "Actually, Bree knows a lot about you people. She's talked about what you're doing over there for a long time. She's just . . . a funny person. If i'twouldn't be too much trouble, could one of you come over and talk to her?" He steps around his brother and places a hand on the truck door, looks in at Claire and Jane. And the pipe smoke visits the inside of the truck, a kind of tumbling and timeless sweetness, especially nice mixed with the tumbling and timeless sweetness of a summer night.

Gordon smacks at first the top of one hand, then the other, now an ear. "Howzit we get over to your place?"

The pipe-smoking guy says, "It's easy."

Jane grabs Gordon's arm. "I gotta GOOOOOOO. Please talk later!"

The brothers give their directions quickly.

Gordon tells them he looks forward to meeting Brianna.

And Jane howls. "EEEEEEEEEEEEE! Let's GOOOOOOOOOOOOOO!"

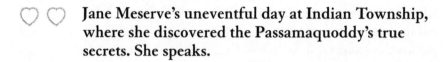

Jane Meserve's uneventful day at Indian Township, where she discovered the Passamaquoddy's true secrets. She speaks.

You would not believe it. No feather hats. No buffaloes. Indians wear T-shirts. And sneakers. Nobody had stuff on their face. Indian kids asked me to play. I stood around with them. I asked them if they liked McDonald's. They said yes. I asked them where was their TV. They showed me. We all watched TV. But it was boring. So I asked where was McDonald's, one that is nearby. But one mother Indian said "not today."

Vandermast is not printed on the tipsy silver mailbox across the road but this is the place.

Gordon St. Onge swings his truck down into the steep yard, house very close to the road. A bird chirruping in the tree over the house. Nice morning, no humidity, shade a bobbing blue-black against archipelagoes of tall weeds painted a ladylike early-day yellow by the fingers of the sun. Pole barn cluttered with the logging biz. Muddy low bed. Diesel pump. Rags of bark everywhere. Battered orange Timberjack skidder inside the bay. A wheel removed. Piles and clusters of needs-repair stuff. And parts. Rust and grease. Metal and rubber. Precious. This is, yes, small time. The bottom of the logging biz chain.

Not the tip-top, not the nice lunches and projections and plots, not the smiles with legislative and bureau buddies-of-the-bosom behind closed doors that stay closed. *Private.* At least inaccessible to us low folk. No, this little barn by the home of loggers is as wide open as a yawn of exhaustion.

Dog barking inside the house. Gordon can't see the dog but it sounds like a collie. House isn't old but not new. A kind of forties or fifties red-shingled frame house with two additions in white metal siding.

He walks up to the door of the larger addition, it has a kitcheny look to it. He drives a homemade toothpick around in his teeth . . . casual . . . no hurry.

Dog is now at the nearest screened window. *Woof! Woof! Woof!*

Gordon doesn't knock, just looks at all the windows, and up at the trees, and around. Two red pickups with no registration. A station wagon with the old-style aluminum registration tags up to 1964, parked deep in the bushy low limbs of a few dozen elm saplings. Fisher plow on pallets. No flower beds.

No spinning-leg Tweetie Birds or bent-over big-bottom plywood ladies.

He tosses down his toothpick, crosses his arms over his chest. Big ol' dog bounds to the other near window. Something crashes inside. No need to knock. Dog is the doorbell.

He waits awhile, a good long while. He studies the gable with his most intense flickering mad-scientist expression, and there a small window of an octagonal shape like a cyclops eye staring back. But Gordon holds the stare, his pale murderous-looking hot green eyes, one squinted, one nearly bulging presently, devilish-looking beard, a man who stands nearly six-foot-five, muscular as a panther. Who in her right mind would answer the door to such a stranger? Even if she had purposely drawn him there.

 In a future time, Brianna Vandermast remembers.

It was different than some believe. I saw not a lamb but a ram. I saw not wine-blood, nor flesh like bread, but musculature. I saw not holiness, but flaw. I saw not God there but all of the broken world, cries, complaints, whimpers, perplexity. I saw the beginning of a long road of trials. Trial by doubt. Trial by love. Trial by loss. Trial by a kind of explainable resurrection. There is no such thing as a savior, but there is a human epoxy that brings innumerable hearts into one hand.

 ### Claire St. Onge speaks.

Finally the savage man, the fist-banging freaking angry one, metamorphosed back into our steadier teasy-eyes goofing-around version and the sky stopped drumming and the walls stopped panting and our meals were commenced with a forthright but unspoken grace. And our food got digested.

 ### Newsroom.

Ivy is alone here. Still cartoon pink on face, neck, arms, legs, fingers, collarbones. But the torture by tickle has eased.

Old-timers have told her how once this was a big open room, blazing with light. Desks all faced north, like one-man or one-woman boats racing along on a sunny sea. There were three papers: morning, evening, and Sunday. Deadlines swooped above like enemy planes. But those were jolly times. "Like a family," Ivy hears them say. And cigarette smoke, ringing phones, the clack of the wire services, the t-t-t-t-of typewriters, and there, raised on a platform like the goddess of the north was Ellen, the operator, poking at her lighted board. "Like a family."

No more. Everyone is in a cage . . . well, a carpeted cage with walls that only go to your chest if you are standing. No more blazing light and cheery hellos. Just shadows so that computers can be seen and concentrated on.

No more Ellen.

Mostly now it's just voice mail or a soft pulse if you are there to catch it.

It is sort of lunchtime, not a cheery merry "let's all go to the cafeteria" lunch hour, but one of those coincidences where the place is empty.

No computer screens are busy. All are "asleep." Even Ivy's. Our Ivy is staring up at the dim ceiling.

There's a sound behind her. Light as a soul. With sound-sucking carpeting, people pass behind you and you might not know it. But Ivy thinks it might be Martin the new reporter, a kid younger and less flashy than Ivy but with more college degrees than her. Ivy believes Martin wouldn't make much noise even if he were walking on crushed rock.

She pictures Martin settling into his textured desk chair now back in his cage. He earnestly listens to his voice mail. Does Martin get calls from people demanding he investigate the Home School? Has Ivy failed to get the dope on the Home School story? Will Martin be sent to replace her?

And Martin would have quotes. Lotsa quotes. Quotes upon quotes upon quotes upon quotes. He would, of course, go to Egypt at least once to paint the setting. And then he would fill it with quotes. The perfect newspaper piece.

Is Ivy's job on the line? Is Egypt Ivy's Waterloo?

Ivy presses and prods her computer awake, checks her e-mail, then pokes around in her computer's files to begin her afternoon's work on her column, which today deals with road construction on Brighton Avenue. What a mess on Brighton Avenue!

 The tour guides.

It is the appointed time.

A few yards up past the old St. Onge farm on the right, Ivy turns off the tar road, heads up the long graveled one, the actual way to the Settlement, first through mucky-green and mossy, black-smelling swamp-woods, then higher into open fields and gardens, up to the clefted plateau where the Settlement hides in its sprawly, tough ostentatiousness. The sky is nothing like blue. More white and creaturely than pure space, like a drooping furry belly getting ready to settle down on its big nest.

"Another hot muggy day," she laments. But she's had several nights of real sleep since the itching quit, so she feels ready to soak up the weird and compelling vibes of this place, which so many of the anonymous callers call the Home School. She hasn't told her editor, Brian, that her status here has changed from reporter to friend. Of course, one could be both. Reporter and reported-on don't need to be adversaries, do they? At the moment, Ivy's left brain and right brain are twirling and stomping around in a terribly old dance.

She parks her sporty red car among a couple of vans, a few cars and pickups, one jeep, and three old farm trucks in the glowing, hot, crunchy lot out beyond and in front of the first Quonset hut, then hefts her shoulder bag and marches in her usual substantial way toward the shady quad. And what does she find but the quadrangle and piazzas and doorways almost as swarming and noisy as before. But different. Not much sitting or scooching. People are standing in bunches. Though griping about the heat, they look so bright-eyed and bushy tailed and enterprising.

"Breakfast, Ivy?" This, the early-gray witchy-haired youngish woman with the high, almost tweety voice and something else that Ivy finally registers, a Chicago-area accent. Lee Lynn.

Ivy says, "Sure!" She smiles around at all the faces of those rather tightly surrounding her. Sentries again?

"We are your tour guide crew," a slim woman (whose dark hair *must* be a wig, so solid and swollen and dead-looking it is) tells her, as if correcting her thoughts. But Ivy still feels guarded. She is still not trusted. And for Ivy this has become her true mission, to be trusted, newspaper story or no newspaper story. She can't bear to be seen by anyone as a trickster. She may be harsh in her columns, well, uh, mean-spirited. But she is not a trickster. It is probably her very honesty that seems harsh.

Everyone notices her change of skin color, their eyes held on her overly long. "I was in a ditch. At night," she says gravely.

She pulls out a chair at one of the long tables. Gordon's ex whose name is Claire, the short, bubble-round, fifty-ish-thereabouts, bespectacled Indian woman (dressed today in a sky-sized aqua-colored T-shirt with badly-sewn seams, but fresh-looking), pulls up a chair across from her. She winks at Ivy in a sisterly way. Many women and young girls are converging now. "Hi, Ivy!" they all greet her. Ivy repeats the ditch-at-night business to each new stare. Lee Lynn, the witchy one, promises to fetch her some Settlement-made poison-ivy remedy, a cream made of weeds. The word "herbs" is used. But *"weeds"* is the word Ivy's brain sees typed out across her mental screen. And *weeds are the enemy,* whether in ditches or bottles, by Zeus!

No sign of Gordon St. Onge. In fact, most of the men have been leaving in droves, turning into shop doorways or ambling out across the quad. Plenty of old people here look awfully settled in, propped in chairs or scuffing by on walkers and canes. One of the tour guides looks at least a hundred. Like one of those cute, sunken-mouthed apple dolls but for her occasional tight-lipped severe expressions, yeah, cuteness comes and goes. She wears an olden-days nurse-type pale-blue pinstripe dress. No embroidery.

All around, hither and yon, plenty of kids, babies, and dogs.

Ivy munches on a fat yellow muffin. She is happy. The women are telling her their various personal versions of last night's rip-roaring thunderstorm.

With merry eyes now, the apple-doll-face woman says, "Man in Kezar Falls has been struck twice by lightnin'."

Another old gal, round of body, electric-white short straight-and-upright exclaimy hair, eyes narrowed, clucks, "Used to be you only got lightning in June, July, and August. Now it even rumbles in January. Ain't right."

A lanky, muss-haired boyish girl or girlish boy Ivy remembers from the morning of the solstice, still shoeless and shirtless, wearing only black lopsided (probably made in a sewing lesson) shorts, appears beside Ivy's chair, holds out to her a violin stained a weird but enticing color, a color that seems not of this planet. Shimmery red-blue-purplish-deep-deep brown. The child declares, "I made it."

Ivy wipes her hands on the clean rag given to her as a napkin. She smiles into the child's face. "You made this violin?"

"Fiddle."

"What's your name?" Ivy allows the instrument to be placed in her hands.

"Tamya Soucier."

Ivy glances around at the faces of the women. "Aurel's daughter?"

Claire nods. "One of them."

"You actually made this, Tamya?"

The kid squints at Ivy's face, incredulous of Ivy's incredulousness. "My other ones didn't work out." She reaches between Ivy's hands and the young fingers press and prod deftly over the graceful neck of the instrument and she confesses, "I can't play it too good. I'm not musical. You would cry if I played it." She withdraws her hands, which are cool, bumping against Ivy's, and she smiles crookedly and

Ivy sees this little girl's eyes are a brown even more tender and grace-filled than those of Ricardo, the young fellow with the Chinese pants who had been her "waiter" at the solstice affair.

"Ivy!" Now someone hurries up behind her and kisses the top of her head. What a coincidence. Ricardo's sister, Heather, Ivy's old sentry. She knows the voice well. She turns in her seat and smiles up into that serious, almost sad face, framed by stiff, short pigtails. Now, turning back to the younger girl, she asks, "What is this stain? It's really different for a fiddle."

With much authority, Tamya answers, "Iodine."

"Iodine?"

"Yep. Just, you know, *I*-o-dine."

"You *really* made this?"

Tamya smiles, then says with saintly patience, "Yes."

Ivy glances at Claire, who, of course, no longer wears the cardboard crown, but just her graying black hair in a large braided knot on her head. And then that *vast* aqua homemade T-shirt. Breasts *vast*. No, not breasts. BaZOOOOMS. Small hands on the table, eyes on Ivy. Those steel-rimmed glasses, resurrected from some old trunk? Yard sale? And her expression seems resurrected from a grim old sepia photograph, back when a person had to hold wearily still for eons before the photographer's black powder flash *poof*ed.

Outside in the speckledy shade and little globlets of sun, hurrying past this long wide porch now, are two women. They both sport cool-dude sunglasses and swinging ponytails. T-shirts with embroidered creatures flocking around the square necklines, also vines and buds and blossoms of yellows and blues and stems of a live-looking nearly buzzing green. They appear so normal! Normal purposeful everyday women. As if extravagant embroidery plastered everywhere was the way of the world.

And see here on this piazza the witchy-looking woman, Lee Lynn, a dress of tangerine, with yet more embroidery, whole platoons of bluebirds across the chest. She stands with a hand on her hip, her other hand on the back of Claire's chair. And in her birdlike voice, she twitters, "Ivy, we'll show you the shop where they make the instruments."

Tamya Soucier tells Ivy, "Stuart and Rick and Vancy and Eric can play pretty good fiddle."

"*Ricardo,*" Heather corrects her.

Tamya's fingers close up around the instrument to lift it away. She says, "Bye!" and lopes off long-leggedly.

And there by the kitchen door, not joining this welcoming group, is the whorish-looking young woman, Bonnie Loo. This time a big, square, solid Rottweiler-mix stands with his side against Bonnie Loo's thigh. His tongue hangs rippling. In and out of his mouth, rippling, rippling, and dripping. His eyes smile into the commotion of people passing, people going in and out of doors, so many leaving, crossing the quad, all with purpose.

Heather tells Ivy, "I love your dress."

"Thank you." Ivy's dress has a pattern of calendar moons in all phases. Yellow on purple. Matches her hair and her earrings of pottery-like plastic stars. This morning as she dressed, she tried to think like a Settlementite. No embroidery to her name. No T-shirts made by three-year-olds. So she went for her celestial second best. The sleeve length of this dress covers her fishy tattoo; the tattoo colors would have clashed with her dress and ivy-poisoned scarlet skin.

"I love everything about you!" cries Heather and again she kisses Ivy's head.

Claire watches this head-kissing with her unreadable, old sepia photo expression. The witchy woman and another woman, a tall, handsome, broad-shouldered, fortyish blonde, confer about "the van schedule for Thursday."

Ivy glances again toward the kitchen doors. There's no mistake. Bonnie Loo is looking at Ivy and that look ain't friendly. Her hands are on her hips now, feet a bit spread. The dark part of her orange-streaked hair is really dark. Her lime T-shirt looks good against her big, hard-looking, dark arms. Golden skin. Gypsy earrings. Big soft shoulders. Big but alert-looking breasts, bare under the fabric. Almost intelligent-looking breasts, pressing out against that T-shirt with creaturely pleasure, with volition. The hands strong, wrists thick. Scary. So many ways a woman like that could hurt you if she does not want you around.

Women are now standing up from chairs, getting momentum. The tour crew. Someone from the kitchen crew takes Ivy's plate. Ivy stands, glances again toward the kitchen door. Both Bonnie Loo and the big dog are gone. *Poof!*

"Where is Jane? Won't she be joining us?" Ivy asks the witchy, gray-haired, youngish gal with the orange dress, whose name she *again* overhears is Lee Lynn, forgetting that introduction. In time she'll forget again. So many names whirling through the hot steamy air. Introductions blurring together like the spotty leafy shadows.

Lee Lynn's high, shuddery little voice says, "Jane," spoken as though the single word were a complete and tragic statement.

 The grays.

As we grays watch this unfold, we are in full study. From our location above and among the dawns and dusks of Settlement life, we have *already had the tour*. But the fierce pink centerpiece of today, the Ivy, the driver of the buzzy red craft, the blue liquid currents of the wrist veins, the jangling curls of the ears, the startling HAW HAW, draws our thundering eyes.

They call her the *Record Sun*. But that is baloney. She contains too many ghosts. Ah, that jostle and elegance and flossiness and orgiastic fun of ghosts.

 The tour.

She takes many mental notes, just in case the Prophet changes his mind about her doing a story.

Today she wears her sandals. Gives her a nice springy walk, though as she is ushered from shop to shop the day's wet foamy heat swallows her whole, presses in on her from every angle until she feels less and less springy. Her mind roams to her shower at home and her favorite towel, the icy nice feeling you get when you swish open the plastic curtain afterward.

And she thinks of the callers: "work camp" and "compound" and "terrible place" and "children worked like animals."

She is led from the shops to the Quonset huts and other locations in haphazard fashion, back and forth, around and around, lunging through the swelter, embroidered flora and fauna in every color of the heart, churning in all peripheries, soaking up the sweat, and oh, aren't Ivy's tour guides proud.

Everyone's faces and necks are shining and trickly. More sweat following other sweat. Waves of sweat. The tide is in! Leaping dolphins! Ivy sees the shops and Quonset huts filled with industry and skill, all at a kind of ambly dabbly pace, lots of yakking and laughter among those who work together, often more adults than kids. But hot. Hot. Hot.

Ivy sees the east parlor. Ivy sees the west parlor. Library teetering, shelves, tables stuffed and bulging. Ivy meets the library crew. One of them on a ladder. One with a loaded cardboard box. One heading out on an errand, book balanced on her head, la-de-da. Everyone happy and gay, as the old saying goes.

She views the print shop with a printing press black and oily, almost dripping petroleum, metal to metal, like a leer. This iron monstrosity dominates the floor while state of the art photocopiers in the corners don't look as though they are up to the humid reality of life here.

Now on to the shop next door, where entries are being readied for the *History as It Happens* books. "These books are important to us," the high-voiced, witchy-looking Lee Lynn explains. "This is *our* history." She is a whirl of orange—a whirl of gray braids—*three* of them. She is a whirl of long arms. Two of them.

A silver-eyed pregnant person sneers, "Oh, indeed."

Claire sighs. Claire of the sepia. Claire of the one enduring tragic expression. Black, black eyes behind the glasses. Mouth a line cut by ugly surprises? Or something.

Ivy is alert now to this pregnant girl-woman who says such things as, "Oh, indeed." Yes, the girl's eyes. Silvery. Her hair is cut quite a lot like Ivy's, the bowl cut, though tapered in back. Not exactly the Ivy look. Not violet-tinted black. Hers is light brown. And no HAW! HAW! She, like Claire, is low on humor. The grimness is waist-deep and rising near these two.

Kids are dashing here and there with paperwork in hand or a drawing clutched to the chest. A young man squints at a typewriter, not typing, just thinking. A tiny old woman, wearing baggy jeans and a T-shirt that reads: *I ♥ My Honda,* her hair a frizzy perm like a dandelion in the white seeding stage, is comparing three similar photos.

"Oops!" A Dutch-boy-haircut, yellow-haired preteen manages to get her elbow in a jar of white paste.

"This is just like a little newsroom," Ivy says with a happy hoot. "I love this!" She glances toward the silver eyes of the pregnant person with the Ivy haircut, but those eyes are squeezed tightly closed, head turning from side to side.

 History as it happens (as recorded in a recent *History as it Happens* book) by Gabe Chapman and Tamya Soucier.

We had to ask more than 8 people to get all this infimation. But here it is. When I was born awile ago (me too) this road was still callet Swett's Pond Road Some people still call it that. Way before ANYBODY was born there was 4 farms One was the Swett poeple. They all so had a blacksmit shop kind of lick we have hear now where we can forg iron only in those days you coulnunt just go buy iron alreddy shapped into things into the store. The Blacksmit shop was a important palce to be.

Down aways was the next farm of poeple name Hanley but it burd in a Fire. And Roberts farm is were Gordie lives now. What is woods now was not then. It was hayfields. And stonwals made for lines whitch are still there thro the woods.

Then poeple had too many poeple and cities got too fat so they cum here fast. They went here and they didnut like Swett's Pond for a name. They was woried it didnut sound nise. They change Swett's Pond to Promise Lake which they said was very pretty and had a very pretty sound. And they change the road. Was Swett's Pond Road turd to Heart's Content Road whitch they say is so PRrety. Also Robert's Hill Road changed to Chrystal Veiw Road. And the Lap Road is Silver Hights. I wonder whuts next.

 Cows.

The fiddle-making shop is closed up tight. Hot and dry. Abandoned but for a treacherous-looking band saw, fiddles in roller clamps, and a tall, many-paned window giving a view of sun-speckled shadows and a supper-table-diametered oak with an orange blush in the rivuleted bark.

Many shops are closed for the day, Ivy is told.

Beauty shop. Closed.

Weaving shop. Closed.

And here's the sewing shop. Just one cloud-gray ancient lady stitching a blue quilt square, says everyone's at the pond and how she loves the quiet.

Then for Ivy and her tour guides it's on to the Quonset huts, which are less hot, furniture-making, shoe-making (including brain tanning of leather to make it as soft as cotton for clothing, an artful *resourceful* technology of America's Indians.) Also there is machining. Then art studios featuring giant papier-mâché life forms and puppets. A pottery shed, kiln, the works. The building under the shadow of the unfinished radio tower is not offered as part of the tour. Ivy eyes it as one would any unidentified object glinting up there in the heavens.

But then there are Christmas tree fields.

Vegetable fields.

More vegetable fields.

Goats and cows. Sheep and cows. Cows and cows. And bees, their white wooden box homes busy as . . . uh . . . bees. And orchards, and the uphill woods beyond all that simmering with blue-green mystery. Lots of enthusiastic woodsy flies on the go. The moist air sags with specks of even smaller life.

Back again in the cool Quonset hut shadows, a solar car of an edible shade of purple. "Our Purple Hope!" is its name.

Ivy is impressed.

 Monkeys.

The computer shop is *REALLY* empty. No computer! Computer none. Not even *proposed*. Not by any Settlement authority figures. So the tour group doesn't bother to enter. The silvery-eyed pregnant person, who they call Lily, is now eating an apple. She whispers to Ivy that Gordon calls computers, "the devil." Apple breath.

"No, not devil." This from a young preteen boy with blond hair and Indian eyes. "Gordie says all technology is just like a stick or a rock, but humans are monkeys and always wind up beating everybody up with stuff."

"Yesssss! He calls us monkeys!" a small, leaping, hopping girl agrees from her upside-down face . . . somersaulting, kicking. A girl with ten legs. "He says we never evolved."

Lily says through gritted teeth, "He told *me* computers . . . are . . . the . . . devil."

Claire seems not to like this conversation and horns in. She talks about stained glass.

 Lily's torment.

Walking out on the boardwalk to the next shop of interest, Ivy again hears one of the women call the silvery-eyed pregnant one: "Lily." Inside Ivy's head, a roaring HAW HAW. Thank the heavens nobody else can hear Ivy's head, but Ivy. She is always so tickled to know that other people besides herself get stuck with a plant name. Too bad the name Violet is fading these days. Bring it back! HAW HAW HAW!

Meanwhile, the guides are chattering about a "town meeting," not as in the Egypt government, but the Settlement government. There are times when even the little kids get to vote. "The most important part of democracy is being informed," one very young girl pipes up in a way that seems older than her eight or nine years. "And understanding how government *really* works. Not the textbook thingamajig. Do you ever read Gore Vidal?"

Ivy is stunned. This squirt reads Vidal? "No," Ivy says darkly. Her face crimsonizes with shame. "Do you?"

"Don't lie," a teen girl with bloated face and extra soggy T-shirt (obviously, heat beats her up) says to the younger girl. "You just spy on our parlor talks."

"I don't *spy*." The younger one spits on the ground. A big creamy-looking louie.

A little boy, also Indian eyes, also light-haired like the other one, grips Ivy's elbow. "We want to be uptominus."

"Autonomous," an older girl corrects him.

"Like the Zapatista villages!" a preteen boy adds.

"In Mexico," the puffed-faced dripping girl adds without thrill.

Ivy sees the silvery-eyed Lily staring at her intensely, less insolence, more a wordless cry for help.

Ivy gives a sidelong quickie glance toward the bear-sized (in diameter only) aqua T-shirt (Claire), then multiple peeks at the other of what Ivy thinks of as the Settlement's "head women" or "women supremes," then dodges (slow-motionlessly and unintended-appearing) between two clusters of yakkety yakking tour guides to where Lily is shuffling along. "You okay?" Ivy asks.

Lily smiles tightly. "I just hate absurdity."

Ivy lets go with a great HAW! HAW! "A woman after my own heart," she says in a hushy way, as if to cover over her loud laugh retroactively.

Hovering near, a wide floppy lime, orange, and purple Hawaiian shirt with a skinny boy inside it, skinny legs with knobby knees and bare feet, sandy hair and exclaimy kind of voice, tells Ivy (with a little accidental flying spit), "Zapatistas kicked the bad guys out!" (Throws out both hands.) "Even kids! Kids pushed the bad guys . . . fshhhhhfffff! (That's his impersonation of the sound of pushing out bad guys.)"

A girl with frizzy brown curls and glasses sighs pleasurably, "Zapatistas have the best hair."

"They never cut it," says another girl, both about twelve, Ivy guesses.

Ivy goes with the flow on this matter. "Indians and Asians have envious hair."

Claire (who by the way is the owner of Indian hair, which is, yes, exquisitely glossy and rich, even the gray) is moving in closer to where Ivy and Lily are hesitating on the boardwalk. Claire tells Lily, "You know, for the baby's sake and your own, you should rest. At least go scope out a rocker and put those feet up."

Lily places her slim arms around Claire's vast aqua-colored blue-green cotton shape; two vast shapes, one pregnant and one not. "I love you, my fussbudget!" She kisses Claire lightly on the lips. "Fretting uses up vitamin B."

 Fretting.

Walk. Walk. Walk. So much to see. Ivy is thinking how amazing it is that a spread like this has been kept so well hidden. Hidden from what? She squints. Well, the media, of course. Reality, so to speak.

Is paraphrasing bracketed with quotation marks reality? Well, yes, so to speak.

Lily is at Ivy's side. Lily. Ivy. The two plants. Haw! Haw! Haw! Lily is done with the apple but still smells of apple. She is just striding along in her pregnant feet-wide-apart way, swinging her arms and smiling. Her kind of sandy soft voice leaps sideways into Ivy's most available ear, "We can talk about *anything* but *him*."

Claire is dropping back again now, obviously bothered, the sad slash of her mouth sadder, her spectacles driving home, square into Ivy, like two powerful telescopes sucking Mars and Saturn, the moon, the stars, out of the night.

Ivy hoists her shoulder bag.

Claire laces a moistly warm arm through one of Ivy's. "It isn't just Gordon who resists the computer craze," she says firmly. "Most of us here know what's good for us. Dependency on computers, TVs, and other grid-like things would not be good for us. There are people outside our community who think these things would be good for us. But we don't think so. Don't you think a people should have the right to decide what's good for their lives?"

Ivy nods, grins. "Most certainly! Free country and all that."

 At last, Ivy observes the sawmill, speak of the devil.

"You like it?" a small voice asks, probably because of Ivy's one raised eyebrow of dramatic amazement. She looks down and sees a snow-haired boy who they call Rhett.

She slaps her hand to her heart, rolls her eyes swooningly, "Oh! Sawmill!"

Rhett smiles in a most beaming way.

Outside the first mill, Ivy stops to pick a daisy. Now she twirls the daisy in her fingers and feels headachy in that high whiney *zinnng!* of the saws at work and the clattery chug and stink of the diesel engines. Sawdust, bark, the powdery dirt of the road, hot people, engines, and Ivy's wilting daisy . . . all this, both fragrant and fuelly, confuse the nose.

There are three mills, actually. One is for rough lumber, one for planed, and one is a shingle mill.

Gordon is here in the rough lumber mill. Too busy. Doesn't pay her any mind. A tall, very narrow, familiar-looking bearded young guy, his purple-checked flannel shirt tucked in, works along the carriage. And here's Eddie, who the day of the solstice wore the toucan head? (Kill the bird! Kill the bird!) And his jazzy bejeweled belt, and all his complaints about hell.

And there is quite a charge of adolescents, both girls and boys, all wearing earplugs or "earmuffs."

Eddie waves to Ivy and smiles showing off all his white teeth in that painstakingly shaved face that shines like glass. He seems mighty cheery for being in hell.

Ivy watches the log gliding toward its fate, the magnificent saw and all the gear works. The tractor-trailer-truck-sized diesel engine looks brand new! She again wonders where these people draw the line with technology, why this and not that? What is THE DEVIL and SEDUCTION, and what isn't? Now she rehears Claire's voice, *Don't you think a people should have the right to decide what's good for their lives?* Maybe this is good for them. And Ivy thinks about how she said "a people," not just "people." *A* people? When do you get to be "a people"?

Now, away from the sawmill area, there is more to see and Ivy notices that by her watch, it is nearly noon, white blazing eye of the sun turning slowly and grindingly upon the little group trudging uphill through steamy space.

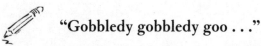 **"Gobbledy gobbledy goo . . ."**

Ivy does another Penny double take. Not her first. There are a lot of handsome people here at the Settlement but Penny is one of those who could easily get a role in any one of hundreds of today's movies. All she'd need to do is memorize a few dozen lines and spend the rest of the time staring into the "eyes" of the camera in a dewy way and therefore melt America. Beautiful Penny. Sort of tall. Late thirties? Nose, Romanesque. Sticky-looking lips. Lips thin, but not thinned. Just awfully English. Streaky tawny blonde locks. And the neck. One of those necks. Proud but not too-proud bearing. Friendly, yet covert. Poster woman for the Settlement cause. She explains, "Seems easier for the Mayans, who still have a culture, an interactive culture, to imagine autonomous. Those of us who have been sucking on the nipples of consumerism find it hard to believe Mother Society doesn't really love us, just *uses* us. And that people have learned to see other people only as opportunities. As tools. It's awful to see that things are—" *Gobbledy. Gobbledy goo. Coo. Coo. Coocoo. Cockadoodle doo boo hoo . . .* Well, this is what Ivy's head now hears. It's the glow of Penny's beauty that holds Ivy's attention, the solidness of the kids, the pregnancies, the quarrels . . . not gobbledies, not for our Ivy, no gobbledies *pleeeze*.

Lily hisses, "It's not like the world will end just because of *one* computer." Rolls eyes. Tsks.

Ivy's villainous blue eyes widen. "Ah hah!"

Now the first aid shop. So small. So cozy. More like a bedroom or little den. Ivy admires everything.

The tour guides tell how there are a lot of celebrations, meals open to the townspeople and trips around the state where people want help setting up the equipment for solar and wind energy independence. "We go and teach what we know. And we learn, too," witchy-haired Lee Lynn's voice trills. Her orange dress, though thin and revealing, makes Ivy hot and tired just from its brilliance.

It is *all* starting to sound gobbledy goo now. Ivy's head aches.

The nearby kitchens rattle and clank and hiss. Mmmmmm. The smell of food is in the air. Cake? Lemon? And something fried in butter.

Also in the air, the sound of accordion and guitar. *In* the air, thin *as* air. Behind some closed door, behind another. Like a memory. *Maybe Ivy only imagines it.*

The tour trudges on, passing open doors. Ivy sees flashes of men, women, dogs, kids, flashes like TV ads that spin the brain. Again some shops are empty. Corners are littered with abandoned shoes and toys. Yes, a white hen is pecking at the rug of one empty room. Only Ivy notices. Another open door shows people leaning over a table with scalpels . . . or . . . something. Another door is closed. Another open. Ivy sees a baby crawling to another baby who is napping on a pile of quilts. A small child, two-ish, hangs upside-down in a man's arms, watches the tour crew pass, discovering the pleasantries of an inverted world.

Another plastic bag of summer heat is shoved down over Ivy's head and neck. Ivy wonders if some people here aren't hankering for air-conditioning. We can pretty well guess how *HE* feels about AC.

 The meltdown.

Back out on the brick walks (the bricks of hell), under the Crisco sky, within the simmering philosophical conundrum, the tour guide crew and egg-collecting crew pass like ships in the night . . . well this is *day* . . . but through the glare, it seems the passing group is soft-edged and surreal. Many children. Many baskets. Many eggs. And one old man.

Okay, not baskets, exactly. Already-used commercial egg cartons of mix-and-match brands lined up in the egg wagons. They wave serenely as they pass.

Yes, and a flash of embroidery.

Somehow Ivy and Lily, the two plants HAW! HAW! weave back into side-by-side position and consider Settlement deprivations, not just computers but calculators, TVs, stereo systems, cell phones, video games, and personal motor vehicles. But take note that *Gordon* has *his own truck*.

"And he does not allow the words "Mom" or "Mommy.""

Ivy's eyes spring open wider. However, our Ivy keeps her head straight forward, as if not really having this conversation.

Lily's pretty and personably bucked teeth spell out distinctly, "It's . . . because . . . he . . . thinks . . . Mom . . . and . . . Mommy . . . came . . . from . . . greeting . . . cards . . . and . . . TV. So *my* baby will have to call *me* Mother or Mammy or Mimi . . . or Mummy . . ." She sounds these out with her eyes squeezed shut. In pain. "Or maaah. It's because he says Mom and Mommy are not mother words but devil words."

Ivy holds her breath.

Lily lowers her voice. What she now confesses is lost. The crunching of so many fiery-bottomed shoes on flaming sands blocks out all other sound in this world. But Ivy believes she hears this phrase, "after it happened," and this one, "Ge-yome the Great . . . is . . . a . . . pig." And she kicks the dirt.

Now a load of hot alternators and converters goes by in a burning wagon behind a melting electric buggy, these having just been repaired in the nearest Quonset hut there, repaired by roasted demon children and demon men who might in *secret* call their mothers "Mommy."

"Hungry?" witchy, orangey, trilly, tweety Lee Lynn asks, approaching from Ivy's other side now, gives Ivy a faint one-arm squeeze and up ahead Claire has stopped walking. She is now a profile, her unsmile now epic, complete; lips corneous.

Ivy blows air up over her face, shifts her mighty mammoth of a bag to the other shoulder. She notices that witchy Lee Lynn wears a wedding ring. Silver. Weenie weensie designs. *Really* weensie, nearly microscope-slide-sample weensie, because the ring is slender. The finger inside it slender. Spiritlike, white, like lagoon steam. Could this Lee Lynn be the merest, airiest, tautest, flimsiest, draftiest, utterest nullified example of the white race?

Ivy admits she's starved. And mean-spiritedness infects our Ivy in times of hunger.

"We'll finish the tour after dinner." Dinner here means the noon meal, the old way. Ivy hasn't seen the kitchens yet but she bets herself a hundred bucks there are no microwaves.

 **Noon.**

The piazzas are not as crowded as the day of the solstice but if this is "the family," *ohmygawd leaping lizard eggs! HAW! HAW!* See mirth and wonder dancing in her never-resting eyes. There's practically a hundred people, including kids. The men are back. But no sign of Gordon. And no sign of six-year-old Jane either. And now no sign of young silver-eyed computer-lusting pregnant Lily, who told of Gordon-the-pig and his devils. Off to the dungeon with Lily, eh?

"Is Jane here?" Deciding not to bring up Lily, Ivy has asked this of Claire, who again is very handy to Ivy at one of the long tables.

Claire frowns. Shakes her head. "Not today." Then says, "That's moose," as she notices Ivy staring at the nearest platter. Patties with melted cheese. Claire (short person that she is) reaches, having nearly to stand in performing this feat, to pull the platter closer to the space between herself and Ivy. "And over here in this bowl, lamb with some sort of sauce. For cold meats, you have the beef and pig over there. And cold boiled eggs, egg salad, and cucumber salad. And as you can see, there is all the bread you'll need. Good sandwich bread today."

"MMMMMMMMMM." Ivy reaches for some white chewy-looking sliced bread.

Claire is now hauling a flying-saucer-sized bowl of ruffly greens across the table toward the guest. "The big meats here . . ." Flashes her dark, dark eyes to the kitchen. ". . . mostly for celebrations, parties, holidays, 'n so forth. The meat today is leftovers." A low grunty chuckle in her billowy neck. "Normally this place is Soup City. Bread, soup, bread, soup, bread, soup." More chuckle. "Today Bonnie Loo likely wants to impress you." Now she makes an almost mooing sound, and a clenched smile. Somehow this makes the day hotter, and a co-ordinated (so it seems) silence falls all along the closest tables.

Moments pass in a humid rattly way, like never-ending train cars.

Ivy strains to be reserved and offhand as she inquires, "Where's Gordon?"

Claire raises three fingers to her lips, as she had oh, so quickly filled her mouth with food while Ivy had spoken. "I don't know."

A woman a couple places to the left of Claire, who has a forty-fivish face of sixty-fivish hard lines, pink green-leafed roses tattooed around her neck. She answers pleasantly and as equally offhanded as Ivy had asked, "He went for a warm swim." She pushes another aircraft-sized salad toward Ivy, this one crowned with wheat berries and seeds, small orange tomatoes, radishes, and other cheery yummy colors. "Eat this stuff, Ivy. The last half of your tour will be *really* rigorous."

Ivy blinks.

Claire snorts. "She's just kidding, Ivy." Munch munch munch munch. Claire is wasting no time in getting herself fed. She is truly a hungry person.

"I'm Gail. I know all these names and faces must be confusing," the hard-faced tattooed woman declares. Her hair brown, shoulder-length, too thin, too careless.

Ivy says, "I thought you might be going to put me to work at the sawmill."

"Not yet," Gail laughs.

Ivy is relieved not to see any sign of Bonnie Loo now, yes, the whorish-looking cook. Thus no I-will-kill-you looks from that quarter. Ivy hopes *she* has left for the sawmill but suspects she's deeeep in the kitchens, her realm of celebrated genius.

Ivy fills her plate with salad and one warm dripping-in-sauce lamb patty. She really is hungry, too. Hot, yes, but not as nervous and tired as the other day. *Warm swim*. She likes the way Gail said that. She realizes she had a heart-hop at this news of Gordon's whereabouts, the reality of him.

 Peak and poo.

Now hurtling into view, an important-looking, arm-swinging, damp-looking group of teen girls settles all at once into the available chairs near Ivy on both sides of the table and the next table, one squashing a noisy kiss on Claire's cheek. One smooches Gail and Gail squeezes her eyes shut in melodramatic thrill. All these girls. So many bare arms, bare throats, and collarbones and summery colors and some embroidery, of course. And heat flush. And smiles. All those eyes on Ivy. Ivy smiles back, vaguely recognizing some of them.

But now more arrivals. A couple teen and preteen boys. Smiling at Ivy. One is stippled with sawdust, T-shirt, hair, arms. He gives Ivy the thumbs-up. For some reason. Hardly matters. It makes her day.

And now more! Tromping onto the scene, running and gasping as if from danger, smelling metallic, salty, a waggly mob of younger youngsters surround the Ivy area of the two adjacent tables, both sides, fore and aft, drawing in tight like a laundry bag string. One boy is nearly naked, bare feet, cut-off jeans, torn, shredded, mended, then shredded again, smoodgy around the eyes, hands black in the seams. Scrappy and savage. In *real* school, his entire being would be labeled *trash*.

One of the older girls formally announces, "Ivy! This is the solar crew! Part of it, anyway. Electricians and painters. At your disposal!"

This girl is about fifteen, has yellow hair swept up in a hard braided knot with big damp worms of hair loose around the ears. Big gray-green eyes. And what are those cheekbones? Slavic? Nordic? Yeah, a Slavic-Nordic princess. Did the old-days' Nordics have princesses?

Viking royalty? Well, here is one for them. Just as there are important-looking women here, alpha women, pivotal women, power women, seems there are some important-looking teen girls, too, and this is one of them. And she tells Ivy, "There are more solar crew members. They aren't around today. Off on a mission. And some are tied up." She wags a finger in the direction of the Quonset huts. "But they're the ones who made the Purple Hope. You need to interview them sometime."

Claire's eyes and Gail's eyes flash at the speaking girl.

Speaking girl has already realized her mistake? Is this why she touches her lips with two fingers? Then she giggles. "You'll love the stuff they figured out. YAY to the Purple Hope!" She throws up a fist.

The crew shrieks and "YAYYYYYY!"s. And there are two ear-splitting whistles.

"Go, purple, go!" cries out a preteen girl from behind Ivy's chair.

Ivy is laughing. Her HAW HAWs fit right in with this rough-and-ready crowd.

Claire's eyes, glittering blackly behind her specs, now remain steadily on Ivy's face. And as she stares, her jaws work, chewing her meal, the jaws stopping for a couple of long thought-filled pauses, but no pauses in the stare.

Ivy has stopped eating altogether. Just dealing with the invasion of all these hot arms, jiggling knees, sockless feet in sassy little homemade moccasins, hot breathing and blowing faces, wet canny eyes, and now more, a few stragglers arriving, the stricture drawing swelteringly tighter around Ivy, The press. Death by clamminess.

"Everything you want to know about solar!" a husky voiced young'un shouts.

"And buggies!" another adds.

"We have buggies!" yet another offers.

"She *knows* that," another one says with a "*tsk!*"

"Hey." (A quiet *hey*.) There is a really squirty little guy at Ivy's elbow, maybe five years on earth. He has hair pale as snow, snowy eyebrows, doleful blue eyes. Some fresh bug bites. Ivy recalls him from the tour crew. It's Rhett. He again murmurs, "Hey."

But an older girl with little square-lens glasses (the latest outside world fad) and frizzy brown hair and a quivery voice is telling

Ivy something physics-esque, about how and why they made the passive solar collectors from scratch, and this goes into an explanation of why homemade labor-intensive solar is king in the way that "force times distance equals work. See?" She is going on about how fossil fuels cannot be beat for work. "Weaning ourselves off of them means more work for people, even with the best known alternatives. So the idea is to make the work part for us humans *irresistible!* To make it like a party! One can't expect individuals and regular-ish modern families to want to take on this thing the way we do."

The girl with the honey braid says, "On a massive scale, such as this nation, it takes fossil fuel to develop the non–fossil fuel transition. If they've started, it's been kept secret, I mean in the way of commercial processes meant to supply the whole population. It's no secret that most regular folks are still using fossil fuel for everything. But it appears that most industry is, too. And the bloated military. This has a mega *uh-oh* factor."

Ivy smiles pleasantly, trying not to appear sleepy. This kid is dishing prime goobledy goo poo.

A golden girl with black, black hair and a vaguely Indian face, age twelve or thirteen, wearing a salmon color halter, compares fossil and solar, adding that "hydrogen is too flammable, and you have to get it with use of the fossil . . . at least as it's developed today. So there's no point in discussing hydrogen as a *replace*ment to the fossil for manufacturing, heat, electricity, and cars in time for the transition we need *now* before *the available and processable fossil* is gone, like . . . you know . . . can't be got. So hydrogen is . . . you know . . . just political distraction."

"Or yet another corporate scheme to outdo the sneakiness of all other corporate schemes," states a girl with earrings almost as wacky as some in Ivy's earring collection. But can you believe this? Earrings made with chicken eggs! Hollow, Ivy presumes. Eggs painted robin's egg blue but no robin could have laid those corkers. Meanwhile, the girl's brown hair is in a fanciful do. From the head up, she looks ready to go to a ball. But her halter is thin and tight and tiny. Red. A real sexy glamour puss, but all sorts of sciency and political goop poop pours out of her mouth. Her bare shoulders are freckled. No tan.

A lotta time in studies maybe? Or in the Quonset huts under cars? Anything is possible here.

She goes on, flicking her sexy little wrist, "You hear that big industry is hot to develop more efficient hydrofracking . . . but that is *still* Peak Oil because the cost of massive water use and ruining prairies . . . and the gasoline used to do this is totally goofball. *Totally!*"

A small-for-her-age blonde in much embroidery (and some tan) intercepts the blue eggs girl with, "the hydrogen thing, you see, it exists chemically bound with oxygen as water or with carbon in fossil fuels. It would use too much energy to separate it."

"It sucks," says a wee soul who stands beside Claire, across the table from Ivy so all she can see is the top of his face. Thick chestnut hair.

An older boy standing behind Ivy remarks, "Hydrogen is definitely overrated. People just don't understand it. If they did, they'd see through all the optimism."

"Meanwhile," another boy says quickly, "It's wars 'n stuff over the last easy-to-get oil and natural gas. And even . . . wherever . . . it's dirty, dirty, dirty."

"Human bee-ings are dirty," a toddleresque person says with a long exhale.

Another small solarist pipes up, "We can't do hyjrin ourselv, so it's not democrissy anyways. So—"

"Hy*dro*gen, Ethan, hy*dro*gen."

"Nuclear is creepy," says another.

"Has vibes," says another.

"*Rays,*" corrects the same voice that had corrected the other kid.

"Radiation," says another small scientist.

"Hey," the snowy-haired little Rhett again murmurs up at Ivy.

Ivy replies, "Hey. Yuh. Hey, hee hoo."

"If nuke power is going to work and they can get all the deadly bugs out of it, fine. But right now, too many bugs," a ponytailed teenaged ever-so-wanly-bearded boy explains.

"Yeah, bugs," says a small kid, shivering.

Several giggles.

Does Ivy look vague? Eyes. Blue. Cold. Vague.

"Then there's biomass," reflects one of the seated older girls (one with that important look about her, not la-la-la-dee-dah *self*-importance but a person who is regarded highly and listened to. A silence happens as she speaks). "It's turning out to be a big gang rape on the rain forests, along with all the other stuff they're hitting on the rain forests for . . . soy and meat. Even in the Middle Ages they depleted their forests over in Europe. Construction and fuel. And the Nazis were resource depleters. Just to name a few. But with the population and consumerism and wastefulness today . . . and all the networks of importing and exporting, and legislative systems with no accountability to anybody but mammoneers, you can just see what's coming. Earth becomes moon. A few woodstoves, fine. But maybe if it were hemp. Hemp grows fast and doesn't deplete soil . . . but even *then* . . ."

"So using miles and miles of trees for biomass is suicide," a crackling crunching future baritone warns. "Whatever they come up with involves the fossil, like for equipment and trucks . . . so we have climate change. That's a huge cost. You have to figure in the climate mess. The peak, the climate. It's all one . . ." On and on.

Ivy's attention *seriously* wanders. The goo poo is running *up*hill. Yes, Ivy's attention is in scan-the-room mode.

Screen door nearest this table has *weeeeked* open and some new arrivals step in. A familiar-looking girl who looks about twelve years old, with a sly, inward smile like people get when they are stoned, only her eyes do not seem stoned. Her eyes are gray, and bright. She is as "big as a house with child," of course, and there's a newspaper under one of her skinny arms.

"Dee Dee! Hey there, good woman!" someone at a farther-over table hoots.

"Oh, no, here's trouble!" another admiring shout.

"Jeez, Dee Dee, what happened to nine o'clock?"

Pregnant twelve-year-old (or so she looks) popular Dee Dee wrinkles her nose. Bows.

Accompanying her are three young guys, one a tall youth with a long, Oriental-type beard, you know, tapered and straight and undercharged. And black. It trickles over the front of his shirt. Ivy's eyes widen. She had just seen him at the sawmills. *And* he'd been at Gordon's farm place with Eddie right after her confrontation with the "strong" coffee. His shirt is a summer weight flannel of purple and black checks. Big, flappy, hot-looking mountain man, felt hat on his head. And again that heavy revolver hanging in a holster from a loose lopsided belt. His hips are narrow as a child's. Shoulders, narrow. Head and face, small. But he's a good six feet, yes, the guy looks like a weasel, a sawdusted-over weasel.

"Hey. Hey." The small boy, Rhett, with snowy hair is now poking at Ivy's shoulder bag, which is on the floor beside her foot. He knows how to get a city woman's attention. Ivy's stony blue eyes flash first to his foot, then to his face. As we noted before, Ivy does not have friendly eyes. The child's eyes are doleful and round. His voice, matching his eyes, says, "You know about Peak Oil and cli-mitt?"

Meanwhile, the rest of the solar crew has been vying for Ivy's ear and eyes, going on about hydroelectric, "a nice idea but displaces people's houses. Sometimes whole towns."

A twenty-something young Indian woman's face floats out of the heat and clamor. "But *small* hydro projects are a must. Like small dams at mills. As long as it's not where salmon run."

A twenty-something young white guy with his arms folded over a muscle-filled, lime green T-shirt, speaks ever so softly. Ever so grimly. More gobbeldy poo Ivy doesn't bother to hear.

A fifteen-year-old red-haired boy with eyes full of sparks, gives more sciency info to Ivy's glazed expression.

"Less consumption!" another middle-teen voice bellers from the edge of the group. "That's the thing we need!"

A nearby face agrees. "A new way of *life*."

"Even if a new commercial discovery or invention works, it'll be out of reach for most people. Wicked expensive," This from *behind* Ivy's head, so there is no face, only decibels. "Think about fracking, just another expense to taxpayers. Corporate tax loopholes. Jobs only for a while."

"Village-sized democracy. It's the thing *we* can do!" Another squealer there.

"Peak Oil," the little snowy-haired Rhett says again. Quietly. Firmly. No doubt in *his* mind. "You know it, Inee?"

Ivy says, "Well, of course," and her cold eyes flash off to the left to activate her memory. Peak Oil. A children's mantra. Little small mouths giving up these empty words to the day. Words that are empty to Ivy. Is Ivy curious? Is Peak Oil worthy of pause? Could it ever be the headline that titillating St.-Onge-as-child-fucker-type stories get? How about somewhere between a sofa ad and retirement of a Nebraska police chief? And what izzzzz Peak Oil? Two empty words trapped in a wee pocket of woods in Egypt, Maine. THAT is not news. If it doesn't come over the wire or from the lips of the governor, it is NOT NEWS. Unless it has "human interest." Or violence. Ivy has thought all this Peak Oil stuff in a flash and discarded it. Leaping Lizards! Droning ducks! Everybody just shut up!

The snowy Rhett is clearing his throat but already two more squeaky voices fill the space like mice in a pail. "The silicon solar panels . . . ones we buy. We'll show you pretty soon." Nod nod nod. Confirmation of this by others, too. All these little nodding heads.

"You can *really* see the difference and besides Mark and Oh-RELL—" This tyke interrupted by another tyke, the interrupter sounds almost angry, little thin angry squeaking voice, "No! She is going to *the mills*."

"*After,*" the interrupted voice insists.

"She has already DONE the mills," a deeper voice intercepts.

"Hey," the little snowy Rhett persists. Doleful finger. Taps Ivy's arm. Little taps of sorrow. "Inee, listen, Inee, hey."

Ivy looks down at his finger and then his face.

"It's awful," he insists.

Ivy turns in her seat and studies him square on.

Voice of a teen girl somewhere in the hot mob, "Rhett, she *knows* about that. She's a *news* person."

Ivy smiles blinkingly. Raises her chin. TRIES not to sound condescending or SARCASTIC. "Peak Oil?"

"It's awful, Inee," the snowy little Rhett tells her gravely.

But heads are turned and more turning. Some chatter in the nearer distances has stopped.

Teen girl voice, "*You* don't know about it?"

Claire's eyes burn through the spectacles, through the heat, through the mists straight into our Ivy's frosty blues, Claire's eyes as dark as past and future, just as a twelve-year-old (thereabouts) gives a nervous giggle and announces, "Hot oceans with acid, dead soils, floods, fires, famine, peak water. It could be the end of the world for millions if we don't—"

An interrupter bursts in, "Wars. The whole world will be fighting over the last little bit. All wealth and resources going into boots for soldiers. Like in *Nineteen Eighty-Four,* that book by the man—"

A voice overlaps, "Orwell!"

The first interrupter goes on, "All resources will go into war. That means millions of people who are just regular people now are going to become bums."

"Homeless, Derrick. HOME-less."

"Or soldiers!" another small eardrum-puncturing voice stabs into the mix.

"Or police!" cuts in another.

"Or dead."

"It'll be feudalism. People will make lace by hand for lords and most of us will get squeezed into barbed wire like Palestine!"

"Cement!"

And now another interrupter-overlapper quite close to Ivy's right elbow asks in a voice full of wonder, "What kind of news *do* you do?"

"Well, I only do official news, not . . . conspiracy theories." She blushes. "I mostly do just news about people, not science anyway. Or politics. So either way, I'm not about . . . *that.*"

"Peak Oil is about people?" a teeny-weeny Minnie Mouse voice sort of states, sort of asks, quite bewildered.

"Dead people are people," a husky boy-man voice plainly states. "Dead from no food, no heat and stuff. The fertilizer that agribiz uses is made from the fossil. From natural gas. No fertilizer equals no food."

Meanwhile, faces all around stare at Ivy dumbfounded.

Ms. Ivy Morelli. *The press.*

 The grays.

WE are NOT dumbfounded.

 Conspiracy theory 101.

Yes, the older kids stare at Ivy dumbfounded, and the women at the table aren't saying anything, but the younger kids have no idea what just went down and continue to squeak and chatter at Ivy about oil.

Oil oil oil oily gobbledy gooo. Pooey poo. Animal sounds. Ivy floats on the hot wet waves of oily mouths, open, close, open, close.

Claire's formerly steady gaze is now lowered to her plate as if the moment has become uninteresting even to her. She lifts a forkful of oily salad and stuffs it in.

Ivy smiles quirkily.

One of the important-looking girls says sweetly, *overly* sweet, like sarcasm, "There are people who have no problem figuring out that what goes on behind closed doors might be conspiracy. Isn't that the definition of conspiracy?"

Ivy says, "Sure."

Girl goes on. Sweeeeetly. Brat. Unblinking silky-white hotshot babe. "Some people believe that learning things is good. It's the basis of democracy. Right?"

Another sweeeet girl trills, "You don't make fun of most science theory, or police investigators with theory? Only science that has political ramifications, huh?"

Several important-looking girls slip out a snicker, but then hold back. *Many* unblinking but lathered hotshot babes. Fucking brats.

Tall boy steps closer. Tall thin boy about seventeen. "But Peak Oil and climate change and acidification of oceans is documented."

"Yeah," says a woman, standing behind Ivy. "But these things are not *announced* through the media by scientists hired by the oil, gas, or coal companies. Just like climate change isn't. And water shortages. Food wars and mineral wars. And serious soil erosion. They'd rather we be surprised. Like *pow!*"

"They want to keep these things as divisive *issues,*" croaks a pimply boy with a nose like a banana.

Important-looking girl dives in, "Independent scientists who aren't on a leash are considered originators of conspiracy theory, right?"

"Theory leads to investigation," booms a deep-voiced man-boy.

Everyone is looking at Ivy. Ivy is all alone.

Gail mutters around her chewy bread, her cheek rounded, "Officials are fascists. Corporatists. Government and big biz and big finance all blended through foundations, campaign finance, revolving doors. *They* aren't going to tell anything. Big media are shills. Madison Avenue fashions the news. All mixed up. Same guys. *They*

call it democracy. *We used* to call it conflict of interests. But there are
new developments in terminology. Look up Fascism in the dictionary, Ivy. You'll see what it means . . ." Gail's voice now has a dusty
surface. Irritated. Dry. *Oh, sweetie pie, look innnn the dictionary.*

Yeah yeah yeah. Fascism. Peak Oil. And flying saucers. Ivy says, "I
see what you mean." She does not want to turn them off. She doesn't
want to lose them. So close now. But the heat is bringing out Ivy's
rough side, her snarly side. Her operating a bulldozer side. She swallows. She thinks of hearts and flowers. Her eyes drift for a moment.
Across all the heads and arms and shoulders of the solar crew, she
sees the bearded and armed (with handgun) weasel-shaped guy with
the big hat and purple-checked shirt holding the screen door open
ever-so-thoughtfully for a broad-chested, big-headed, short-legged
black Scottie dog who hops up onto the piazza and stands surveying
the situation. The dog's head is huge. Eyes dark and gleaming. The
thick erect tail quivers like the tail of a rattlesnake. A child's voice
in a tattling nah-nah mode calls out, "Uh oh, Cannonball is here!"

The young bearded weasel guy's eyes meet Ivy's now. Ivy decides
that these golden-green-brown eyes (which are in the blackest of lashes
and are so lost in the bluish privacy under the brim of his big hat) are
the MOST beautiful brown eyes yet, surpassing all the other glorious
browns she has witnessed so far here.

Someone at one of the farther tables calls out, "What's that dog
doing here again? She bites!"

No reply.

Another voice, this time from a group of men in rockers along
the inner wall, "How'd you wind up with a hound like that anyway,
Dee Dee?"

The pregnant twelve-year-old-looking girl with the newspaper
who has arrived with the guy with the eyes and gun answers heartily.
"Dad stole her. She was tied out somewhere in a yard in Vermont.
Tied OUT. Night and day. You know Dad. He flipped his cookie."

"Hey," the snowy-haired little Rhett grasps Ivy's arm now, his palm
feeling like mailing tape against her skin. He's gaining confidence,
gaining ground. He'll be crawling up around her neck next.

A woman's husky chiding voice snarls, "Well, you don't steal a breed
dog like that. She looks almost like a show dog. Look at those long

whiskers, eyebrows, and everything. Cops'll be at the door. Maybe a lawsuit. Maybe jail."

With quickening blood, Ivy realizes this is Bonnie Loo, standing between the two kitchen doors as usual.

"Hey." The little boy's hot wet fingers knead Ivy's arm.

Other solar crew voices are now murmuring and snickering like frolicking background music. The term "Btus" is repeated many times in squeaky voices, voices that normally discuss teddy bears. Well, maybe not that young. How about Little League scores? Ivy sneaks a peek at the world's best cook. Bonnie Loo's shirt has been changed since breakfast to a fresh soft-looking pink with the Settlement's trademark embroidery, but the large breasts and dark nipples and surrounding areolas clearly defined against the fabric still make her a cheap show.

Ivy tries some pasty stuff that looks like cheese mixed with raw chive. She chews . . . yes, cheese and chive . . . nods toward the various solar crew kids who are explaining more of their theories and some details on their alternative energy projects. In real school terms, they are mixing their current events class with industrial arts. And philosophy. And intro psych. All mixed and mooshed. Oh phew. But it's their *ZEAL* that gives Ivy the creeps. A few facts wouldn't bother her at all. A *few* facts. Short and sweet, like one placid kid at a time at the *chalkboard*.

Bonnie Loo's voice is still advising the pregnant Dee Dee about the perils of dognapping.

Ivy's eyes slide over toward that part of the porch again.

Pregnant Dee Dee has been chortling with great feeling over Bonnie Loo's worries. "Tell Dad that!"

Ivy can't see the dog now. It must be under one of the tables or headed over through one of the open shop doors. Maybe the kitchens.

"I don't tell Willie Lancaster anything," Bonnie Loo says disgustedly. Then *she* laughs. "When'd he ever listen to sane people?"

Ivy's ears REALLY perk up now. WILLIE LANCASTER.

Ivy now has scopes up on this Dee Dee person, quite light on her feet for being so pregnant. Dee Dee hops happily straight over to a guy at the other end of Ivy's table. It's the blue-eyed troll with the carroty beard and hair who Ivy has heard people calling "Stuart." The smiling

Dee Dee places the newspaper in his lap, but not till after she whacks him on top of his head with it and each of his shoulders and pointing at the portion of his belly exposed below his dark green T-shirt, she says, "Cute," then bounds off to poke and prod and humidly love-up half the people on this piazza and then the next.

"Hey, Inee. You want to see my kittens?"

Ivy looks down into the eyes of the pale-haired doleful Rhett. "After lunch," she tells him.

"Lunch?" He squints.

All these hot adhesive-to-the-touch kids still hover and press and prod Ivy, even as solar talk has mercifully ended. The seated teen girls are chomping down food and gulping water or milk. There are certainly enough empty seats on these big porches for those milling about *to sit down* in. Sit! Stay! School is *supposed* to be law and order, correct?

Claire is done. Wipes her mouth on a cloth napkin, which is more like a frazzled rag.

Ivy is thinking how the solar crew enjoys some prestige here, though she wonders how much time they spend on wacky politics. Well, it all fits. Gordon has wacky ideas. Some of the women here talk kind of funny. And so the little critters just sail along in their wake.

Suddenly, Ivy speaks right into Claire's eyes, "Is Lily okay?" (Remember Lily? Tour guide who told of Gordon as computer-phobe. And pig. Pregnant apple-eating Lily.)

Claire's left hand is palm up on the table, a carrot stick in her fingers (her dessert?). She replies calmly, "She's fine."

"Good." Ivy takes some salad and fills her own mouth. She imagines the empty computer room and down below the earth's crust in the flames of hell, the devil and many sticky blue demons are manufacturing computers for humanity in order to steer them wrong. Steer them toward Peak Oil? Whatever Peak Oil actually izzzz *if* it actually is. She wants a thorough explanation. A nonchaos explanation. But chaos is what she'll get from this gang if she sets them off again with THE QUESTION.

Sorting it out, all this that they swear is true, it is this: *Rome is burning and Americans are fiddling. But the Settlement heroes will save the day.*

Hallelujah! The new life. The life of *w* . . . *o* . . . *r* . . . *k*. Never-ending labor. Rickshaws? Pots of water carried on the head?

Whatever. Ivy has to go along with things a bit here if she wants to be a FRIEND. Jolly Ivy.

Ivy smiles down at the little boy Rhett who is still close but not attached anymore to Ivy's arm or her shoulder bag. She smiles at Claire. She smiles high and low, far and near.

Claire and Gail are now telling Ivy about some of the shops they will visit next.

Ivy wants to suggest visiting the secret dungeons. HAW! HAW!

Ivy keeps hearing voices call to Dee Dee. Ivy's ears are perked to the max in the direction of this Lancaster bunch, though her fleshy sweaty corral of solar crew tykes and teens are making some genuine din, making references to names of Settlementites whom she can never keep straight, but Ivy is remembering that soft happy voice on the Lancasters' phone, the voice that would give her no interview because she claimed to be sick.

The tall weasel-shaped young man with the big hat, beautiful eyes, scraggly black beard, and gun doesn't mingle much, just leans himself against the screen door's frame.

"Lou-EE! Food!" Bonnie Loo throws this command toward his shy profile. She points at the table. "Eat up, boy!"

Lou-EE, Ivy notes is, of course, the way French pronounce Louis.

Now Ivy sees the Scottish terrier, Cannonball, who is standing as if she is ready to declare war on somebody but her mouth is ajar like a smile, tongue fluttering. The chest on this dog is like a bulldog. Her tail trembles. Her sagacious-looking eyebrows flicker. Her mustaches and profuse beard are wet. When this dog turns to observe in another direction, it's a Muhammad Ali pivot.

Ivy is studying Lou-EE's gun now. Dark handled. Many ready cartridges on his belt. He looks like a Zapatista–Matt Dillon cross.

And maybe a bit of West Virginia. Johnny-Bob Zapata Dillon. But then there are those green work pants that almost balloon on his long, long slim legs. So hipless. So tall. His expression as he scans the faces of the piazza crowd is hard to decipher. Could be shrewdness, could be tenderness, could be tiredness. Cannonball's attitude is easier to read.

When Lou-EE finally finds a place at the table, he eats ravenously. And he pitches stuff to his sidekick (Cannonball) whose open mouth and white teeth are as large as a Dobie's. Jesus. And again, like an army tank, the Scottie constantly swivels, eyes sweeping the porches for enemies. No wonder this breed is not popular.

Ivy remembers again to smile. Oh, yes. She turns her smiling face back to Claire. Claire is smiling back at Ivy in a sisterly way. Does Claire have to keep working on that smile, too?

"Hey." It's the snowy-haired little Rhett again. He rests his little hot paw lightly but completely on Ivy's forearm. "You like rhubarb pie?"

"I sure do."

"*Ten* rhubarb pies." He points to the kitchen door.

Bonnie Loo makes a special pie for the press. Full of razor blades. (Nobody hears this but our Ivy, of course. She smiles her most huge, painfully stretched smile.) "All for me?"

"Sure!" The boy, now beaming (see what Peak Oil did to him? Now the *Peak Pie* look.) His face has actually changed shape. Eyes crinkled. Eyes full of light. Knowledge makes kids sick. Knowledge makes *everybody* sick. Better to be dumb as a snow tire.

Up on a low stage at the end of the piazza, a little stage that was covered with costumes and papier-mâché heads on solstice morning, classy Ricardo now arranges a little pine stool. He peers down at a guitar as he strums the first chords of something complicated and classical. A gifted boy, yes. Okay, so this place is absolutely rich. But the chaos cornucopia spilleth over.

  The grays.

Today our awe is also captured by the specimen on our study bench, curled and cruel, still alive. Pulled from a ditch. Somewhat vine. Somewhat root. Leaves huddle in triplet, drooping.

Rhus Radicans.

Yes, the three oily scoundrel leaf tips reaching muscularly for human skin, now shrink to discover our rubbery gray.

One of us and all of us suggests the categorizing of this sample with the "Honor Student" bumper sticker, in part because both are green, and in part because of the misery both strew.

The green leaves bleat. We are in sync with its terror and decide to let it go. After all, the ivy isn't as sly as the bumper sticker. No, not at all. The ivy is forthright and humble and plump with ancient ghosts and only fights back when brutelike stomping bears upon it. We open the hatch and gently replace it by the roadside. Such earthly paradoxes cause our heads to spin around forty times.

♡ ♡ **Meanwhile, back at Gordon's house, Secret Agent Jane tells us about HUNGER.**

Bev and Barbara, who are two ladies who don't live all night at the Settlement, talk Gordie into letting me have a few more "healing days." Meaning I don't have to eat the giant meals with all the weirdos up at their "school."

So today I'm still here at Gordie's house.

Bev fixes me lunch. It is the worst color. Like it might be made of something sick. Bev says, "That's just the color of the cheese, dear."

I say, "I'm not hungry." I flop my hands down into my lap. I say, "Probably any minute my Mum is going to call on the phone and say she's going to come get me." I look over at the phone, which is on the wall. Guess what!! It is black. And it is OLD. The kind where your finger gets tired of turning the round thing.

Bev is smiling and she says, "It's good, dear. Especially the cheese part. Try it." She is really cute. A cute round lady like the other one, Barbara. Both cute with their haircuts. They kinda look like two little men. Or two little women. You can imagine either way.

Barbara, who is "fluey" today and stayed home, she knows all the words of a funny language, not like Gordie's cousin Oh-RELL's funny language. It's *another* one. Also Barbara does math. She did number stuff all her life for the government, yes the government. Some kids like number stuff called calcules, but only one likes the physilix stuff. That's Whitney. A kid named Max says if you know physilix, you could make bombs. What if Whitney made a bomb and she let it go off? That would be funny.

I say, "I don't like cheese."

Bev says, "You've eaten cheese. The other day. This same kind."

"This stuff might be made of throw up," I explain. "It smells funny."

"Do you want a sausage?"

I say, "Sure."

She gets up and gets sausages out of the refrigerator. She promises they are store-bought, not the ones made by hands. Those from hands are really big really hard sausages and are wicked hot like hot spice. No way will I eat hot spice. Bev says these store ones are regular "and full of fat." Bev looks so cute and round bent over like that in the refrigerator. Now she goes over and stands by the stove, fixing the sausage. I get next to her and watch and I say, "Don't let a line get on it. A brown line."

But it gets a brown line.

She starts another one. I say, "Watch out. I don't really even want one small line."

But there it is, a little brownish line.

She says, "Don't stand too close," but I have to stand close to make sure she does it right.

She is plopping another sausage into the pan and with my special secret agent pink-heart-shapes glasses, I can see that this is never going to work out. I am starving here at Gordie's cuz nobody can do stuff right and "McDonald's is out of the question."

She says, "Be careful. Dear, you really muss'n't stand so close."

"I'm okay," I says.

She, of course, ruins the next sausage with even a more worse line. Some sausage sparks make greasish spots on my face and secret agent glasses, so I wipe with my smiley face T-shirt.

She says, "See, you need to stand back."

"No, I don't," I tell her. "You've just got it all too hot. It shouldn't be real hot."

She says in a weird way, "I'm thinking of boiling one."

"No," I says. "I hate boiled. I want fried."

"You know, Jane. You can try it yourself. You have got to get started sometime. You'd be a better cook than you are my foreman." She laughs funnyish to herself.

I says, "I told you. I cook at *my* house. Only at *my* house. Guests do not cook."

She says in a real bubbly way, "Nobody will mind, dear. And up at the Settlement . . . like next week, you'll love to cook with the kids . . . they make wonderful pastries and things called birds nests out of toast and eggs, and fun salads made with wild violet leaves and plantain leaf."

I says very evenishly, "But. I Am. Not. Going. There. Ever. My. Mum. Will. Come. Get. Me. Soon. I. Want. You. To. Cook. This. Now."

She is really nice and fries another one. But this next one gets a line on it. And more grease on my face and hearts glasses. She is very, very careful but the NEXT sausage gets a place on one end just as disgusting as a line.

Finally she gets one without a line and we both cheer and cheer. She is getting a bright sweaty look and undoes one of her little shirt buttons. She is a very short lady. Exactly my size almost. I am tall for age six everyone says. Anyway, the perfect sausage makes us both so happy.

But this sausage is cold in the middle. I say in a real nice way, "It's kinda cold in the middle." And I push my plate away and it is a sad thing. As usual I am going to have to starve.

She says, "It's okay. These have already been boiled through for our sauce last night. It's not really raw. You can go ahead and eat a little of it." She smiles. Her teeth are real for an oldish lady. But they are very little teeth. Like a cute Halloween pun'kin. She says, "You know, Jane. There's never any such thing as perfect."

"My Mum is perfect," I say.

She says stiffishly, "If you could just settle for this for now and—"

"I guess I'm not hungry."

"Just try a little," she says.

"No thanks," I say.

 Sun over Ivy.

The last leg of the tour is in slow drizzly motion, the sky, white wax, the sun a flaming pool of margarine. Faces, breath, shoulders, eyeballs especially, voices that squeak ESPECIALLY are all too CLOSE, stuck to Ivy Morelli's forehead.

She trudges from one tour highlight to another, following the wide aqua-blue-green T-shirt point man, Claire. And Ivy feels pissed off at these happily sweaty feverish 78-rpm-voiced kids who shame her with junk science and all sorts of anarchist-sounding politics and with their pale hauteur. Ivy HATES these kids. Ivy hates *KIDS*.

Heft that bag, Ivy. Death. Death. Death. Death by grease. Leaping dead lizard guts. Leaping dead Lincolns. The long gasoline-powered wheeled ones.

And sooooo from solar collectors to sugaring house to MORE gardens and shops, the kidzzzzz, superior brats and their weird mothers or aunts or whatever they are, scrape along, proud proud proud of this world they have made to wrap around themselves, this disorderly, too tooooo sweet accomplished THING. Does it seem all too perfect? Perfect as punch. Yeah, where is the punch? Pow. Ow. Where is verity? Hiding it doesn't make it go away. Where is the PAIN here?

Our Ivy will find it.

 Time to go.

Ivy looks at her watch. Nearly quarter of five. When Ivy announces she has to get back home to get ready for a meeting, the witchy early-gray-haired Lee Lynn takes Ivy's wrist. She humidly kneads this wrist as if to feel for a pulse and she smiles into Ivy's eyes saying, in her keening police car siren voice, "You can't leave here until he talks with you." She's not smiling, but then she is again smiling.

Funny, these people, the way they say things.

Ivy snorts. "An audience with his Highness," she says, testing their humor at this. There are a few smiles but Ivy thinks they aren't the right kind of smiles.

Out on the piazza now, Ivy sees a lot of elderly men and women grouped around doorways and tables in wheelchairs or rocking chairs, waiting.

A trio of white-haired men with stick necks and heads as small as children's are playing cards in total silence.

Each and every member of the tour guide crew and some of the solar crew give Ivy quick, sticky good-bye hugs. "I love you," Heather, Ivy's old sentry, burbles and gives Ivy's cheek (the scratched but scabbed over one) a shy kiss.

A hefty young boy (twelvish) with a not-fashionable-anymore tiny pigtail and a Settlement-made-looking aqua and yellow Hawaiian shirt is Ivy's escort to the west parlor.

 ### The west parlor.

She is left here alone to wait. The boy even shuts the door. It is nearly five o'clock. No philosophical discussions in those big deep chairs now, no talk of municipal law by wee tykes as she had observed early on in her tour.

The room smells strongly of damp aromatic cedar. Ivy looks up. Cedar ceilings. The smell is heady, compelling, dreamy. Like a former life. Since her first visit here, Ivy has had too many flashes of déjà vu.

Most of the rooms and shops and work spaces here at the Settlement have multiple doors, doors that open out onto the piazzas and boardwalks. But this parlor does not. Deep and quiet and secret as a rabbit hole. Ivy doesn't sit. She just gives her shoulder bag another adjustment and studies the two love seats and four divans with torn upholstery and heaps of afghans and old embroidered pillows. A rough, homemade, short-legged crib for babies, also heaped with pillows and afghans and rag dolls with smiles sewed on.

The floors aren't radiant heat tiles here, as they were in the kitchens, but orangey pine layered with hooked rugs and braided rugs. She's never seen so many little rugs. This ocean of rugs is high tide! If you're a foot-dragger, you're in mighty trouble.

A handwritten sign beside a wall of shelves: *DOUBT EVERYTHING. Rene Descartes.*

This ain't Waco, she tells herself with a big sigh and studies a row of tall pictures, variations of a frontal view of the human body. Looks like someone ran a drawing of human organs through a copy machine. The organs were cut out, colored with crayons in personalized ways, then pasted onto identical smiling human specimens. Seems one of these "physiology students" found no need to place the brain in its matching cranium. (There is a maverick in every crowd.) He or she pasted the brain on top, so it is worn like a hat.

Big American flag tacked up on one wall. Really?

DOUBT EVERYTHING.

Ivy goes to the windows, small panes running floor to ceiling. No curtains. She looks out at the thickness of woods and lichen-splattered rocks. That rock-cluttered look of Maine. Even here in this St. Onge-sphere, which seems like another planet, this weird life, it's really just Maine. Her home.

In a far corner at the end of this row of windows sits Godzilla, about nine feet tall if he were standing, but he's sitting, his legs crossed at the knee. He is made of various green floral and dotted fabrics. His wide eyes are yellow. He has a smile you could trust. He is naked, but there are commercially-manufactured sneakers on his huge feet. Leaping big lizard! Something like size eighteen! High tops. Spread on his knee is a book. Ivy walks over and looks down. *The Guide to North American Reptiles and Amphibians.* Godzilla isn't really reading the book. His eyes are on Ivy.

She hoists up her shoulder bag.

She hears his voice outside the door. And another voice. The door opens and then she can see him and Aurel Soucier there in the library talking, Gordon's hand on the door latch, and through the cedar smell and the heat that is as awful as, yes, lizard gizzards, she hears they are speaking French. Gordon has sawdust on the backs of both elbows. Aurel is sawdust-free.

Ivy stares at them. Taking in every detail. DOUBT NOTHING, she says to herself.

Aurel departs, singing loudly. By the time Gordon pulls the door closed, Aurel's song is gone.

She guesses he is six-foot-five or -six. His eyes are on her, coming toward her through the heat and she can FEEL him coming closer, the heat intensifying. Each time she sees him, he's bigger. And he says with that thickened, low voice that big guys with big necks often have, "Sit, dear. Let's talk." He opens a hand to suggest the most deep and comfy-looking upholstered rocker. *"Dear" my ass,* Ivy's brain comments to itself.

She sets her jaw. She turns toward this deep chair. Sinks into it.

He one-handedly picks a wooden folding chair from against a wall, flips it open in front of her, backward, close to her knees. He straddles this chair, facing her. Rests one huge sawdusty and insect-gnawed forearm across the back of it. There are dirty sweaty streaks around his eyes, and sweat glistens through the sparse top edges of his beard. He looks exhausted and terrible but his smile is kindly. He says, "Ivy."

She blinks. She almost trembles. She swallows. She laughs. "Gordon."

He grins.

She lowers her eyes to his thick, stained fingers on the back of his folding chair.

He leans back, eyes on a pattern of afternoon sun splotches on a gold and blue hooked rug, then suddenly looks back into her eyes. "What now?" he asks. He's not smiling.

Maine, Ivy. You're in Maine, her secret voice reminds her.

His weirdly pale eyes are locked on her face. He doesn't fill her unnerved baffled silence with comforting assurance.

She decides she likes the beered-up goofball Gordon better.

He still waits for her answer.

With her hands folded tightly in her lap and her pulse pounding on both sides of her throat, with her own pale eyes more arctic icy than any time in her life, she says evenly, "One question, if I may be allowed. What is the difference between a nightclub and an elephant fart?"

Without even hearing the answer, Gordon St. Onge throws his head back and laughs.

 ## The forests of the planet Earth speak.

What seems, from the blue and tired meridian of today's sky, to be a brown rag below, was once me. Thousands and thousands and thousands of life forms found nowhere else, now dried to a crust, twisted legs, steamy eye holes, lush mosses reversed to the logic of powder. Thousands and thousands of miles of me, the very robe of Mother Nature, have been erased by the power of the dollar bill.

 ## The screen speaks.

See the scrungy bad people in the cities and towns across America! They can hurt us. They blow up buildings, they rob, they shoot, they let their children roam and never read to them, they collect *welfare,* they rape, they piss in front of people and cut people up, they smell and have sores and tattoos and nose rings and nipple rings and swastikas and they never wear pastels. They are dripping in drugs and explosives and have no teeth. They want to hurt *us!* They are filled with envy and madness. They make *our* taxes soar. A lot of them are *illegal* immigrants. Some are not. Whatever, they are COSTING.

And see in the hills! The militias! Oh, god, these crazies have plans to take over the government! They are full of hate and envy and radical right-wing madness and have never been to college and push their women around and teach their children to be like them and they not only have guns, MILITARY guns, they STOCKPILE them, and they will hurt us, oh, this is just so terrible and scary. Oh, but LOOK, see the nice clean pink faces of our president and senators and governors telling us to relax. *Tough* laws will keep all the scrungy people in line or behind bars or put to sleep with humane death drugs. Down with all the scrungy people! Thank goodness for the strong pink voices of our leaders keeping things safe!

And, yes, FEEL the caring corporations, how they keep our beaches so white, our forests so green, and give a helping hand to our crumbling but costly schools. Those lazy rich unionized teachers have got to go. And PO workers. What a bunch of sponges! And Social Security needs to become more efficient. There are ways, once everything is privatized. See how the corporations cradle us all with warm cozy cuddlies, insurance, phone calls to your older brother and your Mom and carefree banking. FEEEEEEL the strength of America's giant businesses and deregulated investment banks getting bigger and more *there for you.*

 After a particularly blistery, hot, thick day, now cooling down to a warm, tree-sweet, field-sweet night.

Even super high-test gasoline is sweetness to the nose on such a night. A night like this, everything we see, hear, smell, and touch, we love it.

Just outside Egypt, on the old part of Route 113, Gordon St. Onge stands against the cab of one of the Settlement's rickety ancient old flatbed trucks, a grip on the gas nozzle, watching the digital numbers flicker across the face of the pumps.

On the back of the Settlement flatbed is a heap of torn up twisted culvert from a "good-neighbor project" in Fryeburg that just about wrung everyone out today. And some pretty nasty bickering. And so here you have aluminum culverting on the way to the dump. Wasn't too long ago, maybe the age of a chicken, that aluminum culvert was the *new* way, an improvement over the old quick-to-rust iron culverts, which were superior to the old stone culverts before them (we were told). Now culverts must be plastic (as in fossil. As in petroleum. As in creeping toward the Peak). Oh, yes, shows how we have evolved. It's the New Age of Man!! The New Dawn!! Doesn't it almost give us a more upright feeling when we walk? Maybe even less body hair?

But . . . but . . . doesn't plastic crack when it gets cold? Next time will stone become the best culvert?

The question stays lost in space.

Aurel Soucier has gone into the Convenience Cubicle. (Note that *everything* is cubicled these days.)

Now half a dozen stripped down Harleys come thundering and popping, passing the cubicle low and slow but there is Gordon, eating a little commercial apple pie lustily, commercial ready-made food being a *no-no,* a kind of broken law in the St. Onge world. And Gordon feels swept along on the highway of human destiny, the rumblings, the shouldn'ts and what ifs, the single-lane bridges, the soft shoulders, the detours.

A newish pickup pulls in, a young man's kind of truck with a windshield visor and jazzy fender skirting and a WBLM bumper sticker on the dimpled chrome step-toe bumper. But the driver is older, late sixty on toward sixty-five perhaps. Little cloth cap. Clean-shaven face, but a nice face. Kinda like you'd expect him to speak your name, your first name, and it would be spoken cloud soft.

And someone else there, a passenger. Is it a big dog? No, it's human. Wild thick hair, deep red-orange, face tipped down like it would be if it were reading.

The oldish guy parks his flashy truck on the other side of the building, goes into the Convenience Cubicle, a medium-to-tall man, big hands, but ever so light and kind of cunning and life-wise.

Gordon laps the sweetness of the apple treat off his fingers, pulls the nozzle from the truck.

When Aurel (Gordon's cousin, yes, and, yes, short instead of
Atlas-sized, and, yes, dark-eyed instead of pale-eyed, but also has
a Tourette's-like squinchy busy face, also has the nose) comes out of
the Convenience Cubicle, he is hot on getting over to Gordon to tell
him something, but turns and sees the oldish guy behind him, coming over to the flatbed, his eyes dark-blue-ringed light blue, a serene
expression, bag of bread and a gallon of milk, one to each hand. He
asks "Howzit goin'?" in a way you speak to old friends.

Aurel gives a gentlemanly tip of his saggy-brimmed olive drab bush
hat, and his dark glittery eyes are one eye wide and amazed, the other eye
squinty and fierce (yes, that look is of the whole St. Onge–Soucier family
passed on and on. Perhaps in the not so long ago, a smattering of French
kings and French peasants, some squinting and wild-eyed, cruel-eyed,
others gentle, got mixed together by passions, thus this complex expression, on a sweet night such as this, while greeting a neighbor circa 2000).

Gordon is trying to place this older guy, which shouldn't be that
hard in a town of nine hundred, but he can't place him so he just
grins and says, "We have entered the advanced age of the petroleum
by-product culvert of which humanity can exult in."

The guy looks up at the slat-sided truck bed heaped with aluminum
culvert and looks back at Gordon and says, "Yep." Then he says, "You
seen any wild dogs around?"

Gordon says, "No . . . just fox." He glances at Aurel. Aurel's fierce-
almost-screaming gaze slides up and down the lean but tough dimensions of this mystery neighbor, and the older guy says, "A lotta rabies
in the area. That new strain. That fast-moving strain up from the
Carolinas, brought up by raccoons. You hear about that rabid fox
ran out of the woods in broad daylight down in Steep Falls? Bit a
lady . . . while she was settin' out with a buncha people at a barbecue.
Tore her leg up. Then a couple of dogs got into it with the fox. You
know an animal's skin goes numb when it's got rabies, so you can't
discourage 'em by no way but dead."

Gordon crosses his arms, ready to settle in for a chat. Mentions how
he knew a family that claimed they ate rabid animals and never got sick.
"Must have been dead for two or three days before they touched them."

Cousin Aurel is bursting with great shrieking poofs of quietness.
His eyes, black as eternity, boom like two twelve-pounder howitzers.

Gordon looks curiously at his cousin but then drifts back into conversation with the chatty guy.

Now Aurel heads back into the store to pay up on the gas while Gordon, who never makes a person feel rushed, is just happily beholding the older man's face and when Aurel returns, Gordon is saying, "so . . . they had to stop feeding birds for all the coons they were drawing . . ." obviously still on the shudderingly wonderful rabies topic, which, like the leprosy topic, always manages to build rather than fade.

After a while, the old guy gives a head-dipping nod and turns to go and Gordon says, "See ya later," and Aurel hops up into the truck cab and settles in, his back arrow straight, munching on a peppermint, and he commands, "Doan' move, Ge-yome. Watch t'iss you."

And Gordon sits straight with his back against the seat as the neighbor's flashy young-man's truck makes a little showy sweep across the lot out to the road and the passenger with the thick red hair is looking away, head and shoulders mostly in silhouette.

Gordon looks at Aurel.

Aurel is unwrapping cellophane from another peppermint. "T'at iss Pitch who t'ere iss some stories off hiss memé and hiss papa in a fight . . . bit him . . . bit somet'ing off . . . like hiss t'umb. Killed t'ree wardens, her people an' wass part Indian an' very smart woods people an' got away wit t'mos' unbeliefable Maine Guide scam where t'ey took city persons off downstate in t'woods and rob 'em wearing bear costumes . . . t'iss I admire sort of, me . . . but you can not belieff everyt'ing you hear. Err . . . t'at is Pitch and t'at iss not hiss truck. Truck off one off his boys . . . t'one t'att has one off t'em lotter-money-union-machinis' jobs. But t'att wass his daughter wit' him in t'truck, her . . . t'kid you are trying to meet . . . kid wit' deform face, her." His most blazing wide dark eye is steady on Gordon's surprise. Then breathlessly, "I seen it . . . t'face. A little while some years ago, me. Fife or six year ol' girl an' my heart jump when I see t'att poor stretch out face." He absently digs at the chin of his fine-looking dark beard.

Gordon says, "Why didn't you tell me who he was?!! I'd've gone over and talked with the girl." He twists the key, revs the engine to life.

Aurel crunches into another mint. "I wass not very sure what wass up. I wass not sure t'girl want you over t'ere pawing her . . . or iff he wanted you to go over t'ere, him. T'iss big school scheme might be juss a secret off t'brot'ers."

Gordon glares. "I do not paw."

Aurel blinks. "Oh, *mon dieu*! You *do* paw! You are like a *vieille mèmére* back home of t'Valley. *T'es comme les vieilles mèméres p'is les vieilles matantes qui mettaient leurs gros tétons dans les faces d'less p'tits enfants quand qu'ys vont visiter!*"

Gordon grins. Big bright smile. "*Mais batège, moié, j'aimais ça quand qu'ys faisaient ça!*"

Aurel says levelly, "T'girl be terrorfy' of big giant nice man who *act* like her *mèmére* on visit."

Gordon hangs his head. "Never mind." He grips the wheel with both hands, looks over at the pumps. "Gas has gone up again. And with Peak Oil at our doors, and Wall Street speculation and corporate hocus pocus . . ." He slips the shift knob into gear and the engine whines its deep low gear voice as the heavy truck rolls away from the pumps and Gordon's voice goes into high gear, "And still *nobody nobody nobody doubts* the news! It's—"

"Stop!" Aurel commands. "Stop t'em complaints! I doan' want to hear it! Tonight iss one off t'ose special nights. I want to remain an uplifting perky man."

 The grays observe.

High noon for those who know the hours one frame at a time. Our craft has no motion as seen from below. We are simply the syrupy sun-less summer sky. But we see *her* and her square silver craft stopping at the old gray farm place where the man (whose real name sounds like Ge-yome, hard G like oh, gosh!) resides by municipal, state, and federal law of this boundaried nation called USA.

She is tall, crisp, crunchy, hair gray at the ears, feet long, fingers long, long arms, she *is* flowing toward the house of Guillaume St. Onge. Rain in the air. Rain on its way, not descending. No rumbles or smash of light. The only invasive sound is of her hitting the door or as humans call it, *knocking.* But there's no crack to it. She uses her palm. Four *flops,* the sound of thrown apples. This is the inside-the-porch door. Maybe her strange palm-knock was in the hopes of the door easing open. Lots of soft tumbling shadows, the long narrow porch too busy with its mobiles, homemade candles, rockers, old couch with a black cat in a curl. Visitor locks her eyes with the eyes of the black cat, whose eyes are locked on hers.

After more "*knocks*" and after some waiting, the visitor leaves her calling card wedged in the inside door. *Joyce Marden, Department of Human Services*.

 Claire St. Onge speaks.

A couple of days a week, I'd be at the university. In the winter, it was three days and meetings with faculty and projects with the students. And a mean blizzard of departmental paperwork. But that summer I just went in to putter and meet with independent study people. Summer seminars and conferences that others were teaching there were quite condensed and intense while the campus was strewn with clumps of strangers with "*my name is*" tags on their shirts, people generally older than the full-time winter crowd.

The office I shared with the other adjuncts was exactly a floor above the office of Catherine Court Downey, who was interim chairman of the Art Department. We were friends.

Mostly she did the talking, good at speaking into a person's eyes, a lot of university gossip, but she also spoke of her marriage and son. She had married at age thirty, waited ten years to get pregnant. "I *hesitated* for ten years," she said, eyes solemn, chin cocked, as if listening to her own confessions. Chagall. She hated Chagall, giving academic reasons why Chagall was not to be loved by anyone, especially women. "Unless you live to be raped by a goat." We both loved our coffees in colossal cups. We both loved peach for a color. Peach sky. Peach walls. Peach fabrics. I loved the old novels, even racist Conrad. At this she would just raise an eyebrow in speechless horror.

Her child's name was Robert. He was four years old that summer.

Catherine loved her job, loved the university, loved most art, was always breathless, always hurried, was bright and positive-thinking. A little peppery busy bee. I had known Catherine for three years but had never met her son. And I hardly spoke of my private life to her. I am not a secretive person by nature. But my life lately is . . . weird. At least in the way modern-thinking American souls would view it. So I skipped around most details and she would gladly steer it back to other things.

Oh, I told her plenty of stories of my life as a kid growing up Passamaquoddy. I explained to her about Indian identity. Indian pride. Indian anger. Indian passivity. Indian honor. Indian memory before memory. I didn't tell her too much about my ex, let alone our *present* new "marriage." Oh, boy. There's too much she would have found unacceptable about Gordon and a lot of specifics would make her feel differently about me, too, as if my present life was something that could be debated. Was my life worthy or not worthy? Pitiable? A failure? Fixable? (*Fixable* being one of her most often used words.)

One time, when Gordon's name drifted into our conversation, whatever it was I said made both of her eyebrows go up and she said sharply, "He's not a feminist?"

I got this really crooked smile. I tried to make the smile go away before I spoke. I touched one of the bows of my glasses professorially and squared my shoulders. I was older than her by only six years but I have seen much life, the wriggling squirmy *un*institutional kind. And here my whole world was being called to the carpet in four sharply spoken words. I said, "Gordon finds today's feminism obscene. He feels it is not about . . . people. He says it is about a system, equality, yes, but equality between men and women within an aggressive elite, and a buffer class elite, an honored group within a subculture of 'success' types in a crappy system . . . a system that defines humanity in industrial terms . . . a system that is a tournament. Like an evil version of musical chairs. He says—"

"Well!" she interrupted. She was looking at me dumbfoundedly. "I'm glad you severed the knot on that one. He sounds like a real shit."

I said, "Most of the people back at the reservation would probably agree with Gordon. You wouldn't really like Indians, Catherine. Most Indians are rednecks."

She flushed. "But of *course* I like Indians!" Her dark, bushy-in-a-sexy-way eyebrows were raised, amazed at such a charge. "Claire, you know that given a chance, Native Americans wouldn't think like that. Education would enlighten them. Why, look what education has done for you!"

I smiled another funny smile.

She said, "If you weren't educated, you'd probably be living with Mr. Dumb Schmuck still . . . living under his thumb."

A car without a muffler roared past on the street below. I glanced at the wall clock. The minute hand was moving right before my eyes, faster than a minute hand should move. I could hear the stomping of feet, fists on the supper tables. "EVIL GROWS! *WHOMP.* EVIL GROWS! *WHOMP . . .*"

I looked at Catherine's pretty face, her lovely and safe outrage, her lovely and nonperilous impatience, her self-absorbed, self-conscious, positive-thinking loveliness.

 Meanwhile, Ivy Morelli in her living room of kooky posters and simple furniture. Her eyes are wide. She had fallen asleep sitting up with the lights on. She had dreamed.

It was a scream dream. But had she really screamed? She's not sure. Maybe a whimper. But in the dream, it was a scream. A field of tawny waving grasses. She was there alone. Miles of grass. No one to help her. A mountain lion, also tawny, trudging along, long-bodied, heavy, and yet, effortless. Big head. In real life, a long dark-tipped tail would be following behind the big cat's body as it sensuously parts the pale grasses. But in the dream she can't recall a tail.

The face fills the screen of Ivy's dream. The face flickers as on a TV with poor reception. The white fire eyes are on her.

Again the reception flickers and is blistered with white dots. But this only gives it more power. The lion's black pupils are trained on Ivy's mind. The tawny jaws clench.

Ivy screamed (or something) then. And so she woke.

She is not a fan of big cats.

 West parlor. Rainy Evening. Bonnie Loo speaks.

Tonight with the rain, Claire and I are looking over the kitchen records, itemizing a bunch of kitchen-type stuff we bought since the first of last month. We do our best. Not perfectly accurate. Not to the penny. But it's something Gordon leans on us about. Once a month, he calls a powwow. And he's hard. He doesn't like spending gobs of money. Fine.

So Claire and I have the books out. And we have our feet up. Shoes around on the floor. Both my youngest kids are asleep on the floor. Very big room, this parlor. Only one lamp is on, bright on our business but the orangey pine walls are peaked and jagged with shadows. And the cedar ceiling is pumping out its cloudy orgasm of scent. Then there is the sweetness of the rain, the sleepy drumming sound of it coming to us through the open windows. And there's the zooming and crashing of June bugs and moths against the screens every time the rain lets up a moment.

And it seems Poon Vandermast just materializes out of thin air, standing by the arm of Claire's deep chair. Rain-darkened brown T-shirt. Jeans. Rain glistening on his arms and face. He never seems to age much, no matter how many years rush away. Poon. Mark's his real name. But we always called him Poon in school . . . you know . . . back in school.

I says, "Oh, hi, Poon. Haven't seen you in a while."

He says, "I know it." Says it real nice. He has a round baby face, little mustache, lotta dark hair, blue worried-looking eyes. Soft mouth, very innocent-looking. Too shy for girlfriends when we were in school. See how weird life is! Beautiful guy like that had no love life. Me, I was a mess, had bad teeth and pimples . . . I *had* a *love life*. All I could handle.

My Ma says Poon has got some married woman over on Morrow Road who reels him in on a big hook every couple months when her old man's out to sea on a merchant ship, and she has kept Poon Vandermast in and out of her bed since graduation, *so the story goes*. That's mighty pitiful. Even now, he doesn't get one whole woman to himself.

I glance at what Poon holds in his arms. Something heavy-looking, wrapped in a black trash bag.

Claire adjusts her glasses, those round kind like Woodrow Wilson's or John Lennon's or whatever. She doesn't drop her feet from the cable spool. But she nods to Poon and says, "Coffee or something? Maple candy? Bonnie and I have a wicked stash of maple candy here. A *secret stash*. Don't tell anyone."

Poon says, "I'm all set. Thanks anyway." And he tugs away the trash bag to reveal a big scrapbook, looks a lot like one of our *History as it Happens* books.

Claire says, "So I suppose you and Bonnie Lucretia here are related . . . everybody in Egypt is connected somehow."

Poon laughs. "Prob'ly."

I says, "Wasn't Kay Benson some relation to the Farnsworths?"

Poon nods. "Sister . . . or sister-in-law. Ma knew all that stuff. I can't keep track."

Claire is staring at the big book in his arms.

I say, "Well, that would make us sixth . . . seventh cousins through Farnsworths, once or twice removed."

Claire says, "I'm from outa town. Fresh blood." She raises her chin, proudlike.

Poon smiles.

I get up from my chair, stretch a little, hug myself, slip into my moccasins, worming each foot in. And Poon is still just gripping the big book and Claire and I just keep glancing at the big book, then back up at Poon's worried blue eyes.

Claire says, "Well, I just met *Poon* the other night on a lonely dark road."

Poon smiles.

I nod. I know all this. Everyone in the Settlement knows. Vandermast boys are trying to get their sister to come hang out with us here. The kid with the bad birth defect. I've not really seen her close up. Sometimes, when we were kids, I got a glimpse when she was waiting for the second-run school bus, but never in the halls. She's younger than my brother Dale, three or four years behind him.

Claire wonders, "Why do they call you Poon? I *like* that. Sounds Indian."

Poon shrugs. "I can't recall. Some baby name, I guess."

"Better than Bubba," she says solemnly. She points at his big book with her pen. "Watcha got?"

He squats down by the cable spool next to Claire and Claire jerks her feet down off the spool and grunts, shifting her wiggly round self into a more upright sitting position. Poon lays the book there on the spool with a flourish.

Claire raises the stiff cover of the big book. The inside pages are grayish rag paper. Artist's paper. Each piece glued to a larger sheet of glossy poster board so that the poster board is the part that is bound.

I can tell you that that artsy paper and the poster board aren't neither one a thing they give away. I rest my hand on the back of Claire's chair, lean in.

We look at the first page.

"Jeepers," I say. I reach over and snap on a brighter lamp.

Claire is silent, her eyes moving over the page.

It is a painting. Not a print. But the real thing. Not some juiceless bowl of fruit like most of us would do. Here are thicknesses of gold paint, gold as wedding rings, which frost the wrinkles of pale blues and brick and maroon and ruby, blood red and pink, dark blue and black. Some of this is oil paint, some of it oily pastels, ingeniously friendly. And then fine hairs of a fountain pen, that fancy real ink. All these things working together as lazily as the hand of Mother Nature. The picture is of the faces of a bunch of kids.

I can't believe those hands! Almost three-dimensional. Probably because the background is a little foggy. The way kids breathe through their mouths, not yet knowing what it means to be a lady or gentleman. And eyes. Too direct. The sleepers and jerseys are in the foggy part of the picture, a sleepy texture. I can almost smell the detergent.

A verse is written beneath with fountain pen in masterful calligraphy:

The little ones are tough inside and red hot. Not at all what you think. Out of earshot, they talk like men, voices deep, making complicated earnest plans for skyscrapers, world travel, and war. Do not underestimate! And do not wish for what you don't want, because they honor wishes.

I can't help but look over at my sleeping son and daughter, Zack and Jetta. Zack on his back with arms open like he has fallen from the sky, Jetta on her side with her whole head buried down under a stripy dirty pillow, disgusting pillow, embarrassing to have someone from the outside world see it.

Claire slowly lifts the page. Her wicked-thick wicked-black wicked hair is in a barrette, swings down across her right side and behind the fleshy arm that draws back from turning the big page.

We stare into the world of the next painting. A dark human figure, a silhouette actually, stands in a window as seen from outdoors while beyond the corner of the building it is all smoke and pink dawn and again speckles of wedding ring gold. And there is a hump of land, stony and treed with black silhouette firs and winter-bare maples and patches of snow and fog. It is the kind of place and the kind of moment I have known all my life here in these hills.

I look at Claire. She looks at me, but only a quick peek. I want to cry. You know, a kind of proud cry.

I look at Poon. Beautiful Poon. Our lives innocently tangled.

I look back at the painting, at those impossible little flecks of gold. How did they get put there by a human being's hand with a paintbrush?

In calligraphy again, the words beneath.

The position for prayer is as a child in the crib waits to be lifted to arms. Submission. This is very common in our world. Prayer's prescription. But my people here, Poon and Dana, Benny and Dad, some mornings alone in the kitchen, not knowing I watch, one of them, usually Dad, will go to a window and roughly take the sides of the framework, one side to each hand, and squeeze as he looks out at what God has made today. Can this be prayer!!!! And his hungry stomach in his waist growls. And the dark morning lays mean on the hills, Egypt and beyond that, all of Maine, broken by cruelties, both earth and human in painful tandem.

I don't look at Poon or his rough hands. I just kinda smile. This is about us! This is our story.

I say stupidly, "Yikes."

Claire says, "Okay. Time's up. Tell us who the artist is. Your sister, right?"

He flushes. "Yep. Wicked, huh?"

Claire says, "You mean your *fifteen*-year-old sister."

He flushes again. Nods a bunch of quick nods. He says, "She's about to bust out."

Claire's eyes spiral all over him. She gets a pretty mean look when she's trying to figure something out. "I . . . can't believe this." She laughs. "Not that you're a liar. I just mean . . . I am jolted. This is . . . wonderful!"

I reach down across Claire's arm and I turn the next page. This one shows two shadowy figures . . . a girl and a collie dog? . . . against a night of heavy woods and jillions of stars, some closer, some far, some so far they are just a gelid smear. Distance beyond distance. Must have taken months to paint all those stars.

The calligraphy verse reads:

In history books, there are no kisses, no back scratches, no first words of babies, no dogs. There are only conquistadors and their blows. Yet in the real past, there has been as many kisses as there are night stars. All forgotten.

 Meanwhile, out in the world.

It is evening in a small Florida town. The streets are wet with rain. Smell that tonnage of tropical sweetness drifting through the trees!

On the gray plastic rear bumper of a chocolate-color SUV that is passing another SUV and a line of smaller cars, there is this bumper sticker: MY CHILD IS A MAE DANIELS ELEMENTARY SCHOOL HONOR STUDENT. There is almost an accident here as an oncoming car brakes, causing the tailgaters behind it to practically pile up. Horns blare. Someone gives the finger to the brown SUV. But the culprit, proud in all ways, just keeps on rolling.

 Meanwhile, back in Egypt, Maine, Bonnie Loo speaks.

Claire hoists herself up onto her little-girl-sized bare feet. Claire, so much shorter than Poon, looking up at the face of the brother of this suddenly larger-than-life fifteen-year-old Brianna Vandermast. She says, "Where is she? Your sister. Home watching TV?"

Poon says, "Gone with Vid and Stacey to the mill." No one asks who Vid and Stacey are, but "mill" means a load of pulp or chips and the snarling and grunting of an engine stout enough to draw it there.

I lift another page, but I feel Claire's eyes on me and look up. Her glossy black tail of hair has found its way over the front of her work shirt, she uses both hands to flip it back over her shoulder as she marches out of the room and then we can hear her beyond the library out on the piazza, calling "SLAVES! SLAVES! ARE ANY OF MY SLAVES STILL ABOUT!!!"

Then the squeakiness of some kid, sounds like a Soucier.

And Claire, "WHERE'S GORDON!"

And *squeak squeak squeak,* is the reply.

Now Claire, "Tell him to come here *now,* on winged feet!"

I look into Poon's flushing face. He says with a shy smile, "Lady of action."

"Yep," I say. I feel like I need a smoke. I peek over at the kids. Zack hasn't moved. But Jetta has one sleepy open eye on us. I turn another page of the big book. "Poon, your sister . . . she's really something."

"She's about to bust out," he says again.

The next picture is of two beat-ta-shit small skidders, one yellow, one orange. One is jacked up in the open bay of a pole barn. Massive tires on rims against the wall. This is pen and ink and washes of watercolor. Arms, elbows, shoulders of men showing at the edges. And feet in work boots and sneakers sort of telescoped through the underneaths of these two machines. This artist has made the peeling skidder cages look like aged porcelain with virtuous little ladylike cracks. I've known skidders all my life. Until now, would I have called them beautiful?

Brianna's calligraphy verse reads:

I work the binders, the chokers, the winch and cables, the pewy scream of a Jonsereds. I am strong. I have gone with my fingertips into the greasy dark stink of hoses, rings, and warm manifolds of my father's bright fleet, and my shirt billows against the skidder's hub as I climb. I climb her all over. Her tire chains come thick as wrists. Always in the company of my brothers and father. We are all genius here. Noesis!

Noesis. What the hell does that mean? You'd never know I had some college. I would've told you Noesis was a Christmas word.

Claire is back beside me. Has her hands on her fat squishy hips. She says, "He's just across in the east parlor." She whispers this part, "He and that Skowhegan solar guy are plottin' up something." Then, "Said he'd be one more minute."

I see Poon is looking around at stuff. He smiles at Godzilla sitting in the chair with the lizard book and the size eighteen sneakers and the big nice eyes. Made by yours truly.

And I really hate sewing. But this was special. Me and lizards have a thing. And rats, too. Smooch! So I did the big G all by hand. Took six months. Except Paul Lessard helped me get those sneakers, through someone where he used to work. Aren't those corkers?

Poon's worried blue eyes move from Godzilla to my face.

Claire whistles, admiring the next page of Brianna Vandermast's big book.

The painting now is of a man standing between a set of gas pumps and a flatbed truck loaded with what looks like old aluminum culverting. Head cocked, the man is listening to two others, one a guy who is gripping a bag and a gallon jug of milk. All three sets of hands are vivid. Almost reach out of the page. But the rest of the picture is soft and dreamy including two of the figures and faces, one a profile. I can tell you without a doubt that the man next to the gas pumps, the one with the clearly-rendered face, is Gordon St. Onge.

The verse reads:

Rabies

I don't get it. Rabies?

Without taking her eyes off the picture, Claire asks, "Is your sister any more interested in hanging out with us up here than she was a few days ago?"

Poon shakes his head once. "If she knew I sneaked this book, she'd throw me against a wall."

Claire chortles in her thick-neck fat-person fashion.

Poon says, "I think if one of you comes over tomorrow morning, you'll catch her home. We're not working till afternoon. Just moving some equipment. We'll be in and out. Bree'll be around I *think*." He is looking intently at Claire. "I can get this book back so she won't notice. Just don't tell her you ever saw this."

Claire chuckles, probably still imagining Poon getting thrown against the wall by his little sister.

Gordon's voice. In the library now, just through the open door. Gordon has a *real* thick-type voice, like talking while swallowing, which *is* often the case . . . ha! ha! . . . but not always. Not now. The Skowhegan guy's voice is also deep but sharper, narrower, more tang, less slobber, err, I mean less vehemence than our dear one. And as they appear in the doorway, I see that the visitor wears a dressy short-sleeve shirt with his work pants. Face shaved. A reserved smile. Like zippered-up lips. Maybe he just needs to warm up to us. Some people take a while.

Gordon is favoring his right arm since he hurt it this morning. No, not the wounds of work. This was a casualty of ridiculous heavy horseplay. He does not need cider to become a twelve-year-old.

Jetta asks croakily from her pillow, "Is it night?"

Gordon directly crosses over the soft complicated layers of hooked and braided rugs to Jetta and lifts her and lets her long bare legs hang down from his hip. She wipes her nose on his work shirt. Oops. At five, she's not a lady yet.

Gordon says, "It is a *dark and rainy* night. Aoooooooo!" Then he nuzzles her.

Claire says, "Mr. St. Onge." She nods to the open book on the cable spool.

Both Gordon and Jetta stare down at the picture with its verse: *Rabies.*

Again I offer the man from Skowhegan coffee, tea, maple candy. The rain beyond the open windows begins to drum heavily. Lightning and quick-on-its-heels thunder speak to us of apotheosis.

 Bonnie Loo, in bald honesty, looking back on that evening, when they "discovered" Brianna.

I felt a sickening wave seeing how beautifully she had re-created him on the page. With pen and brush, she owned him.

 That night, Gordon St. Onge dreams.

He meets a faceless woman with soft white fog for a face, though her body is normal, her hands vivid, the lifelines, branched thick with many futures. He smiles at her. She begins to melt. Just as silver does. Or other metals will do when rendered hot.

He groans.

He wakes.

In a future time, Claire reflects on the summer when Catherine Court Downey became part of the Settlement story.

What I taught at USM were adjunct history courses. So I was not a *real* teacher but, you know, I had *real* meetings. Ha! Ha! But this being late June, meetings took the form of a picnic. Like a toad pretends to be a prince. Picnic phooey. It was a commitment and for me and a few others a long drive. Okay not a picnic exactly, but a kind of cookout thing on the lawn between Payson Smith and Luther Bonney Halls, the only open space that hadn't been paved yet on that campus.

My friend, Catherine, who was an interim department head, left the cookout early. Everyone thought so. But later, I found her sitting in her little metallic mint green car next to my Settlement car, down in the lower parking lot where she knew I always liked to park away from things.

She looked up at me, startled.

I put my hand on her closed window. It wasn't cool enough to be sitting in a car with all the windows up. Unless you have air-conditioning and your car is running. Her car was not running.

I tried to open the passenger's door but she had it locked. She reached over and unlocked it, keeping her eyes on the building across the street, where her office was, as if waiting for a signal from it.

She had recently discovered through mutual acquaintances that I lived at the Settlement in Egypt. Though nothing was written in the papers, word about calls to the authorities about us was burning its way around the universe, no galaxy left unsmoldering. And she probably suspected a lot of things anyway. I don't believe that in the coming days, as she got further into our lives, that she didn't know what she was getting into, though she later would swear it had all been a nasty surprise.

She had tried, just an hour or so earlier, to lead me into talking about him, Gordon, while we filled our plates with gourmet cookout stuff. But . . . how can I say this? . . . I didn't trust her with my heart. I couldn't bear her disapproval but I knew it was coming. This was a woman deeply steeped in extreme feminist doctrine, and I'd seen her at various university get-togethers in full attack mode, scolding male professors and students a hundred times less "sexist" than Gordon . . . and women professors and students a hundred times more "converted" than I.

The first thing she said to me when I had settled into that bucket seat and rolled the window down was, "I'm having some kind of attack. Heart or something. No, really. I just shouldn't have mixed all those incompatible proteins together." Then she laughed and looked at me face on. "It's worse for some people."

I smiled and kneaded her shoulder. She did not really seem at first glance old enough to be even just an interim chairman of her department. Early forties in reality. But a proud chin-up little ball of fire. Her wide black band-like eyebrows almost grew together, but in a most appealing way, and these eyebrows curved up sharply over each eye, like mischief. Her black hair was always managed in a hard frizzy knot on the very top of her head. She had a beautiful small round brown mole near her mouth. She was gorgeous, sexy, but not flirty. A married professional woman and mother who *looked full of mischief*. And *normal*.

Artistically, but for some medium-sized out-of-state grants, she was only recognized in local circles. Work that had feminist messages. Work that reflected one obsession, herself, her undefined spirit. And her body as spirit.

Yeah, she was always pretty queer about food and funny little pains. But I had never seen terror in her eyes as was there this day. *Never* was it out of control.

I asked what was going on.

She said it was "him." I thought she meant her husband, Phan, but she was rambling, pausing, swallowing as if her neck hurt. She quoted some old poets on the subject of being mortal. Then she laughed.

When I got her to be a little clearer, turns out "him" meant Robert, her son, not Phan.

This little guy I had never seen, even though I had stayed at her home at least four times prior. He was always elsewhere. And he never came to the university. I had seen her pregnant. But I never saw the baby. She was gushing now with *very* concrete details about the boy . . . he recently vomited for two days . . . he reads her mind . . . he wants a pet . . . "we can't have pets" . . . he got into her talcs and mixed them together . . . he mixed coffee and bleach together. In the mornings he wakes before she does and mixes things together.

 In the newsroom of the *Record Sun,* Ivy's editor, Brian Fitch, tells Ivy—

that Gil Zaniewski in "Sports" is acquainted with Gordon St. Onge. "Give him a call at home. He's on vacation this weekend painting his house. Also a guy Randy King used to see St. Onge around Portland a bit. See if you can track Randy down. I think he's in Vermont these days. Something to do with their state parks department. I'll have a couple numbers for you after lunch." Brian winks. "Might give you more fuel for this fire."

Ivy goes out on the sidewalk for a few minutes, like some people do to smoke, only she just breathes in the city air: exhaust, and hot cement, hot tar. Fuck the little Settlement bitches and squirts. Ivy *loves* global industry and black grease. Go oil, go! Oil wins. Brats get a D-minus. The St. Onge *story.* What more is there to it? She holds her ears, closes her eyes, turns around. People pass around her to go inside. She opens her eyes. It's all still there. This world. This day. This hour. The smell.

When she reaches Gil Zaniewski, he says, "Yeah, yeah. Gordo was friends with Rich and Di Harbert when they had their big but casual dinner parties . . . before they had kids and dogs and three jobs apiece." He chuckles. "Well, that was before we *all* had kids and dogs and three jobs apiece." Chuckles again. "That was back when us reporters and your average schoolteacher and all manner of people could sit around and toke one up after dinner freely. This was before Nancy Reagan took the stage to murmur 'war on drugs,' and then all of our politicians were screaming 'WAR ON DRUGS!' so you wouldn't notice what their hands were doing, which is an old, old wrestling technique, by the way."

Ivy asks quickly, "Did Mr. St. Onge smoke the stuff?"

The guy laughs heartily. "You mean, did he inhale or just clasp the joint between his lips, quivering with moral indecision?"

Ivy tsks. She doesn't like this Gil guy.

Gil says, "Ivy, we *all* smoked in those days. It was a fad, not a federal crime. We all looked quite adorable. Young and hairy. And patchy. Rags were cheap. Ah, those were—"

"Okay. So what else did Mr. St. Onge do that was noteworthy?" This is patronizing-plus. She really hates this Gil guy. Jerk. *Asshole.* She's *not* five years old.

"He was likeable."

"Yeah, what else?" she presses on, tapping her soft, almost-silent computer keys, with her lip curled.

"At that time, late seventies, he was in the construction biz . . . heavy equipment . . . schools, banks, the *big* jobs. His family were the Depaolos."

"Oh?"

"Yeah, *you* know of *the* Depaolos, of course. And they were . . . *are* political . . . the *family,* you know, in the way any good-sized, successful, monied contracting outfit looks after its interests. Friends in Augusta. Family in the House and Senate. Connections all over the place. And hired lobbyists. The smile guys."

Ivy is typing all this Depaolo info into the computer.

"But I remember that Gordo himself was not political that way, and not the other way either . . . not like we nice liberal kids were . . . not a no-nuker . . . no antithis or antithat. He was just a . . . a . . . a redneck Schopenhauer. You know, he was *out there*. And he was cynical."

"Crazy?"

"No. He just bored a lot of people. But some love that kinda stuff . . . those other 'out there' hate-the-world people."

"What else?"

"He married *very young*. I mean like maybe eighteen. He was *the* kid. Younger than the rest of us. Younger, *much* younger than his wife."

She waits quietly, fingers light on the keys, ready.

He goes on, "To a gal from one of the reservations. Indian Township, or Princeton. Not sure now. But Passamaquoddy, the guys who had the land claims deal. Later, I heard they divorced. No kids."

"What else?"

"He drove a brand-new four-wheel-drive truck . . . with *Depaolo Bros.* printed on the doors. Everyone had a hauling favor to ask of him,

especially when we moved from one shabby apartment to another.
Nobody else had a truck. In those days, trucks were too 'working
class.' We all had Volvos. Old Volvos. Old Opals. Old Saabs. And
VWs. Old, of course. Went nicely with our rags. And hair."

"Anything else about him?"

"He loaned me a thousand smackeroos once to help me out of a
mess." Gil makes a smacking sound with his lips close to the phone.
"Jesus Christ. Think how much a thousand dollars was back in the
late seventies!"

"You pay him back?" Ivy laughs one of her deep raffish HAW
HAWs.

"Yeah. It took me a while. But shit, that little loan really saved my
ass."

Ivy chortles. "So, Gil. You owe him your life."

"In a manner of speaking."

 Ivy Morelli in the newsroom.

On her trusty computer screen in vertical list form, are these words:

> Fiddles.
> Solar gear
> Big ideas.
> Leaded glass.
> Windmills.
> Printing press.
> Municipal law.
> Pigs, chickens, goats. Sheep. Cows.
> Machining.
> Chanting and kazoos. Masks.
> Furniture making.
> Quilts and homemade clothes.
> Sawmills. Three.
> Sap house.
> Water with no chlorine.
> Christmas trees.
> Wood ticks in a jar.

Pregnancies. Too many.
No tractor.
Tree houses. Cute little bridges.
Plays and skits.
Embroidery. Too much.
Hot food. Too much.
A few bruises (normal).
Beer, cider, eggs, Godzilla.
First aid.
Beauty shop.
Warm swim.

Now she says aloud: "No computers. No George Washington. No mommy. One gun."

 Peak.

So our Ivy isn't REEEEEEEL curious about Peak Oil. Peak Soil, acid seas, hurricanes, and Bible-type floods. She still feels the sting of *their* creepy zeal. It was for Ivy a public ravishment, a flogging. Stripped and flogged by a bunch of brats.

But today, while roaming the Internet (*yes, the COMPUTER, the Devil's handiwork, Mr. St. Onge*), she finds a mention of Peak Oil that seems credible. Also Peak water. Peak soil. Peak food. *Leaping cold and thirsty lizards!*

And our Ivy is swept away into the documented official real-life absolute scary.

The hands of the clock move around as fast as used-car dealership searchlights. Somehow three hours disappear and though several people were roaming around the newsroom when she started, she is now alone.

 Wiggling eyebrows.

Next day in the newsroom, Ivy arrives with ruffles and ripples under her eyes. She had lost herself in cyberspace again once she had gotten home last night. Read, clicked, watched to four a.m. Even had a cyberchat with a local engineer who was frantic over Peak Oil and was sending her a book.

She finds Brian at his desk. He is staring into his computer with a small smile, hears Ivy's brushy step on the carpet and turns slightly.

Ivy says in a robotlike voice, "Brian. Peak. Oil. Acidic. Oceans. Climate. Change. Why. Isn't. It. A. Headliner?"

Brian stops smiling. He turns to face her, then he cranks his chair to face slightly past her, his eyes slide to the executive editor's door with the frosted glass window and moving shadow beyond. He wiggles his eyebrows. He moves his eyes back to Ivy's hands, which are loaded with Peak Oil and devil weather documentation and discussion by EXPERTS and OFFICIALS and SANE GENIUSES who are not connected to the St. Onge Settlement.

Then he looks back toward the frosty window and wags his eyebrows some more. Then he says in a robot voice, "How. Are. You. This. Morning. Ivy?"

Ivy squints. She blushes. Her heart thuds. She swallows. She says in a robot voice, going with the flow, "Brian. Silence. Is. Censorship."

He turns away from her and goes back to his screen. Then he whispers, "Remember you were hired because you are a people person. You write about people."

She says, "I was hired because I'm slow." Then turns on her heel, her new earrings, bronzed peanuts (in shells), thrashing stormily from side to side.

 The cruel joke.

That night, Ivy lays spread eagle *on top* of the covers (her quilt of an unconventional insect pattern), too upset to get *UNDER* the covers. She had thought of herself as a sleuth. A Lois Lane. An INVESTIGATIVE reporter. But the *Record Sun* just sees her as what? A Girl Scout? A stenographer? A shill?

If Ivy is to survive, she has to pretend that the Settlement people are all crazy and that the geology and meteorology and environment experts she has connected with don't exist.

If. She. Is. To. Survive.

Trying again (Part I).

The silver car moves like cool water into the St. Onge farm place's sandy lot. Again the long-fingered crisp but fluid person steps out, eyeing the many doors. The leaves of the rivulated old ash with its misspelled sign (OFICE) speak imperceptibly.

Again nobody seems to be in or about, no flutter of a curtain, no running steps respond to the woman's thumps on the door.

Again she presses her calling card into the crevice of the closed inner door.

Again she studies the contents of the screened-in porch, listening, the long fingers of the one hand tracing the edge of the thickness of forms of her clipboard.

Again she and her car are gone.

 Trying again (Part II).

Gordon slows the truck at the tipsy silver mailbox, swings down into the steep yard. A somewhat matted collie dog runs out from the pole barn, and, tail spinning, wastes no time wetting down all of Gordon's tires before Gordon has even stepped out. The truck is one of the Settlement work rigs. Cumbersome thirty-year-old flatbed with an overload of sweet blond two-by-fours and strapping. On the passenger's seat, young Jaime Crosman, eyes closed, billed cap pulled down over his face.

The collie sniffs Gordon's pant legs in a friendly, bounding, light-footed way, making graceful helping circles around Gordon, showing him the way to the front door.

The front doorstep is a stone. A massive chunk of granite like you see at most old farm places around here, though this house isn't really old.

Again, like his previous visit, Gordon doesn't knock. Just stands there, arms folded across his chest.

The collie hustles back to the loaded flatbed, stands on his hind legs trying to get a better look in at the open window at Jaime, but Jaime doesn't stir. Collie's claws squeal against the old red-orange paint.

Gordon looks around. There are no other working vehicles, just a blue and rusty doorless thing up on the tree line across a field, looks like an old DeSoto. And the two unregistered trucks and station wagon here at the edge of the yard. Timberjack gone from the pole barn. A new-looking compressor stands there. He walks around the house, looks up at a little gable window of the tiny attic above the addition. A screened octagon. He sees movement. He steps back to get a better look. Then bellers for all he's worth, "BRIANNA!"

No response.

He again crosses his arms over the chest of his work shirt. He looks, yes, Vikingish. A Roman-Irish-American-Indian Viking. He keeps his eyes on that funny little window a good long minute, waiting.

Another minute passes.

He waits. No cars pass up on the road. No bugs (well, not many). No birdsong. Just that hot ticking sound from the Settlement truck, big engine cooling down. Even the collie dog is quiet.

Another long minute, Gordon watches the window. Then gives up, turns.

A low flutelike whistle floats from that octagon window.

Gordon pivots, tries to imitate her whistle but his whistle just comes out bad. He wipes his wrist and hand across his mouth.

The collie veers back. He barks up at Gordon, coaxingly, his panting mouth looking like a dumb but very nice smile. His honey coat and white chest shake around like a Hawaiian's grass skirt. His head is so long and narrow. Small, funny, slanty, nice-guy eyes. Gordon, not normally an animal person, opens his hand on the firm head and murmurs, "Lassie . . . get help. Get help, Lassie." The collie appreciates this joke and his smile intensifies.

A UPS truck comes banging and jolting along the road, around the curve, then disappears.

Now Gordon tries another whistle for the girl. It's one he knows, one he has always thought since childhood was Indian. It's the call of the mourning dove. Rather dreary. But nice. It says, *I mourn. I mourn.*

The girl replies with her dusky flutelike call.

Gordon again wipes his mouth. Paces a small circle. Once. In pleasant agitation. Now stands squinting up at the little octagon window. The collie sits down next to Gordon's leg, smiles up at him. Gordon sees the lighter shadow of a face beyond the dark screen. He cups his hands around his mouth. He calls, "So, what's the difference between a nightclub and an elephant fart!!!!?"

He hears her giggle.

He drops his hands.

Again, her giggle.

He waits.

The reply is just another giggle. And then a long minute of no sound but for the UPS truck off in a more distant, softer, ring of space and time. Only the space and time between Gordon and that little window and the ten minutes he has been here are clear. He calls out, "The difference izzz one is a barroom, the other is a baROOOOOOOm."

Another giggle, though a pretty fancy giggle. But it's clear that Brianna Vandermast isn't ready for the Home School. Nor is she ready for the Prophet. Because after her giggle, nothing.

Gordon looks sadly at the collie dog, who flumps his thick tail.

 In a future time, Brianna Vandermast remembers.

I believe that Mother Nature and God are both chemistry. The elements. Synapses. The gaseous, the electric, the salt, and the solid. Sometimes fresh, sometimes carrion rotting into a universe of microlife.

I believe the soul is something else. Something unnamable, indescribable. It *feels* nothing. It is spared of tribulation.

I saw him and knew there was a difficult mission, all twisted in the agonies of the body and brain, nature and God. There was a fire over every inch of me. I was young and so the time ahead seemed long. The light at the window looked infinite.

 The voice of Mammon.

Here in America, land of the free, we now have one good job for every two hundred able persons. What indeed is a *good* job? You aren't even a legal citizen while on the boss's property. But hey, you get pretty good pay. Then there's endless low-pay, no bennies temp jobs for all the rest, the losers. The odd men out. They get what they deserve, right? And what does it take to DESERVE?

Bend low, kiss our asses! Hurry now. Hurry. Others are right behind you with more accommodating lips.

 Meanwhile, what is that written on everything you touch?

Made in China.

 History as it happens, as written by Katy and Karma, age five (both). Heavily edited by Oceanna and Heather and Toon.

At breakfast everybody was wet in the hair because of rain that was going sideways. Josee says eggs are coming out of our ears. There is an egg recipe cubby set up "for the duration."

Today Annie B. gets a visit from the beauty crew. She lives in the village and is ninety-nine-and-three-quarters-years old. *Old.* Her street is Pleasant Street.

Also the compost crew gets to go to town to get more buckets. So they were jolly.

Echo is visiting from the Township. We traded Brant for her for two weeks. Welcome Echo!! Brant is on the swanboat crew, which is awfully behind, but he is enjoying a change of scenery his papa said. So Brant is full of happiness and the scenery here is basically the same.

Samantha says there is a rumor that Gordon's stocks and bonds are drying up because he sells them. She says he is *in rebellion*. This will affect the *accounts*.

Benjamin says American flags are now made in China. Beth said why do we need a flag anyway, we know where we are.

Gail says factory jobs are *demeaning*, that she ought to know.

Beth strangled Theodan and he laughed and knocked everything over getting under the table. Slippery eggs slid.

Later, at our philosophy salon, Rachel said she read a book by a positive man who said there is going to be a great transformation, that humans are going to change and peace will prevail.

Kirky said *no way*. "It's easier to put the peel back on the banana than it is to talk monkeys out of being monkeys."

Bonnie Loo who stops throwing up by salon time said, "Picture this. The red-hot red telephone that sets off the bomb launchers and these hairy chimpanzee hands playing around with it. Not to mention all those chimp hands and brilliantly considerate chimp minds who cut you off in traffic and pass on hills being in charge of everything else that hangs over our heads."

Back at breakfast time, Beth crossed her arms on the table and spit a prune pit into her coffee cup.

Evan told a joke he heard at the shingle mill last night. It was wicked funny. An elephant fart that goes ba-ROOOOOOM!!

We got thirty people so far to sign up for the planetarium trip. I've seen it before and they twinkle like real ones in a real sky.

Also while we are so close, Gordie wants us to visit his friends who live at the ocean on *rocks*. His friends are rich but very nice.

Arthur is sick. Something old-age-ish.

Windmill crew has their hands full tomorrow. Lights are out on the lane.

Guess who is also pregnant. (Besides Bonnie Loo and everybody else.) To be announced.

Cindy signed up for the Christmas tree planting crew by mistake. She called it double booking.

 Next day, Ivy arrives at work, swings her shoulder bag onto the floor next to her desk and sees eight calls are on her voice mail.

After settling in with a bottle of blueberry-banana-passion-fruit drink, she runs through the calls. One is from a guy who gives only "Bill" for a name and no call-back number. He speaks slowly and clearly with a Connecticut or New York suburbs accent. He suggests that Ivy Morelli might find it interesting that Lisa Meserve, the dental assistant from Augusta who was arrested in that big marijuana bust a few weeks ago, is the single mother of an African-American child and that child was put in the care of a foster home but was then transferred to a second foster home in three days, and the next week was transferred to her maternal grandfather, Peter Meserve, a widower who owns and operates a service station in Mexico, Maine, but then this child was unofficially transported by Peter Meserve to the St. Onge "compound" in Egypt and several interested parties have proof that the whole marijuana deal has gone through the St. Onge operation, as most likely much drug dealing is, other drugs as well, and illegal guns and illegal gun components, and will continue until the situation is vigorously investigated.

The voice of Bill further explains, "I am leaving this message with all the big papers, not just yours, and with several reporters and editors at each. So whoever does something with it first . . . well . . . you know what I'm saying. It's an *opportunity,* Ms. Morelli . . . CLICK!!!" Dial tone. The next message begins.

 The grays.

See, it's like this: our craft, though undetected by Earthling sensories 99.9 percent of the time, are everywhere, bumper to bumper! All sizes, some of them mere motes. We shift our craft square dance–like or, rather, we flow as droplets of a broad casual river. The skies, the interiors of caves and all structures are made up of our volume, as many of us as there are stars but closer together. In your disdain and erasure of the ghost layer, in your tearing of the gossamer net to replace it with only your VOICE and your FORCE and your TODAYS, you have lost your opportunity to find out that the net of all life is unraveling. Thus we grays are the dulcet antithesis of void. We are not from "another planet." We have always been right here, though once *you* were not, not in your present dimensions.

Do not be embarrassed. In our sorties, we see it all, even up your noses.

 Another night. Quarter to three.

Gordon St. Onge sprawls in his wheeled desk chair in the kitchen of the old farm place, knees apart, distractedly pushing one work boot against the leg of a heaped desk, which makes the wheeled chair go back an inch, then another inch, then another. He stares down at a note in his hands. A note that did not come by mail. Only a few moments ago, just home from late work at the sawmills, he found this note stuck in the screen door. It is written with fountain pen in familiar and flowery calligraphy.

It reads:

Teacher! Teacher! Don't waste time on me. Go beyond the safe margins of these hills. Take courage. Millions have yet to hear the truth. And millions want to be part of your family! Please share with all of America the sweetness of your heart. Take the stampeding cattle the way of the good. Into the embrace.

It is unsigned. But he knows.

He sniffs the paper. Cigarettes. So she is a smoker. He hadn't sniffed the book of paintings. He drops the hand with the note onto one thigh, shuts his eyes. Brianna Vandermast. What do you know about power? What do you know of the world? What do you know about good and bad? What do you know about me?

 During the rest of the night.

He sleeps and dreams. He dreams he dances with a woman. A frenetic dance. Not really touching, but almost. A wild dance of gypsies. Her hair is greenish white, textured like long grass. Rustles drily like long grass. He feels watched in a most terrible way. And this makes him dance harder.

 Tracking Brianna.

Near noon on the Old Dyer Road at the landing of a logging and chipping operation, where miles of skid roads converge. Such a tangled mess and muck, and the racket of machinery at varying levels of "efficiency." And Brianna.

Yes, they say she is here. "There!" one of the men down on the landing points to the forked skid road. And so Gordon nods, thanks him, and starts the climb.

But after ten minutes of ruts and slash and rock, what he finds is one of the Vandermast brothers working alone at a good clip above a high wall of small rock caves. He is dropping medium-sized recent-growth beech trees . . . CRACKLE-CRACKLE-FLUMPH! over and over and over as he climbs higher along the ridge, looking full of purpose, agile as a bug on a wall. Dirty baseball cap. Messy T-shirt. Sawdust-splattered green work pants. Sneakers. He turns now and discovers Gordon. Gordon sees that Vandermast look, round face and worried eyes. Gentle people.

The Vandermast nods hello to Gordon. Finishes a cut. Kicks out the notch. Swings around to press the twenty-pound saw into the heart, jerks the saw away, gives the tree a slap with the heel of his free hand and walks away with the slow descending crackling and crashing behind him. Now he shuts off the saw.

He digs out his ear plugs, slips them into a pocket of his pants, and hops down off the glittery shelf of ledge to where Gordon is still walking up toward him and the sort-of-silence is nice. All machinery now is in the distance, even the skidder that had just groaned past a minute before. Now it's only the sound of feet crunching, a mosquito singing near the ear, and the Vandermast guy saying, "Hey' doin'?"

Gordon says, "I didn't think there were many flesh-and-blood log-gers left in the logging biz, but here you are."

The guy makes no reply to this but Gordon goes on in his chatty way. And as he rattles on like this, the quiet guy sets his saw down and swipes at a half dozen mosquitoes that have taken an interest in the back of his head, ears, and sweaty temples. For a few moments, both men just fight off bugs and breathe in the heavenly green, wood-redolent air. The day is not a bright one. No sun. No shadows. Just a nice even gray. A gray worthy thing. Too muggy-warm though. Earlier, there had been drizzle.

"Think there're porcupines in those caves?" Gordon wonders, looking up at the high wall of dark rock and oven-sized caves and still-standing but badly skidder-barked hemlocks.

The Vandermast's eyes twinkle mightily. "Well, the sure way to know is you go up there and stick your hand in one a'them little holes." He scratches roughly at a mosquito bite on one knuckle, then scratches luxuriously at one on his arm. This is the clean-shaven pipe-smoking taller Vandermast brother, although there's no pipe in sight at the moment. This is Dana Vandermast, although Gordon doesn't know the name yet. He knows only Pitch and Poon, who are really John and Mark. This one, Dana, has never earned any livelier name.

On the skid road above and the skid road below on the left, there are the hurtling groans of two skidders coming closer, none visible.

Dana says, "I need my dinna." He scooches down for his saw and starts down the hill with Gordon alongside. Stepping over and under and through limbs, rock, and root, stump and rain-wet ferns, Gordon asks, "So where is everybody? I saw Cole's outfit down on the road and a couple of your rigs, but—"

"If you mean *where's Brianna?,* she saw you coming. So she took off."

Gordon grunts unhappily. Claps a mosquito between his palms.

One-handed, Dana Vandermast slips his pipe into his mouth, doesn't light it. Just likes to have something to grip in his teeth as he goes along. The two men trudge along the rest of the way without any talk.

Down below, around the landing and along the narrow high-crowned paved road, there are a half dozen parked cars and pickups. And in the bulldozed sandfilled "yard," the vast chipper reigns. This was once efficiency at its near best. A walled-up little room-sized contraption of churning gears and belts and blades, bristling outside with levers, and there's the deafening howl, and the jaws that feed it, all part of the day in the life of this one fabulous *never satisfied* creature. Tomato orange and scarred. In payments and interest and repairs and fuel, would it be worth a quarter million?

Gordon recalls one of the paintings at the end of Brianna's big book. It showed that shimmering wall of tomato orange and an even oranger fellerbuncher, while before it stood a long row of tiny men, smaller than real life, all with empty hands hanging. Even in featureless silhouette, you could see that they were all buck naked. The verse had read:

How can we call this phantasm by the name Progress when all it does is diminish us?

Here in real life, Gordon recognizes the real-life operator of this real life chipper. Larry McMannis. The guy looks a little proud, a little bored. Hands on a lever. His tight T-shirt is light blue. His back is narrow, long, and ribby. Tall guy. Hard hat with ear protectors. Long serpentine-like neck.

The box truck being fed the chips is now nearly glutted. Because you always go a little over. It's the only way. Otherwise, you might as well quit. As the verse to another one of Brianna's pictures asks: *Where is the last honest man? In debt, in shame, begging the grave?*

Gordon walks with Dana Vandermast to the road's shoulder. Dana's pickup has a red volunteer firefighter's light on the dash and, on the seat, a sandwich in a bag. He lowers the heavy saw onto the tailgate, wipes his forehead with a wrist, and says, "She's scary."

Gordon looks harder at this guy's face. *She?* Meaning the business? A machine? A huge tree? Or—

"I don't mean her face. Everybody gets used to her face after a time." He glances across the road at the fern-filled woods, then up the tar road headed toward New Hampshire. "She reads piles of stuff . . . words as long as my arm. For a long time now. Since she was a little squirt. That book Poon showed you, Gordie . . . 'twas just the tip of the iceberg. She gives me the willies . . . like she's not complete' human. Or maybe she's more than one human. Maybe part of her birth defect was *two* brains. Both of them scheming." He smiles down at his feet. A shy gesture. He pulls a plastic pouch of tobacco from a pocket. "She don't want what normal girls want. You can't interest her in a movie or a cute pair of shoes. She's schemy, like I say. I ain't no match for her giant ideas and plots. Nobody is. Not Dad. He's the one that says she might have an extra brain. So I said get an X-ray. Ha-ha. But he's creeped out 'n' afraid it'll turn out true. He says let's just *ride* it. But we want her out of school. They've complained she's taking over, outfoxing them all." He blinks fast. "She's just a kid. That means she really ain't got no sense."

Gordon strokes his mustache thoughtfully, staring up along the trees where he and Dana had just come from.

The crisscrossed heap of hemlock next to the chipper is now only a single layer. Another tractor trailer backs up to take the place of the one that's now headed down the road. One truck is old. One truck is new like a silken newborn thing. The valves of both grunt and chuff and the exhaust from the stacks is baby blue. And both trucks speak the word *debt!* Spelled out in thunder.

The chipper screams.

Gordon says, "I got a note from her. Did she have one of you guys bring it over last night?"

As Dana draws on the pipe to get it going, his worried eyes move over Gordon's face. "She probably come over there by herself. Pulled a sneaky. Since she was about nine years old, she'll take one of the trucks and go riding around by herself at night . . . which of course is when cops are *most likely* to stop people."

"They stop her?"

"Yep."

"What do they do?"

"A variety of things." He laughs a little uneasily. "So what'd it say? The note."

"Well, it's hard to describe."

Dana smiles, nods knowingly. The smoke is a sweet spiraling cloud. He glances again toward the woods, up and down the road. Somewhere Brianna is standing, maybe watching. Slapping mosquitoes. She is, for certain, slapping mosquitoes.

 The screen gooily scolds and cajoles.

Low voter turnout at the primaries. This is bad. We just don't understand you people! It is so perplexing! Voting will turn things around. You NEED to vote. Look at all those poor souls in those countries with rigged elections and dictators and sneakiness. But you Americans are just lazy! Here you have the power to vote and you just goof off!

 The grays.

This morning we captured from the roadside an abandoned TV. It is on our laboratory table now, making noises. It is not plugged in but our large teacup-sized dark eyes in our fibrous-but-flossy faces meld with its essence and hear its voice. Unlike the ivy, it does not cry or show terror. It coos. Blue poofs of loud sweet talk and sticky sales pitches reach out with human hands, smashing through the screen, grabbing one of us to pull into that terrible chamber of hurry-up music, burgers, politicians, insurances, pills, promises of joy.

The one being pulled through the screen gets away, of course. Though we are all slightly winded from pulling.

Inside the screen, tidy odorless fruit-color humans carry on with no apologies as the awful music subsides and the mood relaxes. Now, suddenly, a slobbery lifeless water flings the glasslike screen aside and a waterfall thunders at our feet. Thousands of scarlet fish* zigzag through the deepening tide that rises up to our shins, knees, thighs.

Oh, dear, this contraption is a specimen that we cannot keep. We buzz open the hatch and out it goes.

 In a future time, Claire St. Onge remembers.

Again he was going in and out of his . . . his *spells*. One day he'd just be horseplaying with the kids and working hard and eating his meals with gusto. Just the workings of the Settlement heating his blood. Then snap! He was going on and on about this or that ruthless policy of "America" or "the corporatists" or "the Mammon worshippers." He'd snarl, "The humans are ee-vile!" Then he'd do some charming stunt to jerk us back. His glob of keys jangling, he'd drop agilely to kiss somebody's feet. He was a notorious foot kisser. And he'd call you "my dear one." Hoarse, stirring theatrics.

Many sisters here confided in me that they felt so sick inside and edgy. Which was more dangerous, the world or Gordon?

 The screen explains.

The governor has worked hard to make Maine appealing to FDNA, the credit giant, and now one of Maine's old coastal working class towns, previously "jobless," is host to FDNA. Hats off to the governor! FDNA will employ up to 2,000 people from many area towns and cities in two counties. And there's GREAT pay and benefits. Thank you, Governor. Our hats are off. We should be thankful for these jobs. These jobs could have gone to another state!!! And that would have been terrible!!!

---

* Red herrings.

Uh-oh . . .

While applications were being taken for the jobs, it has been revealed that there will be a policy of NO PERSONAL CALLS WHATSOEVER IN OR OUT. NO EXCEPTIONS. For employees using sick days, A DOCTOR'S NOTE IS MANDATORY. ANYONE EVEN THINKING THE WORD "UNION" WILL BE FIRED ON THE SPOT. There will be STRICT WORK MONITORING. STRICT DRESS CODE. And ROUTINE SURPRISE URINE MONITORING. NO FAMILY PHOTOS ALLOWED IN CUBICLES. ALL MANAGEMENT POSITIONS WILL BE BROUGHT IN FROM OUT OF STATE.

 Concerning the aforementioned.

The screen is blank.

 More to mull.

Somewhere in New England, another family farm is lost. Another one is sold because the grown children don't like farming. Another is lost and another and another. *Crunch. Zoom!! Grrr!* Cul-de-sacs. Foundations. Bedroomy homes. Grass to groom. Another moment passes. Another farm is lost. Another cluster of bedroomy homes. Empty till dark? Always empty but for beds. But no dark. Big security lamps light up the stage. Pink like insalubrious plasma. Another moment passes. Another barn gets made into a studio. Another. Farms dying. Families dividing. Another father looks into his young child's face and sees only the reflected glow of the kid's costly but cheapie computer. Lost in unimagined space.

 Out in the world.

More studies coming in that reveal an increase in America's cynicism. Four major 1993 surveys showed between 15 and 20 percent of Americans were somewhat cynical, more than 10 percent very cynical. In two major 1999 studies cynicism on the whole had risen 46 percent. And 60 to 75 percent of those cynical were deemed to be *very* cynical.

Wedged in the screen door, an envelope. In the envelope, a letter in bold calligraphy.

Dear Teacher—

You do not need to see me for us to exchange a few ideas. I think I saw some of your students today, passing in two cars on the road. I always like to imagine that they are armies of goodwill. Well, I guess that's just what they are!

Oh, I love letters. I can write much better than I speak. So don't keep trying to find me.

I saw some more of the letters to the editor you wrote in 1980 and '81. Six different newspapers. Don't ask me how I got them. Ha-ha. I have friends on the inside (Settlement). But even that's not where I got them.

Yes, I am hiding from you. But I have reasons. But you are hiding, too! You are hiding from the people. I have heard of your passionate mealtime speeches in detail (through my spies ha-ha), so in a way I AM ALWAYS RIGHT THERE WATCHING YOU!!! And I can plainly see that you know what a good leader must do.

Good leaders are not bosses, are not bullies, working with a whip. Good leaders are like sunrises. They stir us from slumber, make our muscles go twitch-twitch and get us all to do what we need to do, what we actually wanted to do to begin with. To be brothers and sisters. To roar.

I have been reading a lot of stuff on the lobbying in Washington and also the Trilateral Commission, Bildeberger, Council of Foreign Relations, IMF, World Bank, W.T.O., Business Roundtable, Project for the New American Century, Chamber of Commerce. These are God. They want everyone in all countries to be in debt. To be slaves. To work with no labor laws, no environmental protections. They want more and more privatization and no laws for themselves. The system has evolved. Poised to enslave the world. There are terrible secrets. But I also like to read Chomsky and Zinn and I get CounterPunch. And there is the little book called Small Is Beautiful *by E. F. Schumacher. And do you know Wendell Berry? There is so much. Have you seen the book* Ishmael? *About a gorilla who talks . . . sort of.*

You want to know a secret? I am really scared.

Your friend,
Bree

She opens the letter, which has come by US mail. The handwriting is large and spiky. The note is written on scrap paper.

Dear Brianna. I have a secret for you. I, too, am really scared.

Your friend,
Gordie
(or Guillaume. That's my real name.
Can you pronounce it?)

Very quickly, another envelope appears, this one *not* wedged in the door, but on the table.

Dear Teacher—

Have you heard about Radio Free Maine? It is a series of audio tapes of lectures. Chomsky! And Zinn! There are others, too. What do you think of the Leftists?

I'll enclose the address for the tapes. They would be wonderful for your library.

And would you tell me another secret about yourself? I love secrets.

Your friend, Bree
Look! See!
RADIO FREE MAINE
P.O. BOX 2705
AUGUSTA MAINE 04338

She sits on her bed in her little attic bedroom and reads the large spiky handwriting.

Dear Brianna—

Yes, I will see to it that some of those tapes go into the library. And we already have the books you mentioned in your first letter.

Another secret about me personally? Okay. Here's one. My life is filled with witches. I am not the big guy you think I am. I am not a world leader. I am nothing. I am a kind of fire-tongued toad. But the witches . . . now THERE is a force to be reckoned with.

Your friend,
Gordie

He stands at the table, rubbing the back of his head, reading with his cheapie drugstore reading glasses, frowning.

Dear Teacher,

There are three witches who go with you at all times. Duty. She is the physician. Dark eyes and silver hair. She rides your shoulders with her canteens, flasks, and contraptions. No doorway is closed that she and you pass together.

The second witch is Passion. She does not ride your shoulders. She carries you. She has neither eyes nor hair. She is the mob, hysterical, and too hot, a thing of blood and fluids and heart's delight. She flies left when you say "right." She flies right when you beg for left. She howls when peace and quiet is needed. She is a troublemaker, especially when she and Duty conspire behind your back.

The third witch is Sophia. She has a thousand eyes. She is Wisdom. She waits at the end of the journey. Though most of us race toward her, almost no one ever really sees the face of Sophia. By the time we reach her, our old eyes are failing, our chests are caved in and our aged muscles flutter. We can't even hear her voice because we have lost our hearing. Oh, poor Sophia has so few guests!

But she will receive you, Teacher. And you will still be young. But you will die in Sophia's arms while Duty and Passion stand near.

Which witch am I?

Your friend,
Bree

P.S. You forgot to answer my question about the Left.

 She reads.

Dear Brianna—

I didn't forget to answer your question about the Left. I remembered NOT to answer it.

You are Sophia. That is which witch you are.

Listen to me. Forget all the reasons you think I shouldn't see you. We need to talk. If you don't want the crowds here, I can pick you up at your house and we can ride around. How about ice cream at Kool Kone? Or we

*can just come back here and find a quiet room. And you can meet Claire.
She knows your brothers from when we all met on the road one night.*

By the way. You are a plagiarist. You've read Macbeth. *Shakespeare's
three witches, you know: "When the hurlyburly's done, when the battle's
lost and won." No, not a plagiarist. Just teasing. Time has passed enough
that we live in Shakespeare's tradition. He won't mind a bit. .*

Meanwhile, I read a review on The Liberty Men and the Great Proprietors, *a book by Alan Taylor on a revolt here in Maine after the so-called
American Revolution. Some of the kids here are doing a series of skits on
that era.*

*You ought to see our library, Brianna. We have collected books, yes,
but also letters and journals, and so much that is beyond partisan, beyond
ideology. It's a vast jigsaw puzzle, this world, this life.*

I also enclose a copy of Macbeth. *Happy reading. I look forward to
yakking with you about all this. This is important to me. I won't go OUT
THERE and be the leader you imagine. I can't. Soon, you and I will
discuss this reality. It's big.*

Your friend, Gordie

 And in elegant calligraphy, she writes.

Dear Guillaume (Ge-yome),
    Wrong. I am not Sophia. I am Duty. I nag. Ha-ha.
    *I am still hiding. Don't ask to see me. It isn't just my face. I can nag you
better this way. Ha-ha.*

Your friend,
Bree
P.S. No, I have never read or heard or seen Macbeth. *Just a
coincidence. The world turns. But thank you for the copy.*
I'm eager.

 **Standing, he writes with a ballpoint pen, using the
wall for firmness under the piece of lined paper.**

Dear Bree,
    *Okay. I understand about your reticence. But if you ever have the
need to come see me, I'll be here. And meanwhile, your spies, whoever*

they are, can tell you what a nice person I am! How pleasant! How
fascinating! Ha-ha.

Your friend,

G.

P.S. Concerning the "coincidence" of witches, I have to say you
spook me.

 Inner voice of the Bureau.

The job of some Americans is to find purpose for the low-use seg-
ment of the American population. Say you have a workhorse that isn't
working to put dollars into your pocket, in this case *the economy*, you
sell these horses for meat. Chop! Chop! Doggie food. Instant purpose.
The economy is saved.

When some horses smell horse blood, they kick their masters in the
face, or *worse,* these horses TALK to other horses and then you have a
stampede that gets in the way of progress. The Bureau's job, you see,
is to go the extra mile and whoa! . . . get these garbage scum groups,
protester-extremist-crud, street-blocking-anarchists, terrorist home
boys, treasonists and whatever other mess-causing-disorderly-useless
types *into cans,* so progress can continue.

It's not as easy as you think, even with the Internet, our eyes in the
clouds. For reasons known to some, there is today a mushrooming
rumble of hooves. Uh-oh. Even what used to be decent people are
starting to talk bad and horsey.

 (The next p.m.) Unexpected visitors.

Bulging hot blank sky tonight, blank as a closed door. Heat and humidity tend to erase stars. The wide open bay of the larger Quonset
hut blazes with frothy muggy light and toward this light, Gordon St.
Onge walks, eating some sort of dried fruit chewy bar (Settlement-
made *this* time). "Hey!" someone calls to him from the clump of parked
vehicles in the sandy lot quite near. Part light, mostly shadow.

He turns, sees a familiar truck and three figures.

He winds his way around the two nearer trucks, brushing crumbs
off his fingers, then reaching up to flatten down his hair. No billed

cap tonight. Just that giddy wild mess of hair that needs to be cut according to the Settlement women, and the lengthening beard, which needs to be trimmed according to his mother (although Marian would rather see the whole thing scraped completely off, revealing his beaming boyhood aspect).

When he reaches the visitors, there's not much talk; Dana and Poon Vandermast, as ever, are closed-mouthed as bread-box mice. Their round faces are silvery on the left side, from the light of the Quonset hut bay, dark on the right, two eclipsed moons. Light color T-shirts. Bare arms. And someone standing between these two, a young girl, nearly the same height as they. She stands in work boots, her legs a little apart. Jeans and one of those old dark green work shirts, old enough to still be cotton, faded seams. No polyester. No scratch. It is tucked into her belt. A shapely girl, noticeably shapely, distractingy shapely. A lotta thick squirmy hair. Frizzed by humidity. The night gives it a blonde-brown look but Gordon knows it is really carrot red. And, yes, that face.

It is the kind of face that was meant perhaps to be two faces, a fertilized Vandermast egg beginning to divide into twins, but somehow changed its heartless mind? Her eyes are great big pale eyes in long, pale lashes, lovely eyes but for the creepy reptilian distance between them.

The mouth. Just an ordinary frowning young girl's mouth.

Gordon feels his own face tingle in sympathy now that he's getting over that first instance of reflexive full alarm.

For only a moment, both of this girl's strange eyes bore into his, but now she lowers her face quickly so that her plentiful hair falls to cover one eye, one cheek, but Gordon keeps staring with his most terrible mad-scientist scrutiny, and he says deeply, "I know you." Only children and Gordon St. Onge stare.

She says, "Yep." Her one word is a soft squishy pelt-like piece. And yuh, a bit cigarette-hoarse.

Gordon now looks to Poon and to Dana, "You hog-tie her to get her here?"

The girl, Brianna, giggles, a full throttle giggle, almost a cackle. One might say ghoulish. Not musical, but a stippled shriek.

Dana says, "She heard we were comin' over and said maybe she'd come along, right?" He looks to her for agreement.

Gordon gazes at her. She is keeping her face lowered, hair sort of damp and clumpy from the day, maybe oily from neglect, too busy with her woods work and her plots? There it hangs. Her one large pale visible eye travels up across his shirt, springs to his face, then lowers again. She giggles. A plain and girlie laugh this time.

To Gordon, the night is now stranglingly hot. He says, "You guys heard we've been going all night on the Purple Hope, right? Three nights . . . and now this one."

Dana says, "Yessir. That's why we're here."

Gordon turns to the great blazing bay with the jouncing human-shaped shadows and yakking racket of a good-sized mob beyond. "The work of dreams," he says, folding his arms across his chest, glancing now over each Vandermast face.

"Drummond said he was going to be here," says Poon.

"Everybody's here," Gordon tells him, glancing over the packed parking lot. "It's my cousin Aurel's big idea to go nights for a while. Usually not as hot. It's been one thing or another an' we've been all fucked-up without sleep . . . makes people paranoid . . . women get bitchy . . . kids bratty, even the easy ones ain't themselves. An' guys go around with their backs up. We even got a rooster now that crows at midnight." Again he is glancing over each Vandermast face. With his arms crossed, one knee bent, he has his usual contented settled-in look, his yakking-it-up-with-neighbors look. He dips his head toward the lighted bay. "Electric buggies. Electric sedan." He laughs. "Next, we do electric snowmobiles!" He winks.

Poon says softly, "Electric skidder. Gonna do one'a them?"

Gordon raises a hand to stroke the graying chin of his beard. He whispers, "Hell, yeah."

Two of the Vandermasts chortle. Gordon throws out a hand toward the light and noise. "Come see! Come on in and check it out."

Poon Vandermast steps away from where he has been leaning against the truck, rubs his hands together.

Bree leans against Dana and says softly, "I'll just stay and have a smoke."

Dana sounds a little irritated. "You gonna pull one of your disappearing acts?"

"I'll be right here." She sneaks a peek at Gordon with her one uncovered eye.

Gordon is staring at her. At her hands. At her bared forearms, the sleeves of the work shirt rolled to the elbows, where there are many dark patches like bruises or tattoos. Or pine pitch. Or paint.

The two brothers trudge along toward the light, stop, turn to glance back.

Gordon, hanging back, tells Brianna, "I'm glad you're here."

Bree tips her head forward so her tumbling hair covers almost her whole face. She giggles. Hoarse and thick, this time a donkey bray but not what you'd call freaky, just a teenager lacking restraint. Her elegant artwork and letters don't match this raw discoordination of youth. Gordon reaches with two knuckles to brush one of the dark spots on her left forearm. "Paint?" he asks.

"Cadmium Red," she replies.

 ### Gordon returns to the parking lot alone.

He finds Bree reading in the cab, slumped low in the seat, one knee up, dome light glowing overhead.

She hears his step at the open window. She snaps off the dome light, lowers the book, drops her knee.

"Whatcha reading?" he asks, resting his hand on top of the rolled down window. He smells tobacco smoke, though he sees no lit cigarette.

"Oh, a love story."

"What's it called?"

"*The Populist Moment.*"

He laughs one big hoot, blinks both eyes.

She says, "It most definitely is a love story."

He looks back toward the lighted bay. He inhales the pussy-willow-thick night. The gray of it. And he is lost for words. He now shoves both hands into the pockets of his work pants and looks at her. All he sees is hair. "If you come back tomorrow at our noon meal, I'll give you a nice tour," he says. "You can check out our library. We have *four* copies of *The Populist Moment*." He grins. "In case you wear that one out."

She seems to be hunkering down lower in the seat.

He says with a kind of don't-be-too-hard-on-me whine, "I ain't got nothing against the left."

She laughs, head thrown back, but quickly drops her face again and covers it with both hands.

"This is harder than I thought," he says.

She is keeping her famously ghastly face hidden in her fingers.

"A whole buncha stuff we need to cover," he complains. "Three thousand years of civilization, our respective outlooks, and more, more, MORE!!!" He gives her a wild look, one eye squinted, one eye HUGE. "And YOU!" he sniffs sadly, "Are making me feel rushed."

She giggles into her hands. A *perfect* giggle. Like tonic.

He stays. He stays right there by the truck the whole hour and a half that the Vandermast brothers are inside watching the photovoltaic crew work. And almost the whole while, Bree Vandermast hides her face and giggles. Maybe a phrase here. A word there. But Gordon does most of the talking. Meanwhile, she smokes three times, hangs her hand out the window with the long cigarette erect in two fingers. Cars come and go. People leave, go trotting past, some carrying kids knocked out by sleep.

As he sees Poon and Dana coming toward the parking lot, Gordon pushes himself away from the truck window a little suddenly and, though what he has just been yakking about was only deer hunting, he now says deeply, "I don't HATE left-wingers . . . nor the right-wingers, notta one. Two halves of big industrialism and finance and empire. Fine. Fine. Together they give us a whole. Lefts, rights. Those are people who are on a roll with their surpluses and maps . . . see?" He pats his chest. "Me? I am a man of questions. No map. No surpluses. Just baby man, see? I am not capable of wisdom 'cause all I do is . . . is whine. Goo goo. Ga ga. Wah! That's me. Baby man."

And he turns toward the two guys, nods, bows to Bree and salutes each of the two Vandermast brothers and strides away.

 In a future time, Brianna Vandermast remembers.

My head was filled with epiphanies that summer. The closer I got to him, the more I loved everything and everyone. Even in the darkness of my little bedroom at night, the inside walls of my mouth moved in such a way as to kiss or to swallow, all the appetites of my living-ness. In my mind I saw, in bright parade, toads and microorganisms and weighty sashaying elephants, sweet chubby babies and my most aggravating relatives and acquaintances, the most fearsome people of history, and my dear brothers, and all the world's rock stars, the fashion queens, and forecasters of weather. All of them blurry, their flesh like fog. Only their eyes were vivid. And I wanted to put my arms around them all. Or at least paint them in colors I'd never seen before. I would invent new colors! I believed I could.

 Gordon St. Onge talks about the girl to others.

He tells how she appeared in the dark parking lot with her brothers. After all that chasing around to find her, she just showed up on her own! But all she did was giggle. Hid her face and giggled.

 Out in the world.

A most recent study shows extreme cynicism spreading into areas of the population where, in previous studies, low rates of cynicism were found. In fact, in some areas of the nation where cynicism cannot be related directly to lowering real wage, it manifests itself in less tangible concerns such as a feeling that the sky is falling or lack of leadership in public offices or no time with family or just no time or a sense of evil in everything or lack of caring in society or fear of violent crime, or everything seems speeded up. These types of cynicism had risen 300 percent in three years.

 Saturday. Ivy Morelli at home.

Ivy Morelli's apartment is two rooms and a kitchenette. Who would need more? She has plenty of space in her bedroom for her computer, worktable, a small television with VCR, and her queen-sized bed with wacky quilt of bugs and spiders that her twin sister, Ida, bought her. Ivy's niece and nephew love it when they visit. First thing when they come in, they both squeal, "Let's go see the bugs!!!!"

This morning, after a long, weird, swirly night's sleep, Ivy lies in her bed listening to the muffled early a.m. clinks and rumbles of construction three streets over. She holds up her hands, turns them.

She turns them more and more slowly, as if to hypnotize herself. Her one slim ring with its wee kernels of turquoise! Her shapely fingers, hard wrists. Peasantish and unbreakable-looking. Mighty Ivy.

On the night tables are scented candles and packets of incense. They smell like pine or vanilla or just weirdly wonderful. She goes through stages of burning these, usually rainy evenings or on those rare free Friday nights when she might have friends over, then the scents are great for atmosphere.

The whole apartment is white-walled and light. A lot of windows for an apartment, everyone says. Nothing like the new apartment complexes and condos with one featured picture window and three or four piteous portholes in the back. Here the floors are polyurethaned, a very light oak. In the living room–dining room combo, Ivy has wacky theater posters on the largest interior wall and a framed photo that her friend Tulani took of Ivy's feet wearing pink high-topped sneakers with double lacings. What a hoot!

No plants. Not even a small, loveless cactus.

No family pictures. She doesn't want her place to look too cluttered, too tacky, too cloying, too much like . . . like an old maid's . . . please forgive the expression. HAW! HAW!

There are two nice, big, pale mauve couches. A beanbag chair. A stereo and another TV (bigger than the bedroom TV) that is often running but which Ivy never sits down for. For real TV watching, her bedroom TV fills the bill.

Her kitchenette is small and cluttered with seasonings and special cooking and preparation devices. She goes through spells of liking to cook. Then for many weeks, she's happy to have a few crackers with cheese spread.

The bathroom is perfect. Everything tile or glass or chrome. No grimy crevices. And though that window is small, she has decorated it with colored tissue to look like a huge green and yellow parrot on succulent jungle boughs, a kind of color-separated leaded-glass effect. Better than old-maidish ruffled curtains!

Nothing is a deal these days. Everything costs. Her full-time job and her freelance articles still pay the rent. She can still get food and bare basics. There's the old saying about paying your own way and carrying your own weight. Well, as her friend Tulani insists, "Today that's *all* you can deal with. Your own weight. Like a herd animal, ready to run. Your fourteen hours a day of accumulated jobs with their accumulated commute-hours support no other life but yours. Go, go, go. Like buffalo. Like nervous elk. Stay lean. Stay ready." And yet all nights are so terribly deep.

Ivy's mother's name is Maureen. Her father is David. They are proud of Ivy.

Would they be proud if they guessed that their Ivy is having a case of voluntary amnesia concerning Peak Oil? Peak food. Peak water. Peak soil. She sighs. *Peak Oil.* The thing that, according to independent scientists and Settlement seven-year-olds, could end their world if not dealt with? Like climate change, which at least has been honored with *some* public debate, not dead silence. Ivy Morelli, no hero is she.

She drops her hands on the sheet. She dreads the newsroom, vendor of people stories. She is thinking up a good way to tell Brian, her editor, that she wants to drop the Home School story, that there is no story. After all, nobody else wants to touch these anonymous calls or even the calls by those who give their names. After all, these callers are just *people.* Seems nobody is interested in strenuously investigating the unofficiated. And the officials are never available to officiate. So let's just pretend the St. Onge Settlement does not exist. Yeah. Does. Not. Exist. We're good at *that,* huh?

That way, Ivy never really has to return to Egypt, to the troubling allure of it, to the big questions, all those questions, especially those ones Ivy needs to ask Ivy about Ivy.

 The screen crows:

We are America! *We* are proud! *We* are number ONE in the world! *We* are on top! *We* are rich! *We* are as tall as the sky! *We* are the fastest, the free-est, the most just. *We* kick butt! *We* are loyal and cheerful and never complain. *We* are about choice and democracy. *We* have merged with the deity of possibilities. America is tomorrow. Bigger TVs for instance, and smaller phones. Soon *we* will invent a cure for death. *We* will never die! New livers and eyebrows will grow with the gulping of a pill. *We* will soon be immortal! Nothing will stop *us.* Get out of *our* way! *We* will kill the challengers with *our* mean machines in the sky, remote control. Yes, these exist! Soon to be unveiled. *We* are the champions. *You* are mere bug splats. Stay tuned!

 ### The voice of Mammon.

Gray suits glide in and out of DC, slip in and out of state houses, seamless as new dolls. These are men and women who are charmingly seeing to it that *interests* are met. I command it so.

Yes, things are changing. Business people, bankers, my reps, and my policies must decide who will be blind and who will see, who will be twisted and prone and who will walk, who will live and who will die. Who is jailed and who walks. Who is elected and who makes the throwing-in-the-towel speech. This can no longer be a matter for others to handle. Only I am capable of these verdicts, being unencumbered by emotions. Only I know what is at stake. Only I can imagine it. What *is* at stake? The planet in the palm of my hand and all the plain human race profitable to me, useful, pliant, robotic. More so even than red oxen under the maple yoke and under the meat cleaver. This is the role of big men since the beginning, this glittery seat on high. Don't you see, human inventiveness has made me, and has fashioned my magnificence. It is meant. There is no *we,* though the writhing billions in their tender skins believe it so.

 Evening, a warm delectable dusk. Cagey DHS* child protective case worker shows up again at Gordon St. Onge's old house on Heart's Content Road.

She steps out of her square silvery car.

Gordon is there in the dooryard.

She puts her hand of long fingers out to him, a small white valise in her other hand, the soft nylon kind with a zipper. They shake hands. She gives her name, adds that she is from the Department of Human Services, and she speaks his real name, clearly, *boldly,* not as a question but as a known fact. *"Guillaume St. Onge."*

---

* Maine's Department of Human Services was not Department of Health and Human Services until after September 11, 2011, when crafty reorganizations occurred high and low.

Gordon understands that this person sees herself as a rescuer. He looks steadily into her eyes. Her eyes are not warm. But they are not the eyes of a machine, either. She is, in her off hours, a very nice person.

Nevertheless, she gives off a business-like industrial consumer smell.

He gives off the smell of freshly milled fir and labor. Blond sawdust powders and flecks his pant legs and shirt front. He has not spoken yet. He has only just stepped down from one of the Settlement trucks, accepted the handshake, while up on the high truck seat, two little boys wait, two small heads with close-cropped summer hair.

As Gordon now smilingly stares into the woman's eyes, having still made no reply to the greeting (is he even now lost in philosophical reverie?), she glances away toward the sign nailed to the ash tree, hand painted: *OFICE,* then around back to Gordon's face. "Guillaume, I have only a few questions. It's important that we talk. I'm only here to help you. We need to clear up some . . . some claims."

A couple of crickets creak from the tall grass. Just two. But a whole platoon of mosquitoes has arrived, touching down on warm flesh.

The truck is heaped with fir two-by-fours and one-by-sixes. Fragrance mixes with the pewy odor of the mumbling truck engine. Gordon's graying dark beard looks, yes, devilish in the near dark, and his thoughts are terrible as he feels the first sparks of another one of his spells of outrage coming on. His pale eyes bore into her even as he smiles, and the mosquitoes whine excitedly now, the woman brushing first at one ear, then another, trying to outstare Gordon who looks, yes, like he might smilingly *kill* her, but his voice, as he speaks now, is deeply melodious and fatherly, "*Tu sais, Madame, la journée est quasiment finit. T'as pas d'famille qui t'attends?*" He smiles on and on. His voice is going soft and poofy, as to a newborn child's ear. "*Tu sais, la liberté, c'est comme eul soleil qui basse, eul temps de la journée quand la plupart du monde commencent à s'endormir. Et liu avec d'la courage peut marcher en confiance vers les ombres qui s'etendent . . .*"

The little boys lean out the window, watching the woman's face, which is looking at Gordon's mouth. Everyone's hands brush and slap at the ever-growing whining airforce of insects. And Gordon's voice just gets deeper, more thickly and hoarsely soft, just a shade funeralesque, but more exactly like something whispered between groans in an X-rated film, so this is confusing to her? and his eyes don't leave her eyes as his steps come closer . . . one step . . . then two . . . his killer look *gone*. "*Sans lois et regimes, y regarde ses champs, ses bois, quelques étoiles gênées, les dos noirs des arbres qui boudent . . .*" He gives the top of his left hand a powerful smack. "*Ces p'tites bêtes agaçant, les bibites sans merci, les moudits maringouins—*" His face breaks out in dramatic eye-rolling despair. Smacks his hands together to end at least one life, then murderously looks around. Then his expression again goes tender. "*Y'ont des bons intentions et y's essaient ainque faire leur ouvrage, mais y's peuvent rendrai fou un homme libre. Oh, be'n, c'est l'prix qu'on 'pay,' pour la liberté. Penses-tu que ces petites piqûres peuvent déranger l'âme d'un homme libre? Et regardes-ça, ça rend les enfants fou, en toué cas.*"

At this point, the little boys are calling out to Gordon in English to hurry, and he turns slowly with a raised fist and snarls, "*Fermez-donc vos mautadits gueules quand j'parle à Madame Maringouin!*"

One little boy giggles manically, whispers to the other and both giggle, then one calls, "*Vas! Vas-t'en, Madame Maringouin-Mosquito! Bzzz bzzz vite dans ta char! On va te donner une bonne claque!*"

The second little boy, giggling almost to the point of choking, calls out something in very old Hebrew, which renders him suddenly solemn, some pronouncement that he has learned from Barbara (of Bev and Barbara) about life and struggle and courage. But then he lapses instantly back to giggles when he's done.

Gordon has gambled on the likelihood that this woman knows no Valley or Maine mill town French or any combination of the two and as her expression grows more and more disgusted, he knows he has gambled right.

She tells him (in English) that she is not tricked. She tells him she knows he can speak English.

"*Ahn? Excusez? J'comprends pas.*"

"Yeah. We no *comprends* you, too!" calls one giggly voice from the truck cab, and then two pale faces in the near dark fall way into the truck's interior, twittering madly, and the horn blows.

The woman calls to the boys. "How are you boys this evening?"

And the answer comes promptly, "Poo poo Swamp Man spits in your mouth!"

It is too twilightish now to see the woman's angry flush. She tells Gordon (in English) that she will return with *others*.

He looks at her in exaggerated puzzlement, then nods and says something in his French, ripply, velvety words, purling along all in one breath.

In a few minutes, the state woman's car is picking up speed on the hill, headed down, headlights blazing in the claylike dusk. Behind her rolls the great flatbed truck, headlights a little cockeyed, Gordon and his assistants headed to a destination three towns away to make a late evening delivery, the unloading being kinda hard work for little boys, some would say, not to mention it being kinda late to be up. No seat belts in the old truck. Children on the edge of peril.

Gordon, driving one-handed now, still not far behind the state woman's car, though she is gaining speed, hears his mother Marian's voice, *You court disaster, Gordon. You bait them. You beg to be a criminal. Someday, when you no longer have friends in high places, because you've turned them all against you, you'll see how hard the law can come down on you.*

 Loose translation of Gordon's words to the state woman.

"You know, Madame, the day is almost done. You have no family that awaits you? You know, liberty, it's like the sun going down, the time of day when most people begin to go to sleep. And he who has courage can walk with confidence among the lengthening shadows. Without laws and regimes, he regards his meadows, his woods, these few shy stars, the black backs of these sulking trees . . . these little teasing beasts, these bugs without mercy, these damn mosquitoes . . ."

Then while he fights a few mosquitoes, "They have good intentions and they're only trying to do their jobs, but they can drive a free man crazy. Oh well, it's the price we pay for liberty—do you think these little picks can devour the soul of a free man? Oh, well, look at that, they can drive the children crazy, in any case."

Then, facing the boisterous kids with raised fist, he snarls, "Shut your damn mouths while I talk to Mrs. Mosquito!"

And one small boy calls out, "Go! Go away, Mrs. Maringouin-Mosquito! *Bzz bzz* quick in your car! We're going to give you a good clack!"

And now, hours later.

In the night, inside a tumbling black sleep of exhaustion, almost dreamless, Gordon hears his own voice answering his mother, *"Certainement."*

 For the second time this month, Gordon St. Onge gets Shawn Phillips on the phone.

"Hey Gordo." A chuckle.

"Very funny, Mr. Phillips. Can't you call off your meat hound?"

"Yeah, yeah. Well, have mercy on me, Gordo. You don't know what it's like up here. There are certain . . . uh . . . appearances one must keep up lest one look like one is not doing his job."

Gordon grunts.

"An' you know the complaints are coming in faster than call-ins to a 1960s music request hour."

"Those summer people again?" Gordon wonders.

"Unh-unh. And it would be against the rules for me to tell you who."

"The neighbors uphill again. About Jane?"

"What can I say?"

"Well? Was it about Jane?"

"This time, no. But yes. All of the above."

"Above?"

Shawn chuckles. "I'm trying to make everybody happy, Gordon. I have so many people to make happy. That's what I'm here for. Kinda like being Walt Disney."

"We have no abused kids here . . . that I know of anyway."

Silence on the other end. Then, "Just a minute. I'm scrolling through your long list of sins."

Gordon doesn't laugh.

"Ah! Here we go. Stacey Christina Kellock of Turner, Maine, Todd Bailey Kellock, age two . . ."

Gordon says nothing as he hears the several names of DHS-targeted women and children he has rescued that have now been metamorphosed into data. He is standing in the kitchen doorway to the piazza, gripping the long-corded phone, one eye squinched shut, watching a group of teenagers (boys and girls) walking by from the tar road, shortcutting to the Settlement, coming back from some-where . . . on foot? . . . from a hitched ride? . . . he knows not. After all, Gordon St. Onge does not know everything everyone here at the Settlement does every waking minute.

Meanwhile, in Augusta, Shawn Phillips, who actually does look a little like Walt Disney, leans back in his chair and chuckles. "That particular child protective caseworker . . . Joyce Marden . . . she's one of our finest. The CIA can't hold a candle to her prowess. She's like the furry thing that is the only animal capable of killing a porcupine."

"Fisher cat."

"Yeh, but I knew you'd deflect." He chuckles. "But next time, I'll suggest they send Jerry Thibodeau. Grew up on Pine Street in Lew-iston. Spoke nothing but the patois till he was five." He chuckles mightily.

Gordon rolls his eyes. Then, swallowing an egg-sized knot of ten-sion, he says in a voice that hunches down now with an unbecoming dog-like humility, "I appreciate your trust, ya know?"

 History (as it happens) as reported by Jane Meserve, age six, with assistance by Jenna Gray, age ten.

In case I die from food, I desidded to get the evidints here, like all writen out. What they eat here is fish. And fish skin. Yes beleev this. Milk squirtid right from animals. Vegtables from the ground. Bugs walk on the ground, okay? It isn't that far they go to need to get on a vegtable. Eggs come right from chickins bums not a clean facotory-truck like you see always.

Bonnie Loo remins me everytime. She says remembr where these eggs come from nah nah.

Mapel candis they make here are good and chocilat Homers. But do you think they let me have some? Only on sertun condishins. Everybody watches me to make sure I don't get enough good stuff. All those EYES. Like mean tigars staring at my plate. I hope you are all reading this.

Another day. Another night.

Ivy Morelli, sometimes fearless *Record Sun* news reporter, flips and
flops under the blankets. Another naked-in-public dream. She's had
three of those this week. Whatever happened to her old flying dreams?

 In the Settlement's print shop, the old press whines and
***ch-chunks* as the Good Neighbor Committee prepares**
yet another flyer blitz. Every few weeks this happens.
"Invitations" go out into the world, tacked on bulletin
boards like at the IGA or fire station, stapled to
telephone poles. Some under windshield wipers. Some
placed in hands. Some mailed. This newest flyer reads:

Come share a nice meal with us EVERY SUNDAY around NOON.
EVERYONE IS WELCOME. Bring a dish if you like but it's not neces-
sary. Okay? We have good things for you. Tasty food, skits about history
and the news and science (the true, actual and investigated kind) and songs
we all sing together and music. You know where we are. Just past Gordon
St. Onge's gray house on Heart's Content Road, up the hill, then turn right
onto the dirt road, keep going. Can't miss us.

The press *ch-chinks* off two hundred of these flyers, then the Good
Neighbor Committee and some of the other committees and crews
draw and color and paint on them to personalize. Such as smiling
bugs and white poofy sheep and brown bulls, smiling flowers, smiling
suns, smiling dogs, smiling humans, little houses, cherry trees, trucks,
windmills, mountains, unsmiling monsters, orange pumpkins, birds.

Every time two hundred flyers go out, a couple dozen visitors will
show up, sometimes less. These visitors always have a nice time, and
usually come back now and then. They are mostly ordinary regular folks
from around Egypt, although "prestigious" friends of Gordon and the
Depaolo family are invited as well; state senators and the Weymouths
(old money), some elderly past governors of Maine, clergy, Council of
Churches, heads of departments, heads of institutions, owners of thriv-
ing midsized businesses. NONE of these people ever turn up.

JULY

 In a future time, Claire St. Onge remembers Catherine Court Downey and asphalt.

We had run into each other unplanned, both headed to the university dining hall. She asked if I'd heard about the latest cuts to the humanities, more celebrating of computers, business, and sports. She said, "If this were a zoo, baboons wouldn't miss the humanities." She laughed.

Sun, getting hotter, following and sniffing after Catherine and me across the parking lots as if it had us especially picked out to fry for lunch!

Then all of a sudden, she froze in the middle of the treeless open tar with oil spots and starry side mirrors and big hungry sky and the yellow spectral eye above, and Catherine's mouth opened, a huge pink square. And her bare arms reached for me. And she wept into my shoulder as at a funeral.

"What *is* it?" I asked, and hugged her completely. She was pulling and twisting my lavender cotton collar. It was ninety-five degrees in the shadows, but out here in this open tarred-over space, body to body, it was going to bring on for me a faint. I was starting to see fairy dust.

Of course, some students passed by and others, politely looking away, veered out around us.

The grays.

We keep at low altitude many moonless nights over the White Mountains and foothills. Human Earthlings publicly despair that we exploit desolation. *What* desolation? Miles and miles and miles of robust precious beings, bacteria, fungi, mites, grubs, dots of vitality, specks of brilliant force, alive and kicking molecules, steaming weak interaction force, all in concert with snow, rime, ice, soil, and leaf. Oh, marvel! The teeny weenie, which to each other are perfectly ordinary in size. And some of us grays in our multitudes of aircrafts are teenier than microorganisms, like those tucked in your cells. *Hi! Hi! Hello! Hello!*

 Bree remembers.

I was being drawn deeper into its thick, black honey. It was, I believed, a place where mind, body, and spirit could come together. I had my spies, Whitney, Margo, and Oceanna, Michelle and Samantha, who had written and called me, girls about my age, quick and rowdy, raised Settlement-style. They came once to my house with Butch Martin, who had a driver's license and was about twenty at the time. They called him their "escort." I thought they were joking. Their *"escort."* Butch was beautiful, all tawny and muscley with dark eyes. He didn't have much to say, but for his jokes and plaguing his charges. He was beautiful, yeah. And maybe that made me just a little bit out of focus.

 Critical thinker of the past. An excerpt.

The war is not between classes. The war is between individuals and barbarian society . . . [which] is rooted today in obedience, conformity, conscription, and the stage has been reached at which, in order to live, you have to be an enemy of society . . . The choice is not between socialism and fascism but between life and obedience.

—Art and Social Responsibility *(1946), by Alex Comfort*

Critical thinker of the past.

J. Robert Oppenheimer, witnessing the first test of a nuclear weapon, confessed to tasting sin. But he and all his colleagues knew from the beginning what lay waiting at the end of the project. And which was the stronger flavor, the sin, or the satisfaction of having stolen fire from the gods?

—*Theodore Roszak*

 ### Critical thinker and scientist of the past.

The real problem is in the hearts and minds of men. It is not a problem of physics but of ethics. It is easier to denature plutonium than to denature the evil from the spirit of man.

—*Albert Einstein*

 ### Critical thinker of the present.

More than any time in history, mankind faces a crossroads. One path leads to despair and utter hopelessness. The other, to total extinction. Let us pray we have the wisdom to choose correctly.

—*Woody Allen*

 ### Stuart Congdon remembers.

Of course I knew who she was the minute she walked in. The face was exactly as I'd heard. Koala bear. That's what I thought of. Not a monster face. But *where* in tarnation was the shyness and continuous giggles? Hadn't our old boy Gordo said that she hides behind her hair? That is *not* what we saw that night.

 ### Rainy (young married Settlementer) remembers.

This was the *east parlor*. Lacy and pastel. Less slop than the west parlor. This room's double doors opened into an entryway of coat hooks on tongue and groove directly off the horseshoe porches. This less-used parlor had a feeling of being *away,* across the quadrangle of trees from the west parlor, library, kitchens, and those porches and piazzas that were plastered with tables and thunderous life. Most of the windows here faced north, so you could see down over the kids' gardens mobbed with scarecrows, some knee-deep or even neck-deep in arcs and halos of lusty sunset green. Others were just standing vigil over yellowed plant death. Then the sloping hay fields between first and second crops. Early evening. Sun still high enough to butter it all. Yeah, dear sun. He was as primary on his knees as he was flying at midday.

 Whitney recalls.

It was Socrates night. For most of the younger kids, it was just nuzzle-smooch time, like our usual salons. Neck rubs. Sometimes hair brushing. You never saw Butch or Evan or any of those guys, but Lorraine, their mother, and my mother Penny, plus Claire and Geraldine were regulars. Gordon rarely came.

Nathan Knapp was our usual facilitator, with his round woeful eyes of molten black. Clean shave. Complexion of a woodsy mushroom. Thin seam of a mouth.

 Margo and Oceanna (*very un*identical twins). They remember.

We heard feet *slisk*ing over the entryway rugs toward the parlor door and then there she was, filling up the doorway on the darker edges of the creamy white room and people turned to look, those of us who had met her and those who hadn't. And for a few witless moments, nobody said anything.

 Lily.

That night, she finally showed up while a group of us were in the east parlor. Her deformed face made those who hadn't seen her before gulp. She was wearing her work clothes and looked like "Paul Bunyan woman," a nickname that stuck for a while, sawdust in her cuffs. But some of us looked that way, too, dusty and defiant. Oh, yes. And her hair was wicked. Frantic red *S*s and *Q*s. The world's best hair. It just goes to show, nobody can have it all.

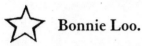 **Bonnie Loo.**

I was there the night she came, the girl who paints and draws like the angels. But. Die Bonnie Lucretia, die, I said to self. I knew she would be the final straw for me, the gunpowder in the cannon, me shot out of the Settlement finally, my ass in flames.

 Benjamin speaks from the future.

I could be a really tough little prick, not Christianly. My mother, Glennice, was a model Christian, a sensitive person, yet in her own way, tough stuff. I inherited the toughie part. But that night the FACE appeared, I almost shit myself.

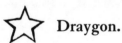 **Draygon.**

I didn't let on, but I was weirded out.

 In a future time, Bree will remember this.

The east parlor! It was just as they had described, but more so. All these faces. Nobody blinking. An almost ceramic scene. Among them my spies, Whitney, Michelle, Samantha, Margo, and Oceanna. And the almost wall-to-wall braided rug of yellows and greens. The antique furniture, high falutin' and dark. And old lace, utterly elegant, utterly dingy.

I sat down deep into a flowery delicately musty couch between Margo and Michelle, my boots crossed at the ankles. Two kisses. Smacking on each cheek of my face, two stamps of approval from my new sisters.

Death! Drink up!

"To Socrates!" shouts a Settlement teen.

"To free inquiry!" shouts preteen Theodan.

"To questions without end!" another shouts.

"To answers that make questions!"

"To questions or death!"

"Death!"

"Death!"

"Death!"

Clink!

Clink!

Clink! The jelly jar goblets go left, forward, right, touching, toasting.

Swallow.

Gulp.

The smacking of honeyed lips.

Each little goblet holds the honey for taste, the hot water for steeping the hemlock sprigs which are for "*death!*" Such commitment to QUESTIONs, as Socrates himself died by the cup, when offered that perfectly fatal choice.

"Death!"

 Draygon remembers.

But of course nobody dies from the *tree* hemlock. But being so young I *was* a little spooked.

 It begins.

Besides the old and mended lace of this room, there is a blizzard of crocheted throws and valances, and a tablecloth to give the long tea table its illusion of classiness.

Yes, Bree is here tonight. She is wearing her logging boots and old but fresh work clothes, her riveted red hair brushed into soft snakes. She is not shy. She seems invigorated by the "death tea," searingly alert, cheeks too pink. After everyone in the many couches and rockers is introduced, she is invited to ask the first question of the night.

She covers one eye while in thought. "Hmmmm. Okay. Uh, is it sensible to die for ideals?" she wonders, studying her empty hemlock tea glass with both of her freak eyes.

Nathan Knapp, legs angled off the stool into the middle of the gathering, always the facilitator for these formal salons, stares at Bree. He does not like Bree, right? Bree feels it. Everywhere in this room is love except on that stool, his worn jeans, some sort of midnight blue slippers, black velour jacket open over a dark gray T-shirt. Black hair slicked back with wettest water.

Bree shrugs nervously, states, "Socrates died for his right to free inquiry. Or maybe the right to argue. Whatever, he had to *steal* that right and then pay a price."

"Death!" says one of the unidentical twins, Oceanna, with a smack of a hand on one end table.

Nathan's eyes move toward the outburst and her short alley-cat brown hair and her oops!-having-too-much-fun grin.

A hand goes up. Nathan nods toward it.

Geraldine says, "Don Quixote died for his ideal of honesty. The ideal of a *kept* promise."

Another hand.

Nathan turns, points.

Margo says softly, "Jesus died for the poor."

Another hand, then, "Poor is not an ideal."

Laughter.

Another hand at which Nathan nods.

With her sleepy young husband (little goatee and glasses, knitted brown vest over his light T-shirt) leaning into her shoulder, pregnant Lily, whose eyes are silvery and sassy, says, "Sancho Panza lived so that his family could eat and live. He lived life for *life*. Some say it was selfish. But coming home *alive* helped his family survive. Is that an ideal? Or—?"

Nathan swivels to face two raised hands, two offerings. He picks one.

"Food is a thing," says a bright-faced teen boy. "What I mean is, food is not an idea. Sancho Panza loved food and his family loved food."

Nathan smiles, touches a finger to his chin. "Let's see." Pause. "But did Sancho Panza also *love* his family? Did he make it home because he *loved* them? Is love a thing, or an ideal, or what?"

"No. Not an ideal. It's a need. Love is a need," replies the boy solemnly, then cracks a smile, blushes, laughs.

Nathan swivels to the other raised hand.

"Love is a *feeling,*" the mother of Samantha Butler explains levelly.

Nathan points to another offering.

"Back to Jesus. He died for the poor? I thought he died for sins." This another fairly young boy.

Nathan gives Whitney the stage.

Whitney: "He died *among* the poor and he seemed to have only a few consistent themes. Mostly he was about poor." Whitney is staring at the yellowy-green world beyond the windows. The picture of bounty. She goes on, "Some scholars ask if Jesus really existed but that doesn't matter; the Jesus *story* is one of the greatest stories of all time. They say different people wrote the different books, the testaments. If he didn't exist then his giving his life for whatever reason was an idealistic *story,* for sure. Some say his death signified the last human sacrifice of the ancient pagan tradition."

"Do you think Jesus existed?" Nathan asks.

"No proof," Whitney says quickly.

"But did Socrates exist?" Nathan asks.

"Maybe Plato made him up!" croaks adolescent and boyish Kirky.

"Maybe Plato's not real, either. Just a pen name," offers a preteen without invitation from Nathan. "Maybe he was really Shakespeare and Shakespeare was really Bob, a poor bum and maybe Bob was really Bobette and maybe Bobette was really a cow—"

Laughter and fond boos drown him out.

"The biblical scholars almost all agree that the Revelation was written in such a different style it was someone else in a much later time," Whitney adds.

Nathan says, "Some suggest it was a poetic cinematic psychic who wasn't *seeing* Jesus in the Revelation, but a Jesus likeness such as the paintings and descriptions people worship today. Jesus seems to evolve with politics and culture. In the earlier Jesus story, Jesus is a political *problem* to the men of Mammon, a scruffy rebel who was sometimes rude to his mother. The Jesus of Revelation is being used as a political *tool* as we speak. Have any of you seen sign of that?"

He selects one of the older girls nearest Whitney on the big couch.

"The Christian right wing! Those guys say no abortions and no gay love. If you do the things *they* don't like, they say Jesus is coming with a sword to bloody the world up."

Nathan bows his head in deep thought, then a young voice behind him bursts out, "The Christian right wing . . . they call conservative and fundamentalist. How's that? They aren't anything like Jesus taught, his giving away shirts and vests. And they aren't conservative . . . such as waste not, want not. They are just . . . mean."

"Words get twisted as we go along," offers a girl with Passamaquoddy eyes.

"Like car wrecks!" a young boy adds.

"And old trees!" another youngster cries.

Nathan wonders of them all, "So what are right-wing Christians? What would be a more accurate title? Right-wing applies to politics, generally speaking. How do politics and religious beliefs get mixed?"

Bree sees his eyes move her way. She launches in, "The foundations, those big organizations set up to protect the interests of the American lords and ladies. I bet they've *shaped* right-wing Christian thinking. Foundations would call it public policy. Through grants and public funding, they infiltrate schools, school books and computer programs, public schools, probably Christian schools. The media, natch. People are easily led. They *want* to follow. We are so much like ants."

Silence.

Small voice. "More people need to drink hemlock and die for keeping their brains straight."

"Death!"

"Death!"

"Death!" the whole room screams except Nathan, who sullenly watches.

Then laughter.

"But they shape the liberals, too!" blonde Samantha snarls. "Liberals aren't as smart as they think they are. They're also a religion. All isms and schools of thought are faiths."

"Indeed," says Michelle, standing near the tea table, pouring more water onto her hemlock sprigs.

"Man, we are an out-of-control pocket of scot-free brains," Samantha says with a hoot.

Someone suggests discussing what Franz Kafka meant by "There is plenty of hope. But not for us."

Nathan rejects the question.

Several young voices screech, "Free inquiry! *Freeeee* inquiry! Censorship is wrong!"

"But most of you aren't familiar with Kafka. I'm just trying to be *nice*." He sort of smiles.

"Okay, let's do the one again about which is better, freedom or happiness?" offers Draygon.

Nathan groans, holds his face, speaks the first two words through his fingers. "You've wrung that one out. Is there anything *new* to say on that? You guys must have the whole routine memorized like 'Oh, Susanna.'"

Giggles. Laughs. A whistled refrain to "Oh, Susannah!"

Bree squares her shoulders, breathes deep of *such* a room. She looks up. This ceiling isn't cedar as she has heard of the other parlor, but grooved boards painted vanilla and milk. She wiggles her toes.

 Claire St. Onge remembers.

Yet another meal where he had come not to eat but to rev everybody up with his latest flush-faced diatribe, this time specifically about the "megamen's" intention to "profitize the Social Security system" and public schools "like big, boxed presents with bows!" working most everybody up into the chant: "EVIL GROWS!" *Whomp!* "EVIL GROWS!" *Whomp!* "EVIL GROWS! . . ."

I went up to my little house, my sanctuary, and stretched out on the bed. No one could be more upset about Gordon's behavior these days than I was. It was Mechanic Falls all over again. The time of the abortion. Yes, I had an abortion. My only child. He had feared for the baby's future *that* much that he'd want him or her vacuumed away. And now was he starting again to see the world as a place he didn't want children to be born into? Was he coming to understand that the Settlement and all the CSAs and co-ops were not going to guarantee a child be spared from the world's horror? It's big, Gordon. It's very big, said I to the ceiling. And all the Settlement children, Gordon, they are already here. *Born*. So, what now, Gordon?

Another evening. Another note left on the table at the St. Onge farmhouse.

Dear Teacher—

 You didn't see me, but I was there last night at your supper tables . . . well, I was with some girls at the far end of the other piazza. And I watched you and I watched them, all of your people, how you and they become one. People outside the Settlement are no different. The longer you wait, the more the evil that you speak of grows. Please help us! Please go outside your gates!

Your friend,

Bree

P.S. Tell me another secret. Not the one about you being afraid. Tell me more about the witches. Not my witches or Shakespeare witches. What did you really mean when you said you were surrounded by witches?

 The grays.

We are warmed by the girl human whose face is a little bit like ours. Wherever she goes we are handy. If she has a stutter, a pause, a need for help in her interior or exterior dialogues, her wonderments, we want to beam to her something special, not the word itself, but the heat, the gist, the odors of her journey. But we are committed to noninterference. All there is for us is to observe, take samples of the human hive's manufacture and try to understand.

 Noon.

Bree puts out her cigarette as she sees Gordon St. Onge striding across the grassy sunny part of the quadrangle, heading right toward her, where she stands with four young women, three being mothers, all being smokers, all together in a loose huddle. Toddlers creep and stagger and tip over under the legs of the giant wooden Tyrannosaurus rex, so grassy and shadowy underneath there, and now the three little ones have disagreed, one pinching and pushing, one whimpering, one screaming.

 The sky is a full and honest blue. Clouds solid, unmoving. They look man-made. Arranged for show.

One mother jerks her young one from the shadowy fray, raises him to her hip. "We're goin' to eat in a minute. You wanna eat? You hungry for yum yums?"

And oh, the air smells of the hot grass! And grass clippings stick to the children and the mothers' shoes. And the stale chemical mix of four cigarette smokes, like the mixing of four uneasy souls, weaves into everything, unsanctified.

"Yum yums go," the rescued toddler tells his mother gravely.

Gordon nods to everyone, scooches under the dinosaur, which is nearly three stories tall, a true focal point among the tall trees of the quadrangle.

He speaks in a general adultlike way to these persons who are babies, and he rubs the palms of his hands together over and over, which makes a soft scratching sound.

A few moments later, Bree and Gordon are walking toward a screen door of the nearest piazza. Their arms are laced, like a lady and a gentleman. But she keeps her head angled so that her face partially hides inside her magnificent wild red hair. He asks, "How long have you been here?"

She tells him she just arrived.

Up on the piazzas, set for dinner (noon meal), the kazoos are warming up. Dishes clang. People calling back and forth cheerily beyond the dark and sun-spotted screens.

"Oh, Bree! Please stay and eat!" calls Glennice from beyond the screen. Glennice, one of the mothers, a kind of tomboy person, much like Bree. Except that Glennice is also churchy.

Bree calls up to the screen that she's definitely staying. She has already promised Whitney and Michelle and Lily that she would.

"Your spies," Gordon says deeply, after Glennice backs away from the screen. "Whitney and Michelle and Lily."

"Yep," Bree admits with a breathless giggle.

"I got your note."

She giggles, this giggle being just a row of gooselike *blip-blips*. She tips her head farther from him, to more completely hide her face. He squeezes her arm. She giggles. He says, "I hope you will let me introduce you formally to some of the family, so you'll know how . . . what good people they are . . . which . . . is what . . . I uh . . ." He lowers his head, trying to see around her hair. He has always conversed best with eye contact. He hates phones. And he hates this hair-hiding thing of hers. He says, squeezing her arm again, "I want you to love them."

 The grays.

We fear for our scarlet-haired cherishling. Oh, grinding merciless Earth! Do not hurt her!!!

 Brianna Vandermast, alone in her little bedroom with the octagon window. She speaks.

Mothers die. They can. Like anyone. People who pass on hills trying to get somewhere faster than someone else, they crash head-on. Their car, made of metal like a war machine, comes into your mother's face.

At nine days old, there is nothing else but that face, while you suck. The universe is in that swimmy face and in your selfish swallowing. And boy, oh, boy you would miss THE FACE if it vanished. But imagine you are nine months. Everything about you responds to everything she is, her scoldings and praise, her hair smell, her hotness. She is your Portland Head Light, your North Star. She vanishes. There is the echo and the reverse echo that precedes the empty thud.

Now at age fifteen, you have photos of her. They are all over the house, on the walls, on top of the TV, in envelopes, at the houses of aunts and uncles. Like thin brown leaves after a season long gone.

Mama, I am my own.

 Editor Brian Fitch with his Virgo coffee mug and an amused smile . . .

Strolls over to the desk where Ivy Morelli is, as usual, talking to herself and mad at her computer. Brian says, "Okay, we've talked with a Mr. Jeff Gerrity. *A name*. And here's his phone number." Hands her a pink While-You-Were-Out slip. "Which, of course, reminds me. How izzz that ol' Home School human-interest *feature* coming along? You. Know. The. School. The. One. That. Bothers. People." The way he says this, it's as if Ivy is fuzzy in both memory and hearing.

"Well . . . it's not amounting to much, really. Just harmless . . . very likeable . . . creative people. No story in it."

"Okay. But I want you to be real nice to them some more. No copy yet. I want a *relationship*."

She looks at his face. She is smiling her get-serious smile.

He laughs. "I talked with Mert this morning and he thinks something *is* up over there in St. Ongeland. There's a guy, Ivan, who *knows* something. Something with the Department of Human Services . . . someone he knows there in Protective . . . uh . . ." He bends to carefully print the name on the reporter pad on Ivy's desk, one-handed. He straightens back up, coffee mug now covering his mouth and nose, his Adam's apple rising and falling with two slow gulps, his eyes held onto Ivy's eyes. He lowers the mug *real* slow, his eyes twinkling. "I think you are a brave gal. If you refuse this story, I'll understand. But . . . if you do it and it turns out to be something we could go with in a big way at just the right time, they—" He rolls his eyes up. "Upstairs will love you. Why not fool with this some more? See what you can come up with, since you have this little rapport with the St. Onge people . . . which I have heard is not something Gordon St. Onge likes . . . he doesn't usually cotton to newspaper people. You know this. I know this. So it would be reeeeeal nice if we had a whole spread ready to go with if DHS or the police or BATF or MDEA or god knows who else he's offended makes a move. Get some pictures. You know. Faces. Group action shots. The whole spread."

Ivy sighs, "Sure."

 The screen earnestly explains to us:

See Lisa Meserve, the drug trafficker, in handcuffs. Brrrrr. Police say Ms. Meserve is no amateur but a hard case, and that the marijuana deal involved MILLIONS at street value, those very streets where your little children walk and play. Good thing this criminal is being held without bail! Our fatherly government will be sure the likes of Lisa Meserve will not be putting potentially dangerous drugs in the hands of your little Megan or your little Ryan. Look! Here we have two politicians and a police chief making *official* statements on the Meserve indictment. Oh, *when* will marijuana and other deadly dope disappear from the face of the earth! Not until we get tougher. We sorely need to erase THIS VERMIN such as Lisa Meserve and make everything NICE. GOD HELP US ALL if we didn't have the DRUG WARRIORS to PROTECT US. Look! Watch this frightening woman as the cops and agents escort her to court. See how she does not look sorry! If not for those handcuffs and leg cuffs, she would do MOST ANYTHING, probably GET AWAY and vanish into THE STREETS to hunt down your darlings Megan and Ryan, holding out to them a huge bag of marijuana, gateway to *heroin*! Which leads to AIDS and shame and death and destruction!

 The voice of Mammon.

Tell me of one properly placed businessman, even at the lowest level, who will not tell you, "There are no problems, only opportunities." And for investment? Oceans of opportunities.

For instance, you hear there's a plague, so you buy up all the coffins and jack coffin prices up to the sky. Tsunamis? You bulldoze what's left of those squashed huts and build magnificent steel-reinforced hotels. And lots of subsidies available to build holding pens and security lights for the ones who used to be in the huts. Supply and demand, kiddies! And friendly brother-sisterhood on Capitol Hill and Madison Ave. It's basic Biz Ed. You see that billions of workers are losing their jobs, losing their homes, losing control over their own destinies (even the most modest control), losing their self-respect, losing their kids. Well, that's all very sad, but hurry, you need to buy up as much of the pharma industry as possible, and even the self-help magazines and books and tapes, audio and visual. You invest, baby, you INVEST in that antidepressant manufacturing. And the jails . . . oh, yes, you especially invest in THE PRISON INDUSTRY. ABOVE and BEYOND all, you buy their DEBT. The frenzy and fervor of all this buying and selling leads them to more DEBT. This makes GROWTH imperative, right? DEBT! Growth! DEBT! Growth! Moola moola moola. You see another man's loss, you make it your gain. It sounds terrible but after all, that's life, that's the way life is. If you don't take this opportunity, SOMEONE ELSE WILL. Don't be a fool. This is what any good businessman or smart investor will tell you. YOU AND I DID NOT CREATE THE SYSTEM. NATURE DID.

 Jane speaks of Lisa Meserve.

My mum! Her eyes like blue stars! Her letting me drive once on dirt! Her cooking! She is more sweet than a billion cakes. If I lived at the jail with her we could laugh about stuff and whisper. But everyone says no way. But it makes NO SENSE for me to be *here,* her *there.* You ever see baby birds, baby horses, baby bears way over there and the big ones waaay over somewhere else? You do not. Because *that* would be sick.

 Ivy's editor, Brian Fitch, moseys over to her desk again.

And when she looks up, he is standing with his hands full of pink While-You-Were-Out messages.

Ivy has just got in. A little late for that staff reporters' meeting (hopefully over with), her denim skirt droops damply around her legs and feet and the wheeled desk chair, another one of those mad dashes through the rain. Her top is a lightweight, light yellow V-neck thing with sleeves enough to bury her tattoo. At her throat a tiny heart locket. This is kind of conservative for our Ivy. But that hair, the thrilling purple sheen of her black bowl of hair!

Brian is squinting at her and continues to squint at her as she flashes him a reflex smile, then she's looking down into her shoulder bag on her lap, feeling for her comb. She touches up her damp hair and says, "I know I'm late . . . for the meeting."

"No problem," he says. "For all I know, you were at the state police barracks or with Jeannine Frazier in her kitchen getting her view on this St. Onge thing."

Ivy's hand with the comb deep in her hair slows to a standstill, then pitches the comb into her bag. She looks hard at the pink paper messages still a thick wad in Brian's fingers. And he still squints. But now he's squinting off into thin air. And now his squinty eyes slide back to Ivy's face and one eye opens wide and his voice speaks ghoulishly, "Pa-gann worship. Satan-worshhhhip."

Ivy smiles crookedly, "Come again?"

Brian drops his arms, sorts through the messages. "A woman named Jeannine Frazier." He places one of the messages in Ivy's hand. "She and I had a nice talk. She said talking with me was okay, but she didn't want to leave a voice mail for you or anyone . . . no recordings. She's sensitive."

Ivy studies the pink slip. Brian has drawn devils and people dancing naked with long streaming hair in the margins. The Settlement's largest windmill flashes and rotates in Ivy's mind. On back, he's written HELL-Oh-WEEN. And he is still talking, "She's a summer person. A decent normal sort. Has property on Promise Lake, which borders the St. Onge experience. She said she and guests were out doing a nice nature walk and got a little off the beaten path . . . a little lost . . . onto St. Onge land . . . we're talking woods here. They found, at the foot of a seventy-foot cliff, a huge, decomposing pile of bodies. Animals. Mostly heads. Skulls. Bones. Some possibly charred. Probably just remnants of butchering. That's my guess. She said she called the state police dispatcher and they said they'd send someone out, but four hours later, she called back and they said she needed to speak to Lieutenant Craigie but that he was out. And then when she called again, he was off duty. For days, he's been out or off and the dispatcher won't give her another guy. I've been trying to reach Craigie myself. But . . . you know, Ivy, these are not human remains and if no nearby neighbor's pets have turned up missing in unexplainable ways . . . or at least none reported, Craigie might just laugh. But then, you know, Satan worship sometimes leads to—"

"That's nuts!" Ivy says with a snort.

Brian folds and unfolds the other messages. "Very," he says.

Ivy says, "What I mean is, I don't think it's true." Now swelling to billboard size in Ivy's memory, the sun-face belt buckle. Pagan, oh, yes. But no. Kids must have made that buckle. Just as they painted the old-country windmill and schemed up the solstice March. And kids are innocence, right? Not pagan worship. No? Yes? No? Ivy's ears crackle.

"See what the lieutenant has to say. Truth is, what *officials* say, remember? But even if he says no, it doesn't mean no. It might just mean not *now* because the cops haven't gotten their warrant or have something BIGGER that they're waiting for, the really big bust. Maybe tortured sacrificed animals is just small potatoes compared with the BIG BAD THING. And you *know* this Ivy, how that works." Brian looks around the city room with a kind of crazy killer look. "Maine. It's such a dull place. We never get goodies like this." He winks both eyes. Strolls away, folding and unfolding the remaining pink slips in his hand.

 Lieutenant Craigie's voice over the phone.

A voice. Bass. Toneless. Not the brotherly, good-buddy voice so many of the local cops have, which Ivy rather enjoys. Local cops are just regular guys. In the inner sanctum of the municipal public safety buildings, they horse around with each other and smile charmingly and tell Ivy jokes and even good recipes for cookies and casseroles and one officer always talks about his old cats. *State* police, being *military*, are never, even in person, more than a mouth, big Smokey hat, a pair of dark glasses, and a hand with paperwork extended out of that blue-gray haze of look-alike platoons. And then there's the flashlight in your eyes routine and the light washing over your lap like you might be hugging a stuffed sack of bank money.

Ivy takes note that Lieutenant Craigie's voice is, yes, deep. Leaping bullfrogs! This means he must be older, one of the originals, the larger two-hundred-pound make and model, from the days before budget cuts. Nowadays, state cops are, just as their cars, almost tiny. Small men with squeaky voices in compact cars. Yes, budget cuts. Less gas. Less fabric in the uniform. Less leather. Less tinted Plexiglas in the tiny sunglasses. More money left over for bazookas, tear gas, door-smasher-openers, tanks. Tasers. Dogs that sniff. Machines that see through your clothes, count your cash, and take pictures of your eyeballs. HAW! HAW!

The deep voice informs Ivy that there has been no investigation concerning Mr. St. Onge.

Ivy asks if there have been a substantial number of calls from the public concerning "legal and/or illegal weirdness" at the St. Onge Settlement or pertaining to the conduct of Mr. St. Onge himself.

There is a lonnnnng hesitation. Lieutenant Craigie says deeply, "We have no reason to investigate Mr. St. Onge for anything,

either civil or criminal. There are no investigations, no warrants
. . . nothing."

"But have there been people calling you reporting . . . decomposed
bodies and—"

"We have no reason to investigate Mr. St. Onge at this time," the
lieutenant repeats. Like a skipping record. Although the words "*at
this time*" weigh like forty cement trucks in Ivy's consideration.

 The grays.

Tonight we decide to capture a newborn beaver. We enjoy cradling
such little bundles, peeking into the mashed little countenance, flattened ears, sucking grunting little mouth. We never place such ones
on the laboratory table, but pass it from hand to hand so that all hands
feel the exploding force within. Such mystery. Even we grays so far
advanced over the primitive human Earthlings never pretend to know
it all. Inside our heads are oooohs and ahhs and tee-hees.

Our lack of illusion of time and the thumping of our multisensory
flylike eyes and several fingers enjoy this sweetie for a year. Such a
thrill! Merely a moment in time beaver Earthlings perceive. And so
when we place her back in her stick hut, no one missed her, she never
became chilled, and will remember nothing.

 At the *Record Sun*.

Ivy stares at three "satin finish" color photos her editor's buddy, Gil
Zaniewski, has sent her. The old Instamatic stuff. Cheesy flash-paled
faces and red eyes. Like a bunch of raccoons caught in a trash can
looking up into a blaze of headlights, four young people on a couch,
then the back of a head of someone standing in the foreground, all
those knees. Couch must have been deep. No smiles. The edge of an
old tiled fireplace shows in one corner. The second photo shows three
faces filling the frame, cheek to cheek, big alligator smiles. *Quite* out
of focus.

A third photo features just a young guy sitting sideways at a kitchen
table, a small, rotating-type summer fan on the table edge, closer to
the camera than the guy's face. Fan blades are motionless.

On the backs of the photos, in round girlish handwriting: *Sept 19 1980*. Names: *Jen, Nick Hardy, Gil, Gordo*. Then: *Gil, Claire, Tina*. The young guy at the table: *Gordo*.

A wave of guilt swooshes over Ivy. She sees that he is the youngest face in the crowd, probably about eighteen or nineteen. The same pale eyes as today. Brown beard. No frosty gray. There's that crease-less baby-fat look across the cheeks that goes with youth. He is either talking or eating, mouth turned in an odd way, eyes not quite on the camera, never suspecting this picture would be used someday in a file on him, a file of *proof* meant to turn the world against him.

 Another day at the *Record Sun*.

For the dozenth time, Ivy picks the Zaniewski photos from her folder, and all the printed-out news articles and photos, spreads them on her desk.

She hunches over them. Only her eyes move. No rustle from the fabric of her chirpy youthful clothes. But her head is roaring with questions. *Would this man brutalize children? Sure, he teases and wrastles them, toughens them with miniterrors and overdoses of fun, but does he punish them brutally? And does he sexually invade them? Does he killll them?*

With each photo image, she studies not just his eyes, but his hands and fingers. At that legislative hearing on school testing, his testimony is punctuated, pronounced, underscored by his hands.

AUGUST

 The grays.

We abducted some purple hair. (Oops! Wrong word. Not *abducted*. We *plucked* a sample from her hairbrush.) She was asleep under her quilt of insect designs. Night or noon. It matters not. We will never be known.

See here's the thing. Time is nonsense. Human scientists say with assurance that it would take centuries or more for us "space aliens" to get here to the Little Round Blue and White Goldilocks planet "from another galaxy." But this is because all Earthlings—ant or anteater, buffalo or boxer dog—can only perceive linear, evenly measured, perfectly paced, tick-tock time and apronlike space with Earth at the center of it all. But that is beside the point. We are *not* visitors. We are the ancient web and to them, we are too fast, too slow, too reversible for them to detect. Unless we decide to give them a thrill. We, too, have our playful sporty sides. And also, sometimes, we screw up.

But getting the purple hair? It was on our lab table even before it left her boar bristle brush. Before cataloging it we watched it awhile. It's ghosty spirals seemed anxious, like the little reporter, who took a prescription pill before bed in order to let go of the day.

 Ivy chews on a thumbnail, not her usual habit.

Of course it was just a dream, Ivy assures herself. Very gray, very bald, fly-eyed men with poor posture standing around her dresser and mirror. They were naked but had no genitals. Okaaaay. These are the dreams of a woman under impossible pressures. This is where a life of approach-avoidance and a crappy low-pay newspaper job takes you.

 The press returns to the St. Onge Settlement.

She begins her trek up the rutted dirt road that zigzags to the bald rock summit of windmills. What looks like flies crawling along up there just below the summit, she has been told, is really the road crew doing road improvements, widening the roadway and building small stone culvert bridges. Their earnest dream is to brick the whole road with golfball-sized stones. To prevent erosion. Man, that's ambition for you.

 And down below it all,

Ivy trudges on.

 In the sky the sun begins to vibrate, its violence nonnegotiable.

Gordon sees Ivy Morelli coming up the grade, flowers in her hand, stopping to chat with the ox driver, Butch Martin, who is not a lot younger than Ivy. Ivy pats the broad forehead of an ox. Ivy and Butch talk and laugh. The wet swimmy heat increaseth by another five degrees.

As the oxen and Butch move on down around the curve, open with only steamy treetops on one side, Ivy turns and watches them and then there's the view of the Settlement fields dotted with sheep, and orchards, and many many small gardens, some terraced, and then irrigation ponds, and then to the world beyond the Settlement, with Heart's Content Road threading through the trees . . . and then in another direction, the summer homes and their docks and boats, gray beaches and the warm blue pond called Promise Lake and its three little tufty islands.

Ivy turns, resumes her hike up the soft rutted road. Ivy Morelli with the steely blue eyes and small pink mouth and robust shoulder bag. Lovely (but cunning) Ivy Morelli. THE PRESS.

Gordon leans on his shovel. Shuts his eyes.

Ernest Smith growls, "Company."

Squishy, overly stout, yes, jumbo Roy Day turns and sees Ivy, gives the waistband of his sagging gray jogging pants a couple of violent hikes and says, "Oh, good. She can have *my* shovel."

Aurel Soucier is quick to unknot the sleeves of his khaki shirt from around his waist and slip the shirt on over his sticky arms and back. He does not believe it is nice to go shirtless in front of women guests.

Giving his shovel a hard pitch into the back of the tool wagon (*clank!*), Gordon stands there in the spotty shade with the dogs and deerflies and mosquitoes and greenheads and dragonflies, unknotting the red bandana from around his neck, wobs it up, and presses the red wob to each of his burning eyes. He doesn't really like this surprise.

Some hoarse Frenchy whispering is bubbling around the peripheries of the road crew. Close to quitting time anyway. One of the understandings here at the Settlement is that hard labor under an uncompromising sun or boring tasks are never committed to for more than one, two, or three hours a day, unless there's some life-or-death oh-my-god-help-us emergency. But the big question now, whispered, of course, is what is ol' Gordo going to do about THE PRESS.

Yes, many Settlement worrywarts have been howling that a town meeting on the *Record Sun* issue is overdue. But Gordon had snorted, "She's gone for good."

Aurel, a close confidant in all matters, watches his cousin without comment, an unusual silence for him.

Gordon looks over at Aurel's face, which is given that crescent shadow by the Vietnam War bush hat, and Gordon just tips his head from side to side, giving his neck muscles a workout while keeping his eyes fixed on Aurel's eyes. Smacks a deerfly. Misses. Smacks again. Misses.

There behind the tool wagon, Ivy finds Gordon. She says, "Hi," trying very hard not to do the BOLD STARE or even the OBVIOUS GLANCE at his chest, with its shameless tornado shape of dark hair that comes to a gentle taper down through his navel then disappears under the sun-faced buckle. And maddeningly muscled-out long, bare arms. And the hands, blackened by pine pitch, calloused by tools, and one very gummy, purple-pink, meaty, raw, dribbly, torn knuckle.

Behind Ivy, Aurel is now loudly advising someone, "T'heat make you loos' yourrr potassium," his voluptuous French *R*s unfurling through the sweet polleny air. And Ivy's neck trickles.

A chainsaw is jerked to life a few yards uphill. A few finishing touches? And the big dogs are trying to get a sniff of Ivy's crotch and shapely bottom while the small, white, puggish-face dogs must settle for her socks and sneakers. Ivy warns them all, "Go on. Go! Get!"

Greg Junkins drags his shepherd mix away. "No! Get!" Ivy tells the others. And they are now being dragged away by the collars by blushing, apologizing owners. Except for the small white dogs, who just lose interest and stroll away.

Gordon is very quiet, just stroking one side of his mustache with a middle finger, eyes on Ivy's short bowl haircut with its outer-spacesque purple cast.

Now a deerfly finds Ivy and she begins to shout at it.

Gordon gives a few swipes at his own deerflies.

Aurel is now loudly urging someone, "So eat lots of bananas . . . orr . . . mushroom!" Then he sidles off into the wagging ferns to climb agilely up into the cage of the skidder and revs the monster-deep roaring snoring stinking diesel engine to life. The skidder churns around in a wide sashaying circle and backs to one of the oozing popple stumps and Rick Crosman tosses his kid, Jaime, the end of the cable and chains.

All this racket. Ivy's questions will never reach ears.

"I thought we were done!" the boy Benjamin whines, kicks a rock.

A young ox turns his head Benjamin's way.

But most everyone is watching Jaime Crosman's shoulders work as he deftly tightens the chokers around the stump. Jaime is as blond as his father, despite his Chilean first name, and Jaime is, these days, nearly as tall and strapping as his father, and the father is one of those very young-looking forty-year-olds, and so they look more like brothers.

Ivy is watching with awful alertness as the father steps quickly to Jaime's side. Can't hear what he says. Nobody can.

The skidder gives another slow deep groan, Aurel up there in the caged-up cab fooling around.

Jaime's father . . . something about his legs and shoulders. Like commencing a cramp. He swings half around as if to leave, then turns back again, closer to Jaime now, almost close enough to kiss Jaime as Jaime stands up from finishing with the chains.

Gordon is looking at Ivy's very thick shoulder bag, her light blue T-shirt that reads UNIVERSITY OF MAINE. Earrings, tiny pewter open books. Shorts made of camo material. Her intellectual military look? She is bouncing on the balls of her feet like a prizefighter, wagging her bouquet of wildflowers and taking in everything. So young, so playful, so pretty. What is he feeling? Does he feel utterly and suddenly afraid of *everything*? Of *life*? He shouts lightheartedly to her over the racket, "You wouldn't be carrying any lemonade in that bag of yours, would you?"

It is hard not to notice, in spite of the barking dogs and dust and clangs and horrid stratas of diesel smoke and devoted blood-lusting flies, that the ever-so-blond Chilean-named boy Jaime sneeringly enounces "FUCK YOU," into the face of his young-looking blond father, Rick Crosman, who now moves fast, smack-punches the son in the mouth hard, hard as hell, and the kid stumbles back, eyes wild, blood dribbling from between his teeth, a lot of blood, which is what you get when your tongue is burst. And several of the men yell, "Hey!" and "Cool it!" or just hoot, unable to latch on to a real word. Greg and Mo step into the space from which Jaime is lunging forward to spit an impressive red blot on the dead center of his father's pale beige T-shirt because you know that although he is as big as his father, he is still just the son of the father, afraid to hit back. But his father smacks him again, the left cheek of Jaime's face now burning cherry pink. And Eddie Martin and Mo and Greg are all reaching for Rick in a sort of silly-looking way, as if to give him little doggie pats, but it is no doubt that they know he's too red hot to touch.

Now Jaime runs. His father doesn't chase, just stands and watches, dust broiling around him. It is done.

Ivy Morelli stares sub-zero-polar-cold daggers at Gordon but he ignores her, reaches for his shirt on the back of the tool wagon, then turns back to her with a big grin and speaks in a Daffy Duck voice, "Despicable!" Then in his own voice, "Come along, Ms. Morelli! Let's go down to the shops and witness some eight-year-olds studying Shakespeare."

Ivy and Gordon.

And they go. Down along the rutted road, out of the noise of that Settlement temple called work. However, spilling from both their faces and bodies their sweat is almost noisy.

Gordon pulls his shirt on, buttons up.

Ivy is frowning, frowning, frowning, slapping one of her shapely tanned thighs with the poor limp flowers.

At last, Gordon wonders aloud, "What are you thinking?"

She replies sadly, "I don't know."

He sighs. With empathy. "Mammals are so unpredictable. All those synapses. All those nerve endings." He hangs his head a minute and looks at her sideways. "We can't always live our good philosophies."

"Some do," Ivy says.

Gordon looks at the press and retorts, "Baby, spare me."

"It's a matter of self control," she says bitingly.

"In air-conditioning with lemonade at the ready, and a nice soft chair, self control is possible."

"Yeah, yeah," she mocks him.

He reaches with a black-stained and gummy hand to touch her moist right ear just above the churning warm pewter earring. She hardly knows what her hand is doing . . . it just claws at him . . . again, like the first time they met, unable to draw blood, but indeed, he does jerk his hand back. Then she pitches her flowers at him, somewhat playfully. And says tiredly, "Oh, I suppose next you'll tell me God said *Spare the rod, spoil the child.*"

He brushes some vetch vine from his shirt. "No, Ms. Morelli. It's all *science*. You see, *your* control just now was lost in a flurry of wonderfully mammalish chemical synapses." He wiggles his fingers at her. "*Sssssssssss!*"

"I . . . I'm sorry," she says. "I am just a hot-blooded Italian . . . and Irish. You're right. It's all science."

He stops walking, beams at her. "Me, too! Italian and Irish!"

She laughs. HAW HAW. "I thought you were all French." She lies.

"French, Maine Indian, Italian, Irish . . . I'm global."

She laughs. They walk again. His work shirt is dark green, but faded. It fills up the whole northeast side of Ivy's peripheral vision as they scuff and crunch along the rest of the way, chatting and laughing, telling Italian and Irish anecdotes. Gordon quotes Heywood Broun, "'The Irish are the crybabies of the Western world. The mildest quip will set them off into resolutions and protests.'"

Upon reaching her sporty red car, parked seethingly in the sun near the largest Quonset hut, Ivy tells him, "The paper is *very* interested in doing a story on your people now. But I promised you I'd drop it."

He looks at her with sudden tiredness. "Right."

She says, "I have in my bag a pad, five pens, a tape recorder, and several blank tapes ready to roll . . . in case you want to talk officially."

He narrows his eyes on the middle of her young throat. "I don't."

"Well." She sighs. Drops her shoulders, glances at the swollen streaks caused by her nails on his right forearm. She leans back against the scorching surface of her car, pulls away quickly, shaking her burned hand. "There are reporters less understanding than me . . . less *nice* . . . uh . . . more professional . . . who . . . are . . . all set . . . for when the authorities swoop in here, which Brian . . . my editor . . . thinks could be any day now."

His face pales.

She says, "Okay . . . now that I have your attention, will you talk to me? I won't turn in *anything* unless I show you the copy first. It's breaking one of the rules . . . they don't like us to do that . . . but . . . that's what I promise you. We can . . . go for a little ride somewhere. Would you—"

"No."

She sighs. She looks around the glistening gravel parking lot and then between the Quonset huts and across the sort of grassy quadrangle with its red brick walkways, wooden dinosaur two stories tall, a sheet-metal-covered spaceship and the larger space saucer with Martians positioned on top, and so many trees, great tall straight trees with no lower limbs, majestic as cathedrals, stirring to the soul, and picnic tables, enough picnic tables for a convention of the entire American press corps. But at the moment it's all abandoned of life, not even a bug-hunting chicken. Sounds of industry in the shadows, the shops, the piazzas, and Quonset huts. The potent secrecy of shadows. She looks down at her sneakers, then up at Gordon's pale eyes. "I'm your friend, Gordon. That hasn't changed."

"I don't want to ride in your car," he says. "It looks scary." He looks over toward the open back bay of the largest Quonset hut. A bunch of people, teens and adults, stand there, watching. One man wears a rag- gedy pink and green Hawaiian shirt and jeans. Hunched. Long armed. More muscle than mind? None present the look of *academic* merit. Not any merit exactly. What does it take to *deserve* being here? Could *that* be the story? Pinning down that which qualifies you to belong?

Ivy says, "Can I bribe you with an ice cream at Kool Kone? I'll pay. I heard you're a cheapskate."

"In *that* car?"

She replies, "Yes, sir."

He turns to the bay with the little group watching, and with great martyrlike dignity, raises his chin and salutes them. Laughing, they all salute back. Then he peels open the little cheapie door of the pas- senger side of Ivy's car, folds himself up into the tiny bucket seat, pulls the door tight, and squeezes his eyes shut.

 Meanwhile, in Southern Maine, on the outskirts of Portland. A maroon "utility sport" vehicle, shining prettily in the perfect center of the short black tar driveway. One bumper sticker on the vehicle. It reads:

My child is a Jack Middle School Honor Student.

♡ ♡ **Meanwhile, as the press has been ascending and descending the hill, Jane Meserve is down at the St. Onge farmhouse, where she continues to reside. She speaks.**

Bev is on her knees getting some things out from underneath Gordie's sink, putting all the stuff inside a cardboard box so she can "organize." She says she could use my help. But I say, "No, thanks."

Can you believe there's no TV here at Gordie's, not even a small emergency TV. And at the Settlement, not one single TV.

No TV. It's kind of shocking if you think about it.

I go over and sit by Gordie's desk in the chair with wheels and all his junk just in case the phone rings, which it has done about eight hundred times this morning, and Bev made messages for the message nail. I did a couple. But it was all boring stuff mostly.

I push the chair around to make the wheels turn and I watch Bev. She is probably trying to make it cozy here. People here, all they do is work, work, work. And they use the word "cozy" a lot. One of the times, I helped them at the Settlement, it was fun. Everyone laughed at how I swished the broom at a spider and he ran fast on his little legs. But work is only fun *once*. You should not have to do it over and over and over.

I says, "Bev, do you ever go to Funtown?"

She says, "No, dear." She is still on her knees under the sink. I roll my chair closer to see what exactly she's doing under there. "Why not?"

She laughs. "Oh, I don't know. I'm not into wild rides . . . and other things keep me busy. We don't go over to the coast very often, Barbara and I."

I tell her about all the stuff they have there, especially the water slide, which actually is too terrible for me. "But you can shop there, too. There's stuff to *buy*."

She says, "That certainly sounds wonderful."

"Gordie would like it," I tell her, just to see what she says.

She doesn't say anything.

I wheel around the table, all the way around, working my feet to get up some speed. I says, "Mum always takes me. When she gets out of County,* she'll want to go. And then we can go shopping. We do all the kid movies and the circus. And the Ice Capades. And then McDonald's and Burger King. And *then* we get videos, which *I* pick out."

Bev is very, very quiet now, under the sink. I wait to see if she has anything to say but she's just crawling way inside there to get one small sponge. Her jeans are made of raspberry-color cloth. Very pretty. But her round rear end makes me almost laugh.

I wheel over to the very bright chimney and I put one of my feet up on it and dig around with the heel of my pretty sandal to see what happens to the shine of the paint. It is very shiny paint. The chair wheels go *squeaky-squeak* back and forth, back and forth. I say, "I'm hungry." I say it soft.

---

* What many of us call county jail.

She finds a clothespin, pops it into the box with the sponge and other stuff, then brushes her hands together, not on her raspberry pants.

I say, "I'm very hungry." I kinda smash my heel on the chimney with my sandal, not meanish, just trying to make something happen to the shiny paint stuff. In a way, it hurts my foot.

"Well, it's only been twenty minutes or so since we ate."

"*You* ate," I remind her. I drop my foot and turn the chair to be in her direction. I cross my arms so I can show her I'm not fooling.

"True. But you said you weren't hungry, dear." All the while she says this, all I can see is her rear end.

"Well, I'm hungry *now*."

Soon Bev is making a jam sandwich for me. I watch her spreading it. It has chunks. I say, "What's that stuff?"

"Plum," she says.

"Oh," I says real smallish. Then, "Maybe you have pancakes. Gordie made me pancakes the other day. I would like pancakes better. And syrup. *And* some sugar."

So she fixes me pancakes. But she puts milk in them. And there's no more flour left to make a new batch. I tell Bev that I hate milk.

"You won't even know it once the pancakes are done," she says.

I narrow my eyes, tap my foot, cross my arms, and I say, "I. Do. Not. Like. Milk. At. All. Ever."

She says she wishes I told her before she put the milk in.

I says I didn't know she was going to put it in. And I says, "Is there some more eggs here? And bread, *white* bread. And sugar, perfect, plain, nothing weird."

She fixes me an egg, but she puts PEPPER in it.

"I told you before how I hate pepper."

The next egg is perfect. The bread is near the heel part but the sugar is perfect. While I eat, she is quiet, smiling with her big eyes floaty behind the glass parts of her glasses. She is so nice.

 Down on Route 160, Ivy passes three cars and a cement truck on a curve.

"Got any suggestions for a better place than Kool Kone?!!" she hollers across the engine sound and wind.

Gordon is feeling his eyes, smoodging dirt and pitch from his fingers across both lids. "Ahhhhh . . . I can't think for some reason."

Ivy takes three curves by hugging the high-crowned middle like a race driver, reaches an intersection, and brakes hard, skids on sand. Then off they go, her sneaker clamped to the gas.

The roads going in this direction get curvier and hillier. Ivy goes faster.

There is silence between them.

Suddenly, a car appears ahead. Seems it is driving backward, coming right at them. But it is really just going *the speed limit*. Ivy mashes the brake, then rides the car's bumper mercilessly. "These people with nothing to do," she snarls. "Jesus, buddy, turn up the heat!" She drums her fingers on the door.

Gordon's hands are welded to the knees of his old frayed jeans. His eyes are wide and wild-looking on the back window of the car ahead. "The ice cream will keep," he says softly. "They have refrigeration."

She glances at him, perplexed. Then tsks. "Don't worry. I'm a good driver."

They plow down through North Egypt, where Kool Kone is situated across from the long public beach of Promise Lake. Ivy keeps going. Kool Kone flashes past as Ivy passes on the straightaway.

Now another car ahead. Ivy sighs.

Gordon's eyes don't leave the back of the car before them. They are close enough to be attached by a tow bar. Gordon imagines his face, teeth, and knees mixed somehow with the face, teeth, and knees of the people in the other car. He keeps gripping the dash and doing a throat squeak every time the car ahead slows on a curve and Ivy brakes hard.

Gordon wonders, "You got kids?"

She snickers. "*You* the reporter now?"

"No. I'm your friend. Remember? . . . the friend thing?" He smiles warmly.

"I don't really like kids," she says evenly. She glances over at his smiling face. Her confession has not changed his expression.

She glances again.

He is gravely watching the car ahead. He grips his knees again and says, harshly, no kidding around in his tone, "Well, yuh . . . kids are like tumors. They attach themselves to your vitals and then proceed to just suck up all your life till they're grown and you're used up."

She looks at him sharply. "I wouldn't have expected you to say that, teacher man."

"Well, we'll just start with that hard and undeniable fact." He wiggles his eyebrows. Winks at her.

Ivy guns her engine, taps her horn.

The brake lights of the car ahead come on. A kind of BACK OFF! message.

Gordon grips the dash again.

Ivy snarls, "These people with all the time in the world. And cars like arks! Always blocking every move you try to make." She taps the horn again. Brake lights flare again. "Jesus!" she snarls. "Why don't they just pull off the road and let us by?!!" She backs off a smidgen.

Gordon leans back again, though not really relaxed.

"So?" Ivy says. "Go on."

"Yeah. Where were we?" He looks over at her, his grease-stained smoodged eyes seeming to admire her purple-tinted black hair, her perfect small ear, the vulnerable back of her neck. He says with tiredness and sorrow, "Where *are* we?" His big frame shifts around, seat belt straining, no place to put his big feet, his knees, his shoulders, the top of his head. "Consider this, Ivy. Consider if you were a cave lady—"

"Cave woman."

"Cave woman. And a bunch of your tribe were frozen in ice . . . but due to something . . . some radioactive force or weird atmospheric changes . . . caused you all to thaw and wake up. And so you open your eyes and this is what you see. Kids raised by one man and one woman and four TVs and some computers, and institutional day care, and institutional school, soon to be privatized and, oh, boy, we get the profits-vacuum-cleaner up the ass and meanwhile, both parents working jobs. The household is a cubicle a hundred feet in the sky with access only to a cement curbside and asphalt street, and then there are some of these, ahem, *families* living in split levels with lotsa 'conveniences' and easy chemically fuelly ways to keep their grass green and short and wonderful blinking timepieces on their wrists . . . mother, father, kids all staring at their wrists as they run, as if from a mastodon, to their wheeled vehicles and race away, all in *opposite* directions." He makes a face. "What would this look like to you?"

Ivy rolls her eyes.

"What about progress, Ivy? Would you call it *progress?*"

"Welllll," she concedes.

Gordon goes on, "Oh, but sometimes there's one woman in the cubicle all day with the baby and one man out there racing around somewhere, maybe one woman with two or three kids allll day with the man out there allll day, or one woman out, one man in with these kids, or the two women thing, one out, one in, or both in, or two men in and out or out and in or any combination of two folks so we have some kind of two parentish thing going on. Then, plenty of day care, the day care biz. And there's the school thing . . . the indoctrination camps. Picture it? Okay, so, Ivy, tell me, what is the purpose of these kids?"

"Purpose?" Ivy repeats drily.

He smiles at her ever so tiredly.

"You say *pur-pose,*" Ivy repeats significantly. "Okay, *what* purpose? Hmm."

He doesn't wait for her to think this through. He snarls, "Kids are just junk. Like old baling twine or rags."

Ivy's own pale eyes grow round with discomfort. "You're trying to shock me, Mr. St. Onge."

He rubs his sticky neck.

She laughs her deep steamy HAW HAW. "Would you be quoted as saying this stuff?" She is already picturing the paraphrasing with the great big fat quotation marks to *represent* all he has said so far.

The window wind is waggling his damp fracas of brown hair, waggling his sleeve, waggling his collar. He gets one of his involuntary squint-blinks in one eye, so ample that his head jerks.

"Gordon, what happened to love? I thought people had kids in order to give them love?"

"Love? What's that?"

She scowls. She has nothing but the ethereal. Nothing but the nonsensical. Nothing but the commercial Valentine-card lingo. Nothing but the rote. Leaping lizard hearts! And besides and beyond even that, our Ivy has questions such as, *Don't you think the planet is overpopulated*

*anyway? Isn't the greatest act of love a nice plump birth control pill? Aren't
you guys thicker than rabbits up there while preaching resource depletion:
Excuse me if I'm BAFFLED, but why? Why? Why?*

Curve ahead. Ivy's sporty little car rides the middle of the road,
anxious for the chance to swing out around the 'slow' car. Her passenger gets a grip on the dash as they are nearing a narrow bridge
with two oncoming cars.

"What sort of purpose would children provide, Gordon, if it isn't
love?" she asks, unfazed as the car she is now passing is somehow
filling the space she is going to need in order to get back into her own
lane in the next two seconds, and the bridge ahead is bringing all this
in tightly, like a throat swallowing.

Gordon's moan is so loud, it seems he is teasing. And yet, he really
is afraid of the fast lane, isn't he? What a baby! He is starting to put
off a bad nervous smell just as our young Ivy slips the spirited and
sporty hot red car back into its own lane behind the car she can't seem
to get ahead of and the oncoming cars flash past in blurs of green and
gray and golden brown.

"Gordon?"

He exhales.

She glances over at him, at his profile, tanned face, the messy hair,
pale eyes, soggy shirt. "I'm sorry. Okay? And I want you to know
how much I appreciate your candor. I'll be candid, too. This interview
means a lot to me."

 Purpose.

They ride a minute through some open farmland, low-slung telephone
wires, a hot weedy wonderful smell whipping in at the windows. For
the moment, Ivy seems to have forgotten trying to get around the
car that is ahead of them. She is actually following at a safe distance.

Gordon lets one hand plop to the lap of his jeans, one arm along
the window.

Ivy says with a squint, "A while back there, you were telling me
that kids are just rags and old wire. No purpose. Something like that.
What was that?"

"Yeah."

"You were saying something like kids don't have a *purpose* today."

"Well, other than their purpose as robotons for the Great Kleptocracy."

"Right," says Ivy, rolling her baby blues.

Gordon looks off across a neglected hay field dreamily. "Children, their purpose, like with smelly, annoying, mumbling, very senile old people, like bad weather, like miserable hard work, like shared land and shared history, kids, when shared by *a people* . . . the family . . . the tribe . . . these kids are the *tie that binds*. At least that's the way it seems to me." He now absently spreads the fingers of his right hand over his chest. Over his heart. "Without this purpose, a kid is . . . is—" He looks sadly at Ivy. "A nuisance." He gives an ugly snort, probably meant to be a mean sort of laugh. "And a commodity, of course. Ah! Such a purpose! Keeping the day cares and child counselors and schools in *business,* eh? But mostly the little critters today are just a pain in the fucking ass."

"So if—"

"Oh, and the CIA and other mobsters get them Uzis. And drugs. And other stuff to sell. In the streets of LA and other places. Useful there. And the military. Kids are so useful at the hundreds and hundreds of all-important US military bases around the globe. Military contractors. Policing contractors. Profits! You know, children, chickens, and hams. And the pharma companies love their little human mice, which are in the laboratories, uh, public schools, that is. But most especially the usurists, they *love* the debt purpose of our kids. And . . . oh . . . well, soon, if all the little rugrats accept the computer promise and become good little vessels of the keyboard and screen realm, the lords of capital will consolidate the tech sector globally, locking in their definition of 'human being,' we the accessories, while *it* will be the plastic and wire heartbeat of the world. You see, if you study it, there's every purpose under the sun for the little dears but . . . not—" He bows his head. "It's no wonder millions of Americans abort them, neglect them, dehumanize them with kiddie fashions, murder them with fists and blunt objects, and—"

Almost too quickly and too pleasantly, Ivy says, "You are *such* a philosopher, a redneck Schopenhauer, only different. No questions. Just answers."

He looks at her with narrowed eyes.

She realizes that she's repeating what Gordon's old long-lost friend said about him in that recent telephone interview. Has she said something to make him realize she's been . . . *investigating* him? Well, of course she's investigating! She's a reporter! No, she is friend. But now, well, yes, reporter, too. She squares her shoulders more severely, swallows drily. She says, "I'm having trouble figuring out where you are."

He is still looking at her. Staring. He. Is. Not. Discreet.

"You are a smart guy," says she.

"In some ways," says he.

"You are smart . . . but some would say formless. And others would say hysterical. Paranoid would be a word." She is bracing herself to ask him some more pointed questions. Her small mouth tightens.

The car ahead almost turns off on Beverly Lane, a road with one little house and a flagpole. A square of lawn in between simmering new-growth woods. But then the turn blinker dies and the car continues.

Gordon has started to rattle on again, reeling out his abundant, iron, no-rest, answers-only philosophy. No, he's certainly not Socrates, or Schopenhauer, or Goethe. But none of it sounds like the stuff of a child molester, either, or quite like a right-wing militia type. But there *are* contradictions. And sharp angles. Whirlpools. Depth charges. Thrashings. Like a man wrestling a bear.

Ivy seems truly to have forgotten the need for speed. Ferns bunched in the culverts by the road's edge are no longer blurred like green projectile vomiting. Between the first car and Ivy's, a squirrel, long-bodied, long-tailed, casually crosses the pavement as if on a slow oceanic wave. Everything about the day seems sane and soft and sleepy. Sort of Valiumized. Ivy steers with one hand, listening to Gordon's voice, and thinking.

He looks down now at her hand on the wheel. She wears three thick silver rings today. Goes great with the camo shorts. "Deep down. Deep deep deep down you feel like a bad person because you don't *like* kids." He reaches for her arm, warm through the T-shirt sleeve, gives it a hard fatherly squeeze. Releases. One-hundred percent full patronizing mode.

She says nothing, just takes the next gentle curve with her eyes on the road.

He says, "Humans don't hatch out. We aren't supposed to wiggle off into the woods, each one of us fully equipped to live. Humans are the group thing! Even introverts aren't independent. We are a *dependent* creature. *Group.* Mizz Ivy, you don't really think those big school systems and big corporations make very good families, do you? But most of us have come to *depend* on these, with some twisted belief that these structures made of fluorescent light, brick, plastic, and their immortal charters actually care. As you know, the devil hath the ability to assume a pleasing shape."

Ivy smiles, her own patronizing mode. "But Gordon, humans adapt. We can do it. We can *become* different, successfully global. The horse is out of the barn. It's too late to gripe. Don't you think it's better to *perfect* what we have? Big *can* work. And *besides,* most of us don't want to live in a *tribe*. I don't. I want *space*. I want privacy. All you're saying is nothing new. It's just the same ol' hippie recipe for social discontent and anger at *change*."

Red wob of bandana has reappeared and he is mopping his forehead and his neck under the short beard. He looks at her. "When the dollar becomes ten cents and cheap oil and gas become not cheap and social security is privatized, thus dead—"

Ivy's foot pounces on the accelerator. She alas passes the other car on a straightaway, but a much too short straightaway, and a, yes, loaded tandem logging truck bursts over the hill, all grille and tall windshield and snarl and teetering weight of its load. But she makes it in time.

 Very, very, very, very close call.

Gordon's eyes are popping.

Ivy is jubilant. "There!" And now her sporty car burns like hell up the road, motor buzzing and the wind roars in at both windows, tearing at Ivy's silky violet hair.

Gordon says, "Any time you get tired of driving, I'll drive awhile."

She glares at him.

"I don't think there's any more ice-cream places until you get to Canada." He says this with a playful little poke at her elbow. "Why don't we just go back to ol' Kool Kone. Who needs more than Kool

Kone? Too much variety is sometimes the cyanide hidden in the spice of life."

She asks coldly, "Do people ever tell you they get sick of you being a know-it-all?"

"Yep."

"Who is Jane? Why does she live with you, Gordon?"

"Jane is a casualty of the drug war. In some ways, a fatality. A human sacrifice. Her grandfather, Pete Meserve, is an old friend . . . lives in South Paris, right in town. You'd like him. The state temporarily gave Jane over to him after the foster parents couldn't stand her . . . but Pete, though a calm and patient man, is a widower, has a service station to run. He felt Jane would do better down here with us, more family-like. More attentive. The state knows of this little transfer. She's on *the list*."

"List?"

"Yeah the list of reasons case workers keep leaving their cards in my door."

"But Jane. Wouldn't the newsworthiness of her mother's crime put more pressure on—"

"I have *friends* in high places with the department . . . helps a little . . . and the state is overloaded, as you know . . . but things can change. Always, things change."

"Okay, you pass the truth test on that one."

He gives her a sharp look. "I see . . . this is the way you treat your friends? With tests? Isn't playing dumb in order to *test* a person a type of deceit?"

"But I thought maybe *you* were deceiving *me*."

Ivy's car comes up behind yet another car that is going the speed limit. Ivy taps the horn lightly, guns the engine, flashes the lights, trying to coerce the driver of that car to get out of the way. The backs of the heads of the two people in that car's rear seat seem *huge*.

"Want me to drive?" Gordon persists.

"*No*. Don't ever say it again."

"Okay, fine . . . so tell me . . . what authorities does your editor hear from that are about to make hell for my family? And for Jane."

"Well, he's actually hearing from people he knows, other editors and people in agencies speaking unofficially and hearing rumors, but nothing definite yet, but he and some of his information sources seem to think something is up. Starting with DHS, the superintendent of schools in your district, the state police, and Gordon, I'm afraid, the Maine Bureau of Drug Enforcement and there was some mention of firearms, the illegal kind." She takes a breath. "And then there's some neighbor of yours who claims there are skulls and bodies of animals at the bottom of a drop-off, some charred. To some people this suggests Satan worship. When I called the state police to see what they had to say about all this, the lieutenant told me absolutely nothing. But your name made him breathe funny. I could hear his thoughts. Your name was a kinda household word with him, I could tell. If ten people a week are calling the paper to report all this *stuff,* and they call *him* more often, his file must be as thick as the one I have on you, and I have a nice thick file on you." She smiles guiltily.

Gordon says, "You're right. This is bad news for my family." He looks at his hands with a dull inward study. "You're a nice person. I'm grateful for your openness."

Ivy turns and heads back to North Egypt.

The sun is high but angled now in their faces. Down go the visors.

Ivy asks, "What about the firearms accusation?"

Gordon laughs.

"What's so funny?"

"Oh, nothing." His pale eyes twinkle.

She wiggles the fingers of her left hand.

He says, "So are we hippies all peace and love and silliness and stuff, as you accused me of, or are we armed terrorists? Pick one. You can't have both."

"How many guns do you people have on the premises?"

He closes his eyes.

"Can I ask how many guns *you* personally have, Gordon? And why, for godsakes, do you have to have a gun?"

He clasps his hands in his lap, his head sort of bowed. He says softly, "This is not the question that is really before America now. The question is how many things can the Friedmanites privatize? Police, prisons, schools, hospitals, Social Security, post office, annnd . . . the Pentagon . . . national intelligence, etc. How much more campaign finance money can be gushed into Capitol Hill from K Street? *And* how

many superfluous American people can America get into the *camps,*
uh prisons, that is, and nursing homes of the shoulder to shoulder sort
without the productive-big-spending-nice-upper-buffer-class people
objecting? How many things can America outlaw that superfluous
people do to enhance this operation, and how much money can be made
doing it? All those antiterror bills and antidrug laws . . . the template.
Next the War on Tobacco and War on Firearms. Ah, the money to be
made!! The intensifying of the great monied network. We used to call
it organized crime. But it's too big now. Aren't prohibitions glorious!"

No he is not speaking softly anymore and his head's at a horns-
locking angle. "And the *debt* of policing the world. Of taking *over*
the world. A new more beefed-up Cold War in the making. And
some actual war, *boom boom.* And you got the CIA-type secret wars,
getting people out there across the seas to fight *each other*. Chaos is
America's finest weapon! And secrecy is a weapon. And those oh so
precious politically correct *nonviolent* sanctions. Starve 'em! Freeze
'em!" He actually growls.

Ivy winces.

He chortles. "Oh, and then, as. You. Know, Mz. News, we have
questions such as climate change, the acidic changes in the ocean, de-
sertification of whole once-fertile regions, and Peak Oil. The climate
disasters and sinking islands are not a hundred years away anymore.
They. HAVE. BEGUN. These are the questions that Americans need
to have in their big fat mouths!"

Ivy has gotten suddenly bleach-white, such as TV faces did when
the olden days' reception went fizzy. Leaping Three Stooges. Again,
she wonders why he doesn't include overpopulation in his list of
mighty questions, an obvious blind spot for the otherwise all-seeing
pessimistic philosopher. And she sighs so hard her teeth whistle.

Meanwhile, none of this has interrupted him. He's been going on,
". . . clean water scarcity, the nightmare of nightmares for all living
beings. These are the questions you need to be asking, Mzzz. News."
He sort of chokes, on the edge of a fatally deep emotion here, but his
eyes just remain on his hands, his head bowed again.

Ivy gives the car more gas, straight into the sun. After a while she
declares, with an indignant raise of the chin, "Guns shouldn't be in
the hands of children."

"Neither should cars," he says, glancing at her ringed hands on the wheel.

She says evenly, "Speaking of the drug war, people are saying the children of the Home School are drugged . . . or are using drugs."

"Baby, we're beer and cider drinkers!" he says with almost squeaky outrage. "And . . . uh . . . maple milk."

"What about the kids? The callers interest is *only* in the kids. Do Settlement *kids* have their hands on drugs?"

He closes his eyes. "This is not the question before America. The question is how many superfluous people can be processed from point A to point B, the coming-soon, local privatized-profitized public schools and labor, uh, *prison* camps. The police-military state. The antiquarianizing of the last remnant scraps of human rights for the nonlords and nonladies of neofeudal America!"

"Gordon, you're evading my questions."

"I'm redesigning your questions to make them intelligent questions instead of baby questions. Your little gun issue, just like that little street drug issue, is another Pharaohic Klepto scheme to get poor superfluous people into the *camps* . . . gulags . . . cages. To throw the book at 'em, you need prohibitions. Thennn you got cheeeeeap labor. And bye-bye labor unions. Ker-*pow!* All they need is food in the supermarkets to run low. Or overpriced . . . same thing. The climate, the water, the oil, erosion, super storms, super weeds, super bugs . . . you'll see it. Chaos! Then out come the government guns. Round 'em up, boys! If they don't have *natural* emergencies, they'll rig up some assisted kind. The stakes are high, baby. The . . . stakes . . . are . . . high."

She looks at him quickly, sees the indignant set of his mouth. Actually, his mouth is a comically dramatic sneer, his eyes blazing. Of course, there is something funny and sweet and appealing about his outrage and fear, at least on one level. The adorable paranoia. What's this with *the camps?* But then Peak Oil wasn't paranoia after all. But. The. Camps. THAT one is nutty.

She presses on. "Do the Settlement kids have their hands on drugs?"

"What about the kids in *public* schools? Do they have *their* hands on drugs? They're loaded with the stuff. They have the four-year-olds stand on carpet remnants in rows to keep from getting the pills mixed up when they pass out the school meds. We're talking off-label antipsychotic shit, which is preferable because the patent is still virgin. The Big Pharma folks got a drug for everything from friskiness to dirty fingernails. Left-handedness to shyness. Maybe the government oughta push a little CS gas into a few public schools, or you know, blow 'em away. With those nice police guns. Nice government guns. Government guns are softer. Kinder, gentler, more sanctified. There's also the electric chair, and the very nice nonviolent socially approved IV death drugs. That would certainly teach all those little public school kiddies to 'just say no.' And then there's the CIA. Remember them? Better chat with *those* boogers. Since *they* are goddamn drug *providers*. But you'll get a bunch of smoke and mirrors there! And 'no comment.' 'Plausible deniability.' And blacked-out files. Melts in the mouth, not in the hand."

She liked him better when he bowed his head, the humility, the sweet sorrow. The red steamy anger pisses her off.

She says deeply, evenly, "My question."

He sniffs with annoyance, picks at the knee of his jeans, squints.

She suggests, "Maybe marijuana is just freely used by Settlement adults in the presence of kids?"

"I don't have any snooping devices in people's houses!" He says around a nasty laugh. "But—" He slouches down in the seat, his knees up higher, and the sun fills his eyes. "I'm not going to tell you that Settlement adolescents can't find a little weed around town. You see, I'm not naive enough to think there are drug-free zones." He laughs again. "It's embarrassing to think there are people who actually believe that, especially with their mass incarceration schools where a couple thousand kids comingle in a nearly invisible blur, and then by god are *allowed* to go *home,* ahem, for a few hours after two p.m." He chortles. "Drug-free zones!?" He sighs blubberingly like a whoopee cushion. "Oh, but I forgot. Now *they* have ceiling cameras in the schools." He shivers. Not a joke shiver. His neck and back really crawl.

A baseball-sized bug splats the windshield. Ivy twists knobs, wipers slash through washer fluid, smearing the greasy syrupy bug remains, which, with the sun, makes visibility poor, but Ivy doesn't let up off the gas pedal. The little red sporty car just hurtles onward into the gray gauzy unseen unknown.

Gordon sits up suddenly, grips the dash. "I wanna go home. I need my Mumma."

Ivy sighs with disgust. She lets up off the gas just a little. The windshield is slowly clearing. There is a visible road ahead, now overhung with trees, a glowing OSHA gold-painted stripe down the center of the black pavement and here and there, pillars of sunlight, as if God were trying to communicate.

Gordon says softly, "I'm not ashamed to say that our kids are curious and adventurous." He watches the blue, green, black, and yellow woods fluttering past through his side window, and now reaches out to open his hand into the wind. He gives her a guilty pup look. "I do too much beer and hard cider, you may have noticed." Sighs. "I . . . am a fuck-up in that way. It's just the way it is. All by itself it pours down my throat." He laughs a little too loudly. "In the 1920s, there was this nice idea on that. To help the fuck-ups walk the line. But the de-fucking-up idea was just—"

"Oh, please," groans Ivy. "Shut up." She smiles a wide professional plastic smile, then her own smile wending through the other smile, small and flummoxed. Tired of his preaching. Thirsty for his personal sins to be revealed. People stories *are personal*. And his closeness to her in the car is tautly personal, his hot work smell, his fear and her hungers are grafted.

When she brings the little car to a stop at an intersection, glancing to her right over his knees, he reaches for her nearest hand, which has a loose grip on the steering wheel, pulls the hand to his mouth, kisses her palm, the beard coarse and sun-warmed. Ivy lets this happen. He places the hand back on the wheel. Now flings his head back against the headrest, jerks his knees up higher, eyes squinched. "Where's my Mumma?" he says sadly. "I need a nap."

Ivy laughs. "Be a good boy now and you can have ice cream."

 Banana boat.

At Kool Kone, the picnic table is a gooey, relishy, chocolaty, birdy mess. They sit very carefully. They are face-to-face, with the little tipsy table between them, four obliging weeping willows and a pine tree above. Two other picnic tables are also sticky and birdy and pine-pitch-splattered, but no people. Just one young guy in a pickup truck waiting across the small sandy lot.

Ivy's cone is lime sherbet "hard serve." The loveliest of pale greens, so cold, there's a little smokiness as her lips touch it.

He has a banana boat, more like a banana ship. Dished up with soft serve. Other cars and pickups pull in. Gordon recognizes them all, waves or nods or salutes them. They holler out, "Hey Gordo! Howzit goin'?!" A few people come over to chat. They come and they go.

The heat of the day increaseth. Ivy's cone was, yes, small, but it had grown larger, swelling out over her hand, over her many rings, had run down her wrist. Stain there in the center of the "o" of her T-shirt lettering. Sweat is sticky. Ice cream is sticky. Ivy blinks through the distinctions of clingy heat and wobbling light at Gordon's face.

"This is fun," says he.

Ivy laughs. "I think you're easy to please."

He grins, kind of stupidly.

The picnic table is really pretty tiny. Gordon is now lapping his plastic dish. "Yummmm," he says. There is chocolate between his fingers, a slimy chip of walnut on his beard.

Ivy checks her watch. "Are you missing a meal back at the Settlement? Are they wondering where you are?"

"Nah," he says, pushing his well-lapped little boat dish away. "They saw us go, remember? And besides, the meals go on . . . for hours." He is mashing his bandana to his mouth.

"All meals last hours? Every day?"

He shrugs.

She hears his keys, sees him looking down and feeling his keys that always hang in a chunk from his belt. But also sometimes when they've been walking together, Ivy has noticed a pocket watch dangling there with the keys.

She holds her eyes on him. Admiringly. "How do you fit so much work and so many activities in with three long meals, too?" Now a raised playfully doubting eyebrow.

He squashes a mosquito with a thumb on his forearm. Again, he grins sheepishly, guiltily. "Highly organized chaos."

She uses the only two paper napkins, already squinched and gooey, works them between her gunky fingers.

Gordon burps softly against the top of one hand. Just a suppressed "*Bft!*"

Ivy smiles. "Tell me more about CSAs. The Community Supported Agriculture. I saw some of it on my tour."

And so there is again his voice and there is this day, both of which Ivy is sinking into. Hot velvet. Chin in hand, she says, "That's nice."

"Yes, 'tis. It's not going to save the world, but it's a good thing, a dear goodly thing."

She smiles. "I mean . . . you're not exactly sequestered up there, are you, Mr. St. Onge?"

"Yes and no."

She drops her hand. "Tell me, Allah, man of wisdom, knower of all life's answers and government secrets, would you say that you and your people are headed for a fiery end? The Armageddon? As prophesied by Revelation 16:16; I think that's the number. Sixteen something."

Another shrug. Another one of his rare *no comments*. And he grooms the long dark mustache on both sides with thumb and forefinger and he stares into her eyes, first one of her eyes, then the other, back and forth. As he does this, raising one eyebrow and raising his chin, he just really is preening away on that big mustache.

She holds the gaze. She fears she might faint (yeah, faint, the thing women never really do). And of course she won't faint. Even though she is overcome with crazy feeling, even though the heat cranks up another notch and the whole Kool Kone parking lot seems to fog over and tip sideways and ooze. No, she won't faint. Yes, those fainting ideas are just throwbacks from the old sexist patriarchal culture of her grandmother's time. Books and films with hundreds of women fainting all over the place.

 During the speedy ride back to the Settlement, especially during Ivy's reckless tailgatings and double-yellow-line passings.

Gordon covers his face and murmurs, "The Armageddon is here! The Armageddon is here!" and grips the bucket seat with both hands and bows his head, "Lord God Almighty, forgive me *all* of my trespasses!"

Ivy says disgustedly, "I read once that people who complain about other people's driving are control freaks."

Back home, she has a message on her machine.

"Hi Ivy . . . it's five-twenty-two. I'm heading out of the building now. I should be home in an hour and twenty minutes. I have a couple stops to make. Call me when you get this message. Call me at my *home** number."

Ivy taps out Brian's home number. She's really puzzled. He has never asked her to call him at home before. Now she gets his machine. She leaves her message. "Hi, Brian. It's me, Ivy. It's a quarter past eight. I'll be around for the rest of the evening. Call when you can. Bye."

Ivy sleeps only on the edge of real sleep. Her dreams are a tangle of Gordon's voice and Brian's voice and her father trying to fix a sawhorse that has six floppy legs and won't stand up. Occasionally she wakes, thinking she heard the funny little pulsing sound of her phone but the phone is quiet. No Brian.

In the morning, she makes toast and sings a melody from childhood.

 As Ivy is pounding up the winding old marble stairs of the newspaper building (never the elevator), Brian Fitch pushes open the fourth-floor door (the cafeteria floor), and, seeing Ivy, points at the step nearest himself, which is the command for her to come to him. And he says,

"St. Onge humps kids."

Ivy, breathless after the four flights, hikes up the strap of her bursting shoulder bag, blows air up across her face to make her dark bangs hop, and frowns, frowns, frowns.

Brian glances out through the caged-looking stairway window to the street. "But don't quote me."

"Fuck the anonymous callers," Ivy says.

Door eases open one flight above and hard-heeled ladylike shoes snap along down and around, on the old echoey marble and metal.

---

* This was when cell phones were even more echoey and sloshy than they are today. Especially in Maine. Thus cell phoning not an option.

Brian says, "Well, but there were *six* calls yesterday while you were out . . . all St. Onge-related . . . some just continuing gossip with Bertie and them at DHS . . . but, yes, mostly these anonymous types. One *did* actually sound like a crank call. Young guy and other young sounds in the background, banging and bomping . . . music . . . maybe street sounds. Anyway, a sporting kind of call." Brian nods at the woman in the lightweight mauve dress and Ivy steps aside to let the woman and the cool tornado of her perfume pass.

Brian cocks his head. "But then Duane at the sheriff's department called to say a woman he knows well called a few days ago urging the department to send someone to the St. Onge property because her sister is in an emotional state about her step-daughter's friend, who is *thirteen* and *pregnant* and not allowed to leave the St. Onge premises alone. The sister says St. Onge has a whole *harem* of twelve- and thirteen-year-olds and that St. Onge is a God figure . . . it's David Koresh all over again, only different. So a couple of sheriff's guys go talk to the sister, but she won't talk. But she was *very strange-acting*, they said. Like *terrified*. Or embarrassed. Or both. Cops are rotten at sorting out civilian emotions, you know. Then these guys take a little drive up to the Settlement . . . which is situated up there in Remoteland, as . . . you . . . know . . . and they talked with a few people and asked if everyone was okay and there were all these *old* ladies and middle-aged women who were all chatty and normal and said everything was just fine. No sign of the Prophet. Just these friendly chatty ladies all friendly to these sheriff's men. More friendly than they are usually to *the press*."

Ivy says quickly, "They are friendly to *me*. But, so, when was all this happening with the sheriffs?"

"Yesterday, late morning."

"I was with him!"

"Koresh? I mean, St. Onge?"

"Yes. We—"

He puts up a finger. He says slowly, squinting, as if watching an ant walking up the wall behind Ivy's head. "Supposing none of these *rumors* are true, suppose there's no Satan worship, no twelve-year-old wives, no forced labor, no drugs, no snake handling, no . . . uh . . . what else?"

"Stockpiles of firearms."

"Yeah, stockpiles of firearms. So let's suppose none of those things are true. Let's say that where there's smoke, there just isn't any fire. Okay . . . but now . . . I'm just so *fascinated* by this. What has come over these people who call us? How does something like this take off?" He swings one arm to loosen the stressed-out muscles of that shoulder and says, "It's unsettling, and—" He rubs one eye hard. "You know? It's creepy."

 After midnight. Big moon. Not a full moon yet. But a moon with a well-fed contented shape.

No big security lights at the Settlement. No welcoming porch lights. No glowing TVs and canned laughter and zippy car ads. A small patch here and there of a single lighted window, somebody up with a baby or a restless old person or up with a page-turner book. But mostly there is moony darkness. And rest.

But Gordon St. Onge doesn't rest. He walks. He washes his flashlight over black shadows. This! The family. So much to account for. To protect. He walks on. To protect. He crosses the quad slowly. To protect.

He steps up to a screen door. Door heavy, well-made. Wood. The strain of the spring always reminds him of the tense aimless singing of the fretted instruments of the Middle and Near East. He doesn't let the door slam but turns to face it and allows it to ease shut against his palm.

He turns. Might there be a smoldering cigarette left in a chair? A gas stove burner left on in the summer kitchen or cooks' kitchen. Maybe one of Willie Lancaster's dogs locked in one of the parlors chewing on a book (this happens a lot).

No rest. Protect. Protect. Protect. Sometimes *protecting* makes him panicky. Sometimes it makes him *insane*. Especially when those moments hove into view that give him the desperation of wishing to protect the whole writhing world. It has started to rot his vitals. Or is that the aspirin?

He walks to an open shop door, swipes the light over the floor and worktables, then trudges on to the next.

There on the next piazza, sitting alone, is a man with a marble face. Or so it seems. Sits very straight, eyes closed. Perhaps praying. Perhaps meditating. Or maybe a little stoned. The shaved pallor of his face is enhanced tonight by the riveting blue-white work of the moon. His hair is wetly black and combed straight back. He wears a black jacket. Hands in the pockets, gripped against his sides. As Gordon trudges toward him, he doesn't look Gordon's way, but he does open his eyes. His eyes are round and slightly protruding. Like piping hot painful restraint.

Now Gordon turns in to the kitchens and when he returns to the piazza, he, Gordon, is eating something. Chomping. He sees what looks now like fear on the man's face. But he knows this is probably just maximized spiritual concentration.

Gordon pushes through a batch of wind chimes, sets them to clanking and donging, some singing in a haunting entreaty, but they go quiet quickly because the air is calm. He eases into a chair beside the man.

Gordon knows that if he says, "Howzit goin', Nathan?" he might not get an answer, as Nathan won't answer you if he's praying or meditating or deeply concentrating. So Gordon figures he'll wait it out. He just chomps away on his carrot and rocks slowly back and forth in his chair, reaches to set the flashlight on the floor.

A steer *murrs* on the nearest hillside. The clock in the library chimes a muffled *thronnnnnnggggggg* on the quarter hour.

When the deeply composed man is finally ready to speak, his voice is business-like. "Hello, Gordon."

"Nathan."

Nathan Knapp. A man of enormous inner geography. Alone in a dark and unadorned cell for years, Nathan Knapp could keep his wits, not scream, "Let me outa here!" He would simply travel in his mind. The kids call him "our peace man."

Nathan Knapp. Mostly a loner. He lives in that tiny, sweet, natural-shingle solar house up in the field there under the moon . . . with Jenny. His wife. She works outside the Settlement as a legal secretary in Lewiston. She is focused, fussy, and uptight. Well, Nathan is focused, too. But in a blooey-ahhh kind of way.

Nathan is well-read. Aggressively well-read, with almost a photographic memory for detail concerning his interests: ecosystems, the macrobiotic diet, Shakespeare, Greek tragedies, ancient cultures including, especially, those that worshipped the goddesses, and then on into the scholars on all religions and all churches, much focus on

Jesus and Gandhi. As a faith, Gandhi is the god, the model for salvation. Gandhi twenty-feet tall, Nathan, five-foot-eleven.

Nathan abhors references to current events. He finds them too rattling. The past is pendulous and in its place. For present-time interests, he looks mostly to the latest discoveries in personal well-being. He is a slave to therapeutic massage, Reiki, and yoga. He speaks the word *pacifism* with an almost *en garde!* challenge, the kind of pacifism where you would protect a child from attack only with a powerful and peaceful stare, eyes into eyes with the aggressor. One of his favorite expressions is "What would Gandhi do?"

Yet Nathan is considered suspect by so many here at the Settlement. He is despised by some. How can that be, Gordon wonders? When disagreement breaks out about his ideas, Nathan never raises his voice; there's no name-calling, no buried insults, and, even as his opponents present arguments frustratingly uninformed, he maintains a fine priestly bearing. He is a patient teacher of the young. Gordon feels both annoyance and respect for Nathan Knapp.

Nathan says, "I heard that the *Record Sun* reporter was here again."

Around a huge cheekful of chewed carrot, Gordon replies, "And you heard about . . . the calls she's been getting?"

"Yes."

Gordon grunts, stretches his legs out, crosses one boot over the other. Chomps more carrot.

Nathan closes his eyes. "Something is about to happen."

"We aren't doing anything wrong."

Nathan looks at Gordon. "Those people who make the laws would disagree."

Gordon chomps chomps chomps. No words of defense.

Nathan closes his eyes. Sighs.

Gordon says, "Those hides 'n' bones Eddie and Aurel threw over the drop-off . . ."

Nathan's total silence is black and thunderous.

Gordon says, "After we got the bears up here . . . digging in the compost bins."

Nathan, still nothing.

Gordon, "You remember, the not-so-good night of the bears and one of Seth Miner's dogs."

"Yes."

"So, that's why the meat-cutting crews stopped putting foody ma-terials in the bins for a while, just the toilet waste."

Nathan nods, but Gordon doesn't see the nod. Gordon wags one foot patiently, then says, "And nobody wanted porcupines. You have bears who can rip the wire, even the boards, and porcupines who can climb."

Nathan nods.

Gordon misses the nod again. "Whatever move we make to do right, the tail of the deed slaps *some* face." Gordon points toward the hills with the thick bad-tasting end of the carrot. "So for a while, they pitched *a lot* of stuff over the drop-off."

Nathan doesn't even nod. He is riveted in some cold iron way.

Gordon chuckles. "Soooo, some summer people over off the back road found some of the bones and skulls."

Nathan leans back, weary of where this is going.

"They say we're into Satan worship."

Nathan squinches his eyes. This eye-squinching is the way Nathan laughs. There is never a laugh *noise* with his laughs. No teeth or open jaws. But this is, indeed, a bitter laugh.

Gordon thonks the chair arm gently with the carrot end.

Nathan folds his hands into one thick relaxed fist on the crotch of his jeans. He looks off toward the long, oblong, fleshy cloud that is unhurriedly swallowing the moon. He takes a deep, deep breath of the night. This night that is of the sweetest kind, the newly hayed fields and the heavy cool wetness beaded up on each leaf and flower and hard green fruit. And in each droplet is a thin moon reflection, being swallowed by a tiny, ravenous, oblong cloud. And he says, "I fear you."

Gordon makes a disgusted sound.

Nathan raises a hand, like a blessing, but he really means, *whoa, let me finish.* "Each and every law you and others here have broken is nothing really. No hurt. They are foolish man-made laws. Some are self-serving laws made by the politicos. And yeah . . . I certainly got my *little illegal stash.* But I'm peaceable. Man, *you* speak sometimes in a way that makes me realize . . . that the law that you hold most in contempt isn't a pale one . . . it's a law that is the law of God as seen through the eyes of hundreds of peoples, of nearly every nation on every continent, for—"

"Contempt is not the word."

"Contempt *is* the word. It's there on your face right now."

Gordon leans forward, arms folded across his knees, buries his face in his arms. "There is no *simple* way of looking at any of this."

"If I tell you I've had a dream about this, a vision, will you laugh?" Nathan wonders.

"No," Gordon says into his arms.

"I ask only that if things become more . . . difficult . . . that if they do come down on us . . . come down with all fury . . . that you'll go *passively*. That you'll submit. That you won't take up guns."

 History as it happens (as written by Theodan Darby age almost ten, with slight help from his sister).

We are almost done with the solar car. The frame was bent then we fixed it. But it is fixed. Then wire stuff went wrong. Brakes next. It is called Purpil Hope. It is the best ever car. Dad said next we make fuel for deezil from plants. That would be better because the solar ones are to quiet. Loud is best. It is good to have POWERRRRRRR!

Dad says the Purpil Hope is a sweet machen.

 History as it happens (as written by Jane Meserve, age six).

There sole car they are so prowd of is a peice of junk. Looks made by hands.

 Brianna's secret book.

Tonight the rebellious little group of teens has really had their heads together with plans to "wake up the world!" and it is past eleven before the first ones leave. "It's just like the radical solar car work in the Quonset hut, the work of any kind of revolution is hard work, long before it becomes a revolution," Bree has said with *joy*. Uh-huh, yes, joy. She sees battle as fun? Romantic? Poetic? Gorgeous?

As Bree and Samantha walk toward the parking lot, Bree smokes. Samantha is gossiping. Nice air. Cool on their bare arms. The great swath of brightness from an open Quonset hut bay and the headlights of a couple pickups leaving is what illuminates their way along the brick paths. Samantha is getting into the really juicy details of Toon Clyde's haircut that turned out "horrid." Seems Jane Meserve (yes, seems like she's getting out a little) had given it the finishing touches, Jane being a new apprentice in the beauty shop. Seems Toon never should have trusted such a little kid with her *hair*. "Maybe brain surgery. But not your hair!" Samantha gasps.

Bree giggles. "Was she wearing those heart-shaped sunglasses Eric just gave her? "

"Ricardo, you mean?"

Bree giggles. "Right."

"She wears them *all* the time. She believes they give her power. She's become a secret agent."

"Oh god," Bree giggles, then moans. "Watch what you say." She blows smoke hard.

Samantha sneezes. "Ragweed."

Samantha is now fifteen, just like Bree. Slim, small-boned, straight white-blonde hair worn long with an Apache-style bandana around her forehead, a homemade bandana of a red and blue print. White blouse that glows contentiously in the night, like her hair. Dark bushy homemade pants. Work boots, like Bree's. And haven't Carmel, Echo, Margo, Whitney, Oceanna, Michelle, Rachel, and Alyson been seen striding around in high-topped work boots lately? Like a skinhead gang, only not bald.

Now reaching Bree's truck, Bree drops her cigarette butt in the sand and crushes it with her heel, jams a hand down into the unyielding pocket of her skin-tight jeans.

Keys emerge. She unlocks the truck.

Samantha laughs. "'Fraida thieves?"

"Tonight I am," Bree says in her smoky low voice. She leans into the cab, tugs at something heavy. When she turns, her so-very-far-apart yellowy-gold-green eyes look into Samantha's darker ones and she commands, "Don't show anyone." In her arms, a huge book. It is wrapped in a blanket. Her wild rippling carroty hair is thick over her shoulders. "It's my very private story, only for your eyes."

Samantha says, "I can't wait."

Bree says, "I trust you with all my heart."

Once the heavy book is placed in Samantha's slim arms, Bree lights up another cigarette and watches Samantha taking the dark brick path toward the first lane of field cottages where she lives.

This is *not* the book her brother Poon sneaked out one rainy night to show Claire and Bonnie Loo in the west parlor. This book has *never* been viewed before by anyone but Bree. It is a bomb, not yet dropped on the Settlement.

 Alone at home in her room, Samantha lifts the heavy cover and glimpses the first page.

"Oh, my god." She jumps up and draws the curtains, although these windows overlook nothing but steep meadow. She worries that her mother will wake up and come find her looking at this. Or Chris, who is still out. She's never wished for a lock for her door before now. This book, too huge to hide quickly. So heavy it indents the bed like a person sleeping there.

She flomps back onto her bed now. Sitting Indian-style, she lifts the cover again.

These are drawings with ink, smeared delicately with oil pastels or watercolors. Purples, yellows, blues. Yellowy cream for skin, skin illuminated by odd light. *There is a lot of skin.* Between the pages of thick rag paper on posterboard (pages of artwork), are thinner pages of calligraphy, bold and ink-black as a proclamation. Names, first names only. Like "Greg" or "Mike." One name to each picture, though most pictures feature more than one man, and each picture is a story. A story of sex.

Samantha tries to remember if Bree had actually said whether these were not *true* stories. Bree called the book "My story," didn't she?

Well, there's not a lot of plot. Just action. Primarily rape or something. *Something.* Different guys. One girl. Always Bree.

Samantha feels watched. She keeps freezing motionless, to cock an ear and to look around her room, over at the window to make sure there's not even a tiny slit between the closed curtains. And is the curtain fabric thick enough? It feels like objects in the room are looking at her, the postcard of a desert scene, a knob of her bureau, the knots of pine in the ship-lap ceiling. She turns a page, her eyes getting bigger, rounder. The edges of the rag paper of the drawings are coarse but the depictions of bodies have the smooth properties of live bodies, filled with oils and fats, water and salt and surges and currents. Samantha has ever-so-gently started to jiggle one leg.

The picture before her is of Bree naked, wrists tied with what looks like dog chain, and several oldish men (what Samantha would call oldish . . . you know, twenties and thirties) surrounding her in the middle of an ordinary kitchen. There's the edge of a supper table, the knobs of a gas stove in fuzzy foreground and background . . . The whole scene is weirdly 3-D.

Samantha lifts the page; it is naked Bree in profile. Samantha quickly peeks ahead. People standing in spaces like a barn with machinery and stuff around. Or outdoors in the woods . . . all seasons . . . even winter, bare feet in snow. But always, the young woman is Bree. And her face is hard to read. What is that in her eyes? Is she flipping out? Fainting?

In the first picture the men are dressed for the outdoors, like they have just come in from a January day, knitted caps or billed caps, jackets, sweatshirts, one with gloves bunched in his hand. Their faces are so real. Their eyes! So real. One man's eyes are dark as night with the overhead ceiling light reflected in them, these eyes on Bree's body, hand going for his fly.

No pictures show Bree face-on. Most are in profile. In this scene, her hands are free. Her feet are apart, pelvis forward while the man works his fingers into Bree's vagina, the pubic hair light and reddish, an ordinary-looking watch on the guy's wrist, so *real* looking, as real as the watch on Samantha's own real wrist, lifting another page. She stares. Makes a funny sound in her nose and neck.

Lifts another page.

Sometimes there's just one man alone. But mostly it's groups. Mean, leering, greedy? One or two guys wear such blank expressions, like faces people have while baiting a fish hook or replacing a cable on a skidder. Some a little squinty-eyed, like threading a needle. Utilitarian expressions. Some are undressed.

In some of these pictures there are guys who look an awful lot like the Vandermast brothers. But they have different haircuts and brown eyes. There are no dark-brown-eyed Vandermasts in the real world.

Samantha turns pages. She finds that in some paintings, Bree stands with pride! And see, in one of these, that *"come hither, I dare you"* expression. In one, a man is fucking her from behind, while another man in front of her holds her wrists together, gripping them in such a way as to make the contours of his arms look strained; while Bree's wrists seem melded, those tender vulnerable squirming heartbeats, pulse against pulse. Is this guy a Vandermast brother? The one they call Poon? But, then, no. Older than Poon.

The face of the man at her back doesn't show, just his shoulders in a dark shirt, unbuckled flapping belt, a bare hip and bare bent knee, his arms around her, just a touch of blurriness to both him and Bree, as though the motion of his hard jabs puts the whole universe into a spin.

Samantha leans away from the book, dizzy. But also sharply focused. Everything beyond and outside her revved-up body now takes on a silly unimportant ticking sound.

 ## The grays.

That hornet inflection, cool to our pulsating eyes, that chattering, sighing, thrill and worry, little-teen-girlfriends of our ripply-haired cherishling, the raising of the big ballast pages, then other hands, then others, and the murmured word: *Bree, Bree, Bree,* lounder and louder, like the confluence of grief and spectacle.

 ## A few Settlement women have gathered.

They have gathered in the Quonset hut where blonde, petite Josee Soucier (wife of Aurel Soucier who is cousin of Gordon) is milking a gangly white goat. It is for that special milk that she likes to take over to old Mrs. Dunlop in North Egypt who has stomach trouble. And for the best Settlement cheese, goat milk is the way.

This is not a planned meeting.

It was just that one remark led to another, one whisper, then another and now the urgent discussion about Bree, yes, Bree Vandermast and her *home life*.

Bree has shown *the book* to three other girls, after Samantha, and like hot lava, the story has filled every room and piazza, every crook and cranny of the whole Settlement except maybe Gordon, who is often the last person to hear of certain types of news.

Lee Lynn's voice is high, really tiny for such a tall, grown-up woman, her wild hair streaming from her head, witchy hair, early gray; she's still in her thirties. She stands barefoot in the mucky hay of the stall area. Long purple and brown print dress. Braless. Big smiling baby Hazel on her hip. "Gail, have *you* seen the book?"

Gail says no.

Josee lifts the pail away from under the goat and sets it on the high corner shelf, a fresh spiderweb under the shelf. She pushes the empty grain pan away with a foot and shoos the goat out through the canvas flap to the fenced-in hillside, where some little girls are rounding up another doe, there being only three who presently aren't dry. The white goat's ribbony tail flutters as she hurries out through the flap. A few *bah-heh-heh-heh's*. Now Josee stands with feet apart, polishing her glasses on her shirt hem, her glasses modern and attractive to all with modern tastes, nothing like Claire's old-timey specs. And Josee's orangey blonde hair is as short as an elf's since her most recent visit to the beauty shop. And her eyes without her glasses seem to crackle today. Something about the engulfing conversation.

Bonnie Loo is kind of sour-looking by nature, her ripply black hair is streaked reddish yellow and knotted into a "tail" with a light blue bandana. Her eyes green-gold, fox color. Some days it is glasses for Bonnie Loo, other days it's contacts. Today it's glasses. Old I-don't-give-a-shit glasses with one taped bow. She reaches for Lee Lynn's baby and settles her onto her own hip, nuzzling her as if she were her own. This means Bonnie Loo isn't depressed today. Or jealous. Or morning sick.

Lee Lynn is describing *the book*. In her tiny voice, she says, "This child, Bree, has been sold like a cow, like you breed a cow. A goat! Who knows how long it's been going on? Maybe when she was a little girl. These things can get pretty weird."

Baby Hazel opens her hand, palm out toward Bonnie Loo's earring, as if to praise a distant star. Yes, Bonnie Loo is expecting again. Due in March. Child will be named after her dead father if it's a boy, her mother if it's a girl. Even though their names aren't that hot. Beal and Earlene. But these days, Bonnie Loo is beginning to be deeply and achingly attracted to her ancestry, her history, her real people. She's having second thoughts about Settlement life. The more she fears the future, the more she loves the past. "The book doesn't *say* these guys are paying. It doesn't really *say* anything."

Gail sniffs indignantly. "Just put two and two together."

Bonnie Loo says, "I think I recognize Andy Churchill in one of those pictures. And Michael Gavin. You know Michael, don't you, Steph?"

Stephanie replies in a quiet voice. "Yep."

Witchy-haired Lee Lynn says, "Fine. But why are her brothers and maybe her dad in that woodsy one?"

Josee finally snarls, "T'at is an excellent question! Why are t'ey involved, t'em? Okay?! Maybe not a sale. But damn kinky. Damn sick!"

Bonnie Loo picks straw from Baby Hazel's sundress. "You can imagine anything. You can imagine almost anything. They are always arresting people for one thing or another you never dreamed of."

Gail puts up a hand. "Okay . . . right. That's what we gotta keep in mind. We do not want this to get beyond here . . . for now. Cops and courts and social workers will make a worse mess of the mess she's in now. They'd put her people in prison. In prison! And she'd feel all twisted up in a weird guilt, sort've like survivor guilt but different. We gotta deal with these guys ourselves. We tell them to lay off or else. We get Bree out of there."

Josee kicks at the hay. Hands on her hips. "T'ey *ought* to be in prison, t'em. Bring in t'Marines. Blow 'em away. It iss too terrible what t'ey are doing."

Cindy Butler, Samantha's mother. She has moved here only a couple of years ago, to be part of Settlement life. She is not married. Not "partnered with." Nor wants to be. Nor does she want to be a modern-world wage slave. She has never felt so grown-up until she came here. Thus she is inexorably defined by this intimate nest of sisters, sign-up sheets, and clockless time. She watches the words fly back and forth between these women, yes, her "sisters." Finally speaks, "If prison solved the problem, fine. But prison is about revenge. Why is that good for Bree? These aren't some strangers. These are Bree's people. Like Gail says, Bree's going to have mixed-up feelings about them."

Josee snarls, "Bad feelings!"

"Bad feelings, good feelings, *strong* feelings, protective feelings, all tied in knots," says Claire. "The important thing is . . . if this is really what we think it is . . . well, Bree has been savaged. We want to put the reins in her hands. Giving it all over to the police and that lot is like giving your wounded heart to a giant monkey. Worse. And I agree that we are a community. We have good instincts. And we care about Bree. Weeee have got this in our laps. We need to think it through very carefully."

Josee rolls her eyes. "Poor Bree will be glad to see t'big monkey toss t'em small monkeys in prison, her. She be glad to see t'em in hot boiling oil. Fix t'ere ass."

Stephanie says, "But guess what. If the state gets involved, she goes to a foster home of strangers. It won't be us. You think she'd be placed with us who on the radio and newspapers they would have us as hippie commune freaks? No ho ho! She'll go to strangers and they'll have all these therapists all over her. They'll make her dependent on professionals! She won't even be able to *think* in her own way, let alone feel! They work on you to think *their* way, the bureau way. The DHS is like the mob. (Tsk.) They say stuff like, "If you don't do as instructed, *it won't bode well for you.*"

"Sounds like Shakespeare," says eye-rolling Bonnie Loo.

"Sounds WHITE," says Passamaquoddy Claire.

A few of her "white" sisters roll their eyes. One gives Claire a rough-house hug. "We fain show the DHS our might."

"And ye shall make haste," Claire adds.

"That was Moses," Cindy Butler chortles. "You *shall* this and that."

"No *that* was God," titters Bonnie Loo. "God lingo."

"English translation," observes Gail.

"White god," says Claire.

Claire's cousin Leona, mother of *many* kids, including one of the teen girls who was given *the book* . . . she has always had this funny little habit in a group, raises her whole arm, like a kid in school. She does this now. She even waves the arm from side to side. "I think," she says softly, when finally everyone is staring at her expectantly, and her arm is down. "That it would be real bad to act now in any way. Bree has trusted the girls with her secret. Trust is important. How can we work around that? Maybe get the girls themselves to ask her stuff."

"They sort've have. Sammy did," Samantha's mother says. "But it didn't go anywhere."

Lee Lynn says, "So we need to get her to move in here with us *before* DHS catches wind of this and makes a move on the Vandermasts."

"Right."

"Right."

Dark-haired thick-legged cherubic Hazel squeals, "Riiiiii!!!" and giggles with nose-wrinkled eyes-skwinched enthusiasm and Bonnie Loo smooches her ear, which causes further Hazelesque enthusiasm, "Eeeeeeee-ya ya ya ya! Ma ma ma!"

Josee fairly hisses (still with hands on hips), "Maybe t'ose horror men not let her move away . . . if t'ey make all t'at money on her, aye?"

Penny (mother of Whitney) agrees. "They sound pretty sick. The sooner we work on getting her out, the better. She doesn't have to know the reason. It makes me so sad. Poor little dickens."

Leona now wonders, "What happened to Bree's mother?"

"Dead."

Lee Lynn sighs her tiny soprano sigh. "We need to tell Gordon about this. He's been getting letters from her. About impersonal subject matter but—." She squints one eye. "He might—"

"Ack!" This is Claire's cousin Geraldine. "Keep him out of it. He'll bungle this. Men can't imagine what to do in this kind of thing, except act stupid, and hormone-ish. He'll probably go over there and get into a brawl and then *he'll* wind up in prison with them. You know, Bree would probably take her brothers' side if Gordon was over there socking their lights out. Then she'll shut us all out forever."

Stephanie keeps nodding as people talk. Stephanie always freezing, hugged up in a big bunchy sweater. Plump sweet face, rosy, even when she's cold. Short swingy brown hair. Brown eyes, stylish glasses. Mother of Margo and Oceanna, the un-look-alike twins. That makes Stephanie one of the old-timers here, like Claire, Leona, and Penny. And so her words now have a kind of sanctification. And she is *heard*. "For now, let's just give her all the love she needs, lure her here with love. And keep her trust. This is home."

Josee squints at each face incredulously. "I'm ready to carry her out off t'at evil place and turn t'garden hose on t'at bunch of lowlifes. I belieff t'slow way iss way wrong, me."

Little girls are now shoving another milk goat in through the flap and Hazel points, "Go!" (short for goat) and squirms polywoggishly to get down and so Bonnie Loo accommodates.

Witchy siren-voiced Lee Lynn hugs Josee. "If it gets to that, you can have the honor of holding the hose."

Josee says, "T'ank you very much. I look forward to it. If you forget, I remind you, o*kay?*"

 ### In a future time, Brianna Vandermast considers.

I do not believe in the damnation of the soul. The thick, chomping body and brain with all their reflexes falter, suffer, ache, burn, wail.

However and ever the soul, part of the mighty, filmy and whole, this huge soul can't feel for it has no physiology. Therefore it can't sin. Nor can it be coerced.

Therefore, death is not punishment. Nor is it reward. And it is *not* nothingness but wholeness. Maybe it is the ultimate embrace.

 ### Riding to the university.

Lee Lynn's dress is orange. Not her harvest orange. Not her pumpkin. And not her *other* orange. But an August orange. Like the billows of orange blooms you see in certain window boxes. Though her braless-ness under such thin fabric can be unnerving to many of those who view her, she never seems to realize. She doesn't do the sexpot thing, gasping between words and licking her lips. No hip wiggling. No chest heaving. None of that. She just gets on with whatever it is she has to do, breasts wagging, like a critter with a litter. Her dark-streaked gray hair, so unnerving and un-self-realized, is braided today and pinned into a careless cabled blob on top.

Bree Vandermast wears a dotted violet sundress over a black T-shirt. You rarely see her in a dress or skirt. Never shorts. So this is fairly "awesome" as the kids say. Like Lee Lynn, Bree wears dark Settlement-made socks and Settlement-made sandals.

Both Bree and Lee Lynn smell good. Lee Lynn has that peculiar scent of Settlement soap and salves, green and prickly, like a walking tree or swamp. And Bree, smelling strong of that commercial talc she shares with her father's part-time girlfriend, Kaye, and the soap in the tub dish used by them all, brothers, father, and Kaye, though along with a bit of cigarette smell, hers and theirs.

Bree's ripply ropy red hair, brushed hard to its full glory, still does its job of protecting half her face, that side where Gordon is driving, though the breeze from the open truck window plays with it quite a bit. She rides, leaning just a little into the door, with her hands in her lap.

Lee Lynn rides in the middle with both long slender arms stretched out along the back of the seat, one arm behind Bree's shoulders, the other behind Gordon.

As the city buildings begin to thicken, traffic slows.

In the car behind them is Whitney, now age sixteen, equipped with her driver's permit, driving a Settlement car loaded with passengers bound for various other Portland errands and adventures. So Whitney is not afraid of risk? A full load of passengers is illegal with a driving *permit*. Is she risky? Or stupid? How do you untangle the consequences of the outside world through Settlement eyes? That ultimate naïveté, where rebellion is accepted and applauded as so darn cute.

Lee Lynn's high siren voice speaks to Bree. "Now, one of the people you'll be seeing is Peter Laskov, who runs the People and Politics course. According to Claire, he's really great. He said you're welcomed to sit in on any of his classes but that the one you decided on is the best one to start with . . . although I noticed it's an intro course . . . and I think you're wasting your time with intros. Maybe he'll get the picture after you guys talk . . ."

As Lee Lynn speaks the word *talk,* Gordon glances past her at Bree and pictures *no talk,* just giggles. When does she ever *talk?*

Lee Lynn adds, "He'll be in his office at 10:15, so we'll yak with him first, then, 'bout the time Gordon gets back from his furniture wheeling and dealing, we'll be catching up with Catherine Downey, Claire's friend in the—"

"Catherine *Court* Downey," Gordon interrupts.

"Catherine Court Downey, yes." Lee Lynn glances at Gordon, knows that he's being sarcastic about Claire's outspokenly feminist friend, whom he has much poorly concealed contempt for, though they have never met. She goes on, "Catherine is interim chairman of the art department until—"

"Chair*person,*" Gordon corrects her.

Lee Lynn's fingers along the top of the seat give the back of Gordon's neck a squeeze. "Quit remodeling my words."

Eyes still on the street of traffic ahead, he leans her way and speaks in a husky way against her snowy ear. "It could save your life."

Lee Lynn sighs. "Anyway, Bree, these are all people Claire knows well, so you can feel right at home."

Bree, raising her face fully from its curtain of thick hair, says softly, "What courses did Whitney finally pick?"

"Pre-engineering stuff. And one that sounds interesting, something about 'architecture as defining space.' And then her second physics course, which, as far as I'm concerned, sounds *un*interesting. Like death by dull. I think when people get too much of that stuff, they start to sound like they've been drinking hot plaster."

Bree giggles and her large strange eyes move over Lee Lynn admiringly.

Lee Lynn says, "There was this other physics-like course Whitney wanted, but she's still yakking with Gerald about it. She tell you about Gerald? That guy in the department she's so fond of."

Bree says, "Yep."

Lee Lynn has glanced at Gordon. She sees the first signs of middle age there on the back of his neck, middle age and exposure to sun, two crisscross seams like weathering on wood, only on him it is soft, nothing like wood. And nothing yet like the deep "cracks" that come next, his fortieth birthday just around the bend. He makes no comment on this new development of the oldest Settlement-born girl being *fond* of the young university professor, added to the other new development of the Nebraskan boyfriend, Jordan Langzatel, who visits on Sundays now.

Yeah, he has not failed to consider that Whitney will probably leave the Settlement. Either on the arm of one of these square-jawed quenchless men, or the big "C." Career. Worse than quenchless. Can *all* of this be blamed on fossil energy? Big industrialism? Food shortages? Polluted water? TV? Fast travel? It goes around and around, the philosopher's brain struggling like an upside-down bug on a hard floor, trying to square up the muddle, trying to shore up the fort's walls.

Bree is saying, "Yeah, I remember she said she might do *two* physics courses, but there was something, a problem with doing that . . . like it came on a Friday. Cars are all tied up on Fridays."

Lee Lynn says, "Michelle is going to just hang out with Claire this year, help her teach history. She loves it. Like you do. You both are a couple of little history shmisteries."

"Yeah," says Bree, her smoker's voice low and rough.

"And probably I'm just repeating Claire on all this, but none of these courses you take are for credit. You have to have a high school diploma for that," Lee Lynn reminds her. "If you want to do a GED, I think you might have to be sixteen. I'm not sure. But it all has to be done just so, to please the institutional *machine*." She glances at Gordon, grades and diplomas being a touchy subject with him. But strangely, he seems not to have noticed this reference now. He has the sun visor down, face in shadow, but across the chest of his work shirt and both arms, the morning sun, light of the east, lies insoluble and fantastic, like sudden déjà vu, while his eyes just follow some guy crossing the street, a guy with a bright-colored shirt and shaved head. He touches the brakes of the truck over and over, easing along with the traffic, a slow river of clutter and lives.

Lee Lynn continues, "Anyway, *then* we meet everyone in the cafeteria. Claire, too. She's got Chris Butler and the Crocker boy with her today helping her move some artifacts. So there'll be a gang."

"Nice," says Bree.

Gordon brakes at a light. He leans on his elbow with one hand dangling out the window, grooming his mustache with the other, distractedly. He likes to peer down into other cars, sizing people up, guessing stuff about them, smiling at those who glance his way, his left boot heel hard on the clutch pedal, his right heel hard on the brake.

Then they are rolling along again, all in silence, the Settlement car behind them filled with smiles and waves whenever Lee Lynn or Bree look back through the cab's gun racks and spotty glass. Lee Lynn keeps glancing at Bree. Something is on Lee Lynn's mind besides college.

Lee Lynn drops her arm from the seat back and pats Bree's folded hands. She speaks Bree's name.

"Yuh?" Bree looks at her.

"How's everyone at home? At your house, where you *live*? How are the men?"

Gordon glances over at Lee Lynn, or rather at the blaze of light that is the sun on the lap and chest of her orange dress. Then he looks back at the congested avenue.

Bree says, "Fine. Doin' good."

Lee Lynn says quickly, "Good. Good." Now Lee Lynn is doing something with her mouth, a small mouth for so long a jaw and chin, and what she is doing with her lips and teeth seems to come from desperately working over much cumbersome indecision. "What's your father like? I've never met him."

Bree giggles. "Old fart. Funny ideas. Sometimes he's a total nut."

Lee Lynn stares intently at Bree's profile. She works her mouth around some more, feels the back of her own long lovely neck for renegade hairs, then strokes the sleeve of Bree's black T-shirt, the shirt Lee Lynn made just for Bree, finished yesterday morning, just in time for this special day. "Well, if you *ever* need to have a woman-to-woman talk about anything, if you ever have any secrets you don't want passed on, I'm at your service. Okay?"

Gordon seems not to hear any of this. They are passing the old Department of Human Services building . . . two glass doors on their left across the wide street . . . he has his eyes narrowed on the yellow brick front, the sidewalk, fifteen-minute parking signs, no-parking signs, now a Harley passing in a tumble of deep sound, now a truck . . . tractor trailer . . . hauling milk. Now more cars. The yellow building is gone, only a crabbed yellow blotch shivering in the side mirror.

Bree's voice. "Same here. I'm good with secrets. If you ever have any to spill." She laughs, a light yet deep laugh.

Two spots of heat and worry blister on Lee Lynn's snowy face. She sighs a tiny sigh.

 University of Southern Maine.

Small grassy lawn with only a few big trees. A *few*. No Ivy League shade here. Some cement rectangular things to sit on. Rectangular shadows made by buildings, and other shadows shaped like the shrubs they are laid out next to. Nothing much here is old or awesome. The architecture here was hatched out in glass and plastic and uniform brick from those recent and current eras of soulless pragmatism, efficiency, and cheesy-is-next-to-godliness resignation. A lot of oil-splotched gray tar. And cars, cars, cars.

As Gordon walks through the parking lots, which are connected by sets of cement steps, he glimpses people staring at him. Not in the old way. Not in the way he has always drawn attention, with his size and his bearing and his penetrating pale eyes and that other thing, solicitousness. No, this is a new way. It hasn't been hard to deduce how there's a tidal wave of whispers and grunts behind the scenes, all those who call Ivy and the agencies and cops, plus all those agencies and cops, and reporters who receive the calls and a lively thicket of gossipers between. Such as Catherine, Claire's friend. Chatty Cathy. Or is Gordon just being paranoid? Maybe Ivy Morelli had exaggerated all the complaints anyway.

Nobody frowns at him or hurls an ugly remark. It's just those open-faced WOW looks and some people nudging an acquaintance to whisper. With some, he smiles, nods. With others, he feels struck with small terrors. He hates being alone away from home, from the Settlement, from Egypt, from his responsibilities, yes, but also from that space and place where he has earned prominence. Here, he is nobody, just a husk of matter, which infamy or fame add only illusion to. The knowledge that some of his family awaits in the cafeteria is a desperately good feeling. But then he feels ashamed that this is so.

Woman is home. Man is world, right?

So they used to say.

Think of the thousands upon thousands of men and women alike, who hold the world in the palm of their hand.

Guillaume St. Onge. Without the greatness of his land, woods, and fields, without the community of his kin, without his work of wielding the seasons, sun, and tuber, Settlement laws and justice, savagery and tenderness, what is he?

And yes, yeah, in some way, infamy feels good. It's better than desolation. And in the end, Gordon really does hold *all* people dear. So he really is very distinctly and utterly two men. Or perhaps a sort of Minotaur, piteous, cursed to live his life part cordial man, part pawing-hoofed nerved-up beast.

The serving section of the newish Campus Center cafeteria is about to close for the day. It is quiet but for small muffled clatters beyond the kitchen doors. A lot of abandoned-looking mocha-colored plastic chairs under giant flags hung like banners from the crisscrossing conduit and otherwise useless space above, auditorium high. Babylon flashes into Gordon's ever-so-sensate heart and mind. A few people stand around, several chunky twenty-year-old guys in oversized flappy knee pants, oversized flappy T-shirts, and white golf caps. All too young-looking to be college men.

Nobody is sitting with trays except the Settlement group, which has a couple of tables together near the rows of royal blue "please recycle" bins, within view of the cash register and the woman who works the cash register, who, yes, keeps glancing at Gordon.

Between the tall windows are early 1900s photographic portraits of formally dressed New England men and women of African heritage. An exhibit arranged by Black Studies students, this explained on a pedestal sign.

Gordon gets right to the job of eating, digging into a huge slimy pile of American chop suey, tearing into a buttered roll, slurping his milk. Little milk cartons. Four little milk cartons all opened and ready to go on the table beside his tray.

Claire appears at the end of the table looking quite nice in one of what she calls her "adjunct outfits:" mid-calf length smocked gray dress and flat shoes. Her sleek graying (just at the temples) black hair is done up in a loose bun, a piece of embroidered Tyrolean cloth, very Swiss-looking, knotted around it. She seems, as ever, in charge, more chairman or dean than adjunct, willing slaves hovering. Chris and C.C. from the Settlement group and two freshman students, introduced as Jake and Sam, are taking orders about leaving three brown paper bundles with security and three with the mailing room. Chris (Samantha's brother) was born with "thin skin" and is plastered with scabby sores throughout his patchy light brown hair, on his face, stick arms, hands, and all over his delicate bearing.

Whitney places her blue tray on the table beside Gordon's, slides her book bag off her shoulder, and grins, flushing. A bouncy, athletic-looking girl, wearing shorts and green leafy print Settlement-made T-shirt, hair in a slithery golden ponytail that flashes as she dips her head to kiss Gordon's cheek above the ragged edge of his beard. And then she kisses the top of Bree's head, which Bree accepts without any giggles, just a nice sigh. "Michelle izzz laaaayte," Whitney tells them in a tattly nah-nah voice. On her tray is a pita bread sandwich and three milks.

Lee Lynn's tray is on the table next to Bree's, but no Lee Lynn.

Whitney sits. "How was the tour?" she asks Bree.

"Good," says Bree happily, raising a spoonful of very bland-looking tabbouleh to her normal, in fact lovely, mouth. Her face squinches. So the tabbouleh is not as bland as it looks.

"The chairperson had a problem," says Gordon around noisy gulps of his chop suey. He has tomato sauce on his beard for too many disgusting moments before he jabs a napkin to it.

"She was sick or something," explains Bree. "Left us a note on the door."

Gordon's milk cartons are all drained quickly. He reaches for one of Whitney's. She watches this theft intently but says nothing. He smiles into her eyes. He tells her, "Bree talks to you friendly-like. And she talks to Lee Lynn friendly-like. She talks to everybody but me."

Whitney looks back and forth between Bree's ruined but noble face and Gordon's striking but pouting face. Then she laughs a little spluttery, through-the-teeth laugh just as there is a burst of kitchen clatter from the double doors opening beyond the cash register.

Gordon says, "For me Bree only giggles, *never* speaks nice. She talks to me like the automated lady on the telephone who says to hang up and dial again. She talks to me like someone in New York telling you how much to pay them for getting on the subway."

Throughout this long complaint of Gordon's, Bree has giggled happily. She now covers her mouth apologetically.

Whitney says matter-of-factly, "Don't blame Bree. She's just having trouble getting used to the company of King Kong."

Now Bree laughs a real laugh, deep and hearty.

Gordon narrows his eyes at Whitney. "That's not the first time I've been insulted with that comparison."

Whitney rests her sandal on Gordon's work boot, a thing she's done since she was little. It is a loving thing, which he does to all the kids and she especially has taken it to heart and returned it. She says, "No, not *compared* to King Kong. You just *are* King Kong. The only one. You been around." Now she whispers to Bree, "Something's going on with Catherine . . . in her life . . . you know . . . Catherine . . . Professor Downey. *Marriage stuff*." She enounces these last two words with a lot of teeth and bottom lip.

The boys hustle off to do more tasks and Claire comes back to the table and says, "I already ate." She pulls up a chair next to Bree and fingers Bree's hair. "Howzit goin', sweetie? This place got any appeal for you? Ready to take the plunge?" Her extra tenderness is, of course, in no small way affected by her knowledge of "the Book." Her steely glasses gleam with motherish authority, her huge breasts and small dimpled hands signify at the moment more power than any man's muscle.

Bree nods. "Peter was nice. And political."

Claire laughs. "Of course! Political."

Gordon frowns. He looks at Bree with one of his blinking, squinting-of-one-eye befuddled expressions. "You *talked* to this Peter guy?"

Bree says softly, "Yes, sir, I did."

Now Whitney giggles. "Yes, sir."

Gordon wiggles fingers to get Claire's attention. "Word has it that the chair*person* is having personal troubles." He smiles thinly. "She canceled on our Bree. With a note. On her door."

Claire gets a stricken look. "Uh-oh. It's been coming on."

"Where's Lee Lynn? I thought she was here," Whitney says, opening one of her remaining milks.

"Ladies' room," Bree tells her.

"Persons' room," Gordon corrects, eyes twinkling, yet another one of his dumb "jokes" inspired by all Claire has, in earnest, told him about Catherine.

Whitney snorts disgustedly. "Gordon, you're so cute." She again pats his foot with her foot.

Claire scans the near-empty cafeteria and doorway, over to the puffy-chair-filled lounge, then looks down at her own hands, gives her silver wedding ring a little spin. "This could be really bad . . . about Catherine. It's been brewing. Not just her husband. Actually, I'm not sure exactly what it is. I'm real worried about her. I might go over to Luther Bonney Hall and look for her in a minute."

Gordon is looking predatorily at Whitney's one remaining un-opened milk.

"Go ahead and take it, Mr. Kong, *sir*. I got 'em for you anyway." Whitney glances long-sufferingly at Bree and Claire.

Gordon snatches the little carton to himself, hugs it passionately against his ribcage a moment. "Thank you, dear."

Something causes Claire to get up quick. Real quick. She is such a short woman, she seems barely taller standing than when she's sitting.

A woman and child have appeared. Almost out of thin air. Quietly standing there several feet away in the open space by the lobby. The woman, early forties, with a soft baggy pale pink top and jeans, no jewelry. Just a wristwatch. Black hair in a frizzy topknot. She has the little boy by the hand. His eyes are Asian. Hers are not. Her eyes are odd. They look as though they've had acid thrown into them. Worse than the reddening caused by puffing grass. This is something else. Many hours of hard weeping? Her brows are very black and thick and shapely. A small dark mole is noticeable over one side of her mouth. She could have been homely, had this or that feature been more or less. But she is beautiful. And the fact that she has been obviously crying is just another fine raw edge to the lovely whole.

The boy's eyes are watchful. He is tiny, not as in tiny baby, but as in tiny gentleman, chin high.

Claire and this woman now grip each other in a hug and Claire commands, "Sit with us, Catherine."

Catherine walks a few paces closer to the tables. She and the boy no longer hold hands. "I'm sorry I wasn't in the office." She looks vaguely around the tables, face-to-face-to-face, but not really seeing. The child now leans into her, his very black hair against her pink top, his eyes finding Bree's deformed face, his eyes widening. Bree doesn't turn her face away but looks down at her own hands.

Under the table, Gordon pushes his work boot hard into Bree's foot, which has only its sock and sandal. She jerks upright, raises her face to look briefly into his eyes. And Gordon is thinking how nice it feels to have Whitney's foot on one of his feet and his other foot on Bree's foot, how if the whole human race could do this for one long moment! He remembers a social science class he took at this very college, that short era of his life when he was in college (six months here, one year at the Bangor seminary). They did an exercise called "Star Power," which involved people placing their right foot on other people's right foot, to force them to make deals with poker chips. It was a lesson in power, class, and . . . as he saw it, revolution. But it wasn't like this, this foot-on-foot fondness thing. This! Kind of like monkey love. He doesn't want to think about revolution now. He looks again into Bree's face. Her eyes are taking in the art professor, Catherine Court Downey. He presses a little harder on her foot. She is trying to hold back a smile. She refuses to look at him. She does, however, push her foot that is under his boot, closer to him, then she flushes deeply.

Catherine is whispering close to Claire's ear, "I need to talk to you alone. Can we?"

Claire takes Catherine's hands, whispers, "You bet." Then turns toward the table. "I'm going to go with Catherine for a few minutes. But first . . . Catherine, please meet my family. This is our Bree."

At the moment, both of Bree's honey-color eyes show, and that nose, flared across the top, the bridge slightly blue-green with veins so close to the surface. Looks like a small cloudy bruise in this sort of light. Her low smoky voice says, "Hi, Catherine." And she smiles.

"And this," Claire goes on, "is Whitney, Penny's daughter. You met Penny when she came in with me for the auction that time. And Whitney has been around here at USM now for—"

"Yes," says Catherine to Whitney. "I've seen you many times in the halls. What are you . . . a niece to Claire?" She looks now at Claire. "You said family."

Claire stands straighter. "Yes. Family."

Whitney, chewing her pita bread sandwich, has given Catherine a little wave and bobbed her head up and down, as to a bee-boppity tune. Now she is looking at Claire, who is saying quickly, "And Lee Lynn is here . . . somewhere . . . women's room, I guess. You don't know her. She has a little baby girl . . . a real doll . . . named Hazel. Hazel's at home." Claire glances at Gordon, who has perceptibly raised his chin, hearing the thunder of Hazel's name. Hazel, who is to Gordon present even when not present.

Quickly, again, leaving no room for questions, Claire continues. "We also have Chris and C.C. with us, but they're on slave duty over at the mailing room. And Michelle is around, too." She hugs Catherine to her side, as they are both facing the tables. "And this, guys, is Catherine Downey, who I've told you so much about. Her work is amazing. I want you all to see it sometime. She is about to transform the Art Department into the dazzling apex of civilization," which is supposed to allow Catherine a cynical laugh due to the funding cuts, but she doesn't, just looks another degree dispassionate and distanced. "And I love her," Claire adds, smooching Catherine's cheek while Catherine stands like a soldier, eyes like blind eyes. Beautiful eyes. Brown eyes. Beautiful brown blind. "And this is Robert." Claire aims a finger down at the boy's dark head.

"Hi, Robert!" everyone at the table sings out.

"You forgot the gorilla," Whitney says around another squishy bite of her tabbouleh and pita sandwich.

Claire has not forgotten. She has just been stalling, disliking the sharp thuds of her heart that have always come whenever she imagined the day Catherine and Gordon would meet each other, the ugly electricity, the opposite poles of the political, social, and class planet upon which these two creatures exist. Claire chortles. "Whit-neee . . . in public, pretend to . . ." She almost says *pretend to honor your father,* but, missing a few beats, fills out the sentence, "to honor your elders." She then dramatically throws out a hand to give Gordon his fitting introduction. "My ex!"

Gordon stands up, always more of him than people expect. Taller than everyone. And right now, no belly at all, and small-hipped, his summer look. And slopy thick shoulders like . . . like . . . well, like King Kong. Dark green work shirt, a little frayed. Jeans. His one pair that fit tight. He, unlike the others, has not dressed "pretty" for Portland. And there, as ever, the belt buckle, copper, the sun's face, the gaze that seems older and weirder than mythology itself, older than all the human story, yes, and all faith, back to a time when the only fire, the only light, the only epiphanies were in the sky and art was brand new. His eyes lock with Catherine Court Downey's bloodshot ones for an impolitely long time. Her eyes, equally impolite, return his gaze. The distractedness and passionlessness of her eyes are *gone.*

Claire squints a little off to one side, thinking, *Hmmm, I should have known.*

And Catherine says, "David?"

Claire says, "No, *Gordon*." Claire suspects David means David Koresh. Waco. Koresh being another head of a teeny nation within the nation called America.

Claire has witnessed Catherine's crackling super contempt for these ways of the world, and so she, Claire, now winces.

Claire also suspects that Catherine has figured out *the whole thing* about Gordon from all the hints Claire has dropped lately like anvils during their summertime phone chats. Too many to count. And if Catherine is anything, she's a gossip, especially if it involves "big bad men." Oh, boy. But whether this speaking the name *David* was Catherine's weary confusion or a sly dig, Claire doesn't know. Claire looks hard at her friend's lovely profile. The overhead cafeteria lights and bright rectangles of afternoon glare from the tall windows across the room slide over Claire's glasses as Gordon takes Catherine's left hand in his right hand, nothing like a handshake, more like a chivalrous man helps a lady from a carriage. He doesn't *say* anything. He just does not let go of that hand, then opens his other hand over the dark hair of her child and Robert is looking square into the face of the copper sun, bewitched. And Gordon looks down at this little kid like he wants to own this kid . . . to shelter him . . . to absorb him, and Catherine murmurs, finally, "Yes, Gordon. I'm sorry. Yes . . . Gordon. Of course. I'm sorry."

Gordon fondles one of the boy's ears while still keeping Catherine's hand in his other hand. The boy doesn't fight off the ear fondling, and he still doesn't look up at Gordon's face, just continues to look at the belt buckle but with one eye squinted now in that silly way of four- and five-year-olds when they exaggerate disbelief.

Across the room, by the open lounge, Gordon sees a man staring at him. When Gordon stares back, the man doesn't look away.

Gordon lets Catherine's hand go. He scooches and says quietly, "Robert." He places both hands on the front center of his belt to undo it, jerks the belt from its loops and, with a twist, the sun is freed. He says, "A boy just about your age made this. He'd be honored if he knew you liked it. You like it?"

Robert holds out his hand. He wears no smile or signs of gratefulness, but he now has a deathly grip on the sun.

Catherine says, "Robert. Where are your manners?"

Robert says, "Thanks." His voice is really high, cartoonish. But not cute. Suddenly shrugging over him is the eminence of great age, old age, vulnerable understandingness.

"Thank you, Mr. St. Onge," Catherine further coaches the boy.

"It's not a gift. It's a trade. When he comes to the Settlement for a visit sometime, he can make me another one. Or whatever sort of thing he thinks would become me."

Gordon stands from his squat, buckleless belt drooping from one hand, sees that the man by the lounge has been joined by another man, who also looks across the room at Gordon. A small sick feeling touches Gordon's stomach. Not paranoia exactly. But the way he has started to dislike that his family roams so freely. All this public, all this hungry hard-assed public, their eyes more like groping hands than eyes. Would he be willing to keep his family in a prison of protection? It has crossed his mind. Yeah, it has crossed his mind.

And now Michelle, the Settlement's second oldest girl, and three young strangers (two girls and a boy) breathlessly arrive, too late for a meal but in time to nibble on everybody's yet-to-be-eaten desserts.

After a few *good-to-meetcha*'s between the Settlement group and Catherine, and a man-to-man squeeze to Robert's right bicep by Gordon, and after Claire and Catherine and Robert walk away, Whitney says, "There's a guy over there with nose trouble."

Now Lee Lynn is back from the ladies' room and her funny tiny Chicago-accented voice, almost as tiny a voice as Robert's, adds something melodic to the conversation at these tables, and her wondrous orange dress is the passive-aggressive focal point of the whole room.

The cashier closes the glass doors to the serving area. A nearby juice vending machine begins to hum.

And now the staring man is crossing the cafeteria, his eyes on Gordon. He is a medium-build medium-height man in a sport jacket, thin hair, shaved face, professorial glasses. Jeans. Sneakers. Gym bag. He puts out a hand. "Gordon St. Onge?"

Gordon says, "Yep," puts out his hand.

"Good," says the man, his eyes glittering all over Gordon's face. He doesn't give his own name and Gordon doesn't ask. The guy says, "Very good. Very good." His eyes laser into Gordon. "Well . . . you give it hell, okay?" And then he turns, eyes grazing with wild appreciation over the faces of those at the table, and walks away.

Lee Lynn stares after him.

Whitney is balling up her napkin. She snorts. "One of Gordon's fans."

 Across the campus ten minutes later.

Catherine stands with her back and shoulders to the door as if to keep out a formidable army. Also the door is locked.

Claire has gone to stand by the window but keeps her eyes on her friend.

In one corner, the boy stands beside a tall rangy silver-gray wood sculpture depicting not a recognizable life form, but a mood or emotion, like nervousness or enthusiasm.

On the way over to this building, Claire had been thinking once again how she has never laid eyes on this child before although she has been friends with Catherine for a few years. Even stayed overnight three times in that Stevens Avenue home. The husband, Phan, she has met. But Robert was at a "friend's house" or on a trip with "my sister who has tourism-a-holism" Catherine had said with a roll of the eyes. But also Robert gets lots of day care. And au pairs. And camp. A busy boy.

Catherine often mentions Robert. "He's a good kid." Or all that trouble about finding his shoe size. And something about his birthday, moving her schedule around for his party, which was "a fabulous party for a fabulous little guy."

Sometimes Claire had the creeped-out feeling that the boy did not exist, was like art, created, rendered fleshlessly but solidly as genius tends to do.

Now Catherine levels her burned-looking eyes on Claire's face. "A counselor is like a lawyer looking for accident victims, like a fungus on a dead tree, like a fly on shit."

Claire says, "I thought you were seeing a psychiatrist."

Catherine nods. "All of the above. Two of each."

"There's a counselor . . . one you mentioned . . . you said he was a friend."

Catherine looks past Claire. "Yes."

"And your regular doctor in Portland?"

"Yes."

"Somebody is giving you a lot of pills, aren't they?"

Catherine nods once. Gravely. "Because I'm crazy and might hurt people."

Claire laughs.

Catherine steps away from the door. "I love you."

Claire laughs. "You're just saying that because my advice is free."

Catherine laughs.

Claire squints one eye. "I have an idea."

In the corner now, Robert is standing with a superhero posture, chest out, arms at his sides, eyes straight down, trying to see how the sun-face belt buckle looks, clasped loosely there to the stretchy waistband of his sporty shorts.

♡ ♡ **Tonight, Secret Agent Jane begins her career in earnest. (Jane speaks.)**

I am in my bed at Gordie's house.

It's him. Gordie. I hear him coming up the stairs. Yes, it's *him*. None of them other ones, Bev or Barbara or Bonnie Loo or Claire, make that many squeaks and *eeeeeks*.

He knocks soft and I say, "Come in," in a sad way.

And he does. He is never mad that I leave the light on all night, even though he says wasting "juice" is killing the world. And he sits on the bed, really squashes the bed down, and he feels my hair and my ear. We don't talk. We both just look into each other's eyes in a sad-feeling way. Although he might not see into MY eyes because of my secret agent glasses with pink heart shapes that Ricardo gave me to be a spy. Mum says they give special powers of vision. I see Gordie's whitish old sad eyes very well.

He is wearing a very wicked-wrinkled black T-shirt washed by the mothers.

Gordie tells me we can go visit Mum again real soon. I say, "It's about time." Jail is far away but Gordie never says it is wasting up all his gas, which is what he says if you say the word: *McDonald's*. Or *Burger King*.

Before Gordie goes back to the stairs, he reaches down into a pocket in his pants and it's a small black notebook, very small and flat.

"What's that?" I ask.

"A spy book," he says and gives it to me. He says, "It's just something I found around and thought you might like."

"Thanks," I say.

His giant face comes down and his mouth smells like Cheerios although you don't see too many Cheerios here and he squashes a kiss on my head, the *side* of my head by my ear. "I love you," he says. And he squashes a long, long hug around me and I wait limpishly inside his arms. When he drops his arms, I kinda laugh and I bend close to him and kiss one of his big round arms which is the pop-out muscle part.

After he is gone, I open the little book. Ah-ha! What a coincidence!!! This is *exactly* what I need.

♡ ♡ Secret Agent Jane begins collecting evidence.

My secret notebook is too full already. I do the reports in pictures. Much faster. Babies lay around in laps or on the grass wagging their legs. Stuff pours from their noses. And pee and poop are like storms.

Big people are all the white kind like Mum but not pretty. Some say they are Indians. Big deal. Nobody even tries to look famous. This evidence is just for Mum to see. *Only* Mum. Mum says she is "Headquarters." I am her agent. Very secret of course.

Now here is a page of me standing in the middle of all the eating mouths, men with hats, no eyes, food on the floor. That's when Gordie makes me go up there to visit instead of staying in his quiet house. But big problem at Gordie's house. Emptiness. See my sad face. Here's one with me answering Gordie's phone. Hello is coming out of my lips and see my cute top with straps. Here's Gordie's evil cat. He scratched Bonnie Loo's tall small boy. Here is Gordie's red chimney. Here is a sponge in Gordie's sink. Here is Gordie's ratty desk. Here is Gordie's empty refrigerator.

Here is Claire and Bonnie Loo telling a secret while I hide behind one of their goopy trucks. With these pink heart-shaped glasses I can hear every word. They say Cherish, my Scottie dog is *not* at a farm like Mum keeps telling me. Nope. Cops killed Cherish by leaving her alone in the hot car with WINDOWS UP!

See this page ripped out. Once it was my picture of cops but I squashed it under my shoe.

Cherish was not some *junk,* not some old snot rag. She was a *dog.* Get it!

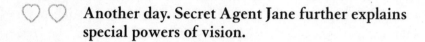

Another day. Secret Agent Jane further explains special powers of vision.

My spy book is loaded now. Here's a picture of Gordie eating *all* the cupcakes, none for me.

 Another day, now midnight. And Bree, witch of duty.

St. Onge farmhouse. Stacks of mail arranged on one desk and in a cardboard box on the floor. Phone messages six inches thick, tightly mashed down over the message spike. Gordon in a rush but ever so tired. He has come straight from the sawmills, his truck parked up on the grass close to the door outside. He snatches the phone off the hook, leaves it on the floor, knowing that the dial tone will turn to the high-tech robot's voice that tries to sound like a professional woman, "Hang up and dial again. Hang up and dial again. Hang up and dial again," and then the high-tech head-splitter. Impossible to ignore.

So then he stands with the high-tech shriek spewing out of the receiver near his foot and he looks up at the ceiling. Jane still resides here at his house instead of at a Settlement cottage though everyone agrees moving her out of here would be best. Supposedly Jane is up-stairs *sleeping,* not spying. And there is, not far from her room, an appointed night watchman (yes, not a companion now but a *watchman* since she has been running off and visiting neighbors up the tar road, neighbors unfriendly to Settlement life. Ooooo does she ever tell those neighbors wild tales. How could an almost-seven-year-old know of the consequences of this almost-year-2000 world? So yes, for now, a "watchman" for Jane.

Something catches Gordon's eye. Envelope on the bare table. His name. In bold calligraphy.

He slips his cheapie plastic reading glasses from his pocket. There is a flyer. CITIZENS ALERT. It is a flyer about seminars being held to discuss "corporations usurping democratic authority." Registration $10. This particular event takes place in Newburyport, Massachusetts. He notes that the date of the seminar has passed. There is an article enclosed as well, made from a transcript of a talk a man named Frank Parenti gave in Palo Alto, California. About citizen sovereignty, about controlling corporations that are not flesh and blood persons, just constructions. *Quo warranto?* you might ask when you believed all that about *the people* replacing the role of kings. And yet the corporation was given human rights (and kingliness) in 1886 in the court case: *Pacific Railroad v. The State of California*.

Sounds almost like the very tirade Gordon gives from time to time. This lefty article sounds, yes, like Gordon's own words but academic, gaseous, abstract, chains of clauses, weeds out any enthusiasm by the everyday person, black, red, white, or yellow. A discussion for the honor-studentesque.

Meanwhile, televisions shout at everyday people. Frantic hold-your-attention noisy corporate sales pitches.

Gordon thinks professional-class lefties are either afraid of insulting the common man with the TV-style hype or they just don't like the common man enough to try to pull them in. Maybe they just want to show off in front of the muzhiks.

And yet, Gordon stares dreamily at the flyer, not "tsk"ing it.

He stands with a shoulder against the cabinet, eyes moving from left to right, and he understands that this is not like his own words in more ways than the academic part, something is missing, something that is sympathetic and brotherly in ways connected to a man like his old friend Rex, for instance. *What is it? What is it? What is it? Hang up and dial again*. Ah, yes, what is missing is HOME. And family. And boundaries. "Redneck" is missing. Yeah, we rednecks are so much like the red neckerchiefed Blair Mountain coal miners of not so long ago. Ah, the tongueless sorrow and homely rage. He understands that these seminar people, lefties, progressives, socialists, professional class activists are not even the same species as himself and Rex. They even *walk* differently. They hide their cards. They ask questions instead of teasing, bragging, and gossiping. They are

always in positive mode. They don't come to this with brotherishness, sorrow, and rage.

When he is finished reading, he feels the edge of the paper . . . the
flyer and the article. Now he reads them again. The flyer. The article.

He flips over the flyer and there in Bree's bold calligraphy. *WE
ARE NOT ALONE.*

He picks up a fresh envelope from a box of a hundred. Addresses
it for the US mail. On a scrap of paper, by the stingy bluish light, he
writes:

Dear Brianna—
    *Thank you for the info. You're right. Looks like something's happening
out there in Lefty Land.*

Love,
Gordon

 **In the little attic bedroom of her family's house, the
room with the octagon window, Bree dips her fountain
pen, her magic wand.**

*Dear Gordon, I bet they would come here if we wrote them. We have
enough people to make up one of the seminars. It would be educational.
And it would be great to meet with other activists. We're activists, aren't we?*

Love,
Bree
(Your Witch of Duty)

 He doesn't write back.

But two days later, a warm, forever-blue sky afternoon, bone-dry,
a hay day, last crop of the year, Gordon arrives at the doorway between the library and the west parlor. This, just as Del, bearded, long,
lumpy blond dreadlocks, wheels out from the committee meeting, his
wheelchair the kind that is worked with the muscles of the hands and
arms and shoulders, his eyes steady on Gordon's face. He says, "We've
pretty much finished the whole mess." This means the clearance applications and so forth, necessary for the Settlement's new Death Row

Friendship Committee to fly to Texas for their visits with Jeffrey, a
nineteen-year-old in Huntsville, Ellis Unit 1, soon to be moved to
the death house. Jeffrey has written his Settlement friends only a few
halting cards and notes in response to the committee's blitz of cards,
drawings, pictures, and group letters, but in each one that he writes,
he ends with "Soon you see me. My teeth aren't good."

Del says, "The tickets are going to be expensive. We can't reserve
till we know when we can go, but the criminal checks take a long
while . . . maybe longer than he's got. He's got two months."

Gordon makes no reply, just gets a hard bitter look. Then makes
a winky clown face toward a Settlement mother listening to a tyke
reading from a storybook, both now looking his way curiously. They,
their lustrous pinked-by-contentment faces, the antithesis of death
row. Stuart and Penny and one of the Martin boys, Evan, come up
behind Del, their eyes also steady on Gordon's face. Gordon ever-so-
reluctantly turns his gaze back on Del.

"We'll be tourists!"

This is Stuart speaking. This is simulated glee. Remember Stuart?
He's the guy who looks like a red-haired troll doll. And now red-faced
with disgust.

Penny says, "Yeah, tourists," big frown, then she heads out through
the library to the piazzas. Gone.

Del sighs.

Stuart says, "Yuh. I wanna get me some execution postcards and
"Scenic Death" T-shirts for the whole family. And I wanna eat in a
restaurant with electric chair, gas chamber, noose, and lethal injection
motifs. Why not? Progress should be celebrated. Let's immerse ourselves. It's really the empire thing, right? Let's not forget the Romans,
our parental models. So no T-shirts. It should be togas for golly's sake."

Seven-year-old Andrea, one of Leona's, sidles up and hugs Gordon,
takes a deep breath of his loose plaid shirt, which smells of today's
haying . . . sweet . . . and not terribly different from the smell of some
Settlement soaps. But also the scent of the tangy spoor of toil.

"You going, too?" he asks her, and pulls her head back gently by
the hair, to see her face, that bright-eyed Passamaquoddy face, her
China doll haircut really too slippery and short to hang on to for long.

She says, "Yep, I am."

Gordon looks at midget-height Stuart, then to Del in his wheelchair who is wagging his eyebrows in a funny Groucho Marx sort of way.

Stuart says, "She'll be okay. We'll all be together most of the time. We'll all talk a lot before and after. You know. This is school, man."

Del shifts a bit in his wheelchair, pushing himself up with his palms on the chair arms. "We could protect them. We could lie to them. Sometimes it's tempting, isn't it? Even for you, Mr. Truth?"

Gordon says, "Yep." And now sees Bree, who is in some sort of huddle with white-blonde Samantha and brown-haired cherry-cheeked Margo and some others next to the open windows, with spots of sun like white coins in Bree's orange hair. She is standing with her back to him. She wears her usual jeans and boots, but a black blouse with embroidery. That hair of hers. It hangs a little below her beltline in those ardent ripples, and Gordon can't help but note the resemblance to Rex York's daughter, Glory, whose *much* longer hair is not carroty like Bree's, but a dark auburn, her face not freaky like Bree's, but perfect (*shudder*), and she is probably driving Rex and the grandmother, Ruth, crazy with her wild Saturday nights, drinking, and fast driving, but you won't hear Rex speak of it. Yuh, Glory is definitely a different product than Bree but if you squint your eyes you'd think maybe this was Glory here now, especially the way Bree is swaying that perfect bottom back and forth as she talks.

Gordon hangs around the doorway, trimming his fingernails with his buck knife, nodding as each person passes, hearing more details of the Texas trip from each. He keeps his grim expression, while only inches away, still taped to the parlor door, the old photo of the Haymarket Anarchists' bodies hung by the necks. "The price of *real* activism in America" is handwritten in pen. Gordon winces. Yep, humans, baboons, hyenas. He sees these in a hectic snarling chattering, biting blur in the dead center of his mind's eye.

When Bree notices Gordon, she does the usual. Hides behind her hair. In fact, she pretends not to see him, keeps chatting and whispering with the others. Until they are leaving, in a bunch, and Gordon says, "A word with you, Mademoiselle Bree."

With a toss of her razor-edged longish pale hair, Samantha whispers close to Bree's ear, "Sounds important." Then rolls her eyes; oh, Samantha, chronic smart-ass.

Margo, a kind of funny-faced girl with that stammering pink to her cheeks and brown hair, not tall, but stocky-framed like Stephanie, her mother, gives Gordon's elbow a little push. "You smell like beer." Then steps around him into the parlor.

Samantha sniffs him. "Hay. He smells like hot hay."

"Both," says Gordon with his full-latitude smile. "You can't do one without the other."

Some of this group are girls from town and Gordon, not wearing a cap, tips a pretend top hat to each of these. And from them the giggles rain down. And of course Bree giggles along. And then in another minute, Gordon is alone with her in this darkly strong-cedar-smelling room, and asks if she'd like to sit down . . . here or out on the piazza? And she shrugs. So kidlike. She never seems like the same person who writes the letters or painted the pictures in that book, *the only one he knows about* . . . the glory and strain of work and horses and trees and rocks and stars.

He points to a soft chair for her, and snatches a small armless rocker for himself. Straddles it backward, facing her. The library clock *chonnnngs!*s four times.

Bree snuggles in her softie chair.

Says he, "Well, here we are. In the days preceding the execution of Jeffrey."

Bree, sidelong, with her shoulder up, no face, just hair, says nothing. Zero.

"Yessireee," he says.

Then a long silence.

Gordon says, "Um . . ."

Bree giggles, her mind *not* on Jeffrey.

Gordon says, "I really like your letter-writing idea. How you and I write back and forth." He gives his little backward rocker a back and forth easy-does-it push. "I um . . . think you . . . are rarin' to go. As an activist."

She raises her face, enough to show clearly both eyes for a split-second. Eyes that are golden. And brownish. And greenish. With that weird panoramic distance between. "You didn't answer my last letter."

"I . . . um . . . couldn't think of what to say yet." He frowns.

"You don't like activism and you don't like leftists."

"I like your letter-writing idea a lot. It gives me a chance to edit out all my ums."

She giggles.

"And you can edit out all your giggles," he says with a pleased shake of the head.

"Yes," she says, and then, of course, she giggles.

"I think you should invite these people to do one of their seminars here. Fine with me. We need to get all the ideas out on the table." Now his face wrestles with itself Tourette's-ishly.

She says, "They have ideas on how to do away with corporate personhood."

He nods. He is looking at his knee as if that's where her face is. He looks up quickly, catching sight of one of her eyes and says grimly, "You don't want to believe I'm a baby man, do you? You won't accept that fact."

She giggles. Shakes her head.

Says he, "I don't even have a diaper. Totally naked of ideologies, faith, hope, and all those grown-up human traits. I had 'em once. But now I'm just a mean-assed baby."

She laughs, big, smoky, husky chortles. She says, "Stop. Cynicism comes with great age. You've got it backward, sir." Then she sighs. "Maybe . . . mayyybe each tempers the other, you know?"

He says, "So go ahead and invite these dudes."

She is real quiet. Just one eye showing, but not looking at him.

And *he* is real quiet.

The Godzilla of floral fabrics and jumbo sneakers by the window is real quiet, too, his hefty tail stretched out over the floor in repose.

She says, "But you hate corporate power. That's leftist, to hate corporate power."

"I hate everything," says he, flicking a spear of hay off of his thigh onto one of the prettiest rugs under their feet, a braided one in wines, pinks, and blues.

"Everyone says you're moody," she offers, then giggles apologetically.

Gordon turns and looks at Godzilla. He smiles. "He's been reading that same book for about four years. Somebody oughta give him *War and Peace*."

Bree giggles. "Or *Magic Mountain.*"

"Or *Remembrance of Things Past*," he says, jerking a thumb toward the library. "He has the arm power to heft it at least." He looks back at Bree. "Okay, so what does saying left wing and right wing tell us? It says we're supposed to think that there are two halves of something . . . or two little rooms of a main room. Like poor ol' Godzilla over there thinks the universe is made up of just reptiles and toads."

"If you liked the left, you wouldn't be saying this."

He squints at his knee. "True. I'd be devout."

"You don't like the left."

He laughs. "I like *them*. I even know some real communists. Old party people. Nicest people on the earth. Nicer than most. And courageous. I mean, these guys are pure people. In fact, between you and me, I think they're the only true Jesus people. I speak not of a communist structure or the structure's elites, but of *them* who are waking every morning believing their ideology will win justice and fairness for all the world's people who have been crushed by those with technoadvantage and resource advantage but wanting equality for all more than anything in the world. So maybe they are the only *real* Americans. If we are to believe Americans are the good guys."

Now she is looking at *her* knee.

Silence.

Something catches Bree's eye. It's Godzilla. The book moved? No, just the late day August sun fluttering there on the book and the broad green floral print reptilian hand. And one of the alert-looking powerful reptilian arms. She says, "But you're right-wing now? Everyone says you are. I didn't believe it, but maybe I do. I don't know."

He says, "In the fall, I go up on the backside of Stackpole and every year I see a buck and I take the safety off my Winchester and I do what I need to do to be who I am . . ." He gets a mean pinched-lip look. "I don't want to be interfered with." He widens his eyes on her. "Unless I were fucking with innocent people. Stealing, dominating, torturing, giving them unrest." His eyes, neither one are twitching now. "*That's* not about left or right wing, except to say that they both do it, fuck people over, whenever one wing is in charge. There izzz only democracy among lords and ladies and the top. The rest of us are just yard fowl."

"So you're about *rights*."

"Don't say rights! Say privileges. There is no . . . such . . . thing . . . as . . . rights. Whatever you have the right to do it's only if the prevailing bully kleptomaniacs allow it!"

Both of Bree's golden eyes spring wide as Gordon now flings himself out of the little rocker. Stands. Begins to pace. Uh-oh.

"Rights are a fantasy! And basically, left wing in America is a fantasy, too!" He paces in a small circle. He trips on a rug. *Clomp*.

"But these leftists who are doing the seminars are just into teaching. I thought you—"

"They're as manipulated as all the ressst," he hisses, pale eyes unhandsomely bulging. "Foundations, dear! Foundations!"

She keeps her eyes on him, no longer buried in hair. How startling, how harsh he is. She seems not ready for this.

He comes back to his rickety little chair, leans his knee into it so that it creaks forward. "Brianna, there izzz no left or right at the *top*. Up there is the unity of ideology. There is only left and right down here among us crawling grubs." He throws a punch into the air (left), then another (right). "It keeps us busy, eh?"

"I know about their foundations," she says. She stands up. "I am *agreeing* with you. There *are* them *up there*. But we have got to organize to fight them." She stands up. She looks ready to wrastle. Logger girl.

He keeps forgetting how tall she is.

He smiles. "Forgive me."

She giggles. "I think the left has some good information." She is fondling the embroidered flowers around the neck of her dark blouse. "It's about *education*. You know, for the sake of *it* . . . education."

He glances at her hand and then her face. There they are. Both of her eyes. Blazing at him. He moves away, says, "So you *should* invite them. Everyone needs to work through the whole thing themselves. We need all the ideas out on the table."

She sees he is pacing a little again. She hides in her hair.

He comes toward her, starts to touch her shoulder, that same heart-bubbling-over way he touches everybody. But she stiffens, her one visible golden eye wide and rounded. He draws his hand back.

She giggles. An apologetic giggle.

He says very slowly, "My dear friend. My dear conservus, trapped here with me in the very pit of life."

She does a shruggy sweet thing with her sturdy logger girl shoulders inside the beautiful embroidered blouse. Then her face is fully hidden again. Head of flaming hair nods eagerly. "Conservus." Under her hair, her eyes scan her memory. "It means *fellow slave*." She rocks a bit, foot to foot, pondering.

He says, "We'll welcome them, your lefties."

She looks up again. "The seminar people?"

He winks. "We'll roll out the *red* carpet."

She misses the joke. Still pondering. Her mind is a wheel. Her *mind*. So maybe she's not a genius. There are no genius kids here at the Settlement, including Whitney who takes the show at salons and so forth. So what *is* it? Passion. In his own image. The lust for understanding, lest you rot while still breathing. He cherishes her.

"But you watch. I bet they won't like what they find here," says he. "Especially the . . . witches. They will not like the witches."

She cocks her head, listening for further clarification on *witches*. But he is only staring at her. She gulps. "They'll only be here a couple days. And not till winter, I think."

He sniffs the air. From the cook's kitchen, something baking, something yeasty, rolls or bread, snaking around the building and in through the sunny screens, mixed with pine and mown hay in their dry hot articulation.

He moves quicker this time, gloms onto her wrist before she gets jumpy, steers her toward the door. "Mademoiselle Bree. Stay for supper tonight. And sit with me." He walks her through the cool library, out onto the piazzas. "You always avoid me. I'm too loud. I know. Everyone says it."

She says, "I'll write you about it sometime. In a letter."

He says, "Write the giggles in, would ya?"

A giggle starts to gush out but a handy swallow clamps down on it.

They pass the kitchen door and Bonnie Loo, cracking eggs at one of the sinks, looks up, sees them, braces her shoulders, looks away, cracks another egg. *BLAM!*

Near 11:30 p.m., a hard rain.

Gordon hunched over one of the desks down at the farmhouse. Sorting through phone messages and mail. Books and notebooks teeter in ramparts about him. He tosses a copy of *Real Good News* into the box between the desks. Written on the box: *To Library.*

Kitchen door that goes out to the screen piazza is open. The mobiles and chimes are still. But the rain really drums and sings.

Headlights. Engine, eight-cylinder. Truck door slamming.

Gordon keeps on sorting, cheapie reading glasses giving him a slightly old-geezer aspect.

Someone raps on the door. This tells him it's not a Settlement person. But he pulls off the glasses and stands. Finds Bree out there in the rain. So Bree must still feel like an outsider.

He holds the door open for her and his eyes sparkle on her face that, yes, does not look that horrific anymore. Time makes adjustments.

But she still cocks her head at that angle that keeps the curtain of hair semidrawn while she clutches something up under her shirt and peers up at him. "I know it's late. I was by twenty minutes ago. Bev thought you'd be here then."

He smiles. A funny sheepish smile as though he were the outsider, or the owner of the deformed face.

She goes to the little table. Pretty dim, being too far from the ring of cheap indecorous blue that the fluorescent lamp over the desk makes. She lays out some paper, and a bottle of ink, some pens . . . the old kind. She flops down a batch of notes, already blocked in with hurried calligraphy. She says, "I have an idea. It's *no-wing.*" She doesn't look up at him, just pushes the papers around a bit, searching. "No left. And no right."

He folds his arms, eyes twinkling. Waiting.

"Let's call it *The Recipe,*" she murmurs, but she still doesn't look at him, won't look him in the face. All that is revealed to him is that perfect bottom in jeans, her shoulders, her thick swingy hair.

He says, "A manifesto? Tonight?"

"No, not a manifesto. That sounds too commie."

He snorts. A double snort, actually. He steps closer to the table.

"We're going to change the world," she says. "Sort of." She sighs. "Well, we . . . will . . . educate."

He says nothing. He wants to bathe deeply in this enthusiasm. This innocence.

He watches her begin. Her wrist. Her fingers. The blackness of the ink to a bolder blackness on the page. For a moment he recalls his dream of an old woman in photographic negative, skin silhouetted deep gray, hair white and weedy from too much winter, but whirling, dancing, outliving him.

He sees Bree now, her lack of hesitation, *scratch scratch slisk slisk,* dip, page after page, and yet not one single idea on how to *fix* America. Why did she call it a recipe??

For several pages Bree's pen loops and unfurls, blaming *The Thing*. It, *The Thing shows itself only in pieces and halves.*

More pages reveal that *our minds are left in tangled dingle dangles straining to simplify, hungry for the slogans, ohhhh, the Thing's management of our airwaves and printing presses and schools, our art! It has penetrated all of us intravenously. No one is spared, but transmogrified into numbered appliances for its use. Nothing can be realized until we get it out of our musculature and arteries and glands, even as it dictates from a cloud of power through all its organizations, media, shut doors, sticky webs, and systems, both private and governmental. Our technology has evolved faster than we have. We are dumbfounded primates. The race is on.*

She writes on and on, never steering right or left, never grasping for hope from any of the offered opiates, gods, parties, ideologies. Just spirals and Ss and dotted *i*s, the calligraphy of despair, the archaeology of baring the hidden, the deeper bone.

We are the outside, the wee flecks, the creaturely. But we, compounding our voices, if we could, are a single HURRAH!! We are the mothers, fathers, welders, builders, growers, cookers, soldiers, teachers, young and hoppity, old with the remembering, nobody must be left behind. We must rise like a hot mountain of red ants, and then our size will be known. The Thing MUST fear us. THE THING MUST FEAR USSSS! Which comes first, learning who we really are and tearing up the myths? Or does our rising come first? BOTH!!! Or The Thing won't fear us. LET US BEGIN. THEN ALL WILL BE KNOWN. Pick up the drum.

Her calligraphy and splashes of rubric, now in a half ream of damp
puffy sheets, ends, but reaches no conclusion. Except that if you follow
this recipe, you will be ready. For what? For war? Of sorts.

What does Gordon St. Onge do when she dries her pen, lays it
back in its box of cherished mates, and looks into his eyes? And no
giggle, just silence.

 **On Ivy's desk this morning, she finds photos, the flat
cheesy metallic digital dull product of the computer
age.**

They show a highway. Deep ferny ditches. Dirty ragged children
dragging or carrying over their shoulders huge bulging fabric sacks.
One shot shows just humped-over backs with several nearly naked
figures standing in the distance, thigh-deep ferns and steamy-looking
pavement. Faces turned away from the camera, profiles of pain and
fatigue. Here's a frame that shows a dirty childly hand with a wood
tick on each of three fingertips. Ivy looks at the back of the pictures
and sheets. Nothing written. She looks for Brian. No Brian. She enjoys
some gossip with Laura, a feature writer whose cubicled desk is near.
A desk plastered with family pictures and her squeaky rubber dog
toy collection of presidents busts, starting with Ronald Reagan, whose
nose is chewed off. Laura and Ivy laugh and whisper for a while, then
Ivy settles in with her computer, snaps through her lined pad for the
slashed notes on today's column, interviews with used-car dealers, a
charming experience, of course. Ivy intends to slam all of them.

A rustle and a little scuff on the rug. She wheels her chair around.
It's Brian. Fresh from the cafeteria. He holds a melon slice with a bite
out of it. He says, "Good morning, Ms. Morelli."

"What are these?" She nods to the picture pile.

"Kinda Charles Dickensesque, wouldn't you say?"

She keeps silent.

He adds, "Or *Let Us Now Praise Famous Men*. Or the coca fields of
South America or—" He flutters his eyes.

"Or what?"

"Or Home School urchins collecting beer and soda cans over the
border in New Hampshire where there's no bottle law . . . just a lotta

bottles and cans . . . the discarded can being New Hampshire's state flower. Live free or die." He waits for Ivy to laugh.

She forces one.

He continues. ". . . Settlement people make their passive solar collectors primarily from cans with the ends cut out, painted black. Takes a lotta cans. You see, Jeff was coming back from North Conway and came across this amazing scene . . . had a little talk with these people."

Ivy flips a picture over. "There are no adults in these pictures."

"The power of the camera," Brian reminds her, in a robotic voice.

Ivy frowns. She flips through more pictures, glances at faces. Maybe there is, yes, a familiar face or two. "What are you going to do with these?"

"Right now? Nothing. You just keep 'em in your folder. For your spread. For when the big day comes. When this all busts open. We can add some of these to the photo of St. Onge in handcuffs. Keep yourself a nice thick file on this. That's an order."

From here, Brian can see the copy "boy" standing by his cubicle. He scurries away in that direction, melon slice held aloft.

Ivy closes her eyes. The only picture she can see with her eyes shut is the torn and gummy knuckle of Gordon's hand as he grooms the grand effluence of his dark mustache and stares into her eyes. At Kool Kone. Not a photo. Just a memory. See that face of a hundred expressions. The one of seduction, her favorite.

 The grays.

We abducted another specimen, the human Earthlings' pride and joy. We placed it on one of our laboratory tables and watched. Tick-Tick-Tick-Tick-Tick. This one is digital. Oh, whoopee. Our speed is the thing. We are too fast for them to see, too slow for them to believe. Their eyes dilate. Rods and cones strain. Their chest cavities are blind. Their devices x-ray and interrupt, delve and probe and record and spy, but never *see*. No, they never *will* see! They believe we will come to master them. But for what purpose? They are just monkeys with toolboxes. Monkey hands. Monkey ways. Monkey lungs. We have no time for pets. Our eyes beat. Our hearts blink. So we now at last study this sample of their greatest achievement. Time. Tick-Tick-Tick.

Almost five o'clock. Tick. Tick. Tick. Like a tongue dragging over a sticky fruit. BEEP!!! BEEP!!! BEEP!!! Rise and shine!

 Ivy thinks about her father, David Morelli.

It's Saturday. She was with him today. Her sister Ida drove behind with her kids and Maureen, Ivy's and Ida's mother. As foggy as a dry-iced rock concert. The two cars creeped along; to Ivy's mind, walking would have been faster. Ivy sighs. Her father, a junior high science teacher in SAD 55, talks. Yes, he smokes a pack a day. But not in the car. In cars, he talks. Talk, talk, talk. He is small, fussy, thin, with curly hair. What there is left of it. Students like him. "Mr. Morelli." After all, Mr. Morelli is a character. All his inventions and experiments concocted with such glee, not always from the textbooks. And his comical expressions. And his funny remarks, some intentional, *some not intentional*. There is a dopey innocence about him. Like how a few years ago, during third period, there was a construction accident behind the school where the new addition was just beginning. A laborer, running to avoid a collapsing crane boom, fell into the open fifteen-foot deep concrete cellar, broke his back and both legs. Mr. Morelli had snatched his little first aid kit from the closet and dashed out, wearing an important look on his face. Nobody in that classroom laughed any big laughs . . . but they made little tsks of appreciation. Of fondness.

Today he is wearing a dressy cardigan sweater, a sunny-day blue. But in winter, he often wears his long-out-of-date dress overcoat and goofy snowflake scarf so he can ride with the window down. "Winter air is healthful," he has always insisted. Ivy believes he is probably *really* cheating, smoking *in the car*.

Sometimes Ivy and Ida are embarrassed by him. As teens, they'd hang way back in stores, use other aisles. Race back out to the car ahead of him.

Even today, as he pulls the square little Buick up to the tollbooth, fumbling for silver change, he inquires of the toll man, "Are you in the mood for this?" Ivy closes her eyes.

But Ivy's mom, who is in Ida's car behind them, has always been proud of him. Being a schoolteacher (or in this case your husband being one) means you have arrived at a height, some acceptable plateau in this clearly casted world. Are the fine details of minor shames not gaugable by Maureen Morelli?

Ivy's mom calls her husband "David."

Ivy and her twin, Ida, call him "Mr. Morelli." *Everyone* but Ivy's mom calls him Mr. Morelli. Though when Ivy is mad at him, she calls him "Father." But the main thing here, the big pounding pink heart-shaped measure of Ivy's life, is the quickening fact that the definition of the word "teacher" to Ivy means sweet bumbler.

And maybe this is Ivy's definition of a man: someone who makes you furious, embarrassed, and who keeps you awake at night with your attempts to analyze him and then maybe there are secrets behind his eyes.

 Settlement assistants Bev and Barbara (both white-haired, both sun-ruddy, both square, sort of terrier-built) are on the long porch at Gordon St. Onge's farmhouse while six-year-old Jane Meserve, after taking a bubble bath upstairs, now stands naked at the mirror doing commercials for cosmetics and shampoo (although there are no such products in Gordon's bathroom).

It has turned drizzly this afternoon, a little distant thunder, periods of light and dark, air of the porch extra muggy, more like sitting in one of a cow's four stomachs. Usually, Bev reads aloud from a magazine or newspaper and Barbara nods her concerns or approvals and interrupts with annoying questions. Or else Barbara reads and Bev nods and interrupts. Right now, Bev is reading to herself, making the sound "Uh-oh," which means she is about to *share*. She says, "Hear this. Willie Lancaster has been arrested."

"Oh, no. What for?"

Bev reads just to herself, whispering just to herself as she reads along, holding a humid turquoise and yellow tie-dyed bandana to her cheek or upper lip, alternating. Then her glasses need wiping. The steam of the day pushes around them in ship-sized billows. She says, "Something to do with *militia*. He's joined a militia."

"Oh, my goodness." Barbara sighs.

"It says *36-year-old Egypt man released from Cumberland County Jail with no charges Wednesday following . . .*" She trails off into a mumble, reading along again just to herself, now positioning the bandana to her forehead. Some sort of coughing sound uphill beyond the trees. Something agricultural. Something Settlementesque. And the rain has begun to wail.

"What's it say!" Barbara demands.

"Well, seems he was in a bar in Portland with another guy . . ."

"I thought he didn't drink."

"Well, it doesn't say he was drinking."

"Then what was he doing in a bar?"

"It doesn't get into that. Just listen, okay?" She reads along a little more to herself. "He was wearing a gun."

"*Wearing* a gun?" Barbara also has a face-wiper, this one a plain charcoal gray fabric. She just leans into the whole spread-out cloth, whole face at once, as if to smother herself.

Bev says, "He was wearing it in a holster outside his shirt. And he was flashing it around in the bar. And . . ." She reads along silently now.

Barbara pulls her chair closer. "Beverly, will you *share!*"

"Well, Russell Heald, the other man who was with Willie, was also with the militia and this man was preaching from the Bible."

"In a bar?"

"That's what it says. There was a fight. But not with the gun, though what Willie was arrested for was the gun. Sounds confusing. But—" She whispers to herself, then, "They interviewed Rex. While he was at Moody's store."

"Rex York?" Barbara fans herself now with another publication. Gray now-damp bandana on her lap.

"Yes. *He's* in this article, too."

"Tsk."

"So he wasn't in the bar, but you know . . . . .at *Moody's.*"
Silence.

"Get this. It says *Captain of the Border Mountain Militia, Richard York, does not condone Heald's and Lancaster's actions, and insists that although Heald and Lancaster were in the uniform of the Border Mountain*

Militia, they were acting independently and irresponsibly by instigating a fight while armed. He also goes on . . . to say . . . that the militia is a civil defense organization, loosely organized . . . to be available for natural disasters and other civil defense situations . . . and . . . then . . . he says there are nearly two hundred members in his militia, but will make no further comment concerning them."

Barbara moans.

"He also says that New England militias are coordinating with all militias nationally. But he refuses to name any. He goes on a little more about Willie. Sounds like he's mad at Willie."

Barbara moans again. Looks off into the rain with a worried motherly expression, fanning away at the right side of her neck.

Bev says, "This article definitely depicts Rex as some sort of nut. I never thought he was a nut. Just a little too quiet and a little too serious."

"Still waters run deep," Barbara reminds her.

"But *Willie* has always been wild. Nothing could surprise me about Willie." She sighs, gives the paper a little shake, lifts to the next page. "Well, the whole business is just a little bit scary if you ask me."

Barbara says, "A big world. Holds a lot of crazy people."

Bev turns another page. "I know it, dear. But Egypt is *small*."

 Ivy reading the news hot off the press.

Suddenly she freezes and her steely pale eyes blink. She leans close, leans back, but the print still reads the same. *Thirty-six-year-old Eygpt Man released with no charges Wednesday following a firearms incident at The Tap* . . .

It's WILLIE LANCASTER

. . . *William Lancaster, member of the Border Mountain Militia* . . .

Ivy looks around. She sees Brian's head, over there in his cubicle. He's on the phone, the soft *Star Trek* light of his computer giving his face an otherworldly warmth, like warm cream or warm snow. Her eyes settle on the rubber Ronald Reagan with the hole of his chewed-off nose, Bill Clinton's head tipped over on its side, nearly at the edge of Laura's desk.

She tries to remember if Gordon had actually answered her question about stockpiling weapons. Yes or no. Seems he gave some squirrelly answer, seems he soared off on a philosophical zigzag, a friggin' crafty detour.

She thinks of all those little white homely push-faced dogs and the Scottie named CANNONBALL . . . yeah, CANNONBALL of all things. Willie Lancaster's dogs. Militia dogs. Militia people. The militia connection. She holds her forehead a minute, blinking, thinking. Then reads the article through again. And again. And again.

 Ivy strikes gold online.

His grayish eyes aren't at all frigid as she had imagined they would be. Nor do they hold that end-of-the-road dimness that all other people in these police station photos have. His eyes reflect *joy*. As if lightbulbs of happiness are making him slightly squint, maybe a store window Christmas tree, the kind that twinkles and maybe dangles with pottery elves, glass balls, little silver bells, and cellophane-wrapped candy canes. He wears a Jack the Ripper sort of beard. He is thirty-eight years old. (The *Record Sun* item said "thirty-six.") No previous arrest. Not even speeding. Ivy has had eleven speeding tickets. But not William D. Lancaster. His teeth are a little bit bucked . . . how does Ivy know? Because his mouth is smiling a *big* happy smile. Ivy thinks the news item on his detainment should have been accompanied by this photo. How its oddness catches the eye! A story in itself.

 Ivy investigates the militia connection, for a quotable quote.

She had called his residence and gotten none other than the very pregnant fifteen-year-old-looking Dee Dee who she'd observed at the Settlement noon meal during her "tour." Dee Dee pleasantly offers to arrange an interview with her father but said it was probably best for Ivy to meet her and her husband Lou-EE down at the Settlement first and they can ride up together "just to be sure Dad doesn't answer the door buck naked. Or worse."

Ivy tips her head. Worse? What could be worse? Bleeding from the eye sockets?

The girl has spoken pleasantly but not laughingly, though Ivy has a clear-as-glass memory of Dee Dee Lancaster St. Onge from the tour day, her grand entrance at the meal, the gray eyes teasing, perusing, smooching, embracing.

And so here Ivy is now. And here is the very and massively pregnant child pumping on the pedals of a wee bitty eensie Toyota pickup, a vehicle born before its driver was, gears crunching, cab sagging on one side, the light of evening revealed through the floor. Ivy compares the speed of the craft to an ox-pulled plow, digging in, biting into late summer's cold earth, willing them backward instead of onward.

Dee Dee admits, "He knows you're coming. He figured it out. I had sorta wanted to—"

"Sneak up on him?"

"Right," replies Dee Dee pleasantly. A store-bought purple bandana girds Dee Dee's lopsided loose French-twist-bun-ponytail. Store-bought gray sweatshirt, too short, revealing the school-globe-sized midriff, collar and cuffs of a blouse of that crisp 1950s country red-and-white check, little pearlesque top button. No embroidery or patchwork. Not much that is Settlement-fashioned about little Dee Dee Lancaster St. Onge, not tonight anyway. And there are the jeans, the fat black socks and work boots. Wristwatch with black boyish leather band. Pretty little hand working the gearshift.

Meanwhile, oh *where* is Dee Dee's husband Lou-EE St. Onge (cousin of Gordon's from "THE County," Aroostook)? No room for Lou-EE. Not in this Lilliputian truck cab, the shift stick on the floor where a third pair of feet might go. So Lou-EE is stretched out in the rusty, almost frothy, crackly, about-to-rip-off-and-away truck bed. Remember, Lou-EE is the guy with the scraggly *lonnng* black beard, the holstered gun, the big-brimmed brown felt mountaineer hat, no shoulders, hipbones but no hips, *lonnng* legs and *lonnng* arms and green-golden-brown eyes with a black-brown outer ring on the irises. Raven lashes. Riveting beautiful eyes but no rivet in his glance, no zeal, no charisma. Eyes, shoulders, long arms ardentless. His beauty is all poetry but no rhyme.

He rarely speaks. Though when he does, he carries a bit of the melodic, the Aroostook, the ending branches of the Acadian tree, going,

going, gone, the way the younger generations always get ironed out
and starched and made uniform by modern school and TV.

He hugs the Scottish terrier Cannonball close to himself, advising
her to keep her mammoth head down in case a lawman or tattletale
should pass and observe the marvel of this yellow trucklette full of
outlaws on the go. It has been twenty years since the Toyota has passed
for a sticker.

Dark is coming earlier and earlier now in the usual late August way.
The tree tunnel they ride through makes the sky a checkerboard, like
Dee Dee's blouse. They ascend a hill, a leveling, then more hill. Dee
Dee sees fine with just the parking lights and the pinky gold twilight,
and that semiradar of being home sweet home.

At the top of the next grade there's an opening on the left but the
glory of the western sky is made inferior by the pinky-green-orange
super progress mercury light on the garage side of a modern house.

Dee Dee nods toward that house. "Both of them are teachers. One
the mom, one the son. Both always trying to teach Dad."

"Teach him what?" Ivy leans forward to try to see through the
schoolteachers' proud cracklingly clear lighted-from-within picture
windows.

Dee Dee shrugs. "Everything. They keep calling the constable on
him." She sets the truck's turn signal (which *works!*) to blinking frisk-
ily, an unnecessary, dutiful action given that there's not a soul around.
Ivy considers this an elderly person's trait, quirky for a person of Dee
Dee's generation.

The vessel now dips achingly and squeakily and squealingly and
putt-putt-puttingly to the right. Ivy can make out pine trees with
trunks the diameters of living room rugs. Just woods? The wee truck
ka-chunks to a stop behind an old tarp-covered snowmobile. It's for
certain there is no light in the Lancasters' windows, their mobile home
wedged back inside the dozens of shoulder-to-shoulder pine giants.
In fact, there are two connected mobile homes. It brings to Ivy's mind
a train of boxcars, ghostlike in some creepy freight yard.

Dee Dee is already out, slamming (and slamming it two more
times) the truck door and she is talking low to Lou-EE, who must be
climbing out of the crispy rust-riddled truck bed because the truck
with Ivy still half in it whimpers and shivers and *boings* all over and

Ivy is now fully stepping forth, hefting her shoulder bag and feeling her right earlobe with the small twinkly star earring, rhinestone and pewter, yes, dressy. And her most conservative newspaper reporterly outfit, gray and black top, khaki trousers, prissy shoes with leather-looking ruffly rumples across the top. A flick of cologne. This is also her funeral outfit, whenever that need arises.

Small dogs are barking inside the trailers.

Dee Dee starts ahead. Lou-EE and Cannonball hover around near the edge of the piney blackness, Cannonball's nose snorts deeply of the six o'clock (though it's not six o'clock) doggy news on grass stalks and pebbles.

Ivy can vaguely make out more vehicles. More buildings. More stuff.

Ivy can't see Dee Dee but as the girl goes along the path ahead, the scrunching of twigs and scuffing of grit leads the way in audio. Ivy follows, feeling with the toes of her funeral shoes. Small dog voices make increased uproar in the trailers.

"That's his shop."

Ivy jumps. She didn't know Lou-EE was so close behind.

Ivy says, "His shop?" Her eyes are adjusting enough to see Lou-EE's pointing hand, the fingers long but muscular. Maybe not ardentless, just wisely heedful. The building to the right that he is referring to is built snugly among the mighty pine trunks. Unlit old windows like a church or courthouse. Kind of cuckoo and eerie when viewed out of context, in this dark unwelcoming.

"That's where Dee Dee and I live." Lou-EE's hand points to a place beyond the shop.

Ivy sees a five-story pink (or yellow?) rocket-shaped house overly close to the shop. No lighted windows there, either.

"Dad! Daaadd!" Dee Dee's voice broadcasts inside the mobile home.

Small white forms surround Ivy. They snort as they breathe in her socks and dressy pant legs. She can't see Cannonball at all. Black against black. Just these dozen white shapes that shift like a Rubik's cube. Ivy recalls how they roam the Settlement but are always referred to as "Willie Lancaster's dogs," yes, rangy, curl-tailed, mash-faced, long legs in back, short in front, no collars, free as the breeze.

"Daaaad!" and "Daddy! Pleeeeze!" Dee Dee's voice lurches through the rooms of the trailer, a light here and there filling a

curtained window, flicking on, then off. The two trailers are connected by a trellis "hallway," which Dee Dee passes through twice,
once each way, calling all the while. And Lou-EE seems to have va-
porized, he's so soundless. But now Ivy discovers his pythonesque
form on the path still behind her, silhouetted by small bands of the
pinky-greeny-orangey light from the neighbor's house as they slant
through the Lancasters' many formidable pines.

Ivy proceeds closer to the door through which Dee Dee went,
startled now by the vague shape of a portable chipper and a sided-up
flatbed truck with lettering on the doors parked close to the steps.
A slash of the space-age light from the neighbors causes part of one
fender to glow. Ivy leans toward the truck and, wide-eyed, works
through the letters. WILLIAM D. LANCASTER & SON/LAND-
SCAPING AND TREE WORK.

Something touches Ivy's trouser leg. She gasps audibly. It's just one
of the white dogs, though most have gone out to sniff further news
from Dee Dee and Lou-EE's truck.

Lou-EE is now *somehow* ahead of Ivy, had slipped by like a fish,
heavy revolver, huge hat and all, and he's on the step of the mobile
home. Now a snapping sound. And Dee Dee is saying from the doorway, "He's here. He's just . . . not here." And most of the white dogs
are now suddenly on the step, too. And the snapping sound again.
Lou-EE says, "Porch light is burned out."

Dee Dee tsks. "Too coincidental. It's one of Dad's conspiracies."

Ivy sees no reason to get much closer to the step. Pretty silly to have
EVERYBODY on the step.

Dee Dee says pleasantly, "If we wait, we'll win."

Ivy says *pleasantly,* "I'm not in a rush." A white dog is snorting at
her foot, a slobbery hoglike snort so powerful it pulls her sock away
by inches. Her eyes are adjusting better and better even as the twilight
is withering from pinky-blue to purplish-slate out beyond this strange
bodeful forest and beyond the brilliantly lit teacherly house. Suddenly
a FACE is floating before Ivy's, a hideous nonhuman FACE. Ivy grabs
at her own throat, sort of strangling herself. Ivy admires the shape of
the body and stance. Jeans. Bare feet down there, pale. No shirt. Pale,
tight, agile-looking physique. Not a burgers, fries, and Coke man. Not
a desk man. She knows that six days a week, William D. Lancaster is a

tree-climbing man. Ivy decides the mask is a mouse or a squirrel. Yes, exactly. Rocky the Flying Squirrel, friend of Bullwinkle the Moose. It is supposed to be a cute mask, maybe? Like the TV cartoon was? But here and now, it is otherworldly and makes Ivy's heartbeats hurt.

"Dad," says Dee Dee. "This is Ivy Morelli from the *Record Sun*. She wants to interview you about guns in general. Ivy, this is my father."

Ivy puts out her hand, "Hello." She had expected *noise*, from all she'd heard about Willie Lancaster. Hooting and tee-heeing and bragging and carrying on. But the eyes in the mask just gaze (or so it seems) into Ivy's eyes, the mask's frozen grin (with squirrelly teeth, a little bit like Willie's real ones in the police mug shot) speaks not. Oh, this izzzz disquietingly reminiscent of Gordon and his yellow horned head and silence. It's not the thing itself but the doubling effect that creeps our Ivy out so that her neck hairs turn into spiders.

But now the big squirrel shifts his bare shoulders, arms raising out from his body just a bit, making him look even bigger. Again the "other" is exhumed; she sees Gordon in the creamy yellow dawn wearing his papier mâché head, big, crayon-yellow, horned. That writhing silence. What *izzz* it about masks and silence that men just love to put between you and them? *Leaping lizard dicks*!

She says evenly, "Out collecting nuts?" Ivy likes how she just said that. She feels his power dissolve like shattered bulletproof glass.

The squirrel's shoulders shift again and he moves closer to Ivy just as Dee Dee is trying to situate herself between them. And several white dogs are also moving along en masse to be part of this important congress. The squirrel's paw looks to be nudging at Ivy's hand . . . to finally shake hands? . . . but something is in his hand and Ivy is recoiling. Willie swivels and slaps audibly the object into Dee Dee's two hands, which she had been quick to position there, like clockwork, she being as quick and fluid as her dad is. And predicting his moves? These are, yes, spooky people.

Ivy has remained two steps back. It seems there can be no normal interviews in this part of the world. Her next flashback is Gordon at the merry-go-round, refusing to talk sense and chasing her to her car with his bull-bear-gorilla routine.

Now Dee Dee is speaking pleasantly and the plastic squirrel face is nodding and grinning. "You got them." She sighs. "All natural."

Voice from the mask: "As opposed to *super*natural . . . oooooooweeeeee. Burn you at the stake when you order from the *Super*natural Vitamin Company." Now the squirrel *suddenly* makes a crackly scream and hops around as if something is burning his feet. The crowd of white dogs bursts apart, then recoalesces pantingly.

"Dad gets deals," Dee Dee says pleasantly, turning to Ivy. "It's some club they all get stuff from through the militia. Colloidal silver-making gadgets and that kind of stuff." Dee Dee kisses the bottle. "Thanks, Dad."

"Don't let Lou-EE eat them," Willie hisses.

Lou-EE remains in the distance. He's squatted down and Ivy can now make out in the gloom the Scottie dog Cannonball receiving ear scratches there. She is said to be Willie's dog. But maybe Lou-EE believes she's his own.

Dee Dee turns to Ivy again, "These are prenatal."

Willie is now also turned to Ivy staring. Can he smell through Ivy's dressy cologne her fear? Or just see her cowering soul with his naked eyes? Or maybe it's his "Willie radar." Dee Dee had chattered earlier on about her father's "radar" for when it comes to his many triumphs of agility and being at the right place at the right time. Whatever it is, Ivy can tell, Willie loves people's fear.

Dee Dee is rolling the big bottle in her hands. Her little silhouetted ponytail shudders with happiness.

Willie steps closer to Ivy.

She impels herself to remain marble firm.

"*You* pregnant?" he asks her.

Ivy snorts.

Willie snorts, too. "I can get you a deal, dear."

"I don't need any, thank you," Ivy replies not as icily as she believes he deserves because she is finally becoming trained to the fact that react-ing is *un*professional, or rather it is unproductive. What would a CIA operative do in enemy territory? Maybe women cuffing and scratching is on par with women fainting? Ivy now smarts with patience.

"*You* are pregnant," he says.

Ivy sighs.

Dee Dee says pleasantly, "Dad, she's here to interview you. Let's go in and sit down. Guns. Remember? Your favorite subject."

Willie's body is still frozen in place, his eyes still frozen on Ivy. "It's war, Nancy. You know? A war is on us. And we all get shell shock. *Some* of us get pregnant. But all of us get shell shock." He steps closer. To Ivy.

She doesn't flicker a muscle. Meanwhile, there is a decisive probing-snorting-grunting around her feet. Seems a tongue is wrapped around one ankle.

"The medic will deliver!" Willie exclaims, then howls wolfishly, grabs for her hand.

Her feet jerk, both of them, but not a leap. He has her by the wrist. His hands are coarse, woody. And dry. And gentle. He pokes a bit to get a pulse.

"He's *not* a medic," chides Dee Dee, her face a heart shape of gray floating near, grainy in Ivy's peripheral vision. "*Daaad,* please. Take off the kiddie mask and let's sit down."

"All the lights are off, dear," says he.

"Well put them *on,*" Dee Dee says with a tsk.

"They're all broke."

"But I had them on in the house a minute ago," she insists.

"They're all broke now. Light is an aid to *spies.*" Revolves his plastic-faced head meaningfully toward Ivy's.

Returning the gaze, Ivy's eyes are slitted, imagining she and Willie are duking it out on a sheeeer rocky sky-high pinnacle. Which one will it be who falls to his death?

Dee Dee sighs. "I'm sorry, Ivy. It's my fault. I *should* have known."

Now Willie is taking Ivy's pulse on both sides of her wrist. "Your heart has . . ." Seems he is squinting at her. "Heat. That means you *are* pregnant. Or—" He moves his pulse-taking up to her forearm under her long sleeve. "You *want* to be."

"Dahhd," Dee Dee says between gritted teeth.

Ivy *almost* hears herself roar: *Oh, shut up, Dee Dee.* The girl's whining is now so grotesque. Ivy's sorrow at the Settlement-militia connection is already making too much toxic babble in her heart.

Releasing Ivy's arm, Willie sneers. "No lights. And I keep the mask. I am *not* interested in departing with my identity to the newspaper, which never ceases to side with the enemy . . . and screw up, no offense, dear" (a nod to Ivy), "but I do have to protect myself. This is war. And I am part of a covert defense team loyal to the Republic *only,* not to the entertainment biz that you work for, which means tonight I am nobody. I am just Casper, the friendly ghost."

Perfectly clear. His goofing around is not play. Ivy nods.

Now Willie places both hands on his belt buckle.

Ivy blurts out, without taking her eyes off the whole of him, "Dee Dee, ask him why he and his friend had Bibles in a barroom. And a gun. Ask him what the significance of Bibles as juxtaposed with guns means to the militia movement. Just a few facts on the militia movement, its goals, its activities, that sort of stuff," she presses on. Because this is what Ivy wants more than anything? To be more than a girl scout reporter, to be a real journalist? To . . . uncover . . . the . . . scoop?

Dee Dee says, "Dad?"

Willie yells, "Watch this!" He makes a dive for Lou-EE . . . no, not Lou-EE, but Cannonball, whose stubby thick legs pedal as Willie transports her through the air, sets her down easy-careful between himself and Ivy. "No. No. This won't do. You *have* to *see* this, Miss Reporter Lady," Willie says, and jogs to the shop building, flicks on a light. The elegant churchy old windows spectacularly lay patterns of ivory and lacy gray across the yard. Everybody is squinting because of its suddenness.

Cannonball's tail quivers. It's plain she knows what is about to be. There's a routine here. The man. The dog. Some hand-in-glove almost mythical fellowship, these Lancasters and their big trees and their pleasant savagery. And terrorism. The terrier's deep eyes under her trollesque brows gleam.

"Don't let her in the road," says Lou-EE in a soft way, spoken it seems to someone behind himself though no one is there. Something about this both warms and breaks Ivy's heart. Gentle, gentle Lou-EE.

"She *won't* go in the road, Auntie Lou," Willie taunts, straddling the short-legged large-headed no-necked sturdy black dog with his bare feet.

In a flash-glance, Ivy takes a mental snapshot of oh-so-young Lou-EE, his oversized brown felt hat now in his two sets of long fingers, his black, black hair, almost baby-fine, parted in the middle on his small head, that vulnerable hair-part, his long black eyelashes lowered upon his becoming eyes. A moment ago he had been a boy and his dog, now he is a boy, bereft. Ivy HATES Willie Lancaster. She didn't exactly HATE him till now. Now, yes, full steam revulsion.

"Now for some militia activity. And militia goals. Biblical, and let me concentrate, *Ultima! Ratio! Regum!* No, I'm not about to fuck this dog." He snickers, shakes his head, squirrel face grinning on and on. Willie leans forward bending low, still gripping Cannonball's massive-for-a-small-dog shoulders with his lower calves and pushes her backward an inch at a time, snugger and snugger between his tightening lower calves. He whispers in golf tournament fashion, "The artillery team is now loading the cannon. This one is a thirty-three pounder." More pushing, another inch. Another, though actually Cannonball isn't progressing backward. It's just part of the great and perfected illusion. Cannonball's eyes get a transfixed focus and all is silent around her. There are millions of merry stars in each of her deep slanted beady eyes.

"Cast iron is what we're working with here," Willie's voice whispers.

"She's really Dad's dog," Dee Dee whispers to Ivy.

Lou-EE says nothing to correct this.

"Shhh!" Willie scolds, "Quiet behind the earthworks."

Willie is now reaching behind, takes the end of the Scottie's stubby (but not docked, just stubby) tail in his fingers. He makes a hissing sound . . . yes, like a fuse. "Ready?!!?" Willie has screamed the question.

"Yes!" calls out Dee Dee.

"Ready Lou-EE!!?" Willie screams again.

"Yep," Lou-EE answers flatly.

"Ready, Nancy?!!"

"Ivy," Ivy corrects him.

"Whatever," he says.

There's a fluttering of one of the layers of light. This is the neighbors across the road flashing their big garage lamp. A warning.

Willie therefore gets louder. "FIVE!! . . . FOUR!! . . . THREE!! . . . TWO!! . . . ONE!!! . . . FIRE!!!" Willie's bare feet spring apart and Cannonball tears off back across the yard, across the front of the shop and into the darkness that embraces the rocket-shaped house, residence of Lou-EE and Dee Dee, into the blacker depths of woodsy black backyard beyond.

Now a squeal and a snarling. And *ki-yi-ing*.

"Oh, no," says Dee Dee. She hurries pregnantly off toward the darkness and these sounds of struggle.

Willie screams, "On target!! The enemy took a hit!!"

Neighbors' light flashes again.

Dee Dee returns waddling pregnantly with Cannonball sagging heavily under one arm and she's pushing a dirty-faced, mashed-faced, pop-eyed panting speckledy white dog along with a foot. Dee Dee explains, "Usually Cannonball just makes a loop and comes right back, but poor Boopie was in the loop. Cannonball's in very serious brawling mode." Dee Dee groans as she lowers the *thirty-three-pounder* to the walkway. Cannonball's eyes sparkle and she gives herself a shake. The white dog turns to face the other way.

"Anything else you want to know about the militia, Florence?!!! Or you Bernice?!!!!" Willie broadcasts his voice to include the school-teacher neighbors, but faces Ivy.

Ivy says, "Yes, the Bible. What sort of religion is involved in your group?"

Willie is silent. Then he farts. Otherwise, no response.

Dee Dee sighs ponderously. "It's my fault, Ivy. I should have known he would act retarded. No sense wasting your time on this *thing*." She flings out a hand toward her grinning masked bare-chested father. "This . . . animal."

Willie's voice croaks, "Chicka Dee Dee dear, I've been up since four. I'm going nightie-night. Lights out." He strides through the brontosaurus necks that are his pine trees, toward his shop. How, Ivy wonders, does this guy combine that trudgy redneck gait with the split-hoof bat-fast agility of Pan? The frothy, too elegant, cathedral-esque light collapses within an eye blink. Now again only the deep sea murk of nearly no light. Except now, seizurelike, the neighbors are working the switch of their big garage lamp.

Ivy assures Dee Dee, "Don't worry. It's been fun You're a sweet-heart. You, too, Lou-EE. Actually—"

"GRASS IS THIRSTY!!!" Willie's scream blares into the mountainy twilit distances as he spins around and heads back along the walkway to the road to go piss on the neighbor's lawn, a broad wake of several four-legged white Boopie-like shapes accompanying him.

"Stay." Lou-EE grabs Cannonball, ever protective of her. She'll never know the sheer freedom the white ill-favored dumpy Boopie Lancaster vagabonds have. Lou-EE scoops the handsome black Scottie up, holds her against his heart.

 Ivy distressed.

The road at night, pouring seventy miles per hour under her wheels in a residential zone, is imaginary. Shadows, limbs, manhole covers, four-way stops sizzle in and out of Ivy's thoughts, which is where the real world is. She mulls the Gordon St. Onge–Willie Lancaster connection. It makes her nauseated. All of it a mystery. Gaps, deletions, ums, and detours. Then there's the Rex York guy, the militia captain. But his number is unlisted . . . or under someone else's name. But whoever wrote the police item has it. Or his e-mail. Or *something*. They interviewed him in the store. Caught him off guard, right? Like a weasel. Willie the squirrel, Rex the weasel.

Meanwhile, there's a part of Gordon, some dark seam, not visible yet. She visualizes him now standing before her, only half: one leg, one arm, half a head, one blinking wincing Tourette-like eye. Is it evil, his "other" side? The crisp masked demons frolic about him with Bibles and cannons and pink pine-tree-size penises, clearly in her mind's eye.

Oh, Jesus! Up ahead the dark roadway pulling toward her at seventy miles per hour. And in it the fluttering and seesawing of small luminous patches. A person on a bicycle on the pavement, Ivy's side of the road! She veers just in time, her heart muscle splitting and shuffling like a deck of cards. *Man, oh, man, leaping hamburger!!*

Why doesn't everyone just stay off the road at night unless they are a wall of clarity? Such as Ivy's sporty car . . . a fire-engine-red blur.

 City hall in Portland, Maine. Ivy Morelli takes on the great Kotzschmar.

She sits in a hunch on a marble step of the wide semicircular staircase, running a pen over the pages of her reporter pad, revising one sentence over and over, not wanting to lose the thread of the sentence but exploring all its possibilities. If she loses the basic *feel* of this sentence, it'll never come back. *The power of the great Kotzschmar and the passions of Bach always make one feel as though the hot core of the earth has been given voice, especiall*—"Shit" she cusses. "Sappy to the max." And wouldn't *as though the hot planet Mars was visited* be better? But wait a minute, is Mars hot or cold? Well, it *looks* hot. But it's probably the Papa Bear planet porridge-wise. Or was it Mama Bear's porridge that was cold?

She tries to start over, somehow winds up with the pen in her mouth. Is there ink on her face now?

Feet. A lot of feet to a crowd. Some *slisking* and *clucking* and scuffing past Ivy up and down the stairs. The marble is cold. Nice. Nice against her rear and thighs and through the near-nothingness of her purple pantyhose.

She glances up to think of other hot poignant places besides the earth's core and maybe Mars, and a better, less sappy word than *passion*, and she sees *HIM,* Gordon St. Onge, dressed in a light blue chambray work shirt, dark blue work pants, his usual work boots, but carrying a dress jacket . . . pinkish gray, tweedy, professorial. His hair and beard newly trimmed. He is wearing cheapie plastic drugstore reading glasses, now reading aloud from the concert program to a group of people around him. Clearly these are Settlement people. Kids, one with bloody-looking sores. Not chicken pox. More like a breaking down of the skin. Maybe leprosy?

And adults. One a really frail-looking old guy with crossed eyes, neatly combed white hair and a hand-carved cane.

A whole bunch of handsome, broad-assed, line-faced women in their late forties or fifties, awkward in "society," but Ivy has no doubt they are all grand empresses back in that St. Onge situation in those hills. And the younger one, Bonnie Loo, wearing a soft pink but tight T-shirt and jeans. At least a bra this time, but not dressy like the other women. Her hair is knotted up in a black floral bandana. Her acne scars are more rough and poxy in this light. On her shapely left hand is a plain silver wedding ring. Most of the other women wear similar silver rings. Settlement-made, you can be sure.

Just as expected, Bonnie Loo does not look happy to see Ivy. Ivy feels the steadfast scorch of Bonnie Loo's orange-brown fox-color eyes.

And lo and behold there is the silvery-eyed Lily, depregnanted, must have left the baby home! Yes, Lily who *believes* in computers and called Gordon a pig during the tour a few saggy hot weeks ago.

And there is another young girl. Girlish mouth. Girlish skin. Hair in a wild, youthful, thick rigmarole, orangey-red. But Jesus. What a face. A strapping hourglass-shaped girl. She wears an emerald knit dress that accentuates her shape and looks really swell with that or-ange hair. But the face. Like a face in a convex funhouse mirror. Is she fourteen or twenty? Ivy never saw this one before. She wouldn't have forgotten her if she had.

She remembers well the ox driver who now stands a bit to the left of Gordon. Handsome-as-hell guy in his very early twenties. Dark. Cocky-looking in a jostly kidding-around sort of way. And a brown commercial T-shirt that reads: ARCTIC CAT. Around him are a few teenaged guys and kids, kids who also look familiar. She recalls that the ox driver's old-fashioned nickname is Butch.

And Jane. The kid now wears a weird dress that surely looks made of plastic, splattered with huge gold stars. BIG gold earrings. And on her feet, commercial, very tall-heeled plastic see-through sandals, the clear plastic filled with blue and pink glitter. Jesus. What a character!

And Ivy can't help but notice that included in this cozy little Settle-ment group, listening to Gordon read the after-intermission selections, are State Senator Mary Wright and Majority Leader Joe Savagneau, whose faces Ivy knows *oh, so well*. Holy shit, she whispers, squeezing her knees together, wriggling her toes. *Holy lizard shit. And leaping politicians.*

She sees now that Gordon is looking up the stairs at her. He shakes his head, an oh-god-please-no kind of head shake, then drops both bespectacled eyes back on the program.

Ivy snatches her camera and, still sitting . . . FLASH! . . . slip . . . FLASH! . . . slip . . . FLASH . . . slip. By the time she reaches that fourth frame, Gordon has thrust up two fingers for rabbit ears behind the dark head of the petite and svelte Senator Wright and the senator looks up toward Ivy with a silly grin Ivy has never imagined on that senatorial face. Ivy waves to her, who, of course, recognizes Ivy, the terrorist columnist.

And the ox driver is thoughtfully feeling his scruffily bearded jaw.

And the voluptuously built funhouse-mirror-faced redheaded gal is looking right into Ivy's eyes, smiling a little.

Jane has struck a pose for the camera, hand on hip, eyelids lowered, the look you'd see if you opened a *Playboy*. Or, of course, MTV, which was probably a companion of Jane's prior to the drug warriors pounding down the doors of her home after arresting her mother on Route 202 and leaving the family dog in the sweltering car to die.

And Gordon's plastic glasses are *not* becoming.

And the dresses the Settlement women wear are home-sewn florals with hundreds of tucks and gathers and every sort of overzealous sewing flourish.

Senator Joe Savagneau calls out to Ivy, "Will the Kotzschmar be on a pedestal or a pickle?"

Ivy chortles. "Concert's not over yet. I'm waiting for one little slip."

"One little flat note, eh?" Joe calls back.

"That's right," says Ivy, rising slowly, knees together, camera over one shoulder, shoulder bag over the other.

Gordon's eyes move over her clogs, over her purple-tinted legs and short dress of an old-fashioned yellow print . . . a fabric like the Settlement women might use . . . except this dress is so short and part of a total effect. Cute sleeves. Cute little old-timey white collar. But that one long flashy earring. Yes, one. Yes, long. It drags back and forth over her shoulder. Made of yellow and purple objects . . . beads, shells, and plastic animal likenesses and one tiny yellow and black crap-type die. A *heavy* earring. She hops down the stairs, earring alive and clonking against itself. She is so very young, agile. She sees that the ox driver and the white-haired old feller are watching her, too. She hops, hops, hops the last three steps one at a time.

Gordon, of course, turns the introductions into a playful mess. Some are laughing. Some are scolding him. Senator Joe Savagneau is more boisterous and cheery than Ivy thinks is his natural way. Has he been drinking? Maybe *drugging*. The possibilities for surprise tonight seem limitless. Gordon puts his arm around Ivy. "Come with us afterward. We're doing coffee and whatnot before we head back to the sticks."

"Sure," says Ivy, her eyes glittering over the faces of the legislators. "I'm fascinated." Then she explains that she has really come here with friends, a married couple with kids who she knows will not want to stay out, so she'll need a ride to the restaurant if they are driving, and then home, if someone wouldn't mind.

She gets several offers.

Gordon grabs her nose. Gently. But it *looks* like he's really wrenching it. "Friggin' newshound," he growls.

She ducks her head, her short, purplishly dark, silky hair shimmering from side to side.

Then he pretends to grab her reporter pad, but this time she's faster. And not afraid. She plops the pad into her bag.

Jane says, "I'm hungry."

Over in the other lobby, the crowd is beginning to churn back through the doors to the great cavernous space of the auditorium. There again, up on the back wall of the stage, are the towering pipes of the organ's grand facade rising well over twenty feet high, painted gold. The velvet seats are maroon. A little hard. Well, okay, *very* hard. But there is nothing to fault. Ivy feels kindly tonight.

☆ **From a future time, Bonnie Loo remembers certain things of that critical summer. Here, she speaks.**

A half-hour or so later . . . after the pipe organ concert, we were all squashed into a corner with two long tables pushed together at a not-too-noisy and not-too-dark place that had a jazz pianist.

I was afraid. Gordon was in the reporter's hand, in her palm, ready to be tossed to the great big fucked-up greedy EYE of the public. Anybody could see that she was just a shrewd little hardheaded, tight-cunted, smarmy, brat-bitch opportunist pretending to be Gordon's friend.

♡ ♡ **Here and now, Jane speaks.**

I only ask Gordie about thirty-eight times if we can go to McDonald's. This place is queeeer. The music the man plays is queer. The walls are queer. The smell is queer. When we get to order stuff, you only have to wait for four hundred years for them to make one little piece of cake stuff. I am trying to be nice about this. TRYING. My secret-agent glasses are in someone's car. I have no power.

Gordie sits beside me, his arm around me sometimes. I say "WHERE is it?"

He says these things to me: "Rome wasn't built in a day, Jane." And "Patience is a virtue."

At McDonald's you do not have to have virtue.

 The pleasures of the outside world.

Everyone orders something nice.

It is a pure kind of night.

Chris Butler's hair is real but seems a crude musty brown imitation, clipped, contrite, some of it in clusters, some of it in scalpy splutters. It crabs along his skull, most of it on the left side. He wears a plain gray T-shirt and trousers. The flush of blood shows through his skin in the small territories between sores, and he is *covered* with sores. "A condition," some have called it but it has dominated his world since birth. It is said to be "not a fatal condition." But it is no way no how a life-fulfilling condition, either. Though tonight he is visibly bright-eyed and smiley. At age thirteen, he is a pretty good pianist. It was his idea to come tonight to hear the Kotzschmar played. Because of his too-tender fingers he can never practice enough. But maybe if he broke his afternoon nap in two, he could work in another twenty minutes of practice before the smarting and stinging begins. Imagine playing the Kotzschmar! Oh, to be that lucky organist!

Gordon looks across the table at him. Gordon knows someone who knows someone who might be able to arrange an appointment for Chris Butler and the Kotzschmar to be together some weekday afternoon. But Gordon says nothing now. Not till he knows for sure.

Plump nearly thirteen-year-old Kirk Martin is dressed in a spiffy, mint green, short-sleeved dress shirt and polka-dot bow tie, his once-fashionable little pigtail viewed with two mirrors for fifteen minutes before leaving the Settlement earlier today.

And Jane, her chin held high, hair in a pile of jittery ringlets that one of the other Settlement girls fashioned for her for tonight. Her dress is made from a slimy synthetic, a pattern of "glamour stars," what Jane knows any self-respecting, husky, growly, hip-jerking MTV gal rapper star gripping her microphone and licking her lips would

wear during her finest hour on a concert stage before those countless blazing cameras and breathless fans with burning eyes. But at
the moment, Jane's expression is long suffering, her beyond-galaxies
dark eyes almost on the verge of tears. "WHERE is it?" she hisses.
Wanting only Gordon to hear.

He ignores her.

While Jane is seated at Gordon's right elbow, Brianna Vandermast,
newest Settlement "student," is on Gordon's left, her hair an event, a
volcano there, in the prophet's periphery vision.

Whitney and Michelle. Look like sisters. Both with almond eyes,
broad faces, one dark, one fair. Both girls are discussing a course at
USM, philosophy, far different from Settlement yak sessions. More
academic. More ordered and formidable.

Butch Martin doesn't tease his brothers tonight, just smiles his little-
bit-smirky but mostly gentlemanly smile and feels his new short beard.
He is thinking about how he hates jazz piano. His idea of going to a
wild rock joint went the same way as Jane's insistence on McDonald's.

This is a tablecloth restaurant. Old brick walls on two interior sides,
brick arches around windows of leaded glass scenes lit electrically from
behind because they were plugged up and boarded up before new
buildings went up right against them. The two exterior windows on
either side of the piano, those frame the street where the clear evening
is electrically lighted a harsh pink-green-purple for "safety." So the
fake scenes are pretty, the real are not.

All the young people watch Senator Mary Wright acting nutty,
giggling. She wears quiet earrings, a quiet brown outfit. Wristwatch,
wedding ring, and diamond are all white gold. She has never once
looked at her watch tonight. She seems to be right where she wants
to be. She has ordered only one drink and is making it last.

Senator Joe is a small man, sandy-haired, dressed really sharp in a
camel-color summer-weight suit jacket and a tie with a fabric of pink
and creamy yellow kites and clouds on a maroon sky. His shirt is a gusty
blue. Did he, too, like nearly-thirteen-year-old Kirk, use the mirror for
fifteen minutes front and back before leaving tonight? He has already
had two drinks. He leans forward, wrists on the table, telling the kids
about the time he and his wife went to hear the Kotzschmar played by
a different organist who, to his and Denise's horror, "never touched

the big pipes. It was just roller-skate music! Toodle-toddle-toodle-toddle. All those wasted big BROOOOM BROOOM BROOOOM! pedals and whatnots. It was awful. But guess what happened. Bells started ringing. Fire alarm. The doors opened onto the sidewalk and outside on that side street, fire trucks were everywhere but . . . no fire. It had been a false alarm. Denise and I never went back in but we felt kinda . . . bad . . . you know, guilty. What if *nobody* went back in. I'm sure some did. But Denise and I hightailed it. I mean, those hard seats are torture if you aren't enchanted."

Everyone likes this story.

The reporter, Ivy Morelli, has a laugh that is deep and raffish for such a small person. Her violet-tinted black hair shimmers in a fairy-talesque way, and that earring with so much "subject matter" really draws people's eyes. Ivy likes wine but has ordered nothing to drink . . . just water.

Whitney asks, "Can we get tapes or CDs of people playing those Bach selections on the pipe organ?"

Senator Joe says, "There's a really good series. I'll get you the name of it and the address and mail it to you."

Whitney looks at Gordon. She knows that tapes of any kind for the audio tape players are okay. He's even beginning to bend concerning the VCR idea. But concerning almost anything hi-tech, the reflex is to check his face to be sure. She and other young people often had whispered discussions about what Gordon would do if he found out there was a television . . . regular old commercial television . . . hoarded somewhere in one of the Settlement houses. What would he do to it? What would he do to *you* if it was yours? *Tantrum,* Whitney always says. *He'll lay on the floor and kick*.

Note that Gordon has not ordered any alcohol.

Jane narrows her eyes. "Where's my cake thing? A hundred miles away?"

Gordon says, "They'll bring everything soon. It's busy here. Remember, Jane. Patience is a virtue."

Jane swallows, turns her face slowly toward Gordon. She says in a sugary way, "Please do not say that virtue thing again. It is not funny." She pushes his napkin and silverware to the middle of his place mat.

Gordon lifts his long arms and makes a big hug with one arm around Jane, the other around the red-haired Bree, enormously tender, a bit protective, a completion, like a circling of moons around planets, and planets around sun, leaving a summer, arriving at yet another summer. And Ivy, who sits directly across from Gordon, watches this with alertness. Whenever his pale weird eyes come around to settle on her face, her feet under the table jiggle anxiously.

At the other table, Bonnie Loo, her hair shuddering out from the squeeze of the small black handkerchief stirs her coffee, watches only her coffee.

Duotron Lindsey International arrives.

The conversation about Bach and pipe organs takes them all until the desserts come. Jane pokes hers suspiciously.

A woman-sized mermaid is suspended high above the bar. Her fishtail is truly convincing, handsomely stripy, black against silver, perfectly mackerel. But her eyes are a little crossed. Her lips shine a carnivore red. And she grins. Her teeth are *real!* Not human teeth, but maybe shark teeth? A red light has been directed on this creature. The bar area therefore is a lot less blah than the eating-at-tables part of the establishment. More like the proverbial "joint," wonderfully creepy.

Gordon has slipped his arms away from Bree and Jane to deal with his Maine Moose Maxi Mousse.

A guy in a dress shirt open at the throat, dark rounded eyebrows, and a rounded nose, clean-shaven with trim dark hair suddenly appears at the table and asks in a syrupy voice, "Everyone having fun?"

Faces turn toward him.

He presses on, "So what are *you* doing in Portland, Joe?" Then, "Hey, Senator Wright. What on earth brings *you*?"

"I live here," she says with a laugh. "It's all right for me to be here."

He pulls up a chair. "Am I invited to join?"

"This is Alan Sutherland." Senator Mary pats the newcomer's hand. "He seems to be joining us." Her eyes glide around to all the Settlement faces. Is she insulting the newcomer? Or is she playing?

Senator Joe smiles in a peculiar way. "Our young constituents . . . uh . . ." He glances at old cross-eyed Reggie Lessard, who
is looking at him intently. "Our *constituents* are all from Egypt. Go
ahead, everyone. Rescue me. Tell him your names."

Old Reggie Lessard has perfect hearing. Keen hearing. But he understands very little English. He just keeps looking with cross-eyed
keenness at Senator Joe's mouth and shoulders and hands. But while
the others speak their names, Reggie gets the idea and when it comes
his turn, he speaks his name *Reginald Lessard* with all sixteen lustrous
rolling *R*s. And now on to the next name and the next, each speaking his or her own, though just before Ivy opens her mouth, Senator
Mary says brightly, "And this is . . . ta-dah! . . . Ivy Morelli from the
Record Sun."

The guy turns his somehow dagger-like but teasy dark gaze on Ivy.
"Ah . . . yes. I *know*. Hello, Ivy." His voice. Warm cake.

About eight tables away and beyond, the piano zigzags through
a kind of thin jazz number, thinner than the last, which was
thinner than the one before that. A waiter passes with a heap
of gory-looking pastries that catch Jane's eye and cause her to
slump in her seat, arms crossed, underlip puckerish, her dessert
dish quite empty. When it is her turn to give her name, she sits
up, smiles a sudden big smile, and announces, *"Jane Miranda
Meserve"* with just a little bit of sensuous MTV-style tongue over
the bottom lip.

"And this is . . . ta-dah! . . . Gordon St. Onge," Senator Joe says,
not to be outdone by Senator Mary. "Gordon is . . . uh . . . headmaster
of a school. Sort of."

Many Settlement chortles erupt.

"Oh, master!" chirps a young'n.

The stranger nods vaguely, eyes on Gordon's face too briefly, then
sweeping around to all the faces, a big, wide smile, then eyes back
on Gordon's face while Senator Joe explains that Alan is a lobbyist
and names the lobbying firm that represents the interests of Duotron
Lindsey. Many Settlement folk are squinting at the devilsome muzzi-
ness of such a universe.

"What's that?" young bow-tied Kirk Martin asks.

Bonnie Loo's murderous golden brown eyes settle on this jolly newcomer. Samantha Butler, her pale hair extra shivery tonight, whispers (not whispery enough) to Kirk, "He is an enemy of the people."

Alan's leprechaun eyebrows wag, dark eyes on Samantha. "Forget that nonsense, Sammy . . ." (He remembers her name!) Now he proceeds to spurt eloquence (uh, nonsense and a tangle of detours and smoke to Settlement ears) in a voice as smooth as strawberry milk.

Settlement girl Aleta across the table from Samantha whispers, "Duotron Lindsey makes parts for bombs and drone computers. What's he doing in *Maine?*"

Another girl whispers, looking toward Gordon, then Senator Mary, who is laughing along with the lobbyist. The girl's voice doesn't reach the other tables. "If the people had as much money as Duotron Lindsey and Alan's lobbying firm, we'd have access to senators, too."

"We do! We *have* access," another whispers loudly, glancing at Senator Mary and Senator Joe, who are getting more pink and animated, drunk on Alan Sutherland's friendly heat.

"Only because of Gordon . . . you know . . . Depaolo Brothers . . . the money wing of Gordon's family." This whisper goes spectrally soft. "They own a lot of guys in Augusta, I heard. But probably not Washington. That's got a *heavier* price tag."

Kirk sighs as if exhausted, plays with his polka-dot bow tie.

Whitney groans. "Washington is worse, of course. But Augusta is a microcosm of the same."

"Do Gordie's relatives own Senator Joe and Senator Mary?" Eyes flash horrifically onto the two. Whispers painfully ceasing. All the kids are quiet as stilled wildlife watching the boyish body language of the lobbyist. So . . . so . . . so *likeable.*

Says Margo grimly, "So if you're poor, you have no representation." She looks at Whitney and Whitney is nodding fast, as to a jazzy tune, *fast* jazz, leaning back, using Michelle and Margo as a cover, like a fort between her and the ugly truth of Alan Sutherland.

One of the younger solar crew kids wonders, "What if you aren't wicked poor but one of the middle ones?"

"Pigeon," says Oceanna. "A working-class nuisance pigeon. A professional-class nuisance pigeon."

Samantha raises her glass of water. "To the pigeon class! Too poor to pay for b'jillion-dollar campaigns. We are all poor in the truest way! Bottoms up!" *Gulp. Gulp. Gulp.*

Whitney continues to bob her head.

But there's no music. Even the sleepy piano music and the pianist have vanished, withered with a *poof!* Practically everybody from the Settlement tables is quietly gaping at the lobbyist, except Gordon, who is making starvingly spirited noises on his Maine Moose Maxi Mousse, his eyes on the center of the table. And with eyes of fire, Jane is glaring at him. And so now Alan the lobbyist's dark eyes are also on Gordon, and Senator Mary says, "Alan, are you with other people?" and he answers, "Yes," but then quickly adds, "So . . . a school. Private, of course." He does another quick take of the people squeezed in around the two tables, all the mixed ages, the billed caps beside certain dessert dishes, the hands of both male and female, both young and old having a certain tonicity, a certain *ableness*. "Is it a Christian school?" he asks.

Senator Mary's light, perfectly mascaraed eyes twinkle.

There's a soft little giggle from Bree.

Butch and C.C. faintly smirk.

Gordon picks up a napkin and presses his heavy black and brown mustache into it, his eyes moving upon each face of his rangy family and somebody whispers a few French phrases to Reggie Lessard.

"We are followers of Socrates," pink-cheeked teenaged Margo offers. "He had to drink hemlock because he got people thinking too much."

"He was an iconoclastic nerd," Montana, a chunky eight-year-old, says. She enunciates schoolteacherishly "But he may *actually* not have existed. Plato might've made him up."

"I think he was a Harvard lawyer," skinny alley-cat-haired Oceanna laments.

The lobbyist is laughing a warm and easy laugh. Looks around at the faces. "Delightful."

Ivy is quiet, mulling over the idea of *not* being the target of smartypants kids this time.

The piano tinkles and ripples but the pianist isn't there. Somebody's two-year-old in yellow overalls is giving the keys nice pats.

Senator Mary brushes crumbs from one sleeve. "Don't laugh, Alan. This school is out of control. It . . . might catch on. The whole state could eventually object to shadowy manipulations of the government and sideshow illusions of the media." She winks at Alan.

"Stop that now!" Alan winks back. He rakes his eyes over Gordon, the work shirt and now the ringless hands. His eyes rest there on the thickened hands, the torn cuticles and bashed nails. Oh, yes, tonicity. Like a racehorse can give you speed. Like a workhorse can pull your plow. "Well, well . . . tell me about your school." Then, "No! Wait! Let me give you a little test." Alan is *such* a fun person. He *enjoys*. He points at Butch Martin, whose Arctic Cat T-shirt is noticeably filled with muscle. And the hands, another two piles of tonicity, thickness, and crusty edges. "Tell us all about the Monroe Doctrine."

Butch lowers his eyes.

Senator Joe gives a hoot. "Hell, what *is* the Monroe Doctrine? I mean *exactly*."

Alan chuckles. "Damned if I know . . . *exactly*. But I just heard on a talk show that most American kids are graduating these days without knowing this essential fact . . . even in multiple choice!" Alan and the senators guffaw.

Whitney, Michelle, Butch, and Bree whisper now. How many loud yak-it-up discussions, even skits on USA imperialism's first blush via the oh-so-flexible hemisphere-gobbling Monroe Doctrine have steamed up the west parlor on cold nights.

From a pocket in his jeans Butch tugs out his kazoo, kind of a mini Kotzschmar.

The lobbyist's eyes rest on the aqua-colored metal tube. Butch keeps his eyes down.

Now other kazoos appear, all up and down the two tables, sheens of various colors, partial lettering on some. These are recycled soda and beer cans. They stand straight up, in various hands, mostly the teens but some of the women, too. So sly, so preplanned-seeming, like handguns in a bank robbery.

The lobbyist is laughing and giving everyone warm squinched-eyed loving looks. You can see that basically this Alan is a pretty good guy. Just a different planet. So many planets in America! And sometimes there are interplanetary visits such as this. These are Bree

Vandermast's thoughts as she sees his eyes come to rest on her, and a yellow kazoo is pressed into her fingers by the fingers of Josee Soucier. Then a kazoo for Ivy's hands. And another, which Ivy passes on.

Now a sort of silence.

Butch lightly taps his instrument on the tabletop. Others join in, matching the tap. Now kazoos to lips but tapping continues with spoons, some gooey. A drumroll. Rat-tat-tat-tat-tat-tat . . .

To our Ivy Morelli this is déjà vu, the beat, the sun, the family. Not a school, no. Hadn't Gordon called it the heart? "It lives!" He had proclaimed.

The melody begins. It's, yes, "Midnight in Moscow" . . . *zhip zhip zhpp zhip zhip zhp zzzzzzzzzzzzzzzzzzzz! Clunk clunk* of forks and spoons, perfectly in sync. Ivy joins in, feeling heady. But suddenly, *abruptly* the dragging, soaring "Star Spangled Banner" begins.

Senator Joe sways from side to side, bumping shoulders with Senator Mary and Butch. His kites-and-clouds tie swings. As some of the Settlement folk bang the table with their palms, he bangs, too, keeping the somber beat. And now three teens whisper between kazoo *zhip zhips,* "Evil!" and then louder and more voices attach to these and then louder: EVIL! *Zhip-zhip* EVIL! *Zhip-zhip* EVIL! A messy throaty beat weaving through the sailing splendorous patriotic starbursts.

People at other tables glance with half smiles or composed irritation at this queer lively bunch. A waiter passes by, nods and winks, not unaccustomed to "party types."

And yes, Ivy Morelli feels the belonging. She is locked in the lava heat of it, between all these bodies.

And the lobbyist's eyes glitter over this while his huge brotherly smile, always at the ready, spans across his face.

Then the racket ends. "That was geography!" laughs skinny twenty-something Niagara, wiping the mouth part of her kazoo on her sleeve.

"It is *one* of the places where imperialism comes to a wall, " even skinnier Oceanna declares. "The great fat eagle and the great fat bear, snout to snout! The highway to the last hour is paved in policies and doctrines. *Many* doctrines! One leads to another."

A rumpus of clanging spoons, several awful ear-busting whistles is Oceanna's prize now. Oceanna (who wears only purple, *always* purple) raises a finger. "We're still working on how to do China, Brazil, and India with kazoos."

"Soon!" one of the Settlement women pipes up amid squeals and bellers of "yesss!" and one "*gonnnng*!"

 Gordon is tested.

Alan, the lobbyist, jokingly despairs, "I don't dare ask any more school questions or we'll wind up thrown out on the sidewalk by a big bouncer."

"Just ask one more question!" Kirky insists, excited, still a little breathless from the last, his polka-dot bow tie now tilted clownishly. "Let's do physics!" He points at Whitney like an emcee. "It's all yours, Whit!"

The wonderful lobbyist turns his grin on blonde ponytailed Whitney.

Whitney raises a finger. "For first-grade physics? Want the four properties of matter?"

Kirky again throws up a hand toward her. "In a nutshell," he says in a jolly way.

Everyone smiles slyly and looks at Whitney, as she explains, "The four interactions of matter, or *events* . . . are nuke force, electromagnetic force, weak force, and gravitational force." She smiles. Though Whitney is a handsome girl in that blonde straight-nosed broad-faced sort of way, her smiles undo it all. Her nose grows preposterously. Her chin disappears. Her mouth goes goofy. All of it glued together with a dog-like humility. "My favorite is weak force, or rather weak interactions. The speed of its reaction is really slow." She grins. "One billionth of a second."

A few chuckles reward her here and she looks over at her mother, Penny, who says, "I wish I could be that slow doing my share of the dishes and floors."

More chuckles.

Ivy Morelli is remembering very well that Whitney was one of the "important" teenagers of the solar crew, one who knew her Peak Oil stuff, and her how-to-make-Ivy-feel-like-a-stupid-ninny stuff. Are Ivy and Whitney on the same team tonight?

Now Whitney says, "When you sit a minute alone and think about the gravitational interaction, which is what holds the earth together, the earth not being a big round ball at all, but a collection of countless particles and pieces of objects . . . thinking about this, you can really *feel* the meaning of everything . . . especially love." She slides her deep-set green almond-shaped eyes around the tables in a way that would put you to mind of the sweep of a lighthouse beam, her chin up. Eyes brushing eyes, each face of *the family* reflects the light.

Alan, the lobbyist, says earnestly, "A very sciency woman, you are."

Whitney snorts and says in a friendly way, "It's just life. The nature of life."

He nods and smiles. "Well, okay. But I guess this school of yours doesn't do Bible studies."

"Sure we do," one of the line-faced women replies.

Gordon pushes his sticky dish across his place mat.

Michelle says, "We learn everything."

Whitney adds, "And we doubt everything. At least once."

Ivy Morelli chimes in, "That's Marx, right?"

Michelle shakes her head, "Descartes."

"They both said it," Bree murmurs.

Alan looks at Gordon with a suspicious squint. "These your best students, or do they all talk like this?"

Gordon says, "There are no best students."

Alan smiles. "Well, you know what I mean. Are these your *honor* students?" He gazes dreamily at Michelle and Whitney.

Gordon says evenly, "You mean like those real schools would have the USDA stamper for their haunches?"

Senator Mary sighs. "There are many lobbyists who are urging even more tests."

Samantha half shouts, "To break the public schools, then privatize-profitize them?! That haunch stamper has turned out to be a weapon and the path to someone's wealth!"

Alan looks carefully over at Senator Joe and Senator Mary. Then back at Samantha, her Apache-Comanche-style head rag tonight a galvanizing blue, her hair, as ever, moon-colored. Then his eyes grip Gordon. "Come again?"

Gordon looks down at his hands a long moment, so Alan, impatiently but ever so cordially, moves on to ask a different question of someone else and the question is answered simply, and when Gordon looks up, Alan's bright dark eyes are again fixed on him.

Alan watches Gordon's hands opening and closing once, then again there on the table like the squeezing of fists while giving blood. Or bracing for a fight. Or what? The big "schoolmaster" guy's face is so tame. So friendly. But there's some inner upheaval it seems. What's wrong with him? Alan wonders. Gas?

Now Gordon lunges into one of his "jags," and all the while, Alan's bright gaze lays hard on Gordon, on his forthright duplicity. The attentive lobbyist swears there are tears in the big boy's eyes.

Gordon goes on rambling. Words like "institutionalized" and "industrialized" and "desolate" boom from his whiskery mouth. His hands are ferociously busy, shaping and punctuating. He has been sucked in. The lamb!

Ivy Morelli watches him as he further accelerates, almost levitating off his seat. She understands everything he is saying but with the lobbyist's eyes warmly and wonderfully cutting through Gordon's jugular, it seems like Gordon is just spluttering out nonsense. His fierceness is embarrassing.

Alan is trying to get in a word edgewise now. Gordon is leaning toward him, over the table, one hand open almost in Alan's face, fingers spread like a big pink star. And on and on, Gordon overflowing. Now he leans back, placing an open hand on each thigh. He squints at Alan, wags his head in that fawning and goofy manner Ivy has seen before. His apology?

Other restaurant patrons rustle past these tables but seem far away. Piano music has returned. It's tinkling is so earnest.

Alan takes a gleamy-eyed hospitable shot at Gordon's world. Another query darts straight out of Alan's world, his insistence on "assessment" and "excellence" and "globalism's opportunities" and "keeping up." Gordon says in a friendly snarl, "This education thing . . . it's not something for a test score. It has more to do with . . ." Gordon flounders, drowning in emotion, ". . . with *life* and *death*!"

Alan stares at Gordon. Something moves across his smooth cheeks, a kind of series of pulses. He says, "In other words, you're bad-mouthing progress on an obsessive level and you're . . . dragging down *truly* gifted people by burdening them with those who aren't smart, in order to create a totally worthless society where everyone is mediocre?" He has stopped smiling.

Senator Joe busts in with, "Let's take this outside, boys!" He laughs, fingering his colorful kite-cloud tie, then gives Alan's shoulder a soft playful punch.

Ivy's lips and teeth almost form the words, *Let me write this story! Let me give you a forum, Gordon. And I can condense your rambling! And . . . uh . . . paraphrase it. Yesssss!* And she turns and sees the rows of Settlement women along the other tables . . . their home-sewn outfits, smocking and embroidery, all staring at Gordon and Alan. Ivy thinks Bonnie Loo is the best, those fox-color (yellow-brown) eyes really glare at the fun lobbyist and ol' Gordo both. It is the greatest of all to have Bonnie Loo on your side!

Meanwhile, old, old Reggie Lessard glances from face to face, smiling cross-eyed. None of this tense conversation has interfered with what's in his own head, those imploring brass sounds and tumbling deep monster notes of the Kotzschmar, which still push and pull, seethe and pound and breach the infinite. His shoulders are squared. He has not ordered dessert, only black coffee. His shaky hand raises the cup for another deep swallow, which jerks along down inside his rumpled neck.

And the restaurant's piano tinkles on witheringly, like falling stars, like the universe folding up again into a reverse bang, now more like a barely existent gray flicker.

And Chris Butler, he, too, is seeing, hearing, being with the Kotzschmar at city hall. Before him, the golden facade rises as if from mists, the organist's back in dark gray pumping, feet pumping, small man together with the great beast and a greater god, all moving together in an orgy of spiritual muscle. He does not hear the restaurant's piano, nor the conversations near or far.

 The fringe.

The forlorn trickle of piano keys seems to be struggling to get out from behind the brick walls, captured there, scant ghosts of the unwanted.

Gordon is flushed. "We have Ayn Rand's novels in our library. We offer all views."

Alan smiles. "But then you smash them, the views not suitable to you, that is."

Gordon smiles, a bigger smile than Alan's. "When you live with questions, weak assumptions fall by the wayside in a natural way."

"You sound born again."

Gordon leans back. "You could say that about your Milton Friedman and his Chicago boys. And the usurers. A certain belief. And Hitler! And the bankers who financed both sides of *that* scene. And the other slavers . . ." The Settlement women at the next table look anguished. A couple of them are trying to catch Gordon's eye, turning their heads from side to side to signal to him to lower his voice. Seems he doesn't notice this, nor does he catch one of them making "calm down" hand signals.

Suddenly, Ivy feels surrounded by WEIRD PEOPLE. There *is* a born again glow around Gordon. His passion. It's too sticky. While the Wall Street religion is spanking clean and pleasantly cool to the touch. More American.

Ivy looks down at the table, at her half-eaten dessert. And then at her shoulder bag on the floor. Inside it are pens and reporter pads. There's no story here. Just hyperbole. RAVING CULT LEADER HOLED UP IN THE HILLS is a story, a great story. Ideas and processing ideas are not. She fingers her earring, all the wacky shapes dangling there. Her earlobe aches.

Alan flutters his eyes. "And you say that you . . . ah . . . don't let people leave? Did I hear this? You don't *allow* eighteen-year-olds to seek better opportunities outside your little snug community? Are you saying they're not free to leave? I'm not clear on this. Could you explain that to me?" He leans with his elbow on the table, a palm cupping his chin, fingers open across one side of his face, his dark eyes now on Christian (C.C.) Crocker, who looks in every way like Huckleberry Finn, freckled and friendly and most notably restless.

Jane whispers to Gordon, "I'm bored."

Gordon speaks again with pious softness, "Our kids understand that serving one's community is one's greatest achievement, a great *honor,* that the combined gifts of each of us will multiply into healthy *inter*dependence. In this way, you best serve the world."

Alan drops his hand with a thump. Looks directly at Gordon. "A little xenophobic, don't you think?"

Gordon holds his stare. "Tell me how you come to that conclusion, my friend."

"Well," says Alan, fluttering the fingers of his right hand to erase a thought. "I call it xenophobia because essentially this is what you're teaching. All those nervous paranoid boundaries." His eyes get big like a doll's. He inhales deeply, greatly burdened by the air around him, as if the atmosphere *smelled* of bad philosophy, bad policy, and wrong turns. "Maybe provincial is a better word . . . for now." His kindly smile returns.

Gordon's left eye is widening, the eyebrow raised, the right eye squinty. And there it is, one of his violent facial twitches. But he says absolutely nothing. Just sighs. His face and neck have gotten damp. He folds his hands prayerfully and says, as soft as silk, "In America, land of the *freeee,* it should be acceptable for a people to find their own way, right?"

Alan looks at his watch. "Yeah, sure, sure," he says. "Sounds like progress. I wish you all the luck in the world."

Ivy is thinking how a *real* reporter would be like this lobbyist. He or she would reach out of the modern no-nonsense professional vacuum and . . . well, just not take Gordon St. Onge seriously. Not for one split second. What is wrong with Ivy that she hears Gordon's drum?

Leaning into Gordon's side, Jane commands, "Shut up now." And she reaches with one long bare golden brown arm, takes his lips into her long fingers.

"So how is Carol Gibbons?" Senator Mary flutters her eyes at the lobbyist. "Have you seen much of her these days? She wasn't around last session and I thought I heard it was health-related."

"Moved on up to better things. A regular tiger," he says, his bubbly voice fully recovered. He again glances at his watch.

"Hmm. And what about Doug Griffith? What happened to him?"

"No hope," he says with a smirk. "No hope there. Everything he touches leaves a slime like the oozing of a garden slug. Caspar Milquetoast all the way. Even in soft mud, he wouldn't make a footprint." He pretends to shiver. Now he glances around at all the faces, Settlement faces that have turned away now, mostly engaged in conversations among themselves. Butchie Martin is fussing with his kazoo, poking something into place with the little finger of his right hand.

The *Record Sun* reporter is staring at St. Onge, kind of in the middle of his shirt. Is she doing a column on these crazies, Alan wonders. Good to see it. The merciless bitch will toast 'em.

But what are the esteemed senators doing here? The puzzle of puzzles.

Young Jane says painfully, "Are we going? Or spending the night here?"

Alan turns his big smile on the senators. Senator Joe smiles back. They share a life in that teeming world under the grubby green but august dome fifty-five miles away. Sometimes a smile is worth a million words. Or a million dollars.

Jane pushes closer to Gordon now, almost in his lap. She fingers his newly trimmed beard, the long untrimmed mustache, feels his ear like he often feels hers, stirs her finger around in his dessert dish. "Gorrrrr-deeeee. Let's gooooooo."

Alan rises, holds a hand up, says to all, "Be well," starts to turn, then, on second thought, swings around and reaches across the corner of the table to shake Gordon's hand and Gordon stands up out of his chair, all six-feet-five inches of him, and offers his hand, and both men have a tight, overly long grip and Alan says into Gordon's wild never-to-be-forgotten pale eyes, "Peace."

 Good-byes.

After he is gone and the two legislators fill everyone in on the humongous and ruthless corporation Alan's firm represents, Gordon asks Whitney and her mother, Penny, if there's room for Jane in the car they came in, or do Bonnie Loo and Patricia have space? "Or Butchie, what about you? You got room for the secret agent?"

"Nooooooo," Jane protests. "I'm going with you, Gordie."

Gordon says he is going to be in town late, needs to give the press a ride home.

Ivy is fondling her earring. It looks like the weight of it is setting her earlobe on fire.

Gordon is whispering something nobody else can hear in the fifteen-year-old Bree's ear. She giggles. He smoothes the scrambly miracle of her thick hair back, so that both sides of her face show. She pulls her head away from him so the hair slips back again. Her shoulders are squared though, her breasts high. She is comfortable with all of her body. After all, her reptilian face is one story, her body another.

Everyone gets up. They crane their necks around like seeing the place for the first time.

They call for the check, but the waiter tells them smilingly that the check has been taken care of, compliments of Duotron Lindsey International.

"That shit head!" snarls Senator Mary laughingly. She seems flattered by Alan's prank. What is the right way to feel? Normally a gift from Alan would be *from Alan*. This mention of Duotron Lindsey seems to be Alan needling Gordon. But Gordon just looks tired and goes ambling off to the men's room. When he's back, he bows low to kiss little Senator Mary Wright on top of her shining black hair. Then he bows abruptly to his right and lifts the end of Senator Joe's tie of clouds and kites and then he kisses it. Are the senators corporatists like all the rest? Let us recall how Mussolini once said corporatism and fascism are the same. Seems the senators tonight are duly forgiven.

Lots of goofing and screeching and cackles and fun and the passing of caps and purses. Someone presses Reggie's ornately carved cane into his smooth shaky hand and people at other tables watch this all from the corners of their eyes or they just stare outright.

Gordon smooches Jane on both ears. She ignores him, pouting, arms folded.

Gordon hugs Whitney and Penny. He hugs Bonnie Loo. He whispers something to Bonnie Loo. She looks up at him gravely. He whispers again, not into her ear but close between her eyes. She whispers something back. He laughs. She laughs along but her eyes aren't laughing and instead of glaring at Ivy now, she simply doesn't look at Ivy at all. Then she takes old Reggie's arm and helps him through the narrow channel between table and wall.

To fifteen-year-old blonde and happy-faced Whitney, to Oceanna, to Butch, to Montana, Gordon says in a soft way, "You made me proud tonight." Then Whitney assures him, "You made us proud, too, Gordon."

Now he gathers up Bree and lifts her, her feet leaving the floor. A big squeeze. A cheek smooch. "This is only the beginning," he tells her. "Do you love us yet?"

She giggles, "Yes."

Obviously, this Bree is not a Settlement old-timer, Ivy observes.

And then he is hugging Kirky's head, little going-out-of-style pigtail contorting between the big fingers; Kirk does not flush or fight this like you'd expect. He has wrapped an arm around Gordon and pats Gordon's back.

One of the strapping broad-faced thirteen-year-old boys actually gets a light kiss on the mouth from Gordon, and then another steps up for his quick on-the-mouth kiss and head hug from Gordon. Would you think this a family reunion or a wedding? You would, wouldn't you? Not just a "see you in the morning" kind of thing, which is what it actually is.

Now Butchie Martin is out on the sidewalk playing a kazoo solo of "Midnight in Moscow." Every time the door opens, you hear the enthusiastic Old World buzz of it.

One of the quiet, stern, lined-faced, handsome women has Jane by the hand. Jane glares at Gordon now, her eyes filled with beautiful, sorrowful, light-flashing tears.

Gordon picks Ivy's bag and camera off the floor next to where she had been sitting, hands them to her, and murmurs deeply as he stuffs a big bill under one of the plates, "Tonight, baby, *I* drive."

 Ivy Morelli uncovers the facts of life.

Up along Congress Street, Gordon mashes his face to a store window and says, "Guess."

She says, "Dickens."

He wags his eyebrows at her. "Close enough." He grabs her arm. "To the High Street parking garage," he commands with a shake of three fingers in that direction, then nods and tips an imaginary top hat to anyone on the sidewalk who will meet his eyes. He hugs Ivy's arm tight against his side. He sings and Ivy joins in. They sing without trying to sound good. They sing in all kinds of horrid funny voices. They dance around. People pass them, groups divide around them, ignoring them or chuckling. There's a cool oceany smell tonight mixed with exhaust. And the smell of treelessness.

Now they turn down a dim side street, no cars coming, shortcut to the parking garage, and they run like robbers. They cut down another short side street, then, while tearing across the next street, its wide swath of empty one-way lanes, a car turns from a street above and its headlights splash over them. They lunge up onto the sidewalk, Gordon swinging his professorial jacket over his head like a lasso, "*Yip yip yip* where in tarnation are them doggies!!"

"Was there anything in those suspect desserts?" Ivy wonders aloud, with her low raffish laugh.

"Morrrrrrrrr morrrrrrrrrrrrrrrr! Give me more sugarrrrrrrrr!" Gordon screams, rolling his shoulders against the parking garage wall. Pretends to cry. He stands straight now and says grimly, "Jane Meserve does exactly this."

Ivy shakes her head. Her earring of objects casts about.

A car passes slowly. *Abby Road Taxi* along its expansive side. Yes, slowly. And quietly. You'd know in a moment (waking from a faint) that you were *not* in Boston or New York. And that nobody as modern and earnest as our Ivy was at the wheel.

Gordon trudges on. "My gawd," he says in the same grim manner. "Us rednecks just do not know how to act right . . ." He looks at her. "In this here civilized place. No more running, dear. No more fun."

Now heading down toward the bright entrance and ticket booth where a few people are walking up from the other direction, many of them dressed formally, a man follows this group. Alone, he trudges along the sidewalk as though he carries something on his back. But there's absolutely nothing on his back. Up close, he is younger than you'd guess. Full lips but bad teeth. Gray sweatshirt and winter-weight wool shirtsleeves showing under that. Checkered polyester old-gentleman trousers. His eyes are blue, like Ivy's. But not dark-lashed as Ivy's are. He is quite fair. Smoodged and dirty and fair. As

Gordon and Ivy approach, his eyes widen on Gordon's face. He stops. He stares. Gordon breaks his stride, turns toward the guy, puts his hand out and the guy puts his smoodgy hand out and Gordon clasps his hand, brings it right close to his chest.

The guy asks, "You Pete?"

"Gordon," Gordon tells him. "Are *you* Pete?"

The guy nods slowly, his hand still clasped in Gordon's hand against Gordon's shirtfront. "Pete," Gordon says softly, then backs away and trudges on with Ivy hurrying at his side. Ivy says nothing.

Gordon looks back.

The guy is watching him. The guy doesn't follow. The guy, of course, *might* have followed.

Gordon waves to the guy with a childly wave. Nods manfully. Then turns and doesn't look back again.

Now he and Ivy climb four flights of stairs to the level in the garage where Gordon's old Chevy is parked.

Ivy is thinking that Gordon's impulsiveness is . . . breathtaking . . . scary and breathtaking. Impulsiveness or policy?

They get all settled in the old pickup, windows rolled down, Gordon fingering the wob of keys from his belt loop, key into ignition, Ivy's camera and shoulder bag arranged on the seat, but the truck won't start.

Gordon gets out. Throws up the hood. Wiggles wires. He cries out, "Mumma! Why is life so hard?" Cementish echoes answer him with his own question.

He gets back in. He heavily jounces on the seat, twisting the key to try again. Engine does not respond. "Ivy, dear, get behind the wheel. We're gonna push her down that mighty fine grade. You know 'bout poppin' the clutch, huh?"

"Refresh my memory."

He explains the steps and, yes, it works, and he runs like hell to catch up and hops in, slams the door and says with a feigned near-faint, "Was it coincidence or our Almighty Vengeful Lord God who put you back behind the wheel again?" Covers his eyes.

Ivy cackles like a witch, then while she hands the garage attendant the ticket and cash, Gordon tells her, "Down on Park Avenue there are lotsa opportunities to pull over so we can switch places."

Ivy cackles even more witchily. She plows on down Park Avenue, shifting and careening the old truck, passes a car on the right, a right lane that is not actually a lane but empty parking spaces.

Gordon murmurs, "Lord God, Heavenly King, Almighty God and Father, Lord Jesus Christ, only Son of the Father, Lord God, Lamb of God, Son of the Father . . . Thou taketh away the sins of the world, have mercy on us and receive our prayer." And now he whispers, almost inaudibly, *"Domine deus, rex caelestis, Deus, Pater omnipotens, Domine . . ."*

Over the crotch of his work pants, his hands are in a single tight fist of prayer but his eyes are wide on the street ahead, the changing lights, the railroad overpass seesawing its way from fore to aft.

After they are out of the heart of town, Ivy pulls the truck into a variety store, parks up close to the plate glass window, the truck's two headlights blazing back at them. Brilliance is everywhere, left, right, and above, floodlights, "mercury" lights, fluorescence, and a bombastment of sunny signs. She jounces on the seat triumphantly, her earring leaping. She looks at him, her chin high and says, "God knows best."

Inside the variety store, Gordon pays for a six-pack of cheap beer while Ivy stands next to him, her thumbs hooked into the big pockets of her short dress, glancing around, eyes drifting over the rental video tapes, magazines, and other flashy trashy stuff. She hopes people will see her with Gordon St. Onge. What is it about him? Even these people, none who know him, their eyes spring to him and linger. Sometimes you see them actually doing comically sudden double takes. She thinks of the kid word: *Awesome*.

As Gordon and Ivy walk back to the truck, he proprietarily plucks a piece of lint from the shoulder-blade area of her old-fashioned yellow dress. Then he is swinging the six-pack up into the truck bed, arranges it snug against the cab. She doesn't even pretend to fight him for the wheel. She wants the feel of him driving tonight, of his cautious navigation while she closes her eyes against the sharp unnatural city lights. Yuh, all the most cheap and foul manifestations are chosen to be the best lighted here, it seems.

The engine clamors to life. As he backs the truck out of its space, as they roll along slowly (the speed limit) toward her home, she watches him, can't take her eyes off him. He scratches his left ear, then his short beard and long mustache, stroking, stroking thoughtfully with his dirty (from fiddling with things under the truck hood) fingers.

She tells him some lefts and rights. Her street comes up fast. Parked outside her apartment, he is standing now at the side of the truck bed, staring at the six-pack, stroking and stroking one side of his mustache. He looks at her. His eyes turning on her like that cause her to give a nervous little hop, her glossy black bowl of hair shifting, her earring pirouetting. He opens the cab door and tucks the six-pack carefully on the floor with his rolled-up sport-dress jacket. She watches all this little business with held breath. Puzzled. He locks the cab. Looks at her again, holds his eyes on hers, then laughs. "I'll walk you up."

They walk up the one flight of stairs at the back. There is that old apartment house smell. Dusty varnish.

She holds the door open for him and he steps past her and she is going a little crazy now, every inch of her pounding with fast blood and readiness.

She offers him coffee.

He says, "*You* have real coffee? *You* who is subject to the great abandon of performing Elvis's top two hundred hit songs?"

"I've had this coffee here for two years. Just for you," she tells him as she plunks the teakettle on the stove. Never mind the microwave. The teakettle is more romantic. She kicks her tallish-heeled sandals into her bedroom, then pads around soundlessly, shorter now, and he is, as ever, the towering Viking.

She ushers him to the living room area with its art posters, the white walls, the long curtains closed against the street.

He looks gravely and tiredly at the room, then at her face. Her pretty face. Her twenty-four-year-old, creamy, flustered, beaming little face. He presses his left hand fingers against his mustache, hard, as if to sooth painful teeth or erase unspeakable words. She goes over there and stands right in front of him as he slowly settles there on her little couch with his knees apart and she, even on her feet, is not a tower above him. She steps closer. Another step she will be between his feet and knees. She bends down to him and takes his face in her hands. He stands up quick, causing her to step back. He grabs her to him, gives her a hard bear hug, not foreplay to sex, more like the bear hug of a brother or dad. She breathes in the smell of his shirt, the shirt so many have nuzzled this evening. She cannot believe the feel of the mass of his body inside his shirt.

She pulls back to see him better, looks up at him, her dark hair slithering in and out of its professionally clipped perfection. "Didn't you come up here to go to bed with me?" she asks, a little hysterically.

He gently shakes his head.

"But you are so solicitous!" she accuses, sharp and high-pitched, almost the voice of another person.

"I'm sorry."

"Sorry? You bastard!"

He exhales very, very slowly, looks down at his right work boot and her rug underneath. "Making babies is . . . it's for a man and wife . . . I believe."

She cocks her head. "I have birth control possibilities here. I have, yes, a microwave, two TVs, two VCRs, a push-button telephone, a phone answering machine, a computer, and birth control."

He starts to smile over this wit and to speak, but she keeps talking.

"Are you telling me, Gordon, that you don't believe in birth control? Are you Mr. Fundamentalist Born Again after all?"

His eyes squint-blink, then one eye widens, his crazy man look. He looks down at his hands, rubbing his hands together, hands so toughened and callused they hiss as he rubs them. "Naw. I said it wrong. I just think a man oughta keep his pecker to home."

Ivy chortles huskily, her voice back to its old self. "So if I was at your house on your property, you'd make love to me."

"If you were . . . committed."

"Sounds like a mental institution."

"Forget committed. If you were *devoted*."

"Like worship?"

"More like . . . if you were happy and involved there . . . and there was your *love*."

The teakettle's shriek gives Ivy a jump. She twists around and heads out to the kitchenette, her hands shaking. Snaps off the burner. He follows her. He watches her dig something out from a little apple-shaped canister. "What's that?" he asks.

"I'm making myself some warm relaxing mint tea . . . to calm the nerves. I am upset."

He wedges around in back of her in the tight space of this not-quite-a-room. "I'm sorry." Takes her shoulders.

She swings around and claws him. Draws blood. *Really* draws blood.

He presses a thumb to his wound. "You're getting better at this all the time."

"I'm sorry." She closes her eyes.

"And for a woman who preaches nonviolence!" he scolds.

"I said people shouldn't punch children in the mouth."

He looks at *her* mouth. Small, the top lip almost pointy, pink childly mouth. He takes a step away from her, sideways in the narrow passage, and he breathes in the mint of her gentle tea and his hard, hard tireless coffee, both cups on the counter steaming pleasantly.

"How come you don't have kids, Gordon?"

He has turned away now and keeps his back to her, lingering, considering, mulling, his eyes blinking like one of those quick thinks, like when he decided to leave his beer in the truck and, still with his back to her, he says, "I have children."

"I don't mean figuratively . . . bonded by interdependence and all that stuff. I mean *blood* . . ." With a single *shhh-ing* finger, she touches her lips. "I'm sorry. This is a personal and intrusive question. It . . . popped out."

He turns around and she is looking at his ringless engine-greasy hands, not his mouth of twisted bottom teeth and kind of savagely long mustache that covers the top teeth of his now cautious smile, as he says, "I am not a monster, Ivy. Okay? You hear me? I am not even David Koresh . . . who was also not a monster." He pushes his fingers through his hair. "I . . . am just in an odd situation. It would seem unpleasant to some . . . you know . . . it would seem wrong. But . . . you know . . . America, land of the free. Well, I believed that when I was growing up. To me, it meant your personal actions are not guided by the fucking cops and courts and Congress, and, uh . . . Wall Street and Madison Avenue . . . and media but by what your loved ones need. And from a sense of rightness that comes from inside you. I always figured that to comfort and protect my loved ones was the only law. Breaking *that* law was punishable by the unbearable feeling I would get inside me. There were cops *inside* me and—"

"What are you getting at?"

"I . . . have children. Blood children. I have—" He shrugs and flushes. "—a *lot* of kids."

She widens, then narrows her eyes. "Like how many? Give me a rough figure. More than ten?" All her limbs are hardening, face hardening, back stiffening, eyes on his mouth.

He says, "I'm not on trial here, baby."

"Someday you will be on trial, baby. You got some weird stuff here. So . . . it turns out people were right. The anonymous callers! They TRIED to tell me! Now, every day another piece of what they told me comes true! I just don't quite get it! I mean . . . there's still the missing link! Or maybe that which is yet to be revealed. *The Bible.* The goddamn Bible! How is it we have a horny prophet in this picture, but no Bible studies, sermons, and wild preachings!!! What makes your followers believe they have to succumb to you?!! No Bible, just weirdness. At least you could have the decency to thump a Bible while you hump 'em!"

He breaks into a fine, handsome, huge grin, eyes twinkling, folds his arms across his chest, leans back against the little heaped counter. He is laughing. Yes, laughing.

She pours her steeped tea through a strainer into a second cup, her hands shaking.

His smile is gone now, his pale eyes fixed on her hand pouring the hot tea. She jerks a jar of honey from her cupboard and steps away. She won't look at him. She looks into the sink. She says, "I am going to throw up. I mean it."

He says, "It's not a philosophy . . . it wasn't an order from the heavens. It . . . it just happened."

Her lip curls. "Oh, yeah . . . like that boy Jaime getting smacked in the mouth . . . *punched* in the mouth. It just happened."

He frowns. "I'm familiar with a lot of the Bible. I've studied it and I've read and met and conversed with a lot of serious Biblical scholars. I've studied the scholars on many religions, *many* religions and practices and beliefs . . . their histories . . . the customs and languages of the peoples who . . . well . . . you know, shaped those religions. Mostly I did this study on my own . . . but . . . a while ago . . . back a while ago, I did two semesters of theology school—"

She looks at him in a startled way.

"—but not as a man of God. But as . . . a friend of someone who taught there, who understood me, how it is with me . . . the thing I feel."

"Yuh . . . what's that?"

He shrugs. "I feel . . . you know . . . I have a response to people that is always alert. Well, you know . . . some people are alert like that to every breath and heartbeat of every living person. It's dizzying and tiring . . . especially with so many people on the planet." He snorts, shakes his head. "If you're that kind of person, you're plugged into a kind of life force . . . a current, without which you will die. Like dialysis and yet *with* it, you will die of so much heartbreak . . . and so much fuss. Spread so thin. And you need to be alone so much . . . to get away from all of it . . . to shrink it somehow . . . in your own mind's eye . . . to rest a bit. Because it's impossible to not hurt somebody. It fuckin' hurts."

She seems not to be breathing, just watching his mouth for more surprises, more ugliness, whatever it is that lays beyond all this philosophical justification. Which is what it is! Because man, oh, man, leaping lollipops, there *are no* saints.

He goes on, "Whoever or whatever created the universe and all this squiggling writhing mean ol' life, created in all of us thousands of needs so complex, we humans are too stupid to name them all. And you see, Ivy, many many many people get left out. They are called 'less.' But they're not 'less'! Without them, we're only a partial picture—"

"I've already heard this, Gordon. You're repeating yourself."

He nods. "Yes, repeat. Repeat. A garment with only ornate buttons but no fabric. The only place some people, the gentle ones, can shine, is within the protection of a family, not out in corporate America and not in the friggin' streets! Not in one-room apartments with not a soul to knock on their door but the landlord collecting the rent. Not forced to work the three-dollar-an-hour job, institutionalizing their babies in day cares. If society only allows the winners to love and to live, the winners will find that a society of only great 'achievements' will be a society that dies a death by laughing gas!" He strokes, of all things, his belt buckle, the ancient face of the sun *gone*. Now it's an even quirkier image, a sort of voodoo mask, eyeless, awkwardly and yet magnificently rendered in *wood* stained red and purple and mustard yellow by, yes, probably, one of his many, many sons or daughters.

And she is thinking, yes, when he bought that beer, he was about to lose control, he was planning to come here for the night, to drink, to fuck, to sleep it off, then changed his mind. Changed his mind. *Domine deus, rex caelestis . . . have mercy on us and receive our prayer.* She stares into his face, watching the words come, his deepening voice, that thick-necked big soft voice, "So . . . okay . . . God spoke to us at the Settlement, in a manner of speaking, and said, 'Do what you need to do to get by.'"

Ivy spanks her hands together with a crack. "You fucking coward. You're not going to take any blame. One minute you tell me it's not a message from God, but somehow you weaseled it around to be all God's fault!"

"Yeah, right. *Everything* is God's fault because everything is God."

She says, "Get out."

He looks at her mouth.

She points to the door. "Go away! Go. This is horrible. What you're telling me is you have something like twenty-five or thirty kids. Next you'll be admitting that some of your wives are fourteen years old, young virgins that your grown-up followers give you as gifts . . . out of gratitude or something. Or maybe a protocol of the militia, your Willie Lancaster and Rex York connections. Onward Christian soldiers!! And it's not your fault or their fault, but God's fault. Right? It's sick! You make me sick!"

He murmurs, "Okay." And he goes.

She leans against the frame of a curtained window to listen to his truck door slam, down there in the street. The engine starts sluggishly. Truck chugs away. She feels as though a hundred warm arms have withdrawn. She feels the vitality and noise and carnival colors of his world diminish to a hot speck, then gone.

  About the days of her youth and Gordon's youth, Claire St. Onge speaks.

We were just two kids. Married young. We were never needing for anything. His share of the Depaolo family business was certainly what

I would call wealth, if you put it next to reservation life, if you put it next to *most* people's lives. The Depaolo family even had a cousin in the Legislature to . . . to rely on. And several dozen "friends." It was working-class rich. Rich and getting richer. So much construction in those years, especially for those well-organized and shrewd low bidders, big enough to bid good and low or do sneakies for no-bid contracts, yeah, big, like the Depaolo Brothers.

But Gordon and I weren't happy.

In front of his mother's family, those Depaolos and Gleasons, his uncles, aunts, and cousins, all this devout Catholic swarm, Gordon was spirited, full of sudden fun-filled antics. Plus, he worked like a fiend. And they liked that.

But when we were alone, he would say to me, in the most ugly and dark way, "Do not conceive." Funny, huh? Was this a mean streak or a streak of panic. Well, when Gordon gets panicked he can be nasty. Rumors of his sainthood are greatly exaggerated.

I understood this. With my family in Indian Township and his father's people in decimated Aroostook (*the* county), it was a thing you could understand. Most of the world was not the Depaolos, with their fleets of equipment, big roomy houses, and their own state senators. Okay. So most of the world suffers, then gets mean. Fact of life. "But our child will have opportunities," I insisted.

He said, "The mega-Mammoneers will bury the next generation."

Okay, so I say we were kids. I was almost ten years older. I was twenty-nine, nearly thirty. He was twenty. *Twenty.* He was lean, almost bony in the shoulders, like a colt. Small hips. And that dusky Italian-French-Indian skin. And no gray in his beard then. And I was this little smooth golden thing with a head of hair like a wild mare and a wiggle when I walked. A little on the hippy side. A little. And a little bit nerdy, too. I liked to eat history in whole volumes. And I liked current events. But I liked to eat my current events sunny-side up. And here he was flipping books into my lap, what he called "The Other." Or he'd say, "Here you go, baby. Another one the ministry of truth hasn't blessed yet." And he'd say, "The mega-Mammoneers will bury the good."

What could I say to that? Could I say, 'We'll raise our child to be bad.'?

Well, of course I got pregnant. I tried some birth control devices. But as we all know, sperm are small and ingenious and frisky.

We didn't live in Egypt then. His mother still had the place on Heart's Content Road, still called Swett's Pond Road then. She had been widowed for several years but she had friends in East Egypt. *Ladies*. Reading club ladies. Church women. Do-good people.

In Mechanic Falls, we rented an old place converted from a store. It was an odd space. The front yard was a tarred parking lot.

Rex York was still coming around a lot in those days. Yeah, Rex, the one you may have read about in the *Record Sun*. Captain of the Border Mountain Militia these days. But back then it was the tail-end of a heavy-duty hard-drinking every-weekend brotherly relationship between those two. Rex York. Always a gentleman. A quiet, gloomy well-mannered person. It wasn't a fight or anything that ended their intensity. They just both got married and brotherishness gradually took the backseat.

And there were other people coming around, Gordon's people, my people. We've always had a lot of people.

But this night, there were no people but us. And this night I will remember *forever*. It was early dark. Winter. Snow shovel in the snow bank by the step. He was just coming in from work, dropping from that brand-new company truck he drove in those days, armload of groceries. And I said it fast that I was pregnant. I stood with my feet apart, a fighting stance. Like I say, I was a trim little person then. Trim and fit as a little bantamweight boxer, only, you know, with a *figure*.

I couldn't see his face, just his vaguely lighted shape in his heavy jacket. And the bag crinkled. He was shifting the bag. He didn't say anything. I waited. Waited. He didn't say *anything*. I said, "Please don't ask me to get an abortion."

"Yes, I'm asking you," he said.

"I can see this baby's face, the way it will be," I insisted.

He said, in a most gravelly way, "Yep. Abortion is killing. Yes, it is *izzzzz* killing. That's not debatable. And a fetus is a person, sure. *That's* not debatable."

"Not debatable," I repeated. I wanted so badly to see Gordon's face, the generous look of his eyes, his playful smile. Or even his sorrow. But the winter dark was his veil.

What was his voice that night? A gray stone. Then his unseen face said, "There are all kinds of killings. Killing for food. Killing for self-defense. Killing for anger. Killing in order to rob. Killing for resources and territory. Killing for revenge. Killing for political expediency and political bluster. Then there's ethnic and class cleansing, the aggressive kind and the passive-aggressive kind. And then there is killing for mercy. This would be killing for mercy."

"Yes, mercy," I repeated.

"You see a coon squirming in the road, spine crushed, bowels smeared from one side of the pavement to the other, you bust that coon's head with a rock! The old dog goes lame, deaf, and blind, you shoot him. Coons, dogs, fetuses are honored with the right to escape torment, if a helpful killer stands by. Ah, that you and I should be so lucky, aye Claire?"

"We would be lucky," I said. By then my argument of mother love was a skirling vacuum.

Each day, Gordon shed more and more of his youth, the good humor he seemed so blessed with when I met him, it was only part of a funny mask he wore for the Depaolos on holidays. Between him and me there was still sweetness. No name-calling. No fights. No game playing. None of that shit you hear about with others. But the books and journals and newsletters piled around the house all testified to the cruelty of our species. The cruelty of life. And the doom of life as we know it. Doom would be soon. Oh, boy. After reading, he would pace the house. Or slam a door. Or go into a diatribe at breakfast, spitting food out with his words. Eating and yakking and yelling about the increasing peril of the world. It was all true. I could hardly eat. His yelling and muttering made me actually sick. But it was *all true*. Then for a few hours, he was sweet again.

I actually considered hiding all his books. And the TV? He didn't want it on when he was home. He called it "the box of torpors and created needs." He called their news "the Six O'Clock Follies." He said he would shoot the TV. He had a few rifles and I said to myself *he might really shoot it*. But then he would love me up, hard kisses and hump hump humping and all the hugs I could want and sweet talk in the patois and bits of mangled Blake or Shakespeare and in those eyes his right of ingress in buttery green-blue. And wasn't he one for bouquets and hemlock cones and pretty rocks and teasing and wrastling.

A lot of people we knew, people with less resources than the Depaolo family, were getting pretty deep in debt. This was the early eighties. Hallelujah. Things looked rosy. People talked rosy. But Gordon cautioned them. "It's all an illusion," he said. "No money. Just credit. Just bubbles."

He photocopied articles for all our friends. Articles that would curl their hair if they'd read them. Nobody read them.

Of our friends and family, of the people who mattered to us, none knew what Gordon knew. Not even me. I couldn't stand reading all that stuff. It depressed me. I would even try to shut out his angry complaints at breakfast . . . try to nod and *look* interested, but not hear it. Somewhere out there in the world were strangers who knew what Gordon knew. But they were there. He was here. Alone.

Someone said, *The truth will set you free*. Was it Jesus? Jesus was nailed to a cross.

  ## Claire's love-hate.

I agreed to the abortion. I wept and wept and wept.

In the nights, that whole week before the appointment, we both lay awake, me with wide eyes and tossing, him silent as frost.

The abortion was hard, both the pre-appointment and the day itself. The whole time was full of snowstorms we were trying to drive through. And blood. And hot cramps. And hollowness. And then there was the niggling question I asked myself again and again. What next? I loved Gordon. Gordon was forever. What next? Another pregnancy? Another mercy killing?

I went through the whole business. Got my tubes tied. Yeah, they had vasectomies then. And there were times I knew he was thinking about it, like when the word vasectomy was mentioned by someone in conversation. There was the word like a roar and flaming letters VASECTOMY and he would lower his eyes. Vasectomy was not an option with him, I'll tell you that. After all, Gordon was, and is, when all is said and done, just a great big proud redneck man.

Okay, so now you hate him. I hate him a lot.

Claire's story of the birth of the Settlement.

Get ready for this: a year or two later, his mother, Marian, moved closer to some of her family in Wiscasset and gave us the house and 920 acres of land in Egypt, some of it farmland, and a lot of it well-managed woods. Gordon's father is buried on the land in one of the fields, a windy grassy-in-summer high spot. And Marian also gave us more than half of her shares in the business, and all of her shares in other businesses, which meant a heavenly sum of money. And around the same time, Paul Lessard and Gordon had their heads together with half a dozen solar and wind schemes. And even Rex York was back to coming around a little because he was only just down the road. Rex. A great little plotter, that one. Yes, as I said, I am speaking of he who many now call Mr. Militia.

And so the Settlement formed, first a bunch of St. Onges, Lessards, and Souciers, cousins and friends of cousins of Gordon's father from THE County. Then my cousins, Leona and Geraldine and Macky from the reservation and Chuck, a distant cousin of mine who had been living in downtown Bangor since graduation. And his wife, Dawn. And their friend Carol. Macky didn't get along here. He went back to the Township. And Carol left for other reasons. But then others from around Egypt joined us and brought their families, even their old grammies and various other elderly relatives, and our sweet sweet community came to be, and we all pledged to make a dignified life for ourselves and we taught the children how to *be* a community, and Gordon started to believe that all people could have lives worth living if they lived like this. He finally had others who understood about the growing high-tech oligarchic system, the terrible dilemma. He was no longer *alone*. And so he believed in the possibility of an epiphany on the part of people. The great ideal. That people could then take power, *make* a "we the people" government and society out of many, many small interdependent and variedness-of-character communities.

And here we were, living proof of the part of it called community. I say it again. It was sweet. There were good days and bad days. There were smooth sailing times. There were ugly glitches. But the dark horrors of Mammon and its tyranny were less of a concern now for us who could make this good thing work, we believed. Me, too. *Of course*. Sunny Claire. Don't laugh. I'm not one to grin and coo. But my heart is almost all the time full of good heat.

 ### The revelation. Claire remembers.

It was exciting to be part of this. Within six years, we had organized a solid network of fifteen little solar-wind communities around the state and in New Hampshire, including two groups around Augusta that were experimenting with making turbines and inverters and alternators and photovoltaic collectors, all the stuff you usually depend on the big guys for, the systems, the grids. And humanure composting systems about which Lee Lynn always loves to twitter, "It's really about keeping our water clean and our rye fields green." And we were devout collectors and savers of old "grandparent seeds." There was a growing network for that, a "seedy web" (another of Lee Lynn's repartees).

When I refer to some of the other *communities*, I do not mean as large or as tight as ours, but they are working out well, yes. And some of these are combined with the CSA farms. That's Community Supported Agriculture, where residents in a given area altogether invest money or time in a crop in return for a share of the harvest. We travel the state back and forth for shop talk and noisy feasts with communities that are usually built around home-schooling, three of these fundamentalist born-again-style Christians. We learn a lot from each other and sort through *a lot* of differences. Yes, I tell you, good hearts are everywhere.

Meanwhile, our Settlement grew and the hammers rang as more little houses went up on the hill, some with building permits, some without . . . depending on Gordon's mood. And Gordon was tireless. He would go in and out of spells of drinking but he was always tireless. He was not one to drown and go *down* in his drunken tears. He worked. He watched over us all, even while goofing around and gabbing people's ears off, and his other distraction, which I hadn't realized yet.

Meanwhile, he started to organize a network of little family-owned furniture factories around Maine, middle-grade pine. He said it was evil to take a log that could be made into a locally sold supper table and chip it all up for megaprofit global market biomass or paper. From those little enterprises came our one big cooperative Maine-made furniture exchange, which was actually the idea of a guy named Mo Petre, who lives in Patten, a friend of Rex York. The exchange and warehouse was set up in Gray, near the turnpike exit-entrance.

Energy. Food. Keeping the water clean. Furniture. Trade. Low-profit trade. Good trade. Community. *Dignity*. It can be done. There was even talk of community banks. One and a half percent interest. And why not some based not on debt, but on services and commodities.

But you guessed it, there was that something else. Behind closed doors. He didn't tell me this at first, but there came to be women here who welcomed into their hearts and beds this man, a man so many people naturally acquiesce to, a man who, being part of so many minds and hearts, had taken on a salience . . . a size larger than life . . . a, yes, power. Like fame. His unraveling weaknesses were all in the past, or overlooked. He had become the perfect being. Desirable. Oh, indeed.

 Claire continues.

As far as any of us knew, Gordon never touched other men's wives, even though he was stupidly solicitous with everybody. He always managed to *stop short*. But also there were living here women who were not "wives" of Gordon. There were unmarried and divorced women with no kids, women who society had kicked, ripped, and mangled because of their gentle ways. Some women arrived here with plenty of children. They simply wanted to be mothers, not "workers" and "servers." Meanwhile, those who had gone to Gordon willingly, left their doors open in the night, or waited in the tall grass under a sugary moon and lather of stars, here in the safety of this loving place, and started making *a lot* of babies. Most of these mothers even gave the children the last name of St. Onge. Whitney and Michelle, for instance, are his two oldest daughters. Quite a few of his children were young teens by the time the *Record Sun* set time ticking faster. They were all ages. Down to crawling babies and a few brand new. Natty was due real soon. And Vancy was showing. And Bonnie Loo had started up the "morning drools," as she called it. This, her fourth child, the third by Gordon.

There were many families, married and unmarried couples (one a lesbian couple), and a lot of very old people who lived here. There were kids and various adults who came to work with us during the day. So you see, not everyone was a St. Onge "wife." And there were a few women who wore that silver wedding band for Gordon, women who lay with Gordon and knew all those special whispers of his and his bear wrastles and his *moods,* but did not want or could not have pregnancies. I tell you this to let you know this wasn't just a breeding ground for Gordon. It's wasn't just that.

Okay, so I might have been able to handle the "his having sex with others" concept. Barely, but maybe. The women, most of them, were like sisters to me. But the babies! All those children with his face and those tall robust bodies. Especially those with Passamaquoddy looks, my cousin Leona's bunch, for instance. Today, I can almost see my own face as a youngster in the face of twelve-year-old Shanna St. Onge.

When I first got wind of his other relationships, I said to him, "Don't ever touch me again."

And that was it. I filed for divorce.

He didn't want the divorce. He made a few small scenes. But he backed off. Did his sulking alone in the big old farmhouse he no longer shared with me.

After the divorce, I lived with Sonny Estes in East Egypt Village for two years. But of course, Sonny Estes seemed small as a fruit fly after what I'd had. And a lot went wrong. Sonny ridiculed fat people, and I was getting fatter every year. And Sonny had a relationship with TV. TV! The very thing I once wanted so badly and defended against Gordon's TV wrath. But Sonny was a real TV man. How do you respect a man whose face every evening and weekend has that mindless palsied TV stare?

A few other St. Onge "wives" left the Settlement because it is hard to share a man. In some cases the fur was flying. Some stayed but shut Gordon out. Some even paired up with a different Settlement man. What Gordon's reactions were to these events varied.

Meanwhile, he certainly collected more than he lost. And day by day, we made it work. Yeah, it was weird. I agree. And sharing a mate is harder for some than others. So I'll speak only for myself.

I came back. And I was happy to have him in my bed on those nights when he came around.

 ### The voice of Mammon.

The company is family now. The company appreciates loyalty! The people work. And they work and they work and they work. Heigh ho! Heigh ho! There are seminars now where big-business–minded people go to discuss finding *the soul of business*. At these seminars a luncheon is served by college-age waitresses and waiters in maroon or green golf shirts, so Ivy League and wholesome. These waitresses and waiters are called servants . . . oh sorry, we mean *servers*.

Meanwhile, the speakers have well-managed hair and skin without blemish or chafe or too much age and they are conservatively uniformed, a boon of identical grays, and they are beaming with know-how. Lots of beaming. One of the speakers is going to the podium now. She adjusts the mike. Everyone smiles, smiles, smiles. Such a positive concept! Finding a business's soul. Like warm lips in the night and a whisper of love. Behold the trembly breath of the corporate thing floating up sweet as a child's prayer.

 ### In Ivy Morelli's Portland apartment.

The phone rings.

 ### David Morelli. Ivy's Dad. Only forty-seven years old.

Too young to die. But yes, he smoked. A pack a day.

Ivy knows "Mr. Morelli" didn't look right that day they all drove to their cousin's camp on Moosehead. He walked funny. Funnier than usual. And his eyes looked . . . reddish . . . or was it yellowish? "You okay, Mr. Morelli?"

And he had quickly said, "Doing good."

Too quickly.

He wants for you never to feel even a slight inconvenience or worry, let alone pain. Did he think he could keep liver cancer from them forever? Is she right to believe that even her mother didn't know about the liver cancer?

So she had put it out of her mind. Her questions had melted.

This morning, her mom told her over the phone, "He has known for three months." She didn't say "we." She said the doctors thought, with the treatments, he'd have more time.

Treatments. Step right up and get your snake oil. Only $14,000 a whack or whatever ransom figure they can pump out of you. *Was* Mr. Morelli getting treatments?

"Oh, yes," her mother assures her. But maybe she really means, *Oh, yes, I think so.*

"And you knew?"

Hesitation. "I . . . do now."

How could he have managed SECRET TREATMENTS? Secret vomiting, secret baldness? No, no, no. He no doubt put the treatments off, needing time to figure a way to carry this creaking, bristly, foul harvest by himself, to traverse the great epic of terminal cancer without his dears noticing!

On the way to the hospital "at home" upstate, Ivy hardly sees the wet road, traffic lights, cars with their left- and right-turn signals. She plays the screaming thumping radio, feeling it only on her skin, not in her ears.

When she gets there, he is in a coma. Or something. He opens his eyes and shifts around. But sees nothing. Eyes close again dreamily. He is VERY yellow and VERY small. Even his head. Weird now (and partly bald from age) and doll-sized on the pillow.

She cries in her twin sister's arms. She loses it. She is screaming. His death will be nothing after this, the dying part. The little head on the pillow will be taken away.

She goes out to her car in the big parking lot and holds her face. The rain closes in around, thrums on the cheap tinny roof.

Days later, back at her apartment, in the pile of sympathy cards, one card from a person she hardly knows . . . met once at a party (somehow they have stayed in touch), a wacky artist type named Sarah. It's not even really a sympathy card. But it is being used by this Sarah as a sympathy card.

It is a drawing in yellow, pinks, and turquoise. Feminine colors. No, Easter colors. *Fun* colors. Sassy.

It shows a hallway of wild ripples, the walls wackily decorated in spirals and diamonds and ferns. The ceiling is stripes. A door with a jazzy fan light window over it. Beyond the door, a stairway leading upward into darkness that is adorned in Hollywood-style stars . . . not like gold teacher stars . . . these are chubby stars. Kind of jokey stars. Ivy stares and stares at this stairway, tears pouring from her eyes, but she's kind of smiling, too.

If *that's* where Mr. Morelli has shuffled off to, then okay.

 ### Back at her desk in the newsroom.

She is transfixed by her screen. Which is off. Blank. The future is blank, yes. The past even more incomprehensible. She moves her clover-color lips in her paler than ever face, pale as though lighted by the science-fictionesque glow of the screen, *if it were on*, that is. Her lips speak voicelessly. Her throat gets an "apple" in it, clenched to circumscribe great unplumbed grief.

Teacher man, you lied!

 ### Ivy getting even?

Today Gordon rides a Settlement horse. Arkie. The trail is old and the first half mile is worn brick-hard, except where it is occasionally dank and fleshy. Two small recently reinforced bridges. This path unbraids up through the trees to the old camp built in the 1920s on the southwest top side of the mountain. The horse is old, too. All is old today. Horse steps along in a clompy but ladylike fashion, up, up, and up. Trail's not overly steep but no leveling. Lofty bank on left, mostly rock, but lichen and mosses and twining roots have metamorphosed the rock bulges into faces and shoulders of great gray spooks and beasties.

There is a branching of this path you need to avoid like the dickens when taking a horse through. Some bridges "there thattaway" have rot. And there's a very black mucky hellhole that sneaks up and sucks you and your mount toward the earth's creamy core. Or just glues horse hooves and fetlocks in place. Then, if you get past that, low limbs plot to poke your eyes. And too many partridges. They explode from your chest it seems and this makes certain horses take to the sky.

Kids have made signs at this juncture. *Path of Life*. And *Path of Death*. Though horses can't read they never fail to make the right choice, whether you rein them in that direction or not. Arkie chooses "life."

Gordon's face is seamed with rocky sorrow. He has worn an old stained felt crusher, once a forest green, his riding hat today; other days, this hat gets to be his logging hat. No resemblance to the big modern cowboy hats of the Southwest, more of the old, old hat style of log drivers and cowboys pre-Hollywood. The saddle is old and it has an old voice; more snivel than creak.

Oh, yes, the day is mighty old.

Old Arkie is officially a pinto but almost entirely the color of a used-up yellowy bedsheet. A face like a skull; let's say "spirit." Black splats on his eyes and ear tips and black whispering along through the yellow white of his tail. He's too old to dance or prance, buck or churn. Gordon is not that sure a rider, so the two are a perfect fit. Gordon could have walked, since he isn't really going anywhere, not all the way to the old camp, just in the direction of deep people-less void. But he wanted someone along, someone who wouldn't be bothered by his stature turning to pudding today. For what if he should sob?

He hasn't toted along a copy of the *Record Sun* his little daughter Andrea pressed into his hand about an hour ago at noon. One of her important errands, Settlement life so always glutted with weighty comings and goings, the swarm of the thing.

He left the paper behind, carrying it only in his head.

Here comes a tunnel of hemlock boughs, a black firmament with which to merge one's wounded incorporeal self. The man closes his eyes, hears and feels the horse's hooves pad like a cat's paws across the moss. Arkie has no expressed opinions on this place, as ever his rider's sturdy slave. His ears turn, but not worriedly. An overcast embraces both beings suddenly, giving the forest darkness a deeper, more silent seamlessness. Arkie's pupils open in his apple-sized eyes but his great old head remains directly face-front. Gordon reins him up.

There's a leveling off here and so they stand together going no-where, the crusher hat low over the man's eyes, the horse's black pinto splotches around his eyes, which the kids call his "cool sunglasses," though the skull look is what Gordon always sees, a damn creepy-looking animal, actually.

The sun rips back out through a mouth in the purpling sky. Man and horse both stare at sunny polka dots and lacy gloom of manifold trunks, fern, turkey-tail fungi, the dust of spores, mist, and fallen limbs caught against the standing mass, altogether reaching out as ghoul arms begging the man and horse "come hither," "come to Hell's gates," "you belong."

In his mind's eye, Gordon sees the columns of what Ivy has spilled, a full spread, photos, the works. It is plainly not an attack on Settlement life, just a baring of it. There it is. Dangling. Buck naked. *Out there.*

There is no reference to his "more than twenty" *wives* nor to the face-smacking of the boy Jaime in the heat of that day on the mountain. But—

Can this silence and woody August sweetness help organize the chaotic terror inside him, the terror that increaseth in his gut every day, the militia-connected and polygamous master of the Settlement, soon to rip out onto the stage of America in truth and in exaggeration, beyond, *far* beyond the intentions of Ivy's pretty little pale hand?

 The newsroom.

Ivy, diddling with her column, this, her belated Kotzschmar review, still trying not to sound too passionate, too corny, but she is *feeling* both passionate and corny about this most grand instrument, sees something scarlet in the corner of her eye, sees two substantial figures, understands in the way they move, even in the feeble blur of her periphery sight, that this is Gordon St. Onge and someone who has inherited Gordon's way of standing, and the same way he holds his head. She wheels around fast. Yep.

She goes to them, leads them to her desk, Gordon and a Nordic-Slavic-faced blond teenaged boy who calls her "Ma'am" and holds his cap by the bill against the outside of one thigh, as his father does. The boy wears a scarlet chamois shirt and jeans. Keys on his belt like Gordon. Maybe only age fourteen or so, not bearded, just fuzzy, but an air of self-sovereignty, of mastery, of capability, which Ivy knows by now is learned but also shared.

Gordon does not make an introduction. He just looks at Ivy with an unflinching pale gaze, none of his usual twitches and squints and such.

She offers them seats. "Coffee? Juice? An apple?"

"Naw," says Gordon. "But thanks." He looks toward the boy. Boy is now looking the other way, bright-eyed, cap loose in both his strong hands, looking around at all the computer screens, and from both this boy and Gordon a smell of the Settlement, their strongly scented prickly almost stinky herbal soaps, their food, so many smoked meats and smoked fish for "holidays," herbed soups, maple desserts.

Ivy's dress is a plaid of many grays with an old-fashioned patent leather belt. Very short dress. Bared legs. Sandals. Her hair, shimmering purple-black. Both hair and clothes flounce around stylishly as she asserts how happy she is to see them. And yes, animal crackers dangling from her ears! A tiger and a zebra. Cookie-colored and crunchie-looking. Are they real? Fresh from the little circusy box? Both critters leap and lunge, as Ivy won't hold still. She is nerved up. Almost squeaky. She is very, very nerved up.

She offers seats again.

Gordon sits. The boy, still staring around, says, "Yes, thanks." But he is slow to comply.

Gordon's eyes slide over Ivy's computer screen with the Kotzschmar story glowing passionately and yes, cornily, there.

Ivy promises them that she'll give them a tour before they go, that it's a great educational experience. "Girl Scouts and Boy Scouts come through here a lot."

She has never seen Gordon so devoid of expression. His color is stony. Makes the gray on the chin of his dark beard look white-hot.

She takes the plunge. "Gordon. It was a sympathetic piece. You know it was. I made it clear that . . . what I heard and saw was exemplary. And . . . magical. And good and right. And revolutionary! You know it's true. I didn't slam you."

Now he lets go. He squint-blinks mightily, his bewildered look. "Yes . . . i'twas a beautiful piece."

"Please, Gordon. Don't hate me. I did it for you. From this end, things look different."

He looks at her mouth.

She sighs.

The boy asks about newspaper pictures, how it is those are done.

Ivy says that it is mostly now by state-of-the-art computers and digital cameras. No more real photo developing in the photo lab. "That will be part of the tour!" she tells him with gusto.

Gordon turns in his seat, places his arm over the seat's back, glances across the tops of cubicle walls, over heads, over glowing screens, glowing faces, the strange slightly dim new look of an almost twenty-first-century newsroom, then again his eyes fall on her screen with the Kotzschmar story which, only days ago, was filled in brightly with the Home School story and the lives of Gordon's loved ones in a nutshell and breathlessly about to be made public.

Ivy says softly, "I broke your trust."

He looks back over at her.

She is on the edge of violent weeping. In the grief and loss side of her heart, where she has spent so much time these past few days, it is all pressing to stumble out, like a wire cage tightly and mercilessly packed with eye-rolling panicked animals. Into her wheeled chair she slowly sits. She looks down at her fingers, wiggles them.

Gordon is deathly silent, eyes on her fingers.

She says, "It had nothing to do with the other night . . . about us . . . honest."

He looks at her face again.

She says, "Gordon . . . it's just a matter of time. There's a lot of smoke . . . you know . . . the rumors and complaints. I heard the state is poising itself to really go after you on a few things . . . child-protective stuff. They've figured out you have Jane . . . instead of Pete Meserve, who is supposed to have her. It's all hush-hush but Shawn Phillips has been accused of being lax, and the governor is asking questions. This stuff . . . the complaints . . . the accusations about . . . you . . ." She glances at the boy. "Are ugly." She winces, her voice terribly grave, no HAW HAW. "Several agencies have begun compiling reports . . . casual reports, they *say* . . . whatever that means . . . reports . . . about . . . your . . . wives. They say some of them are too young. And *that* could mean prison and the whole sex offender registration bit."

Gordon flushes. Definitely the look of guilt. He snorts out a little laugh. He says, "The state machine. Slow. But . . . big. And . . . hungry."

Says Ivy, "My feature on you is, if anything, a favorable character reference."

Gordon's face is still stone, in its color and how it would feel if you touched it now.

Ivy stands up abruptly, almost a leap, which catches the eye of the person at the next desk and a couple of people just coming into the newsroom, and they stare as Gordon stands up quickly. Tall and, yes, bull-built, powerfully built, and *demoniacal* when you consider the worst of the rumors.

Ivy opens her arms and leans into him, and with his billed cap in one hand dangling from his fingers at her back, he hugs her up hard against him and she cries without sound, just huff-huffs, and puts a big wetness on the front of his old patched green work shirt and her words audible to a few of the nearest desks, "I love you. I love you. I love you." Gordon rubs his beard across the top of her shimmery head and the boy gets up from his chair and thumps his billed cap against his leg embarrassedly and all the newsroom is poppingly hotly alert. Ivy's editor, Brian Fitch, is stepping out of the managing editor's office with an armload of old folders and printout sheets, and Brian looks to the face of the copy editor nearest him, who throws up her hands and grins with the great marvel of this, everyone in the newsroom knowing who Gordon is, knowing from the rumors about pagan worship, the Satan worship, the child labor, child lust, child death, stashed weapons, the militia connections, the "forty" wives. So what does this make Ivy?

Eventually the tour. Then good-byes. Good-bye forever. Ivy will not ever go near that *place* or him again lest she go mad. After he and the boy amble away, she breaks into unsuccessfully suppressed wild sobs, hurries to the women's room where she stays for over a half hour while the newsroom buzzes and bubbles with this, the kind of news it loves best.

 For two days, Ivy tries to reach Gordon by telephone but nobody knows where he is "at the moment."

But then he calls her.

She tells him in a rush, as if time counted, "I found out only a few minutes after you left the other day that the story went AP. I'm sorry,

Gordon, but they added in *things* . . . like . . . that there has been con-
troversy around you . . . which is true. Seems there's been a lot of calls
to their offices, not just ours . . . and AP's been interviewing people
right and left . . . including grandparents and ex-teachers of some of
the Settlement kids who've come to the Settlement more recently, or
recent teachers of kids who left the Settlement a few years ago. AP just
says you are 'controversial' and mentions 'passionate disapproval' by
'many' . . . then, of course, some emphasis on kids lacking 'education'
and lacking a 'competitive environment,' these as quotes."

He hears her small *tsk!* He inhales, holds it. She rushes on. "Even
with all the changes, the AP version is very short. Condensed. Really
condensed. It . . . changes the tone of the piece from the way I wrote it.
And the picture we never used for *reasons*. They seem to like that one
a lot. In all the papers that are using the piece, they rewrite the copy
and use *that* photo. One of the ones of you by the merry-go-round.
Like I say, not the one I used. And it's cropped. It's this slightly fuzzy
whir of creepy beasts in front of you and your face in sharp focus. You
look . . ." She swallows. "Pretty scary."

 **From a future time, Penny St. Onge tells us how it
went.**

The whole business with Ivy Morelli and the feature article she put
together had brought the media-cheap side of life down on us. Gawk-
ers would drive right up in here to look. They'd park out just beyond
the parking lot and Quonset huts and stare. Or maybe not stop at all,
just circle around slowly, then head back down the hill to the tar road.
There were those who greeted us and were interested in our solar and
wind projects and the community supported agriculture. But there were
those who greeted us just so they could get inside the buildings. Then
they'd gape at everything and probe us about the polygamy experience
that was rumored and the "stockpiled" guns. We were a cheap thrill.

 Josee Soucier remembering.

It was not t'e big article *itself* t'at was t'mess. It was t'world. The article
opened a big lid on t'a whole sick world.

Lorraine Martin.

It was really sickening to look up from your work and see a person leaning against a car, raising a camera or shouldering a camcorder, the lens stroking you ever so lightly yet ever so deeply. In your own home.

 Beth St. Onge.

Our nice smiling faces were as twittipating to the poplace as twisted-necked corpses and squashed towns with airplane fuselages sticking up. Holy fuck!

 Claire St. Onge.

Gordon had the kids go down to where our dirt road came off Heart's Content. They made a gate with a pole and signs saying KEEP OUT. So then the media gets a few shots of the leafy lane, dappled sun, and unfriendly sign, announcing to the world that we were shutting ourselves in. And those publicized photos drew *more* media, which exploded into more sightseers, more phone calls, more mail.

 Bonnie Loo.

Nobody should have been surprised.

 Ellen St. Onge.

Gordon was pissy. More than usual.

 Glennice St. Onge.

I prayed and everyone at church prayed, too, that the Lord would offer us a lesson in this and we'd all be better off. Mr. Baker, who leads our Wednesday night study and Sunday school, suggested with a giggle that we should charge admission. Meanwhile, Gordon's mood miraculously changed from old grouch to Mr. Bright Eyes because he was adding lots more wind project people and CSA people to his rotary files. He was on the phone yakkety-yak every night going on about a world made up of little communities, local trade, good food, and "poop composting." That's what a lot of little kids loved to call it. Some of the worrywarts here thought the phone thing was too much. "He's not eating," they said. "He's acting toooo happy," one said. Too happy?

 Geraldine St. Onge.

You couldn't make a phone call pertaining to our needs here, calling a doctor, for instance; the thing was either ringing or stuck to Gordon's ear. And once the "gate" was up, the sightseers would hang around down there waiting to catch us coming and going. Made you want to cover your head like mobsters do when leaving court. I started wearing my sunglasses a lot more.

 Gail St. Onge recollects.

Radio shows talked about us. Newspapers in other states picked up the story but there the story took a different turn. Even the pictures looked inside out. We were whacked at like a piñata. Strewn all over the place. Hands grabbing.

 Penny St. Onge.

We had always been good neighbors and enjoyably connected with people around town and beyond. Our businesses of wreaths and Christmas trees, maple syrup, meat cutting, the CSA and so forth depended on this. But also we did weekly, sometimes daily, field trips (all ages) to museums, concerts, lectures, the State House, and there were our cooperative windmill projects and the pine furniture exchange. What I mean to say is, our road in and out has always been busy. We were *not* separatists!! But because of Ivy Morelli's deceit, because of the media's glossy edge of fantasy in all of this, we now *were, ta-dah!* separatists.

Leona St. Onge.

I don't think Elvis used to get as much mail as we did. The mail crew, mostly kids, were under a blizzard of envelopes, mailers, and boxes. "Don't eat any of those cookies!" us mothers warned. God knows who these strange gift givers were. But most correspondence was sad stories of the lives of people *out there.* Some of the kids took these to heart.

"Don't read 'em! Just sort 'em!" bellered Bonnie Loo. "Not if you haven't the guts to share in a little agony!"

 Busy at the bureau. Federal Building. Special Agent (S.A.) Kashmar scrolling over the *Record Sun*'s "Homeschool" story and all those stories and photos that have sprung from it. His thoughts.

Ain't he pretty. Network television is going to yum him up. *If* we go that way. For now, we wait.

 History as it happens (as dictated by Kristie).

We saw Randy Graffam at the IGA. He has a new potbelly pig who gets to live *in the house*. Pig's name is Ghostie for some reason. Also he told us details about what happened this summer, which was bad. The social workers busted in at night with FIVE police at his sister's and they held her down to get her baby. His sister is Rachel who works at the variety. She hung on to the baby but they pulled harder and the police said she better let go or else. But she screamed and screamed. Baby must've screamed, I bet. The baby's name is Megan. The police got her baby and took her and then Rachel was on the floor in the corner rolled up in a ball. Her neck ripped from crying. Her boyfriend Aaron came home just as all this was going on and he got his gun and shot the cops' tires so they arrested him and it was all in the news that he's crazy. But everybody knows him how he's nice, usually.

The DHS said the day care people saw the baby had sores and said they were cigarette burns. On her legs and arms and everyplace. But Randy said those were bug bites, which get sore, even his mum's friend's kids have that happen when mosquitoes and blackflies bite them. Me, too! Bug bite allergicness.

The social workers said "even then. Bugs aren't supposed to bite babies." In their heads they have plans. It doesn't matter about what is nice. The judge believes the DHS guys and never checks. At first I felt scared because we have one trillion mosquitoes here. Beth says all us kids look like we have the pox. But she said ha-ha about DHS. We are lucky. We have a *gate*. And *lots* more guns.

 In a future time, Claire remembers when Professor Catherine Court Downey became part of Settlement life.

In the middle of all this "fame," which we were trying to push away, I invited Catherine to come stay awhile. To help her get off the pills. And to have a real gangly sort of extended family for Robert, less institution and less au pair. Her husband, amazingly, had had no idea about her drugs. And she didn't want him to know now. He was gone a lot during this time. She would just need to close down her house in Portland, transfer her mail.

Let me tell you about my cottage here at the Settlement. It's small. It is surrounded by birch trees. White birch with bark like velvet, which always gives my yard a magical silver light, except at night when it can be as black as pitch, and in springtime a thousand garden variety purple violets and white violets that started themselves out there in some puzzling way, and in winter, the whitest snow. But always there is something about walking around in those birches that makes you feel like a self-satisfied spirit.

I have a real tiny sunroom, mostly full of plants and baskets and those two-foot-tall bright red ceramic cats my mother-in-law Marian gave me years ago. The ceiling of the sunroom is too low for most people to stand under. There's just room enough for two rockers and a little table carved in the shape of a toadstool, just right for two cups of coffee, or one cup of coffee and a paperback book.

Oh, yes, the baskets. These are from home. Princeton. Not Princeton, the college. Princeton, the reservation. Tough baskets, made the old way, like tough lives. Immortal, sort of. In the memory of the mothers and fathers, grandmothers and grandfathers. Worthless in the way of the new way. The American way. Immortality of the spirit, I mean, is worthless. Not cost effective. Not part of the forward motion. Not part of the flow or the GDP. My sunroom: a gentle cessation of the GDP. And my baskets breathe.

In the kitchen on the west side there is a wall of colored glass. Not stained glass. Just colored glass squares. Like an old English church. I love the mix. My home, the mix. All peoples since the beginning have striven to *make* beauty, not content with the moon and the wild clover, spiky blue lakes in a summer wind. Nope. They must *make* godly things. Baskets. Glass. Stone. Wood. Textiles. Glossy "well-bred" animals. Cleared vistas. And see, admit it, our beauty is equal to God's. See, God made us, so what we make is God-made. And our destruction? God-made. God is all beauty and love? Ha!

But there was only one place here at my home for Catherine and Robert to sleep at night . . . my small bedroom. So we made it two bitty rooms using a hanging curtain. She did not complain.

Most nights we talked for an hour or two through the curtain, and then some more on the way down to breakfast at the shops. She talked about Phan a little. She said he was easy. She said he was never home. Then she'd laugh. She said he was always *under*.

"Under what?"

"Under our feet . . . on the other side of the world."

Phan was a businessman. Vietnamese American. His people were still in South Vietnam. His English was excellent. But he was not a chatty guy. Maybe he was a good listener. Attentive. The time I met him, I recall that he was. And he told a few little businessman jokes. I thought his springy sort of zingy-zoingy accent betokened an inheritance of tenacious honeybee-like industry. Yeah, immortality of spirit, as I mentioned before. But Catherine now seemed happy to erase him from mind.

I figured now it was safe to tell Catherine about *my* husband. I finally let it all spill. I confessed that I was one of *them* . . . one of the wives. I told her almost EVERYTHING there was to tell. She was good-humored about it! She said she understood.

A few days passed. It was not cold turkey. She eliminated medications in stages. Starting with the spooky Zolpidems. She napped a lot, in a restless way. We all shared Robert. The whole family welcomed the two of them gently. At this time, Catherine seemed so vulnerable. All the women wanted to mother her.

She said once, "You're right, Claire. Out in your yard it feels magical. It feels like an extension of oneself . . . a better self."

"And light as a breath," I added.

There was a little stone bench out there, and from it you could see for miles. She sat out there to meditate alone while most of us were off with our crews and committees and errands.

Then I suggested that we find space in one of the buildings here for her to paint . . . or meditate . . . whatever. Her own private workroom.

"A room of one's own," she said with a smile. And yes, she would like it very much.

 In a future time, Catherine Court Downey remembers.

His face. His size. The way he stood and the strength in his hands and arms. Even his neck. He was six-foot-five but appeared even bigger to me that day at the university.

Yes, from my Internet search, I recognized him. A newspaper article where he spoke at the legislature on education had been posted. He seemed to be speaking with his hands. Like a foreigner. So in the cafeteria, I knew him instantly. Those eyes. Penetrating, like Rasputin's. Have you seen Rasputin's eyes in the old photos of the royal family's court? And you are familiar with the havoc the shabby monk wreaked on the Russian empire?

The first morning I was there at the Settlement, Claire fixed a little breakfast for Robert and me, just she and I and Robert alone in her tiny crowded sunroom. She made up a little tea and toast with homemade bread, homemade preserves. And an egg thing with cheese that neither Robert nor I could eat. It was all too much.

The rest of the day, I slept and didn't eat another meal. I didn't want heaviness. I wanted to drift.

But the next morning, Robert and I went with her down to what they called the shops. It wasn't even light yet. But the place swarmed. The huge kitchens, one the summer kitchen, not in use that morning but the cook's kitchen and winter kitchen, were basically one town-hall-sized room in sections fluttering with light from dozens of glass lamps and candles. It was all true, children everywhere who looked like HIM. And women at the stoves and sinks, looking like the laborers of hell . . . hot crackling sounds, hissing, big roiling steam. Water was pumped from tall green *hand* pumps over the sinks. And everyone spoke with a kind of weird satiatedness.

And HE was there, horsing around with some young men. Arm wrestling and taking bets and laughing in ways that sounded sexual. One of them knocked over a pitcher of milk. Dogs and cats lapped it up. Women raced around with wipe-up towels.

When he saw me, his eyes widened. After a time, he came over to me and scooched down in front of my chair and asked me how I was feeling and he admired Robert's new belt buckle (yes, the copper sun face) and got Robert into a conversation, Robert looking a little too intense. Then this strange man, Gordon St. Onge, looked back up at me and it was like his eyes were eating into my face. I noticed that he was younger than I first thought him to be. I had expected him to be Claire's age or older, but he was nine or ten years younger than Claire. He was even younger than me. What was he thinking?

He looked like he wanted to take me to bed. And make ten more babies. But he just said, "Get strong, Little One" and patted my hand as though he were my father or a hotshot religious cult leader, which is actually what he was.

 Lee Lynn St. Onge visits the sick.

I gave a little rap on Claire's cottage door. Claire was not around but it was Catherine I came to see. She didn't answer my little rap so I hustled in. She was in Claire's bedroom stretched out, not asleep. She sat up. Her pallet was behind a curtain of hot, almost hurtful colors. She rubbed one eye with a hand of stubby nails.

I said, "Hello," then, "I'm Lee Lynn," and I bent to touch her arm.

She froze but smiled as if to apologize for the semirebuff.

I offered softly, "And you are Catherine?"

"What can I do for you?" she asked. Like a cool bureaucrat on the phone. Like someone *not* feeling embraced. Or safe. Or cozy.

"Nothing," I answered. "Nothing at all. You are to rest. I have brought you remedies. And I can work with your energy. Help refresh you. And give you a foot massage? Or head and neck?"

She squeezed her eyes shut to stop this line of thinking.

So I explained the contents of the basket that I was lowering to the floor for her to inspect, my back to the curtain, the space only for her pallet of quilts and blankets, not for visitors.

She raised her eyebrows as if hearing a loud *BANG*! "I can't buy anything. I don't do . . . that sort of thing." Whatever *that* meant. I heard she was a zesty shopper. And that she was no stranger to Reiki and other energy therapies.

I hurried to correct her. "These are *gifts*." And reached again in a sisterly way for her shoulder which was skinny but iron. I couldn't read her wounds. There was a blankness against my palm.

She covered both eyes as if an awful flash had filled the room and beyond. Then she said, "Sorry, I'm not good company. I'm not well."

"You will be soon, Catherine," I offered cheerfully. "You're in good hands here." I had several herbal liquors but mostly teas, salves, all calming and meant to boost the immune system. I took them out and, one by one, held them aloft just so. "But my favorite," I went on, as hushy as possible, trying not to cause those dark eyebrows to jounce up again, "is goldenrod." I enthused how you "don't really need to enlist a gang of Settlement slaves, ha-ha, to assist you because you can gather quite enough by yourself with a couple of big baskets, making a few pleasant trips."

I described how we "gather it, hang it up in an out-of-the-light place to dry. This would be early fall."

Then "in later fall, you break it up and store it in large or small jars, leaf and flower."

I praised it as an immune-stimulant antiseptic tonic if you make a tea from it, "but also tasty; it would remind you of chamomile. It calms pain. Cures wounds. Astringent, diuretic, antitoxic. Anti-inflammatory, a urinary antiseptic. Used for cystitis, urethritis. Used for indigestion." All this time I caressed the jar , just a nice old canning jar filled with the green of miracles.

"If you stop by at my place, I'll give you some of the salve made with the crushed flower and lard and clove, also in jars. Jars are so pretty, some of the glass blown by my small witchy assistants, not slaves, *really.* I was only kidding." Smile. Smile.

During my description of this blessed healing goldenrod, crown of our September hills, her eyebrows must have shot up fourteen times.

Slowly her hands slipped to cover her ears.

"Oh, dear," I said.

"My eardrums hurt," she whispered.

"Oh, dear."

She sank back into the pillow. I covered her up, gave her dark hair a pat, left the basket on the floor, and tiptoed out.

 ### In a future time, Claire St. Onge remembers.

She slept a lot. She was fussy about food. But she grew stronger. She drove to town in search of some herbal treatments to replace the prescriptions. St. John's Wort and ginkgo, but there was nothing like that in or near downtown East Egypt except Lee Lynn's homegrown or home-scavenged stash, which Catherine seemed distrustful of, so the next day she drove farther and stayed away all day. Returned with a lot of bags. She laughed, said shopping always makes her high. Robert hadn't gone with her. He stayed at the Settlement shops, busy as a bee, the kids already treating him as a brother.

 ### In a future time, Catherine Court Downey remembers.

It didn't take long to figure him out. He surrounded himself with weak and injured people or the crazy. This made him a big man. This gave him an almighty position.

The second time I showed up for breakfast, that next morning, again before daylight, again the big kitchen noisy and chaotic, the light beautiful and eerie, the food all over the three long tables in pans and trays, in HEAPS! . . . some people singing "Happy Birthday" to whoever, I couldn't tell . . . there *he* was at the head of the two longer connected tables, his hands folded as if for prayer. He smiled at me. I sort of smiled back. This time he was surrounded by elderly men, like bishops and deacons, like lords! They had that sort of look about them, their chins up, old raggedy necks, small eyes lost in collapsed lids, all watching the room as if God had given THEM some special privilege, special rights, above the women and kids who brought them coffee and cold juice.

Robert and I were invited to sit with a group of young mothers, girls actually, with their children older than Robert.

I looked toward the end of the table and saw "the Prophet," some here called him that as a joke, referring to the recent newspaper and radio publicity with lightheartedness, not the shame I would have imagined. And there he was looking right at me. His eyes were white! Almost like he had no eyes. Light from nearby glass lamps were dull in comparison. He was magic. He was beautiful. He was the patriarch who gathers you into the heat of his harem, then owns you. I almost stood up and went to him. I was so susceptible! I was easy prey. The newspapers and radio call-in shows that now discussed him didn't know the half of it.

 ## At the merry-go-round at the tree line just above the St. Onge farm place.

Short, square, ruddy-faced, gray-haired Barbara who almost daily visits the Settlement but actually lives in a house in East Egypt Village, sits on the edge of the unmoving carousel deck while a Settlement child climbs on and off the saddled monsters. The child has a bad heart and tires easily. Short, square, ruddy-faced gray-haired Bev, Barbara's "dear one" who lives with her, stands with hands on hips glaring at the old generator, which is silent.

Barbara, the *Record Sun* on her knee, reads aloud, "Hyannis. A trucker who held a load of potato chips hostage returned them yesterday but police say he will be charged. Charles Monahon of Ohio delivered 1,153 cases to the New Hyde Park, NY, distributor that expected them August 8. Monahon called the *Fitchburg Sentinel and Gazette* on August 7 to say he was kidnapping the chips because his employer, Kitco, Inc., based in Townsend, owed him and fellow employees over $6,000 in bonuses and vacation pay, and vacations that were promised but never happened."

Suddenly, there is the sound of gunshots in the distance.

Then nothing but the forlorn *creak-creak* of tall grass bugs.

Bev looks across the two-headed golden merry-go-round beast to the boy, who has no reaction to the gunfire. His back is to her, he's sitting sideways on a yellow and black striped creature, swinging a foot, and murmuring to himself. Seems content.

Now the *brrrrrrrrrrrrt!* of fire from full automatic rifles, then just the cheery tall grass bugs.

Bev says, "It's them. The militia. In the pit down there on Boundary Road."

Barbara shivers.

Bev says, "The whole world . . . it's flying apart."

Then again, *Brrrrrrrrrrt! Brrrrrrrrrrrrt! Brrrrrrrrrrrrrt!*

 Beth St. Onge remembering.

Well, there he was again. His old "brother." Richard York. Alias "Rex." Rex's militia had been in the news. Gordon got himself in the news. So there you have it. They were both stars now!

 Claire St. Onge remembering.

They weren't real brothers, but years ago they were two bucks on the loose. After Rex met Marsha, and Gordon and I were settling in, the "brothers" drank less, roamed less, but voilà . . . the Settlement happened. And Rex was in the thick of it, welding the steel towers for the wind plants, wiring cottages. And some of the time his little girl came here instead of public school. Her name? Glory. Glory indeed.

 Bonnie Loo St. Onge speaks.

Yeah, the thing that rattled Rex's cage and got him re-enthused about the Settlement after a few months of his being under a rock or something, was Ms. Purple Hair's feature on us, which she had *promised* she wouldn't print without Gordon's approval. I guess things must have been a bit sizzly in her little purple-haired tattooed hollow heart, *hot for the man.* The way Gordon came off in that feature was like some god. Well *that* was a stretch. But Rex, in the *Record Sun* article that quoted *him,* came off as looking like the Son of Sam. Charles Manson maybe. No, wait, Timothy McVeigh. And *that's* a stretch. And Willie was also in the article, being Willie. Goofing around in some bar with a militia crony, a gun, and a Bible. Spent an hour in the slammer. The man doesn't drink, the man doesn't shoot, and I can't believe he's ever been in a church. But for the record, the *Record Sun* . . . hello! . . . seems our whole Egypt municipality was bent and recolored into a baaad thriller movie. Soooo Rex and Gordon must've felt they needed to share their pain. But you put two heads like those two noodles together and soon we were all being swept down an even darker road through a grimmer fairy tale.

I should have moved out of the Settlement then. I had already stored a couple cardboard boxes of my stuff at Ma's. But, well, I wasn't ready yet to riiiip my heart out even though as things were, *all* my guts were being turned over fire on a spit.

 They met several evenings this way. At the old farm place. Gordon rocks the child to sleep while he himself gets revved up. Rex is usually seamlessly silent.

Tonight Gordon has a beer, Settlement-made of course. Rex has empty hands. He is clean in every way, not even an imbiber of desserts. Has a stiff military bearing like there's a shovel handle in his back. The dark mustache creeps down to his jaws. In brighter light there's a haggardness in parentheses, the mustache less dark, more of a jaded brown. He removes his army cap by the visor. Eyes as pale as Gordon's but more of a blue, like fairer skies, but their purpose is not to transmit love and moods as Gordon's are, but to be meters, to gauge and measure you. Is this leadership? Or fear? Is Rex, like Gordon, getting hotter with fear each day? One might wonder if most unmonied American men are, especially those with the chillest eyes.

See Rex's hands. He doesn't play with the cap. His fingers are simply unfurled. If Rex could tell you why he wears the gold band on his left hand, he would tell you through this kind of stubbornness, where after six years of divorce, after a woman has left you to go somewhere else with someone else, not a bitter battle divorce where people do calisthenics in court over who gets what, nothing like that, just a heart-wrenching quiet throat-choking tight-jawed miserable severing of two lives . . . he could tell you how this feels and how this is against God. And how if your wife can be lost, *anything* can be.

He has been told by some that God will hurt his ex-wife bad for this, though he sees it more the other way around. That she has hurt God. He sees God as the strong silent type, distant and hard to communicate with, but generous and genius and huge and flabbergasted at this ungratefulness of Marsha's. Someday, when Marsha realizes her mistake, her very bad mistake, she'll come back to complete this marriage, this holy plan, cemented by her first wedding vows to him, Richard York, and by the conception and birth of their daughter, their confused wild daughter . . . and so . . . Richard York waits and waits and waits. He waits in a kind of vacuum of purity. Cool, righteous, flabbergasted. Strong, silent, and desolate.

Yes, Marsha York is her name. Her new married name, Marsha Stevens, is against "The Law," the only real law, God's law.

For Gordon, this pain of his "brother's," expressed only indirectly, as statements of more general law and order, is pain to Gordon. Gordon feels what Rex feels, pulse to pulse in sync. Gordon is now swinging his head like a bull. Yes, the verbal arc of their brotherishness comes with the enjoinment to remain only on the perimeters of consolement, as evidenced tonight by Gordon, who after fifty minutes of political wrangling, bellers "Yeah! Yeah! Anthropology! I'm guilty! History! Guilty! Some of us *are* obsessed with concepts. Others with little doo-doos!"

Rex winces. Slaps his soft olive-drab cap back on his head.

 In the meantime.

Secret Agent Jane is, as most always, now equipped with her pink-lensed white-framed heart-shaped secret agent glasses, which give her the power to understand even Gordon's sweaty socioeconomic-political philosophy and Rex's crusty counterpunches.

The night beyond the porch screen is almost as dark and quiet as a closed hand. Mosquitoes want in. They scream for blood.

Gordon is snorting at something Rex has just declared. Yes, Rex declares, Gordon snorts. Rex states. Gordon interrupts. Gordon raves. Gordon thunders around and around the subject he can't shake off tonight. The world's children.

But the word "children" causes Rex's mind to graze over the faces of the younger "men" in his militia, always on *his* mind. Mickey, fifteen, scrawny, somewhat orphaned. Six-foot-one Thad, fourteen years old. Tires easily. Needs more outdoors. The rugged kind of outdoors. Rex does not like to dwell on Jane, whom Gordon calls "war torn." Rex almost sighs. As usual, kid-made candles that smell like hot fields, almost like marijuana at times, give unworthy light to the long porch diluted with chairs, mobiles, little round rugs, wooden toy trucks, embroidered dolls, and papier mâché monsters. All this in opposition to Rex's fondness for simplicity. Yet, this to him is his other home.

And *yes,* Gordon is his "brother." Gordon ten years younger than he. Gordon a kid back *then.* A kid with a twitching-eye-big-puppy grin, fun and clever, more of a strategizer than you'd first notice. Rex just home from "the conflict" wanted nothing but a very little little piece of America. He joined the "volunteer fire department," he got his electrician's license, and he and Gordon lathered themselves in the confusion of the remainder of the 1970s, Rex to ascertain that his terrible initiation was finished, while Gordon searched for the sacred.

Yeah, Gordon would be one to see the sacred in the act of tonguing a stripper during her performance at the fair, evermore profound because he and "his brother" took turns, and so it seemed that she, a queen rising out of the stage in a greenish light and tinfoil-like music, was the issuing authority.

Oh, yes, there is always an issuing authority in America. And this one was here to permit brotherhood. To under-twenty-one-homeboy Gordon, this was sacred. To "the vet," it was just another muddy river, but it was *home.* And he allowed that it was good.

Neither man will forget the sound of her bare feet stamping the wooden stage, side to side, with that swinging long hair . . . *thump!* pause. *Thump!* pause. *Thump!* On and on.

But now life is lived differently.

On the hill below, on Heart's Content Road, curvy but tarred, is the buzzing of a small car engine.

Over the last couple of weeks, THE ARGUMENT prevails. Gordon has called Rex a right-wing fucker. Rex has suggested Gordon reads too many "commie books." So Rex, the worldly vet who has felt deeply OUT THERE, smelled what's OUT THERE, bled OUT THERE, looked into *their* eyes OUT THERE, seen their running backs and worse, their creeping-up shadows, has heard the yong and phong of their speech, has now come to this: a world cut down to size. No, not a "world." "World" is the wrong word. A *spot*. Small enough to stand on, and the necessity of walking its boundaries, to stand sentry beside. A spot that he wishes not to see unraveled. And here's Gordon full of all that is undefined, all that is too big, all that is teetering like the tin globe on the seventh-grade homeroom teacher's desk. All that is *every*where. So maybe Gordon is the enemy? Eh? Maybe Gordon is not his "brother."

The engine on the hill perseveres. Gordon cocks his head. It's the same engine sound that belongs to Ivy Morelli. Gordon, still raving about the frightening future for the world's kids, yes, stops midword. Jane raises her cheek from his shirtfront, her pillow.

Churning up into the dooryard a low car, yes small, yes red, same as Ivy's.

Rex turns from where he stands to view the face of a woman with handsome, thick, dark-streaked, mostly gray hair in a professional-class cut, appearing.

This woman pulls the screen door wide with familiarity. This fairly tall large-framed woman is not a bit slope-shouldered, like some tall large-framed people tend to get; for instance, Gordon. The woman wears well her white round-collared blouse. Pastel print shorts. Lo, she is no stranger to Rex. Nor to Jane. Jane gives her special glasses a little one-fingered adjustment.

In a show of gentlemanliness, Rex pulls off his olive-drab army cap again as Marian St. Onge steps into the porch.

When this woman recognizes Rex, she closes her eyes prayerfully, gives Gordon a long-suffering look, and heads in through the doorway to the dim blue-lit kitchen. She seems not to have seen Jane at all whatsoever, zilch.

Jane, referring to the one and only time she has met Marian, says with a sad sigh, "Gordie, your mum is still upset."

Gordon just grunts.

Jane says, consolingly, "Your mum looks so pretty tonight, though. She has herself fixed up good."

The candles tonight have been made by Jane and the soft fleshy light that fills the porch is significant and owned.

Rex and Gordon are looking into each other's shadowy eyes, which they have been doing since Marian Depaolo St. Onge walked so brusquely between them, and Gordon's eyes now get that slightly crazed look he often has, one eye wide, one eye flinched narrow. "My mother," he says reverently, "worries me. She drives too fast." He lowers his bottle of beer to the floor.

Marian St. Onge has driven a long way for this surprise visit, at least an hour and a half. Although Gordon visits her in Wiscasset almost every week, it is rare that she darkens this door. It is almost as if she knew she'd catch Gordon at some new and deeply troubling nose dive into further debasement, each debasement being a full level lower than the last. And Gordon says, "I'm still thinking of bringing some kids to one of your meetings. It's in the works."

Rex squints at his black military boots, soft rose-colored reflections of Secret Agent Jane's candles there across the toes. He is now standing with his back to the screen, his olive military cap loose in one hand. Behind him, that old porch screening breaks the gray night up into pepper-sized gray pieces.

In the kitchen, there's a scary silence, worse than an angry smash of dishes or a slammed door.

Jane commands, "Gordie, tell me a story about when you were little and she was your mum."

"Not now," he tells her, tightening his arms. "You have had a full hour of stories, *yours and mine* and none of it worked getting you to the land of sweet dreams."

Phone rings.

"Cuz *he's* here." She nods toward Rex. "He is inlegal."

Rex shifts a bit.

Gordon says, "You said that before and you mean *ill*egal."

"Whatever," says Jane. "Milishish are in the news." She fingers the stems of her pink-lensed glasses, one hand to each stem, holding them tight as if to steady them against a sight that is accompanied by a big wind.

Rex doesn't shift a second time, but he *radiates*. His pale eyes lock to Jane's heart-shaped lenses, the two powers testing.

Gordon says, "You don't have a TV anymore, Jane. No more red herrings, lies, and crap from that source."

Jane reaches to possessively pat Gordon's whiskery mouth. "Some people still have them. They tellll."

"Of course," Gordon replies on a beery burp. "But the Oklahoma City bombing was rigged by the government, big banks, whatever. They own big media." What a sucker. He's taken her bait. Just like he fell for the bait of the Duotron Lindsey lobbyist.

Gordon's face turns to watch his mother's shadow swaying through the sickly blue kitchen light at the window beside and behind him. She is mumbling to someone.

Says Gordon, "Look, Lady Jane. It's time to nod off. Think of sheep. Multiply and divide 'em."

"Gross."

He resumes a bit of chair rocking.

Rex fits his cap back on, more *meticulously* this time.

Now they all hear Marian St. Onge's voice talking, the only words audible being, "Rex York," clearly spoken three times in a most distressed and crackling way.

Suddenly Jane queries, "What . . . do . . . you . . . mean? . . . Oklihomish City?"

Oops! Now Gordon sees. The trap. He sucks in the sweet weedy late summer night, nose whistling, lips under the mustache sealed.

Jane snickers to herself. "Well, *everybody* knows that Willie guy, went . . . to . . . jail. *His* friend." She jabs her pointing finger at Rex. "It was about gunzz. In murder they use guns a lot."

Rex had, himself, just arrived, not quite fifty minutes before Marian. Not enough time to get his muscular ideology fully tangled up in Gordon's loud bottomless zigzagging. And he has zero reaction to the husky bluster of Secret Agent Jane. He turns a little toward the screen door, then back toward the chair he had picked out to possibly sit in for a spell before he felt the significance of Marian's cold shoulder. Years ago, she had thought of Rex as a "good model" for her confused and only child.

Gordon says, "Sit, Richard. I want to hear more about that patriot group in western Mass. The ones with the *tank*." He doesn't say this softly. He says it like maybe he *wants* to jab Marian with this? Is this Gordon's mean twisted side leaking out? Or would he see it as mere teasing? Or is he unaware of how his big voice and his sensibilities sweep in all ears within a half mile, and how it could someday be his felo-de-se. The otherworldly candle flames flutter and twist. And from the kitchen, his mother's voice speaks again, words unclear, tone clearly distraught.

 After Rex's truck turns out of the yard, sleeping Jane is carried upstairs to her bed.

The wind picks up. It brings a coolness that speaks at every open window. As the mobiles and chimes come to life out on the piazza, there is the symphony of shimmering metal and tinkling glass and the *thot . . . thot . . . thot* of wood to wood.

He stands at the kitchen sink, one knee jiggling against the cupboard door, which causes a nearby tower of books to sway, the kind of books with footnotes and uh-oh nasty no-hope-but-fascinating facts in a variety of disciplines. He gulps down aspirin with water. Yes, this kitchen that has more unanswered mail and phone messages and books than food, a kitchen of cheapskate low-wattage fluorescent light, which he insists on because the house is still on the "corporate grid," not wired to converters and batteries yet. No microwave here, no automatic mooshers and mashers, no *bing*, no *whirr*. A kitchen of "resistance." A kitchen with a handsome woman, Marian Depaolo St. Onge, rewrapping a little dish of cold, cooked, frozen, and thawed, and recooked dandelion greens. "Here's this and I brought you some éclairs. Also, I've started getting a lot of mail at the house . . . mail addressed to you in care of me. And one call for you. A stranger. Even though I'm unlisted."

"Where'r the éclairs?" He lowers the water glass, looks eagerly about with his penetrating, too-keen, crazy-looking eyes. Hers are the eyes of restraint, of earned virtue.

She replies, "In the refrigerator. They must be kept chilled."

Happily, he says, "Let me look at 'em." Swings the refrigerator door wide.

She flutters her eyes. "I wouldn't waste them on children. A child would be just as happy with a cheap Tootsie Roll."

Gordon lets the door ease shut by itself, which makes a mashy rubber-edged sound, just as old Lucienne, the elderly woman who looks after Jane many nights, appears in the door to the front part of the house, making no sound, then disappears, never seen by Marian, and now something big, almost unmanageable is going around inside one of Gordon's whiskery cheeks. He speaks in a muffled way. "I will respect your wishes." He swallows. "Who was on the phone tonight? Anybody we know?"

At the sink now, she is rinsing off a plastic lid, squinting, holding the lid close to her face, her glasses reflecting her nebulously lighted hands. "Your wife. She was calling from Portland."

He stares a long moment at this word *wife*. He almost blurts out *which wife?* But gives himself another three seconds to remember that Claire is spending the night with Catherine Court Downey in the big city. Catherine is packing up her art supplies and some other gear to bring to the Settlement, has trouble with concentration, wants Claire to be "close by." So it's Claire whom Marian is talking about. And Marian is not in the dark about the wife situation here. It's just that Gordon's "polygamy" to Marian is like the "corporate grid" is to Gordon.

Gordon swallows again and works his tongue around his chocolate-and-custard-covered teeth and gums a bit. He leans back against the fairy-tale red chimney, one foot out before the other in that Viking-at-ease look Ivy Morelli was so amused by. "You're looking good, Mum," he says. "You must be feeling a lot better. Back pain all gone?"

"How can you say I look good, Gordon? In this awful light, you can't really see me."

"You mean in better light, I'd see things about you that would worry me?"

Her expression is almost military, a repeat of Rex York's. Her fashionable glasses with large frames nicely enhance her high cheekbones, the light-colored almond-shaped eyes, something enduringly well-favored about that Irish-Italian mix. She says, "I don't know what I'm saying." But she knows when she gets home, she will bawl for hours. Her fine face will cave in, will swell and discolor.

Gordon asks himself why it is he can never make her happy. His father Guillaume did a better job. His father Guillaume had the magic touch. Gordon *wants* to make Marian happy. But what is the key? Guillaume Sr. from Frenchville was not a gift shop gift giver or book club, garden club, church club social schmoozer. Marian's family are the ones with the big flashy cars, wardrobes, and colognes, and professionally attended hair, thick wall-to-wall rugs, appliances of every gleaming beeping sort, and big jewelry worn on every appendage, much show. Guillaume was so naked! No rings. None. Not even a wedding band. His reading glasses had frames of almost boiled-looking black plastic, which made his very dark intense eyes look sad and introspective. He wore a Saint Christopher's medal, but under his shirt.

How could Marian stand Guillaume? He was just this little slouched person bumping around doing little carpentry jobs and feeding birds. He had been a power shovel and crane operator when she met him! His English was awful. He sometimes licked his fingers at meals. His best and only friend around here was Stan. Stan visited every weekend. Stan had a reedy voice and a banshee laugh, always at the wrong time. Stan told gruesome hunting stories and hog-killing stories and stories of hoochy-koo girls at the fairs LOUDLY and this made Guillaume be loud, too, and giggly and *manly*. And Stan was always farting. Marian was not thrilled with Stan. But Guillaume was her "dear Gary."

Gordon sighs darkly now. Trying to figure out the ways of another person's heart! It can drive you bonkers.

He looks at his mother in a most tender way. Now his voice, getting a tweak high, getting urgent, says, "Mum . . . I beg you. Get rid of your TV."

"Gordon, I'm leaving."

He rushes past her, blocks the door with his big damp body and those maniacal eyes. "First hear me out."

Her chin trembles as she looks at his face. "I just realized who you look like since you've decided not to shave."

"Who?"

"Fidel Castro."

He opens his mouth, then shuts it. He fingers his jaw. "I haven't shaved clean since I was nineteen! And all these years, you've been working that thought out?" If there were more light, he'd see she is losing color, as one might before fainting. He says sheepishly, "Well, thank you for the compliment."

She says thickly. "It was not a compliment. And you know it wasn't." She pushes her fingers up under her glasses. She seems to be squashing her eyes to blind them. She whispers, "Next time I see you, you'll be on TV with the FBI trying to shoot you and Rex and those other crazies out of a bunker. I . . . I can't believe I raised . . . a . . . person who would . . . would stoop *so low* as to socialize with that sort of element."

"Black Elk. You ever heard of him?"

"Never," she says. Proudly. Defiantly.

"Well," Gordon tells her hurriedly, "he was a chief, a sage. He said these words: *It is the story of all life that is holy.*"

Silence between them. She is unmoved. Her pale eyes on him are wide, as though witnessing a horror feature from a seat too close to the screen.

Gordon repeats, *"All life."* He waits.

She says nothing.

He says, "Black Elk never saw TV. He never saw the eyes of his family glazed over by cheap transistors, mountains shrunk to the size of cupcakes, skies the size of envelopes, and the lives of real people and their struggles, even the lives of their own neighbors, grated and mashed into passive-aggressive political garbage so a brother would turn away from brother and a neighbor turn her back on her neighbor."

"Let me out, Gordon. I'm leaving."

"I love you," he says gruffly, yet ravishingly, but does not move his hands from the door frame, does not reach to caress her ear or shoulder.

"You love everyone. Your love is easy. Not very special."

"You mean . . ." His left eye squints. Incredulously. "Is Marian St. Onge making a statement that *love thy neighbor* is a sin? That *As you have done it unto the least of these my brethren, ye have done it unto me* was a stupid thing to say?"

She pushes hard around him. "YESSSSSSSSSS!" Betraying her promise to herself to not cry until she is home, she is bawling before she's pulled open the door of her beloved little car, the sporty car that she's told her friends and family "is me," has given her "a new lease on life," has made her feel young again. So sleek, so fast, so red, so easy to park.

 As Marian's car speeds away, the phone rings.

It's Claire.

Gordon listens to her speak, the phone in the crook of his neck, watching a freckle of Settlement light up there on the hill, flickering through the wind-churning leaves of that patch of woods behind this house. The mobiles and chimes bash themselves violently on the piazza. Claire is saying, "And she said you told Rex you plan to take a couple of the kids to one of his militia meetings."

"Sure."

Silence. Just the clamor of hissing crackling trees and the racket of the mobiles and chimes.

He goes to the refrigerator, stretching the phone cord too tight, fetches the big Saran-covered enamel pan, stuffs another éclair into his mouth.

Claire is, yes, laughing. Or something. Sounds like laughing.

He laughs. Laughing is catchy.

She says, "Rex has lost his noodle. Everybody knows it. The militias are crazy and they hate hate hate and are . . . paranoid. It's one thing all the fundamentalist folks we deal with in the cooperatives. We've done okay because most of us don't let them engage us in conversation concerning the Bible realm. That's worked out. It's been *okay*. But the *militias*. Get real, Gordon. For children, I would say this is a little little little not okay. Gordon, some militias *bomb* kids."

He has listened, chewing, dragging his tongue across his chocolatey thumb, slurping, slisking, the phone amplifying all this over the miles down to Portland right into Claire's ear. He says, "Tell me how you know this."

"Oh, shit, you know. Conventional wisdom."

"Ah-ha!" He unwraps another éclair. (Yes *homemade* by Marian. Custard deluxe.)

She listens to the crinkling.

"And conventional wisdom these days originates from . . . from what?" He laps the waxed paper first.

"Oh, stop it! School's out. This is your media-is-at-the-root-of-all-evil lecture again."

"Geronimo said *I think I am a good man, but all over the world they say I am a bad man.*"

"That was *before* TV."

"But not before Big Money owned the USA. And counterintelligence was in its seedling stage. You need to read up on COINTEL-PRO. Especially what it did down on Pine Ridge. You—"

"Is it just me you use those Indian quotes and references on? Or do Leona and Geraldine have to listen to them, too? You know what I mean, us folks from the reservation?"

"Oh, no, baby. I use 'em everywhere. Why just ten minutes ago, Black Elk was speaking to my mother. My mum just loves Black Elk."

Claire snorts. Says wearily, "Jesus, Gordon. Please don't get the Border Mountain Militia involved in our lives."

"So you're suggesting we begin a list of untouchables? Could you call this place a home then? A community? Erasing people? Especially our old neighbors?"

"Sure! If they hurt us. If they're dangerous! We can still wave at them when we pass their houses in our cars. I don't mean we sh—"

"Tell me, when did Rex York or Stan Berry or even our illustrious Willie Lancaster ever bring injury or *any* sort of harm down on you or anybody we know?"

"Not yet."

"You know the worst hurt our people have ever known has been from the outside. The *outside,* baby. Rex is inside. And Willie . . . he's *really* inside. We're related!"

"Through marriage."

"Third cousin . . . Lou-EE is my third cousin. *BLOOD.* So when Dee Dee has the baby, the baby will be my fourth cousin. But also, through Dee Dee, the baby will have militia Willie genes in him or her, so the baby might start using explosives on the toy box—"

"You're talking stupid."

"I dare you to find a television so we can have our first militia act of terrorism. We'll all dress in camo and sneak up on the TV, during prime time, and then I personally know where there's a whole case of 1-F and I personally will blow the fucker up—"

"Your poor mother. I can imagine the way it was for her tonight." Claire is quiet a moment, listening to the ghastly sounds of Gordon eating the last of six éclairs. And outside the wind, which blows even harder in Portland. Over the phone, the anxiety of the piazza chimes and mobiles can be heard in miniature. "We need to talk about this some more, Gordon. All of us. All the *adults*. Of course, everyone will eventually give in to you. They always do. You're convincing in a way that scares me. And then there's your bullying." She tsks. "But I hope you're right about the militias. I'm feeling very tense about it. I think there's such a thing as being too trusting, too open-minded . . . too nice . . . too . . . too something. It has to do with boundaries. Like sex. Some people will sleep with anyone. And then they say that incest victims, for instance, develop a sexual promiscuousness tha—"

"That's feminist bullshit. Professor Ms. Catherine Something-Hyphenated-Something is poisoning your mind."

"Should I erase her?"

"With a wet diaper."

She laughs, but not for very long. "That's an exceptional imitation of a classic asshole. A person, I, myself, wouldn't care for. Where'd you learn that?"

No reply.

"Okay, hotshot. I just need to say a little more. DO NOT INTER-RUPT. I'm sure that if polled, ninety-five percent of the people in this country would agree with me that militias, even if not *dangerous,* aren't *wholesome*—"

"They do food drives for flooded Indian people in the Southwest."

"DO NOT INTERRUPT! Okay . . . I know . . . ninety-five percent of America is misinformed. But if something happens, something bad happens to one of our kids, your apology will not be enough."

"I realize that," he says somberly.

"How has our Jane been today?" Her voice has changed to something softer.

He holds his forehead. "A strong, self-conscious, selfish woman. Your friend Catherine Blah-Hyphenated-Blah would approve. Jane is going to grow up and be a CEO for AT&T or governor of Texas or some-such and execute manacled prisoners and move vast sums of capital through the outer stratosphere while wearing lavender fingernail polish and . . ." He goes on and on while Claire, at her end of the line, sitting in Catherine's pretty green and white summery decor alcove den, is smiling a kind of pained smile and she says, "I'm going to hang up now, Gordon. I wish life were simpler. You know I do."

"Yep, I know."

"See you tomorrow at supper," she says firmly.

"I love you, woman."

She sighs indulgently.

After hanging up, Gordon laps his fingers some more, paces a bit. Wind slams a door upstairs. A limb crashes outside. And the chimes and mobiles on the long porch are no longer lovely or haunting. The violence that is upon them now just hurts them, tangles their strings.

Now as he goes about the house, shutting a few windows, he says to himself sadly, "God is bad."

 Breakfast at the Settlement.

Big cold wind. Big cold sky. Soon to be a blue extreme, abyssal and thrilling, like prehistory, like before memory. Soon the cold white sun will come. Breakfast is in the winter kitchen this morning. Long sleeves. *Real* socks. Fuzzy sweaters. Closed in like this, the breakfast smells so good. Bacon. It's smoky force satiates you just by wandering up your nose. Yeast breads. Corn breads. Molasses breads. Molasses out of bulk tins, yes. Preserves from every Settlement tree and vine. Butter. And maple. And coffee. Store-bought coffee, yes. And cold strained juice of the tomato. A lot of tomatoes this year, cultivated from saved seeds of old neighbors in the valley of North Egypt. Platters of sliced tomato. Slathery seedy red piles. Fried green tomatoes and cheesy omelets. A plain egg for Jane. An egg that somehow came out perfect on the first try, even with Jane's nose inches from the pan. Jane still refuses to cook the egg herself, insisting she is "a guest." But at least she is here this morning, her white-rimmed pink-heart-shaped lensed secret agent glasses swiveling in all directions from where she sits. Gathering evidence.

The mothers stare at Gordon all through the meal, or at least glance his way frequently, while some make a point of avoiding his eyes. Most mornings, Gordon and each woman he is "wedded" to will, across the mobbed kitchen, exchange a look. A kind of two-second accounting for. Nothing erotic. More like checking the gauges in a plane before takeoff. Life and death. Dearly beloved, we are still a strong unsurrendering people. Dear one, hold fast.

This morning the eyes of the wives, especially the mothers, are different.

It's one of those times when Gordon sits at the head of one of the two longer connected pairs of tables. He sits hunched a little, the sleeves of his jazzy yellow and red plaid Settlement-made flannel shirt rolled up, big, good-looking smile on his face. One woman, *not* one of his wives, a woman named Ann, not a regular kitchen crew person, but a musician and scholar, does a lot in the library with kids, mostly sciency stuff, birds, bugs, microorganisms, geology, meteorology, a *real* weather expert, and mother of two teens, not a fan of militias, is pouring Gordon's coffee, pours a little over his hand as his fingers lay loosely around the cup. He snatches his hand back fast. She doesn't say, "oops!" or "I'm sorry." She just moves on to the next cup, old blind Mrs. Morse's cup, Mrs. Morse brought up here for the day from town, Ann pouring Mrs. Morse's coffee oh, so carefully.

Another woman, also not one of Gordon's wives, comes along and takes his full cup away.

"I'm not done with that yet, dear," he says with his big ol' nice smile.

Her eyes steam into his, her eyes hotter than the burn on his hand. "You're done," she says, then keeps walking away with his cup.

This goes to prove that bad news travels like wildfire, as the saying goes. But Claire is right. If he wants to take some of the kids to an armed militia meeting, it will be so. Whatever Gordon wants badly enough, that is the way.

And so throughout the day, you can see his bright shirt and thick slopy shoulders across the quad, or up in the gardens where the trucks and solar buggy wagons are being loaded with bushels and crates of summer squashes, zucchinis, corn, beets, small mild pale turnips, and late greens, early parsnips, more tomatoes, herbs, and late toughened kale. Piles of potatoes. Potatoes ever so dear, sacred. Without the potato, how much of humanity would have been erased even before calendars. And now as the singular and global food trade system shows spots of rot, might the little locally adapted potato receive back its dirt-caked eminence? Settlement-wise this is already so!

Meanwhile, with his arm around one of those commanding middle-aged mothers, talking down at the side of her face, Gordon is gesturing with his free hand. Rex's militia is an educational experience! A great opportunity! See history in the making, right? In the cases of those real narrow-eyed mothers who argue a bit, he acts silly, wags his head, covers his ears or leaves them for later, for bed, where they are more easily influenced.

He works side by side with some teen boys and girls, all armed with knives, hacking some early blue Hubbards free of the vine, hefting them, so satisfyingly heavy and polish smooth, handsomely lumpy, grasshoppers and crickets plunking against pant legs, sun hot but dry, shirts around waists, billed caps pulled low. To kids Gordon says nothing about the militia. He means well. He *wants* to respect the wishes of other adults here. Yes. He. Means. Well. He really does. But—

He whispers to his wife Glennice while heading back for supper, walking up the dusty road. She closes her eyes, a tear on one cheek. "Yes, sir."

"Don't just say yes and not mean it!" he implores, almost squeakily.

Glennice, who is normally so cheery, so upbeat, so Christian, produces another tear, and says, "okay," even less enthusiastically than her previous "yes, sir."

It's different with the other Settlement fathers. There's no objections, verbal or nonverbal. A couple dads even want to go with Gordon to "see what it's all about." Is there militia in the heart of almost every working-class man? The servant? The peasant? The slave? The system's cogs? The rich person's ox? Even here at the Settlement, the memory of OUT THERE never washes away but is spurred into the bones.

Over the next couple of days, Gordon moves from shop to shop, Quonset hut to Quonset hut, hay field and sawmill, like hot fission, pushing to fill up space, large objects quivering, nobody left unconvinced.

 Now, out in the Midwest.

Another dozen family farms auctioned off yesterday, another dozen today. One suicide.

Some experts speak of job training, food stamps, medications, all to help these families with the "change."

Depression. It's like anything. It can be fixed! Right? The system takes. The system gives. It crawls high and low, growing. Growth! Growth! Growth!

And la la la la, the sun will shine on us all. And the electronic bluebird will bow and chirp and bless.

 And—

The militia grows.

 Out in the world.

In dozens of French cities, tens of thousands of jobless people are demonstrating. In many cases occupying unemployment offices, welfare offices, utility companies, and repossession agencies, they push their way into pricey stores and yuppie restaurants and make raids on superdooper markets.

Soon, the Paris Trade Center and elite École Normale Supérieure are occupied. Police arrive and use varieties of force to solve *the problem,* but the heroic mob charges on to take over an amphitheater at nearby Jussieu University.

Now months have passed since the riots. Leaflets! Assemblies! Talk of revolution! Even those with jobs join the jobless. If you look at a map, you will see the shape of France but its angry voice is matched by angry, writhing voices all over the planet. Australia. Argentina. Japan. Kashmir. Haiti. Britain. Egypt. Sudan. Yemen, Tunisia, Syria, Libya, Colombia. Though, of course, in most cases, each one's common people never know of the other's shaking fist.

Screens far and near . . .

are blank as a floor concerning the aforementioned.

 In a small town in Indiana, a woman is preparing a quick supper for herself.

She cranks open a can of clams, those small kind that look like "newborn" clams. The woman presses down the loose lid now to squeeze out the water. She gasps. There's only a half inch of clams on the bottom. Each time she buys these things, they cost a bit more and there's more water, less clams. She sighs. Trying, yes, really making a brave effort to accept that she has been robbed. No, better to think of it as a *good* thing, the "green" thing, cutting back, saving the planet. Indeed, if you get angry about things, you are like those types on TV being dragged to jail . . . shabby and low-class. She takes a deep breath, lets it out, thinks positive . . . yes, a positive thinker. She smiles, opens a second can of clams to make up the difference.

 Denise's Diner.

While out on an errand, Gordon sees Rex's YORK ELECTRIC van parked outside Denise's Diner and so he decides that today is the day he will eat his noon meal at Denise's Diner.

Inside, there is only one visible empty seat. Conveniently, it's the stool at the counter right next to Rex York.

Gordon spreads his legs and, from behind the stool, lowers himself onto the seat and Rex looks up at him, then back at his half-eaten crab roll, then at the three coffee pots on the burners in front of him.

"Good afternoon, Mr. York."

Rex nods gravely at the three coffee pots.

The waitress, a big-built long-faced girl with acne scars, some relation of Bonnie Loo's, flips to the new page of her pad. "Hungry?" she asks.

Gordon smiles. He looks up at the list of specials on the wall with a look too wild and too passionate and too lunatic for such an ordinary list of greasy, salty, fried stuff. "I . . . I want that baked bean thing . . . no . . . wait . . . I want that macaroni and cheese."

"Red hot dog comes with that. You want corn or peas?"

He rubs his thickly bearded chin a long moment, staring passionately into midair. "Peas."

"You get a roll with that, too," she says.

"I'm glad," he says.

"Coffee?" She flips his upside-down cup upright.

"Yes, ma'am." He looks down the length of the diner. A hand waves. He waves back. Another relation of Bonnie Loo's. Then another hand. Now, nodding once in a manly way, Jeff Johnson, who has just recently married and is "struggling," they say. Everyone looks familiar. Everyone. Now he looks the other way and there's more nods. No strangers. No passers-through. He sighs happily. Turns his creaky stool from left to right, right to left, restlessly. Looks back at Rex, who is chewing food in a most dignified manner, no food whatsoever hanging off *his* mustache. Gordon can never be sure of his own.

The late summer sun, blasting in at all the big windows, jumps and wags and flickers as people walk through it or stretch out a hand for a relish jar.

Minutes later. Gordon and Rex now eat side by side without much talking. Eventually they discuss and agree to both order pecan pie, even Rex, who never eats dessert . . . Gordon pressing him to "lighten up."

Then, at last, outside in the sandy lot, Rex has something for Gordon. First a copy of the (outdated, sort of) FBI *Project Megiddo* report, which defines all the ways an American, (certain difficult Americans but also including just average people . . . people who own firearms and surmise the government doesn't want them to . . . or people who believe there is a new world order) . . . how these people are probably terrorists. Terrorists, yes. That is the word. And "paranoid." This is what you are if you do not believe the big-business-owned and "intelligence"-guided government is your friend.

Gordon gives this a quick scan, then tucks it under one arm.

And stapled together are two Internet printouts, one from Australia, the other a photocopied article from a publication that Gordon has never heard of. Some sportsman's magazine that details a suggested plan for global citizens disarmament, presented by a Japanese delegation to the United Nations and supported merrily by US delegates. It doesn't say it becomes official policy but . . . but it *feels* real. You can *feel* the cold hands of lords and ladies stretching in through your front yard gate, into the rooms of your home, down your shirt front. If you aren't rich enough to be a legal "person," that is. *Rights* for the rich, retractable privileges for everyone else.

Now a whole folder stuffed with clippings and printouts of intrusive gun laws and bans in Canada and England, with delegates to the United Nations' "positive" remarks on these underlined in pen or yellow highlighter. Some include the statement by the attorney general of the United States that guns in the hands of citizens are bad, citizen disarmament "timely." None are *bills* or impending laws. Partisan rhetoric, for certain. Some of this stuff is taken from sources like the *Washington Post* and *Los Angeles Times*. Gordon tucks the whole thickness of reading material under an arm and watches Rex standing there looking at the road, which is momentarily quiet.

Gordon swallows. "Maybe I owe you an apology, Brother." *Sort of.* At least honor a brother's fear, right? How many hours have they argued the last few days, Gordon accusing Rex of silly paranoia.

Rex turns his icy blue-gray eyes on Gordon. Now he reaches in his pants pocket for his wallet, picks from one of the little plastic photo sheathes a laminated card. On one side, it is a photo. Geronimo with what looks like an old trap-door rifle. The stock is kinda blurry. Hard to tell. But the man's face is clear. On the other side of the card, in cheapie-style computer print: BORDER MOUNTAIN MILITIA/625-8693, RFD2, Box 350, Egypt, Maine, 04047.

Gordon looks back again at Geronimo. Firm set mouth, eyes boring right into Gordon's. He is remembering the words that go with that face, words he offered Marian just a few nights ago: *I think I am a good man, but all over the world they say I am a bad man.*

Gordon says nothing, just quietly returns the photo card to his friend's hand, keeps a grip on the folder.

Gordon now feels the door swinging back. *Slam!* All his new hopes to fight the thing, for instance, Bree's and his *THE RECIPE*, are so embarrassingly childly and dopey and sweet, while the militias have known all along that the only possible outcome was glorious defeat.

He swallows, then says, "I'm still bringing some people with me to one've your meetings, Captain."

Rex nods, slipping his wallet back into place. "Maybe my men can meet at your place before long. Check out some of your goodies. Your shortwave. And they might like the photovoltaic stuff. Don't get me wrong. I'm not against that stuff. It's not that I'm against it."

Gordon says, "I would be honored to have you all."

Rex says, "I'll see what I can do. Why don't you just come over to the next meeting at my place and we can work out the details."

"Hey. Yuh. Sure. Let's give it hell."

 He is slouched in the one upholstered chair in the cool parlor of the old farm place, door closed. Silence as tight and unstammering as the innermost room of the sepulcher of a dead Bible-days hotshot.

Overhead, the old-timey frosted glass light fixture, suspended from its thick bronze chain, gives off a raging hundred watts. All around him the books in leaning towers, academics and their end notes, glossaries, introductions and afterwords. Stuff of the philosopher. Stuff of thought. Stuff of the informed. While spread open on his thighs, the *Project Megiddo* report, its first page flashing the seal of the Department of Justice, Federal Bureau of Investigation: Fidelity, Bravery, Integrity.

This first page reads: *The attached analysis, entitled Project Megiddo, is an FBI strategic assessment of the potential for domestic terrorism in the United States undertaken in anticipation of or response to the arrival of the new millennium.*

He turns to the next page.

BOOK TWO: WOLVES

It begins.

Settlement trucks are crowded between a mound of split firewood and the Yorks' glassed-in porch. Indoors, eight Settlement men are talking "militia," talking of being "prepared," bursts of laughter, rolling grumbles. Not much of the husky loud voice of Gordon St. Onge. These nights he is less argumentative, stares down into a galaxy of new thoughts just above his folded hands.

None of "Rex's men" are on hand, unless you count one meager wordless fifteen-year-old, Mickey Gammon, outfitted in a camo BDU jacket with the Border Mountain Militia's shoulder patch embroidered green and black, a mountain lion in midsnarl. Olive-drab pistol belt. Hair in a streaky blond ponytail. More of a mouse tail, thin and bewildered, not overly shampooed, it's length probably *meant* to display manly rebellion.

 Jolly.

On the third night, as they linger in Rex's dooryard, a small car burns up the driveway, lurches to a stop in billows of dust behind Rex's gray work van. And out hops (like a cricket) a fellow whose multiple cameras all flash at once. In the stricture of dying green evening light, these bursts make a sort of war fire in everyone's eyes. But the man is so smiley and white of teeth, so jolly, then poof, he's gone.

 ## In no time . . .

Independent photographer Cal Alonsky's shots of the infamous "Prophet" Guillaume St. Onge and his militia connections creep like bacteria throughout the state of Maine and then outward into America.

These will be referred to by thousands of worried souls as "angry white men," which is true if you don't count dark-skinned Cory St. Onge. All of these guys are *angry* for sure because they really didn't like Mr. Alonsky's style.

 ## At the Settlement, the mail arrives in even bigger bulges and billows.

The black old-timey phone in Gordon's kitchen jangles long into the night.

Radio talk shows are REALLY at it, squealing away at such words as: "right wing" and "militia terror" and then plain "terrorists" or extra fancy "baby-raping terrorists" punctuated in other instances by "socialist" and "communist," even "environmentalist." And "needs to be a law against" and "we need to think of the children" and "I heard they have a bomb."

Ah, the magic of Ivy's pen. How it had torn open the future and out slithered *this*.

 ## Thicker.

He meets again and again with the girl down at the farm place. She hears him out on all the wild things he tells her. Primarily Rex's fears. She picks up her magic pen and with his passion she merges her genius. The *Recipe* spumes its evermore improved, deluxe version, as an asteroid would wrap its red-hot tail around the endless bickering between Gordon and Rex, where primarily Rex never says more than a few words.

It dazzles.

Now the mail comes in bundles and boxes.

Letters and cards from all over the country. More folded clippings of the St. Onge-militia-connection photos. Old friends asking Gordon, *What's this surprising development, our old philosopher? And Is this really you?*

But mostly strangers now. A couple of white-supremacist types. But some without any supremacist reference or racist blatherings, but the letters feel white, white and angry. Mostly men. A few women. But oh, they *loved* Cal Alonsky's photo. To them it was a warm *hello*!

Gordon scribbles down their addresses, adds them to the file. He writes a few short cautious notes to as many as he has time for, laps the stamps.

Meanwhile, no comments from anyone about his and Bree's (mostly Bree's) "no wing" concoction, *The Recipe,* though he has sent out dozens of copies to acquaintances far and near, those with a political bent, mostly those who would be best described as "liberal," "liberal" being the Gordon of yesteryear, *sort of.* "Liberal" means open-minded, right? So, he is certainly that. But he was never *quite* one of them.

Bree had asked the print shop crew to do the first page of *The Recipe* on fluorescent-orange copy paper, blaze orange glowing, like a hunter's orange vest.

With *The Recipe*s Gordon has sent out, he includes a short personal *urgent* note.

Eventually, a few replies. Like, *I haven't had time to read your opus. But thanks. I will soon. And how are you? Still doing the alternative energy stuff?* And blah, blah, blah. And, *Still with the militia? Bang! Bang! Ha! Ha!* The progressives can knife you in such smiley ways.

One old friend sent a seven-page typed letter talking about every damn thing BUT *The Recipe.* Then a scribbled P.S. *Thanks for the missive, Gordo. Looks like you've been busy.*

Gordon has a vision. Nearly a hundred *Recipe*s in nearly a hundred homes, the top orange page dazzling, straining unsuccessfully to catch the attention of someone who cares.

In his dumpy, musty, farmhouse kitchen, he reads aloud to Brianna the letters and cards of friends who just aren't getting around to reading *The Recipe*. Nobody is reading *The Recipe*. He reads their excuses in comical voices to make her giggle. And yes, she had giggled for him.

 Brianna Vandermast's most recent artwork is placed in Gordon's hands.

It shows a robust hairy creature with big feet, big mole-like nose, beady eyes, standing with hands on hips, legs apart. The epitome of defiance and invincibility. It is the "Abominable Hairy Patriot" and he (or is it she?) is pictured at times with a three-corner hat, other times hatless with different expressions. But mostly just one expression. Kindly militance. And mostly he (or she?) has no clothes. Just his (her?) very THICK white fur, which Bree explains, "is probably actually brown in summer."

The Abominable Hairy Patriot versus The Thing!! The Thing is portrayed as sort of a sea anemone (side view), and the two opponents help the reader along with a condensed version of *The Recipe*. This is two sides to one sheet of paper. A ready-to-print flyer.

All the no-wing concepts are boiled down in a chatty language, more alluring than the language of the first *Recipe*. Less lyrical. Less rant. More lovable.

A bit of woodstove fire, a windy cold tumble of rain outside. With his cheapie unbecoming glasses on, Gordon reads through both sides twice, he sitting, Bree standing. Now being breakfast time in the winter kitchen, Settlement people munching, or helping a child to cut up a sausage or to pepper eggs, a small boy spitting food across a table, displays of embroidery strutting by, a mother angrily jerks a kid from his chair, kitchen sink hand pumps clank and squeak and the dear good water explodes into pottery, someone never tiring of "Goodnight, Irene" sailing through another refrain with cheeks full of food, a door slams, laugh, laugh, candles flick and whisper like newborn hearts, the drone of several men just arriving now, every chair filled. Many eyes watch as Gordon takes off his reading glasses and stands. The new *Recipe* lies brightly on the table. Gordon crushes

Bree HARD against himself and she lets him, pressing her horrific face into his shirt.

 Yes, this is all very sweet, big molesque cartoon, gift to the Prophet from earnest, shy (or something) Bree, but secretly behind his back the plot thickens, in no small part due to Bree's scheming.

This, while Gordon is off (miles and miles off) on a delivery of two-by-fours and two-by-twelves and boards. See spread flat on the clothes-making shop floor a full-sized dark blue flag. Handmade, of course, but resembles the state of Maine flag, except for the addition of golden yellow letters along the top. It says: THE TRUE MAINE MILITIA. One Settlement girl fusses (fumes actually) over the "Dorky lookin' moose!"

Eight more girls crowd into the room within the hour. The moose is discussed.

"It's his eyeball," one young seamstress whispers. "Too square-shaped."

Work on a replacement eye takes a couple of hours. The serious-ness of the task gives each girl's face a grimace. Then the flag (and hornbeam pole with mighty eagle on top) are sneaked through the velvety cloudy blue-black of a late August night to "Bree's" truck to be hidden "until it's time."

SEPTEMBER

 Privacy.

A building crew begins work in one of the Quonset huts, making one of the lesser-used upstairs storage rooms into a double studio for Catherine and Bree. Hammers pound, saws zing and there's the cutting away of metal roof for two tall round-roofed dormers. Big fans for ventilation of artists' paint fumes. Big PRIVACY sign on the one shared door at the top of the stairs.

Inside the room, a temporary wall of store-bought corkboard dividing Catherine's space from Bree's space. Temporary because apparently Catherine is temporary. "I'm not really Settlement material!" she says laughingly on various occasions. "I need to be close to things." But for now, this time and place, her space is treated as reverently as Bree's.

And isn't Catherine as fragile as Bree? Some here think so.

Inside the PRIVACY-marked door is a small shared entry space, then two inner doorways, hung with tarps. Again, that temporary feel.

Catherine says with delight, "Our own artists' colony!" yet she, herself, begins no work. But she teaches Bree wonderful things, like how to stretch canvas and build frames for canvases.

While Bree has painted large, mural-sized canvases and has drawn tirelessly several hours a day on her side of their "artists' colony" all the first week since the studio was finished, Catherine either goes out,

or meditates, naps, or digs into university paperwork while listening
to soft tapes and CDs of spiritual new age music or atonal symphonies. She asks Bree if the music bothers her. Bree assures her that she
doesn't mind.

Bree asks if her cigarette smoke is flowing over the twelve-foot
temporary wall, over the open top, what isn't sucked out by the purring
fans. Catherine says, "Not in a way that bothers me." This isn't really
true. Catherine hates cigarette smoke, even if it didn't stink and kill.
She hates everything it personifies: "patent stupidity." But Catherine,
so far, has been angelic here at the Settlement. Her chin a little high.
Her quirky beauty having a shockingness to it whenever she enters a
room or group. Her knot of black frizzy hair is the size of an acorn but
has the texture of those wiggles of heat that come from a hot biscuit.
She glances at her watch almost continuously. She dresses in jeans,
camp shirts with patch pockets, and cuffed short sleeves. All in the
most gentle colors. But she often goes barefoot. Not a tough barefoot
look but a casual urban indoors barefootness. Claire watches her like
you watch the sky for weather, weather being such a stunning range
of possibilities.

Meanwhile, Bree and Catherine honor each other's space, though
sometimes Catherine calls Bree into her part of the studio to talk.
Catherine tells of her marriage to Phan. "Our life . . . our love . . . it's
like being two really small hardworking little bees inside a huge white
flower filled with total stillness. It has been sweet."

Bree looks impressed. "Sounds romantic."

"So much on his mind, which . . . well, makes him quiet at home.
Whereas, when my work is going well, it makes me chatty, his work
doesn't make him chatty at all. At least, not with me. He's like a general studying his maps. He's gone for weeks, then home for a day or
two with a tongue of stone."

"I'm very sorry to hear that," says Bree.

"Oh, it's really okay. It's not painful at all. I don't *depend* on him
like that."

But each time Catherine tells the story, Bree says she is sorry.

Meanwhile, at the university the new chairman of the department
is in place so the interim chair, Catherine, is free of that load and
Catherine celebrates it by being gone somewhere for a few nights.

And then Catherine's classes at the university begin full force. But also she is shopping or seeing friends, or back at her house in Portland, collecting things to bring to the Settlement, so she is gone more than she is here, yet she is edging closer. And Robert is always here. She thanks and thanks the mothers and teens and men who spend time with him.

Bree returns to her painting each day, her booted feet spread apart, arms at her sides like a gunslinger, studying the filled and yet-to-be-filled regions of her huge canvases. She works with her roaring red hair pinned tightly back, exposing all her face (a little bit of Catherine Court Downey influence?), her spaced golden eyes narrowed, her nose with its flat flared pale blue bridgeless bridge looking less like a birth defect than the courageous scar from a war she has been on the winning side of. Her physique is limber, as when she works in the woods with her brothers and father, the untroubled swing of hips, thighs, and arms, her mind only on *the job*.

Bree shows Catherine long and short versions of *The Recipe*. Catherine reads the short version aloud. She does not praise the "Abominable Hairy Patriot" cartoon, artist to artist. She just smiles a knowing professorial smile and says, "It's healthier to focus on personal growth. It's so hopeless out there." She waves a hand to the tall arched dormer she has already filled with glass and pottery from home.

Bree says, "I didn't do this alone. Gordon and I did it together."

Catherine raises an eyebrow. "Yes. Claire says he is a regular Mr. Revolution."

Bree says, "Well, I don't know about *that*." And she sighs.

In another two days, Catherine's side of the studio begins to heap high with stuff, a lot of stuff, but no "works in progress." She has shown Bree slides of her old work, holding them to the light. Watercolors. None of the actual pieces are larger than eighteen-by-twenty-four inches. They are like bruises of blue on cream, or blue on gray, as shadows would hesitate on a vertical plane of dimpled sand. At first, so mysterious. But when you look with a knowing eye, you see Catherine's own face ghostishly apparent, sometimes just one side of her face, as if she hides behind a doorway, a silvery hand at the edge of the door frame. And there, a bodyless transparent gray dress against frosty space. And there, hands and feet but no head . . . just a figure of smoke . . . but no, see there on the chest area, look close, Catherine's face, like a face photo printed on a T-shirt.

In another one she is dancing. Her face and head recognizable and placed where they should be. The body naked and starved. Bare of living tissue but for skin and skeleton, the anorexic nightmare. And what is that on the pelvic area Scotch taped on, as if by a child? The uterus and ovaries.

Catherine brings a few Settlement women one at a time up to view the slides of her work held up to the big dormer's shouting light. Bree can hear them whispering beyond the wall and sometimes she joins them, sometimes not. Three different times she hears Catherine say how much she misses her TV, and then the other person explains the no-TV rule here, Gordon's biggest rule. And each time Catherine says, "Now isn't that silly." Not an exclamation. Just a gentle observation.

Bree is surprised when after all this, Catherine tells her, "When I bring my little TV here, I'll show you the tapes of my opening shows. You'll get to see Gus and Candice (friends she has so often spoken of). I have all kinds of tapes . . . safe things. Nobody will mind. Nothing to upset anyone here. All very good educational material. I *promise*." And she gets an extra mischievous look, a look that's quite becoming on her unconventionally beautiful face. "I'll pick up a bottle of Chardonnay and you and I can have a little party! And then an open studio when your work is ready! Really, we do need to bring some of the finer things to this . . . this . . . *farm*."

Bree laughs. "Oh, boy." Then mimics the very same mischievous look which, on her deformed face has a different effect.

Meanwhile, Catherine continues to heal, has taken the last of all but one prescription, still sleeps at Claire's place with Robert, shows no sign of ever fully leaving the Settlement. At the early breakfasts, the only meal she is a regular at, she places many bottles around her plate of toast. She has always taken ten million vitamins and trace elements and minerals and homeopathic remedies for every sort of cramp or hitch or unpleasant sensation or to prevent disease, but now she's added a few more, including the St. John's Wort (which Gordon points out can poison a cow) and ginkgo and some other sort of "healthy" capsules that smell like glue.

Robert roams the tables, sometimes sitting with his mother, sometimes not. At times, he just stands beside her with his hand on her arm like riding on a subway, a pleasant look on his face, his sun-face belt buckle hanging heavily from the stretch waistband of his shorts or jogging pants.

In the meantime, Bree's mural-sized canvas paintings (her art now released from the confines of her rag-paper books), bulge with power. They take up all the generous wall space of her studio. She thrashes away at three all at once.

The paintings are crowded with human figures. Anguished people in events of brutal confrontation. People up against lousy odds. Religious and Renaissance-like. Much flesh and tortured trees. And whipping streaked skies. Masterfully rendered. Most include mythical creatures, too, something like a Minotaur and plenty of angels. Devils and goats with human torsos and striped enamel-looking horns, hooded spooks with ancient faces and pursed lips and wary eyes. Fire. And rage. Devastation. Hundreds of undiapered babies, plump as cherubs, but without wings, no wings necessary. They pour lavalike from a fissure in the rocky treeless mountainside. Angry babies.

Catherine has seen none of these. No one has. Catherine promises never to look at these works in progress without invitation. Between young Bree and the beautiful degreed, distinguished, *mysterious* Catherine, there is a trust. "I definitely understand your need for privacy," Catherine tells her. "We artists know these things."

 One afternoon.

Gordon and Rex in their respective trucks pass on the road. Both stop. One on each side of the road.

They talk of a meeting Rex has planned with a guy from a Virginia militia. "Not sure which weekend yet," Rex says.

Gordon asks, "What's he about?"

"He seems to have inside info on something not meant to be leaked out. We're talking video tapes. The MJTF and FIN-CEN. FEMA. The whole thing. The camps. Maps of the transshipment locations."

"Concentration camps," says Gordon.

"Correct," says Rex.

Gordon squints. "Well, keep me posted." Then he shuffles through papers and bags and jackets on the seat of his truck across the road and presents Rex with the new shorter version of *The Recipe*. "Don't read it now. Just sometime when you're bored with your breakfast or something. This can't be speed read. What did you think of the other one? The long one?"

Rex folds the paper up without looking at it. "I haven't read it yet."

Gordon smiles. "This one is shorter."

Rex flushes. "Well, I'll read this tonight. Thanks. I appreciate it." He says this warmly, though the sun is in his eyes and he is scowling against the light.

 History as it happens (as recorded by Gabe St. Onge).

We went to a militia. At the Rex man's. We did first ade and how to drag people out windows in a fire. We alredy knew the stuff on CPR. Next they might come see our shotwav where they wish they could do shows wich peepil can here for miles. Dee Dee's Dad is Willie Lam-kastir. Iv seen him before but not his shotwav setup. Ours is bigger than Dee Dee's Dad's but Mum said DO NOT BRAG.

 Out in the world.

A little convoy of Settlement cars and trucks driven by seventeen- and eighteen-year-olds sweeps into the parking lots of post offices and IGAs in four nearby towns. The flyers are of both the typed wordy kind and the cartoon flashy kind, many touched up in crayon or Settlement-made weed and berry and beet paints to give that personal feel. Tacked to telephone poles, stuffed under windshield wipers, placed smilingly into hands, it is a busy day. Most flyers entitled REAL HISTORY. NOT BORING.

 See there among them.

Riding along in one of the trucks is redheaded Brianna Vandermast, a small cagey smile on her young normal-looking mouth . . . yes, her pretty mouth. On her lap are two bundles of what she calls *The Recipe*.

One pile is the fifteen-page version. These are in case she runs into someone who shows an interest in reading more than the shorter one-page flyer. Over the last few weeks, she and Gordon decided not to waste them on people who will just toss them into a corner, or in the trash! Heavens! See Bree's strong tanned hands grip both bundles lovingly, like a mother with her children.

 The following letter arrives wedged in one of the many saggingly full boxes of St. Onge mail.

To the Principal of the School on Heart's Content Road, Egypt, Maine 04047

Hello—

I am a teacher at SAD 78. I have in my hands here materials that several of your students were passing out at the post office here a few days ago. Today, America's children are subjected to so much violence and cynicism as well as drugs and parental apathy. I feel obligated to stand up for today's youth whenever I can.

And so now I'm going to tell you it is wrong to teach children this awful stuff (which I hold here in my hands) about our government. They need to grow up with a healthy attitude about this country in which they live.

I certainly hope you will stop this <u>crap</u> before you poison the minds of your students any further. <u>This might fall under the category of child abuse, at least to my way of thinking.</u> And you can bet the right-wing terrorist element you people are immersed in would put you at a disadvantage with the Department of Human Services should there be a complaint. My advice is to soft pedal your antigovernment lessons to your youngsters. Teach <u>respect</u>.

Sincerely yours,

Mr. Keith McKinnon

 In a future time, Claire St. Onge remembers that late summer. She speaks.

He was spending a lot of time alone with her. Alarms went off in the hearts of us women who knew of Bree's "secret" book and what that meant about how fragile Bree might be if Gordon made one of his moves. I can name you eight women who wore his ring who were only seventeen or eighteen when he made *the move*. That's not a big difference from fifteen, is it?

It was this little project they had going, called *The Recipe*. Perfecting and perfecting it. You'd see them at one of the piazza tables after supper with their heads bent over their papers. You'd hear him getting loud. You'd hear her low, smoky voice and her giggles. With him, she giggled a lot. Early before breakfast, they would sit in one of the parlors. Or sometimes they met downhill at the farmhouse. And sometimes it was very late. I mean like two-thirty in the morning. He seemed to be in a very good mood during this time. And we knew this mood was because of her, this very special child. Then we knew it was time to tell him a few facts of life about the Vandermasts.

 Gordon and Penny St. Onge alone, taking an evening walk over the bristly, newly mowed field northeast of the Settlement.

The late summer chill draws dampness into the short stiff grass. Crickets are creaking mightily. The sunset is a pile of flabby blue-purple clouds lined in headachy-to-look-at gold. The foothills are close and spiky and blue-black. This Penny, mother of teenaged Whitney, is "prettier than Whitney," some have said. Penny wears a long dress, as she would out on a date. Her blonde hair, the kind that looks baby fine and bunny soft, is held back with a large, fresh, powdery strong-smelling maroon and orange marigold. She looks forward to evenings alone with Gordon, as few as they are. Even when he's overly warm and yakky during the nights he spends at her little place, the little cottage she shares with her daughter. But she loves the evenings and nights he is *not* there, too. She has a lot of social life here with her "sisters" and others here, and outside the Settlement, too. She loves to read in bed at night. She is nourished by silence.

As they reach one of the irrigation ponds, glassy with reflected gold and cumulus blue and the ripples of feeding frogs and fish, Gordon puts an arm around Penny, tightly. And it's as if his name were squeezed out of her, "Gordon."

"What?"

"It's about Bree."

"Yuh?"

She leans her face against his shirt, places a hand over that place where his heart is. "As far as any of us know . . . you've only seen Bree's social comment drawings, the ones her brother brought here."

He says nothing. Just a suspicious grunt, sensing something not very handsome, a curse, perhaps, coming soon from Penny's handsome mouth.

"You *have* seen only those, right?"

"Uh, yep." He narrows his eyes, knowing, yes, there's been one of those keep-it-from-Gordon conspiracies among the women. This would not be the first time.

They are still walking along, though slowed a bit, and the ground is rough here, where the old tractor and the electric buggies have made ruts in the spring, all hidden in the tall weeds and grasses. You have to feel with your foot as you go.

Penny says, "You haven't seen the pictures of what her family does to her . . . the forced prostitution."

He drops his arm. Stops walking. Turns away from her, looks off toward the "view" of Promise Lake, which is all in dark shadow now, blocked from the sunset by this very hill he and she stand on, this the part of nature that is powerfully pleasant, unlike the part of nature Penny is describing to him, which is foul.

Penny describes the book in detail. She sort of chokes on some of those details. And he flushes, more red a flush as each detail is laid bare before him. He scooches down on the stony edge of the pond, stares into the glassy water.

Penny relates all the conclusions of the Settlement women who have conferred. She remains standing, her arms crossed under her breasts, such flowery dress fabric, thus flowery breasts.

Something in the pond splashes once. The ripples roll out softly and the gold and blue reflected sunset shivers.

"We . . . her new mothers . . . decided not to tell you at first . . . or any of you guys . . . because . . . we thought you might overreact."

He snorts, rubs one eye with the heel of his hand. "Where is she right now? She told me it was her turn to make supper at home. But there's a philosophy salon tonight. Maybe she had some other things—" He cuts off his own sentence. Sighs. He stands but still doesn't face his wife.

"Who knows what's going on . . . at the Vandermasts?" Penny says darkly.

He rubs his palms together. Slowly.

She says, "No cops, Gordon. We need to be in control of this, not—"

He waves a hand to dismiss the very idea of cops. And his eye flinches violently as if whacked by or pepper-sprayed by the aforementioned.

"Gordon, all the time you've spent with her, has she hinted in any way about this?"

He squints. "I don't know. I've got to think."

Penny wades through the tall weedy-smelling goldenrod to get closer to him, steps to the stony edge of the pond. She looks him hard in the eyes. "You haven't been messing with her."

"No."

She touches one of his work boots with her toe. "Just checking."

But he looks stunned and embarrassed and something else. Guilt. Yes, guilt. It's as if he were the one who had wrapped the girl's wrists in dog chain so she could be enjoyed by customers again and again and again. How many times? How many years? Penny knows how it is with Gordon. He often takes on in shards, in conscience, the sins of other men, wears the guilt, and then tries to speechify his way clear, and he will also confuse Bree's "heart" with the "hearts" of other women. His grief can never be sampler-sized, only jumbo. Right now, he seems pretty dumbstruck, avoiding the eyes of his pretty wife, this wife who has known just gentleness since she came here in her early twenties. He takes Penny into his huge arms now, as if to protect Penny from the Vandermast men and "customers." Yeah, he is pretty quiet, just hiding his face in her clean-smelling hair. And that pringly, zingy, aggressive odor of the marigold pinned there, sort of awful, sort of nice, so naturally a part of her, her handsome womanly sunny ways. "I love you," he whispers. Then, "I'm sorry."

"We need to help her, Gordon."

"Yep."

"We need to figure out how we can get her to come live here. Away from that. And you can try to remember things she has said. Clues."

"Yep."

Around 10:30 p.m. on a summery September night.

Claire's little house.

Only a thin Settlement-woven, Settlement-dyed tapestry is the wall that divides the ell bedroom into two skinny bedrooms, Catherine and Robert sharing a pallet made of quilts and sheepskins on the tiled floor there on one side, Claire's big bed rammed against the opposite wall on the other side. Gordon has arrived for his "prearranged night over" in spite of Claire's insistence that he now wait till after Catherine has gone back to her life in Portland, when she is "healed." Usually he's sensitive to this, the decisions or moods of his wives, their various schedules and cycles, the way at any given time they either want him or don't want him in their beds. And he is careful not to seriously fondle one woman in front of another. Or in front of anyone, for that matter. He understands these dynamics, the hard-won semitranquillity of Settlement life. So this, tonight, in all ways is out of character for him. He appears in the bedroom door, makes a point of not looking to the right side of the tapestry, steps to the left, and opens his hand around a bedpost.

The rosy light of the small lamp blushes through the thin tapestry, a lamp Catherine Court Downey can't sleep without. She is not afraid of the Settlement dark, just sleeps better with light, she has said.

"Go!" Claire commands in a whisper. "Not tonight. Get!"

Gordon imitates the whine of a chastised dog. He sniffs the air, short quick sniffs the way dogs do. He sniffs the bedpost. Cowers a little. Not at all playful, Claire sighs. "Okay then. Let's talk. Something's come up."

Gordon eases his weight onto the edge of the big bed, a bed he himself has made from pine with every sort of lathed and carved embellishment, one of the hundreds of almost desperate ways he pays homage to Claire, his old friend, his first and only legal wife.

He twists around to look down at her; her golden face, which, without glasses in this dim rosy light, holds two very dark, very dangerous-looking eyes. No-nonsense eyes. No ha-ha. There is one thin blanket and a sheet to cover her up to her nearly bare shoulders. Fat. Behind the tall ornate headboard, there's an open screened window. Two distinct sounds, a close neighbor not far beyond the birches, sawing away on his fiddle, and thousands of tall grass bugs sawing on theirs.

"Gordon."

"What?"

"About Bree."

"What now?" He looks at her hard, her darkly and rosily lit face. And she says, "You're going to be honest with me, okay?"

He stands up, his keys jangle. He unbuttons his shirt fast, like a shirt-unbuttoning race. Tosses it to the floor. Then the T-shirt. Facing her, he is half black, half red. One arm in the darkness that Claire's side of the room makes, his other half, which is nearer the colorific tapestry, glows.

Claire pushes herself up, sheet settling around her tremendous middle, her summer nightie a massive plain of wee flowers. She says, "There's more than just *the book* now."

He arches his back, scratching himself between the shoulder blades, turned now so that his back is bright, his front dark.

"Gordon, it's her paintings. Big ones. Nearly big as the walls. She's so gifted, it's . . . creepy. Catherine saw them this morning after Bree left to . . . you know . . . to go work with her . . . her *family*."

Gordon eases tiredly onto the bed.

Claire goes on, "She's, artistically speaking, left Maine and gone on to a Dante's Inferno sort of place . . . mythical . . . or biblical . . . whatever . . ."

One boot falls and there's the hiss of sand from a sock.

"A Minotaur. A seraph. And a devil . . . to name a few. As Catherine points out, they're primarily male creatures, representing Bree's own repressed energy, and her abuse. There is extraordinary attention to anatomy. Most artists take anatomy *courses* to get that good. Bree obviously hasn't had that luxury. She's been forced to be more than face-to-face with the real thing."

The other boot falls. Sand. Sock.

Claire's fingers close on the velvety hard muscle of Gordon's left upper arm . . . *huge* left upper arm. "In every painting, the central figure, the focal point of the event, has your face. And . . . your body. I mean . . . the body is *exactly* yours. Chest hair. Everything."

"It's summer."

"I don't mean just chest and arms."

"I thought you said they were Minotaurs."

"Seraphs. Devils." She stresses the Ss, F, and V. "Devils with horns, your exact beard, writhing in blue fire. Shows the whole body. Some front. Some back. Feet. Ankles. *Toes*. Your toes. The way your middle toes are long. And private parts . . . the way yours is. Uncircumcised."

He sniffs indignantly. "Probably a good guess."

"She's fifteen."

"But experienced, remember? Remember *the book*?"

Claire tightens the tips of her fingers into his bicep.

He snorts. "Dictionary is loaded with uncircumcised peckers. All those Greeks."

"Not exactly like yours."

He says deeply, "She could have had an instructive huddle with any one of you women here. That's all you women talk about anyway is dirt and smut. Why, she could have asked my mother! Same shape as I used to be, just bigger. Bree's good at math."

Claire is not amused.

With an edge of irritation, he says, "In every other way you've accepted that this girl is more intellectually keen than most fifteen-year-olds. Why not this? And sex and bodies aren't something that takes a lot of intellect to figure out—"

"Exactly! What it takes is experience! You just boxed yourself in on that one!"

He grips his face with both hands. "She's just a normal horny girl," he insists through his fingers.

Claire's eyes widen. The fiddling in the house next door has taken up the weird old tune of Polly Vaughn, or is it *Swan Lake*? Both unnerving.

He snickers. "She's obsessed with men."

"Abnormally."

"Oh . . . right . . . if she hadn't been raped, she'd have no interest in men. Well, hell, I've been obsessed with women since I was twelve. I guess I musta been raped by a buncha hags—"

"Shut up."

"This doesn't sound like you," he says wearily. "You're really stretching the space between nonexistent dots on this one."

"Well, we've turned a corner on this."

"What are you getting at?"

"Because these paintings . . . are you! And—" Now she covers *her* face. "It all feels so sleazy!"

"And you say Catherine saw these," he asks quietly. "But you describe—"

"I went over and saw them after."

"That's Bree's own private space. You didn't honor it?"

"It was an emergency! If someone is having a heart attack in the bathroom, you bust in."

He hangs his head. "I thought you all had decided to take it slow . . . not to make a crisis out of it. I thought that that was quite wise."

"Have you, Gordon? Have you been intimate with Bree . . . fifteen-year-old Bree?"

"No."

"You lie, you son of a bitch!"

He snatches up her hand. "I don't lie," he says in a hard ugly way.

Beyond the thin, ever-so-slightly swaying tapestry, only a small distance from Gordon's bare feet, Robert's thin voice. "Mommy?"

Catherine's clear not-at-all-sleepy voice says, "It's okay, sweetheart. They're just talking."

Robert speaks now in a conspiratorial whisper. "Gordon's here."

"Yes, it's Gordon. Gordon's here tonight."

"Why?"

No answer. Just the giggle of the boy as his mother distracts him with a light tickle or a nuzzle, their dark silhouettes fluttering upon the glowing tapestry.

Gordon unbuckles his belt *loudly*. Throws his work pants over the nearest bedpost, dives into the covers, throwing an arm and a leg over Claire's great soft body, which is now turned away from him, and he bites the back of her neck and *growls*.

"Ouch!" She turns toward him, laughing a little but also gasping in that short-winded way of the obese. "I'm sorry," she whispers against his forehead. "It's just hard to figure. This with her family, if it's true, is . . . is . . . driving us all crazy. We want to save her from that, to lure her out of that. Abused women and children are trapped, not just physically but by their *attachment* to the perpetrator. Invisible chains. They're the most insecure people in the world."

Gordon breathes against her ear, "I hate the chair*person*."

Claire ignores him. "And she goes home to these monsters every night!"

He now takes one of Claire's small hands and presses it into the hollow between his jaw and neck and shoulder.

"And as you know, Gordon, she's not showing any signs of quitting that job with them in the woods."

"Claire?"

"What?"

"If the paintings of me are imagination, a great imagination of a natural *master,* why are you so sure the ones of her family are real?"

She wiggles her fingers against his neck. "I think you'll find that most of the women here and some of the guys would say that that part about you is also true. You're alone with Bree a lot. And she acts differently with you than anyone else. That giggle would be seen as a knowing giggle, a lover's giggle."

"What about you? What do you think?"

She simpers. "Well, my dear. Natty is only eighteen and big as a house with your progeny and Leona was not even *seven*teen when she came here and had her first wrastle in the pickup truck with you."

"With Leona that time, I was only in my twenties!"

"But what about Carol?"

No reply.

"She said you were pushy, that you made assumptions."

"I've never touched Carol."

"She said you haunted her."

"How?"

"She said she didn't want you. No glow. You were a nice person, but no glow. But *you* must have thought *she* had plenty of glow. She was uneasy enough to go back to Princeton. I called Bob F. and he and Macky came and got her. And Geraldine said *some* would call your assumptions about *her* rape."

"But—"

"Yep, but . . . okay . . . but I also know you are a sucker for . . . for women who want you."

"That's—"

"Hush up. I know you keep confidences when someone has asked you to. And yes, I know you don't lie. But keeping confidences and telling the full truth are contradictory. I—" She falls silent, cocking her head as if to enjoy the fiddling of the neighbor and the tall grass bugs, then says abruptly, "Everybody was just here."

"Everybody?" He sighs, eyes narrowed.

"Everyone who's been trying to help Bree through this. Lee Lynn, Lorraine, Vancy, Penny, Leona, Glennice, Bonnie Loo, and . . . uh . . ." She taps her fingers counting. ". . . Patricia. And Ann and uh . . . Stephanie and . . . ummm . . . Geraldine. Also Josee. Suzelle and Jacquie. Gail couldn't get up here. Misty couldn't. Did I say Cindy?"

No reply.

". . . oh, and Bev and Barbara, of course. Lucienne came for a moment and left. Adrianne and Cathy. Natty. Diane. Terry. Donna. And Fran."

He grins hugely. "Here? In *this* house?"

"You bet."

He grunts. Rolls away from her, covers his eyes with a forearm as if her voice saying "*you bet*" was a terrible light in his face.

She presses on, "You know, darling, you tell outsiders all that pretty talk about democracy, democracy, democracy . . . for a better world. And all us Settlement folk love our little so-called 'town meetings' here, which . . . were your idea, yes . . . and they feel sort of like democracy. But you know . . . this is no democracy. You're a dictator! A benevolent dictator. But a dictator. One *could* say it's because the Settlement is on your *property*."

Gordon's chest muscles clench.

Claire laments wearily, "This place is like medieval patriarchy, oh, feudal lord . . ." She trails off.

Toward the silent glowing tapestry with Catherine beyond it, Gordon raises a hand, middle finger up. Holds it that way for several seconds.

Claire grabs his arm, pulls down the hand with the offending finger. "No, Gordon. You're wrong. I've been thinking this myself for ages. All by *myself*."

He shifts abruptly. Makes the bed bounce. Takes her left wrist. Mashes his whiskery mouth to the top of her hand. Kiss. Kiss. Kiss. "That is total unabridged bullshit, Claire," he now whispers, and then mournfully, mostly to himself. "I am everybody's *slave*."

Beyond the rosy tapestry, the cartoonish voice of Robert. "Mommy?"

Gordon tsks. No, he never liked the word *Mommy*. As everyone at the Settlement has heard him preach over and over and over, "Mommy" is a TV word, a greeting card word, which has worked hand in hand with other cheap words to tear down everyone's true culture, everyone's regional *real* cultures, with the epitome of the commercial culture, the commercial industrial capitalist fossil-fuel-driven satanic mother word, Mommy! Indeed, he has pressured all mothers here, even those who are not mothers of *his* children, to keep the Mommy-word from the children's vocabulary. Mum or Mumma or Ma or Mother, as beautiful and strong as four million New England hardwood trees. Momma, if you are Southern, fine, also beautiful . . . "in its place, place is the thing, where you are or grew out of, Mammy, too. And then there is Maman, ah, music! Anything but Mommy or Mom!"

No TV.

No teenage girls or women out alone after dark without two full-sized watchful Settlement male chaperones.

No grades in college.

No Mommy.

"Go to sleep, Robert," Catherine's voice whispers.

Gordon stares at the glowing tapestry, one eyebrow raised, his best-so-far unhinged look. "So. What was the unanimous decision of the council on my guilt or innocence? *Was* there a unanimous decision?"

"No."

He chuckles. "Well, there. See where real democracy gets you?"

 On the road out of town, Gordon and Rex run into each other at the Convenience Cubicle gas stop, Rex ahead of Gordon at the pumps.

Rex putting gas into his York Electric work van. Gordon stands there with the thrumming hose between them, dumping change from one hand to the other. Back and forth. He looks in and sees the little Bible in there on the van's dash. Bible on the dash, service pistol under the shirt, or somewhere near . . . under a jacket on the seat, maybe. Rex tells him that the guy from the Virginia militia will probably be up for the Preparedness Expo in Bangor and will stay at his place for that night before and the night after.

Gordon nods, "Just one guy?"

"Maybe three."

"You get crowded, we've got room. Let me know."

Rex is watching the digits flash on the face of the pumps. Gordon watches Rex as though numbers, or something even more critical to this universe, were flashing over his profile. Rex is not wearing his sunglasses. They're on the dash with the Bible. And no floppy green army cap. He is dressed in blue Dickees for work. Bare-headed.

Glass door of the Convenience Cubicle swings open and closed a time or two. It is a *very* small store. Guy on the other side of the pumps finishes, goes in to pay. Another car pulls in, takes the space at the pumps. A truck pulls out. Another car pulls in. Late summer song bugs chirring and cheeping in the tall grass down the embankment behind. A distant crashing; tailgate of some dump truck slamming back into place. The change in Gordon's hands almost melodious. Back and forth. Back and forth.

Gordon says, "You read the short version of *The Recipe* yet?"

Gas nozzle jerks once. "The what?"

"That thing I gave you the other day. Shows a furry thing, Bigfoot. Drawn by one of our kids."

Rex is watching the digits, squeezing the gas nozzle nice 'n' easy to round out the figure to $9.50. "I haven't had a chance."

"What about the other one? The orange one?"

"What about it?"

"What did you think? Good, huh?" Gordon doesn't expect Rex to be charmed by the piece. It doesn't speak much of martial law or of common law or *any* detailed solutions, just the bit about all the red ants rising against The Thing, so lyrically told and tale-like, a literal person such as Rex would *skim*. But wouldn't its urgency speak to any militiaman's bristled-up spirit? "You haven't read it yet, my brother?"

"I've been out straight."

Gordon watches Rex shove the gas nozzle into its cradle. Capable hands. Wedding ring. Military black-faced wristwatch. Now reaching to replace the gas cap. Reaching for his wallet. Eyes now come up, meet Gordon's.

A black wave of despair washes over Gordon. Gives him a stony expression that matches Rex's.

Rex says, "I'm going in to pay."

Gordon says a bit loudly, "I've been reading those articles you and Art and Doc've been burying me with. *Long* fucking articles about Russians being trained as spies in Massachusetts collecting welfare and Gorbachev in California who, by the way, is a capitalist, not a commie. *Tsk*. Then you got gay men poisoning the world with some weird new dis—"

"I didn't give you anything like that."

"Well, Art and Doc did. And Willie with his welfare state obsession—"

"But *I* did not." Rex's steely eyes are fixed on Gordon's face.

Gordon shoves his hands with the change deep into the pockets of his new Settlement-made jeans. Then looks at Rex. "This stuff in *The Recipe* is important, R—"

"Okay, don't cry. I'll read it. Every word."

Gordon pulls a small bottle of aspirin from his pocket. Works off the child-proof cap.

Rex watches Gordon toss three aspirin into his mouth and chew them up. Rex looks disgusted. Then, "I don't know where I put that long one you gave me. The one with the orange. I was going to give it to Thad."

"I'll get some kids to bring over another copy tonight. One of the committees for saving the world." Gordon grins.

Rex snorts. But a friendly snort. Turns away.

 At breakfast. Winter kitchen.

In the wildly fluttering candlelight of the tables, rose and yellow, green and blue, Catherine Court Downey has chosen the wooden chair at the opposite end of one of two connected tables, and this means she faces Gordon, who is sitting at the far-off other end eating lustily from a plate of hot buttered applesauce and eggs.

Beyond the wide archway to the cook's kitchen, the incandescent light is bright and important. Steph, one of Gordon's wives, smashes walnuts in a plastic (yes, plastic) bag with a rolling pin while Jacquie Lessard is talking to her from the sink. And two preteens are helping a four-year-old break and separate eggs. No eggs have landed on the floor. Yet.

Back at the tables, a toddler, blonde, with a huge cheery-looking mouth, reaches for Catherine to pick her up and Catherine, yes, picks her up and the child snuggles into Catherine's big floppy white boat-neck sweater. "What's your name?" Catherine whispers.

The child simpers, whispers something back.

Catherine is trying to figure out if this is one of Gordon's. She decides that she's not.

Ricardo, wearing a flashy gilded paisley 1960s Nehru jacket (frighteningly out of fashion) and a red neckerchief and funny pants, pours Catherine a glass of juice and pats her head and pivots away with a flourish. He could pass as a Parisian waiter if he didn't also seem so much like an auntie . . . too loving to be a waiter. He is always kissing people on the head or ears, sometimes passing by with a baby under each arm. She keeps studying him to see if he looks like Gordon but there's no resemblance. Though tall, the boy's face is too narrow, foxy almost. And none of that significant St. Onge nose.

She sighs happily. She glows. Some of the young mothers are settling in the chairs around her, asking if she slept well.

No, she didn't sleep well, she tells them. But how she glows! And her light brown eyes reflect the vivaciousness of the life of these rooms. Catherine the Vulnerable is gone. Here sits Catherine the Sagacious, Catherine the Up-'n'-at-'em. The toddler on her lap stares at her face. The child is mesmerized by Catherine's face. Catherine gives this little one a really squeezy hug and again sighs. She is anxious to deal with the "Bree issue." She glances around for the girl but Bree is nowhere this morning, not at this meal. She knows that usually Bree has breakfast with her brothers and father back home, and the father's girlfriend sometimes stays there. Nobody is clear on John "Pitch" Vandermast's exact living arrangements with that woman.

When Catherine speaks, all the young mothers listen attentively. "We need to get Bree to some professionals." She details her plan to approach Bree this evening while Bree is painting up in "the studio." Right after "dinner" (she means supper). She looks down through the long tunnel of fluttering candlelight between the dozens of seated people to Gordon, who is now wearing his old man reading glasses and studying something written on a small square of brown paper, frowning. A chubby young man stands next to him, glasses, no whiskers, but a long brown ponytail. He passes Gordon another piece of paper, which Gordon takes hesitantly from his hand.

Ricardo with the Nehru jacket and neckerchief brushes past Catherine's chair, carrying two big canning jars of dark stuff on his head, using his hands, of course. He is singing loudly, "Riiiiide the snake . . . toooo the lake! The snake he's lonnnng! Seven miles! He's ollld! And his skin is colllld!"

The mothers tell Catherine how hard this whole Bree situation has been, that everyone feels their hands are tied.

Catherine glances again down the long, long connected tables to Gordon as he is writing with a pen on one of the scraps of paper. "Well," she smiles at the mothers. "Today we will be taking step *one*. There is no excuse for enabling."

She understands that the girl must be in a great spiraling space of aloneness. And now the footsteps of her rescuers will enter that space and bring her OUT. Tonight!

 Late afternoon.

Catherine is coming up the Settlement's gravel road in her car, a little metallic-mint-colored thing. She sees up ahead a flatbed truck pulling out from the sawmill yard, and as it approaches her, she sees from its driver's side window an arm waving to stop her.

It is Gordon. Dark hair a mess. Metal-frame cop-style sunglasses and all that beard. Nothing showing of those eyes, those pale eyes usually so unsettling in his dusky face. Then she sees Robert's face. And two somewhat familiar men. She shifts her car into park, hops out, sees that Gordon is opening the truck door, but then he closes it as he sees her coming.

He pulls off his sunglasses, lays them on the dash. Catherine sees that the guy holding Robert is in his twenties, sunglasses, no beard, thick brown ponytail, a shirt of some awful plaid, unbuttoned to show off a T-shirt that has some sort of awful advertisement.

But now, even as she takes that last step up to the truck's open window and that sweet smell of freshly-milled pine . . . or hemlock . . . from the high load strapped on back, she hears a sound. A whomping. From the south.

Coming closer fast, then slowing, surrounding them, it seems. WHOMP-WHOMP-WHOMP-WHOMP.

She sees that Gordon's eyes are raised, fixed on this thing in the sky behind her head, and one of the men is leaning forward, the one who has Robert on his lap and maybe Robert was trying to speak to her . . . she sees his mouth shaped around the word *Mommy,* but the sky is now really opening up with the deafening WHOMPING and the aircraft is now really *in* their space here, swinging around the treetops on the nearer mountain of the St. Onge land. Now it hovers exactly above this truck and car. It leans in and away. It's wind gives the row of oaks along the road a thrashing. They crackle and hiss like fire. She watches the white star on army green, the side of the aircraft, lift again and angle away farther. All the while, its maddening racket beating straight down. She can feel her hair move a little, even now. She sees that Robert is excited, thrilled actually. Mouth open. Pointing.

Now the horrid thing is back. Like it wants to play. Like it wants you to throw it a stick or a soccer ball.

Then it is departing and Gordon says something Catherine can't hear and he grins weirdly. He and the other men laugh. Together. Loud. Ugly laughter that seems completely sexual to Catherine, and in some way about *her.* Worse even than her suspicion that he has seduced-raped a fifteen-year-old already-damaged girl, is *this,* the blustery hilarity of three men, their open mouths, opening, closing throat muscles, thick necks, the ultimate macho arrogance.

But what Gordon is really doing now is quietly noticing how strong Catherine Court Downey looks. Self-contained. He can't imagine being like that. It doesn't ring true. *Self-containment.* It's an eccentric concept to him, in man or woman. It has such a reptilian ring to it. But she is also radiating something else. That mischievous arch of those brows. A let's-play lightheartedness? The disgust for her that he felt especially last night is gone, as he lingeringly studies her face, the small dark shapely mole by her mouth, and then the mouth itself, and her throat. The throat. He is stirred. He reaches. His arm is long and his large hand enters her space, fingers almost closing in on her shoulder but she's not quite close enough. He lowers his hand, lets it hang outside the warm truck door. He says, "Howzit goin'?"

She says, "Very well, thank you." She stares directly into his eyes.

He says, "Well, you look good. Claire says teaching this year has started off pretty smooth . . . for both of you."

She steps close now, almost against the idling truck, within his easy reach. "Yes. *Smooth*." She smiles.

"Mommy! The helicopter was loud!" Robert calls, stretching his neck to see better out across the edge of the high truck door from where he sits on the young guy's lap. No seat belt. No car seat. Soon she will have to ask them not to put Robert in danger again like that but now isn't the time. She is trying *so hard* to feel the family's embrace and not recoil from every prickle. In this moment, the Settlement feels like a deep bath in perfectly warm water. The only wrong note is coming from her insides.

"Yes." She nods eagerly. And her smile. A professional smile. Almost a magazine smile, which lasts long into the growing quietness as the thwomping-chomping of the helicopter gets farther away and nobody in the truck speaks. "Wait!" she cries.

She suddenly remembers something. Steps back to her car, bending in to sort through crackling bags.

Behind her she hears Gordon shifting into neutral, setting the brake, settling in.

She finds what she wants, gifts for Robert. She passes them up to Gordon now. Glow-in-the-dark figures, one green, one yellow, one blue, one pink, one gray. Not a monster-faced muscley warrior. Not a Yoda. Not a Troll. But something of the latest personable creature epidemic. Big-eyed, cute, asexual, and plastic. And shrink-wrapped in more plastic.

"Neat!" says Robert as Gordon hands each one over.

Catherine nods, the smile unstoppable. Yes, like a picture, and yet a too desperate hardworking paddling-along eagerness in her brown eyes.

"Thank you, Mommy," says Robert.

Catherine looks into Gordon's eyes, which are terribly green and scrutinizing. Benign scrutiny, yes. But scrutiny nonetheless. And the late afternoon sun on his face, a reckless September gold. Brings out those two or three red hairs among the brown, black, and gray of his short beard. It brings out his age. Almost forty.

He asks, "What are you planning for Robert. Is he expected at school? In Portland?"

"Yes, he's preregistered in Portland, but—" She sighs. "We're not ready to go back there yet . . . to live."

Lightning quick, Gordon looks her up and down. "Take your time, Robert's okay here. He's my Mr. Buddy." He looks around at Robert.

Robert's high voice giggles. "Mr. Budeeee! *You* are!"

"I mean it," Gordon says, looking back at her. He reaches for his sunglasses. "Take your time. You're important to Claire. You're good for her." He slips the dark glasses on, and sort of reaches again, as if to touch her shoulder but now again she is out of reach. He sees her smile is still in place. But her posture is bracing against something, like weariness. He draws back his hand, this time into the truck, fingers folding around the wheel. "Are you coming to supper?"

"I thought I might."

"Sit with me," he says, his eyes behind the dark glasses unreadable. "We need to talk." He shifts the truck. The emergency brake thumps free. The truck rolls forward an inch or so, making the sand crunch sleepily.

Catherine tells him, "That would be nice. Yes." Then she says cheerily, "Have fun, Robert!" And waves to him. He says, "Yep" in a manly way. *Yep* is his new word, almost *a-yup,* probably *a-yuh* next. Even his *yep* is now spoken with a distinct Maine accent.

Then the truck rumbles along downhill. Now something like gunfire . . . a spray of heavy acorns raining down on the truck cab and on the load of lumber as it moves under that row of high oaks.

Catherine's heart is beating too fast, like tachycardia. And this worries her. Her heart. Her lungs and organs. She worries that the antidepressants mixed with all those downers have harmed her, and maybe all the wrong things you eat over the years adds up in your body. All those toxins, those *poisons* that so many experts say you store in your fat. But she is afraid to think "diet." When she has dieted in the past, she went too far. Right now, all she wants is moderation and a clear head.

She thinks of Bree. Poor Bree. Tonight when she gets Bree to talk about what men have done to her, she'll not only bring other Settlement women with her for that important women-only assurance that the girl needs desperately, but some gifts she shopped for today, things that will go with the girl's stormy red hair.

 At supper out on the piazzas, a warm weedy sweet September evening, creaking with the lusty rhythm of tall grass bugs, so stirring and restive to humans.

There are two new faces. Brady and Sadie. Brother and sister. Both with dark eyes and silvery blond hair. Silvery complexions. Long necks. Elegantly swanlike in their physicality, their breezy substance, professional-class in speech and in their teeth, perfect as mathematics. Sadie is healthy. Brady has the DREADED IMMUNE SYSTEM ILLNESS. Early stages. Sadie is eighteen. Brady is twenty-three. He lived in New York for two years. The parents whom Brady came home to live with again can no longer take the neighbors' AIDS hysteria abuse anymore. They dread the phone ringing, dread cars passing slowly by the house. Brady offered to leave. But Sadie is his shadow as she is almost his mirror image. And so this morning they arrived, knowing no one, looking like two silvery Christmas card angels. Now Sadie and Brady are here, at the table, one on either side of Gordon.

He has welcomed them both. With shrewd reasoning, he understands that all in the Settlement will learn best this way. Love. AIDS. Stigma. Politics. Hysteria. THE WORLD. Grief. When the young man dies, doesn't a healthy community grow even healthier from shared grief? The temple of Life raised from Death. How coldheaded! Would you say coldhearted? No matter, he had said to them, "Welcome."

Before supper, Catherine and Claire had talked. Catherine said, "I'll pick up all the literature I can get my hands on tomorrow . . . HIV positive, AIDS, spirochete virus, all of it." She meant at the university, where she would have a full day of classes, including one night class. So many of her days are really packed.

Catherine knows many an HIV and AIDS story, from students and friends of friends . . . there are enough of their stories to make it clear that Brady should keep his secret quiet for a little while. Not tell more than a few folks here until everyone loves him as an ordinary person first, an identity separate from his disease. When she suggested this to Claire, Claire hesitated, then agreed. She and Catherine hugged. Then they walked to supper together, Catherine with her little basket of vitamins and healing herbs. And in the other hand hung some of the bags of little gifts she had bought earlier that day for all the children and for Bree.

She goes straight to Gordon and he sees her coming and reaches back to another table for an empty chair and, with ease, he one-handedly swings the heavy chair to the corner of his table, smiling at Sadie. "Scoot over, dear. Make room for Catherine *Court* Downey." He stresses *Court* playfully and when Catherine settles in tightly between the silvery swanlike girl and Gordon, Gordon introduces the brother and sister to Catherine and then whispers close to Catherine's ear, "I'm glad you remembered to sit with me."

She places her little basket on the table, arranges her shopping bags under her chair. AIDS. AIDS. AIDS. AIDS. She is ever so *drawn* to the young Brady's pale profile. She is ever so *bothered* by the young Brady's pale profile. AIDS. AIDS. AIDS. AIDS. She feels a bit faint. Her sympathy is a perfect white fire.

As the three long tables (and several small tables) of people eat strips of moose steak and onions, new potatoes, huge beets (sliced), chopped kale, pickled five-bean salad, golden rolls and some sort of weedy bread (better than you think), and three kinds of pies, Gordon rambles on and on to Catherine about education and the community, a "family community." And he talks about Robert. He talks passionately about Robert. He talks coaxingly about Robert. And once Robert comes from another table and buddies up to Gordon, they swing at each other, play pokes. Catherine watches, smiling. A queenly smile. The great velocity of discord in her eyes barely detectable.

Gordon's right hand almost touches Catherine again and again. She's in easy reach but he is a complete gentleman with her. And maybe he is even trying not to sound like an oinking pig when he eats . . . for her. He is so good with the two young people, Sadie and Brady. Asks

them questions about their interests and their dreams. So fatherly. So
THERE for them. He laughs quickly and loudly at their little reserved
almost-businesslike jokes. And you can tell Sadie and Brady really
like Gordon. Reaching behind Catherine with his long arm, Gordon
touches Sadie. Once. Playfully. Her startling pale hair. The hand, the
hair throw sparks in Catherine's eyes. How disorienting!

Focusing back on Catherine, Gordon has that same fatherly expression. Well, he surrounds everyone who comes near, doesn't he? Like
a boa constrictor but different. Hugging and fondling young and
old. Well or sickly. Soaking them up. Owning them. Staking claim.

Catherine watches all this with her restrained but flickering smile,
chin high. And Gordon looks like the merry king. Or is it the Prophet?
That is what he has been called on the radio, isn't it? And the papers
as they were quoting a couple of townspeople. And Catherine, floating
and freefalling in confoundedness, is detoured into territory that has
no markers for her. The disarray is only in her "right brain," because
in her body and heart she feels blessed. And she is thinking how this
amazing and cuckoo Settlement situation becomes ordinary once you
are inside. Could that be called brainwashing? Now she is breathless
with a moment of panic. No, not a moment. A half moment. Now
she is back to body and heart.

Bree is nowhere in sight. They say she is painting, really into painting tonight. No supper for Bree, neither here nor at home with her
father and brothers. Just the muse. Her escape from life. This, Bree's
life, the problem that will be addressed this evening.

 **Tools. Brooms. Boxes. Cabinets. Jackets on hooks. Two
trash cans. An acorn on the floor. Dim light. Fifteen
watts. Thrifty watts. An industrial-looking space.
This is the upstairs hallway of the Quonset hut where
the studio is. Main door to the studio is open. Privacy
sign on the door.**

Bree stands, smiling sort of, her hair tied back tight to expose all of
her face. "What are you all roaming around for?" She asks this with
one of her giggles. Paint on her hands. Paint on her work shirt. Black
and orange. A twinkle in her wide-apart freaky honey-color eyes.

The women aren't really roaming. They are standing. And staring.

"We came up to check on you. We missed you at supper." This is Vancy. Age twenty-five. She is very pregnant. But also she is a fat person to start with. Huge square face. Brown tightly-permed short hair. Tiny little pig eyes with nearly no lashes. She has just finished helping three out-of-touch elders with their soupy suppers and has one small splat of color, like pink watercolor, like the makings of art, on the rounded-out middle of her white maternity shirt. She also wears a prominent heart locket, a wristwatch, and the plain silver wedding ring of Gordon St. Onge.

Catherine, hugging her shopping bag of gifts to her chest, says, "Maybe we can get a little peek at your work, Bree."

Bree laughs sharply. "No way, José." Then giggles apologetically.

Catherine clasps one of Bree's large paint-covered hands. "Bree, there is not a person here in this hallway who doesn't love you. You can trust us. Let's sit down. Let's talk."

Bree looks past Catherine at short, round-faced, bosomy Claire, and then to Lee Lynn and Gail and then at the several young mothers who are not Gordon's wives. Catherine still hangs on to Bree's hand even as she shifts a bit to manage the loaded shopping bag.

In the dim hallway of light, Claire St. Onge's eyes behind their steely specs look fiery. "Gordon's birthday is next week. His *fortieth*."

Bree whispers. "Oh. I see. You're planning . . . uh . . . *scheming* something for him."

Catherine squeezes Bree's hand, then releases it.

"Forty spanks!" laughs Bree, wagging her head playfully. Shifts to her other foot. But her feet in those high-topped leather work boots of hers are still set apart in a way that means nobody is getting past her into her studio.

Claire says, "No, Bree. That's not what I meant."

Bree's eyes turn down to wide little Claire's upturned face.

Claire finishes her thought, "We mean, we know a girl of fifteen who knows the facts of life. That's good. But a forty-year-old man knows more, *should* know more . . . should at least know enough to keep his hands off."

Bree looks a little stupid, mouth ajar. Lee Lynn, skirling high voice, Chicago accent, hair of a gauntly lovely witch, addresses the girl.

"Bree. We need to talk. Can't we *please* come in and see what you're working on?"

Bree stands taller, her stance more iron-like than before. "You guys think Gordon and I have had sex?"

"It's a thought that's occurred to us, yes," admits Catherine, looking up at Bree, who is so much taller than everyone present. Catherine is giving Bree's elbow a slow consoling rub.

Bree snorts with disgust. She raises her eyes to Vancy, who stands close behind Catherine's shoulder and then to the row of faces beyond. Says Bree, "Don't worry, you guys. Maybe you haven't noticed. I'm not pretty."

Vancy says, "Haven't you noticed, Bree? *I'm* not pretty."

"You are not a freak," Bree says evenly.

Vancy sighs. "Freakhood is how one sees oneself."

Catherine says firmly, "Pretty is beside the point. We're talking about a man taking advantage of someone who is young, susceptible, and already a victim of violence. Bree, this is my studio, too. Let us in. We'll sit over on my side if you wish. We won't look behind your tarps."

Bree doesn't budge. "Something tells me you already have." The hallway where they all stand seems to grow even darker, the lights over and beyond the hanging tarps to Bree's space blaze like suns.

Claire reaches to put her arms around Bree and Bree responds with a little slump, her cheek to the top of Claire's glossy black hair. Claire tips her head back, Bree so tall. "Okay. You're saying Gordon is clean. But your fathers and brothers . . . is there something you want to tell us about them? About—" Her voice softens even more, a hitch of sorrow. "You know what I'm talking about, don't you sweetheart?"

Bree stares for a long moment into thin air.

Claire says, "What about the others, sweetie?"

Now Bree glares straight to the back of the group at the one young woman she had most recently showed THE BOOK to. One of those she trusted. *With her story.* Bree's bottom lip trembles.

The young mother looks down at the floor. Guiltily.

Claire continues gently, "Your brothers have been monsters, Bree. Haven't they?"

"No!"

"Yes, oh, yes!" insists Catherine. As Claire hugs Bree harder, Catherine scoots around them into the studio, Vancy following her. Catherine pulls the tarp to Bree's side of the bright room aside. She throws out a hand toward the canvases beyond. She announces, "See *him! Them.* All of THEM being HIM. Are *THESE* not monsters?!!!" She backs up to the tarp, holding it open with her back, still clutching the shopping bag, her lovely chin high. "Please come in here and tell me I'm not crazy. See for yourselves!"

The younger women reluctantly but obediently file toward the lighted room, Catherine's teacherly voice a crowning force, and Catherine turns to Bree and cries out pleadingly, "Bree!" Then accusingly, "You depict here every sort of beast. THIS is how you view men!!! Because this is how you've been subjugated! It's . . . oh . . . yes . . . spelled right out here. You can't deny it!" She pushes the shopping bag into a chair, keeping her back to the tarp bunched behind her against the Homasote. "And your father and brothers . . . oh, yes! I *have* seen the book." She rubs one eye hard, as if to make that eye forget. "Until you come to terms with that whole rigmarole, until we get you to some good professional help . . . dear heart, you can say all you want but—" She looks over her shoulder into the blazing light and color of Bree's studio space. "These paintings are, without a doubt, the work of a young woman damaged, if not by the act, then, at the very least, by the basest patriarchal environment anyone could imagine. It makes me sick! It makes me angry! And I tell you, if this *has* been done to you, the perpetrators must be punished!"

All the other women look sharply at Catherine as she speaks the word *punished*.

Bree begins to half-squeal, half-howl. "Get out of here! Everyone get the fuck out!"

Lee Lynn's urgent shrill inquiry, "You really haven't had sexual intercourse with Gordon? Be honest. Pleeeeze be . . . it's okay."

"No! Never. No! Get out!"

And then Claire, "We're not going to punish anybody. And we do not need to get professionals of any kind involved. But Bree, it's best if *we* know . . . we're your *family*."

And Lee Lynn, not giving up, "All those men in the book?"

Bree laughs. Quite a beastly laugh. Makes her hands like claws. "No! Nooooo nobody! Nooo-body! No-body!" She now shrieks with laughter, then hunches her back up, gripping Lee Lynn's thin lovely face, then tips her own face up as if her neck were twisted, rolls her eyes, and says in a low gruff scratching voice, "The bells! Hear them!" Then backs away, lunging at another woman who stiffens, wide-eyed as Bree, hunchbacked and shaking a fist, bellers, "THE BELLS! THE BELLS! HEAR THE BELLS!" She laughs heinously at all their stunned faces. She hops around, back hunched, head low and twisted.

Now she looks up at Catherine, and, still in her low scratchy ani-mally voice, asks, "You like that, dontcha? That's my Quasimodo imitation! He's in special ed." She snickers and stands up straight, then bursts into tears, strangled wretched sobs, holding her face. The women begin to move toward her to comfort, while staring down on them from every direction, the pale green eyes of Gordon St. Onge, face, beard, throat, navel, cleft hoof, wings violently constricted or spread, feathered wings, lashing tail of a bull, here falling into flames, here steady in the turbulence of countless babies that are fat and green-eyed and powerful, boy babies and girl babies, POWER BABIES. And there are other figures, men and women . . . but Gordon is THE FIGURE, the epitome of perfection, sexuality, power and transcen-dence, damnation, exorcism, and forgiveness.

Bree doesn't wait to be hugged or soothed. She strides proudly (it seems) out, down the stairs, out of the Quonset hut, across the sandy lot, hops up into her truck, driving that truck neither fast nor slow, just driving out of there, bye, bye.

 Catherine that night, head on pillow, eyes wide. Silently she speaks.

My god. My god. What is it, Bree, if it isn't that? Your sweet raw soul biting the rescuer's hand! If not that, Bree, what is it? What *is* it? I don't understand.

 Six-thirty that next morning at the Vandermasts.

Dark green Chevy pickup with white cab rumbles down slowly into the Vandermast dooryard, parking lights glowing. A dreary cloudy morning, just a moment here and there between long drizzles and cruel gusts. Not full daylight yet.

Claire St. Onge and Gordon St. Onge head for the kitchen door of the house, Claire gliding along in the lead with her arms crossed under her huge breasts, brown button-up sweater, her hair down, which makes her look young . . . sort of. Gordon wears one of his billed caps, which he takes off when invited into the kitchen by Bree's father. Bree's father wears his cap in the house. Soft-spoken man. Blue eyes. Hands crusty as fossils. Welcomes the two visitors. One of the brothers is at the table with five cereal boxes of five different cereals around his one bowl. Collie dog swishes around happily, no longer barking since John "Pitch" Vandermast has pointed at him.

Pitch explains that Bree has gone to stay for a few days with his deceased wife's younger sister, June Shaw, in Belfast. "He used to live down this way till his work took 'im" (*He, his,* and *'im* meaning the woman's husband?).

"Was Bree upset?" Claire asks.

Pitch Vandermast raises an eye. "Well—" He tips his head down, digs at the back of his head luxuriously a moment, which causes his billed cap to flop forward a bit, covering his eyes. Then he quickly readjusts his cap, screws it on good, and smiles. "She's awfully cross with you folks."

They talk about Bree awhile in the kitchen, then are still talking about her out in the dooryard while one of the brothers loads up an orange Timberjack skidder onto the low bed and the groan of the engine and low low low gearing punctuates every sentence and then the Vandermast men have to leave and Claire steps up to the father and hugs him, and he's not much of a hugger, but he doesn't fight it.

 Saturday, sweet, warm, late a.m. Catherine at *home*.

She decides on fresh air, some wholesome exercise. Dressed in her white sneakers and loose pants and sweatshirt, she explores the roads and paths of the Settlement, nodding and smiling a bright-faced, "Hello!" to people she passes. Her eyes under their handsomely thick eyebrows seem the color of green olives in the sun, eyes that have that way of color coding the day, the place, perhaps even the ambience.

As she comes to a narrow gap in a stone wall, she sees the woods here have been recently and brutally logged. Sometimes the Settlementers don't live up to their eco-friendly maxims? She studies the nearest opening between remaining oaks. Oaks with manly girths, saplings, suckers, and russet-color slash. The lane beaten and rutted. Rocks and slippery stumps, roots, yellowing ferns in bunches, elbow high. She sees this area has also been recently fenced. Double-strung electric fencing through the white eyes of old outdated insulators, above a fence of wide and battered horizontal boards, larger than any pigpen she's imagined. The fencing disappears beyond this sunny opening up into the thick blotchy enigma of undamaged woods. Looks like half this mountain is reserved for pigs. Though she has been told "pigs and hogs" are here, she can't seem to catch sight of one.

"Pigs!" she calls, "Here, pigs!"

No response. She decides to come back later. She'd really like to see one.

She is starting to feel deeply for this place.

 At breakfast the next morning in the muffin-warm, coffee-hot, kazoo-zippy, baby-back-thumping, flame flickering winter kitchen.

There Gordon sits at one of the smaller tables. Empty seat at his side. Catherine carries a cup of coffee and her little basket of herbal "treatments" to this seat and makes herself comfortable. There is a kid a few feet away, playing a guitar softly, playing quite well. Catherine notices that it is Ricardo, who isn't on the kitchen crew this morning. He wears a baby blue cowboy shirt. He sits squarely under several trophy-sized stuffed paper fish, painted in bright tropical colors, which churn and bounce prettily on strings, as if tripping the light fantastic.

Gordon tells Catherine that he heard she enjoyed seeing the pigs last evening.

"Yes! They were wonderful. I asked Aurel to show them to me. He's such a nice man. The animals are well-treated."

"Yes." He smiles.

She sees that he is drinking beer. For breakfast. One untouched piece of buttered toast on a Settlement-made plate of blobby red and white stripes and boxy green clovers.

She does not plan for this subject to come up. It just pops out of her. She tells him she plans on picking up a few more things at home after classes today. Including her TV. She wants it in her studio, for watching videos mostly. Educational. "And the news. Which is important."

He shifts to fully face her. The smell of the beer reaches her, like unquestionable eminence, not trespass. "We have a rule here. No TV. It's an important rule."

Catherine smiles, looks down, flushes prettily. Looks back into his face. "I understand that institutions have rules. But not families. Yes? No?"

He looks at her oddly, reaches for the brown beer bottle, label-less, filled with *homemade* beer, of course . . . hoists it up. Swallows once, twice, three times.

She answers her own query. "Well, yes, rules . . . families do . . . but they are for *children*."

He smacks his lips once, wipes his mouth and mustache with his thumb and fingers once, drops his hand. "This is a big family, you understand. We desire to survive."

She smiles. "Are the rules posted on the wall here or do you just make them up as you go along?" She unscrews a bottle from her basket, two capsules roll into her palm in a frisky way.

He watches her hands. "I'll write them up for you if you want."

"YOU'll write them up. So YOU write the rules here?"

He smiles. "Okay, I'll dictate. YOU write 'em down." He laughs. A nasty laugh.

Catherine *appears* unflustered, her off-brown eyes steady on his face, her curved naughty-seeming eyebrows raised. Little pretty mole by her mouth. Mouth a hard line of certitude. Shoulders squared. "Wouldn't it be nice to have a VCR here for tapes? I know you all have tapes here. Why have them if you don't watch them? And there are so many available that you'd be interested in. Films particular to your causes."

The guitar music seems to be climbing, becoming lighter. Feathery. Breathy. But in the foreground, Gordon's voice, thick and substantiated. "Yes. We've been talking about having a TV, just for the VCR. Only we would sabotage the antenna works if necessary." He laughs. "Maybe break the channel thingamajig. Pull it off or something." He laughs again. Playful, but in a vinegary sort of way. "Reception isn't so good up on this road anyway. It's the hills. That's why you see so many elaborate antennas bigger than the houses themselves on the way up here from town. Some have those dishes. No cable around here yet." He narrows his eyes at the wonder of all this, the craziness of it. "Probably we'll do the VCR thing eventually. But *this* isn't a good time. We've *agreed* on it. And when we do, there would *not* be a TV in each home."

"I can't see why this would be a bad time," she presses. "What's so different about now from, say, next year?"

He just smiles.

"*You* probably would have the last word. Even once *you* have given in to a VCR, *you'd* have control over what people watch here." She smiles.

"Could be." He smiles.

While she is taking her capsules, Robert, her child, yes, hers and Phan's child, comes skipping from the opposite table, where a squiggling gang of kids are planning their day, going over committee and crew lists with Gail St. Onge, who is "clerk of the house." Robert pushes in between his mother and Gordon and flomps his face and arms onto the table as if he is exhausted. Catherine rubs his back, the feel of his Settlement-made brown sweater bristly as life itself. "Coming down with something?" She touches his shining hair.

He sighs. A *big* manly sigh. "I was just hired to be on the soda panel check crew."

"The what?"

"Solar," Gordon whispers, then swigs more beer.

"The soda panel check crew," repeats Robert, standing straight now, his superhero stance.

Catherine smiles. Again she both hates and loves this place. *This place!*

"Congratulations, Robert!" She shakes his hand.

Bree and the nature of art.

Alone today, she makes a fire in the woodstove though the day has turned out clammy and too warm. She doesn't need heat. She needs a vanishing point.

She begins to tear up THE BOOKS.

The collie dog steps around, excited and happy over the fun sound of tearing rag paper. The interesting smell of colors and the whites and blacks with weighty names a dog would never appreciate such as titanium and zinc.

Bree does not feel attachment to this old work, only blistering shame now that there is no such thing as privacy or trust. NO such thing as a sister.

Her large hands work as well as paper shredders or wood chippers. Fast. The books she shared with them are not the only books. There are others. Never shared. The book of Bree and the Civil War soldiers, so handsome! So romantic! She had only been twelve then and the soldiers were kissing her hair or smooching her neck. No wild sex yet. That would come to mind later. Thank heavens the Settlement bunch never saw the pirates! Bree had been reading some history on pirates, how they had been sailors, slaves actually, and brutalized by sea captains on the British empire's corporate ships.

But as soon as pirates manned their own vessels, they were into democracy and all voted on things. And they performed plays! Bree put herself on their ships, sometimes as a girl pirate, sometimes as a hostage but a hostage who sympathized. The sex was great. A real seething brawl. Bree had the whole crew to herself. Not *her* slaves, exactly. They were always willing. She could always imagine them, their breathing, their livingness. The ship rolled. The sea was a wall. The decks were slick. All those tough bare feet. Hands missing. Hooks. All those beards, tattoos, and scars. Men of all races, slave ships often overtaken, the "cargo" enlisted into liberty. Stolen rum. Stolen food. Stolen gunpowder, enough for suicide (of the whole ship) when needed. Bree would be there. Girl pirate in the crow's nest, the great mast, the phallic symbol. What's wrong with phallic symbols?

And yeah, there over every tilting ship is the lilac-color cast of justice, fairness, whatever you want to call it, the only thing Mother Nature never *gives*. You have to *steal* that. You have to get mean in the process.

And pirates sang a lot. Ho hee ho hee! And they would fuck. Fuck Bree.

So much noise. Wind.

Wapping sails.

Chains and winches.

Bellers and hoots.

And the flag of DEATH.

JOLLY. Death would come like party time.

MEN. Like Maine men, shy and serious, or loud and bragging, drunk and in your face, unforgiving and pissed off at lords and enemy captains, pissed off at phonies, and pissed off at suck-ups. And at God.

All of this goes into the odd-smelling fire, torn first, shredded small enough to fit.

The beautiful faces. The beautiful bodies. The fire of a young girl's freedom to imagine, transformed by the fire of a match into ash. Images shriveled. Calligraphy words gone as if they never were. Bree bereft.

Bree sighs, weeps, howls, screams, down on one knee at the little woodstove door. The collie laps her face. Dog. Best of souls.

 Bree, the incorrigible doodler.

Another day. The sky a wizardly blue, deepening, the sun a red closing eye beyond the fields.

She knows she should be in the kitchen helping her brother, Dana, make his "Mexican Special" because the mess he makes when unattended would take twenty people to clean up. He tries, oh, he tries to remember all those splats on the floor, drizzles over the counter. He sometimes claims he's color-blind. She doesn't buy it.

She can hear through the open windows the pans clunking, lids clanking, hears the can opener cranking, hears the refrigerator door . . . ominous sounds. But she stays where she is, in the early evening light. Outside. Under the world's most human-looking tree, colossal old maple with a face and arms. Its being radiates against

Bree's shoulders and the back of her skull as she leans back, resting her eyes. On her lap, her drawing pad. She has drawn a picture of "souls." These are random souls. But as she looks down now, she notices how the faces look like her brothers, her father, her aunts. She thinks perhaps they look like herself, had her face not been deformed. And like her mother, had her mother not died. She understands how it is that the artist's hand conveys from every cell, from the DNA of generations, the self. Yeah, conveys the self. The artist unconsciously constructs a child of his or her SELF.

She frowns. Wondering. She understands that, yeah, all her work is probably like this, every face preexisting like a ready egg tucked in her ovaries . . . every face having a soul. And yes, no wonder the Settlement women and Catherine believed mistakenly that her fantasy pictures were of her brothers! She feels a pang, deep, like something bursting and stinging, a grief. How long will Catherine be dead to her, Bree's own heart steeled against her beautiful friend? Had Bree resisted mothering?

 ### An old-fashioned late summer day.

A lot of late-morning traffic using the bridge in East Egypt, bridge of arched stone colonnades, and a too-narrow passage for those who need to *push* through a day.

Today's sky is a blue to marvel. Roar of the falls. And seeming to float on the edge of the falls, the hunkering woolen mill, shut down for almost ten years now. *Everything going to China*. Part of the empty parking lot and loading area is nearly under the bridge, and from there the bridge is laid out up there against the sky. Though it is not a tall bridge, quite level with the road, it remains true to the fact that here in these hills life is a series of God-sized stairs.

Howie Stover's Dodge is having trouble. Had to coast it down into the empty lot from the road and bridge area above. Gordon St. Onge helping, leaning over the engine, his back to the bridge, saying stuff that makes Howie laugh. Now Gordon ambles over to his own truck to find a smaller wrench . . . Howie facing the bridge, looking up at something, a tactless stare.

Gordon turns and sees, his eye that flinches doing so in its most stark-raving mad-looking way.

Bree up there on the bridge. Bree up there in the sky.

Yes, bridge so narrow. Made in those days when you had an old horse and wagon or a Model A and time to be polite. Bree on its skinny sidewalk, standing against the stone and mortar "rail," hands in the pockets of a longish yellow print dress that Gordon has never seen her wear before, a soft gosling yellow with wee flowers or dots, hard to tell from here. Not sleeveless, but almost. Just at-the-shoulder cuffs. Lovely young arms. And some sort of *shoes,* not work boots. He can't tell for certain from so far. The eyes of her wronged-by-the-gods face stare into Gordon's.

"Hey!" he bellers.

She lifts one hand from its deep pocket for a wagging-of-the-fingertips-only wave, rather girlish. The bridge rumbles and thunders with each crossing.

Gordon feels in his whole person the million and one dangers that could tear at her, some to tear her body, some to tear her heart. Traffic! Dirty air! Deep dammed-up river! Cruel people! Misguided people. How such a face can lead evil out from evil's deepest tunnels and chambers.

A tractor trailer, hauling fuel, hisses and groans into the curve, up onto the bridge, too fast, lifts her hair.

He turns back to finish with Howie Stover's car, replacing the last hose, finger tightening nuts, reshaping a clamp with his fingers. Howie: *thanks! thanks!* Now slipping in behind the wheel, he starts the engine. Gordon at Howie's car window, a blackened hand resting on the roof, leaning down, talk, talk, talk, talk. Then as the car putters away up onto the roadway, heading north into Egypt away from the bridge, Gordon sees Bree is still standing there, hands in pockets, hair lifting, then settling around her face again to hide it, and when next the air is made violent again by a rumbling UPS van behind her, her yellow dress dances, wraps tight around her hips and legs.

He goes up the curbed tar lane that leads to the road, then onto the bridge, loping, his chunk of keys making their music, and as he gets close to Bree, he says breathlessly, "Hey." And as he steps very close, she tips her head down so her hair does its faithful work of covering her face from him.

"What brings you back to Egypt . . . ah, specifically, this spot?" he asks, wagging his head, pale eyes full of pleased twinkles.

She points toward the little white ranch building next to the brick P.O., *Phillip Pap, D.D.S.* printed on the white Colonial-style sign.

Gordon sees parked there Pitch Vandermast's pickup with chains, gas cans, and tool box in the bed but no one in the cab. Bree, driving without a license as usual. Driving around like that since she was eight years old, as he has heard.

A tractor trailer passes, a load of biomass chips, and Bree's heavy ripply red hair lifts off her shoulders.

Gordon turns and watches the truck swing around the curve, close to the bank, fast, too fast.

Now a load of pulp. Brakes hiss deafeningly. Driver shouts down from his open window, "BEEEE VEEE!"

Bree turns and gives a manly abrupt half-wave. She says to Gordon with a giggle, "That's Kenny."

He narrows his eyes, "Kenny who?"

She leans forward deeply, as if to check one of her dressy Settlement-made moccasins for a loose lacing. Her hair fully covers her face now and inside that hair are low almost tuneful giggles. "Kenny Levasseur. Helped do Dad's lots on Richardson Pond."

"Somebody you're sweet on?" Gordon asks.

She keeps her face down, poking the cracked cement sidewalk with her right moccasin, ramming it, ramming it, so like most nerved-up fifteen-year-olds might do, and her dress again churns around her legs and Gordon steps against her, catches the back of her hair with one hand and pulls it gently back, which causes her malformed face to raise up to him. She promptly covers her face with her hands.

"Don't cover your face like that," he says.

He keeps ahold of her hair, waiting.

Eventually she drops her hands. Eyes shut. A big closed-lip smile. "Now I have to look at you," she tells him. *Giggle, giggle.* Opens her eyes; blink, blink. "It's sinful. You're almost forty."

He reaches back around to the back pocket of his work pants and tugs out a bandana, wrinkled, red, turns her slightly, ties her hair back, tight.

"You take liberties," she murmurs, then *giggle giggle*. "They say it. And it's true."

"When's your appointment, Brianna?" he asks.

"Twenty minutes ago."

"Bad girl."

She looks down, smiles again, lowers her face some more but her hair does not accommodate. "He's very nice. Kinda cute, tells good jokes." She giggles.

"The dentist? Or that Kenny guy?"

"Dentist." She laughs. "Who's remembering Kenny?"

"We need to talk," he says. "Your Dad's truck is okay to stay there?"

"Sure," she says.

They walk down to his truck parked by the old mill's loading zone, boarded up lower windows, and a KEEP OUT sign on each iron column of the dock.

As they pull open the cab doors, Gordon remarks that her dress is too beautiful for the dentist. "So what's this with impressing the dentist?"

Giggle. Giggle. "It's the hygienist, Ariel, I'm going to see today." "Yeah?"

"Auntie got this for me. I just came down from there. It was Goodwill. Deal of a lifetime." She swings her hips to make the soft skirt flutter.

He closes his eyes, seems to chew on his tongue, then turns and raises a leg to get into the truck.

The truck starts up without a hitch, unlike *sometimes*.

They ride along out of town, truck windows down, the dappled light of sun and trees slipping across the hood and windshield. The road is dirt, recently graded. It leads into New Hampshire and higher elevations. Under the tires, sand and loose stones kick up and *thwonk* at the fender walls. "We saw a fisher cat on this road once," Bree tells him. "Broad daylight. His head looked red. Red ears. But actually their ears are sort of gray. But . . . they were *red* . . . see . . . the sun transformed him . . . big black and red . . . like a demon. He was really something." She wags her head, pulls on her ears. Sighs. "And he was a long one." She opens her long work-tanned arms to show. (Yes, some redheads *do* tan.) "He stopped and defied us as we came on but then

got himself into the culvert in the nick of time. Dad had his revolver
with him and was reaching for it. Dad doesn't like fisher cats."

The dappled light dances everywhere.

"They can jump sixteen feet," says Gordon.

Bree asks, "You ever seen one?"

"A couple live ones. A lotta dead ones."

"Dead? How?"

"Trappers feel entitled since fishers have such an interesting rap."

"Wipe out the fishers is what *they* say." She sniffs.

"Yeah, they say that."

"Fishers kill pet cats."

"Pet cats, on the other hand, kill *everything*." Gordon sweeps his
hand across the horizon. "Or play with their victims."

"Yep."

"Juncos. Swipe 'em right out of the sky and then pop on the thumb-
screws. That's the kitty-cat motto."

She giggle-snorts. "It's not funny but it's the way you say a thing."

Now a half mile or so with no words.

A small plastic green Godzilla swings from Gordon's rearview
mirror. "I like that," says Bree, giving it a little tap with her freckled
fingers. It spins gaily. "Smaller version of your east parlor one. Maybe
this one is actually Gorgon. From the movie where Gorgon was a
mother."

Gordon sighs. "This one is big, dopey, well-meaning, and
misunderstood."

"Yeah," she says with a low laugh.

They talk and ride into the day, over the miles of roads leading to
Gorham, New Hampshire, and around down through, back to Maine,
South Paris, and Norway. A lotta road.

She is talking to him in a normal way for the first time. In her husky
low smoker's voice. How many years has she smoked? Someday he
will ask. She talks not as a genius and not with the idiotic giggles.
She tells him about herself. Confessions like gifts, like little boxes
unwrapped. Gifts for him. And he tells her something he has never
told anyone before. About his worldly fears, yes. But also about obsession. Compulsions. How he fears *himself*. And she hears him. She
nods sagely. Then she gets so silly again, like a kid. Making funny

noises, a couple of illogical uninformed conclusions. A moment later she is near genius. And her intuition borders on the creepy. Like she has a third hand, a ghost hand that feels his thoughts, giving them little squeezes. Now she asks, "Okay if I smoke out the window?"

He looks at her.

"I need it."

"Of course. I have nothing new to tell you about the stuff."

Then more miles. *More* fossil fuel. *Another* cigarette. Day getting late. On a crumbly tar road somewhere beyond the main drag of Harrison, Maine, he shifts down, takes another road, eases the truck onto a solid-looking shoulder, drives cracklingly into dense ferns, brakes easy, shuts off the engine. "I'm going to love you up," he tells her. He knocks away the buckle of his seat belt and gets up on his knees over her and, a hand on each side of her face, kisses the straining blue-green area where the bridge of her nose sets between the eyes, that space that didn't form right, the nose, her face hot and salty.

She has a grip on the batch of keys that hang from his belt, fondling them in nervousness. But he now drops one hand to grip both of her hands together, pressing them against his crotch, and he kisses her mouth. Through all this, she is agreeable, but not reciprocal. He kisses her throat. He takes her throat between his hands. This throat is trusting. *Of course*. He has never known a woman who did not present her throat like this. TRUST. He thinks that it is this way with most men and women, trust, full trust. Most. Yeah, he can't imagine it any other way. He erases Claire's scoldings a few nights ago about his assumptions. Assumptions? Nothing that brainy. Just the steering wheel of the body. But it is true—no woman has ever said no. All of them pushed back in that way that means heat, in that way that cannot be misunderstood. Though Bree is being awfully . . . uh, *complex*.

He says, "They told you . . . about my situation?"

She sort of smiles. "The ugly polygamy word?"

"Yes. So you know."

"Yes, sir. It's public knowledge, isn't it? The people's airwaves and so forth."

"Well, I would not deceive you. I want to be sure you know it's true. So much shit. So much gossip. I want to cut through that."

She lowers her eyes to where his hands are now dropping from her neck to again grasp hers and jam them against the hard glut of his crotch. And he is thinking how by law, he is now a true criminal. Now the radio callers are correct. Now the gossipers are right. Catherine Court Downey is correct. His mother's fears? Bull's eye. This is what he really is. Sick. But why does it not seem sick? He feels he and she are a hundred years away from this culture of . . . issuing authorities, legislators, social workers, and incorrectness. He, Guillaume St. Onge, has created an alternate universe, Settlement life, Settlement allowances, Settlement devotion. The fear of the law, of police, that he *should* be feeling, is trying for his attention but falling away.

He says, "You're beautiful."

She says, quietly and reasonably, "I am the abominable, the fiercely deformed tormented one. Your compassion empowers you."

"That's pure analytical liberal bullshit."

She laughs.

"Did the chairperson tell you that stuff?" His blackly lashed, bleached-out devil eyes narrow.

She laughs again. Shakes her head slowly. The hard knot of his red bandana tied around her hair hurts a little, clumped there between her head and the cab's back window . . . and something else there, close to her head, a jacket hanging from one of the gun racks, jacket with stuff in the pockets. The truck, cramped and awkward, neither Bree nor Gordon being small people. Now Bree isn't laughing, just passive again, waiting for his next move. A scared-looking fifteen-year-old kid.

Police! Police! Where are the police?

He flings open the truck door.

Outside, he leads her by the hand through waist-high ferns. Song bugs are deafening. Bree's body is as powered and limber as when she works with her saw or operates a skidder, her climbing and balancing, bending, kicking away brush . . . on the job. The woods. She is at home here. That easy swing of her hips. Even in dressy moccasins and swishy soft dress. He keeps leading her along, however, as though she were dainty. And she *does* ever so tightly hang on to his hand. And now a fistful of his shirt she grips, she standing behind him, waiting, as he stops to piss out coffee into a rotten thickness of downed birch. He has a little trouble pissing from a penis swollen for its *other* use.

When he turns, still zipping himself, she looks away.

He says, "They say you've already seen *it*."

She flushes.

He says, "They say you've been with me, that you *know* me."

She flushes an even deeper, very unpretty red.

He takes the one step even closer, now rubs his crotch against her, makes a low sound, steps back again, says, "I haven't seen the paintings. And you have never seen me undressed. But . . . a witch is a witch is a witch." He breathes fully of the warm layers of leaves, layers of seasons, club moss, princess pine, berry bushes. "In the old days, people would have burned you at the stake. Today . . . *everybody* gets burned."

"I'm sorry."

"That's not what I meant. I didn't mean you were to blame."

"Once you told me you were *surrounded* by witches. Must be rough." Her voice is sort of teasy, but melancholy.

Now she looks away. A buzzing yellow jacket swings around and around her bright ripply hair and red knotted bandana. She closes her eyes, soaking up the terrible possibilities of *the tiny,* the knowledge before transformation that tells you that every penetration of your soul, every tentacle reaching in, large or small, is really you . . . always was you . . . you are just unfolding . . . pain and pleasure, you and he, you and them and you . . . consummate.

Again he presses closer. The ferns swish and whisper, dividing in yellowy-edged green knee-high waves. He mashes nose and beard against her cheek and ear, sniffs her ear and neck, *sniff sniff,* putting the nerves under her skin there into a frenzy like effervescence. She giggles. He runs the fingers of one hand through her long hair at her back. He whispers against her forehead, "And neither are they to blame. You see, we people don't get more grown-up with age. Baby girl, you know this? We will always act on the commands of our chromosomes, enzymes, the wishes of chemical synapses and blah blah blah. No one is ever old enough! It's all dust anyway."

She leans into him, and this is an embrace, her official permission, both sets of arms locked around the other, both faces in the hair of the other, no words, an aloof though singing stillness all around them as they rock back and forth, back and forth ever so slightly.

And now another bee. This, a bumblebee, fat and fuzzy and drowsy and potent, traveling slowly past them. A worker bee on her way.

Gordon takes Bree's hand again and leads her a few yards farther toward the slanted sun. Whenever he looks around at her, she giggles, or smiles, her carroty hair parted primly in the middle of her head, tied there in back.

Here he stops walking, glances around on the ground around their feet, pitches some sticks and pine cones away. Begins to undress.

Bree doesn't move. She averts her eyes.

He says, "Come on. Get yourself ready."

She slides her eyes back to him as he makes a pile of clothes at her feet, slinging them with rough abandon almost right onto her dressy moccasins. His gift.

Now her eyes are moving over his nudity in a most unnerving way. Her weird eyes, like the eyes of the public. A whole Milky Way of eyes. Now *he* flushes. "Need help?"

"No," she replies, pushes her moccasins off, then backing up to a little hemlock with low secrety limbs around it, she takes off her dress and underthings, but hugs the dress in front of her as she steps out.

"Let's use all our clothes for a pillow," he suggests.

She shakes her head.

He laughs appreciatively. And maybe a little impatiently. "No pillow? Fine. Okay." He comes around to stand behind her and again begins to rub himself against her, against her hip and buttocks.

And Bree? She can feel *it,* yeah *it,* spear-like and velvety, rubbing there as if to coax her into something besides sex. Something more like jumping off a cliff into the unimaginable and indescribable and unretrievable.

"Okay," he says, sort of to himself. Starts pushing her slowly down, so that she winds up on all fours. And she is quiet through all this, stunningly quiet, not even a small intake of breath as she receives that darkly haired belly against her spine and *it,* his penis, seeking, helped by his own hand, and finally he is ramming again and again through the virginal tightness in a way that seems deeper than natural to her, a deeper place than she knew she had.

He doesn't expect wild shrieks of ecstasy from a fifteen-year-old, but maybe *something,* like his name whispered. But there is nothing. She is rather studious, even as, at last, his thighs buckle and he groans, and his cry, almost like an angry complaint, "Jesus Christ!" falling to her back with all his weight, his own heart pounding audibly in his ears.

No police sirens. There *will* be police sirens, right? They are on hold, but the eye of the true issuing authorities is always turning, probing, entering. It shall not miss this, a hot spot on the national graph. Nobody in America can hide from it. There is *no* alternate universe. There is *no* secession from the true power that blossoms from every hemisphere, and Gordon St. Onge is not really that special.

Done, he remains, keeping her buried under him, she flattened out onto the ground. Nuzzles her neck and hair. "You're beautiful."

She doesn't argue. How can she not believe it now?

A car passes out on the road. The wonderful terrible ancient late summer song bugs chant. *Creak, creak, creak.*

In time he stands up, shaky in the knees.

Bree flips around to a sitting position and says in a buttery voice that surprises him, "Do me again. Do me pretty. Not doggie." And she reaches to bunch his pile of clothes up into something like a pillow.

He smiles stupidly. "Again?"

She looks him up and down. "Yeah."

So, okay, he goes at it again, with her laying out long and pale on her back under him, knees loosely apart, her dress in one hand. But with the too-soonness of doing it again, he can't keep hard, just gets slacker.

"I'm sorry," he says at last, walking backward on all fours, brushing his beard straight down the middle of her whole length . . . and then *there* between her legs, drives his teeth and tongue deeply, quickly.

"What are you doing?!!!" She yeowls, horrified, gripping him by the hair of his head, ripping his head away from such business.

"Going to give you a good thing," he says mournfully.

"Gross! I hate that!" This "gross" word makes her sound so . . . so kiddie, so cute.

He draws himself up off her, so full of regret but chuckling, too. He squats at her feet, looks at her while fussing with his beard, drying the ends of his mustache with the thumb and forefinger of one hand. The setting sun, chilled blue and gold, barred by trees, falls to Bree's arms and shoulders and large swingy breasts as she sits up, draws her knees up, wraps her yellow dress around her legs. She whispers, "Don't look sad."

He grunts. "I'm not sad. I'm abashed."

She is watching him.

Now he rocks slightly on his haunches, a restless gesture, still grooming his mustache, watching her. And she watches him. She watches him. She watches him. He smiles sheepishly, and reaches down between his legs, unaware at first that he's doing it, tugs on his shrinking limp penis, to dry with his fingers what remains of the fluids mixed together of himself and Bree, then looking off thoughtfully into the chilling-down jungle of sumac at his right, says worriedly, yes, and sadly, "World without end."

 Bree's thoughts as she climbs back into Gordon's truck cab for the slow ride home.

Then we are not alone. Not in our bodies, not in our soggy self-shaped ghosts.

Oh GLORY! We are not alone.

 Glennice St. Onge speaks.

I am not a young woman. But I'm not complaining. I am grateful to God for my health. I see those in wheelchairs, those in iron lungs, those in countries where they can't pray, and I say "Thank you" to Him.

My first husband, Barry, left me. He, too, had accepted Jesus Christ as his personal savior, but had turned his back on the Lord when he chose to go against our wedding vows, against the laws put forth to us by Him.

He said, "Jinny and Justin are grown now."

I said, "God marries us forever."

We had a terrible argument. He said okay, he'd stay. But the next day, he was gone. He sneaked away! Took his car and some of our photo albums, his records and tapes and guns and the dog . . . little beagle pup. He left me money on the table, his whole week's pay, but he didn't leave any note.

I was alone for a year. I prayed to Our Heavenly Father that Barry would come back. But God brought me Gordon instead.

It was through Harry Drake's brother I met Gordon. He took my hand and put my hand in Gordon's and said to Gordon, "I'd like you to meet a fine woman."

I know I am special to Gordon. I know that to his soul, I am really the only one. When we are alone, he will kiss my eyes and the palms of my hands and if I ask him to pray with me, he will. He will do anything I want him to do if I was selfish enough to ask for that impossible thing, whatever that would be. But I care too much about him to take advantage. We are not married by law, but by God. I know this because when I asked God, He sent me a sign. Just as I was asking, the sun moved in the window and struck my praying hands, and my silver wedding ring looked gold. I am happy here and they all need me here.

I have a real knack for farming. I love garden work and I don't mind dirty hands, dirty knees or backaches. I have taught the ways of growing food to most of the children here, not just to my Benjamin, my boy by Gordon, but all of them who come to me on the "garden crews." I am good with children. My thumb is green. My heart is young. And the Heavenly Father WILL take care of you and give you everything you need in this life. All you have to do is ask. And to believe.

I have my heart set on another baby. The others say, "Don't do it when you're over forty-five because it'll turn out retarded." But God loves retarded babies as much as regular ones. In the end, it is what the Lord God wants, what He chooses. I leave it up to God. God is grace. God is love.

 Beth St. Onge speaks.

I ain't complainin'. Shit, I'm too busy to complain. Work your ass off from dawn to dim in this place. Run like a rabbit. People here are pretty funny. A lotta noodle heads. You gotta keep right on 'em and give 'em a hard time but people like Suzelle and Bonnie Loo will find out your worst weakness and rib the hell out of you.

My parents visited here a buncha times. And they think they wanna move right in. Probably will as soon as Dad retires. He has two more years. He likes all the gadgets and machiney stuff that's here, always somebody's new inventions. You wouldn't believe the wild ideas that fly around this place.

But I'm pretty sure my folks don't know how Gordon is, about what he has so many wives. They think he's all mine. It's crazy. The whole country knows. But it's somehow gone right over their heads. Maybe they're just not lettin' on. They'll shit a brick when they finally get it. But I'll tell them how it's so obvious who his favorite is. Obvious to me. Maybe not so obvious to the rest here and I never say nuthin' about his wicked wild passions for me, what he manages to do to my body. A thing that is probably against the law, I heard it was in the state of Virginia. A crime right up there with masturbating a donkey. And also his little gifts to me like wildflowers and memorized stuff in FRENCH. I don't say nuthin' 'cause these are my sisters and I always wanted a sister and now here I am with this swarm of sisters and that's like gold and apple-sized diamonds to me. I don't mind torturin' the piss outa've 'em in fun . . . you know . . . ride 'em. But I ain't never been one to wanna put sadness into other people's hearts. You know how tender hearts are. It's the softest weakest part of a person. So that I am Gordon's favorite is just between you 'n' me.

 A night of horizontal wind and hot rain.

Misty St. Onge's cottage. Her big bed is splattered with every-which-way human limbs, mostly Gordon's because he tends to sleep splayed out. And all over and between is a pleasant-sounding quilt of Misty's purring kneading cats. Cats of every color. Any of them would squall terribly if Gordon should shift. So he doesn't.

But this isn't exactly so, now that Gordon is missing from the bed.

"Gordon?" Misty's tremulous voice. Her long fingers scrabble for the chain of her bedside lamp. The scene is shellacked a damning yellow. The entire purring blanket of cats freezes, a stillness that is more bloodcurdling than an air raid alarm.

"Gordon?" Misty's voice again, this time directed solidly at his bare back, which is near the windows that are full of rainy night. And the wall to his left papered in marching along old-fashioned daisies. And there, Misty's gram's chest of drawers. Propped-up photos of Misty's parents, brothers, and past cats.

Yes, Gordon is standing. But he is not alive, so used up by the bulky custody of him by Settlement land and Settlement lives. His oversized pledge to it all. *Till death do we part.*

"What are you doing over there?" Misty gets up from the bed, her rosebud print gown flicking from side to side. Cats are interested in *the puddle,* but disdainful. They wrinkle their noses. A spotted orange and white tom, who has never liked Gordon, almost speaks, "He's pissed on the wall again."

Yes, Misty is a romantic person. *She* doesn't say, "You pissed on the wall." She doesn't say the word "peed" either. She just cradles her husband's face in her long fingers. His heart is still thumping from his weight being moved by that spooky force of sleepwalking. His whole head yearns into Misty's hands. He has nothing to say, either. He recognizes her, Misty, luminous on the map of his life. But he doesn't know himself because this is himself not standing in a display of power and provision, but of shame.

Misty's fingers drizzle down over his temples.

Some of the cats are self-launched from the rug back onto the bed. They fill in Gordon's shape, still warm where he had lain. They don't recommence purring though, because they are bothered and prickly.

Misty, age thirty-one, dark hair Peter Pan short so her long creamy neck is the thing you notice. She never becomes pregnant by mistake or on purpose. Cats suit her, so why go further? Why gum up and smash up this wee home with childly extortions and scrimmages?

This is not the Gordon, this puddling Gordon, not the Gordon she once thought he was, not the man she wanted. No, he's not the person she thought he was.

 Claire St. Onge remembers.

Time passed. Everything that before this hadn't ripened and been picked, eaten or canned, was now ripening and being picked and canned. And eaten. Or saved. The air was odd. Not the usual for September. A lot of days that seemed to arrive from Brazil in a jar. The sun often rose much too red, but it wouldn't rain as you'd expect.

The day would just sort of slide down the sky at evening time in an exotic lather and no promises.

 It is blowing rain. Sideways rain. The windows of the old church shake. A leak on the sill of one gives forth jewels that race to the edge and drop to the floor.

The bride's hair is wet on the ends. Her man is looking into her queer set-apart eyes as the reverend speaks. The reverend is small, not straight-shouldered though he may have been once. Which is older? Him or the church? It is not a full-time church. No furnace. No lights. No downstairs kitchen. The outside paint is coming off in chips, as lead as bullets. Today the wind and rain floats a few of the white chips down the driveway. The stained glass is lilac and yellow. In this light what bride isn't lovely?

Beside the reverend stands a stout woman in a scarlet suit. She has something in her hand hidden by the folds of her suit jacket. She is the reverend's niece-in-law, Celia, witness.

The reverend asks the scarlet-haired bride the questions and she answers the way brides always do, staring into her true love's eyes. She doesn't giggle.

The style of the ceremony is not one of those creative types you hear of these days. The words of the vows are not "corrected." The promise is time-honored, classic, a sturdy ripple of a river of nuptials out of the past, out of maybe pre-America, that came across the longitudes in a big boat.

The bride wears her newish yellow dress, which radiates as if she stepped right out of one of the church windows, and so nobody misses the sun.

In her hair, a store-bought scrunchie that gathers a thick braid from the sides and lays upon the rest of her loose roiling red hair. Pinned to the scrunchie is a kind of gommy blossom she has made herself with paper and splats of paint, dark yellow and blue. In her hands a bouquet of goldenrod. From this wild flora explodes an ardent smell.

Gordon's tweedy sports jacket is very wet. Hair very wet. Beard wet. Boots wet.

When the promises are all made and the ring is in its place, Gordon grips Bree's head as though it were food to a hungry man, and kisses her perfect mouth and there's a splash of light, Celia taking their picture. She takes a few others and explains she'll send them to Bree when they're ready. She has done this for all of Gordon's "brides." And yes, the St. Onge "weddings" are all the same, same ninety-nine-year-old Reverend Andy Emery, same "witness," the reverend's niece-in-law. The same absence of a license. The same broad empty pews. No one to fling confetti, no rows of teary smiles. No presents with white bows.

Celia now steps huffingly forward because she's so fat, fat to superlatives, fat deluxe, and so the yards of red dress shiver around her panoramically. She takes both Gordon and Bree by a wrist and says, "May you both travel forever in today's glow." That's when Bree's eyes fill with tears and she hugs her husband, one side of her face kind of rubbing his shirt front, his rain-wet sort of wooly smell swishing through her nose. And he inhales her bouquet, which is being crushed between their bodies by the hug.

The camera flashes again.

Something bangs against the building and the wind screams and the old church sings in its walls. Bree's silver ring doesn't sparkle or make a golden impression. It is homely and snug. Homemade. By *him*. It is exactly the same as the ring that each of the other "wives" wears.

  Claire St. Onge tells us:

But two nights after old Andy Emery "married" Gordon to Brianna Vandermast, there was a slight twist in the routine.

Suppertime, looking all chesty and cocky following his "honeymoon" at the old hunting camp on the mountain, Gordon came into the doorway of the winter kitchen and stood looking at Catherine Court Downey, who was sitting at the near table across from young Brady and Sadie. Catherine was close enough to hear his little sniff of triumph. I swear his neck looked thicker! And he kind of swung his arms in a real hard-assed way like I'd never seen him do before, and he said, not to Catherine, but to Beth and Lorraine, who were sitting on either side of Catherine, "Tell the chairperson that what wasn't true before about Bree getting messed with by the monster, *is* now true."

Penny St. Onge's apprehension.

What Gordon had done could be called twisted, if seen from the crisp center of modern culture. It was soooo impulsive, looking at the risks. It could be seen as arrogance. It could be seen as cruelty, as exploitation. It *would* be seen in all the bitterest ways.

 Ellen St. Onge.

Basically, he was getting himself hung. Firing squad. Whatever.

 Cory St. Onge.

It was just the usual. Just another day. You grow up with this, you don't get all twittipated and you don't faint. It's just life. Man, we had more road work, some straw to bale, a new roof on the sap house, extra orders at the sawmill and shingle mill, firewood to stack, and new CSA people to meet with. My mind was *not* on this thing with Brianna except to appreciate that she was a pretty okay person.

 Margo St. Onge.

Bingo! It was happening. She and Gordon. It meant she'd be ours forever. Personally, I was tickled pink. But what did I know? I was fourteen. A kid, right? Dumb, right? The "justice" system was like a fat spider poised, motionless, all those legs, all those eyes. Me, I was only able to see hearts and flowers.

 Gail St. Onge.

His recklessness was breathtaking. It made me tremble.

 Lee Lynn St. Onge.

I stopped eating for days. Scared. Scared. Scared. Sips of warm mint tea, my eyes on the moon through the curtainless windows of my cottage. Praying to one special star. Closing my eyes. Whispering to all the stars. No sleep. Though our baby Hazel slept her baby sleep in her crib a few feet away. Hazel with his dark hair, his sturdy frame, his kooky smiles. Then I'd "see" police coming for him. I screamed. Hazel woke. So okay, when I don't sleep nobody sleeps.

 Josee Soucier.

I was sad for Bree. You have to be at least thirty-five to decide whet'er it's a good idea to get into a rip-roaring polygamy mess. And I wouldn't blame t'em now t'at *t'ey* not turn out to be child molesters, that t'a Vandermasts come here steaming wit' t'eir fists and t'eir guns and bruise up t'e big monkey name of Guillaume St. Onge.

 Secret Agent Jane.

Gordie says his house isn't safe anymore. Too many meteor snoops, which is people who want your face in the news. And the "DHS birds" Gordie calls the people who take kids away in the night. But this morning, they packed my stuff, which I didn't lift a finger but watched with glaring expressions. I do not want to live with Oh-RELL and Jo-SEE. My room at Gordie's is the best, right exactly over where the phone rings.

So now I don't live at Gordie's house anymore but *you know where*. I keep my pink spy glasses on day and night, and I keep my glaring expressions. I show them how this they are doing is *not* going to be easy.

 The weather, New Guinea. The place, Rex York's kitchen. The day, Sunday. Bree is here. Darling Bree? Or dangerous Bree?

Not many show up for this meeting. It is like that. Sometimes a packed room, sometimes almost no show. Three of Rex's men stand against the counters and the corner cupboard. Rex sits at the little chrome-trimmed table turning a large map. Under his fingers, it is like the earth sliding out from night to dawn as Oxford County eases out from the shadow of his arm.

In the doorway to the living room a small muscular teen boy in T-shirt and jeans that look exploded, he stands without comment though his appearance growls. As if this young creature has already been wrung by war. His blond hair makes enough for a twig-sized ponytail. His gray wolfy eyes are fixed upon the map. He doesn't look as sweaty as everyone else. But he radiates a rotten god-awful smell. He must not live very close to water.

Another of Rex's men is at the table, wears only a denim biker vest with "the wings" spread over his narrow back. His tattoos are frolicsome. His watch is like Rex's, black-faced, a source of much data, compass and all that.

And there also at the table is Gordon, another Settlement man John Lungren, and Mrs. Bree. Tomboy Bree. Her usual heavily-laced work boots. Her work shirt and jeans. Sweat trickling down one temple. Her face is showing, yes. Her hair pulled from the sides is braided and bunned at the back of the head while the rest of it tumbles everywhere. She has an expression that means her brain is a hot coal. And much faster than Rex's muscular fingers turn the map.

Gordon is in a Settlement-made T-shirt, one sleeve noticeably baggy. Probably fashioned by a five-year-old. Maybe even Secret Agent Jane, who has begun to be involved in Settlement life when she's not slithering around behind doors doing her spy work. If you look very very closely at the little stitches along the shoulder of Gordon's red T-shirt, you can almost see where she stopped to consider redoing it better but flicked her lovely elucidating wrist dismissively and went on.

And so Secret Agent Jane is present here in this way. And her mother, too. Maybe the essence of *the cage* is why the militia movement grows. It can be laughable to some but the chances for loss and enslavement are clearly seen by the low rung man, woman, and child even without heart-shaped glasses.

Bree says nothing. If anyone looks at her, she smiles, but otherwise she's chin up and soldierly.

Gordon is quiet, sort of. He's not raving and butting in. He has kept a promise he once made to his "brother" to remember that the Border Mountain Militia *Rex* is the "captain." And that he, Gordon, will not behave like a gorilla (why do *so many* of his people notice the resemblance?).

There is a clatter and thump and voices on the glassed-in porch. Butch Martin and a Settlement man in his sixties, Davey, both flushed by the not-very-Septemberish ninety-five-degree weather.

Bree turns her head. Small smile, not enough to reveal teeth. Butch nods to her, then to all.

Davey gives everyone a one-finger wave, the hand lifted almost to his forehead. So maybe it's really a salute.

The meeting goes until suppertime. It *seems* as though nothing has happened. But there is a burnishing of what already was, deep in the eyes of Brianna St. Onge . . . people versus The Thing, *her* way.

 In a future time, Claire St. Onge recalls.

Though all the arrangements had been made for Bree to travel to Portland with the college crew a couple times a week, and she had seemed so enthusiastic in the beginning, she very apologetically and very sweetly and ashamedly and thoughtfully and politely said she now wanted to "wait awhile." Our sharp-as-a-tack, bright-as-a-penny Bree! Wouldn't she like to hang out with college people?

But Bree had *big* things on her mind. *Bigger* than college. Bigger than sky, you might say. Bigger than being just one more wife of Guillaume St. Onge.

 Ivy comes trotting into the *Record Sun*'s "city room" a bit late.

Brian sneaks up on her like a purse snatcher. But really he stuffs something *into* her shoulder bag, then veers away, not looking back.

Ivy is sizzlingly curious. Let's see, it's made of paper, it's smaller than a breadbox . . .

She flumps into her swivel chair and sighs, catching her breath, pretending not to be curious. She glances around to see who else is at their terminals. Checks her watch. Her look of nonchalance is beyond the pale. She considers faking a yawn. Glancing across the short wall to the center terminals Ivy sees Brian standing there listening to the clerk, Ray Peters, but flashing glances at her. Their glances glance. Hers. His.

Time's up. She slowly draws the mysterious papers from her bag. They include a three-page computer printout from Bob Drown's desk (Bob, the Sunday paper's op-ed editor). It is in progress, apparently slated for this weekend. Separately, there are pages of notations and artwork from the authors of the op-ed, not the *Record Sun* art department, but many names of a St. Onge nature. Names Ivy knows all too well.

The article begins:

Some of you may have the idea you are in danger. Let us be more specific. Some of you can clearly imagine that in the not too far off future, "they" will come and put you and your family out of your home. All you have grown up and worked for is threatened by some large conspiring force.

And the article goes on with many skin-chilling details, then in bold print:

YES, OH, YES . . . SOMEBODY IS GETTING READY TO TAKE EVERYTHING AWAY FROM YOU. EVERYTHING.

We are members of the True Maine Militia, not to be confused with the "plain" Maine Militia, or the Border Mountain Militia, or the Southern Maine Militia or the White Mountain Militia. But with those militias, we do have a bit in common.

Like them, we are not ostriches.

We are angry.

And we know the government sucks.

It is not a government of We, the People, but one of Organized Money, of Big Faceless Transnational Financiers ruling through their shrewd tool, the corporation, the lobbyists, the foundations, the prohibitions, the spooks, the military, the media. And money laundering and fraud and other creepy stuff.

Welcome! We welcome EVERYBODY! We are not a right-wing militia. We are not left wing, either. We are NO WING. We are everybody's militia!

Now there is a cartoon of a stern-looking Bigfoot with hands on hips standing on a mountaintop. He wears here a 1700s tricorn hat, camo spot vest, and army boots. Behind him waves the American flag. (Remember, this is BEFORE September 11, 2001, yes BEFORE we were all completely sick and tired of seeing the damn thing.)

The op-ed finishes with:

The True Maine Militia already has a lot of members but not enough. Our goal is a million for starters. Because we are planning the Million-Man-Woman-Kid-Dog March on Augusta (for starters) and we will all be armed. With brooms. We will arrive at the doors, all the State House doors, and begin to very very gently sweep the great floors of this, which is our house . . . yes, the People's House. We will sweep out every corporate lobbyist. Corporations OUT! We, the People in!

And if this doesn't work, we'll be back next time with plungers!

If you are interested in joining up, it is totally FREE. No dues. Just promise you will be angry and you will be nice. Get in touch with us today at militia headquarters, RR2, Heart's Content Road, Egypt, Maine 04047 or call 625-8693 or find us the old-fashioned way. Sundays are best. We'll open the gate for you! We love you! We are your neighbors. Keep your powder dry and your ear to the ground! Let's save the Republic together!

The article is signed.

Militia Secretary, Bree St. Onge

Recruiting Officers, Samantha Butler and Margo St. Onge

Other Officers, Whitney St. Onge, Michelle St. Onge, Dee Dee St. Onge, Oceanna St. Onge, Carmel St. Onge, Kirk Martin, Tabitha St. Onge, Liddy Soucier, Desiree Haskell, Scotty St. Onge, Heather Martin, Erin Pinette, Rusty Soucier, Chris Butler, Lorrie Pytko, Jaime Crosman, Shanna St. Onge, Alyson Lessard, Rachel Soucier, Christian Crocker, Buzzy Shaw, Theoden Darby, Josh Fogg.

The list goes on—another dozen names, all girls.

And just in case readers need help making the connections, the *Record Sun* editors will helpfully place a box at one side with a lively little rehash of the Home School–Settlement–Border Mountain Militia relationship. And there are two photos already in place on Bob Drown's computer. One the never-to-be-forgotten more unsettling of the merry-go-round shots, the one the AP used, with Gordon's scary weirdly-lighted face and upper body, St. Onge-as-madman. And one of the "gate" and KEEP OUT signs. Editor leads in with: *GATES OF ST. ONGE SETTLEMENT WILL COME DOWN IN A BIG WAY.*

On that day that the *Record Sun*'s True Maine Militia op-ed appeared.

There is something they want to show Bree. Something she's never seen.

And so Bree, the newest St. Onge wife, has been led here across the darkening quad by children, children not being at all startled by Gordon's badness in "messing with Bree." It's the Settlement adults who buzz of the impending doom. Meanwhile, evenings come so early these days, fat acorns responding to the perfect retreat of sap, banging on roofs in the near distances. The small hand that holds Bree's is damply warm. They have led her to the Quonset hut where her studio is, but they take a different set of dimly lighted stairs. Bree looks around her at all the mostly preadolescent and younger faces, faces she can match with names now, Stacia, Miranda, Fiona, Gabe, Michel, Lindsay, Katy, Spur and Max, Montana and Seth, Kristy, Dara, Rhett, Andrea, Draygon, Graysha, Theodan, Benjamin, Oake, and Cymric, perfectly formed faces with wonderful noses and perfectly placed eyes, *his* eyes, most of them have the eyes of *her husband*. Does this somehow make them *her* children?

Chirping and giggling, they reach a door with barely a froth of light under it.

"We have alas arrived!" The always forcefully eloquent Montana calls at the door and swings it open wide.

It is more like what you see when looking out of an airplane window, a plane you are riding on in the night over a city, the city below, a stirring and flurrying of puny lights.

What it really is, is Kirky Martin on a chair, a table before him . . . a big table, six sheets of plywood in size, covered by a miniature nighttime city, both urbs and burbs.

Yes, *the* Kirk Martin, the twelve-year-old who despises *real* roadwork, wearing big glasses and crewcut with a little pigtail in back, man of the dashing bow tie when he's out on the town in Portland. But this town before him now puts a silvery-pink glow on him, giving his face the important luminescence of a planet in the heavens.

There is no other light source, so only the city makes light, which also gives life to the greenish freckles, dots and splashes of comets and stars painted with phosphorus paint on the room's black ceiling above.

Kirk says, "Hi" to Bree in a kingly way. He is working remote control panels like the TV channel kind, his eyes on the traffic of his town, tiny metal cars buzzing along avenues, alleys, and parking lots. There are bridges, too. Houses and churches and four-story apartment buildings all have electrically-lighted interiors that glow from their hundreds of windows.

Bree is struck silent.

Outside the burbs, a field of tiny cows. Their tails wag!

A pond. Made from a glass mirror. Crowded with mussels. These, you see, are made with real mussel shells, purple and black and crusty, and so to this wee world, mussels are menacing, monsterific. Their mouths open and close, open and close. And they have voices! Friendly little creaking burping voices, though to the teensy residents of this town, the little voices would be roars.

Now there's the wee blue flutter of a cop car pulling a speeder over, someone perhaps speeding to escape the giant mussels.

All around Bree are the gasping wet mouths and noses of the St. Onge children, all eyes round with the never-get-used-to-it wonder of Kirky Martin's city. And his subtle humor.

Bree says, "Where'd you get this?"

"Made it."

"By yourself?"

He nods, gives one of his remote panels some squeezes, and a line of traffic surges across a bridge.

Hands now in her jeans pockets, Bree leans close to study all these moving parts, the lighted windows, smaller blinking red lights on the radio tower high on the highest hill.

"Neat, huh?" This is Gabe speaking. Bonnie Loo's oldest, her child from the first husband. He stands closest to Bree. His hands are in the pockets of his jeans, like Bree is doing.

Bree murmurs, "It's breathtaking."

Kirk says, "It's electronic, powered by that solar-charged battery." He dips his head to point.

She looks to the dark shape low in one corner of the room.

"Kirky's an electrician," Max tells her. Max in gray sweatpants, loose plaid flannel shirt, face ghosty.

"ElecTRONICS," another small boy corrects him.

"Obviously you are a woodworker and wood-carver, too . . . and a little papier-mâché there, maybe?" Bree observes as she stares into the whizzing traffic, and then the dark areas of woods, impossibly detailed tiny trees (wooden?), wee creature eyes glowing among them. A church with a cross. Catholic. Then a couple of white churches. Protestant. And there the Star of David. Synagogue for Barbara (remember Barbara and Bev?). Little tune playing from one of the white churches. Music-box-like. "Amazing Grace," yes.

The undulating bubbly buzzing creaking of the table city is . . . well, it's profound. Bree looks at Kirk's businesslike face. She slowly shakes her head. "Amazing grace. That's what you are, Kirk."

He flushes; the flush, however, barely detectable in the wondrous light.

The children all around Bree titter.

Bree wishes that for a few hours, she could shrink to be a tiny person and play among the tiny tail-wagging cows and above her, the dignified kindly God Kirky would never let anything bad happen, a world where even the monsters are lovable and stay put in their pond of rigidly serene water. She sighs.

But now appearing in the doorway to the dimly lighted hallway is six-foot-two, fifteen-year-old Cory St. Onge, Gordon's oldest son, who has the thick black Passamaquoddy hair of his mother, Leona, and her eyes, and his father's everything else. He wears a forest green Settlement-made shirt, a 1770s French workingman's smock pattern, what Jacquie and Josee and Suzelle call *habitant*. And now behind him, Paul Lessard. Paul, small and dark and pointy-faced, sees Bree. He turns away quick. And now stepping around them is Gordon, with a section of newspaper in one hand. Has a look like he wants to thwonk somebody with this newspaper. As you do to housebreak a dog. (Well *some* people do that to dogs. Jerks.) He sees Bree. "Everybody but Bree clear out," he commands in a-don't-dare-argue-back fashion. Paul Lessard is somewhere out in the hall, not visible now. Cory hovers. Bree can see a shoulder and elbow of his green shirt just beyond the door frame.

As the little kids and Kirk Martin leave, they aren't quiet about it. They whine and groan and the eloquent-*most*-of the time Montana runs her tongue out at Gordon as she passes him. Bree smiles at

Gordon but he shakes his head at her smile. Now Bree hears all the doors shutting downstairs, the kid voices trailing off.

She says, "We could have gone someplace else to talk."

Gordon just says, "Brianna."

She knows now not to smile. And she quells a nervous giggle.

Gordon looks like he wants to break her, kick her, KILL her. He steps closer. "Something tells me you never, in all your fifteen years, ever got a good strapping with a goddamn belt, though my guess is you've been driving your family nuts with your pigheadedness for a long time." He pushes, slowly but hard, the newspaper into her hands.

She shrinks back a little. But then she stands taller and one little scornful spitting snort escapes from her nose and pretty mouth.

He looks hard at her mouth a long time. Loooonnnnnng silence. Kirky's town twinkles happily, Kirk's stars glow, the mussels creak with their tiny terrible threats.

Bree says, "I'm not your kid. I'm your wife."

Gordon turns away, steps over to the big table and seems to be staring down into the heart of civilization with a wish to end it. He says, "Our home here is in danger now, Bree. Because you have taken so much into your own hands. You are smart, yes. But you are young . . . and impulsive . . ." and then he stresses. "*With too much freedom.*"

Bree frowns. "You want the Puritan thing here?"

Gordon looks up at the wall, still facing away from Bree. "Yes!"

"You don't really mean that. Cuz you have done things Puritans would give *you* the strap for. Maybe *hang* you . . . uh *burn* you."

He says nothing.

She pipes up, "Following all your teachings of democracy, we all decided together to do it."

"We?" He turns and looks at her.

"Yuh, all of us. We took a vote."

"You mean you and the other *kids*. You don't mean you and the other women and men who live here. You mean you and the other *kids*." He turns back to the town, running a hand through his hair.

Bree sees Cory is still in the doorway, like a guard. His back against the hallway wall and door frame, an arm and foot visible. She supposes he and Paul are just waiting, had been with Gordon on their way to join one of the evening crews working at the sawmill, or that other big thing that's been taking the men and some women and youngsters away from suppers, the planning of the new machining Quonset hut. There's always some chattering bunch of Settlement people bent on some mission of importance, no matter the evening hour. But nevertheless, she has an ugly flash that these two men have been recruited by Gordon to help hunt her down, and then guard the door while he thrashes and smacks and bonks her around a bit.

But . . . of . . . course . . . not.

Bree says, "The older people are . . . too stuffy . . . about some things. And you know they hate *militia*. Your other *wives*."

Gordon says, "One minute you insist you be treated like a wife, an *adult*. Next minute—"

Bree says, "Some could say that about you." And she smiles. "Part man, part big kid." She sighs. "Well, by law I'm a kid. Maine law. Maybe USA law. And some people here say that you having a relationship with me was rash and childlike. And you yourself called yourself Baby Man, remem—" She giggles. "So here we—"

He turns. "This is not a discussion," he warns her.

Bree's face drains of color. "What *is* it then?" Without taking her eyes off Gordon, she calls out to the hallway, "Cory?"

"What?"

"He ever use a belt on you?" She knows the answer is no. She knows Gordon is just pissed and bluffing.

Cory shifts slightly. Cory's voice. "Yep."

Bree looks exaggeratingly shocked.

Gordon is back to glaring angrily at the town, neck muscles hard and hurting, palms and fingers open on the table's edge.

Bree giggles, steps toward Gordon, his dark shape and glowing face. "What about a wife? You use a *belt* on Claire?"

Out in the hall, Cory laughs.

Bree smiles.

Cory's voice says, "Might be the other way around."

Gordon says, "What do you think is going to happen now, Bree? To us? Our family?"

Brightly, Bree replies, "We have work to do, Mr. Man."

He pushes down on the table with his fingers in a way that makes his hands stand like spiders.

Bree says, "I never knew you hit kids."

Gordon raises his left hand over his head, like a classroom student asking a question but with two fingers up. "Two times. Two times I lost it." He keeps his eyes on the town, hand dropping with a slap against his thigh. "Two times and nobody forgets it. Or forgives."

Bree says, "I thought you'd be proud of what we did. Kind of a little birthday present to you."

"No, Brianna. You did not think that."

"Oh, okay, yuh, I knew you would be worried . . . but that *duty* would speak to you."

He shifts. She can see that befuddled business of his face, the way at times he'll squint-blink, one eye wide, one eye narrow. His psycho look. Now he shifts again so that none of his face shows to her. Yes, he had taken his belt to children, though it has been some years now. All the family knows this. And they've seen him drunk. And they've seen him wrastle and act out too playfully, knocking over furniture, acting stupid. But they have never seen him break into tears. Tears now, running, twinkling with the table town's fantastical light, streaming into his beard. He keeps his head turned away, lest these tears be seen, *and remembered.* For when you break, you have betrayed all the people who count on you, and now more than ever they must count on him, for even at this moment back down at the old farmhouse, the phone is ringing and more cars are parking along Heart's Content Road, pulling right up to the KEEP OUT signs nailed to the gate. For a moment he *actually* visualizes running them all off with his .32 Special.

 At the university.

In the art department, in Ms. Court Downey's office, the desk has been getting a little heaped. Ms. Court Downey has been distracted these days. Not drugged out like before. But something else. A plain unadulterated sadness.

She is alone. She takes out some university stationery and begins.

Dear Phan, Yes, I have received all of your messages on the machine at
home and from the department secretary and from Nan. Yes, yes, yes, yes,
American Express, Mastercard, Citibank, Fleet Bank, Sears. Yes, yes, yes.
You are the machine. You have no understanding. Perhaps my writing
you with this cold pen on cold paper will appeal to you. Better than my
voice, always crying, my "mush-heartedness," as you like to call it, is at
the core of our troubles? That I am without CONTROL, without your
brand of CONTROL? But you would live in a bare hotel room with no
homey touches, happy as a pig in shit. It's all an issue of needs, isn't it?
Some need, some don't.

I am staying with friends. There is fresh air and peace and Robert is like
a new child, a whole child.

You hinted to Nan that you have seen an attorney. Oh, yes. So have I.
No problem. Carry on. Go away.

Catherine

 In a future time Claire St. Onge remembers the days
following the article.

Well, *kaboom*. The dam breaks. Dozens and dozens of someones calling, asking about the True Maine Militia. As soon as it was back on
the hook, the phone would come alive again. People harried. They
weren't apt to use the word "revolution" or call themselves radicals
but they were "coming out." A few professional-class leftists and progressives. But mostly working-class, small city, town or rural Mainers lured by the militia word. Some would probably call themselves
middle class, whatever that meant. Whatever. The silent presence.
Until now. Surprising to me, actually. I never realized how many
people were ready once you put it to them in a way that touched them
personally . . . which Bree and the others, mostly Bree, had done, the
losing your home stuff hit home, no pun intended. Our kids were red
hot *and* contemplative. So young! Our darling insurgents.

So now the call-in talk shows were about nothing else. "The True
Maine Militia." Radio listeners wanted in.

Those warning of "the mad prophet" and references to "his blatant polygamy" and "child abuse." These accusations were vague.
No particulars. No naming Brianna. Some called the True Maine

Militia "crazies running through the woods with hand grenades." Some referred to them as "men" so they obviously had never seen the article.

But here it was, the people were stirring. Democracy was in the air.

But Bree had disappeared again. We knew where she was. But the Vandermast men said even they couldn't get in. She seemed to have "about forty locks on her bedroom door."

 The voice of Mammon.

This is the room. No way for you to know anything about this room because this is *private property.* No way for you to whine for FOI applications because one should never forget that the corporate charter that is made of paper is really "a person," while you the common worker, the taxpayer, the consumer who is yolky and greasy to touch is really a resource. All are in their places like concrete and sky.

Meanwhile, the revolving door goes *whump! whump!* Steve in. Bob out. J.T. in. Steve out. Bob in. Jenny out. Les in. J.T. out. *Whump! Whump!* Sometimes Paul is both in and out. Or in two important places at once if you know what I mean. No law against it. Virtue is the word.

Today we discuss some ugly mooing, oinking, and whinnying coming from the masses (sorry for the commmie word).

As an example, Phil passes out copies of an op-ed article from a paper in Maine. Everyone skims, gets a chuckle, then back to work.

 Inner voice of the bureau.

You see, hotshot, if everybody stopped shopping and started oiling guns and loving their neighbor and wiping their noses on *progress,* there are people bigger than you who would lose. And losing is not their style.

You know we're not really mean guys. Some are real sweethearts to their wives and kids and pets. But there are always people we need to answer to on a regular basis. If you chafe them, definitions of words apply where *they* say they do. But also, remember, you are gold. You will make their train go choo-choo if you can be used to terrorize

America. As things are looking now, we'll have all green lights before the month is out. Then the patsies will have their day in the sun.

 Next day, late afternoon, metallic mint-green-color car comes buzzing up into the lot.

Having a couple of young mothers in her confidence, Catherine has help getting the television and VCR up the stairs of the near Quonset hut, and into her studio.

 Next afternoon. Brianna reading about international banking. Banking bubbles. Banking lobby.

She is on one elbow. Bed made up in an old scarlet and black quilt, razzy and scratchy. Octagon window opened inward. The sound of a mean rain, all sticky fists and sleepy drumroll. It has kept the *clop*-pause-*clop*-pause-*clop*-pause of metal-shoed hooves on pavement from reaching her ears. Even the collie dog downstairs hasn't heard or suspected.

Bree turns a page. She is a slow reader, stopping to underline and "talk back" in the margins. "Right, you clowns," clowns being the kind of people who would fund both sides of wars, design a dollar born from debt, and debase *all* life into stark figures on a spreadsheet.

She tosses down the pen, the book, sits up to dig her feet into her boots, lace them, still digesting the latest banking deregulations. For instance, the annihilation of the old sentry Glass-Stegall Act.

When she stands, a presence out in the yard catches her eye. Her own eyes, that raw honey-green-brown-yellow, widen. It is an old dirty wet white horse, a pinto horse without much "paint," black Rorschachs and apostrophes and splats only on his face and one fetlock and hoof. Also streaks of black in the tail. Big ears, clownish, mulish, sad in the rain. Head hanging. There is a wet man in the saddle. A wet crusher hat, looks black, probably started out dark green before he set out to ride here. Brim of hat awfully relaxed, but not enough to cover the eyes, which are hot and grating, driving into her honey ones. He wears a darkened work jacket, cuffs too short, possibly not his jacket, the Settlement shamelessly communal at times.

Bree clicks open the little octagon screen.

The eyes under the crusher watch. Horse's head comes up, big ears revolving to try to understand the sound of Bree flinging some shredded paper pieces out. Horse's shoulders shift. A little stumbly stepping back.

The flakes of paper fall. "Snow in the forecast!! Better brush up on your winter driving skills!!" Bree calls through the drumming rain. Then she giggles. What has she torn up? Recall there was no marriage license. So it is not that.

The man remembers her *old* giggles. Shy. Nervous. Horny maybe. These new giggles are different. In such a *short* time she is someone else. He watches as her hand withdraws.

"Going to hit me?!!" she calls, her perfect mouth more tremble than tease.

He calls back in his big-necked voice, which carries through the downpour like a ship, "Going to beat the wickedness out of you!"

Now the collie barks.

Bree giggles.

The green eyes under the drip-drip of the crusher hat brim still stare, like true threat, but really this is a spark of teasing. But the spark doesn't carry to the octagon window.

She screams, "Fuck with me, Mister, and see what happens!!!"

He drags a hand across his mustache and mouth, now turning his head to something interesting out there on the nearest cold blue hill.

The collie down in the kitchen commences a frantic "shout."

A skin-crawling, squeally, bray-bawling pours from the little window. Bree's wounded laugh.

"All this stuff about beatings! That's no way to get forgiveness!" Bree calls. "A bouquet of flowers is more traditional. Norrr-malll people think that waaay. But for you, you—"

"This is *not* an apology!" he booms. "Would you rather have a stake in the heart!" Again, twinkles of teasing in his eyes.

But those are gone in the rain as though down a drain. Again he looks toward the distant misty wooded mountain. Then raises a pleading hand to the queer little window. "Get down here *now*, Brianna and get your lickin'! I'm too busy to screw around here with talk of flowers!"

"Then you shouldn't have ridden old twinkle toes! You shoulda taken a jet!" She giggles teenagerishly. Slams the screen shut. Slams the window.

Gordon and the pinto gelding remain hunched and motionless, a mini mountain.

 Out in the world.

The people work. The people shop. The people hurry. The people wait at streetlights, grumbling. The people now talk on phones *while driving* . . . and chewing, swallowing, on their way. Work, shop, drive, talk, chew. Tinted windshields. Flashing mirrors. Automated voices and hidden cameras. The people are on their way. Credit cards. Interest. Faster money. Longer days. Lighter meals. Memories of no past. Catalogs. Packaging that crinkles. Packaging that opens faster.

 History as it happens (as dictated by Benjamin St. Onge with the help of Rachel Soucier).

The world is scary. It could happen anytime. Look out when you answer the door. Butchie says insurance men are scary too when they come to look in your house and catch you with a broken smoke detector. Then there's Drug War. They bust in and smash everything and take your mother and kill your dog. Like Jane. Mother gone. Dog gone. House gone. All her stuff gone. Nothing left but Jane. Then there is IRS which takes your money for rich people. And schoolteachers who have GRADES for honor kids and "*trash* you." I used to *think* that means they put you in a big trash bag. Finally I got the difference. Here it is safe. We have a GATE. And a sign that says: KEEP OUT. Evan says we also need to get our own army. That's pretty funny.

 Next day, an even colder meaner rain.

One of the Settlement flatbed trucks, boarded-up sides. Cow, hay, oil, lumber remnants mixing into one smell of hard use, that trucky smell. It stops not down in the Vandermast yard, but out on the shoulder of the road. Engine goes silent. Resembles a siege. Gordon slides out into the rain, work boots, jeans, sleeveless black sweater vest over plaid, no hat.

Headed directly for him through the sheets of straight-down icy rain, Bree. Her jumbled hair and green T-shirt flatten and darken. She seems to be about to embrace him. And she sort of does, her fists bunching up the upper arms of his jacket. She gives him a stout shove, then draws him forward to her again, snug. Not a fighter, this man. Perhaps his restraint is due to her sex? Fairer? Weaker? But no, this is our preview to his submission in blood. This is rehearsal for a future of trials.

Rain blows and tugs his and her faces, carrying everything down.

He squeezes his eyes shut, shakes his head.

She tightens her grip on his jacket sleeves.

His eyes are *old* eyes to a girl of fifteen. His eyes that are filled and fluttering with the beating rain. Her semigenius cannot behold what his captivity within time gives to his sight. He pleads, "We need peace! *Not* the True Maine Militia! We don't need more hordes, dear! We need to stop and *think!*"

Her hands hold fast. She sneers. Her pretty mouth not pretty. "*You* can have your *boy* militia! You and your Rexy! Oh, yeah, yeah, you *were* sweeet! You *were*! Until somebody else has an idea!"

"That's not it, Bree! I love your ideas!"

She tightens her grip. She's strong. Logger girl. She shoves again. His back smacks the truck grille.

He hollers, "Rex York's group isn't about publicity or—"

"It isn't!!?"

"Well."

"Yuh, 'well' is right! And Rex's militia is just a prawww-duct of great big conservative foundations and their turds on the shortwave and wherever! Rex's militia is a *toilet!* The True Maine Militia is *people,* not political parties, not a movement to help out Wall Street! The True Maine came right out of *here!*" She draws back one hand as if to punch him but punches her own heart.

"We can't have all these *crowds* at the Settlement, Brianna! That's all I'm saying!"

"We *will!*"

He grasps her wrist, the wrist of the hand that was lowering from her heart. Perhaps his grasp seemed like aggression because her wrist within his work-stiff palm melts to nothing, withered, gone. And also magically, her teeth are now closed around his empty left hand. She *chomps*. He swears he hears crunching and alas flings her away.

She loses balance. Goes down. She's on one knee. She begins to rock, arms around her knees now, sitting in the pebbly road shoulder sand with small rivers of rain, nodding weeds, and there she can view his work boots close range. All those snakes of her wet hair sluice her shirt front and arms. She is not talking now.

His thumb trickles a little blood but oh, how numb and stinging. And his dear one, his Bree, very very quiet. He wants to hold and stroke her, yes, the father thing. To comfort. To cause flourishing, not this, this wound. But he hesitates. Something in the way she is staring at his boots, her muscles tensed. There's twitching along her right forearm. No, not twitching. Flexing. He turns, squeezes the door handle, jerks open the truck door. "I'm going now!"

"Good," says she. "You stupid piece of turd!"

He sits in the seat a minute thinking how that last remark was so childish. But of course!

He slams the door. Waits. His thumb smears blood onto the plastic steering wheel. The windshield is dreamy, covered in silver spangles and gray ribbons, gauzy tendrils reflecting his own fucked-up stupidity.

 ## In a future time, Catherine Court Downey remembers.

For me, television has always been two things. It is an educational tool. And it can be soothing in the evening after you've put in a long day with students and meetings, especially meetings. So I had brought my twenty-four-inch screen and VCR to my studio at the Settlement. Does this make me a bad person?

We were all facing the TV, a little group I had invited to my studio to watch the AIDS tape. Understand that this was a really moving tape on AIDS victims and at this time only a small core group of us knew that Brady had AIDS. This would prepare the others. Brady wasn't present. Of course not. I didn't want any remarks, if there were any of those kinds of remarks, to hurt him. Nor was flashy Ricardo there, whom I suspected was gay.

The room smelled strongly of acrylics, which I had begun working with. My new series. Myself with AIDS. No, I didn't have AIDS. But in the work I did. I wanted to deeply identify, to FIND OUT. This is the artist's job, to explore all those mortal dreads. And I can't tell you how much knowing sweet Brady and Sadie affected me.

I had several twelve-by-fourteen-inch canvases stretched and ready to begin. Unriffled, welcoming, dazzling white, yes, *blanc* and blank, oh possibilities! Thank you, Gordon St. Onge, for this new world! For this frontier! This is what I was saying to myself as the pale TV light flickered and glided over the canvases that were lined up on my big worktable.

The little group of teenagers, both boys and girls, and some young women I had invited were all quiet as mice, faces tilted up to that big twenty-four-inch screen. We had made popcorn. I was serving wine to the adults. It was a sweet and important evening and I was glad to be able to do this for them. I regretted losing Bree. I was more stunned by that than I was by what was coming down between Phan and I. Phan and I had ended too many years before. And the contests between Gordon and I. It had started to feel GOOD. He was a bastard right from the start. Okay, fine. It was a game. And I was ready to play. Or so I thought.

Meanwhile, it seemed that I'd win Bree back someday when she understood that it was only with love we women tried to protect her. I shiver now to imagine that big groping man with his hands on her within days of our reaching out to her. Didn't he realize the power that people whom he had offended would have over him? He was committing what used to be called statutory rape! A worse crime today. He'd be registered as a sex offender. And there were other "wives" of his nearly as young as Bree. He was walking on thin ice!

So strange that we could all sit there like normal people watching television, a normal family-evening-type activity, with so much brutality and insanity going on around us.

The documentary was nearly over when we heard him on the stairs. You could tell it was him. He was six-foot-five and all muscled up from all his self-inflicted hard labor and he was rigid with venom for me. His keys wailed against his belt. And we could hear those boots. Clodhoppers. All this is no lie, what I am about to tell you.

When he pushed the door open, I swear I could smell cow manure, yes. He had both hands bandaged, one that we heard he had injured repairing something on the manure spreader. Yes, there is such a contraption. A manure spreader! Blood spotted the bandage and in that dimly lit studio room, blood that looked black, like tar or oil. Some inhuman substance. How the other hand was injured was a mystery.

He seemed to take up the whole room with his size and he looked at young Christian Crocker and young Jaime Crosman, which you are *supposed* to pronounced Hchheye-me, but they do not, of course. And he said to each of them . . . yes, he said it two distinct times, "Unplug it. Take it out. Destroy it."

I stood up and shouted, "Are you crazy!" and then to Christian and Jaime I yelled, "Don't." I tried to reason with Gordon. "This tape is important. This *AIDS tape* is important." But Gordon wouldn't look at me. He just looked at the two boys . . . a look of threat, like this was their fault, like they, the young males of this Settlement Republic, should have kept this enemy woman in hand.

Do you know what total lunacy is? *That place*. You will never know *that place*. Feel grateful!

The boys stood up, really red-faced with embarrassment. And who knows, also maybe terrified of being beaten. They went for the TV.

I said, "That is *my* property."

The boys hesitated, the fluttering blues and pinks of the documentary's final credits passing down across their faces.

Gordon said, "Get it out of here and destroy it." Again, he said this to the boys, not acknowledging me, or any of the young mothers either, though most of them hardly turned from facing the screen, even after Jaime reached up and pushed the *off* button. Only Vancy and Misty and Nova were Gordon's wives, the others were not. But they all acted the same. Passive, acceptant.

Jaime looked hard at Gordon. He was a blond swaggery boy, a toughie, really redneck, cruel in some ways. But he had been interested in the tape and now seemed upset at how we all had to bow down to Gordon's shit, excuse me, to Gordon playing Big Man.

I thought for a moment Jaime was going to attack Gordon but after a few seconds of this bold resistance I saw the boy's shoulders sag, already defeated.

I said, "Don't anybody destroy my television. Just place it in my car trunk, would you?" I went over to the table by my napping-cot and found my keys.

And believe this, Gordon St. Onge said, "Jaime. C.C. Take the TV to the bank at the back of the killing shed. Fetch my Winchester. It's still in the cabinet shop area, over by the small lathe . . . yellow door, check the boxes for .32 Special . . . there's also 22s and 45s. Don't fuck up." Then he, too, held out a key that he picked out from that bunch of keys that bristled there on his belt, and he said, "I'll be along in a minute."

The boy, C.C., took the key from Gordon's hand even as I kept mine outstretched. The two boys disconnected the VCR as I watched, dumbstruck. And scared for my life.

The boys ambled out into the poorly lit hallway, each with a piece of equipment, and then down the stairs.

And then Gordon walked to the wall and snapped on the blinding overhead lights, giving everybody the squints. Then he stepped out, closing the door behind him.

I untied the twine I used to hold open the tarp, let the tarp drop so that we now sat in this smaller space, like scared baby birds, our hearts in our throats, whispering. The women who were Gordon's wives kept still. They looked sad and sickened.

A few minutes later we heard the shots.

Claire, the friend.

I heard the shots. Well, I suppose half of Egypt did, the way this mountain leans out over the open lake. Before long, Catherine found me over in the furniture-making Quonset hut where a bunch of us were setting the pedals, rudders, and little paddle wheels in the latest pair of swan boats . . . each swan different, as a real swan would be who had cracked his way out of an egg into this wicked world. The night was almost cool and was all sleeves and buttoned-up collars, thick socks. My nose *felt* red. Next thing this hot, moist sobbing dear one is in my arms. She was cracking wide open to let out the hurt.

"She's a snooty frigid cunt," Bonnie Loo had grumbled once. But Bonnie Loo had a low view of a lot of people. Catherine was not a cold person. Does a cold person weep? Maybe we owed her a more teeming-with-warm-hearts welcome than this?

Of course the reason behind the gunshots reached our Quonset area before Catherine did, thanks to those Settlement tongues of fire and their tinder pathways! They seemed to enjoy this human sacrifice! That night I had such a revulsion for the whole family.

Catherine and I went briskly past the faces of the other swan makers into the narrow "brooms and coat" hall that connected the two main workrooms and which supported two sets of stairs. It was lighted poorly. One of those little pink four-watters. We cleared the bench of cultch and held hands. I said nothing (nothing that I can recall) while she described what Gordon had done. Her cheeks were flushed to fruit red, her lovely eyes narrowed.

Was I betraying her not to speak more? I nodded, I listened keenly. I kissed her trembling-with-fear knuckles. I listened on and on but I didn't praise her bringing the TV here. I understood her arguments, the way a TV *can* be useful. Oh, yes. But also I saw the dangers. She may not have understood that most of us here had voted on the "no TV" ban year after year. Gordon was just a lot more vocal on it . . . his passion colored all his beliefs. Now Catherine's throat shook. She kept checking my eyes for something, flickering glances. I was betraying her by not calling Gordon a nut, a dangerous man, a criminal. She was on her own with this. I was just a woodchuck on the median strip in the middle of the Maine Turnpike. Either way I go, I'm going to wind up a pancake.

 Same night, Claire remembers more.

I now had my little house to myself since Catherine and Robert had begun sleeping nights in her studio. Some of her belongings were still stacked against the bedroom wall here and by the kitchen door and she had accumulated a lot of stuff, mostly new stuff, since she moved here.

Later on that night, although it was not his scheduled night to be with me, Gordon came to my cottage and sat on the edge of the bed, fully dressed. He would often come in like that, in the dark, feeling his way along the walls, getting to this bed without any light whatsoever. And then sit there. He was so at home in my bed, my space, no need even to say, "Hi."

My head was deep in my pillow. I listened to the night with one ear and waited it out, letting him do his thing. It *seemed* like peace.

He didn't move. I was sure peace was not what it was. Such a lot of time passed. I couldn't stand it. I was bursting.

"Gordon."

"Yep."

I spoke from my pillow and he just kept staring out the window, a faint grayness to his face from a partial moon and all the usual stars. "I know she doesn't belong here but—"

"You're right. She doesn't belong here."

"But she needs to be here. We've got to make this work. What about Robert? You're doing this to Robert, too."

He swallowed drily.

"She could hurt you, Gordon. She mentioned that she has actually looked up all the statutes about a man your age with a fifteen-year-old. And the punishment. But guess what. She won't do anything about it. I explained to her that it's different here than out there . . . that this is a way of life. That nobody is traumatized by your . . . by . . . growing up early. I hope that's true . . . for Bree. And Gordon, Catherine is a *good* person."

He said nothing. He would concede not even that one thing.

"You have never been so hard on anyone here before." I didn't learn of all the details of him and Bree's discord yet. Or the real reason for his bandaged right thumb. He was cloaked up in more than one smothery silence.

I sighed.

He was still facing the window.

"Even when you caught Macky stealing when he was here. And when Esther used to argue with you about putting Gretel in public school!"

"True."

"This, what you're doing to Catherine . . . there are better ways to handle it. You certainly have your cruel side. Couldn't you just *talk* to her? Can't you *talk* for godsakes? Or do you just love running that barbed hook through the tender worm?"

"Tender worm?" he sneered.

"Whatever. I can't see why you and Catherine can't communicate. I . . ." I then realized I couldn't imagine Catherine talking, either. Not at this point.

"It's not her fault the way she is," I pressed on. "She has more needs than you realize and she's *my* friend!"

Silence.

"She's just used to another kind of world," I pressed on further.

"True," he said huskily.

"She's not Settlement material. I agree. But this situation between you and her is not all her fault. You are acting like a very little boy."

"True."

 Gabe Sanborn recalls.

They shot the lady's TV. Pow! Pow! Pow!

 Bonnie Loo.

Yeah, we heard the shots. I had no idea what it was at the time. I wish I'd known. So I could have *enjoyed*.

Misty St. Onge.

Yes, I was there when he had the boys carry the TV out and shoot it. Catherine didn't know Gordon. You could tell. If she had, she'd know that the Settlement was created by his scary tireless will. That whole night made me nervous. His will. Her will. Eeeeeeeeeeek!

 The screen tells us.

The elections are coming! The elections are coming! See the elections in living color!!! Tweedle tweedle deeee! Tweedle red. Tweedle white. Tweedle blue. Tweedle Republican. Tweedle Democrat. Pick one! Only in America do you have the power of this choice!! The power of your VOTE! VOTE! VOTE! VOTE! Tweedle tweedle doo ding dee deedum. Lucky you. Lucky, oh, you doo dee doo! Democracy!

 At the St. Onge Settlement.

The mail increaseth.

 Claire St. Onge remembers.

First it was just daytimes she was not around. Then nights. She asked me if I'd keep Robert at my place at night. He wanted to sleep in my bed with me, and that was all right. He didn't seem afraid of sleeping alone on his floor pallet. But maybe lonely. He was just so meticulous. There is something more tidy about *one* bed, two beings, I suppose. Whenever she visited, she unloaded bags and bags of gifts. As if she was a visitor, one of those you haven't seen in thirty years. Gifts for Robert. Gifts for all of us. A lot of gifts. Nice things. Not trash. Nothing Wal-Mart-ish. She looked good. Rested. Had had her hair cut. And straightened. Short. Cute.

But once or twice when I ran into her at the university, she was prickly perfect and peculiar . . . like she might have started to be fed up with me. That I didn't stand up to Gordon enough in her defense was no small matter. Maybe she was about to take Robert and ease on out of our lives completely. But the next time I saw her, she was her old self. I mean she really was. There was no way she could pretend that well, her funny, gossipy, busy, blurry, mischievous artist self. My heart sang.

 ### Brady dreams.

It is not a dream of terror of the Stygian and endless realm. Nor one of his ostracism dreams, dreams where the word *fag* or *faggot* and *AIDS* aren't spoken but the jeers or fear that is hitched to them usually shapes the drama. Lots of jeers. And, no, tonight's dream is not of a precious and arousing tumble with Kennard on the nighttime beach of the lake camp with the camp's Indian name on the end-of-the-road sign that was sawed out in the shape of an arrow. Nor is this a dream of Kennard's two dark hands holding out to him the surprise gift of a Himalayan kitten. (Though in real life, Kennard never gave him a kitten.) Also, this is not one of those disorderliness and weirdness dreams he has had lately, that incomprehensible idea of more than twenty St. Onge wives and the pounding running feet of the Settlement children horde with their oftentimes filthy faces, cowlicked hair, and jars of bugs. Their inventions and highfalutin talk mashed in with the swears and the ain'ts.

No, this dream is just shadows of the softest velvetiest kind, a twinge of perfect blue. And within this velvety blue, Gordon's *baritone* speaks in its matter-of-fact across-the-supper-table way: "*Nothing's* wrong."

 ### Claire.

One morning she asked if I could have Robert call her at the university for little daily chats. Only once to her cell phone, which made waveries and slush sounds and harbor tunnels and coal mines seemed to hove in around every other word. Thereafter she insisted the university number to her office was where he was to call. Only later I learned that with a cell phone, you get charged both in and out. Wow! What can I say?

We arranged times. Uh, the chats were pretty long. Robert talked. He wasn't an introvert at all. Only when things were wildly tense, chaotic, or too new. So, he talked some. But Catherine really chatted away. Even Lisa Meserve, who was in jail, kept her talks with Jane short. Lisa fretted over our "doing too much" for her, not wanting to be a "burden." But Catherine seemed emergencyish with phone in hand.

Uh-oh.

I started to *worry* about the phone bill. Phone bills weren't something Gordon bothered with much. Only a few times, like back when my cousin Macky lived here . . . shifty, shady Macky . . . and then a couple of other times the phone bill became a problem. If people made long-distance calls, we had a timer and a money can for that. It was all about trust. And Gordon wasn't the bookkeeper. Bonnie Loo, Lorraine Martin, and I did that.

But THIS phone bill was going to be . . . uh . . . plump. And Gordon did check the bottom line of various pages of our accounts, and this time he'd sniff out something REALLY OFF. See, we had different categories. He always checked these in a cursory way so he could figure, including income, for instance, how well the CSA thing was doing, or the fall meat cutting, or Christmas trees and wreaths, and the sawmills or furniture, so then he could project expenses, like what we were going to be able to handle over the next six months, or over the next year. That sort of thing. And without exception, he was the one who signed the money orders and made up all of our allotment-shares envelopes, which were cash.

So I was feeling a little edgy.

But Bonnie Loo and Lorraine and I talked. We decided that once Catherine got her divorce settled and got herself resituated in Portland, as it now seemed she had plans to do, the phone bill here would not take this beating. She and Robert would both be in Portland and that would be that.

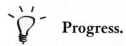 **Progress.**

Jeanne Tull, an old lady in Maine, just outside of Biddeford, is looking at a pale plastic object in her hands with tears in her eyes. It's the third telephone she's had to buy this year! She recalls her solid old rotary that was a pleasant shade of dark green. Never broke. Does a chunk of granite break? The repairman came from the company when the one before that lost its dial tone. No charge to replace it and give her a longer wire too!! Now this little thing you have to buy yourself, made to expire routinely. A milk jug cover is ruggeder.

Living on Social Security, which never goes up much, you do not have much of a sense of humor about being stolen from.

Whenever she calls (the unknown company on the phone's wrapping) to complain, she doesn't get a person. She gets a recording and a "menu." The menu is too fast and causes her to feel *very* alone. And yes, robbed! Like a sociopath cleverly talking his way out of whatever it is sociopaths do, chaos and ruination on regular nice folks!

Anyone would say what a sweet old lady Jeanne is. Not a wild or mean bone in her body. But right now, she has a terrible thought, which she must keep to herself and never tell a soul. There it is, just a thought. A picture actually. She pictures herself tossing a stick of dynamite at the main offices of the Blue Booger Corporation or whatever outfit's name is on the latest cheesy phone.

Now she feels really awful! Gosh, she just lost her head for a moment. Just a quick passing flash of insanity.

If she goes and puts on the TV for her show, which starts in eight minutes, gets the teakettle started, gets her mind off THE SUBJECT, she'll do just fine.

    Waste management.

Yes, I am speaking to you. I am the inexorable fact, size-of-the-sky pile of used plastic foam, wrap, boingy and cracked forget-me-nots, remnants of your washing machine, tires of your car numbering as the stars, all of which will become your new scenic mountains, going up, up, up, just as the old mountains are razed down, down, down for our helpful coal.

What? Someone of you just squeaked, *Can't appliances and vehicles be made more stoutly, nourishing a mighty army of repairpersons singing as they work like Disney dwarfs?*

Whoa! But I, the heap, make jobs, all those trucks lugging the squashed cars and upside-down TVs, computers, cell phones, and egg timers hither and yon, folks in plants sorting through broken mercury bulbs and motherboards, manning the furnaces, the transport of ash to the heavens.

Sorry dears, but repair is outdated, old-fashioned, possibly commie, definitely NOT PROFITABLE. Repair is the wish of fools.

 ### The coalescing of wolves. Oceanna St. Onge speaks.

Bree would be joining us for the Lincoln trip. Hurrah! We had gone over to her house a few days before and hugged and smooched her and yelled and crabbed at her and Samantha got military on her.

"If you go AWOL," said Sammy in a husky sort of way, "it's a hundred lashes."

Most of us laughed but Bree cocked her head with a pale smile.

"Firing squad," said Dee Dee.

And besides, this thing we had strategized we truly believed was going to stop entrenched corporate power in its tracks. Boyzo, did we ever feel wicked influential. Tsk.

 ### In a future time, Whitney St. Onge (oldest daughter of Gordon) thinks back on that day, heading out for Lincoln, Maine.

When we left the Settlement, I was driving the Ford we always called "the Vessel." Now it was our "Command Car." The caravan headed down Heart's Content Road through the dark and darker trees, the rocks piled in miles of loose ferny walls, unseen or barely seen. But the sky was brightening and so the woodsy mysteries were quickening. And we, too, were quickening, we the officers of the True Maine Militia.

 ### Margo.

Samantha had her corn-silk blonde hair wrapped in a black and brown Comanche-style head rag. She was all snuggled down in her black military BDU jacket in the backseat feasting on the stuff addressed to the True Maine Militia, which we'd gotten out of the message box by the Settlement gate as we drove through. There were notes, business cards, letters scribbled onto receipts (the way emergency messages are usually left).

There were too many of us all to use our seat belts. The taillights of the Settlement truck ahead of us seemed to brake a lot. It was the truck with the turbine chained on back. That was the overt mission. *We* were the covert mission.

 Steph St. Onge speaks.

We got there late in the day. I remember how sweet it was, the Settlement guys there with the Lincoln guys, inspecting the pylons together. Cement pylons they had set earlier on. These Lincoln guys were Bible-hard but smiley. Yeah, flushy angelic smiles. And it seemed they were all chubby.

 Michelle St. Onge.

We got out of the Command Car. I remember how Samantha looked so cagey and strategic, eyes narrowed, studying the long field, the straight tar road below. Plotting. She looked SO OBVIOUS, I warned her that she might give it all away.

 Claire St. Onge remembers.

The Lincoln families apologized for their water having a metallic taste and some of them apologized for the ground being hilly, and profusely apologized for the weather being muggy.

 Andrea St. Onge, seven years old at the time, recalls later.

The Lincoln kids really LOVED the fart pillows we brought for them.

 Rusty Soucier, fourteen at the time, remembers something of the first day in Lincoln.

Well, you know that was a buncha years ago. I kinda remember this kid with glasses who really loved the fart pillow we gave him, a pillow that makes a fart noise when you sit on it. He kept calling it "the thunder pillow." I remember Mimi ordered me to sit in the truck but I can't remember what for.

 Steph St. Onge has a memory of that first evening.

When it was clear that the fart pillows were being used as weapons, they were confiscated. "You don't chase people with these!" Leona screamed and snatched one of these pillows from Gus, who was taller than herself.

 Claire.

There were three houses up on that hilly field, three families. One old house with a barn. Two newish solar houses built up back sort of, but also in the open. Not many trees. The families were all of that same church and their Christian school, and Pastor Rick was mentioned about forty times before he finally arrived in his little white car and he, Pastor Rick, of course, was fat and smiled an ear-to-ear smile.

 Penny.

For the first couple of days, I don't remember much. Seems it was sweet, kind of going along there. They had their Pastor Rick. All of them very churchy. They apologized a lot for stuff. And we've talked about it since how our girls, the True Maine Militia, looked so innocent.

 Michelle recalls.

There was a mad scramble setting up the tents and cookers. The water tasted funny. Samantha kept whispering, "We're going to die! We shoulda brought our own water!"

 Whitney.

Bree and I were scooched by the door flap of our tent looking down across the tufty short-cut hay and she says, "He isn't going to like it."

I could see she was looking at Gordon, who was back to and goofing around with some kids. Even if I couldn't see who she was looking at, I knew who she meant. I said, "We won't let him blame you. We'll protect you."

She kind of laughed. Then her eyes moved again toward where he was, quite a distance away.

I looked down there at him. He had his big gorilla arm around one of those Lincoln Christian ladies and she was laughing all shrieky like a kid.

 Geraldine St. Onge.

The first night passed. It was pretty uneventful, I think. We slept in tents. Some slept on the truck seats or in the vans and cars and three homemade campers, but mostly the tents. We had pretty good tents because we did this sort of thing a lot . . . the community wind-solar thing.

I remember the air the next day was *thicker*. I remember as work started, some of the other people from their church stopped by to watch. They parked down along the road and hiked the mowed part of the field. Some stood with their hands on their hips taking it all in. And smiling. I never saw a bunch smile so much. At one point, Bonnie Loo said the smiles were getting on her nerves.

 Penny.

The temperature wasn't over seventy, but it was muggy. Like mid-summer. The grasshoppers and crickets were deafening at times. And they hopped high, striking people's pant legs and bare legs, landing in cups of coffee and toolboxes and baskets where babies were sleeping. Everything *seemed* normal.

 Gail.

It always gave me a little chill . . . you know, a chilly thrill . . . like hearing the tune to the "Star Spangled Banner," to see one of the wind towers beginning to rise against the sky one piece at a time. There were groups of men and strong teens and a couple of gals lugging the steel sections from the Egypt flatbed trucks. The windmill co-op jobs are always fun, and something else . . . gives a self-concious edgy person like me a feeling of being part of something big. And warm. No, not a party. Better than that.

 ### Glennice.

Well, what we planned was for some of the Egypt teens to show the Lincoln teens how to build a ten-foot mechanical windmill, the kind that pumps water, and one smaller version of the one the adults were setting up, only theirs would charge a *small* battery. And for the little kids, ornamental windmills. This was what we hoped. *But.* Through all this humidity here were all these sweaty shrieky kids lugging rough pine boards and conduit from the trucks while others were crawling all over the trucks, even jumping on the cabs and hoods, *whomp!bang!whomp! bang!* . . . and kids were sorting through tools. Mostly kids were losing tools in the grass.

 ### Leona.

I remember how the men and older teens, mostly boys, were taking turns bolting sections of the big windmill together.

I could hear Aurel yakking up there. There's no place where he was ever quiet for long. Not even forty-five feet up in the sky! "Juss like a big erector set, aye?" he says to the boy who's up there with him, one of the Lincoln teenagers. And the father was up there, too, father of that boy, both of them on the chubby side.

Then I could hear the boy asking his dad, "Scared?" And the father was laughing as if to deny it.

Aurel scoffed at the very idea. "T'iss high-up part iss not t'danger. It iss far more off a danger down t'ere below where you got to keep dodging t'tools t'at we drop from *here*."

Meanwhile, Gordon looked tired, though once we had to get a fart pillow away from him, which he was going to plant in this nice Christian lady's lawn chair. Yeah, and he was his usual solicitous self with these women, all married women, these Christian ladies, our hostesses. But it didn't seem to annoy the husbands whatsoever. Sweet smiles continued.

 Bonnie Loo.

I think it was that third day, but no, it might have been the second, the muggy one, that one of the smallest Lincoln kids wound up with an opened can of turquoise paint flipped off the high flat bed of a truck onto her head. But that's just par for the course. THE BAD THING was still *on the way*.

 Claire.

Uh-oh. So here we go. I think it was the afternoon of the second day that three people showed up who were not part of the Christian group. I gotta say they acted strange . . . like . . . like suspicious. Observers, not socializers. I don't mean that they didn't say anything at all. One of the men told our Ray Pinette, who was especially red-faced and damp-looking from his work, that a windmill still stood in his father's field near a pond in Milo. A mechanical windmill.

But otherwise, none of these unbidden visitors had much interest in the project. I watched them, saw their eyes move in sly ways over the Settlement's old beat-ta-shit trucks, the half-finished child-made smaller windmills.

All the embroidery on blouses, jackets, and floppy skirts seemed to daze them.

And then they studied Bonnie Loo in particular, standing there with one hand on her hip, sucking a cigarette, with her orange and black hair rip-roaring out over one side of her head from its bright green embroidered "rag," talking with Ellen who was probably wearing that above-the-knee tent dress, and who had a real bad cough. Oh, and yes, how could I forget her black eye. It was a stitched up blood-red mess, a surgically removed benign tumor. These strangers looked at her a lot. Yes, Ellen St. Onge, one of "the wives."

And boy, did they study Gordon. I remember another carload had pulled up and these people *really* drilled Gordon with the old eyeballs. This bunch were too much like the sightseers we had had coming

around at the Settlement before the pole gate went up. I looked over
to see exactly what about Gordon intrigued them so much. He was
standing alone, arms folded across the front of his work shirt, staring at a dribbling sun in a dribbling turquoise sky freshly painted by
kids on our one-ton truck driver's-side door. He reached to pick off
a grasshopper that was stuck in the paint. Grasshopper covered with
paint. Mercifully, he crushed it. And then he reached into his shirt
pocket for a small bottle. Aspirin, yes.

The families we had come to work with had promised not to tell
too many people that we were coming, and they understood this, Gordon's media infamy. And now the kids' op-ed. Maybe for a moment
or two some of us suspected the Christians had broken their promise.

 **In a future time, Penny is remembering Lincoln,
Maine.**

After supper, there was a prayer and during this I was one of the ones
who peeked. Like kids were doing. I saw that Gordon was sitting on
a board bench with Ellen and Whitney.

His huge hands were clasped, the bare forearms, his carefully buttoned work shirt, his hair wet from the comb. Yes, Sunday school–like.
It made me smile.

 Lee Lynn.

Before we opened our eyes from the prayer, Pastor Rick began to
sing. I could feel that singing voice on my retinas, thin and high. It
soared right up into the darkening sky as he gave thanks to God for
everything from good food to good friends.

 Bonnie Loo.

That sky in Lincoln was big. Unlike Egypt, no humpy mountain
blocked the west. There was a pissed-off-looking red sunset with
purple worms over the top edge and a bottom layer that looked like
human organs, veiny and orange. HELL. Where the devil lives. Except that it did not roar or hiss or gurgle. And no screams. Just, you

know, an unsullied silence and growing chill. I hadn't seen Gordon
and Bree even acknowledge each other at this point. Meanwhile, it
was plain something was up, another one of Bree's schemes. What
else?

 Margo St. Onge recalls that evening.

There was a sunset made up of every color. We were all politely praying with the Christians. I peeked at my father. He had his head hanging, eyes closed, fingers laced. Well, if you knew him, you'd have
known how he had this side to him . . . this God thing. I think he
really was praying. There was something there you couldn't fake.

 Penny St. Onge.

Now the colorful sunset deflates and, gracefully and driftingly, stained
a hundred shades of blue, falls parachutelike into the dark, and the
next song of the evening, backed up with kazoos, harmonicas, jaw
harps, guitars, three fart pillows (sad to say), Settlement-made fiddles,
and one small accordion . . . a "squeezebox" actually . . . was "The
Log Driver's Waltz," then some of what Gordon called "complaints,"
sang in valley French, memorized by most Settlement kids, and then
came the hymns, most of which the Egypt people knew very few of but
were happy to learn. I will never, never, never forget that evening. It
is now a part of my past but also a wish for the future. Being *a people*
with other Mainers. Peace and good will.

 Dee Dee Lancaster St. Onge.

Lou-EE, my hub, and I were sitting together kinda arm in arm in
that deep cherry color dusk. Everyone was grouped around, mellow
you know, just enjoying the cooling air and deep mood. We had Cannonball on a leash cuz she attacked a Malamute the minute we got
here. Now I peeked over Lou-EE's shoulder and there was Samantha
over there a ways, standing with her arms folded, listening to one of
the Christian ladies singing in a very beautiful way. Sammy's pale hair
was so wicked. It just looked so central to the scene.

Yes ol' Sam was looking forward to the big True Maine Militia surprise. I could tell. Me? I was uneasy. Gordon was not my father and he wasn't head of *my* household. I didn't live at the Settlement. But maybe I feared him a little bit. I feared messing with his security, his little world. Dad likes to talk about being "point man." He calls it "walking point." That's war talk for when you are the lead guy walking in dangerous territory. Well, that night as I sat there, pulling my sweater around me (and my pregnant belly), the thoughts of the next day seemed like . . . well, like one giant minefield.

 Claire St. Onge remembers breakfast time on the fourth day.

It was very cool. You could see your breath. There were muffins, coffee, and juice which the Lincoln people unloaded from Pastor Rick's little white station wagon. Pastor Rick was bald and shiny under his Red Sox cap, which he took off and held in his hands whenever he talked with a woman. His hair around the sides was a little long and quite fair and as soft-looking as a baby duckling's. I remember there were a few moments where he was standing with Paul Lessard, you know, *our* Paul from the Settlement, the two of them looking uphill at the fifty-foot tower. Pastor Rick with a steaming coffee in one hand, Red Sox cap on his head. Paul was wearing a black corduroy jacket, hands on his hips, kinda blending with the shadows of the new day.

The pastor spoke in his cheery high voice, "I heard most people assemble these on the ground first, then, with the turbine in place, they use a crane to raise it."

Paul Lessard was quiet a moment. Then, playing off some insulting old Frenchman joke, "Err, yes, I herr'tat, too. But we do it Frenchman way, you know? Jacques and Pierre do tiss'all ass'n backwarse, t'em."

The preacher laughed kind of weakly, not knowing how hard one is supposed to laugh at a Frenchman joke when a Frenchman tells it.

Both of them stared quietly up at the tower in that dim morning sky. Then Paul turned and stared at the flatbed truck with the wind plant chained on back, and he said with silk-soft momentousness, "Four hun'ret pounds." He looked at me again and I winked and then we all looked slowly and momentously and grimly back up at the top of the tower.

And boy did that preacher giggle. And then he added happily, "I'm sure you folks have it all figured out."

And then Paul glanced around at Eddie Martin, you know, our Eddie from the Settlement, who was strolling toward us with his own steaming coffee. Paul asked Eddie, "Where's Bree?"

Eddie smiled sickly (he was never an early bird), which made his bony, carefully shaved face sort of ripple around the sides of his mouth. And he covered one eye. "Oh, around. She was helping them up at that house there. Some extra tables. Bree said they're putting a lot more tables out in case of *crowds*."

"Crowds?"

Eddie shrugged.

Preacher noticed me about then. I admit, I had been quiet, just enjoying the morning, trying to wake up. He tugs off his cap and nods at me.

I winked at him.

Paul says, "Little girl named Bree, her going to put t'win'plant up on'tat tower, her."

The preacher giggled almost explosively. Nodded fast, "Sure. Sure."

 Bree recalls.

As the sun picked its way over the trees and the building up at the top of the long humpy drive, I was readying myself for the job, which on the first day we arrived, Aurel had asked me to do, saying, "T'logger girl expert wit' a truck and 'quipment. When we'rrre ready to go, will she do t'honors, her?" So this was it. Day Four. I slammed the door of the truck, checked both mirrors.

Uh-oh, there they were down below on the tar road. A few cars. People with binoculars trained on the tower, on those of us drinking coffee and chewing on muffins. And on that array of little child-fashioned windmills, all painted up in dribbling carnival colors. Oh, how exotic we were! And two windmills somewhat taller, made by the older kids, which would, by the end of the day, be ready to each light a one-hundred-watt bulb, providing there would be some breeze. At the moment the whole Lincoln landscape was raw silence. My hands were loose on the wheel.

After a few minutes, there were many more carloads of "unexpected" people. Then more. My heart popped popcornishly.

I could hear one of the Lincoln women chirp, "Oh! More visitors! Let's welcome them!"

 Lorraine Martin.

I could see Gordon watching the little groups of figures move up the shadowy hill and then a couple more cars, easing up onto the shoulders. He was eating a muffin, chewing, then pausing, his jaws frozen a moment, then chewing, then again a pause as he focused hard on the invaders.

 Bonnie Loo.

Boy, they were coming, cars and cars. And more cars. A lot of cars. They were coming from both directions, so they were not in a procession, but they sure did yessiree seem to be brought there by a signal in common, like the green flag in a stock car race, or some sort of widely advertised sale. Or you know who. I never did buy that rap about her innocence. She was always finding some new flashy way to make the Settlement into a three-ring circus.

 Leona St. Onge recalls.

Gordon was looking over at the cheery fat frosty-breathed faces of the five Lincoln men and women standing nearest him. Then he looked over at Pastor Rick, who believed that "man is basically good," that goodness will triumph, and I know that Gordon wanted to believe that, too. He wanted to believe that what was happening to his family now was in God's hands, not his own. And not the hands of children. Indeedy.

Today, as I look back on that cold, skirling, shadowy morning, I think he was reaching a point where he was, at least for the moment, resigned. You could see it in his face. Chin up, ol' boy.

Pastor Rick.

The thing is, that when you give yourself over to the Lord, you will feel wonderfully weak. Yes, I remember Gordon St. Onge. We worked with him off and on, on solar and wind projects. And some fellowship. He was a man who wrestled with demons. But there was many a time you could see great peace in his eyes, perhaps greater than most who claim they are in a right way with the Lord.

 Penny.

The first clump of strangers reached the top of the hill, cameras in hand.

Linda, one of the Lincoln women, spoke in a manner of much pleasure, "I'll get more coffee!" and she headed up toward the nearest house, which had solar panels on the roof and geraniums in the window and was gotten to by a series of steep rock steps. Her brown tightly permed hair and frosty breath took on the deep gold of the rising sun. Now several of us Settlement women followed, ready to help.

 Steph.

More cars, bunching farther and farther back on both shoulders of the road.

I watched Gordon joining a group of men and teens, and Beezer, a woman from the Settlement, who were all hustling now to start the final work on the windmill.

The women at the tables said "Hello!" to the many strangers, and our hosts' dogs, old Malamutes, were sniffing the new arrivals over. Cannonball, the Scottie dog, was condemned to a leash due to her combat zone attitude.

A man and woman approached Bonnie Loo, whose youngest, Zack, was wrapped around one of her legs, looking sleepy, while Bonnie Loo herself was wrapped up in a big green sweater, her pregnancy not showing when she was dressed that way, but with her continuing morning sickness, her face had a nasty lime green cast to it, and the man and woman asked her if they had come to the right place, "is this *it?*" Bonnie Loo was not the best person to ask in any condition. A lonnnnnnnnnng pause, her golden-green fox-color eyes dizzling up and down their personages.

Then they told her that they heard on the radio "what is happening here."

I asked, "What is it that the radio said is happening?"

"Doing your thing, spreading it," the man replied warmly.

Bonnie Loo's eyes widened. With her contacts, her eyes *shone*. "Spreading what?"

The woman laughed. "The True Maine Militia."

A woman with a camera steps up. "What's that you're putting up? A radio tower?"

Another offered this evidence, "We heard about your event on WERU. We came up from Bangor."

"I heard it on public radio," admitted a young professional-looking-and-sounding woman behind her.

"You'll probably have a great turnout. It's supposed to be a pretty day," another stranger offered. "Less humid."

Now another, "What time does the meeting start?"

More and more and more cars.

A mob gathering.

And the big cold morning sun hiked up another notch.

 Bonnie Loo.

We were in the middle of nowhere and all of a sudden there's enough people to cram the city of Boston, Massachusetts.

 Claire.

I remember our elfin Josee's eyes tightening behind her always-polished pretty glasses. "Radio people heard t'iss about a meeting wit us, t'em. Funny t'ing, *we* didn't. I did not know off a meeting!"

Steph took one of the unexpected guests by the hands. "Want some coffee?"

From the group of ready-to-work men in the open field, where some strangers had wandered, Aurel was hollering, "From here on

t'ennertainment and chi'chat iss off limits here in t'iss *dangerous place*!
Everybody stay back! Excep't'crew putting up t'turbine! OUT OFF
T'WAY PLEASE T'ANK YOU!!!!" He had whipped off his Viet-
nam War bush hat and was gesturing with it for a serious clearing out.

More cars down there on the road.

 Penny.

A group of people in their twenties thereabouts were just arriving.
Collegy kids. I remember this very well. They asked Leona breathlessly, "Where is he?"

She said, "You mean Gordon, right?"

They said, "Yeah."

"Well, keep your eyes peeled. He's here. Get your cameras ready.
He's very photogenic." And she snickered.

I rolled my eyes.

And Bonnie Loo lifted Zack up onto her hip. He felt all over her
chest, hunting for a pocket, and when he found the pocket he was
looking for, he carefully placed inside it the dead grasshopper he'd
been holding. And he told it, "Rest." Bonnie Loo wasn't paying any
attention to this, but was squinting crankily at the tar road down at
the foot of the field, where a Caravan SUV thing, big enough to hold
a dozen more strangers, was easing to a stop.

 The work of dreams.

Aurel begins to climb the tower. Hatless, just that head of dark hair,
little gentlemanly beard, small scrawny quick little person in khaki
work shirt and Settlement-made jeans, small feet in small boots. Unencumbered. Unstoppable. Unequivocal hero of the moment.

Down in the vast "audience," a lot of held breaths and silence,
while into this silence stray a few oooooo's and aaahhhh's, one big
gasp and a whisper.

Aurel is screaming orders to his helpers and yes, accidentally drops
a screwdriver, which narrowly misses a head below. No hard hats here.
A whole box of Settlement-made fart pillows made it to Lincoln but
hard hats were forgotten.

Aurel hammers away quite some time, erecting a wooden tripod on top of the tower. Under the tripod's peak hangs a pulley.

The crowd slowly but surely thickens. And through it moves, with deliberateness, all the officers of the True Maine Militia (except Bree), recruiting.

Each new recruit writes down his or her name, address, phone. And checks off whether or not they are interested in "The Million Man Woman Kid Dog March" and other actions, perhaps some meetings at the Settlement. And each new recruit gets a True Maine Militia membership card pressed into his or her hand, a little blue card with the person's name scribbled in over the tiny American flag and then signed in impressive calligraphy by the "secretary of offense," BRIANNA ST. ONGE, and the recruiting commander, whose handwriting is just regular and girlish-looking, SAMAN-THA DALE BUTLER. Then there are flyers, as well as copies of *The Recipe*. Both versions.

Samantha really moves. Obviously, this is her element. And she is hard to miss. Hair like corn silk stirring around the shoulders of her camo BDU shirt. Her pants are tight and black. Black military boots. And a dynamic-looking black-band black-faced wristwatch. A rascally smile. No one can say "no."

Meanwhile, back up on the tower, Aurel is calling down to those below, "Get Bree!" and there are many adolescent shouts of "BREEEEE!" and "BRI-AHHHH-NAHH!"

And in the truck cab where she has been waiting, Bree shifts into gear. Now she deftly backs the flatbed flush to the foot of the tower, wild grasses under the tires hissing.

This is the truck with the dribbling sticky sunshine and the dribbling sticky words SUNSHINE ARMY on the door.

"Turbine crew!" Aurel bellers.

Egyptians Joel Barrington and Butch Martin and two young cheerful Lincoln men slide the inconveniently shaped four-hundred-pound wind plant to the tailgate area of the flatbed truck, now easing it into the hands of four teens and twenty-year-olds, who ease it to the ground. Jaime Crosman and a short smiley Lincoln girl quickly knot a thick cable around the thing as Bree pulls the creaking rumbling truck ahead a few feet.

Meanwhile, the other end of the cable rope dangles down, where it is threaded through the pulley more than fifty feet above, up there on the tripod. The free end is now fastened underneath the truck to the frame. Four approximately hundred- to hundred-and-fifty-pound beings leap aboard the flatbed for extra weight.

Bree *seems* casual, waiting at the wheel, smoking a cigarette, watching her mirrors.

Down on the road, more strangers, a quarter-mile of parked vehicles on one side of the roadway, a shorter line on the other, a bit of a traffic jam down the middle.

"Ready driver?!!!" the Settlement's Ray Pinette hoots.

Bree waves an arm.

"Well, then go!" calls a young Lincoln guy.

Bree kicks in the clutch, shifts to first. A man attached to the turbine by a strap climbs the tower in tandem with the turbine as it rises slowww and easy and Bree eases the old truck along velvety-smooth, the cable ever so taut.

Aurel waits at the top to receive the turbine, his dark gleamy eyes taking in every move of his helpers, the truck, the pulley, the cable, the guy wire, the wind plant.

When the wind plant arrives, he works quickly, bolting it in place, the sun in his face at times, too much sun.

And now, wrench in hand, Aurel waves to all in triumph and screams bloodcurdingly, "She's up!"

The mob applauds.

Now a single delirious kazoo.

And somewhere, a St. Onge baby bawls.

Again, from a future time, Geraldine St. Onge remembers well.

Aurel comes down the tower charged up. His eyes are like mirrors. A chatterbox in everyone's face. Josee brings him a huge glass of water and he takes it with both hands. Even though the water there at the Christian folk's property tastes like telephone booth quarters, he drinks it right down and his beard looks like a wet dog's. And Josee puts her hands on both sides of his face and she says slowly and deeply, "You big and nice."

 After the work.

Bree has found a clump of good-sized maples and for a while, she and Samantha Butler are alone, sitting under them in two webbed lawn chairs, hungrily eating their sandwiches and whispering. The lawn chairs feel good and when Samantha gets up to "go scoff up some root beer," Bree remains, flapping her stained and empty paper plate like a fan.

Whitney comes up behind her, pushes a knee into the back of her chair playfully.

"I know it's you," Bree says.

But now in the sun, with "Witty" and "Sammy," one on either side of her lawn chair, Bree can hear Gordon standing not very far away, sloshing and chomping. She sees it's a ham-cheese-pickle-looking sandwich. She places her paper plate underneath her chair on the grass and smiles at him. She feels lazy and good. Some of her carroty hair is pinned back with barrettes. The day is too bright and triumphant to feel fraught by a man who *tries* to govern her.

Suddenly, her lazy happy expression changes. She sees eight men.

They wear jeans or work pants but their camo BDU shirts are identical . . . well, some are tiger stripe, some woodland camo, but each has an embroidered patch high on the left sleeve, olive green with black BORDER MOUNTAIN MILITIA lettering around the form of a mountain lion.

The people who had been staring at Gordon all morning, or at Ellen St. Onge's black eye, these people, as Bree does, now stare instead at the eight uniformed men.

One of the eight wears the patch of captain, which is more elaborate, with an additional crescent underneath that reads: OXFORD COUNTY.

Wise-ass Samantha's voice from quite nearby calls out, "Gordon, see . . . it's your Rexy!"

Gordon doesn't reply.

Young Mickey Gammon (who is homeless, they say), age fifteen, is among them, dressed in the camo shirt and patch. Shirt fits him well. Looks spiffy. And he wears an expression of what seems like exaggerated dignity. Several men wear camo or plain green army caps of various styles, but Mickey just wears his usual tiny tail of streaky blond hair. Rex, bare-headed, steel-framed sunglasses and a flash of noon sun off his elaborate black-faced watch, walks over and stands next to Gordon, just stands there looking around, and Gordon has one eyebrow raised, the other eye squinted, his ultimate deranged look. He digs furiously at his bearded chin and finally says, "Could you tell me why you just happen to be in little Lincoln, Maine, when I just happen to be in little Lincoln, Maine?"

Rex says tonelessly, "We had business."

"That's not possible, I believe in coincidences to a point." He is staring with his eyes like pale green arrows into Rex's.

Just now, Aurel Soucier is hurrying past with five arm-swinging preteen boys, and Rex nods and Aurel nods back.

Gordon presses, "So you and the militia were just on your way to the Yukon when you looked up and saw us up here on the hill."

Rex *almost* smiles, eyes shadowy behind the dark glasses.

Gordon looks into the remains of his sandwich, which is dribbling pickle juice through his fingers. "Something secret, huh?"

"Not at all. T'was the preparedness expo in Bangor. We talked about it before, remember? And I gave you the flyer about it. And as I recall, that M.O.M.* article. But you don't really read any of the materials I give you." He looks away now, stroking one side of his dark mustache with good-humored irritation. In the brightness of the day, close range like this, Gordon sees his old friend is getting, yes, old. A few less hairs at the temples, five or six gray hairs in the sideburns. A line across the forehead, harder lines around the mouth, and a thinness of the lips, a softness under the chin, settling, leaving a bony line along the shaved parts of the jaws. And what's behind those dark glasses? More age, yuh, and fifty years of disappointments, yet the guy still stands like a fighter.

---

* Militia of Montana.

Gordon sees that Bree has hung her head. Resting her eyes? Tired? All the teenagers up late last night giggling and whispering, drinking more sodas (soda being against the mother-made rules at the Settlement). Noticeable how Bree spends less and less time with the Settlement "grown-ups." Her eyes are closed but Gordon knows she's listening for all she's worth to him and Rex.

Rex says, "All the New England militias were represented, Maine, Mass, New Hampshire, Vermont. Everyone well represented. Maine militias were *very* well represented. The Virginia Militia, the man I mentioned to you who you've probably forgotten, since you never listen to me . . . they never made it after all. But there was representation from Virginia. Mostly just New England, of course. They have expos elsewhere as you would know, if you had been reading the materials I gave you."

"I recall now about the gentleman from Virginia. Brother, I've had a lot on my mind."

A Malamute walks directly toward Rex, but stays back a few yards, staring up into Rex's face, then growls at Rex and moves on.

"Funny," says Gordon. "He's liked everyone else." Now he pushes the last of his sandwich into his mouth, says with his mouth full, "Help yourself. Lotsa food. Lincoln people churning out the goodies."

Rex nods.

Gordon swallows, says, "Bangor is still a long ways south. Nice of you to . . . uh . . . stop by."

Rex looks around, sinks his thumbs into the pockets of his work pants. "There's weirdness going on right now." He looks at Gordon. "Something in the air. A lotta talk."

Gordon chews faster, noisier.

Rex says, "People using your name at the expo."

Gordon nods.

"Patriots want to know you."

Gordon flutters his eyes exaggeratedly, presenting the look of a person everybody wants to know.

Rex says, "And everybody seemed to know you were here . . . in Lincoln. They've been paying a lot of attention to you. Keeping track of you. Checking you out. Mark Bunn asked if I knew you, you and me living in the same town."

"What did you say? Did you say you knew me?"

Rex is really into his militia mode now. He speaks tonelessly, which strikes Gordon as both funny and sort of neat. "I told him I knew you."

"Did you tell him we used to suck pussy together? You know, at the fair?"

Rex flushes. Gets clown cheeks. Remains silent.

Gordon asks, "Okay, so what did they say about me?"

"They think you have a militia . . . you know . . . that which your kids wrote in the paper. And all that other newspaper foolishness prior to that. It confused them. They think you're . . . you know . . . a militia. They think you're sympathetic."

"I am! I *am* sympathetic!" Gordon chokes just a little, and something half-chewed flies out of his mouth just past Rex's sleeve.

"Well, in a twisted way," Rex says grumpily.

Gordon looks through the trees at the group of camouflage shirts that are circled around the food table. The notorious Willie Lancaster with the slightly bucked front teeth and Jack-the-Ripper beard is here. Willie hasn't warmed up to his surroundings yet, isn't his usual frisky self. He just skulks around, smiling like a cat that's just swallowed a whole jungle of canaries.

Gordon says, "I see your main man is staying out of jail. Talk about *twisted*."

Rex says nothing to this.

Gordon notices that Jane Meserve is over by the table that has the big cakes on it. She isn't wearing her secret agent heart-shaped glasses at the moment, but she is staring at the militiamen in a way like she's memorizing details.

A stranger, a short woman, mid-thirties, with glasses and a T-shirt that reads: *I ♥ My RADTECH,* approaches Gordon. Just behind her is a man with glasses and a close shave, a baby in a baby sling, and another man with no baby, both men in pastel knit shirts and khaki shorts and sandals, one shirt the color of a rose, the other the color of lemon sherbet. Neither man seems to be with the woman or with each other, just kind of trailing along. The woman looks into Gordon's face as she steps closer and closer, steps in front of Rex but not facing Rex, not acknowledging Rex.

Rex raises his chin a notch, drops his hands behind his back cop-style, keeping his feet apart, and surveys the crowd as the woman asks Gordon, "Are you Gordon St. Onge?"

Gordon smiles boyishly, "Yep."

"It's wonderful to meet you," she tells him, her eyes fixed on his eyes, which are, in person, even more striking and more chillingly pale than in newspapers. And his lashes and brows so dark, kind of Shakespearean and dramaesque. Rex's eyes are rather pale and striking, too (which is probably why, years ago, "The Fly," a very nice reefer dealer in a bar, thought they were brothers), but his are behind dark glasses and staring down at the tar road, where more cars are arriving.

Gordon asks, "What's your name?"

"Peggy Moffett. I'm here with a bunch of us from work. We thought we'd come over and see if you were still here. Some said it was Sunday, some said no, it was today." She glances back over at the crowded tables.

Gordon wipes his hands on the ass of his work pants and then takes the woman in his arms and kisses the top of her head. This is all quick and playful but the woman shrieks and is now all quivery and hoppy and high-colored, like the winner on a game show, and this draws her friends, who hurry from the tables, several women in jeans and T-shirts, funny hats that read *Bert's Fried Clams* and they all line up for hugs and Gordon hugs them all and smooches their ears. They all shriek and hop around and laugh. Gordon turns to a lost-looking man wearing a snowy T-shirt with the Bert's Fried Clams logo written small on one side of his chest. Probably Bert himself. Gordon clasps the man's hand hard, saying, "Good to meet you. Where do you live?" And the man tells Gordon about his situation, which is harried and hurting, and how it seems lately he is up against a wall.

 Willie Lancaster in the background.

Gordon proceeds to smooch three little girls who have hurried here moments ago to find out what all the squealing and hopping was about. The group here by the maples gets bigger. There is some conversation about wind plants and solar energy. And organized money usurping the rights of human people, the obscenity of money buying access to our national and state capitals.

A few yards away is the soft click of a 35mm camera, somebody capturing the moment. Several distance shots of Gordon St. Onge and

Richard York standing there together, and perhaps in these photos part of Brianna "St. Onge" will show there behind them, one knee and a leg of her jeans perhaps.

Now, more people are coming to Gordon, two or three at a time, wanting to shake his hand. They look up at him in that way that says *You are much taller than your newspaper pictures, but boy do you really look just like your newspaper pictures. We'd know you anywhere.*

Such a preponderance of pastels. A man wearing a knit shirt and tuck-waisted shorts the colors of bananas and whipped cream stands near reading a flyer. A woman a distance to his left. Collared knit shirt of lilac, shorts palest khaki, hair cut at satisfying angles. She tips a cup of coffee to her lips. Beyond her two women together. Cantaloupe and celery shirts. Two cups of coffee. All edging nearer to "the Prophet." Here they come. Peach. Vanilla. White and chartreuse. White and white. Little polyester fanny packs around their waists. White long-visored golf caps.

Rex says in a low voice, "This is weird."

Gordon groans his agreement, then steps back and behind Bree's chair, places both hands on her shoulders and her shoulders shrug lovingly against his palms. Gordon, always playful and affectionate with all women. You wouldn't know which ones were wives if you didn't know. He almost never publicly makes *serious* passes at any of *his* own wives, nothing, no serious caresses to one wife in front of another. And yet *this,* whatever it is that is between him and this girl, is it definable? Bree lays her head back against his belt buckle and his fingers knead more deeply into her shoulders, neck, and skull, her red hair gushes and exclaims through his fingers.

Notorious Willie Lancaster, gray-eyed and sly, yes, known to be boorish and lewd, yes, known to be merry, he is quite near now, standing with another militiaman. He watches Gordon's hands on Bree, then he looks at Bree's face, in profile to him, as she now draws her head forward, her expression triumphant.

  More strangers.

A great thickening and layering and mixing of faces, clicking cameras, shoulders and elbows, all ears trying to pick up on the subject of talk, and Gordon's reflex to their attention to him is to get unnecessarily louder, "Any of you hear of the Oglemobile?"

A voice in the back layer of the crowd yells, "Yessss!"

As Gordon rattles off details about an ingenious car mechanic, "a real tinkerer who wanted to make a four-cycle engine run longer on a gallon of gas," a good half of the crowd just starts to bemusedly watch Gordon's teeth and tongue as these mesmerizing words fall from his mouth, words like "micromesh screen," "carburetor jets," "brass fittings," "alley ways," "intake pinhole," "atomized effect," "screen below the main jets," "four half and halfs," "twenty-five hours straight on a pint of gas," "one hundred plus miles to the gallon," "making kits the average person could work with."

They watch how his thickened fingers illustrate and shape these images. Yes, a few guys add details to this, as they had heard the Oglemobile story before, while cameras click, camcorders sweep, one pausing on that young Settlement mother not far behind Gordon, changing a baby's embroidery-edged cloth diaper on the grass in the dappled shade of the trees, baby waving a flower, baby's hand fat and dimpled, baby quite noisy in her ease and joy with the moment.

Now Gordon is shouting to the crowd, "This feller, this inventor . . . guess what he does!"

"Gets a patent!" one of the strangers calls out.

"Yes! Yes!" Gordon shouts back. "And then . . ."

"Gets rich!" someone exclaims with a single punctuating clap of her hands.

Jane Meserve, who has come to stand close to Gordon, is now facing the crowd. Such commanding dark eyes. And see her floofy movie star hair! Given extra glamoury touches by the Settlement beauty crew the evening before the trip. And a Settlement-made jumper, a plaid of powdery pinks and grays, precisely smocked. Lots of perky buttons. Black tights. Her beloved difficult-to-walk-in thick-heeled sandals. There is just *no place* where glamour isn't a must. Now as another camera clicks and another camcorder sweeps around, Jane strikes a sexy pose and smiles lushly and MTV-ishly. And now, seeing that so many eyes angle away from Gordon's face down onto her, she lifts her skirt just a little, to show a bit of her black-tighted thigh.

"Yes! He got rich!" someone off to the right calls.

A couple others yip and yahoo over this delicious scenario of instant wealth.

'Welllll, maybe he did, maybe he didn't." Gordon's eyes blaze over the crowd. "That's the pivot here. That's the basic deep-most philosophical really-screwed-up American faith reflex, that the purpose of inventiveness is to get rich!"

People squint with bewilderment.

Rex surveys the crowd. Behind his dark glasses, those eyes brush over dozens of hands, waists, pockets with cigarettes or reading glasses, the way a shirt hangs on a certain guy, the way some people walk, the suspiciousness of some people's mannerisms. He has folded his arms across his chest, feet still apart, black military boots shined impressively. He exudes a meticulous, all-in-order, machinelike countenance you would not be inclined to mess with. And this expression of Rex's never alters one iota over the next forty-five minutes as Gordon preaches to the crowd the things that cause him to be *more* animated, *insanely* animated, shared fears and hard truths that pull more and more and more and more lives toward his own.

And so, Bree is satiated.

 Pushing through the crowd.

A woman with a long, neatly trimmed braid, jeans, dressy jacket, glasses, nice green eyes, and a tape recorder reveals in a professional schooled, nonaccent which newspaper it is that employs her. "Tell me, Gordon, what is it that has brought you people up here to Lincoln today?"

Gordon is on one knee, wiping mustard off the face of one of his young sons with his own red bandana. With his face trapped in his father's grip, the child's eyes can only roll up sideways to the face of the woman.

A lot of questions coming at Gordon at once. People are pushing. Good-natured but urgent. Noisy.

The woman asks her question again, louder and somewhat rephrased. Gordon stands slowly to his full height and looks down into the reporter's face, his own face reddened from having had his head down, his eyes bloodshot from the unrelenting sun of three days, of mixed-up sleep, and too many people pulling him too many ways, and yet he is charged, faster and faster, head humming. "You mean you want me to kind of condense what I already just said for the last . . . uh . . . forty-five minutes?"

She laughs pleasantly. "Well, sure."

"I'm sorry," he says softly, not hostile, just soft. "I can't. I can't condense it."

"Just a few words?" she begs him pleasantly.

And he wonders, "Are you the only reporter here?"

"I'm not sure. But—"

He turns and looks toward the windmill, the three blades as motionless as a tired face with too many dangerous secrets. He looks back at her.

While people take this as their opportunity to hit him with their questions and suggestions and fears, saying, "Gordon?" and tapping his arm, the reporter slips from her big canvas satchel a handful of papers and pushes them into Gordon's hand. It's the condensed form of *The Recipe*, and the thick one that he and Bree had worked on together, their plot to save the world. And there are several flyers he's never laid eyes on before. The familiar bigfoot creature, the Abominable Hairy Patriot, is plastered all over each, wearing different outfits, patriot hat, or sometimes a wide singing mouth where usually the creature's face is all just white hair. He sees that one of these flyers is actually a song sheet. "This Land's Not My Land," a skewed version of that Woody Guthrie favorite. Another: "The No-Wing Militia Song." At the bottom of each paper reads: SEE YOUR TRUE MAINE MILITIA RECRUITING OFFICER TODAY!

He looks up into the reporter's eyes, and at the others standing around, looking eager but patient.

Reporter tells him, "The recruiting officer of the True Maine, a Ms. Samantha Butler . . . and Ms. Whitney St. Onge, both called me at different times last week. They said you'd be here today . . . and that you'd be interested in speaking with me."

Gordon glances over at the trees where he last saw Bree but she's gone. Now he looks down at his feet.

The reporter is talking. "Well, I've already met these girls here today, interviewed them . . . already. And they were kind enough to supply me with all that great stuff!" She laughs a friendly in-collusion sort of laugh. "So now I'm wondering what kind of comments you might make, if not about your wonderful speech here today, then about the True Maine Militia and its goals. And perhaps the Border Mountain Militia, which is also here today, I see. You're a member?"

Gordon studies her a long moment, then, raising one eyebrow over a crazed-looking green eye, slowly raises a fist and bellers, "GOD SAVE THE REPUBLIC!" Who but she would have seen square-on the razzy twinkles in that one wider eye, but she was not familiar enough to decipher his joshing from nonjoshing and it wouldn't matter anyway, for a bunch of cameras click and the reporter gently scrawls across her lined pad, nods, and says, "Thank you," then again laughs pleasantly.

 Lorraine Martin recalls.

I guess he was goofing around.

 Steph St. Onge.

Oh, boy.

 Beth St. Onge.

He came off as a fucking nut with that fist business. Hitler. Stalin. Mussolini. Ready to do a send-off with the big tanks. Maine the Republic, ha! ha! More like Maine the dot.

 Claire St. Onge.

He was doing it for Rex, I guess. Rex mattered so much. He would beat up on Rex during their front porch and kitchen debates, then make it up to him with *this*, whatever *this* was. The republic? The fist? A war? The good brother?

 Gail St. Onge.

I understood Gordon completely at that moment. It was like he was winking all the while.

Glennice St. Onge.

He had his reasons.

 Butch Martin looking back to that day.

Well, um, you should've seen the reporter's face. She was lappin' it up. They're all alike. They're like pigeons. Eat your popcorn, then gone. Only a couple days later they fly over and shit the popcorn out on top of your head. So Gordon, man, he feeds 'em shit.

 The very last night in Lincoln.

With leaf crunchings and branch snappings, he trudges up into the woods to piss, which is cheating and thoughtless because the Christians have a rented kept-spotless "porta potty" close by.

He is nearly finished when he hears someone coming. He half turns in the twilight and makes out two pale circles floating toward him. Gives his heart a creeped-out hop. Yeah, it's her with some of that putty-like turquoise war painted around her eyes, that paint the kids spilled instead of prettying up their small windmill models as planned. He groans, stuffs himself back into his fly, zips.

She arrives with a sigh, a poof of breath smelling of soda pop and donuts, all that fun Christian food. It drifts serpentinely around his head.

"Imagine being Adam and Eve," she whispers with a happy shiver. "No one else but these trees and us."

"I'm sorry. Really—"

"Sorry?"

"I'm sorry, Brianna, that we aren't a *real* couple."

"I don't mean *that*."

"What *do* you mean?"

"No bones and no weeping." Her whisper has that usual smoke-harshened edge to it.

"I don't get it."

"No tools. No slaving. No birth pains. No hell. Just peace. And mushrooms. And nuts. Ede*nnnn*."

"Right."

She plays with the hemmed neckline of her T-shirt, trying to decide something, her pale hands appearing as brutish spiders in the dark.

He says, "Hear it?"

"Hear what?"

"The woods."

She is listening.

He says, "The silence, you hear it?"

"Yup."

"That's fear. That's what that silence is. That's what peace is."

"Sure," she says.

Says he, "There are hundreds of creatures but no sound. Only sneaking."

Says she, "Well, some of the silence is stalking . . . you know, hunting."

"But even the hunter is afraid. If there's a miss, there is terrible hunger."

"Sure," she admits.

"And," he goes on, "In the spring . . . the birds . . . that birdsong isn't joy. And the woodpeckers beating on ladders. It's not play. It's *strain*. Trying to beat the other guy at winning the lady lest you become the end of the line. It's all fear. All strain." He squints to see perfectly her turquoise encircled eyes, less clown, more primal jubilation. He touches her cheek, one rough finger against the still-wet putty-like paint. "Why'd you do this?"

"Kids did it. Kids are the thing, remember?" She giggles. "Winning the lady. Building up the population."

He draws back his hand. His heart begins to pound. He has learned to truly fear her.

She explains. "It had to do with round things. Eyes first. They were all fascinated with my face. First they felt my eyes. Like research. The kids that live up here said they never saw a face like mine. So they painted me. To make me pretty, they said."

His sadness rocks him.

She laughs sassily. "*Kids*. Kids are the thing."

He listens to his own fear. And his vapidness. How unplayful he has become lately. He listens to his plunking heart, not the rich silence around him.

She strikes a match.

He takes one step back, away from the stink of cigarette.

The sound of her lips and lungs, teeth and nose and audacious throat, are mixed with the silence like a big lake lapping its beaches. Not even one single giggle. She smokes. And smokes. Ashes fall to her boots. She bends to smoodge them out on the leather. What is there to say? Moments fly off in smoke.

Then he leans into her, a hand at her back. "Who are you, Brianna? I *need* to know."

"One of your wives." She giggles. Finally. She stomps out the cig. She takes his free hand and kisses his palm. "I'm still mad. So don't take this for forgiveness."

He bear hugs her. Then, "Don't take this for forgiveness, either."

She coos against his worn-softest chambray (leaving turquoise paint?), her voice forced into high melodious register, like poetry. "Once you and me, it was perfect. And clear. Now it's complex."

"Muddy," says he.

Her painted goggle eyes hover not far below his for she is, yes, a tall young woman. "Yeah, muddy."

In a few moments she turns to go back to the shushy murmuring tents, one kazoo now pitching out into the consuming dark a melody that would be painfully sweet if it were on fiddle or flute, but the kazoo gives it a tickle.

Gordon still alone in the trees pats his pockets for the aspirin bottle.

 History as it happens (as recorded by Jane Meserve, edited by Alyson Lessard).

Lincoln was fun. People took pictures of us. A girl got a whole can of paint on her, which fell off a truck and messed her hair and outfit. We stayed late because people wanted to tell Gordie their troubles. Some losing their houses. Some with too many jobs but poor. One man cried.

But Gordie hugged him a long time. People wanted Gordie. Some weren't crying but they wanted hugs anyway. I ate FIVE brownies and guess what. There was Coke.

 The mail increaseth.

A brown paper envelope from Bangor, stuffed with a full-page "feature" arrives in the St. Onge mailbox down at the farm place on Heart's Content Road. Color pictures of the smiling sun on the truck door and dribbling words: SUNSHINE ARMY, and then a close-up of three painty, dirty children. One of Samantha Butler and Margo St. Onge passing out flyers into outstretched hands. One of Gordon with his arms raised, yes, looking like a prophet on the hill, a bit higher on that hill than the crowd before him. And the windmill shows up there behind him on the higher hill, and some seamless sky, all framed by the dark lethargic boughs of a hemlock behind which the photographer stood across the tar road. This was when someone pestered Gordon to do his speech, though he didn't really hesitate. His cup runneth over.

Meanwhile, there was a great close-up photo of the sea-captain-bearded hefty militia guy and two Lincoln area teens picking deep fried zucchini slices (as good as potato chips) from a platter on the goodies table. The photo clearly shows the Border Mountain Militia patch on the man's sleeve. In fact, the patch seems central to this picture. And then, of course, one close-up of Gordon with Rex.

It's the photos that take the stage. The article is short, the size of a cracker, riddled with misquotes and misconceptions, not necessarily intentional, mostly just the way things are viewed through the eyes of people who see the world *in a certain way*.

Gordon tosses this article into a cardboard box under his desk, sits back down in the old oak office chair and swivels away from the desk, puts his face in his hands, listening to the silence of the dimly lit farmhouse kitchen. The phone rings on the wall behind him, maybe the fortieth time today, and beyond the screened window, the tall grass bugs sing their ancient same song, over and over and over and over.

Geraldine St. Onge (wife of Gordon, cousin to Claire).

One night at our big meal soon after Lincoln, Gordon stood and banged a jar with a fork to get everyone to shut up. He made this announcement. "If media and sightseers show up to look at us when you're coming or going, like out by the gate here, this is not cool. Hey, nobody talks to a reporter, okay? Even if one lays down in front of our wheels. There can't be any conversation. This craziness with the press has gone far enough. Okay?"

He even had a couple of youngsters go down and nail up another sign on the gate. It read, ANYONE TRESPASSES WILL BE SHOT. TRY IT.

I told him this word choice was a bad mistake. Aurel and Eddie and Raymond and Paul and Stuart and John all told him it was a bad mistake. Maybe "mistake" isn't the word. Maybe it was something already out of our hands, a future already written and Gordon was just a tool of destiny.

 Rex.

At first the dream is ordinary, the usual illogical chopped-up flutter of memory but Rex senses it is about to swerve. Like horror movie music, but not, it sets the stage. In the dream there is simply *a window* and he is lying down. Gordon's face glides into view and stops. No, but it is not Gordon's big face filling the window. Well, it was, but now it is a planet that has gone off course and hovers within inches of the glass. The thing is all lighted up as the moon is, only this one is swirled in blue and red on white like a prized knocker marble. So it's not Gordon's face. It has no eyes. No mouth yakking away. But, somehow *it is* Gordon. Rex's terror-knowledge tells him so. And it is beyond humankind to stop it, this vast mass of rock, gaseous seas, and light bouncing off Rex's house. And what comes next is unknowable. You can't *prepare* for what is buried by night daze. Heart belting out blood, he wakes, having already made his usual girlie scream. The shame of his daughter or mother waking to such a sound.

Carmel St. Onge, one of Gordon's daughters, almost thirteen at the time, recalls from a future time.

The True Maine Militia intensified. But Gordon was back to red light again, soured over the Bangor action, even though HE WAS THE ONE who messed it up, so our plans for a State House siege were *secret*. We met *in the woods, at night*. We made contact with Senator Mary, who would give us up-to-date intelligence on when the governor would be in his office. We had almost every little kid at the Settlement recruited. Their mums were to help with costumes and protest signs. A bunch of older boys were coming along and we stole one of Rex's men, fifteen-year-old Mickey Gammon, stoic as ever. Gawd, those predator gray eyes!

So we were ready and waiting for when Senator Mary would give us the word.

OCTOBER

 The plot thickens thicker. Down in North Egypt Village, Gordon, on his way home from out-of-town errands, sees the old farm jeep owned by a neighbor, Danny Wicks, parked outside the new Egypt House of Pizza, and decides to stop now to settle some business.

It is about the sale of sheep. Four sheep Danny wants to buy. He and Danny stand next to the jeep, under the lights of the pizza store's entrance, while inside the jeep, Danny's wife waits, stroking her little dog and smoking. Danny has strawberry-blond hair and clean-shaven businessman looks from the neck up. He's wearing a blue and gray plaid flannel shirt and has farmer's hands.

Two diagonally parked vehicles away, in front of the blazingly lit but closed real estate office, a group of young people stand in a fat, thick, sly little cluster. Gordon likes "loitering" young people better when they are loud. The car they lean and slouch against is small and white. Nondescript. No bumper stickers. And then he looks up, right into the eyes of Glory York, who is among these young people. Rex York's only child, the face, like *the face that launched a thousand ships,* whose kiss, just one kiss, could make men immortal. Or damned. Nineteen-year-old Glory York. Chewing gum slowly. Staring at him.

Danny Wicks is now relating to Gordon details of the theft on Mushy Meadows Road, Elmer Hanson's heart attack, Ron Brackett's son joining the Masons, and how next year there will be an epidemic of brown tails.

Gordon has heard how wild Glory has become. He hadn't heard it from Rex. Rex never talks about life, only strategies.

Gordon feels it is necessary to give her a little friendly smile, wiggles his fingers hello, looks away again, nodding as Danny fills him in on the two site possibilities for the proposed town salt shed.

She used to be pudgy. With clammy little hands and a happy smile. A million freckles. Sweet-natured. She loved games. She was good at board games; outdoor games, too. Not always a winner. But dogged and good with rules. A cheerful loser. Her dark auburn hair back then was in two short fat sawed-off ponytails. She was a good swimmer like her mother, Marsha. Often in summer, Marsha and Glory were there at Promise Lake with dripping hair and towels around their shoulders. Glory was likely as not goose-bumped. But chattering happily. Not complaining.

He looks up now to take in more of this picture. One of those little strappy tops cut short to show the belly. Mostly unbuttoned. In fact, he thinks it isn't buttoned at all, but there does seem to be at least one button. At the bottom. And between her semi-exposed breasts, a twinkle. Some sort of crystal on a delicate chain. And "across the eyes," she looks just like Rex.

 Two nights later. At 9:45 p.m. Parking lot by the Quonset huts, Gordon and Aurel get out of the cab of the flatbed truck that puts off the almost smoky scent of the just-delivered load of cedar shingles.

Aurel, ever quick, lunges off toward his house with a cardboard box under each arm, some stuff neighbors left down at the new gatehouse.

Gordon stays behind to see why there is a light left on in a nearby car. Then he hears weeping. And Alyson Lessard's whisper, "I think it *is*! I can't leave you like this!"

Gordon smells reefer. He walks closer.

He sees Alyson scooching down by the driver's door of the car and he sees it is not a Settlement car. He sees that it is a small white car and now Alyson is hopping up. "Gordon! Please come see! She's hurt her ankle bad! It's swelling!"

And now stepping around Alyson, he sees Glory York. All that tangly dark auburn hair. Never wears makeup. Still a bit freckled, as when she was a kid. Blue eyes, very blue. A face that displays no range of expressions but seems cast. Classically handsome. No makeup needed.

But that's not what catches his eye now. Not her face. But her two long legs, and her flouncy rose-colored skirt hiked way up. A chilly night. Cold leather-like seats.

"She fell," Alyson explains. "She hurt her ankle bad. It's swelling, isn't it?"

Gordon now realizes that Alyson is holding a chicken in her arms. A black sex-link hen, the one that has become such a pet with many of the Settlement kids and adults, too. It's one of those birds with "personality." He sees that Alyson (Paul and Jacquie Lessard's girl) is nothing like the fast-lane Glory, but such a softie, the hen held tightly against her oversized jacket. Long skirt. Thick socks. Moccasins. Little pixie haircut. Small cheery face . . . well, usually it is cheery. Brown eyes that tonight are worried.

Glory's voice, "I'm so embarrassed."

"Which ankle is it?" he asks, putting a hand on the back of her seat.

She raises one of her silky-looking tanned knees. Draws in her breath sharply.

He doesn't smell any alcohol. Just another little whiff of the marijuana smoke, which seems more outside the car than in it.

He scooches down and takes the foot and ankle into his hands. Glory jerks now, cries out, "oooooo," then laughs a little. Nervously. "I'm so sorry. I'm so embarrassed." And then, "Do you think it's broken?"

He works the ankle joints a bit and again she howls, prettily. He thinks she is faking this for attention but the ankle does feel thick. He takes the other foot and ankle in his hands. In order to compare, yes.

He looks up to her face, lighted by the dome light that is a cheap sort of light, a thin gray, and he asks, "Where are your shoes?"

She laughs. "I hate shoes." She does this little shivery business with her arms and shoulders that draws his eyes to her unbuttoned little jacket and black little short shirt thing, mostly unbuttoned. No bra. Something that looks like an old coin twisting on its long delicate chain between her breasts. "I can't really bear shoes."

But she loves shoes. She loves clothes. She's a dresser.

He asks, "What happened?"

"She tripped," Alyson answers quickly.

"It's so dark out here, Gordon!" Glory scolds. "You need those big pink lights like Shop 'n Save." She laughs. "I promise I won't sue you." No pouting of the mouth, no scowls. Her beautiful face remains strictly composed. "You *know* I wouldn't sue you."

He suggests she wait before seeing a doctor, till morning at least. "Just keep the foot up and use ice."

"Ice?" She stretches her leg, worming her foot out the open door, her knee brushing his arm. She points her toes. "Owwww." Then, "Oh, I just don't want to bother any of you guys! This is so embarrassing."

"Is the old man home?"

Her face softens. "Oh, Bumpa gone nighties, all poopy out from big hard day."

Gordon tries to remember. How many years since the child sat nowhere else but on her father's lap, snuggling, eyes cast down, doing this baby talk thing and Rex's arms around her, sometimes tightly, his face like stone but he would, yes, he really would whisper back to her lovingly, something possibly not quite language.

Gordon shakes his head, smiling. He says, "Well, the hospital will *cost*. And for something like this, you'll be there all night in the waiting room watching people cough. I'll get somebody to drive you home and if you can get through the night, your regular doctor can look at it cheaper and quicker." He stands up. "You sit tight, okay?" He turns away, takes a few steps.

Behind him, Glory has burst into tears. He makes a disgusted face to himself and Alyson shouts, "Gordon! Come back! Pleeeeze!"

Glory's crying is real. Nothing fake about those sobs. He feels horribly guilty that he has doubted her. He reappears at the open car door beside Alyson, who is still hugging the quiet hen to her jacket. He

says, "Hop over, Glory. I'll take you home. Alyson, get in the back.
We'll swing around and tell your folks so they won't miss you. And
we can get rid of the hen."

"Pooky," Alyson corrects him. Then she's in the backseat in a flash.
With Pooky, the hen.

But Glory can't seem to get up. She sobs, "You hate me!"

Gordon squints an eye.

"When I was little . . . do you remember this? You kissed my nose
to make it better. I never forgot that. I had a nosebleed. So you kissed
my nose and it stopped! And I have always loved you for that . . . but
now I hurt and you hate me. You act funny and cold. You. Hate. Me."

"It isn't that," Gordon says, patting the top of her car.

She tries to sniff through her tear-stuffy nose. "Alyson, he's gotten
so mean! Fame has changed him. He used to be nice."

"Come on outta there," Gordon says. "If you get in the other seat, I'll
drive you home. See, I'm nice." He speaks this in a warm playful way.

She sighs, "Alyson . . . help me reach my bag. It's on the floor here
. . . in front. It hurts to reach."

With the hen still in her arms, Alyson clambers out the door opposite the one she got in, opens the front passenger door.

Glory says, "I came here tonight special to see him, to show him
something." (*Him* means Gordon.)

Alyson positions the corduroy shoulder bag daintily on Glory's lap,
on that little bunchiness of her hiked-up skirt and much bareness of
the thighs. Glory paws desperately through this bag, sniffing back her
tears, her nose seeming even more plugged now.

She finds a little book.

Gordon squats down so that he is lower now and she is higher,
up on the seat. The poor dome light makes the little book show
up unsettlingly significant there in her fingers. Like a declaration
that could crush a nation. Turns out it is only a little journal filled
with Glory's handwriting, a book Gordon gave her years ago, she
explains. He can't remember doing this but supposes he did. Like
with Jane. Only instead of the spy stuff and the drawings of Settlement misdeeds, Glory would have kept track of joys, visits to her
grandfolks, friends at school (mostly public school), favorite TV

shows at home, visits to the Settlement, especially the two Settlement ponies (gone now) and board games, and the skits that she was too shy to be part of, but she would definitely write about them. They mattered to her. Her handwriting is large, with little round bubbles for dots on *j*s and *i*s.

"I was eleven," she explains.

Now, getting closer to her, he smells the beer. She tells him to keep the book awhile. "It's fun to read about the past. Mostly stuff I forgot all about."

He sees one Budweiser can sideways on the floor. Empty.

He slips the little book into his shirt pocket, then tells her playfully, "Come on, leap on outta there and let me behind the wheel. This chariot's going to roll."

"But I'm stuck here forever!" she laughs. "Poor ol' ankle!"

So he has to help her out of the seat. She hobbles along with him to the other door, *ooooo*ing and *owww*ing.

He is reserved, cold? None of his usual ear fondling and bear hugs. Not with this one. There are possibilities here that fill him with terrors small and large. Terrors in every shape and texture and malignant pose. Something that keeps coming to him in the manifestation of Rex's eyes.

  Next day.

In some moment alone, he reads Glory's tiny journal, written in her bloated curly handwriting, that nevertheless tries to fit so many words on each page, margins gorged, every space filled with her abundance. And the word LOVE always in caps. Love is, indeed, a certain kind of genius, of hard intelligence, a way of organizing information, a way of analogy . . . "this" means "this" so "that" means "that" . . . and *the world is precious and thrilling and I trust it*. Yeah, Glory trusts this world. She has no nagging doubts. And thus she shall celebrate! Unlike her father, Rex, she sees no set traps, no deep holes, no more than what you'd have if you sat home and watched TV and died from the inside out. And so all Gordon's protective instincts rise.

He slips the little book into his shirt pocket again. If only she were that tiny. That easily swathed in safety.

The vow.

And he whispers wearily to that which is in his mind's eye, Rex's hardening face. "Brother, you don't have to worry. I'll never touch that little girl."

 Whitney.

Yeah, we had finally reached Senator Mary again and she had given us the "go!" on our State House plan. Got the governor's schedule for that whole week, which was the key missing piece up till then. The True Maine Militia was bracing for action. The next day would be D-day. "D for democracy," we said. Agents and operatives would not have to beg to get one of our blue oak-tag militia membership cards. The sky would snow down membership cards. *Welcome!* was *our* militia motto yodeled out to the wide world.

 History (the very recent past)

"Maine is no longer a warm place in the heart. It's a line on a spreadsheet."

—Governor King, speaking in Bangor
circa 2000 *Bangor Daily*

 Oceanna St. Onge recalls the next day.

We marched along the old State House tunnel and up the winding stairs to the Hall of Flags. Hup! Hup! BAROOOOM! Hup! Hup! Hup!

It was sort of like our solstice march. Only no mountain and no sun. We had all the littlest pipsqueaks from home and basically kids of all ages. Even Butchie, Evan, and C.C., Cory, too. Jaime, Seth Miner, Steven and Eben and Jakey Savage. They offered to help out, you see. Though I caught a few smirks. Mickey wore his Border Mountain Militia jacket. But mostly it was tykes. The whole thing was Bree's idea. She kept saying, "Kids are the thing." Flags. Banners. Big drum.

Squirt guns. Kazoos. Brooms. And one never-before-used plunger. Big cardboard signs saying stuff like BOMB THE CORPORATE CAMPAIGN FINANCE SCHEME. SPARE THE HUMANS.

 Rachel Soucier telling what she remembers of the "siege."

There were public schoolteachers and their "best" students with science displays. Boy, these teachers went into cardiac arrest to see "bad" kids like us on the loose in a place of such high order and majesty.

 C.C. Crocker looking back.

Some of the True Maine Militia were eating the school people's donuts, which were on a big tray for the public. *We* thought we were *the public*. They thought we were rats and mice. Only corporate lobbyists got smiles when *they* plucked a donut from the tray.

 Aleta St. Onge, who was a preteen at that time recalls.

They didn't like our message.

 Samantha Butler.

It was the Maine State House in Augusta, *the people's* house. The office of the governor was upstairs. It was the True Maine Militia's first offensive and official action. We had a grand speech on democracy written out on a scroll. Lots of signs demanding the lobbying industry and other tools of Mammon be banned from *our* government. We had drums. We had kazoos. We had badly played bagpipes. Loads of signs, buttons, camo, robes, helmets, feathers, face paint, body paint, and joy! Even the toddlers learned how to say "co-putt!" (corporate slut!) with expertise.

We all said it together: "Corporate slut!" at the governor's door, which nobody inside seemed inclined to open. We were in sync. It was like thunder. It was a sunny vista. It was like candy. It was like cake. It was beautiful. We were beautiful.

Mickey Gammon.

They kicked us out. Cops in suits like bank presidents. But for once I was leaving with a crowd, not alone. In school you are alone on the moon. You are the big, the bad, the *one*. It was a kind of high to be shoulder to shoulder now. Souped up. Like twin tailpipes. That's how a rebel army works. Only in this case, no one had to bleed. After that, you want more. I knew the minds of certain ones were already cooking, the True Maine Militia. Pretty silly. Girls throwing orders and doing little jumps like cheers on the way out into the rain. But when you are a guy you have the instinct to protect. So you just hang around like a ghost in case things get serious and the girlies fall apart and beg for help. That's why I was there, with C.C. and Butch and the others. In case things got out of hand. You just can't believe how jolly those girls were in that weirding-out place. They just didn't know life. The enemy was not going to laugh off their making a mess of even *one* of their days of business as usual. Eventually you knew there would be the pain of the knife. Pepper spray. Whatever.

 Whitney St. Onge looking back on that October.

Stirred things up in the papers again. And talk radio was turbid with hysterical jibber-jabber over abused Settlement children, pedophilia, Nazi men, terror, illiteracy, polygamy, gunzzz. Even the squirt guns the little kids had at the State House were discussed as promoting terrorism.

Yes, we had a not-so-secret radio in the summer kitchen to "monitor the media" as Claire called this. Not a peep out of Gordon. By then, he had his own militia sins developing. How could he bitch about ours? Our militia. Or our little radio. I loved my father completely but he had to grow up!

 In a future time, Claire laments on another matter.

Yeah, I knew of Catherine's shopping obsession, the browsing, the selection, the euphoria of filling the backseat of her little green car with crinkly bags of gifts and clothes, video tapes, herbal remedies, sweaters. She loved to buy sweaters. She was not a clothes horse, really. There were only a few things she actually wore. Then there were her memberships, like aerobics and the gym and the pool. She had a calendar full of appointments: massage therapy, nutrition therapy, acupuncturist, shrinks and counselors, music therapy, dance, psychics and astrologers. And the shopping. Every day. *Every day* another carload of bags and that smell so particular to new merchandise.

I was starting to suspect there was something death-defying going on here. And later we would know the whole piteous picture. That she was doing something sly and desperate and messy with credit, first exhausting her batch of credit cards, then overextending the credit line of her equity loan, then selling off stocks, and then forging her sister's name on her sister's credit cards, which she *stole*. Though her sister would forgive her, her husband Phan would not. It had been what started all the trouble between them in the first place, but now it was worse.

Then I heard from others at the university that she had been making long-distance calls at the university's expense, some to Phan to argue for hours in whatever hotel room in whatever country he might be installed in. Europe, the Middle East, Canada, Indonesia, Mexico. And nice newsy deep-feeling chats with her friends in places where she had once lived, and chats with her sister, and her dead mother's best friend. The provost was wild. This especially wasn't good for Catherine's position. But since she hadn't done this with the phone before, it could have been chalked up to stress and a temporary emotional breakdown, which perhaps the provost would agree a good treatment regimen and repayment could fix.

But then there was the Settlement phone. Yes, I had been taking Robert down to Gordon's house to call his mum at her office but there were those times when Catherine breezed in here with her gifts, sitting in for a noon meal or supper, but she herself was also stopping down at the farmhouse for a while, warming the phone with calls to Phan in Europe, the Middle East, Canada, Indonesia, Mexico.

 Robert Court Downey Xiem

He is four years old. He whispers, "Are we shepherds?"

There was a biting wind yesterday but it has died. Wind has so much push and noise but this new whispery silence feels holy.

Gordon whispers, "Real shepherds would sleep outside with the sheep. We're half-assed shepherds."

Robert gives a manly single snort of a laugh. He keeps glancing at the way Gordon's right fingers and thumb are locked around the forearm of the rifle. Then he glances back up at the sky. They are looking for a sign of the missing lamb, hopefully a live lamb, though Gordon is not expecting a live lamb. Mainly he is looking for a small piece of mottled evidence.

The sun is stuck in the trees up along Hanley Brook Hill. It is a small white, weak sun.

Down here are five acres of balsams planted in factory rows and pruned. Some are chest high. Some are hip high while others are small as bouquets of clover. There is a sense of strenuous order in this, of too much human touch. A *rat-tat-tat-tat* unhearable drumroll of perfection. Robert and Gordon walk abreast here, Gordon taller than trees, Robert's dark eyes wide, concerned only with comparisons.

Somewhere, some coyotes or an eagle or someone's pet dog knows the answer to the mystery Robert and Gordon mean to solve. Robert knows wild animals and other sneaky types are like ghosts with special powers. He glances at the rifle, gray worn iron and dark worn wood. It too seems supernatural. He looks at Gordon's fingers, the green cuff of Gordon's shirt, the raggedy sherpa-lined vest. He looks at the weak cool light of the sunrise pressing between the tops of the special trees It is all merging, weakness and power, beauty and fright.

 Steph remembers.

At noon Robert sat with Gordon at dinner. His eyes sparkled. John Lungren who was sitting on the other side of Gordon asked Robert if he wanted to help him rewire a lamp. Robert squinted.

John said, "You'll be an electrician before the day is out."

"Robert can do anything," Gordon said. "He takes to details."

"Can you fly?" Montana asked him, Montana who was a bit of a beast, a wordy beast, when she was seven. Beth's oldest, one of her two, one of Gordon's many.

Robert lowered his eyes and shrugged.

John said, "We'll get the lamp fixed. That's good enough for today. Leave flying to turkeys."

Robert laughed, then sighed.

Gordon placed his hand on Robert's glossy black hair.

Montana said, "Your fingernails are dirty, Robert." She tsked and her eyes crawled all over him, looking for more to mention.

Gordon lowered his hand slowly and held it out across the table to Montana.

Montana's eyes widened. "Gawd, *your* fingernails have buckets of dirt. You men are hopeless."

Robert squared his shoulders, his Settlement-made hand-woven shirt laying upon his small shoulders like the kisses of many, many, many fans. I will always remember how Robert looked around at all the tables and, keeping something to himself, that indescribable small power of being part of *a people,* not to repeat the idea too much, but that is *the* idea, right?

 In a future time, Claire remembers the day when Gordon saw that month's phone bill.

He was rip shit. He came into the winter kitchen at noon and just stood there in the doorway with the envelope in his hands, staring at Margo. And then Samantha. And when Whitney stepped in through the door around him, squeezing one of his arms affectionately, he turned around and said, "We need to talk." He wore that new store-bought vividly scarlet chamois shirt that his mother, Marian, had given him for his birthday. That red took over that whole huge room in every way. Everything except his face, which was bloodlessly furious.

So the girls stood with him out on the piazza arguing. They denied making the calls to Mexico, Canada, Indonesia, Israel, Pakistan, India, Poland, and Russia. "Well, then, who *did* make them?" he demanded. They shrugged. And Samantha, looking insurgent with her feet apart in her black military boots and that black jersey and camouflage vest, flashed her pale, pale corn silk hair and said indignantly, "You always blame everything on us." She looked to Margo for agreement and cherry-cheeked Margo made a squinchy face that said: *true, true, true.*

In the nick of time, I was there to the rescue, took Gordon by the hands, looked him in the eyes, and whispered who the real culprit was.

He flushed. Now his face matched his red shirt. He left the kitchen, returned with a handful of tacks to pin all seven long-distance pages of the bill up on the wall by the stoves. And a small sign, scribbled in marker: *Anybody who puts their hands on the Settlement phone again to make a bill that looks like this will have their hands hacked off with an axe.*

For the first few minutes of the meal, he sat along one side of the table, drinking beer and glancing at Samantha, who was almost exactly across from him. Finally he said, "I'm sorry, dear."

Samantha smiled. "Apology accepted."

The rest of the day was quiet.

Although later that day I did overhear through the doorway of the print shop a loud voice saying, "Jeepers, did he really think our militia had gone global? Don't I wish!"

    And then—

I can't recall how many days later. Maybe the next day. Catherine came around. Beautiful and breathless. Her sleek new haircut, even shorter than the last cut. And some more hair straightening, too. Her pretty mole remained. The little car bulged with gifts.

She was bustling from one building to another and did not seem to be anywhere near the phone bill tacked on the wall with its accompanying scribbled threat.

And nowhere did she cross paths with Gordon.

I figured before something happened, I should talk with her. I didn't fear the axing off of the hands. *Deo volente*! Just more heartache. But I couldn't find her. She was gone, Bev told me. Turns out one of the young kids *had* showed her the tacked-up phone bills and sign. He didn't realize the sign was written FOR CATHERINE. I was told she read it quietly, made no remark. She just got in her little car and drove off back to the world.

With Robert.

I'll tell you this right now. She wanted Gordon. She wanted *us*. The whole deal. She wanted his approval, his intimacy. She wanted the nestling of all these shoulders, hands, long tables, rumbly buzzy voices for the rest of her life. We were a writhing grounded modern tribe. But Gordon had only two arms and a head of snakes. A boy Medusa. And what had she really done wrong other than be needy . . . yes, the addictions . . . but wasn't Gordon a sucker for need? He had hated her *before* the TV incident a while back and now the phone bill, so it wasn't the TV and phone bill. *What was it?*

 Farewell forever.

When Gordon notices Robert Court Downey Xiem missing at supper, he asks for him. He is told that Catherine is gone. Robert is gone.

Gordon leans back on two legs of his chair, stares gray-faced out through the low many-paned back windows into the early October darkness.

"Gordon?"

He looks up. It's Penny wearing a lovely square-necked black jumper. The straps and neckline embroidered in pink roses, that dainty effuse work that had to be at the hands of one of the elders here. But in Penny's hands now there it is, the copper sunshine belt buckle. She folds it into the fingers of his right hand and says sadly, "*She* said to give it back to you."

 History as it happens by Draygon and Tamya edited somewhat by Heather.

A bunch of us picked up the mail. The postmistress Cookie said our mail is making her tired. We explained it is letters from all the people in America who are scared. No place to live! Land Lord and Land Ladies who own it all! And banks! Jobs are masters cause the union stuff is outlawed! Slavery doesn't always mean real chains and whips. The people are freaking out! Help!!! Help!!! When they write us it is with screams in their hearts.

The postmistress said, "Good thing there's a zip code."

 History as it happens as written by Vancy St. Onge.

All day, all night, the phone rings. If you answer it, it'll be somebody, usually Maine or next door, but sometimes Kansas, Oklahoma, North Dakota, North Carolina maybe. "Is this the True Maine Militia?" they ask.

If I'm the one to hear this, I say, "Wrong number," and I hang up. I am not the one to get involved in anything political. I don't understand what half of it's about. That's why I vote so the real experts can run things.

 And the mail increaseth.

More mail this day than the day before. Then even more the day after. And yellow cards from the postmistress declaring: *TOO BIG TO FIT.*

So somebody always must go fetch. Cardboard boxes piled behind the PO desk. They load them up, feed sacks lumpy with unraveling hearts and wits from all over Maine and beyond. Sometimes a crew heads for East Egypt on horseback. "The pony express. Goin' through Indian territory now," whispers Oz, one of Leona's teen boys, himself more Indian in the eyes and nose than his father Gordon's Frenchie-Indian-Italian-Irish mixed-up aspect. The saddles creak, the hooves clop. A new house on the highway, a pit bull runs at them. One of the younger horses goes bananas. But a woman comes to the door and hollers, "Molly! *Come!* Molly *now!*" The Settlement mail crew salutes the dog, the woman.

 Another day.

Even *more* heft to the mail. And more notes at the gate. More phone, its old clattery jangle most breathless now. *Hello! Hello!*

 Suppertime at Vandermasts.

It was Dana's turn to cook, so of course it's spaghetti.

Their father eats with no words but blue eyes twinkling with many, many, many stories. His stories are always short. He has hundreds, all on hair trigger. But he's moody. He has two moods. His exuberant mood. His tired mood. This is his tired mood. So stories remain represented only in eye twinkles. His cap is off. He stretches an arm over Dana's plate to get butter. His work shirt cuff is frazzled. Grease. The skidder-breakdown kind.

Poon is reading the *Record Sun* to himself, having pushed his plate away, pokes his teeth with a toothpick. Behind him, the bread box and Dana's new computer, two equally kitcheny type devices in many a small rural home. Computer shows colorful fish images swimming past, then repeating. The computer is "asleep." But the fish trudge on and on, reminding all that that is not the bread box.

Poon makes a slight and sudden chickeny noise, his way of laughing when the thing has snuck up on him. He says, "B.V., you look at this. You're a liberal lady. See how to save a tree." He gives the paper a lift over to just short of Bree's full plate. The paper is a bit sideways. Bree hasn't tugged it completely from Poon's reach. So she's sideways, neck crooked. Poon taps a finger on the spot. It's an op-ed. It says that women need to use less toilet paper. "*The* one-tissue tinkle," is suggested. The writer has a woman's name.

Bree laughs. "A female elf wrote this. A dehydrated female elf."

Poon laughs through his teeth now, shaking his head, his dark-haired blue-eyed round face flushing sunset colors, pulls the paper back to himself.

"What?" Dana pipes up.

Bree sighs. "Why doesn't she piss in her hand? Or wipe with her sleeve? Why bother with *one* sheet?"

Their father laughs, just because he is in tune to what is meant to be laughed at from his daughter's perfect mouth, which is below her freakishly spaced, now alarmed eyes. Her eyes do not look at all freaky to him because a father's vision that frames his child is as transfiguring and sanctifying as cathedral windows. But he is just now taking note of her alarm.

Dana sucks spaghetti, long pieces, and points at the paper. He, too, has not seen the op-ed, nor seems to be under its power enough to try to wrestle the pages from Bree.

Bree says, "Why toilet paper? Why not junk mail?"

Poon groans, "If I were to make a list of things to give up, junk mail would be one of them. That shiny stuff especially. *Not toilet paper*."

"Junk mail," says Bree around a full mouth. "Wastes our time, wastes gasoline. And water to process it. And it uses electricity. And why not trim down newspapers . . . the sports and lifestyle and big business sections are so fat!"

Dana now has a toothpick in his fingers, though not working it yet. Stares at his water glass. His hair has that squashed on top look from wearing a cap while sweating. He says, "Hotels, resorts, restaurants, airports, airplanes . . . *they* use a *lot* of paper. Cardboard 'n' stuff. Paper place mats. Vacation land has to go."

Bree swallows. "Biomass chips for all the electricity used on everything stupid. *That's* a biggie. How many tons've we hauled to the transfer?"

Their father shakes his head to represent the overly stupendous figure of trucked chips chugging past his weary experience.

"The rich won't give up travel," says Dana. "They'll tax *us* for our trips to town."

"The *system* won't give up travel," says Bree. "Think about it. The *system*, the *thing*, won't give up travel. Salesmen and soldiers and businessmen in planes and ships full of stuff. It's all built on travel. This spaghetti traveled!"

Under the table, the collie groans.

"Gimme the paper," says Dana. Holds out a hand. Alas, he is bothered enough.

The paper is flappingly transferred over the smeared and gunky plates to that hand. Then silently, Dana is reading the op-ed. "Too stupid," says he, flinging the paper to the nearby empty seat.

Bree says, "They'll put the price up anyway, or at least make the toilet paper thinner, smaller, less sheets on a roll . . . the poorer you are, you have no choice. The *half* tissue tinkle is for the *poor*."

"Then an *eighth* of a tissue tinkle as the dollar loses more value," Poon chortles.

So Bree and her family joke and razz the article a few minutes more. And Dana leans back to touch a kitchen match to his pipe. Bree's posture feels heavy. It's suddenly too much work to hold her shoulders up. Such an ordinary evening. The smell of spaghetti and the wood heat and dish soap. And Dana's cherry-sweet tobacco. But Bree thinks about those who set the priorities. And shape the debates. These waves of approval and disapproval and then regulations. Regulating the *folks*. Never the system. The system, the *thing,* steamrolls on and on, its drivers free and well supplied.

She is laughing and blushing and slurping seconds on spaghetti but realizes that though her stretched-between-the-eyes face has made her feel bad at times, *this takes the cake*. By using enough toilet paper to do the job, she's a planet wrecker. And this is *the* moment where she wishes she was never born.

 Extinction.

Bree scrolls along the many columns. This computer of Dana's makes Gordon's shadow lay muscularly and remindingly upon the walls. Too bad. Inside this house is off-limits to her "husband's" wrath. The Settlement, ah, yes like diving under the sea to witness the force of miracles, phytoplankton choreography, that dear source, and the bearded crowned Neptune shaking his trident. Yes, a certain deeeeep perfection. But here in this bright little kitchen, one can breathe without oxygen tanks.

Bree now scrolls down and up, her wide-apart eyes reflecting the world beyond. *Is* there intelligent life *out there* on earth? Well, yes. And here's the PO address for the Human Extinction Society. She paws around for a pen, keeping her insatiable eyes on the screen. Here's the paper pad. Now she scribbles. Not calligraphy, no need. This is just in case somebody else at the Settlement would be interested in making the pledge to never, never, never procreate.

She pictures the two brothers who live at home here, their round faces, soft mouths, and their tender awfully quiet ways. Only their oldest brother, who lives upstate, Ben, has kids. She stands up and the collie is up, too, stirred by Bree's urgency.

"The exponential descending swarm stops here," she whispers as she raises a hand of pledge to the Bree reflected in the kitchen window over the sink. Her mutinous hurricane of ripply orange hair pours livingly down over her back and chest. So much hair, that which Mr. St. Onge loves to nuzzle and yet insists on tying back with his sometimes sweaty bandanas. She has kept them all. Her treasure.

Out through the glass pane, she sees the sun looks baggy today in its prison of humidity overly excreted from so many clever human schemes. She knows she cannot *give up the life* of modest riches, toilet paper, and little trips to the Settlement in the pickup. Or deodorant. Or books! Or dental floss!

She sees the child she might have had, its whirling hurling fat hands, grasping truckloads of toilet paper. She hears the infant's cry coming from the mouths of the ghosts of the mighty ceiba trees. And the topsoil has mouths and the dying oceans have mouths. The bats and bugs, fish and plankton, thrushes and frogs. They wail to Bree in their reverse exponents. Oh, dear, it's not that the human critter's infestation of earth is a new idea to Bree's brain. No ho ho. It has been stuck there a lot these days. But gosh, *toilet paper!* It's intimacy. Now her internal shout, "This is the last straw!" This demand by the op-ed writer, bearer of virtue and correctness, has put the neck hold on Bree. Killing herself would solve the toilet paper problem . . . that no tinkle, no tissue solution. But Bree isn't going there. Can't.

Again, she imagines the baby she would have had, round-faced like her family and broad backed as Gordon St. Onge, but the tyke transforms now into a thick spotted snake, thrusting through more deep tunnels of self-aggrandizement.

She recalls the antiabortion bumper sticker she saw once. *SMILE. YOUR MOTHER CHOSE LIFE.* What does that really mean? Bree has wept over her use of toilet paper!! Even a one-sixteenth-sheet tinkle means DEATH to a world of existing life if Bree is multiplied by future–future pissers.

They say Bree is a genius but she knows she is no genius. It's time to simplify. Like the Shakers nearby in the town of New Gloucester, the ones who only adopt, the opposite of the big spout of St. Onge multitudes.

   The dangers of continuing education.
Butch Martin speaks.

Um . . . so, things were getting more sticky. And weird. Cory and I had the flatbed out, coming back from Gray, had had a big load of furniture and lathed porch posts, truck bed empty now, sunset boring into my eyes even with the truck visor down and my sunglasses, made no difference. Cory was riding shotgun, window down, elbow out, cold as Moses, but Cory's showing everyone he's immune.

So, um, we pull over into the Convenience Cubicle for gas and I recognize Jaxon Cross off to the side, two little ten-year-old cars, one his. Well, actually the one he always *borrows*. So I swerve the truck over to that side of the lot. Set the brake so the old beast wouldn't roll. Piss-poor compression, couldn't trust it. Needed some serious work but hated to tie her up.

Cory and I dropped to the tar, stretching and grinning and getting our landlubber legs back. Sun was cowering lower, everything this side of it phasing into dark blue. Big chill. I grabbed my jacket off the seat, expecting to stand around some.

So there was a whole carload of Jaxon's anarchist buddies, the Black Bloc, tree huggers, tree sitters, Earth First!, vegans, that entire society of cut-loose young guys and chicks with a keen sense of uh-oh about this too-well-ordered world. That night in that high contrast orange and blue light, they all seemed dust-colored and secondhand black. Their car was all ready for takeoff but they cut off the engine and piled out, stuff falling on the pavement, clothes, backpacks, books, flyers, food wrappers, a withered lemon, a gas mask. The stuff was mashed back in and everyone was smiling these small smiles, some as tight as, you know, jar covers, sealing in the holy didactic, right? That was what Gordo would say about them.

Their car had bumper stickers. Jaxon's didn't. But his looked pretty crammed with stuff like the other one. Sleeping bag zipper pressed against the glass. Brown paper bags. T-shirts. Cardboard with the words THIS SIDE UP.

We do a back-of-the-shoulder punch-hug, him and me and him and Cory. The others were just smiling on and on in their slouchy rodent-ready-to-scurry ways.

So Cory Guillaume St. Onge had been letting his thick Indian hair grow out that summer and was wearing, of all things, his camo BDU shirt with the Border Mountain Militia patch, olive and black. Mountain lion in midsnarl. Cory had the showiness monkey on his back as his central tribulation like some guys can't say no to a big fat drink. Or women. Or driving too fast. Except that it was impossible in this case to say for sure if this would be Cory's downfall. He drew a lot of stares across the parking lot and through the plate glass of the Cubicle, stares that seemed familiar, that very thing that had always given Gordo a place in this world of . . . what's the word? Uh . . . deference. So Cory was carrying that gene along.

One of Jaxon's buddies had at least one Indian parent. And this guy wore his dark hair long, too. Small patch of black beard, just on the chin under the lip, wholly distinctive. He wasn't real tall but you'd not think short. He was familiar-looking but I didn't really know him. He'd probably been over to Jaxon's father's once or twice when we stopped in there. Him breezing in and out maybe, like all of us always did. But here in the darkening lot, I catch someone calling him Winter, which was possibly a tree-sit name. They often had tree-sit names which were also good for street protest, withholding their legal names from arresting officers while talking to each other as Blinky or Blue. And they almost always had accents from other states, right? All of them were pretty much my age, twentyish, but they'd been around. Cory, who was sixteen by then, but as tall and powerhoused as a bear on hind legs, and at the moment quiet for a change, he could pass for twenty . . . he must have taken into account Winter's Indian hair.

Meanwhile, two of Jaxon's friends that day were girls, or should I say *women,* twentyish at least, and were looking Cory and me over. Both were dark-haired, one Topper, one Munch. And Cory and I were looking *them* over, especially those goldy-white bare necks showing there in their open-zippered hoodies and now the short girl, Topper, had . . . ahem . . . *breasts* that mattered. Also she wore a big floppy black hat cocked like a mobster, worn over the hood of her hoodie, and the dark front part of her hair. We were all doing these looking-by-glances and smiles, right? Hell, no matter how alert you are between the legs, you never turn into an ass-sniffing dog. Rules are for a reason, even within anarchy. You keep your upright posture, you mainly study faces, and maybe their car tires, and you can make conversation about tires and other car talk, keeping to those sort of wide-open spaces. And you can admire their bumper stickers, like my favorite: AMERICA! YOU CAN CALL FACISM FREEDOM IF IT MAKES YOU HAPPY.

☆ Cory tells of that day he first thought of blowing up bridges.

Jaxon passed around a joint. Brazen, being right there in the parking lot of the Convenience Cubicle with the big pinky green lights on a timer having just exploded to life and, no doubt, some security cameras and also all those rush-hour windshields watching. Well, you know, rush hour in Brownfield isn't Boston. But still, there we were . . . on stage.

So the reefer was slowing my blood while the night chill was goosing my blood . . . heh-heh.

One of Jaxon's buddies, Winter, he had the look . . . like the Township. Like Claire and Ma and Geraldine and me and the rest and that always interests me. Munch, one of the girls, was like 3-D, sort of Jewish, sort of Scottish, sort of Japanese . . . or Indonesian maybe. The Maine Frenchie accent was the trick there. Her whole person was a havoc and that sort of twinkly True Maine Militia enthusiasm, heh-heh. My eyes were sort of Scotch-taped to her. My wicked happy eyes. She wore her black bandana peasant-style, there on her black hair. This was the mark. Black . . . bandanas, masks, and sometimes head to foot. Black meant anarchy. Or maybe it meant clean slate, like now it *begins*.

Well, whatever, Munch and the other g— . . . uh, *woman* . . . were looking good and I couldn't tell who was with who. Meanwhile, except for Winter and Jaxon, the guys were weighted down with dreads, light brown, no variety there. And they were all skinny, like big elves. And they smelled of garlic and time. And arduous travel. And war. Street war. War on America, the place that so many people think exists like one of their bumper stickers pointed out. And here's another. *America's not a place, it's a corporate lord's wet dream.* And here's another: *The Maine Blackfly. We breed 'em, you feed 'em.*

One guy had the hood on his hoodie so tight, his especially solidified sort-of-cardboard dreads stuck out on the sides of his face like wacky ears. I never learned his name but the tallest guy they called Roast.

Jaxon announces in his North Carolina accent, "We're just back from the city of brotherly constipation . . . copwize I speak thereof. Good to see the drawbridge open up over the moat and allow us back into this here honorable land." He jabs another freshly lit joint into my fingers and rocks on his heels. All these people wear sneakers so their feet look big and light gray and squishy, heh-heh.

We all work the reefer seriously down to a sort of smithereen. Winter, the Indian guy, calls it a "safety break," the thing we're doing. And there's soft talk, lazy talk, secrety, with eyes scanning and taking in the larger public scene but nobody is really saying anything that important, although being sixteen at the time, I thought it was all mega-cardinal, heh-heh.

And oh, how I remember myself being so deep-augered into this place and time. I saw the big honking orange sun drowning in its purple hilly suicide, its fingers of fire still hanging on to the edges of the White Mountains. We were all on the edge of tomorrow, you see, fighting front and back. Then the sun let go. Gone. Just the mountains, like blue tombstones. But here the bunch of us stood in the razor pink-and-green big parking lot light. On display. Like products. Like bad inventory, a going-out-of-business sale.

"Well," says Winter in his sort of upper New York state accent, or something.

So now they were squashing themselves, body and hair, back into their little car. All of this group but Jaxon presently lived up the turn-pike, an hour or so ride, and it's close to an hour to the pike, and Winter himself lived up on the coast. As they putt-putted away, their exhaust smelling like old donuts, one of the girls driving . . . and the last thing I see through the spotty glass of the window with the busted turner that could not be rolled down, is her big nice smile.

Jaxon seemed in no hurry and neither did Butchie and since Butchie was our driver, it was fine by me to stand around some more. I had layers enough under the BDU shirt to do an Antarctic expedition. But no gloves. And, shit, the metallic pink parking lot glare always seems to intensify miseries if you've got them, hot or cold.

Meanwhile, Jaxon had been to the front, IMF and World Bank protests in the city of New York. Lots of Philly protests, for instance one for Mumia Abu Jamal on death row who was framed for being a radio host and Panther, too noisy about "institutionalized injustice" against poor people, a *reeeal* heavy dose of it on people of dark skin. And there were the politicians and their conventions, which needed the attention of chaos specialists and other bodies volunteering to a state of imbrication in the streets.

And then it "came to pass," to use Jaxon's own words, that Jaxon and others with fake names and black masks, in flowing anarchist form, smashed blocks and blocks of windows of business chains, *after* the cops, clad in Kevlar and other moon-man gear, teargassed and pepper-sprayed the pacifist folk who were not doing anything but saying hello to the empire, to *The Thing* as Bree V. called it. Cops had even teargassed and pepper-sprayed the faces of little kids and rubber bulleted the knees of the white-haired people, some in wheelchairs and leaning on canes. You ever see a rubber bullet? About as rubber as a bowling ball and the size of a claw-hammer handle. Many of the Black Bloc and others had locked themselves together preventing the corporate critters from getting into their closed-door murder-the-world plans. So *after* the cops waddling around in their moon-man suits bashed and burned flesh and eyes, the A-boys, admittedly unsurprised, admittedly on hair trigger, began to turn glass into falling stars.

I could see Butch's eyes. He had that glimmer. Pink. From the parking lot lights and from the reefer and from the lure of the class-war stories and just the zing and wildness of Jaxon himself, showering over us like, yeah, like stars of beautiful broken glass and his rose-color courtly manners oozed. He would call even us "sir" and the girls "ma'am." Okay, so see, he and his father and sisters were from the South. Well. Heh-heh. There you go.

Well, it was easy to see that Butch had already marched up the plank of this ship with its black flag and would go wherever it was going to float him.

Butch remembering.

Man, um . . . did Cory's eyes look bright to hear all the gutsy shit Jaxon and his buddies had been up to. And Jaxon was really reeling off the tales, some repeats from times we'd been up there to the hill, his father's place. Cory was maybe memorizing the stories but the picture of Jaxon himself in that present moment was worth keeping. He looked a lot like his dad, the gray eyes and face shape, but his dad dressed like a middle-aged carpenter, not a pirate. Picture a pirate and you see Jaxon, except unlike guys climbing masts, and unlike the other anarchists, he wasn't spidery-bone-muscled. He had a little bit of pudge. Not fat. But stocky, okay? Very short beard like a cool movie beard, black knit watch cap with ends of a grayish-black bandana sticking out in back, and one around his neck. One gold earring sort of like a doubloon. His brown hair was not long, not short but good and scruffy like cut with kindergarten scissors. He'd been the victim of bad scarring acne, and there was this hard criminal smile. If you didn't know he was our wholesome good-guy Jaxon, you'd think he was about to cut your little throat and smile doing it.

And . . . um . . . let's see, he wore cargo pants like all the others. That's what they called them. Cargo pants. A million pockets to carry all your cargo in, ha!

His father wore glasses. Jaxon didn't but when he wasn't smiling, he looked at you funny, so maybe he needed them. He was average height. Me, too. So Cory was the towering one in this unplanned cold night meeting. Boy was I wishing I'd remembered my damn gloves. Blew on my hands. Made use of pockets, the few I had. I see one of our CSA people going in to pay for gas. We nod.

So . . . um . . . then Jaxon whips out a toothbrush from one of his pockets, plucks out the lint from the bristles, and starts brushing his teeth. Funny guy.

For more pockets, his all-black BDU military shirt has . . . yeah, a slew of pockets. And under this heavy shirt, more like a jacket really, is a gray hoodie, there's thermal sleeves at his wrists so he's got at least that under the hoodie and under everything is a thick layer of tattoos that I'd seen before in T-shirt weather. Some standard dragons, vines, gremlins, and such shit but also, on the forearm, a red cross that he had explained goes with the idea that he and one of his local buddies are licensed EMTs. At the big protests they serve as medics for fainting people or people with other heat problems, heart attacks, strokes. But when the cops are sicced on the crowd and people get pulverized, you are cordoned in or out, not just with yellow tape but by a thick line of helmeted Kevlared moon men, so you can't assist anyone . . . the whole matter becomes battleground and rules of decency are off. But I can see Jaxon and his sugary manners of "ma'am" this and "ma'am" that helping stove-up lady protestors off the hot tar and they would feel comforted and safe in his hands.

So that's the red cross, right?

On the *palm* of his hand . . . ouch . . . is the tattooed telephone number of a legal aid volunteer. "One of my souvenirs," he called it. The original was in magic marker on the inside of his forearm.

So maybe you can picture Jaxon Cross. Now picture him brushing his teeth and around this he is insisting, "No change has *ever* happened without fear in the hearts of the elites. If you think so, the history you've been immersed in has been doctored." He spits into the stooping weeds at the edge of the tar. Already a plastic baby diaper curled there and some fast-food soft drink cups. "You need . . . this is proven historically . . . chaotic out-of-control protests and all-out property damage. You can't scare an empire with prissy-pants obedience."

I saw Cory blinking a bunch. Like the kid that he was. Sixteen years he'd been in the world, right? And this war talk might have been too much for him. There he was in his militia jacket and mighty mountain lion, and I'd seen him take the X out of a lot of two-hundred-yard targets, his fingers like silk, like a river, like shadow over the mechanisms of old and new guns, lever action, bolt action, semiauto. BUT cozy brimful Settlement peace and love was all his bones knew. Kazoos and blueberry pie. Road work and sawmill work with ten million breaks.

Well, yeah, me, too. That was the stuff I was made of, too. And I'm kinda with my brother Kirky on the idea that humans can never get it right. And wasn't this anarchist antihierarchy shit just another religion?

Nevertheless, I had been thinking hard in those days about the difference between standing up or lying down as the red, white, and blue bulldozer track crunches along over other folks' bodies, their lives, homes, livelihoods, headed in *my* direction. I'm not into glory. But dignity is a kind of instinct, I think. I resent being *used*. Fuck! What *is* the right thing? Just to take it as they dish it? To just lie there warm and wet? Like a fat whitish-green loam grub?

So Jaxon turns with his toothbrush handle wagging in front of his mouth, no handed. Then he whips open one of the back doors of his little shit-box car and just like the other guys, all this stuff falls out, paper bags and a sneaker and a cell phone, or part of one, and he stuffs his toothbrush away and gets to pawing through the insides of several backpacks and finally finds a little soft-cover book. He purrs, "The book I told you about last time. Churchill. I told you about Churchill, right?"

Cory and I both give little grunts. Yes, Churchill. And he doesn't mean Winston Churchill.

Jaxon is smiling away, his best cut-your-throat smile and all those pox scars and black bandanas and the doubloon spinning, brimming woozily with shit-assed parking-lot light, and the beard cut in a way as to only surround the cold clean smile. And now here's the little book.

At some point in all this, I remark, "I have a Winchester. I have no plans of shooting anyone. But . . . it would be a really idiotic thing for the American people to holler for gun control for many reasons . . . like how many more poor people would be stuffed in prison . . . for . . . um, you know, *just being armed*. Like the drug war. It's war on the poor! Concentration camps for the poor. Millions of human beings in . . . um . . . in cages. That's what we got with prohibition now! Fuck! . . . and besides . . . I can't see . . . I don't get it . . . I can't understand . . . people giving up the *right* to . . . you know . . . the second amendment . . . because . . . um . . . because we may need it tomorrow. Things change. Giving up amendments . . . messing with the Bill of Rights . . . making ourselves more like loyal subjects . . . surrendering by mass consent our fucking rights! *Any* of our rights. Just givin' 'em up! So passive. Like dogs! But especially . . . um . . . self-defense. And . . . you know . . . revolt against tyranny. Today is today. You never know what's around the corner."

But there's Jaxon standing there facing us with the little book in his two hands, like a preacher about to bless us, no, like a pirate, no, like a young man of his time. His sinister grin is gone. His eyes are squinty but also kindly and EMTish and rescuing and committed. Voice edged with husky sorrow, "Yeah, Mister Butch, sure. But what about dynamite? It's already illegal."

 Cory confesses.

Over the coming days, Butch and I had this between us. This that if nobody fights the system and its handful of suited-up lords, then the vast majority of people are fucked, these people of the world. Oh, yes, pretty small world, like a smelt, BIG high-tech net for the little bug-eyed smelt.

But if you *do* fight them, heh-heh, unspeakable punishment befalls you. Little windowless high-tech dungeon cell, twenty-three hours a day would be the *best* you could hope for. Till you die.

But for the *worst,* torture with a capital T, that's the cold-hot nerve kind and the water up your nose kind, you'll get *that* till you die.

Either way, you will know helllll till the end of time.

Think of it, the courage it would take to *bait* a beast like that, The Thing, with its eye on you, those atrocities that the United States of America is ready and equipped to commit on *courage*.

Well . . . heh-heh . . . Butchie and I would go around and around with this. Courage? Or coward? Either way, we were damned. It was, each day, the both of us going to a nice breakfast in the Settlement kitchens, food for the gods, an act of shame.

 Butchie confesses.

Yeah, if I stayed only with Rex's kitchen militia, no courage necessary. Just Stonehenge patience. If we diddled around helping the girls with their theatrics, no courage there. No risk. No damnation. So after a while, Cory and I stopped hashing it over because we were both embarrassed in front of each other.

Um . . . maybe Jaxon Cross was himself just talk. Just philosophy. So all his high moral ground in honey and hush was probably his own way of fooling himself, because he really could not risk the agony of a live burial, America's prize for its *real* soldiers.

Maybe we were all just waiting. Waiting for what would be around the corner. The day when The Thing gave us no choice. We'd just be on reflexes and high holy adrenaline.

It has been said, it has been *shown* from history, that many atrocities for scaring the public are done with set-up patsies, events bright and shiny, media as tool, bombs, bangs, assassinations, sinking phantom ships, twists, turns, big red lies boiling right out of the cold genius of the top most humanity, then broadcast over and over until people's minds *believe*.

I'm no reader, but others are and they share with us that don't. And man, the Caesars and Napoleons, their ghosts are just like socks, passed on and on and on to like souls, decade after decade, century after century. The others, the holocausted-on souls, the slave and servitude souls, they are recycled socks, too. It's the swarming model. We all move together to protect our oppressors. But somehow, I'm a fluke. On TV and in public school I'd be called sick. Cuz yes, sir and ma'am, do not fuck with my answered and unanswered questions, the then and now and how the world works. Some out there would *not* call me an A-plus, no diplomas, no degrees. But to me, the jewel of my mind is mine. Do not ever fuck with my mind, ma'am, sir. Do. Not.

 In a small town in Ohio, not far from Youngstown, it is evening.

A man sits in a chair and pulls from a crinkly bag some new socks. Big sale. SIX pair inside a paper adhesive band. He unlaces his shoes, eager to see how well these fit. He's been discouraged with socks in the past. They seem to run a bit smaller than the stated size. He holds a pair up. They look large enough. They are dark blue. He wanted black but these only came in dark blue. He pushes his bare foot into one of the socks. Kkkkkkkchhhhhhhhhrippppp! His foot goes right through the heel of the sock. It's like the sock was rotten. But new. The man realizes it's not rotten, just cheesy. He swallows. Closes his eyes. "This is thievery," he whispers. "I've been robbed!" He feels anger banging all through his various organs and arteries like nano-thermite charges.

 At the beauty salon in Portland.

Ivy Morelli, *Record Sun* reporter and columnist, holds her dog biscuit earrings in her hands while Sandra cuts away. She can see Sandra in the mirror but she can't really see her own hair. She has to trust that the outcome will be right.

 Ivy's new hair.

It is the same violet-black but instead of that shimmery bowl-do, it is now shorter and fashionably spiked. Chaos hair, Ivy likes to call it. Ten-thousand-volt hair. Wonder hair. Ivy just LOVES her new hair. What *else* is there to live for?

Lily Davis's computer lust unabated.

It was one of the few times Gordon and I were across the table from each other at a meal. It was after Pryor was born, so I wasn't working my fork and spoon, just rubbing Pryor's back as he gurgled and grunted there on my shoulder, trying to eat my hair. Okay, I plunged in. I brought up the subject once again of getting on line, just *one* computer, *one* for all to share. "It saves money on mail," I pointed out.

He slowly shook aspirin from a bottle, put them in one cheek, then stuffed almost a whole yeast roll in the other cheek, then chompingly mixed it all together, swallowed some of it, then, around the rest, he said something like this: "In the future, *they'll* implant very dinky little computers in babies, right between the eyes or maybe the brain stem. And this will cause the entire population eventually to raise their right hand all at the same time, or wiggle their toes, or shout this or that, turn their heads all the same, maybe sleep all at the same time during certain events. These computers will be *free of charge*. In fact, they'll be the *law*. Why not wait for then and be a model of compliance?"

I picked up a vegetable, pea or something, and tossed it into his plate.

He laughed. "Bombs away!"

 The prayer.

The dining room, like the parlor and the kitchen, is cluttered with books in towers, plastic milk crates of files, bags of yet-to-be-answered mail, and is also wallpapered in blue but no gray clipper ships and anchor patterns repeating. Or orange flowers and pink parrots . . . the kitchen decor. Just a white-dotted sheer blue; except that the big maple beyond, aflutter with breezy purply-red leaves (what's left of them) and the blinding yellows of the woodline beyond that come to invade through the glass and turn the walls into wagging, bouncing, watery squares a thousand shades of lavender.

You see there is the table. Coffee cups and papers. Every straight-back dining room chair occupied by a man. Even the several extra chairs, captains and rockers. The corner hutch, as we know, is emptied since long ago of Marian Depaolo St. Onge's best china.

But some of her homemade ceramics remain, wedged and mashed between Gordon's journals, newsletters, and files. Boarded up as all the others, another small fireplace. The room is cold. Rex has not brought any of "his men." Only these Settlement guys on hand, now wear *the patch*.

The boy Mickey, being both one of Rex's men and a new Settlement resident, got swept along by the grave whispers of Cory and Jaime and Butch at meals. And so he is here, eyes open on the ceramic cherub he remembers from an earlier meeting here, up there in the catty-corner dish hutch. Bubblegum pink, the cherub's skin. Would his nephew Jesse, so recently dead, only two years old, limbs just twigs and vapor, having sort of starved to death (or is it that cancer possesses you and its invisible mouths suck out your fat?); would Jesse already look as dreamy as that winged one? Would he have that little curvy pleased mouth? Mickey isn't paying any attention to the prayer that the New Jersey militia guy, "Pastor Lon" is rattling off.

But Gordon is. You can tell. His eyes are open, too, but squinting at his coffee cup. His shortish-longish dark brown hair has burst into a bunch of cowlicks for no reason.

Rex's eyes are open, too; you can always be sure of that.

Cory and Butch just look at the middle of the table, one set of eyes Passamaquoddy black, the other that brimming mix of THE County. And his, Butch's, eyes seem more public, less cryptic these days, now that he has that gallant Rex York mustache to compose his mouth with. And all the thin smoky soups and war drums (inverted white pails) and covenants of his hoodied brothers and sisters in anarchy, make revel in each of his light-brown irises.

Pastor Lon had started his prayer by promising God he will join others in keeping (Mexican and Somali especially) immigrants out of America. "They are breaking the laws of the Constitution, which is God's law and God's will, because they *themselves* are illegal."

Mickey notices the tip of the chubby too-pink cherub's wing has been chipped off. A gritty white spot shows.

Pastor Lon goes on in a pleasant voice, his mouth and cheeks practically match the cherub's, sort of curved up at the corners. "And God, the Father and Creator, power of all powers, You call us today to enact Your *will* and *law* concerning sodomizers. We know your *wrath* at those who wickedly disobey your *will* and your *law* against sodomy . . ."

Mickey's eyes slide to the faces of Jaime and Butch and Cory. All three pairs of eyes are now politely closed, hands folded. He glances at Eddie Martin, Butch's dad, who is putting off an explosion of smell, like marigolds but probably not marigolds. But then maybe, yes, marigolds. Settlement people never see commercials to guide them out of embarrassingly smelly homemade soaps and greasy salves. But if you are wearing Old Spice (which Mickey is not but smells like a goat in rut and rat piss and ferment); but let's say you smell like Old Spice and you are among Settlement people, you will stand out like a madly twinkling Christmas tree.

On with the prayer. Pastor Lon's hair is as thin as scribbles and it is white. His tiny mustache is gray. He has taken off his army cap. He's a gentleman in stuff like that and his voice is honey. He is maybe ninety years old, though Mickey hasn't reached the age where he can judge ages of those over sixty. But the turkey buzzard neck is a clue. Meanwhile, Pastor Lon's honey voice slides through the prayer. "Sodomizers will head the line, two by two, into Lucifer's gates . . ." This sort of prayer is usually screamed by a sweaty guy in a suit and he'd be jumping around with his arms raised and everyone yells, "Amen, brother!" but this voice is tender and nobody at this table is making a noise, either. Everything is floaty.

Mickey sees two of the guests from upstate Maine both sneak peeks through partly open eyes at Gordon. They are officers of the Knox County Militia. They seem to really admire Gordon. In a restrained manly way, of course. But Mickey figures it has been the news and talk radio that has got them twittipated, which is extra funny since Gordon smells like weeds and so forth due to his lack of news and commercials. It's a total one-way street St. Onge-wize.

Pastor Lon's voice (and Mickey now notices one missing tooth near the front) rolls on in its warm wave, "Into Lucifer's gates will also be forced those wicked who defy the Constitution that Your hand has written using the hands of the divine founders of this great and Christian nation. Who among us does not recognize the Constitution as a page from Scriptures?"

Mickey thinks Pastor Lon's old eyes might fly open now to take count of those who have a problem with "recognizing" whatever it was he just said. But his eyelids stay mildly closed. He seems to feel real comfortable in this room and probably everywhere he goes.

"Now," the pastor speaks with weight on each word, not louder, but just good 'n' solid. "The true sons of the true sons of the true line from the seed of Abraham must prepare for battle in accordance with Your *will* and Your *law* and in Your name. Amen." He opens his eyes. Brown old shaky eyes that now stare straight ahead out the window into the glow of the October trees.

One of the Knox County guys says time is limited and he'd like to get on with everyone coming to some agreement about the e-mail that will be sent to the governor as well as a hand-signed "snail mail" letter.

Mickey had seen the document; Butch showed him last night. But Mickey cannot make out written words. At the moment, this meeting reminds him of school a little bit.

 The squares of window-shaped pinky-purple-gold tremble more contemptuously on the blue walls.

Rex's body shifts but his face and eyes remain frozen upon all details of this scene.

The guy asks if everyone received a copy last week. "Have you all had time to study it?"

Rex doesn't move and none of his men (outside the Settlement) are on this guy's mailing list, nor did Rex, as we know, feel they should be at this meeting, and so they aren't. Rex is here, though, like the enamel cherub. A gritty spirit image.

The Settlement men have had a chance to meet hurriedly after breakfast on this. Gordon had showed them the one copy the Settlement received. He had already scribbled changes on it in his forthright barbed-wire-looking handwriting. John Lungren added three words. Then there was a vote. Beneath the hands of Settlement men here at this table are photocopies of the one that was changed.

Gordon says deeply, "We offer some revisions."

The other guy from Knox says, "Yeah? Like what?"

Old Pastor Lon is one of the three New Jersey militia members. All three are positioned with their copies of the original on the table before them. One of them, a guy with shaved head, says, "We have sent this very same document to the governor of our state. Before your changes, that is."

"The same?" This is John Lungren, gray-haired, no camo jacket or patch today, but a sherpa-lined hunting vest over dark "chamois." His light eyes under raised eyebrows target the upstate Maine guys who are pushing for the letter to go out. "Is this a nationwide thing?"

"Sure is," says Pastor Lon.

"Who wrote the first?" John studies all the guests.

The upstate Maine guy shrugs. "Got it off the 'net."

John grimaces. "And who put in *on* the 'net?"

Gordon has pulled more copies of the Settlement's version from a folder and passes them around, one first to the guy beside him.

Rex has offered no revised version. He accepts a copy from Gordon's hand and looks at it almost sideways, then drops it on the table, folds his hands.

The New Jersey guys read slowly through Gordon's bouncy handwriting.

The shaved head guy looks discomfited. "What's this stuff you put in about corporations? It's the commie government that's the problem."

Gordon looks up at the ceiling, big mustache flicks, crazy eye flicks. How can he begin to unfurl the last twenty years of his hard study of the global system, the reading and thinking and seeing in, say, five minutes to people who are . . . are what? He refuses, even in his head, to use all the words overused to describe these men. He *wants* to love them? To respect them? To honor them? To own them? To redeem them? Deliver them?

"My brother," he says, "the shadow government of big finance and bottom lines and intel agencies, which controls all the media and finances all our elections, which is set above our observable national and state governments, is a fake god that challenges the god that most people of the world see in the blue sky and in the blue sea, and in the two-leggeds and four-leggeds and winged ones and in the woody and grassy beings who photosynthesize." He throws a hand to the window.

"Well, whatever," says the shaved head guy, *slightly* sneering.

The New Jersey guys are quiet. Pastor Lon's eyes are closed, his chin shaking, his neck shaking, all his old self shaking. The skinhead now looks hard and haughtily into Gordon's written words.

The third New Jersey man, a white-haired and naturally balding fifty-year-old, looks at all the faces around him, then settles on Gordon. Yeah, he admires Gordon, it seems, even if the Gordon-philosophy is silly. Gordon, who has been reprinted in patriot newsletters and patriot web sites shouting "God Save the Republic!", arms extended, a crowd pushing to get closer, closer, closer. This Prophet who is a thunderbolt, and the liberal press hates him.

One Knox County guy says, "We have at least four other outfits here in Maine who will sign the original version. Before it goes to Augusta, I'd have to show it to them again . . . if this new stuff goes in."

Gordon says, "The document was great before, just not complete. Takes a lot to round out a good thing." He had almost added his Maine-seceding-from-the-union idea, which he has begun to feel stirred over and because he believes that that's what he sees in Rex's eyes, too, along with the ice and snow, and doesn't he want to please Rex, his brother, who at the moment is receding away? But still there is that hot extravagance of feeling in Gordon's chest for all these guys, their darker edges, their vicious little edges erased by his wish to do right. And to please his effervescent kids, which would include Bree. Certainly not to save the world. Save the world from what? From life? But then . . . ahhhh. A great red roar there in Gordon's head now. Once again, he has webbed himself up, tangled in the thickety woolly wholeness of the great Mother and her cruelties, logic subtracts logic and multiplies the deep-most, the bare-assed verve. He at last looks at Rex. Rex seems to be chewing on one side of his tongue.

Pastor Lon's eyes widen. Something in the window there.

Gordon turns sideways to look. Nothing. Sighs. But what he now sees is a bundle of papers on the floor, several boxes of old .22 ammo and some black markers. Those weren't there before this moment, or before today anyway. Who has been messing with him? He doesn't look at the faces of these strangers yet to see who looks shifty, though he hadn't seen *shifty* exactly before, just fucking right wing. But now he is sure he will see a betrayal in one face. Maybe.

Again Pastor Lon's eyes widen on the window, then squint.

One Knox guy says, "What's out there?" then turns to see for himself. Everyone turns, even Rex, who is still chewing on his tongue. Or something.

Gordon again sees nothing.

Pastor Lon shakes his shaky head slowly.

"What?" asks the skinhead.

"Light. Like *orange* light, " Pastor Lon says gravely.

Gordon says, "Trees. Sun on the trees." He opens his hand to the walls, but at this point the lavender glow has moved on, sun headed west, blocked by the house.

The fifty-year-old New Jersey guy with white hair on the sides says, "Well, gentlemen. We're being watched."

Butchie laughs. "You guys aren't planning the overthrow of anything. Let 'em watch. We have nothing to hide."

Cory smiles.

Rex's eyes target each face of the New Jersey guys. Then looks at Gordon, sort of sighting between his eyes.

Gordon tiredly grins. He realizes Rex has said *nothing* this whole time. He can feel the man's wrath placed squarely on him, even though Rex was all for this meeting until *now*.

John Lungren says, "The media can take the thing you aren't hiding, the thing that is not even air and create a masterpiece as solid as pig iron."

"Amen," says Pastor Lon.

"And agents," says the skinhead.

"Take your pick," says the younger Knox man, blond with a goatee. His army jacket is solid olive drab, so popular in the 1970s. Maybe a hand-me-down from his old man.

Eddie Martin snorts. "There are a lot of magic wands out there."

Gordon stands up, edges between the blue wall and the row of elbows and the booted foot of Pastor Lon, who is at the end of the table.

The yard behind the house is full of arched leafy canes of raspberry purpled by frost. The raging red maple, now a bit less sunny but still frisky from breeze, stands alone as ever.

No sign out there of Secret Agent Jane or NBC or some guy in a trench coat (Gordon's idea of an agent). But Gordon is bothered by the bundle and .22 shells on the floor. And he is bothered by Rex because he cannot read Rex's ugly silence.

Gordon is disoriented. Too many unfamiliar clues. Too much that buzzes. His darkly bearded green-eyed face wrenches around, the Tourette's-like and poltergeist's possession of his countenance, bewildered lunatic.

One New Jersey guy slides the Settlement version of the document into an envelope.

The older Knox County guy sees and folds his in half. "I think the stuff you guys put in is okay. I'll let you know what the others say."

But now someone is standing behind Gordon at the windows. It's Pastor Lon, who is, yes, shaky, but not stooped, and wears a camo vest over a blue-white dress shirt. Gordon steps to the side to let the guy press his nose to the glass.

"Weird," Pastor Lon says. "I was *not* imagining it. There was a column, a beam, maybe like a laser, straight down from up there." He points to the sky between the gnarly big-armed redheaded maple and the house.

The room feels instantly refrigerated. Drafty, actually. Januaryish. Like a door left open in January, yes. Just like that. Gordon looks needlessly at the closed door.

 The grays.

Whoops! It happens. A lull in our speed of motion normally slower or faster than any Earth being's rudimentary eyes can see, becomes synchronized, and the translation of colors collide so that as we observe their witty bitty earthly efforts (our scouting for possible samples to abduct) one or more of those beings will detect the streamy airy aura'd pull of our goof up.

 The spy.

Gordon goes back to the table, standing over his copy of the document but not ready to sit, just staring into the print.

Pastor Lon is still searching the sky. But then he cocks his head, head turning slowly on his buzzardly neck like a cheap-made kitchen appliance. "What's this?" he asks, not in his honey voice but his voice of alarm. "Did you hear it? Something's in that cupboard." He takes a step toward the corner hutch. "*Somebody*."

Rex breathes audibly, like a reverse drag on a cigarette.

Gordon turns back and approaches as Pastor Lon tugs on one of the knobs at the bottom. There's a giggle. All eyes widen as Gordon hauls Secret Agent Jane out and she is trying to keep her glasses of white-trimmed pink heart-shapes lenses from going askew and giggling and her rough velvety voice scolds, "You guys are sooo bad."

The skinhead is extra stunned. "Where'd you come by one of *those*? Here in *Maine*." He means "nigger."

Gordon lifts Jane to his shoulder, caveman style, and she whines, "Noooo, Gordie. Let go!"

All eyes are on Jane, except Mickey Gammon's and Rex York's, these two just staring into their private tunnels of frettings.

Meanwhile, Cory and Butch look at each other, eyes twinkling utterly. Cory clears his throat, now runs a hand along his lengthening tail of blackest hair and yes, it has grown an inch today. And his shoulders are broader today, broader than Gordon's, Gordon his father. And he had reached page 80 of *Pacifism of Pathology* last night and he is not tired at all. He never needs to sleep anymore.

The skinhead adds no more to his little joke, just smiles thinly around the table. Pastor Lon says nothing, indeed nods into the child's eyes with gentlemanly bearing.

Jane's legs, longer every day, dangle with ease and trust. Her Settlement knitted sweater, pants, and tunic thick with cable stitch, a fir tree green.

Gordon's massive camo-clad arm, the one with the olive and black mountain lion near the shoulder, presses her in place as her heart-shapes gaze memorizes faces and camo or olive caps and coffee cups. For inclusion in her spy notebook, of course.

"This is even worse than I thought," she shudders.

All the men (but Mickey and Rex) pleasantly laugh. Such a cutie. Such a gorgeous little spy. And Gordon feels the *power* of fame, or so it seems, that maybe he *does* have something, what it takes to change the world, their stinging trust and admiration, though fame came to him accidentally. Whatever, it seems to bring an extravagant blush of sweet justice to this room. Or so it seems to him. He raises his chin, the short beard scratching Jane's cheek.

 But then an hour later. Jane gone upstairs to her old room to "find things."

As all are standing around the hallway and kitchen, working their way out, Rex stays behind and draws Gordon's eye.

Gordon turns back. Only then does Rex rise from the table, slipping his cop-looking sunglasses on even before he's anywhere near the light of outdoors. But this is better, maybe, than the coldness of his eyes. He hisses, "Nobody who wears the Border Mountain Militia emblem is to sign that piece of paper . . . to . . . the . . . governor. And nobody here at the Settlement is to ever again make these decisions. I never saw that stuff you wrote until this meeting. Are you trying to take over?"

Gordon nods. "I see your point, Richard. I'm s—"

Rex interrupts crustily, "*Do* you, Mr. Democracy? You can start your *own* militia if you want but don't fuck with me in this one."

Gordon slumps his shoulders, his chin. "So the document bothers you because of the changes? Or the one even before the changes?"

Rex's eyes are unseen behind the glasses. His mouth tightens, the crawling dark mustache rises and falls over a clenching of the jaw. He loses all remaining color. He mutters, "Some guys of the Border Mountain Militia have indicated that they believe you are a stupid fuck. I don't want to believe that." He adjusts his sunglasses and pushes past Gordon out toward the kitchen, past Mickey, who was hovering near the hallway door.

 Hogs eat snakes.

Pastor Lon with the crepey version of the Mona Lisa's smile has repeated his prayer as before, but adds a thanks for the abundant food. Glennice wearing her plaid flannel of two shades of blue unbuttoned over her dark T-shirt and a fly-sized gold cross has been leaning in just as the old fellow opens his eyes. "Coffee?" she wonders. Note also that Glennice's hair tonight is in pigtails. And here we are in the warm winter kitchen.

"Oh, yes, thank you." He raises his chin, gives her a wink.

Glennice pours coffee so well, she need not look at the opening of the cup but into her husband's eyes. "Gordon." She speaks his name swallowing a perfect squeak. "You must say *your* prayer."

Gordon looks down at his hands.

Glennice says, "I myself love the part of the Bible *and Gordon's prayer* where Jesus our Lord teaches about giving away one's vest and *then* one's shirt." She gives Pastor Lon's quilted camo vest a tender pull.

The noise of dishes and chatter and chair-scrapings of the big room all drowns itself out.

Glennice stares into the eyes of the shaved-headed younger militia-man. She giggles.

Little blond child, maybe four years old, name Rhett, pulls at the sleeve of one of the Knox County Militia guys and asks, "Do you like compos' toilets? It's sawdust. You like it?"

"You want to see a hog eat a snake?" Rhett's buddy, a dark-haired Passamaquoddy girl (of the same age as Rhett) asks the militia guests.

Gordon laughs too suddenly, the release of a tight throat.

Glennice says, "More coffee, just holler," and moves on.

Now one of the pies arrives, too hot to handle, Tante Lucienne's own raisin pie with the fleur-de-lis cut into the center of the buttery-looking crust.

Rhett says, "Pigs eat acorns." Rhett's face has the one expression he always wears. Balefulness.

"He *meant* com*post* toilets," Eddie Martin chuckles two seats beyond Gordon. "Rhett is proud to be a tour guide when the opportunity comes up."

One of the Knox County Militia guys reaches with a hand and covers the dark head of the girl and grins. "I saw a snake eat a hog once."

Lots of laughs at the table but the tykes, in deep reckoning, frowningly study the goateed face that has spoken this marvel.

"Well, not a hog. It was a newborn pig," say the lips in the stranger's face. The hand on the girl's head is kind but the eyes are hecklish.

☆   **Cory recalls.**

Before breakfast the next day, the New Jersey guys got a tour of a few things, including the radio setup causing them to go ripe bananas, even though it was a long way from any use, the building itself just a flying squirrel and bat motel.

Our John Lungren listed all our languishing plans for starting a shortwave situation, for spreading our small scale solar and wind ideas and the CSAs . . . the community stuff. But Pastor Lon just waved that away, saying the only real thing for patriots would be to use radio for broadcasting "the movement," the constitutional stuff, the militia stuff, the right-wing thing. "Radio needs to be in the right hands. *Ours,*" he said, his eyes all whirly with feeling.

Gordon said in a gravelly significant way, "The . . . people's . . . airwaves."

Eddie Martin had a smile as big as the blue sky. He added his two bits, "The FCC is the golden gateway to the *real* radio scene. It's them and the big money between people's ears and the people's voice."

John Lungren laughed. "All boils down to the fact that only a small percentage of Americans were ever legal persons."

Eddie: "The more property you had, the more human you were . . . like, you know, gold, acreage, and slaves. Today it's gotten more abstract . . . big organized capital . . . Wall Street . . . how many senators and reps you can own and—"

Gordon interrupted him. "The paper person was born. The paper person, the charter, the corporation, a system, no legs just wings, has a big grip on everything including the media, any media that matters. This little operation here . . . well, I won't say they'd ignore us, but—"

"Whatever," said the shaved skull guy, Bob, squinting like we Settlement guys had just gone off on comparing baby bootie knitting techniques.

Pastor Lon leaned into our group to more centralize himself. He sort of snarled, but gentlemanishly, "I don't care about any of that. What we need to focus on is how in *our* hands, radio is firepower."

All in a rush, I felt both warm and cold in the roots of my hair.

A letter received by the governor of Maine. Though Rex has not signed it and Gordon and other Settlement guys have not signed it, the revisions shown in handwriting discussed at the meeting in the St. Onge kitchen remain.

Greetings Governor,

A request by the leadership of eight Maine citizens' militias submitted to you this spring was ignored. As you may not recall, we asked that we could meet with you to discuss the possibility of Martial Law being imposed on the US citizenry in a future time, particularly in the event of an emergency such as real or government-staged terrorism.

Another request, this one in early summer, was denied by one of your aides, stating that you were too busy.

Do not mistake these requests including this third as TREASON, INSURRECTION, or THREAT or as any other CRIMINAL ACT under the color of law. For the record, we have no CRIMINAL INTENT. We do, however, under the US Constitution and Bill of Rights, as expounded in the Federalist Papers, have the right and the duty to defend against OPPRESSIVE, TYRANNICAL, ARBITRARY, FASCIST (*the merging of government with huge business organizations**) or TREASONOUS GOVERNMENT.

You, Governor, and members of the Maine Legislature, are hereby notified that any and all declarations of Martial Law, to include, but not limited to, the ROUNDUP OF PATRIOTS, MILITIA MEMBERS or ANY CIVILIAN POPULATION, *in groups or individually,* BANNING OF FIREARMS and WEAPONS or AMMUNITION for same, DEPLOYMENT of any FEDERAL or INTERNATIONAL TROOPS, AGENTS, or POLICE, the use of DYNAMIC ENTRY to remove leadership of Militia *or any other Constitutionally-allowed group, assemblage of persons or family*, and/or the use of Martial Law, YES, MARTIAL LAW IN ANY FORM WHATSOEVER, WILL BE MET WITH MILITIA RESISTANCE.

ASSASSINATION under the color of law, the SEIZURE OF PROPERTY, PAPERS or ASSETS whatsoever through the use of

---

* Italics are Settlement-created additions.

bogus instruments or executive orders, INJURY or LOSS OF LIFE due to CIVIL OR CONSTITUTIONAL VIOLATION or under the color of law, the ushering in of a NEW WORLD ORDER, will now and without question be met with any and all resistance necessary to regain *the freedoms of all flesh and blood people under the Constitution and Bill of Rights. Legal fictions (corporations) not being flesh and blood persons by natural law will not be recognized as worthy of protection by the following militia units signed on to this notice.*

If at this time you people see that you would like to talk and iron out the aforementioned issues that concern us as a *Sovereign American People,* feel free to contact any of the following:

Rob Carr, Knox County Militia
John Phinney, Militia of the Cumberland Interior
Don Garland, Great Gluskap Militia
Jackie Farrington, Pine Tree State Militia
Terrance T. Thibideault, Mars Hill P.M.
Chris Brace, Oxford Minutemen
PHONE/FAX/EMAIL on Label

Respectfully,
Rob Carr

 Discovering America.

It is night. This room Cory shares with his thirteen-year-old brother Oz isn't dark. Oz sleeps soundlessly as Cory reads soundlessly, the lamp shooting in all directions one hundred ardent watts. Oz's thing is horses, those he takes care of but all horses are his passion, all of horsedom. Perhaps he is dreaming of them now, though he doesn't even twitch. Besides, his head is under the pillow. Outside the pillow is one long rangy arm holding on, and a red T-shirt sleeve and his birthday wristwatch, wrist portending of thickness, wide hand, skin still toast-color from summer.

Meanwhile, Cory's pages are lifted, swept along, and dropped with the lilty snowflaky silence. Ward Churchill's *Pacifism as Pathology,* very old ideas made to newly rip across the sky, rip, tear, awaken. Such relentless logic, while Cory at age sixteen just becomes more and more and more astonished, riveted, mortified, and the lighted lamp and the book and the early a.m. hour occupy the small room with perfect radiance and surrender.

 Nearby, through stubby white fences and the disembodied tree whirrings of October, in another rangy many-roomed cottage, lies Butch Martin.

This room has beds and brothers, too. Butch is not a book reader but he lies awake with scenes of possibility played out on the palpitant darkness. He sees them so vividly, not the Border Mountain Militia or the New Jersey Militia, but elves! Yes, hooded creatures, human-tall, vegan, light on toe and heel, able to float-sail-somersault when necessary (so much is necessary), dun and slate-swathed, drab as birds, no sparkling, no suspiring, just the tick-tock in the blood, the oily efficiency of their togetherness in their locking of arms, prone in the streets, the wealth of their reckoning, the genius of their thrift, the featherweight scurry and rush of those who are never never never cowards, setting their dynamite in a precision cranny, immune to high order and high rank commands. Like breezes. These elves hove into the cranny and split it.

He groans.

 Back in the other cottage, Cory reads on. Is his education a sunrise? Or a sunset?

Done with the Churchill book, he reaches for another, one of the new three he got from Jaxon today. He just wants to see what the afterword says, no plunging into this big baby tonight. *In the Spirit of Crazy Horse.* Here now at the end where the author goes into the aftermath of an FBI lawsuit, that a publisher should be so un-American, so ballsy as to print a book such as this!!!, say they, the prosecution.

Well, yuh, it opened windows on the agency's shit, their unbeliev-able SHIT against the people of the Pine Ridge Reservation out west, these being nowadays people!!! People you might know and love. T-shirts-and-sneakers people, grammies in aprons, dads in Dickees. Cory's dark, dark Passamaquoddy eyes blink with his own revelation about the person cleaving to his towering and still growing bones, *inside* his skin, *behind* these eyes, the revelation that each book he gets from Jaxon makes him, Cory St. Onge, more warlike.

No wonder truth must be swept under rugs, for only fibs are gentling. He wonders what is it about those who are not gentled, such as the hushy drawly Jaxon Cross.

What makes them soldiers of pointed questions while others are soldiers of official fibs? How does that work?

His eyes keep blinking. Cory, who is a soldier for neither. Cory. Coward. He stands fear-frozen before the cage.

He believes that for most young American men, joining Uncle Sam is not courage. Most of these guys cannot picture their own demise, or what will be asked of them, can't imagine it because everything so far is sport and play. And bravado. Nothing more setaceous or burred than that registers with them yet.

And now, you, official hero boy, are transformed. No matter anything except that you were THERE. And now there is only to bow down under praises, kin, and public alike, even if on a mission somewhere you explode, to be lugged home legless, armless, you have the sweet warm-as-kittens cauldron of those praises to stew in, the nourishing, neon wholeness of God and country of which you are one beautiful legless armless decorated bee.

How does that measure? And do note that the solider for the anti-empire cause, anarchist or militia, whistleblower or hacker, is free and clear and purified of any of that mob praise. *That* choice, *that* sugar deal is off for you.

 Cradles.

Promise Lake, late afternoon, the sky of the east as gray as ghouls in the cave of death, but pleasantly peach in the west. Hither and yon are swan boats, some single file, some abreast, a few in lonesome zigzags. The lakey-smelling water bells and laps from time to time but it is mostly plain-out flat, a courtesy to swans.

Only three ordinary white swans. One cream. The rest bridal colors, nothing carnivalesque, nothing to shame a swan. It is this dreamy creamy sleepy fantasy of it all that has made swan boats one of the Settlement's most popular co-op pine products. Scowlike and sedan-sized, they are not likely to turn over, even with the swan's grand arched neck, even if passengers stand or lean out over the upraised paddle-shaped wing feathers. You get stability. You will know peace, the obtuse thrill of it, unless you are one of the peddlers. In that case, you will know exercise. Even though the gear works running along inside the hump are ingenious, they still require the enthusiasm of the whole range of calf and thigh, buttock and belly, heart and lung. *Huff. Huff. Huff.*

Here comes a little flotilla of the custard yellow, bobbing violet, and bachelor button pink and blue. Cantaloupe, a color almost juicy, lilac, and clover. Presently they are moving imperceptibly. The pilots and passengers all rising and settling in unison with the breathing of the lake. Some kids. Some adults. Nice time. End of a long day of Settlement bustle. This is the reward.

What's up ahead there? Viking "ship." The one and only. Totally experimental. Same size and shape in the body as the swans but far different spirit. For theatrics only is a short mast and striped red and yellow terry-cloth sail, the size of . . . well, yes . . . two towels.

Two ten-year-olds are pedaling this one. One pilots as he pedals. Behind are the ruffled watery Vs of the craftily made paddle wheel and rudders.

"Axle!" the copilot has memorized Viking words and they are called out from time to time.

The "ship's" head and neck, the whole dragony thing, is the deepest best-ever green, with devil red eyes and what's *meant* to be a snarl. Looks more like a bored yawn.

"Skull!" calls out the boy copilot.

The boy pilot steers around bleach-bottle buoys that mark a rock and sandbar. He has learned his way on Promise Lake with rowboats and swans, but this maiden voyage of the one and only Viking "ship" is his finest hour.

There are passengers. The back bench is loaded. Brianna. Claire. And old Dorothy wrapped in her blue and gray sashed wool coat. Claire has Dorothy in a one-armed lock. Dorothy is not in full appreciation of the moment.

"Bloom!" calls the copilot in Vikingese (which in this case is also English).

Old Dorothy's eyes are blue, the way the lake ought to be but is not. Not now in these last daylight hours. Over Dorothy's coat is a floppy oversized life vest.

The ship is headed for Turtle Cove.

Bree laughs. "Shall we raid and burn North Egypt? Steal all their jewels and piggies and virgin men? Make history?"

Silence.

"We could make up Viking songs since we don't know any," she adds. "You guys study about their musical instruments? Gotta make at least one of each."

"That would be good," one boy pants out this remark as he pedals into the curve. He's not the pilot, but has an aspect of *very big* pride, he believes he's not the pedaling slave he actually is. He is one of Gordon's and Leona's sons. The other is a Soucier progeny.

Bree looks into the water, which is getting grayer to match the creeping ghoul clouds, and getting sloshier, the air showing some emotion now. The good lake smell goes up Bree's nose. The water itself bites her fingers. Her life vest fits perfectly. Ah, Bree.

Claire stretches her short legs. The craft is, yes, roomy. Her long wool jumper is patched with scarlet on the hem and near one knee. Also on the skirt, paint, grease, pitch, and ink in streaks, paws, and heart shapes. No ho ho, she did not dress up for this cruise. Her boots are worn out mightily along the toes. Her life vest fits tight. See her knitted cap of baking-soda-box yellow is new and bright, sort of blinding. Serenely, she says, "The swans got thirty-five orders this fall. They win hearts. Viking ships . . . hmmm . . . what is their future?"

"Better than swans," advises the pilot, then snorts manfully.

Bree speaks in her smoky tall-girl voice, "Well, the people with the money to spend on such artsy pleasures are the professional class. *They'd* want *swans*. They would say swans are for peace, even though a swan raped Penelope or somebody . . . maybe it was Persephone . . . whatever . . . it was before the first Viking was even born."

"Born to rape," says the pilot.

"Hush up," scolds Bree. "You can't use the *r* word or discuss the . . . uh . . . problem . . . until you're twenty-one or something." (Bree is almost sixteen).

"Agreed," Claire says, her tone matching her forbidding-as-ever black eyes and specs, the specs reflecting watery gray like two elfin puddles.

Both boys tee-hee and reposition their hats manfully, then whisper. Bree's lovely mouth smiles.

"People who would like pedal boats would pick swans," considers the St. Onge boy. "People who would like Viking boats would want turbo engines on the sides, even the Vikings when they were Vikings if turbos were invented already cuz Vikings needed to smush and blonk everybody and take over. Pedals are wussie. And *today's* Viking types would hate this *toy*. They'd want stealth bombers and lasers."

Claire squares her shoulders, proud of her logical boy cousin, even if he's treading a bit heavily on reverence for life.

Meanwhile, in old Dorothy's eyes is the look of a captive abducted by Vikings, uncertain of north, south, east, or west.

Bree wants to smoke but of course that's out. She taps the ends of her fingers together. "Kirky and Seth want to make the Tree of Diana but one of the metals is mercury, so the whole thing's off."

"Tree of Diana?" Claire squints.

"Like a silver tree that grows branches. Sort of. It's alchemy. Medieval doin's."

Claire rolls her eyes almost playfully. "Our kids are wonderful. They'll probably succeed."

Our kids.

Bree says, "Kirky especially. He has a gift." (Kirky who isn't aboard. Kirky of the electronic table town and bow ties and no-hope philosophy. Yes, *that* Kirky.) She makes the sound of rockets going off and mewling popping fireworks and this gives her a childly aspect. Bree the child, yes.

Claire glances at Dorothy, then says velvet-soft, "I told them back home that she shouldn't come. You take her from her familiar surroundings, she'll be mixed up for days. Her world lately has shrunk to the size of one of the kitchen rockers."

Bree eyes old Dorothy. "Well, let's hope she likes fresh air."

Claire tightens her grip on the hunched old woman. "You like this fresh air, Dot?"

"Oh, yes," Dorothy replies pleasantly but her eyes are still great bulges of bewilderment.

The boy pilot-pedalers are conversing in brawny forced voices about the beachy island owned by friends of the Settlement. They begin to languidly circle it. The bored and yawning Viking beast oozes in through the shadows and stripes of orange sunset leaving its sequined wake.

Claire asks, "You warm, Dot?"

"Oh, yes."

One of the boys calls back. "You cold, Dot?"

"Oh, yes," she replies.

Claire and Bree look into each other's eyes. Then Claire is staring in her steely way at the backs of the two youngsters' heads, her cousin Leona's and Gordon's son with that thick extravagance of Passamaquoddy hair and billed cap, the other, Austin Soucier, brown hair too short to be warm but no cap. So his ears are rosy. And while Claire studies those ears, she absently strokes Bree's jacketed arm.

"I'm glad you're here," Claire says.

Bree's wrongly spaced eyes of yellowy-green-brown regard Claire awfully, then the eyelids slide down, eyes closed loosely as one would enjoy a round hot sun overhead, if the sun were there.

Claire has a quick consideration of the science of red hair. What voice in one's genes orders, "Red!" and then it shall be. How impossible red seems, its insatiableness.

Claire notes that now something stirs under Bree's skin. A tiger under her skin? Or a bag of kittens left to die? Claire crosses, then uncrosses, her legs at the ankles.

As the impossibility of red hair, so is there this impossible thing of five people and a box with seats in suspension over the deep watery chambers of would-be suffocation and slimy rock. And there is sureness in these children's hands. And those who have taught them. Teachers, tools, and the audacity of the unfledged all fused, making this day float.

Bree is wistful. Is she, too, considering these wonders?

And so the "ship" is now turning, the sea monster's ho-hum face and snaky neck leading the way around a sharper bend of the small island. Soooo slowly. One could imagine it as predatorily, looking for villages to plunder. The boys's faces are a mix of strain from pedaling and glorious evil imaginings.

Bree bows her head.

The effusive *tat-tat-tat-tat* of a downy woodpecker on the island fills Bree's and Claire's silences. And the pedals and churning paddle wheel combine clicks, clunks, and slurps as water separating at the bow lisps. Old Dorothy's fidgeting goes *scruff scruff*. And Claire stroking Bree's jacket arm, less scruff, more wispy. Bree's eyes are closed and also her ears are shut because this is just the husk of Bree. Her true self is in the seam between the pages of the booklet she is presently reading on corporate chartering sent to her from the leftist group she hopes will return here soon to do a workshop. She is considering renting the town hall meeting room, more centralized, to attract those who get twittipated and wet themselves over the word "militia." She visualizes a table of healthy snacks, no uniforms, no guns, nothing to scare weak Americans.

Then she has some ideas on an invitation to the Human Extinc—

"Bree?" Claire's voice barges in, her right hand still fussing with Bree's sleeve.

Bree's overly spaced eyes seem woozy.

"Bree, hey, we are *sisters*." *Pat-pat. Pat-pat.* Fingers on the sleeve.

Bree's head turns toward Claire. Plainly, "sister" is not what Bree sees in the bespectacled age-fifty round face, Claire's as-ever unfriendly expression. Bree says urgently, "I'm going to get fixed. I'm going to get my tubes tied."

Claire blinks. She whispers, "Gosh." And what is Claire herself but "fixed" behind her harshly disguised overflowingness?

Bree says, "It's my duty. To the world." She then rushes on to share with Claire the statistics on overpopulation, the reality of shrinking resources. "So there's no need of me adding another mouth to feed and . . . and rear end to wipe."

"Yes," says Claire. "I guess you're right." Claire frowns, then cocks her head, keen to a certain sweep of time, of years evaporated. Of that time when she had wept for her . . . uh . . . duty to the world.

Bree gazes straight ahead, then to the left of the island's stout lichen-blistered trees, the vista opening as the "ship" comes "sneaking" out of the snug cove. The boys' jolly conniving for "ship" improvements goes on. Could turbo engines be *made*? The boys are tiring, eyes wet from October's hard stinging air.

Ah, dream on. Engines are the "soon past," Gordon and Aurel have said.

The paddle wheel's and rudder's watery surges and shivers match perfectly the energy pulses of their feet, beginning to drag slightly. But they persevere. They commence circling another island. Teeny. Not big enough to build a camp on. A hemlock tree. A boulder. Some weedy tufts. A gray plastic pail split up the side, having floated ashore. Doubtful that there's a message folded up in it.

Bree frowns. What *does* she see in Claire's face? Bree has no paintings, sketches, or calligraphy verse to define or box-wrap this afflicted matter. Father, brothers, and, recently, sisters, yes, impulse, gossip, giggles, schemes. But what of the hardness in Bree that still resists mothering?

"Bree?" Claire slings her right arm around Bree's shoulders.

Bree sort of swells, sort of shrinks, mashes her cheek into Claire's bright orangey-yellow knit hat. And Bree is hugging her back. No, Claire is not just another sister.

Claire, though, cut and tied to prevent procreation and who is such a short little person, is Gordon's only *real* wife, isn't she? She straddles it all. If there were no Claire, there's no Gordon. Claire, the glue. And Bree supposes that all is perfection between Gordon and Claire, decades shredded, washed away but rich with branches, roots, and vines, like twin mountains resisting erasure.

Bree remains with her cheek on little Claire's head, and Claire remains with her one-armed embrace of her, and the other arm around Dorothy. Claire peers at that old dear one and finds her asleep. Now Claire looks at the sky, straight up at all that golden and purple October congestion, like the sky needs to sneeze.

The ship ponderously changes course, aiming for open water, back to join the flotilla of pastel swans all progressing earnestly over the face of the "sea."

When the Viking ship penetrates the great swan flotilla, the boys give it all they've got, and soon the race is on. But swans are no sissies. In fact, a pink swan wins the race.

History (the past).

They vilify us, the scoundrels do, when there is only this difference, they rob the poor under the cover of law, forsooth, and we plunder the rich under the protection of our own courage.

—*Captain Bellamy, pirate*

 Old sedan, squatted down with the weight of so many.

It mutters up Horne Hill, past the erect pine post and tidy mailbox of Jaxon Cross's father, L.N. Cross, Box 990. Then it mutter-mutters up the wide dirt drive to the destination, so many inside the car glass, painfully dignified of face, looking out, these young fellows of the Settlement, altogether homing in on that plume of smoke moiling up behind a set of barn-red sheds. Since the old car already knew where to go, it made a fluid bend around to the rear of the sheds, no pause for bearings. Then here we are!

Two bird-lean young woman and one little kid are already close by, even before the doors swing open. Kid has white upright hair like cartoon fear. One woman has close-together miss-nothing light eyes and a lonnnng narrow nose. A falcon woman. She is known by the name Sip, and she's old enough to have rocked and nested and soldiered *Earth First!*ishly in the towers of old growth, holding the line, she and they and the towers as one crackling endangered thing. And now here she stands, plain. Serene. Her eyes and long nose, forehead, swivel to scan these younger friends being sort of choked out of the car. They are all buttoning up or fluffing out their layers as the wind now coolly sniffs at them, their peculiar Settlement odors, and the two young women and child also put off odors, theirs being kippered by the tribal fires and close private spaces made up from blue plastic tarps and tents, down over that back field of bouncing October grasses.

Falcon woman informs them that they are late for the "christening," meaning their garden just below the tents and tarps on the rock-crusty hillside, garden ready for next year. "Christening" means the garlic is in the earth now, for which there was a ceremony. These, Jaxon's resident friends, can now call themselves a "farm collective."

Cory explains that this is the first they could get away from Settlement work, though they rushed all day.

"Never rush, never rest," says the falcon woman, quoting somebody literary.

This day has never once known a sun, just slobbery dank cloud, sometimes moaning, and now in the west a travail the color of cole slaw.

The zingy-haired little kid's face is calm and a smile is forming on one side of her mouth. Maybe she takes for granted that there will always be groupings that come and go, assortments immune to gravity; travelers, busy folk, all tired maybe, from a nation that never settles, and they, all so enthused, all part of what matters, all eventually erased by the terminus of another event or season or perhaps there was an arrest. She, tyke, would have serenely watched as such groups have arrived *hello!*, the prize gained, the story told, the meals, the two-day sleep, bye-bye, then wiped away by the huge hand of the ever-continuing process. But by her side always, her tall windswept mother.

The house on the grassy crest above them all is cedar shingle with black trim, well-kept, tight, no drafts. Just ghosts. And Jaxon's kin of his birth and of some disagreement. This is no longer where Jaxon lives with his father and siblings and ghost mother. Maybe Jaxon lives outside now, like a gray dog, self-plunged into all these blowing-around souls hunched up to the bonfire, night coming on, steadied only by the intimacy with the little red barn and little red shed buildings and bright tents.

All these people! Like an egg-throwing but loveable audience to the ugly never-ending story of kings and moats, turrets and dungeons. These, the darling hoods, the "dreds" in some cases, nose rings, which one woman has three of. All so young. Just beginning. All in wonder at themselves. Well, one woman and two guys less young, the woman's chin tucked into her zippered sweater, eyes watering from the smoke and cold. Her eyes, as all eyes of these well-smoked and chilled young people, shimmer with regard to the arriving Settlementers, Butch, Cory, Oz, Jaime, C.C., Rusty, Jeremy, and Seth. Nods go both ways. Some raised hands, that three-fingered hey-friend how-do "wave."

"You just missed Jaxon," someone says, pointing to the kettle of soup on the fire.

A husky laugh from one of the hooded, zippered-up, gloved, and sneakered women.

A guy with dreads enough to muffle his ears and almost his eyes, gives one warning strum to a guitar.

Another guy, long face, chin shaved and pointed in profile like a smiling quarter moon says, "We raised him special for this soup."

"Ha! He's in that soup!" howls a shadowy hooded figure by the larger shed, not far from the fire.

"No-o-o-o," laughs the someone who had started all this. "I *meaahnt* Jaxon isn't here but would you please stay and have soup."

Merriness prevails.

The sky clots further, now damper. Hunting for jointed bones and other predictors of storm.

Now the guitar and harmonica go in tandem up against the smoke and flames and the crackle-pop of it all. And around goes a bag of cookies made with that special butter. And a plate of rubbery celery stalks and then raisins in a very nice red pottery bowl.

Someone swings another noisy tangle of hemlock onto the fire.

Now voices hooting and shouting and some better at *actually* singing, a Phil Ochs song, he who these days you could maybe call a forefather.

As the cold unhomey sky more deeply purples and bruises everything and the fire expands, all eyes are gold like treasure. One guy and two women blend voices as an old old old Irish ballad wails and sighs all by itself it seems, sorrowing of a sturdy people, of strained harvests, of strangers with swords. With his ever-so-stoic expression and Rexlike mustache and muscular fingers, the magically-appearing always-trusty kazoo, which normally has the taint of fun, now shivers with firelight and eminence in Butch's fingers and lips.

These people and this place are no longer strange to Butch, nor to Cory, nor these others who have come. They have begun to merge with Jaxon and these wanderers with tree-sit names and outlaw postures, and these last few nights have merged even snugger, tonight dishing soup, hands pressing along many skimpy joints, eyes tearing to the pontifical fireside smoke.

Impotence becomes witchery. Poor is rich. Young is ancient.

Oh, but Butch's chest and neck are tight with his worriments, eyes dodging to the littlest red shed, which seems to contain a very dangerous thing. But he isn't trusted enough to be part of it, so it seems. Thus, his wonderings buck-kick him. How cherry pink is the color of his failing. Full blush shame.

 ### When Jaxon materializes, it is full night.

Six-pack of brew slung down to the group by one fist. And the stranger with him, short stocky in-his-thirties guy with dark blond ponytail and red cap, another six-pack there. "Still plenty of soup left," they are told. Soup, hot, thin, weenie bits of veggies and rubbery grain things, potatoes in crap-die size, exotically herbed. And the star of all things, garlic. And around goes a big brown bagful of popcorn, butterless, heartlessly vegan. At one point Cory and Butch and Oz, who is age thirteen and ever-so-smiley, find themselves with Jaxon inside the largest shed. This interior smells strongly of cold apples. A guy sleeps on a sort of cot, his sleeping bag zipped, just hair and a nose and an ear pierced with a pencil-sized spike.

"Works nights," whispers Jaxon, nodding that way, nothing more said. This interior is colder and damper and ruder than *out* was. On a workbench, bowls of grapes, a package of crackers, bowls of seeds from which Jaxon tears handfuls and laps from his palm. And, ever the hospitable Southerner, offers the same to others.

On the gray board and studding is a poster of black-masked Subcomandante Marcos, camo shirt, crossed bandoliers, a bulky black military rifle not familiar to these three Mainers. The famous Zapatista reads from something maplike in his hands. His reading holds his eyes as if each eye were about to be born into a revised world. This image, this wall of only studs, is scantily lighted by the bare low-watt bulb over the sink.

So sudden it jumps the three Settlement guys, the somewhat disembodied voice, Jaxon's voice, his drawl but no honey. Full-throated, each word a billboard-sized thud of threat to someone who isn't here in this cold shed. Jaxon's eyes are closed loosely for he must see clearly his foe now. "Treat . . . us . . . like . . . dogs . . . and . . . we . . . will

... become ... wolves." His killer smile spreads like butter over his face, eyes opened. "That dogs should dare this botheration of them with our little weapons and little words; we haven't got a chance they say. But dogs of the world are on the move, even here, boys, even here in this nation where it is dearly believed a booger is a rose, a rose is a booger."

Now Jaxon is rustling around trying to root out a book from the many books and *stuff* here. After a while he shrugs and out they all go from cold apple to cold smoke. He explains that, "it will turn up."

The singing plunges on into the subject of rain and the highway, ever so melancholy, which causes Butch to reach again for his kazoo. He sees through the fire one girl's face metamorphosed by the spitting untrustworthy light into a skull wearing a hood. He holds the instrument away from his mouth. He grooms his Rexlike mustache, his eyes drifting, sees Jaxon's nasty smile spread over him, Butch. How the fire draws all these beings, *some* with chattering teeth, the skinny blonde patient child moving closer to her falcon mother who stands with a blanket about her shoulders and can, winglike, wrap the little one up in both the fabric and comforting murmurs, for this night testifies as part of no scanty evidence, these people are homeless.

Jaxon keeps standing, his back to the fire, eyes now on the smallest reddest shed, shed of mystery. Shed that is perhaps more central than the fire, the real magnet to these souls. He asks about the True Maine Militia, reports that he heard about it from friends in Augusta. He speaks in his lush North Carolina warm-blooded way, "I'm amazed I haven't heard about this from you boys directlike."

Butch shrugs.

Cory snorts. "Theatrics mostly."

Jaxon's scary smile expands. "Yeahhh. Guerrilla theater." His eyes leave off their characteristic squint, almost popping, then drill each Settlement throat.

Cory and Butch glance at each other, marveling.

Supple still, Jaxon's voice tells a story. He repeats over and over the theme of "diversity of tactics." Then promises more books and articles on such. He unwraps something from one of his ten million pockets, stuffs part of it into his whiskery mouth, smiling, chewing, smiling. He says around this chewing and smiling, "Before ya'll leave,

I'll load you up." This *loading up* always means reading materials. "So whatever you do, don't sneak away without telling me, hear? Like that time when I was working on Fetus's car and you boys left literatureless." He has about five black bandanas bunched around his neck this night, gives his neck the bulk of a storybook lion. One might suppose his endless smile derives its power from its resemblance to a warning sneer but especially just from its endlessness. And there's certain power in the lighthouse flash of the doubloon spinning from his ear. He usually rocks back on his heels while talking, now it's more side to side, not as a rubbery-legged drunk would but as, yes, a pirate would while on rough open seas . . . his experienced no-worry reflex to the sea's vaster power. "All you Mainers and your young'ns over there at your Settlement school situation ought to be familiarized with Mr. Taylor's *The Liberty Men and The Great Proprietors*. It's Maine in the late 1700s, early 1800s. Man, it's your roots. Rebellion. It's your inheritance. And now it *portends*." He rocks on his sneakered feet, in the to-and-fro mode, not nervously, just an easy, generous shift of his not-scanty body weight. "And y'all seen the new one by Doctor Martin Luther King Junior's lawyer buddy Mister Pepper about how the state did *it*. I've got you your own precious copy to curl up with. Just think of me as y'all's librarian, hear? Those books *are* all set aside for you. I did it with my own hands. But somebody must have cooked them in the soup." He chuckles, getting very straight in the shoulders. "More soup?"

"The soup that has everything!" a hooded woman laughs from the cold dark outside of the fire, nearer to the largest shed.

"Soup of champions!" screams one guy with dreads, throwing up a fist.

For a while now Jaxon mopes around pleasantly, eating from the passed-around bowls and boxes and bags. Though he brought beer, he doesn't drink any. He mostly talks, listens, punches shoulders, ambling around and around the fire like clock hands. The Settlementers watch him with admiration and in return *he* watches *them*; in spite of his sneer-smile, he seems to be honorably amazed by them.

A light goes on in an upstairs room of the real house up on the rise. Jaxon eyes the house carefully, then stuffs more of the going-around-the-fire food into his mouth. Music has stopped. Lots of gaspy ha-ha talk of friends and doings. Stories of very recent arrests, something about organizing Maine loggers in a border protest against the big-biz controlled Labor Department, and the way some funny cops handled that, and the total hilarity of taking over the Labor Department office, the upcoming hearing on that. Yes, it seems there is a lot of flagrante delicto in the shared short history of these somewhat homeless, fairly cheerful, totally durable, vegan wraiths.

And the True Maine Militia's State House doings come up, bringing brightness and giggles and breathy praises. Another skinny joint comes around, dispelled into the dampness of the low-hung black sky.

When he is back in their space, on Butch's and Cory's side of the fire, more dry hemlock, brown needles and all, being heaved onto the flames by two sedate hooded figures, Jaxon purrs, "Yeahhh, we all have to find our own way. It's like this. Some feel that you have to make fear in the consciousness of the elite gentlemen and ladies, that history shows there's no change without that fear. Others just want to nicely lie in the street and get arrested and jailed and released and hope for the best."

His squinting eyes play over some of those of his resident friends still gossiping by the shed. "But better to do *something* than nothing at all. We all have to do it our own way." He keeps smiling but looks down at the ground. "It's just that if us of the working class can't rise to the occasion, who will? You got the professional class with their lighting and holding candles . . . which is . . . very nice and what they are willing to do . . . and they do the ten seconds in jail thing. It's all important. Lectures, slideshows, letters, all of it. It gives breath to the resistance. But y'all know what, Mister Butch, Mister Cory? The professionals, the . . . uh . . . honor students . . . are always critical of whatever *we* do . . . they won't support us. If they could just look at actual history, they could see how important *all* tactics are, and they would at least *support* serious tactics, not always be standing there trying to *please* the system by pissing on *us*. It's not *us* that's the enemy, man!" He's *still* smiling on and on, gold doubloon swirling, in rage? Or as they say *in love and outrage*? But his voice is so creamy. No whine. Bushy-tailed and breathy, he goes on, "It's more than that they don't want to risk their hides . . ." He pronounces this *haahds*. "It's that they're still looking for that gummy star on the forehead from the big hand. They were always plastered with those and that feeling of pleasure carries through into their adult lives, and ratting on us bad kids was part of how they became teacher's pets *then* . . . and now. Ya'll see what I mean? It's the class war. I have nothing against *their* tactics but I wish they'd find it in their hearts and minds to not deter the decisive tactics of their fellow dissidents."

Cory, not realizing he's doing it, has leaned in closer to Jaxon, and now a step closer, Cory ever quick, believing suddenly that he is getting nearer to the moment before the pact where Jaxon holds his gaze and Butch's gaze and asks, *"Will you?"*

So Cory's limbs go evermore icy, his lightbulb-bright fist-sized heart not huge enough to shove his blood out to the edges of ruder possibilities, of being dragged out of the thickness of the weald to the realm of the lost, where you are cut off, where they will lower you into the windowless, sunless, cloudless, moonless, starless, scentless, soundless, textureless, inculcately bright and breathless hold in a prison in this land where more people are locked up tight and airless than any other nation in the world. This like the fires of hell while the star-honored professionals are holding their candles and feeling goodie?

Cory steps back from Jaxon and all this while Jaxon is rocking to and fro luxuriously. Two hooded guys are positioning a couple of white plastic pails upside down, drums, though the guy with the guitar goes on ahead, solo, with "Sloop John B." And yes, Jaxon, yes, takes Cory, yes, by the sleeve and nods to Butch and, yes, leads them away from the friendly guttural flames. Butch is way too dignified, too chin-up. And sixteen-year-old Cory with a beer in one gloved hand, is still chilled no matter how warm the beer and hot the front of his jacket and knees, no matter what, now led to that farther shed almost to the first line of tents and tarps. And Butch, now even more solemn, so chin-up that his throat can't hide its wobbling swallows of emotion even as the eyes are so distant and Jaxon looks back toward the fire, only half smiling, toward a certain hooded face it seems.

And yes, two figures rise, two of the leanest guys, both with black knitted caps. And the falcon woman makes a motion to follow. And Jaxon purrs, "Y'all are my friendzzz, Mister Butch, Mister Cory."

Cory doesn't realize Jaxon's eyes are so squarely on him so when he looks back it jumps him, especially because in the high contrast-licking light, Jaxon has got more granite and more razor to that hard cut-your-throat smile. And then he lifts his fingers off Cory's jacket sleeve and opens the shed door.

No flashlight, but Jaxon finds the bag of promised books by ESP or something and he says in a gravelly way that the stash includes about three years' worth of *CounterPunch*es, a bit smoodgy with underlinings.

And Cory sees stacked satin surfaces. The other, the feared, the real reason he and Butch have been brought over here.

Jaxon whispers as he leans toward the blurry glowy shapes, or you could say toward the precipice, "Y'all see this," and tugs now on Butch's sleeve, then Cory's, moving them deeper into the wheeling dark. His syrupy whisper, this maybe not so trustworthy a thing of his voice, "Y'all see what the Anti-Rich Society has been up to so far, its humble efforts to help turn the empire upside down and . . . uh . . . inside out."

Cory's black restive Passamaquoddy eyes widen. Butch's chin lowers. Both faces are draining to the perfect white of lard. And with both, a whirring deep-most tremble inside their clothes. Both of them are *seeing*. But . . . but . . . what *is* it that they are looking at?

Well, it's a bunch of electronics . . . uh . . . equipment . . . yes . . . wire, which Jaxon always pronounces "waaahrr." No full auto military weapons, no stuff for bombs, no dynamite. What Jaxon whispers, close and steamy, and dazzling is, "The people's airwaves. Empire stole them. *We* steal them back." He is smiling at Cory and it's not the outlaw smile now but a sort of church smile, a full churchy smile, maybe a lover's smile swollen and glazy, though Cory realizes he has seen layers of this onion before, Jaxon the complex, but also Jaxon the basic, because Jaxon is just another of the species, human and deeply shivering, eyes on a promise. Cory now fears Jaxon Cross. Because, well, being plain ol' human is a thing to fear, right?

And Butch grooms his mustache, head cocked, hearing in echoes the New Jersey Militia and all their fuss over radio. Radio?

Yeah, the thing EVERYBODY wants their hands on. Yeah, everybody wants to crawl into their neighbor's brain and scream.

A hand on his arm. Like a shotgun blast to his insides. One of the skinny women, long-limbed, lightweight as old celery, elf princess, but has this old-time-actressy self-assured voice, *very* deep like a guy's, scratchy, maybe damaged somehow, but also sexy, god, yes, sexy, says, "The FCC could bust in here now and smash this all to kingdom come. Whenever we set up, we have to stay on the move. We travel around, set up, move on. Right now, the Anti-Rich Society is having a sweet slumber till the posse loses our trail." The hand squeezes the arm, Butch's solid steady exploding arm.

 And then Butch home too late, quietly places himself in his bed.

His mouth remembers the smoke and the watery soup. The seeds. The popcorn. Though he hasn't eaten for hours since, he's not hungry. And not tired. But oh, his head has been launched! Like a sixteen-pounder cannonball fired over into the enemy's fortifications. His sense of duty so perfectly cast iron, yes, but the projectile is so high in the sky it is not arcing. It is a little bit missing from earth's atmosphere. He thinks only of the very wrongness of the masters of this empire, their plots, ah, yes, conspiracies, but so much that is blatant like a creep flashing his pecker from his open trenchcoat, their intentions to build their thrones and their fancies on the pain of peak oil, peak soil, peak water, peak climate, peak ocean life, starving peoples, refugee people, new slavery, and all ruin. Yeah, it is their sneaky, noisy unrestrained wickedness with no Sherlock Holmes or Batman or wizards to stop them! But the smell of bonfire smoke on himself, his pores and follicles, this takes on the consequentiality of deepest oldest brotherhood, of secrecy of the moonless plot, of being. Plot versus plot.

Okay, so kings and lords and power piled high with big rocks is natural but also natural is the emperor awakening with a knife to his throat. And all of this nature knots up hard into a single juggernaut . . . that big dreamy faithy smile over a tiny pile of radio broadcast equipment . . . or guns . . . these someone somewhere else will fall on for hope, while the millions of skull cups, ancient vessels of their once ever-turning eyes boil over now with empty air and dust of those people who once hoped, under other empires. So what? While they stood they were *beautiful* in their insurrection! And all the layers and layers in all the ages of "man" shall be this beautiful lost star! The sky tonight has been blacker than he can stand, but—

Crunch! Munch-munch-munch-munch. Smunch! It's Kirky in his bed, three feet away. Smells like one of his slow-dried zucchini rampages. Often devours them by the bucket, sweet and crackly. Some nights it's the less-racket but more-zoom-to-the-blood maple candies shaped like leaves. Blizzards of those churned out by crews, stashed in hiding places, then found. Yumm.

Kirky's crunching and munching and pleasure intensify, faster, louder, surrounding Butch's head and robust heart, heart of a soldier, bouncing and braced, on hair trigger, waiting for orders from the *right* authority, that which is licit *to him,* waiting, held-breath.

BOOK THREE:
BLOOD
BROTHERS

At the *Record Sun*.

Ivy Morelli and her new hair. She bustles into the newsroom carrying a big box of apples. She stops at each desk, saying brightly, "Help yourself!"

Her editor, Brian Fitch, who is just returning to his desk from somewhere, pretends not to notice her unreporterly hair. He just looks into the box.

Ivy says, "I picked these yesterday."

Brian says, "I want a banana."

Ivy laughs her deep raffish laugh.

As he passes by, Bert Williams, copy desk man, cuffs Brian across the arm with the rolled up sports section, paws around in the box, then veers away, munching on his apple.

Ivy hisses to Brian, "You're spoiled."

Brian frowns. "I want what I want."

"These are Red Delicious," says Ivy.

"Ack! Red Delicious taste like a cross between a pear and a tennis ball."

Ivy rolls her eyes.

He wiggles a finger to draw her to a window. He looks out the window at the other building and the sunny street at one corner. He speaks gravely, "St. Onge people are having *an event*. The gates are coming down."

Ivy lowers the box to the floor, ruffles her choppy hair into a greater storm with one hand, sighs.

Says he, "They are forefront in the news these days. In a *way* I hadn't predicted. You know . . . with the True Maine Militia and all those precocious pretty little adolescents. You know . . . *cute. Sweet. Disney-ish*, sort of. So . . . it's hard to say where this is going. But . . . if something *does* happen . . . even if it's not another Waco, Texas . . . even if it's just the social workers taking a kid—"

"Are they taking a kid?"

"No. But if."

She looks down at her apples, touches the box with her toe.

"Wanna go chat with them again, Ivy? *Before* the event."

"You know it's not easy to get in there now."

"*You* can."

"I'd rather not, as you know." She looks off toward the executive managing editor's door, which still has the old frosty window and moving shadow beyond. In spite of all the changes here, cheap modernity that smells like a chemistry lab, there are still a few nice old touches. "Why don't you send one of your real reporters. I'm features. Remember? Cute people stories. Remember? Why not send Tommy. He's hard-assed enough."

"Sometimes hard-assed isn't hard enough. Sometimes sweet and soft is actually harder."

Ivy looks like she's about to spit on Brian. Maybe the scratch routine. But she smiles and flutters her eyes now. "Then send in a bunny."

 With a groan Beth St. Onge recalls.

Oh, yes, they couldn't let it lie. Not these kids. It 'twas another big hoo-ha, With another buncha pictures and stuff in the *Record Sun*. Oh, but this time the crowds were invited to the Settlement! All of them strangers. Any number of them could be carrying lice.

"Lyn" Potter. Agent. (Actually, he's just an operative, very low on the Bureau totem pole, almost no face at all. Just a black line in the text of your dossier.)

Whole box of Wheaties. Hell, I'm a big guy. So it's like eating air. Normally, I eat only a can of plain tuna for breakfast. But today it's tuna *and* air. The whole spread. They say there will be lots of food where I'm going today. Willpower is the thing. Long as nobody has a tray of homemade macaroons. Those boogers are the only thing that could make me bend.

The funny thing about this crowd shit is you wonder sometime if most of them aren't cops and such pretending to be the enemy. It was in Philly recently that three cops got their kidneys pulverized by other cops who didn't know the guys who they had down were cops cuz only those with the sticks were in blue. But that was different. War on protestors always gets ouchy. You got a protest, you have a potential mob. You have to show force. You have kidneys to bang, the press being elsewhere if you do the right job funneling everybody in different directions. And you don't want a picture on front of the big papers with some teenage girl having her teeth ground into the cement. Too much color. Oh, boy. But generally speaking the big networks, big papers, what have you, won't get you for that these days. Cop death gets the bright lights.

But today the only cop death I can foresee might be that pan of macaroons, *if* there is such. Today it's going to be a little girl tea party. I just need to show up wearing a harmless smile. My contact has me looking for certain people, rating potentials. A certain babe is top of the list.

 Busy at the FCC.

They've relocated again, Bob. We just got a call. We're on it. It's easy to follow ants. They always leave a little trail of vegan cookie crumbs.

 Secret Agent Jane observes.

Some people can't believe their eyes how many stranger people are showing up. Some people's eyes pop out. Bonnie Loo says it is the reporter lady's fault. Then she says it's Bree's fault. Beth, one of the *other* mothers, tells Bonnie Loo to *please* shut up. Bonnie Loo is putting actual *red* frosting on a big cake. Geraldine says red food dye causes cancer. Bonnie Loo laughs and says, "Yeah, mass suicide!" She squirts a whole lot extra in as she says these words.

 What we observe.

Streams of humans, then a high tide of humans. The one they call Guillaume knocks over a vase of goldenrod.

 Leona St. Onge remembers.

Gordon fondled the ears of children who had come with their parents. His pale eyes were intrusive. Maybe some parents felt afraid. Others felt blessed. Healed. Made new. Depending on what they came here looking for.

 Whitney remembers.

Two vans. They were backing slowly through the crowd. They braked flush with the high plywood stage, which crews had built it in a hurry that last week at the end of the piazza on the south side of the horseshoe. The vans were spiffied up with purple and lime green fleur-de-lis and yellow musical notes and, in big print, BAND FROM *THE* COUNTY.

More people were hiking up the dusty Settlement road. No cars allowed inside the gates except "officials." Gatekeepers were assisting visitors with parking down along the paved Heart's Content Road, lining that road for *a mile*! The day seemed so perfect.

 Penny St. Onge.

All of us who wore Gordon's silver ring also on this big day wore a red sash. The sashes were *wool*. They were thickly embroidered with suns, vines, flowers, what Brianna called, "colors of bounty." She had made the first one and got all the rest of us, the *wives,* to make one so "we'd be woven together by the color red, color of hearts." Bree's words.

This pretty much shamed a few naughty mouths that had been gossiping of Brianna's tendency to hang out with only Settlement teenagers.

 And so.

Eventually, Gordon reaches the end of the last piazza, temporarily connected to the high temporary stage. There is a little temporary set of stairs there made of short Settlement pine culls. So good to see his old friends and distant cousins from Aroostook, *THE* County. He embraces them all, a smooch or three, some partylike yeowls, then he and they chat, catch up on some things. Gordon swept happily along in that cheery hoarse back-of-the-throat Acadian-English mix, the patois.

These people, these words that his mother, Marian, wishes to deny him to this day. And yet he loves Marian. And so these musicians with their effervescence and frequent yips of joy are a category of outlaws.

 And behold! There is Rex. Is Gordon forgiven for his transgressions?

He and Gordon both stand with their arms folded across their chests, watching people, hearing the cackling tangle of voices within the confines of the horseshoe of porch-fronted buildings, moss, grass, and trees. Rex's boots are shined, military bearing, but no olive cap. Work pants. Brown T-shirt. No dark cop-like glasses to cover his ever-frosty eyes.

Strangers' kids love the huge hollow dinosaurs, purple cow, and spaceship, a childly face showing in every little opening and hatch of these fabulous bright creations.

A pair of college professors and their families pass through, looking for Claire and the "college crew."

Gordon has absorbed Rex's solemnity, his own face now a mirror of his friend's. Big cold blueberry muffins go by. Settlement-made, heaped on a platter. Cold whole milk in big jars. Milk with a good cow taste. Makes the palms of your hands cold when you hold one of those jars, which makes a really nice cold feeling bust out on your forehead even though the rest of you is a little too warm from the bustle of the day.

Quite a bit of fried chicken left. More people coming, laying down food from their own kitchens outside the Settlement, from other towns, from other states, salads of vegetable or macaroni, chewy bars, cookies, brownies, pies, biscuits, muffins, breads, and beans. And ice cream. And fruits. And soda. And beer. And chips.

Rex's eyes narrow on the uneasy sight of the radio "studio" building and its coveted stout tower swarming with skinny black-gray-and-salty-blue-clad strangers. Gordon wags his head and smiles with all those even and uneven teeth. "Friends of my kids. Horne Hill. It's the Anti-Rich Society." He smiles a great big tickled smile.

Rex's left eyebrow twitches. His brain, which never skips over, never slobbers, is quietly processing these sudden and awful specifics.

Meanwhile, the musicians scurry around up on that temporary stage, setting up the sound system that looks brutal enough to knock people over who stand close. Several men. Three women. One guy in his early fifties, soft dark beard, soft, sparse, latent-like hair on a child's arm. He moves furtively and schemingly. Jeans, very wrecked. Red T-shirt catches the eye. It displays the three chimps of evil revised to show one chimp with binoculars, one with hands cupped behind his flabby chimpy ears. The third chimp is using a megaphone.

Rex says, "There's at least three hundred here."

Gordon grins. "Girls did this."

Rex says, "There's trouble here." His gaze rolls over to the radio tower and studio and the wrongness of the many light-stepping young people there. The wrongness of their ingress. His suspicions that "friends" is too small a word to contain them.

Gordon's face flicks and clenches on one side. "You already said that."

"And like I said, I'm going to get some men in here. Just to watch." He points to the top of one Quonset hut. "Like there and—"

"Watch? You mean like snipers?"

"Just have people positioned. In uniform. Has a corrective effect."

Gordon watches another little mob of folks arrive. The sort who don't bring casseroles. Just cameras.

"You got agents here," Rex says.

"You said *that* already, too."

Rex grunts, a gentlemanly grunt, not the big animal grunts that come out of Gordon. Gordon likes the brotherly protector thingy Rex is about today. Gordon knows he's forgiven. The letter to the governor and all that. Gone into the ghosty past. Right?

But now Rex is eyeing the radio tower again, the figures so light-footed, so possessive, so *strange*.

 And then.

A lot of eyes watch Gordon walking through the crowd, among the tables under the trees. He shakes the hands of three young men in their twenties, billed caps, bashed or chewed nails and stiff palms, wives with nice shapes and pretty hair and clear eyes, two in jeans, one in shorts. Also a child. Gordon reaches to open his hand over the head of this little girl, plastic barrettes warm against his palm and her dark hair slips between his fingers and the tops of her ears are so cool and funny and tender. To her parents he says, "The weight of the world is no longer on each man or woman's shoulders. Today we are a people."

 And then up on the hillside.

Young Lou-EE St. Onge rolls a small deck cannon down the ramp of boards at the back of his little seventeen-year-old yellow pickup. He has a modest crowd with him now. Helping. Lou-EE's small shoulders and small orange felt crusher hat show above all other heads, as he stands to his full and lonnng height once the cannon is where he wants it. Now for stakes and bailing twine, to rope off a safety zone. He gives orders quietly.

On the seat of the little truck broods Cannonball.

Lou-EE keeps his cannon's black powder charges in the folded papers. He uses 1F, 600 grains, thereabouts. The gun he always *wears* is a Ruger Old Army revolver, six shots. Also black powder. Black powder is the thing. Lots of mess and stink and fuss. And old-fashion care. Also over his old plaid shirt Lou-EE wears a powder horn on a rawhide string and a patchbox on a strap. Patchbox is black leather and reads: *US*. He has various other little pouches and a possibles bag all dangling from him. His scraggly tapered black beard is long. From far below where the crowd is, reporters and photographers have caught sight of Lou-EE, and maybe they notice, too, his beautiful green-brown golden eyes. Their cameras go into a frenzy.

One reporter wonders what time the cannon will be fired today. Lou-EE gives a droopy little shrug. "When the True Maine Militia gives the order. I don't know when that is," he tells them sort of sleepily.

The several reporters scratching this info down look disappointed. As we all know, reporters never witness whole events. They stay five minutes, grab a few . . . ahem . . . quotes. Then they evaporate.

 Stopped for the flag man of a road crew down along Promise Lake, a motorist's eyes widen. Yes, it's *pirate radio.*

One minute the radio was playing the usual, then . . . "*Hello!* All you out there in Radioland! This is once again the Anti-Rich Society, with . . . well, you know what the weather is, but do you *really* know what's going on? ? ? Hello! Hello! We're on the air! One! Two! Three!"

Young voices laughing along with this young fellow's voice. Then a young gal voice, mild and trustable. She could sell water to the proverbial drowning man. She speaks like a fragrant flower but the news she gives is quite bitter, while also quite funny and too proud of itself. Then too suddenly she is doing an interview with, of all people, Gordon St. Onge! Right here in Egypt! Live! No messing with footage. No cut and paste. Just the real and actual and perfect time deep inscrutable voice of the Prophet!

The motorist is still staring into the radio, bewildered, weirded out, doesn't see the flag man dancing and waving to get his attention. From behind, a horn blares. But the Prophet's voice is as clear as if he were *inside* the car, which, in a manner of speaking, he is; his warm-mush concern for you crawls over your bones.

 Claire St. Onge.

And so on and on it went, the True Maine Militia event, yes, the welcomingest militia in all the world.

Alyson Lessard's friendly pet chicken.

Loves the stage. Keeps flapping back up there to shuffle and peck among the fallen maple leaves and feet of the band members and crisscrosses of speaker wires. The sun casts horizontally razor-edged gold unsticky webs you can put your hands and head through. The chicken's comb blazes true red in one single strand of this webby light while all else around is ever so blackly blue. Little red crown for a little feathery queen who then marches forward among shadowy drums and becomes one hundred percent blue.

Whisking up and down the keys and buttons and front plates of the readied instruments, there is still gold in wobbles and stars. There is a counting to ten to test the mikes. Spit out from the nearest maple tree, leaves seesaw down, like badly rowed wee boats.

The wonderful hen lands on the drummer's left knee.

Alyson appears in her usual sheepishness and blush, to take her stagestruck bird away.

There are splats of applause.

Next Samantha Butler announces that a surprise speaker and "speech for you" will take place later tonight. The crowd responds with crackling applause and cheers. There she is in all her sassy splendor, bush hat jammed down over swishy white blonde hair to supplement the military costume, boots, red Blair Mountain war–style neckerchief. Mouthy showy Sammy. But she, too, rushes offstage in sheepishness and blush.

Nobody introduces the band. But suddenly the last swollen edge of the going-down-sun turns full devil red, the high clouds pulse impossible inflamed colors no one (but the grays) can name and the hulky treed mountains in their own stew of October purples burn themselves out into black.

 Band from THE County.

The music begins with the bloodcurdling scream of the first fiddler, who wears jeans and the red T-shirt with the three chimps of evil.

Four fiddlers. Two accordions. One large accordion. One very small squeeze box. Two acoustic guitars. And a sax.

Drums. The whole nine yards on drums.

This is not the kind of French music you hear as background sound in a big city French café. This is some hectic beast born of the marriage of hard-livin' St. John Valley loggers and farmers with rock 'n' roll.

While some fiddle bows jerk and chop, others wail like factory lunch whistles, and there's the smash of drums, blood-rhythm, deep-gut rhythm, accordions and guitars played with scrambling fingers, faster, faster, faster, faster, faster! FASTER!

Hard to sit still. Those who aren't hopping around on the quadrangle or in the parking lot and fields, those who won't give up their piazza chairs or picnic table bench, jiggle various parts of themselves, like a foot or a knee or an elbow.

And then more and more songs. For slow songs, none. Only this exhausting hop, hop, hop. And shake'r up. And heave hove!

Many are clapping and whistling as Gordon dances with a UU minister, spinning, hopping, gripping hands to fling each other around. The reverend's graying Cleopatra-style hair flaps like wings.

The red-shirt fiddler screams in Aroostook French that is studded with American English clichés.

People in the crowd scream back, whistle, laugh, or simply dance more frantically, waving their arms, shaking themselves like something hurts their feet, like dancing on hot potatoes.

The drummer is a kid in his twenties, bright green T-shirt with the message BOTHER ME across the chest. His arms are skinny, almost girlish. He is a wild-man drummer, never tiring.

And strangely (to some) this music is blasting out of home and car radios all over the Egypt, Maine, region.

 The last of the golden-orange light haloing the mountain withers.

Two hours of nonstop music, except a brief space when a crew of Settlement teens come out to light all the lanterns and colored glass candle globes hung around the stage, which make a haunting devilish light on the band, while the band burns through another set of wild stuff, half the crowd already slunk off to fall onto the grass or lean against something.

Drunk and stoned Glory York and her various drunk and stoned partners do not dance fast to this fast music, but something glacial and dreamy and barely breathing, slow and close, and maybe a little bored, rings of people hopping and shaking around them, makes Glory and her partners seem motionless, like trees or picnic tables or the corner columns of the many crowded porches lit now inside by soft rose and ivory-colored glass candleholders Settlement-made in forms like ghosts and goddesses.

 And now.

More people arrive. Dressed in jackets and sweaters. Fresh-looking. Not hot or exhausted from dancing. They stand out along the gravel road and field, unable to get close for the old crowd is unyielding, keeping its thickness, keeping its hold on the Settlement quadrangle and high stage of flickering lights. A very few of the old crowd leaves. Those that do stay will say things like, "Let's hope the car's not boxed in."

 And so.

Big applause and whistles when the crowd sees Gordon walking up the stage steps, walking to the mike. Crowd moans. A chant plumping out and exhaling, *Truth! Truth! Truth!* More applause, the pounding kind.

Gordon stands with his arms across his chest, one eye wide, one eyebrow raised. He's far enough away from them all that most can't tell he has an alcohol buzz. But how green that face! Dark beard streaked with green. Throat green. This greenness a gift from a nearby glass candle globe. The opposite side of his almost plaid shirt snickers in plucky yellow and pink.

The accordion player ambles away. The set of drums that spans the back of the stage blushes in candlelight colors.

Talk! Talk! Talk! the crowd calls. *Truth!* some others scream.

Gordon bows his head over the mike, adjusted for a much shorter man. His voice is sore and husky from too much yakking all day. And yet how fast his words tumble, run on, almost choking, no surprise to those who know him.

Claire recalls.

He could easily see his mistake, couldn't he? Even as he was exploding with adrenaline, being his hammy self, throwing up a fist in honor of what should I call it . . . peasant power? Yeah, he was getting us peasants all so "pumped" as the kids would call it. But his dream was that people would stop seeing the system as god. Okay, so maybe some were but they were just transferring godliness from the system to *him*! And maybe he liked this? Maybe something very ugly was playing evil sorcerer with Gordon.

 God for a day.

Yes, he goes on and on and on and on in the usual way. But whenever he stops to breathe, the twilight and candlelight tremble to the crowd's sorties of screams, agreeable jeers, and smashing applause. Then, in a gap of their multitudinal voice, he digs in once again.

"It's all just in your silly head, right? Economists say the economy is glowing! Okay, pal, to hell with the word *economy*. I don't wanna hear how the economy is, I wanna hear how LIFE is 'cause, pal, I ain't in YOUR economy I'm in the Land of Life! That's what you are thinking, right?!!!"

The crowd's response singes the eardrums, then spatterings of the words *Truth! Truth! Truth!* Now a shadow at Gordon's left. Whitney has stepped close and pushes something into his hands. She cries out something but it is dissolved by the crowd noise. Seems she is saying *Put it on!* because it's his camo BDU shirt for Rex's militia, and there the wide woven green pistol belt with rows of metal-trimmed holes. He hesitates because he thinks maybe he does not know Rex anymore.

He looks back around down to the connected piazza where Rex's face is just a spot of utter gray. He knows Rex won't like him wearing this shirt tonight. Mr. Secret-Hide-In-the-Shadows York. He who does not write letters to governors, who will hurt you with his eyes. His eyes are pikes. And sometimes his words are, too. But tonight . . . Gordon . . . is . . . God.

He thrusts an arm into the sleeve.

Truth! Truth! Truth! the coaxers coax.

Shirt on, belt fastened with a twist, olive green and black mountain lion on the shoulder declaring its place, declaring BORDER MOUNTAIN MILITIA, the army of peasants, fright to the lords, yeah, this low rogue army, mere kitchen army, close warm kitchens breathing family, breathing threat. Lords beware, the crowd goes nuts, catcalls and croaks mixed with every possible human sound magnified by hundreds. And now, one voice somewhere near yells, "Give 'em hell!" Another yells, "KILL 'EM! Kill the president! Kill the governors! Blast 'em all!"

Gordon waits it out. One hand on the mike. One hand raised to mean *Quiet,* but it has no effect. It just goes on and on, this whatever it is, the stinging edge of revolt.

 More speechifying.

Yes, he is allowed to go on. And he does. He warns that the sly rulers that look so small and hamsterlike on the TV set are really something *else* all together, a system. The transnational neo-feudal privatize-profitize-everything system is "Evil!" This makes the mob lash its great tail and growl. And during this ugly sound and the stage vibrating under Gordon's feet, he sees ten-year-old Theodan Darby and almost-seven-year-old Jane Meserve, lighted by floating flickering colors, one on either side of him, Jane wearing a black tricorn hat and Theodan bareheaded . . . they unfurl flags, one the flag of the True Maine Militia, the other the Stars and Stripes. Now the crowd is making purring sounds but also indications that it might rise as over a levee up onto the stage and embrace or drown the new god with too much worship.

Gordon's one most lunatic eye finds an open bottle of beer behind the drummer's seat. Full! And so now Gordon is convinced that the old god still loves him. So he gives more speech, then spits on the stage floor. The crowd condones. So then he drinks and it is glorious, all that roaring approval out there in the lively dark, the hot, almost flat brew tumbling down into him and then with a True Maine Militia song sheet he twists up a giant pretend joint and pretends to smoke it. "EVERYTHING WE ORDINARY PEOPLE DO IS BAD," he observes.

It rips into his eyes.

Too sudden. Then more. Great layers of brilliance and blindness, and ashen shapes skating behind it all like fish. Gordon understands that several network television channels are moving in closer with their equipment to grind away on him, cut him down to, yes, hamster-size for the little propped-up boxes of nearly every American home, simultaneously stretching him out larger to be a nation-sized object of terror? But he is feeling like a big bird in the sky.

The crowd thunders its love, its single violent prayer and breath so brisk he can feel it disturb his hair. Uh, his *feathers*.

 The screen is on the scene.

Wow! You will not believe how laughable people are when they take matters into their own hands. Here we'll show some fat ones in shorts so you can be entertained. Here's a quick shot of a sourpuss with a . . . ohmygoodness an assault rifle. See the scary Prophet yelling extremist goobledygook. See his jacket! Sinister! The thing is, how do you *feel*? Scared? When people who aren't officially sanctioned or modeled properly try to do things *themselves,* they are a threat to democracy. Okay? Got it? It's funny but it's scary. Right? How does it make you feel? How . . . does . . . this . . . fringe . . . extreme . . . wacko . . . weirdness . . . *makeyou* . . . *feel??* Feeeeel *it!*

 The crowd is expanding, its thunder blacker as another layer of white TV light springs into action.

Gordon is *almost* squinting. But no, he is not fully squinting. He stares them down. He taunts them with jokes. But the dangerous light fumbles into his pores, the fabrics of his clothing. It is *investigating*.

He draws an arm back, swinging a leg forward as if to throw a mean fast ball, then pitches the imaginary ball to the nearest TV light and the crowd rages and then rips into applause, then comes synchronized labor union–style claps. Now it chants: *OUT! OUT! OUT! OUT! OUT!* Into this chant, Gordon screams a scream of a ghoul, "DISMANTLE

THE BEAST!" and while throwing up his fist, howls, "GOD SAVE THE REPUBLIC . . . OF MAINE!"

The spasming crowd repeats *GOD SAVE THE REPUBLIC OF MAINE!* almost perfectly in sync. Does Rex like this? What does Rex *want* of Gordon? Indeed it matters. Rex, the brother. And what do the kids want? And the others, all his dear ones? And Bree? Is everybody happy? Happy. Happy. Happy.

One of the distant TV lights blackens. Did it get trampled by the immersifying crowd? Now another light draws back, swaying, then shrinks away.

And then: BOOOOM! Lou-EE's St. Onge's toilet-paper-wadded deck cannon up there in the field making a *wooomp . . . wooomp . . .* through the distant hills, and thanks to network TV, all of America.

 Bree.

Gordon, the ram, my teacher, my myth, finally you have given yourself to the people.

 Lyn Potter. Operative. Yes, low on the Bureau totem pole. In fact, you could say he's only ether. No face. A cloud man. But with a little camera, he's a wizard, you see. He speaks.

I got maybe eight hundred frames of the speech. The lighting was a problem at first but I got him so he is recognizable. See him wearing the camo BDU jacket and pistol belt. Patch of the Border Mountain Militia. See here he's chugging beer during his speech. He rolls a gigantic pretend joint from a newspaper or something, pretends to smoke it, just to make some point, the point being he's egging Americans on to disrespect law. He got people worked up. Here, see, about four hundred shots of people being worked up. And plenty of guns around, guys with arms folded, a pistol on the hip or see this: gun against the ribs. And a guy on that Quonset hut roof with a rifle. He has been identified as William Daniel Lancaster. Sharpshooter. And his brother, a sharpshooter in 'Nam, died there. So this live one wears the brother's dog tags. So the live one has a grudge against America seems like.

So meanwhile, St. Onge has America under his spell. And his militia buddies got us in their sights.

 ### The end.

Just as liquids evaporate, the crowd and its cackling and piping and peppery din doesn't do a fast bye-bye. An hour later, there are still dark clumps of chatter all over the quad and in the sandy lot and downhill along the road. Yet another forty-five minutes, the black sky of ferocious stars presses down and all of it is cold. Then there is mostly emptiness, the last of stranger voices gotten tiny beyond the downhill woods. Voices still becoming farther, hear them? They're mere peeps.

 ### Gail St. Onge thinking back.

And then it was over. No heart attacks. No fights. Just one broken garden gate. And litter. We could deal with that. But then actually it wasn't over. The part that changed our lives forever was yet to come.

 ### Brothers.

Out on the quad just beyond the porch screen behind where he sits are voices. Settlementers, Rex's men, and beyond that the band dismantling wire and drums, and beyond that more Settlement people, his family. And Butch's and Cory's anarchist friends occupying the radio building for a few more days. Only two or three strangers still. Three fellows: Mr. Sea Dogs cap, Mr. Wizard-of-Oz-Lion-laugh, and a guy with beach-boy looks who's used his camera the way a ten-year-old does. You know, not afraid to waste film on people's feet or people with their mouths full. He's got the band guys in his crosshairs now, a great shot of those tangled wires and a fiddle case full of maple leaves.

But Gordon is alone. He's inside one of the big porches, in a rocker, leaning forward, holding his face with one hand, beer in the other. The chair has hand-carved bear heads on the back, the wooden faces look to be singing; assuredly there is mirth.

But now Rex materializes and he is standing erect, a cemetery corner stone. He is looking down into the world of the stealthful mountain lion of the Border Mountain Militia patch on Gordon's left biceps. Cheery candles on either side of the rocker ripple and scribble pink and white light over everything stuffed into this moment of silence. Then Rex's iron voice, "The FBI is watching you. They like to know what your vices are so they can twist you up in them and push you over. That wasn't smart, getting them to know you think pot is okay. Even beer. It's sloppy. But when some guys yell 'kill the president,' you say 'No way in hell.' That was an operative setting the mood . . . or trying to. You can't leave that hanging. You don't just let them take over."

Gordon's big face, one eye stuttering, the other a flame, looks up. His huge hands drop to his knees. "Right. The FBI." He snickers. He snickers because he is drunk and because Rex is . . . is . . . corny? That melodramatic tightness around that crawling-to-the-jaws mustache. Now there's something Gordon has never seen before, a look crossing Rex's face and body, far exceeding the hostility over the letter to the governor. This is all concentrated in Rex's jaw and all the teeth locked to prevent saying more, because Rex is an officer and a gentleman, right? He makes no goof ups. But somehow the jaws and the teeth and the unsaid words are all braked against something that is trembling around and outside him as if he were blanketed with biting flies.

Gordon says, "I guess you're right, brother."

"Self-control is what you have to have if you want to represent the Border Mountain Militia."

Gordon looks up and gives a couple of jerky nods.

The light around them gets blotchy, one of the pink-glass Settlement-made spirit faces going out. Just an embery orange piece of wick left. A puny glow. Then not even that.

 Two a.m.

The musical cousins and their musical friends from THE County are pretty revved up, not ready for bed. They have brought a present. A cooler of long-necked Canadian beers and four scary-looking oversized bottles of bourbon, as golden and gloinky as the river Styx.

Late night news. See!

Crazy extremist throws something at the camera. What is it? Just pretending? Now he's screaming. No way to make out what he's going on about. All wobbly and a few extremist followers making sounds on top of his sounds. Now the so-called Prophet is shaking his fist, eyes on the camera, "GOD SAVE THE REPUBLIC OF MAINE!!" You know these racist hate-filled militias. Time to speak to experts now on what to expect and whether or not authorities should be sent in to save the children. But first a close-up of the Prophet's face. See his temples throb! See his perspiration. Fear for your darling Heather and Josh and your dog and your stuff!!!!

 Vaughan Hill Road. The old farm place with "updated" windows, the biggest one covered in fiberglass drapes, sort of green. Glassed-in porch. Wood plaque shaped like a pointing hand reads: ENTER.

The glass porch door shivers as someone knocks. A body-builder-type platinum blond guy. Tanned. Older in daylight than he would look at night. He is shaved totally and as fresh-scented as morning. His truck plates say: MAINE.

Rex's mother Ruth swings that glass outer door wide.

The big guy says, "Hi. I'm Andy. I need to see Rex." He adds that he and Rex are friends.

Ruth leads him in past the wooden hand plaque, into the kitchen that smells of sausages and eggs and one of those dish soaps that is advertised to break down grease but stinks like some mild form of nerve gas. And the house smells of its own tender oldness.

 The magic of photography.

There is the stack of prints in Rex's hand. A "bad hand" you'd say if it were a deck of cards. Rex only looks at the top one, if you call it looking. His eyes turn ever so oily and hollow and just drip over the edge of his thumb. He hands them back to the stranger, Andy, no friend.

Rex is now very still, himself a picture.

In a voice as high as a woman's for such a brawny fellow, the stranger says, "There are more." And another thing about this voice, there's no accent, or rather there is an accent, every voice has an accent, but not the kind of accent you could locate on a bright map. There's no indication of a childhood. It's as if this figure in Rex's living room were manufactured and plugged into the wall. He speaks toward Rex's now iron profile, "I just thought you ought to know."

 Next day. Shortly after noontime in Denise's Diner parking lot.

What is that large human-shaped object on the dirt? Put you to mind of the Vietnam War era Buddhists who set themselves on fire with gasoline and a kitchen match. They would, just this same way, eventually slump forward or to one side, life still roiling deep inside the crust. No face or fingers, just an overroasted black. But here today the figure isn't black crust. It is running down in slippery falling solid red sheets of paint. No, not paint. Warm blood. The figure moves, but how can it be alive? No face. No ears.

The crowd of people that has scurried from the diner or stopped their passing cars is all shouting at once, so many who witnessed the making of that gleaming red thing slumped now so quietly in the sun.

Police wearing latex gloves push Rex York into the cruiser. His knuckles are a little shredded. Some of the blood on his hands and clothes is his own, some Gordon's. Mixed. And where is the rock he used to blind his foe, to crunch the skull, make knots of the ears? Everyone wonders. But everything around is perfectly matched, a tarp-sized circle of red around the melting red man, rocks, sand, little poofs of grass and plantain.

And wasn't there a gun? Someone said gun. But maybe that was cast aside. Maybe Rex forgot how to make such a thing work. When Rex came looking for Gordon and found his face at a table in the diner, how did Rex navigate, his own musculature wobbling with creatureliness, with savagery, with something older and rawer and less negotiable than a loaded gun?

The sacrificed figure is moving a little, perhaps wondering on some wiffy forgotten question. But then it stops moving.

 After Brian calls Ivy to tell her the news.

She is just outside the State House where she was going in to get more grubby stuff to feed her column. Still in her car, parking garage so stinky, echoing, groaning with other vehicles whipping into those narrow slots around her, she now pushes her extra jacket into her face. She is weeping, of course, but there's ever so slight confusion concerning which teacher man is being carried in to MMC. David Morelli's little head? Or this swollen head and face bigger than a bread box, this Brian described, this that showed in the photos the *Record Sun*'s Jamie Knowles got as the rescue unit was unloading.

 Glory York remembering.

These guys I knew were having a late-night party on the lake. I was surprised to see Gordon show up. Him and his Aroostook County cousins and some guys I never saw before, all of them revved up after their big-kid-militia event. And everybody was full of beer or Jim or Jack. I was so sloshed I almost don't remember any of it, except that in those days Gordon had become as famous as the Beatles. Therefore, I had a crush on him. I was nineteen years old and full of crushes.

I danced naked. For him. Though it seemed I danced for everyone there, so the legend goes.

Gordon and I wound up together in the frosty grass and cold sand and in the jillion pictures some weird mystery guy showed dad. And my father became someone none of us knew. He became the mystery.

And then Gordon was brain dead.

What happened between Gordon and me at that party could have just floated away like a funny little soap bubble, with all my other wild party memories of those years, if it hadn't been for those mystery pictures stuck to my father's eyes.

The family.

Sitting, standing, they crowd several waiting rooms. They line hall walls. Some are designated to press the nurse's station for news or call home to the farm place to those waiting and worrying there.

Newspaper reporters and even radio interviewers, they come and they go. Some say in a sincere hush *how sorry* and *how terrible*. Others are twinkle-eyed with amusement or there's something too sugary in their awe as they speak and as they scan the St. Onge gathering as though the family were made up of dancing poodles and elephants wearing tutus.

Dark-haired Senator Mary Wright appears in a brisk red coat, striding along in flat quiet shoes, her face not just grave today but gray.

The reporters clamor, "Senator Wright!" and "Senator, what brings you here today?"

As brisk as her red coat, her words to them, "Same thing you're here for." But her smile is one of true sorrow. Then she turns sharply to the approach of a pair of St. Onge teenagers whose cheeks she pecks and then as more approach, her petite scarlet presence is swallowed in a group hug.

At the same time, Gordon's mother, Marian, walks, almost runs from the elevators. No one moves toward her but Whitney, who is already in her path between a laundry cart and clutch of reporters, does not step aside. She faces Marian's approach square on.

How handsome Marian Depaolo St. Onge is, gray-streaked dark hair clipped just above the collar of her stylish belted brown jacket. And Whitney with her messy slept-on-last-night honey yellow ponytail, not a homely girl, but Gordon's corkscrew grimace gives one of her Slavic-ish Nordic-ish green eyes a one-second bulge, eyebrow high. But see up close, Marian's green eyes are knotty and pink and terrible from hours of off-and-on wailing.

Face-to-face now, both women are equally tall. Oldest of all the children of Guillaume, Whitney opens her arms. She is not rebuffed. Neither one speaks, just the long, long straining crush of their embrace. Then Marian moves on, past all the other teens and tykes, no stopping, no glancing from side to side. So many have that look. The look of *him*. But even today in its heat of feeling, Marian cannot manage an enfolding that diametric or that complicit.

Senator Mary is back-to so Marian is unaware of her old fond acquaintance and vice versa.

The nurses repeatedly insist they cannot permit everyone to visit the patient, even though there's a five-minute limit and big no-visit time between to keep the bedside clear. "Only the im-med-i-ate family."

What's that?

Well, Marian for sure. *One* mother. Easy enough. In she goes.

When she's finished and comes out of that ICU doorway, she is crying infantlike, a wide-mouthed *wahhh!* and hurries lopingly and unladylike in the other direction from the family, the senator, the media. And around the farthest corner, a wider corridor, she vanishes.

 Inner voice of the Bureau.

Your bewilderment is becoming on you. Yes, just as God has his reasons so do we.

 Conscious.

Then there is the morning that the surgeon wearing a pastel-stripe short-sleeve shirt like a businessman meets the earliest arrivals of the family and some who had spent the night here. Doctor has a wall-to-wall smile.

He brags that all the surgeons involved did a remarkable job with the blah blah and the blah blah blah and the blah. He explains that Gordon, now conscious, is stirring. He is not paralyzed, has no numbness in the extremities. He remembers who he is and aced other basic quiz questions. No memory of recent events, though. That's pretty common, due to blah blah blah of the blah blah. And of course, in these cases of blah, the speech will be bungled for a while. Therapy should help. But his speech is pretty amazing all the same.

The doctor never speaks of the missing teeth, which are not his specialty. Teeth? What are those but decoration. The brain is the center of the universe. No brain, no universe. But here he brags up the work of Dr. Lofchie who will be in later today to examine Gordon's eyes, especially the surgery done on the right one. He speaks further on trauma of blah and further brags up the new procedures used and how "we" pulled it off.

At some point in all this Bonnie Loo has dropped to the floor in the middle of the little listening group, sort of on her knees but more of an around-the-campfire style sprawly-leg thing and her hands folded like prayer. She is sobbing in relief but soundlessly, and all this so fast no one has time to wonder if she's fainted. She's whispering "*Jesus Jesus Jesus*." Her floppy orange-streaked black topknot goes from side to side in *front* of her bowed face. This praying is not a Bonnie Loo thing.

The doctor advises in an unchanging upbeat way, "She shouldn't be on the floor."

 Another day. Claire St. Onge speaks.

When I go in to see him, he raises an arm *hello* . . . so I know he can see me but there is still only a small wet slit for his "good" eye, the other one bandaged, and a voice that's croaky and thick.

Aurel comes up to the other side of the bed, taking off his red felt crusher hat, his favorite hat for fall. Aurel, looking especially fit. His short dark beard. Every hair. *Shining*. He smells of the outdoors, the big cold outdoors.

I yearn to be alone with Gordon. I yearn for this terribly. But I can tell Aurel wishes for the same. He and Gordon have always been as close as it gets. In fact, when we told the nurses Aurel was Gordon's half brother in order to get him in for his ICU visit, we didn't have to lie much.

I pick up Gordon's good hand and stroke the palm and wish for all I can never have, though I had it once upon a time. Then I scold myself . . . ye gods, Claire, you have more now than you had yesterday. Yesterday Gordon was in a coma, ten million miles away, a tiny star.

Aurel's eyes. Glittering. Dark. Predatory (in looks only). He pats the covers of the bed beside Gordon and says softly, "*Guillaume, vous savez, mon vieux, on a besoin de vois chez nous.*"

I stare at Aurel. I know what he wants. He wants to touch Gordon. Hug him up. Two Frenchies. This is the way. But Gordon looks so broken. Gordon's head is turned toward Aurel, though there's zero expression in the bloated shaved weirdly purple face.

I turn and study the four people behind the waist-high counter of the nurses station. I'm still so distrusting of Dr. Tureen's telling us that Gordon has "made it." Gordon hasn't really said anything intelligent yet, not to any of the family. And what about his eye!

Aurel outdoes himself with nervous chatter, less soft now, urgent, newsy.

Gordon's one visible eye (crimson), is fixed on Aurel and I feel his hand pulling from mine and I let go and he carefully grasps the red felt crusher hat in Aurel's hands, tugs it away, presses it to his chest for a minute, then pretends that he is about to squish it onto his own head and says croakily, "*Chez nous!*" and nods twice, then flings one of those long legs out from under the covers like he's ready to go, and a sharp-eyed nurse comes on the run to punish us.

 Translation of Aurel's words to Gordon.

Ge-yome, you know, my old one, we have need of you at home.

 At the *Record Sun*.

Ivy Morelli stops at Ken Meyer's desk and stands behind him watching the screen as his fingers almost soundlessly run over the keys, messing around with the York–St. Onge update, getting it in shape . . . front page . . . deadline in twenty minutes.

So far it reads:

> Dispute-1 TK+ DISPUTE SETTLED THE MILITIA WAY
> *St. Onge remains in critical condition+++*

Egypt—
  Richard "Rex" York, leader of the Border Mountain Militia and self-employed electrician, is being held pending arraignment in Oxford County Jail since yesterday on charges of assault with attempt to kill, following the alleged brutal attack on Guillaume "Gordon" St. Onge.
  St. Onge, known as "the Prophet," the charismatic anti-government

preacher and father of several dozen children by numerous wives, remains in critical condition at Maine Medical Center. The attack, which witnesses describe as "a blood bath" in which York used a rock to disfigure and possibly blind St. Onge took place outside a local diner while as many as 17 witnesses looked on, police said. Three witnesses report the presence of a handgun, while others suggest only a rock.

State police spokesperson, Myra Guthrie, said that the incident may have been instigated by militia infighting but one witness on the scene said it was "over a woman."

St. Onge is also reportedly a member of York's militia.

The St. Onge family includes as many as twenty-eight "wives" and many children in what is known as "the Settlement," a compound on 900 acres of land owned by St. Onge, the injured man. A sign on the single entrance reads: KEEP OUT OR YOU'LL BE SHOT. TRY IT.

Ken Meyer inserts another word, pushes *police said* to another sentence.

Ivy walks back to her own desk.

 Two weeks pass. In the newsroom of the *Record Sun*, Ivy covers the mouthpiece of the phone to prevent sounds from entering it.

Through the window at her left, she could see part of the hospital complex where he is, if she could see through several blocks of stone, cement, structural steel, and brick.

"Could I have the room of Gordon St. Onge, please?" she had asked the hospital operator and then, immediately, the extension to his new room purred in her ear.

Several rings now. She imagines an *empty hospital room*. Another ring, another. *Empty bed. Empty world.*

"H'llo."

It is his voice.

She says nothing.

Heart pounding ever so painfully, she hangs up ever so reluctantly, ever so gently. Now she covers her face with her hands, pretending for a few moments that she is alone. She smiles. Yessiree, it is true, he lives.

NOVEMBER

 In the newsroom of the *Record Sun*, Ivy Morelli is at her computer. To fully picture Ivy, you have to remember her purply black hair is now spiked.

She is going to be late with the feature on toxic waste dumped near yet another river in mid-Maine. Her fingers trickle over the keys but she is not aware of fingers. Or the fact that one of her earrings (a red feather) is lying on the carpet. She hears someone behind her. Of course it is her editor, Brian Fitch. That's his walk, the way he approaches.

"What?" she asks without taking her eyes off the screen.

"Ms. Morelli." He calls her this as a nickname, not a formality. When he's being formal, he calls her Ivy.

She wrastles the mouse a bit, eyes squinting at the last three lines now. She has lost her train of thought. She turns in her seat and looks squarely at him. He has ordinary brown hair, gray eyes with fun in them, and a short-sleeved pinkish-beige shirt, editorish pants. A wristwatch of white gold. A cup with the word VIRGO written in leafy vegetation, bugs and birds. As we all know, VIRGO is one of those earthy signs, fertility and all that. But also persnicketiness.

Ivy again says, "What?"

Brian says, "York is out."

Ivy blinks. She pictures New York.

"Richard York . . . Rex . . . the one who mutilated St. Onge."

Ivy swallows. "Let him out? You mean on bail?"

"No, on technicalities."

"Like what? There were twenty witnesses."

Brian shrugs. "So far, it's vague. Vaaaaaague. Oh, maybe the rock was a piece of quartz in the report, but tested out in the lab as feldspar."

Ivy stands up. She is a short person but Brian is not a lot taller. "That doesn't make sense."

"Suppose York is FBI?"

"HAW HAW HAW HAW HAW." (Ivy's big laugh resonates cottonishly through the carpeted and semisoundproofed city room). "Brian, you are starting to sound like a conspiracy theorist!"

"I'm a systems analyst. There's a difference. Systems behave in a certain way."

Ivy swallows again. "Rex York loose."

"He's been out five days."

"How'd we miss that?"

"Ask Tony."

She looks toward the hallway, beyond which is the clerk's new desk. She swallows again. Stunned. She moves her foot. She steps on her earring. *Chrunch!*

 Ivy's epiphany.

It doesn't come to her as a question, a reporterly question or a philosophical one. It comes as a little groan. She *knows*! Mystery solved! Gordon had dropped the charges. Gordon the great big all-forgiving noise. Gordon too soft and in that way a danger to the world?

 In the night.

It's never dark here. Never quiet. Never fragrant. The sound of little wheels in the hall. Gordon has tears on his mangled face, staring into the hungry schemy shadows of this room's corners, the broad open-curtained window with its brick and breathing city beyond. The two TVs. Off but ever-ready. And what are those at the other end of the bed sticking up under the blanket? He can't remember exactly the words. *Hooves? Handles? Claws?*

 Butch Martin remembers Jumbo.

Um . . . a bunch of us came across the quad from the meat-cutting shed, headed for the kitchens midday. This included Blinky, real name of Ryan, one of those eleven persons who had come to live at the Settlement from Jaxon Cross's place, with Gordo's blessing a few days before his demise. There weren't many sitting around on the piazzas cuz it was a bitter rotten day. High winds and the sun; I remember it winking so there must've been some small clouds hot-rodding along. But also it was bone-damp. Gordo and my father Eddie were braving it, both in rockers there on the first piazza by the kitchen doors, like a welcoming committee, but both were dressed big like bears. Flannels and wools, mucho layers. And then there were the two wool felt crushers, one for each head, which stand out in my thinking because they were store bought and were that eye-splitting hunters' orange.

We all tromped up onto the porch, holding the door for each other, feigning extreme manners and laughing, Cory especially bloody, his denim chambray and thermal sleeves light, so it showed. No blood on the hands, though. That's part of the rules of clean meat. Hands have to look like snowflakes. And before heading across the yards to the meal Cory had even taken the rawhide out of his hair and brushed it. Longer every day. And never a tangle, in part due to so much primping.

I hated looking square-on at Gordo. It was hard to get used to. The way he no longer filled up a place, you know, like he used to sort of blind you, even without the orange hat, more like when you are steering into the headlights and you can't see anything *but*. A true force. But now different.

My father, Eddie, Dad, was reading to him something, I can't recall what, but it would be, for instance, a parts list for, for instance, our main turbine.

So see, Dad's voice was just poking along informationally.

But also coming along the porches from one of the shops were Lawrence and Jill, these other real new Settlement citizens since just before Gordo's "accident." Neither one had teeth. Both him and her were . . . um . . . skinny except her rear was wide. But man, from the waist up Jill was a skinny girl and Lawrence was pure sticks and twigs. He kept his head shaved and cold and hatless, but his head was . . . um . . . skinny, not a skull you'd want to show off, right? His eyes were dark so they sort of jumped out at you from all that white. Well, he had a beard. Small, sort of reddish, I guess. Like a stain.

They had a little kid that would crawl when they lowered it to the floor. And an older kid. Named Jumbo. He wasn't rugged or round so the name Jumbo must have only went with his voice. He was only about three years old, maybe four, if you were looking at him, not his voice.

Under the jacket and shirt Lawrence had tattoos covering him like another shirt. And every one of those tattoos was a race car—street rods and speedway classics and Daytona stuff. But that day all you saw was the jacket, neck, skull, and skinny face in dead-body white. These were poor people and everything about them was hard up. This is why Gordo had arranged for them to be here, because they needed to be, but they didn't yet do much here to participate. Very . . . um . . . clammed up. They'd just hunch up together at meals and talk soft to each other and nobody else.

You couldn't help but notice how the poor of America, by the dead end of the 1900s, were pretty much being hung out to dry. America was and is now barren, like a desert, man, when it comes to brotherly love, right? But Gordo, in this way of throwing open the door for refugees, was a fucking high priest. Therefore, what happens next purely pisses me off. I *try* not to BLAME. But for about three seconds I wanted to kick the little fucker across the yard, little Jumbo.

Soooo, see, that day, Jill was carrying the crawling kid. Sometimes Lawrence did. I gave him, Lawrence, a friendly poke in the shoulder and he looked at me, nodded, then hunch-huddled up as if the cold wind had just blown all his clothes off, even his tattoos.

I noticed Gordo was looking up at them from his rocker . . . he's looking up at these two he had rescued from OUT THERE IN THE ROTTEN WORLD and then their kid Jumbo runs out of somewhere and in his deep-for-a-three-year-old voice, his tubalike voice, blasts up at Gordo, "Yoooooor face looks like a butt!!"

This made Gordo get one of his eye squirm-squinch things and it's the eye that's been all stitched and sagging so there's all this effect, and so then he's staring at the kid with this EYE in a way that would creep me out if I were a little kid not used to the way of things around here, but not Jumbo, he's just inflating to a more dangerous version of himself, eyes fixed without a blink on Gordo. Well, Jumbo's TV-watching legacy personality traits were already famous here. And we all figured he was having TV withdrawal on top of his TV reality show courtesies.

So my Dad, Eddie, he's looking at Lawrence and Jill to see how they'll deal with this latest but they just keep an even trot toward the door, which someone who has gone ahead holds open, door of the kitchens, with heat and foody feasty smells rolling out and then inside they go.

So Jumbo is staring Gordo down. He's still out there with us and so I guess he's our problem, right? Normally, there's a pretty free-ranging spirit to kids here, fine. So yuh, okay. Here's what. This is all in a matter of cold hard seconds, this skinny kid, hair clipped almost as bald as his father's, no hat, but wearing his nice new Settlement-made duds. This is what he does next. He spits at Gordo, aiming for his face, but the spit fans out, and some seems to go on the big black and red wool sleeve of Gordo's jacket and some seems to stick to one of the carved bear heads of the back of the chair, maybe some down inside Gordo's collar, but sort of like dewdrops. Cory, yeah, all blood-smeared from skinning and sawing on that deer, this bigger-than-Mr.-Maine Cory Guillaume St. Onge, grabs the little motherfucker and Cory's long totally black hair flash-whirls and tornadoes and full-rushes around himself and the kid. And the kid is like freaked, right? He screams bloody murder, baring all his little white teeth, wrenching and twisting and this is stretching out his new sweater cuz Cory's hold is not being reduced.

So then Gordo's head is turning. Looking at Dad. As if the spit and insults and screams ejecting from Jumbo's little wet animal mouth were nothing at all. And Gordo's face had all that disfigurement, floppy eyelid and fiery red scar all the way to the corner of his mouth where his broken-teethed situation was like a bucksaw and beard growing back funny and one ear like a knob and this is what he says to Dad in a weird flat monotone, "Who were they?", jerks his thumb at the door where Jill and Lawrence had just gone.

Now Jumbo is calling Cory "pig!" as Cory stuffs him under one arm in a casual way and heads into the hot kitchens. I'm thinking that Gordo asking who Lawrence and Jill are, even though he *ought* to know who Lawrence and Jill are, means Gordo's brain, man, it's pretty near the same as the brain of that buck whose about-to-be-taxidermied head is in the cardboard box back in the cutting shed with the customer's name marked on with tape.

 The screen (marching music in the background) commands:

You must vote! It's all in your hands! You have the choice! It's your duty! It's profound! Wow! Wow! Wow! America the best!!!

 Slipping into a quietly idling long cream-colored car with tinted glass is Gregory Allen, Madison Avenue public relations brain-muscle for certain goliath corporations, national and transnational, whose interests must be secured in this year's presidential, congressional, and gubernatorial elections. Yes, Gregory Allen is one of those who sees to it that the elections go as planned. Settled into the back seat now, with a wink to the man next to him, he remarks—

"It's certainly easier to put it over on the public these days, but a *lot* more expensive."

 Over and under, left and right, inside and outside, hither and yon—

Corporate power grows.

 The voice of Mammon.

Growth! Growth! Growth! Growth!

 The Anti-Rich Society.

Motorist slows at the narrow bridge that crosses into Egypt by the abandoned woolen mill. On the radio is pleasant jazz piano tinkling harmlessly.

Suddenly and awfully, young giggles and gasps cut off the tinkles and the motorist's hands tighten on the wheel as one of the young voices speaks. "Testing. One. Two. Three. Testing."

More chatter and one chortle, then a hushy womanly ever-so-slowly-speaking voice: "Hello. This is the Anti-Rich Society's high tea and literary hour. Coming to you from that secret undisclosed location in your heart."

Young male voice, less touching and breathy but equally earnest, "This poetry reading today is especially for you out there in Voting Day Land where you probably believe you are citizens . . . but . . . you . . . are . . . DOGS."

"Yes, Bill," says the wonderful womanly voice. "Our listeners will therefore be especially inspired to hear you read today from your famous poem." The sound of tea being sipped.

"Thank you, Miss Munch. It's a privilege." More tea is sipped.

Womanly voice says, "Yes, we have on our show today, William Blake brought back from the grave to read to you from his oft-misunderstood poem, which, no, is not about a big kitty but about what was once known as 'the hydra,' the dangerous revolts of slaves and sailors all over the world where they used the only weapon uniformly available, *fire*. They knew tyranny when they saw it and they weren't going to lie down and beg . . . or vote." Tea-sipping sounds. "Okay Bill, you're *on the air*."

An old-time fog-cooled London accent it is not, but an accent of steamy North Carolina begins to recite: "Tyger, Tyger, burning bright, in the forests of the night; what immortal hand or eye, could frame thy fearful symmetry?"

The motorist is squinting, not especially impressed with the tea sipping?

The Carolinian Blake voice rolls on, "What the anvil? What dread grasp, dare its deadly terrors clasp?"

Miss Munch interrupts, "Oh, terrors." More tea sipping.

Blake's revived corpse finishes up, the words spaced drumlike and dirgelike, "In. What. Distant. Deeps. Or. Skies. Burnt. The. Fire. Of. Thine. Eyes! On. What. Wings. Dare. He. Aspire? What. The. Hand. Dare. Seize. The. *Fire*?" And the word fire spoken in this drawl is *fiarrrr*. You almost hear and smell its orange licking terrific swallowing roar.

Then after a long silence, pleasant jazz piano returns tinkling in its calming watery way from the normal broadcasting network.

 ### At the voting place.

Building has clapboards painted white. Floors inside are tipped like a ship on a nasty wave. Wonderful, old, old smell. A place of enduringness, the Old Towne House. *We in America are a people!* it enthuses, whether or not it is true, it feels so, thus it *is* so, today.

A Settlement car packed with elders approaches, a big squishy-looking stubbornly maintained old gray (and green) car chugging past the leafless row of November maples with creased rotund trunks, uncountable arms and witchy fingers. Stonewalls, the Maine kind, piled, not absolutely squared. And now the cemetery of 1700s and 1800s slate markers, some tipped fore, some tipped back, there on the heaved ground as if underneath it all there was a joyful rumpus.

Fieldstone and maple, lichen and slate all in complicit grays. Thousands of grays that work together as one, like robust tissue merely resting its brute force.

But what is this ahead? Who are these people with the signs? And faces like skulls! Face paint, a greasy sheen. Terrible. Black grim reaper robes with hoods. Some with old scythes. But mostly signs. But some are wearing suits such as lawyers do. Or maybe lady governors. Or senators. Or those who tell you the news at six if you were a TV watcher out beyond the world of the Settlement. But these faces are bare of greasepaint. Suspiciously young. And suspiciously familiar.

Some signs read: THE SYSTEM IS RIGGED while others say: ONLY MONEY VOTES . . . PENCILS ARE JUST FOR PRETENDING.

The young grim reapers and young senators bow and smile and wave their signs and scythes. Some are playing kazoos. It is so very confusing to the people in the car. "I thought they were *for* democracy," one says thinly.

So the True Maine Militia lives on. And maybe they are a little too close to the voting place and the constable will come or the *state* police and lock them in prison! This is worse than misbehavior. This could be crime, the old dutiful Settlement voters observe.

DECEMBER

 The thread.

Today Jane wears an alarmingly yellow jumper, yellow and green plaid flannel with a spider-web-thin red line shooting up and down and across. This fabric matches shirts and outfits of dozens of other people here because it had come to the Settlement in bulk, several hefty rolled bolts. Her dark fluffy hair has been brushed and brushed by the beauty crew. So clean and smelling like weeds, yes. She is melding with Settlementness, while this other thread, the tight looping interstate telephone company cable is all that connects this child with her mother now. Since Lisa's case became federal, she has been "transported" away away away away.

Miles and miles and miles of such slim thread between Boston and Maine makes voices tired. And faces are erased, except in memory. But when you are six years old, memory has no pluck. Memory is jelly.

So here we are today, the *now* of it. Lisa seems to no longer have much to say. Her lips mostly just breathe. And Jane? Just gasps and sighs. So there is no actual conversation tonight.

Jane keeps her face to the wall, like shame, here where she sits at Gordon's largest desk, her oh-so-elegant long fingers flicking the cards of one rotary file, although she has no idea her fingers are doing this.

Eventually, the six-year-old and her mum say "bye-bye" and "I love you" and "call you soon." What will there be to say next time. The mothers here have promised to fly with Jane to visit the California prison where Lisa is being sent to soon. This has been discussed drearily. Many times. It is losing even its thin clarity. Maybe Jane will become somewhat bored in time, bored by this thing against her ear, this barely warm plastic appliance.

 From a future time, Clair St. Onge remembers.

There wasn't much hoopla about Lisa's fate in the news now. Lisa's lawyer told Lisa's father Pete (Granpa Pete to Jane) that the drug bureau and FBI had begun playing this one down, fearing that Lisa's little Scottie dog's bad death from heat when the police left her in Lisa's car could make a lot of bad press for them.

 The voice of Mammon.

Growth! Growth! Growth! Growth! Growth! Growth! GROWTH! GROWTH!

 Rex York revised.

No computer. No "patriot movement" web searches. No Border Mountain Militia meetings on the kitchen calendar. Lost a few customers due to what the whole world knows of him now but he still has enough jobs to go him. And the steers that he shares with his brother Bob next door. He and Bob and their back and forth favors.

Hurrah! The 'Nam dreams are gone. Gonzo. Because he does not fall asleep. No sleep, no dreams. In his La-Z-Boy with the TV blathering on, he drifts. At the supper table with his mother Ruth's many-ringed hand reaching to lift away the empty biscuit pan, Rex's eyes are blistered with tiredness as some people's are after too much fun.

Rex has had something *like* dreams. They are paper color. But that sleep-eye we all have between our daytime eyes, *his* will not shut. Over the white starkness of this new so-called dream's background, numbers crawl laboriously, like math problems in fifth grade. And his brain is crammed with "tin foil." Crackling. Oh, maybe that's just the clean sheets as he tosses himself over again.

So Rex is not going to land in prison for attempted murder, aggravated assault. Or manslaughter or murder which COULD have been the case had Gordon crossed the river, if he hadn't so stoutly hung on. *And then forgiven.*

But Rex knows one thing for absolute and perfectly certain. This torture of sleeplessness is God's hand at work. God does not forgive.

 And so the world turns through another cold crunchy moon, several snows, and much hot soup.

Five men enter the first piazza and shake and stomp themselves of snow. And apologize for being a half hour early. The Settlement man who leads them to the cook's kitchen says that early is okay.

Gordon is in his usual rocker, asleep, maybe a little too close to the largest cookstove with it's kettles of simmering water for keeping the air moistened. Most other rockers are empty. One woman with a baby on her shoulder nods to each stranger, her eyes holding their eyes until each of them looks away, even the eyes of the older guy with the steely glasses, his bravery must only extend into territory more dangerous.

He, this older one, stands as most alphas do, not bristly, just something in the shoulders, a certain angle of the chin and the way the four younger men glance at his responses to all the dimensions of this kitchen and the words that rock between teenaged pot scrubbers and way too many women. And this kitchen is overly warm so one of the men pulls off his jacket, another unbuttons. A tall skinny old lady in apron, jeans, and moccasins, is quick to point out the coat hooks on that same wall that the archway of cubbies makes.

In both kitchens, along the back wall, the tall floor-to-ceiling windows of small panes frame the majestic slow-motion descent of the thickening snow. Almost simultaneously, like an orchestra, several tall hand pumps at the sinks squeal and slosh into action. A rack of loaded canning jars, so seedy and tomatoey, a winter comfort, borders one set of sideboards. And underfoot, hand-painted tiles, each one different, the many loud colors toiling away there are, as a teenaged voice explains, warmed almost hot by the copper tubing underneath.

Another visitor's jacket is slipped off and the lightning-quick frizzy-haired old woman finds another untaken coat hook to hang it on.

Mostly the men's eyes are riveted on Gordon's face, which is different from when they last saw him. Torn and tracked with stitch marks. One eye covered in freshened gauze. An ear that is a cupboard knob, so it seems.

The visitors had very little to say to Gordon the day of the True Maine Militia event. You'd never have guessed they were impressed with Gordon or anything about that day, so cautious they were . . . faces stony. They just wandered around in their camo pants, dark T-shirts, and military boots, their faces looking as friendly as bricks. Today, wools and flannels, their hellos just a knot of restraint.

The Settlement man who stands with them, murmurs, "Gordo. The guys that called are here." Even as this moment unfolds like a hand of individually familiar cards, full house or royal flush, many others like these guys are roused by their impending ruination to stop in on the Prophet. When Gordon's one unpatched eye lazily opens, the visitors don't look at all familiar to him, nor *un*familiar. But he understands the need for dignity in their just-flickers-of smiles.

They are offered seats and soup by "the family."

The replies are *yes*.

The soup is thick, brown, and weedy, lumpy with potatoes. Some corn cakes come around in yellow saucers. Coffee, some black, some creamed.

The visitors' rocking chairs are now a constellation around Gordon. Another jacket comes off. These men have plenty to confess to that one green eye. His decimation seems to be of no consequence, his queer pauses and silences, no matter. In fact, to them, his agonized presence emanates a perfect sacrificial thunder. And he calls each of them "my brother."

♡ ♡ **Secret Agent Jane observes other observers.**

Due to my powerful secret agent glasses, I can see a thing spinning. I am underneath. It is up there. Actually only part of it is spinning. It is partly black like new shoes. But also some dull. Sort of rough. Like the tall tombstone things in the cemetery for olden days' people with names and stuff. You would never believe this. Out sprays some light sort of blue but pinkish if you wear these secret glasses. It is not *real* dark out yet, nowhere near supper. So why lights? I mean really, I can see for miles, all the snow and frosty trees. But I think The Thing is flashing me a message.

"Hello!" I call up to see if anyone's listening.

A cracklish noise like when you open presents and even more wonderful blue light swooshes down and covers me, blue and pink and *warm*. You would love it, too. I put up my arms and dance and laugh wicked. This is so funny. Scary and funny. Honest, this is a real flying saucer thing. Next comes sparkles soooo powerful and soooo many they lift me up totally off the ground about a whole inch! Then I drop back. Both feet. I have a feeling this is top secret. It is not something I can *tell*. Cuz this is so wicked pure and precious and important and scientifish. My lips are sealed.

 The grays.

Actually we took the little human aboard but she won't remember it.

 **Secret Agent Jane in the privacy of her tiny room at the Soucier home.**

. . . ten, eleven, twelve. Okay. So twelve whole pages of the flying saucer in my secret book. I drew them exact. Except the stuff that doesn't *show*. Like the way the light *tickles* and *tastes*. Like sugar. I'm serious.

And then no way can I draw the way the big thing flew back to the mountain and into space or whatever. It was wicked quivery and floppy like a bat but faster than nature. *Quite* perfect. At first I thought it might be cops, so of course I was terrified.

 Penny St. Onge recalls.

One night we had a meeting with Gordon in the library. Adults only. A lot of parents but others here, too, who had no kids of their own. Like Bev and Barbara. And Stuart, who is one of the single men here.

We talked. Gordon mostly listened, his one eye with the loose bottom lid moving all over each one of us, that look that meant hearing too many words was a strain on his injured thinking. It was a look that said we were . . . well, not poisonous snakes but that we were a people the likes of which he'd never seen before. Our discussion was about getting on the Internet. Most of us thought it best. We understood that droning out on system-manipulation TV was destructive. And more dependency on the grids. But this! A source of information! And there would be just the *one* computer. Down in the unused shed way behind his house. We could fix up that shed way to be a really comfy Internet shop. It would have to be down there because it would have to be connected to the phone line.

He admitted he had, himself, been thinking over the pros of getting "online." BUT, for REASONS, now, reasons that he stammered to articulate, then stopped. Then, "We should be shrinking, not expanding our . . ." dependencies. But instead of "dependencies" he searched through the ruined connections of his brain and blurted words like "nipples," "litter," "weight," "bags." Nobody laughed.

He looked us all over again, his hands in a prayerful pile on the table, those big hands, those wronged, still raw, forever marred pale eyes for the moment chilly.

He stood up from the long library table where all of us were still sitting. He reached for his cane. We watched him. We were all humbled.

Above the filing drawers, up on one wall, a little picture on thick Settlement-made paper, little houses, smoking chimneys, smiling sun, floating hearts, and a childly scrawl: CHEZ NOUS. Our home.

 History as it happens (as recorded by Lorraine Martin).

Something new is coming to the Settlement. It is the Internet. Should be installed by the end of next week. We are all very happy about it. I think.

 History as it happens (still handwritten by the way) by Katy St. Onge with help from Harry and Theodan.

Kirky and his Dad got into a big fight. His Dad is Eddie in case you read this 100 years from now. Kirky is one of the big kids in case you read this 100 years from now. Eddie said Kirky is very smart about ~~electrines~~ electronics and is wasting all his ~~jeanus~~ genius on the fucking computer. He said a fucking computer. He said once Kirky loved the fucking windmills and the fucking solar cars and inventing things like his fucking table town. Now it's just the fucking computer. He said that. Those words.

Once people here shot a TV. It was the lady who lived here once, her TV. Everybody was talking about it. Next they will be shooting the fucking computer.

 Ivy Morelli.

Slouching before her computer with the soft-but-annoying pulsing of three phones at her back, other desks, other cubicles, other concerns, she picks open the manila envelope with the Egypt return address at the corner and the name G. St. Onge above it.

Out from the envelope a reporter pad flops into her hand. She thumbs it open. Yessireee. It's the one he stole from her last spring. A small scuffled-and-scrumped-looking piece of paper taped to the back reads: *Greetings and stuff. Warmly, your friend, Gordon.*

Ivy frowns. Some might see this as a friendly joke, an apology, a courtesy, or just what it says, greetings. But to Ivy, this feels like a gentle good-bye.

 The grays with more testimony.

Again and again we have wooshed the little human aboard. Almost every day. One word we have picked up (through eavesdropping) concerning this action is "abduction." But that word is flawed. We place the creature on the laboratory table. During the first "abduction" we were astounded by her face, how she looked back at us with seeming savviness (or caginess) through her strange eye protectors that were shaped like none we've ever observed on humans before.

One of us asked her, brain-to-brain, in a voice she would perceive as the vocal cords of the gentlest of men, if we could get a look at her eyeballs behind the eye protectors.

With her mouth she made sounds to match the consent that wove through her brain and also cautiously nodded. Undulating in her heart valves was a tune we recognized as b*sΔk and veeop. She was enjoying herself!!!

She took the eye protectors off by herself. Her eyeballs warbled and oozed us. Such eyes! The anguish! The lovely! Black as the farthest space travel! She considered each of our faces. Monster faces to her? She managed her fear and repugnance quite courteously, inside and out, for her heart still frisked like fun or perfect interest even though we had slowed our speed of motion down to match hers so that she could see us as clear as the world that was hers because we were terribly curious as to what her response would be.

She re-covered her eyes with the white and pink device after only a few moments, saying, "I need these. Without them I don't have *the* power." She tapped one of the pieces that curved over and behind her ears. She did this rather expertly and had certain adult human mannerisms that intrigued us.

Such a specimen of an Earthling! Our best ever.

She was covered in woven materials that keep warm blood warm and organs functioning in Earth's remaining sputtering ice age atmosphere in the short-span solstice-time. But how her woolly colors whistled and percolated! Sticking out of pockets were mittens the color of Mars. But better. Her cap a thunderbolt of titillation factor that breaks all our records. She had a frilly collar sticking out, a sort of scrappy mushroom pink that burned our nerves.

Meanwhile, as we are ever-snooping, it is no secret to us that this is one of thousands of little humans whose mothers and fathers are sealed alive in cages. The cage-vault surrounds the parent who is on the inside and the little human is left behind over much distance in Earth measure. The reasoning for this is not complete as we eavesdrop upon the reedy vapors of human voices. Humans as with their warm, feather or fishy counterparts are not steered by reason but by that which is bigger than their will. They are pushed along by the magnificent Mother Force, the forces of nature, that is. It is humorous to watch the humans strut about as if this weren't so. But today we don't laugh. The damage is too close and for a while we stand still in awe of the pain behind the eye coverings.

"Would you like something tasty? For your mouth?" one of us inquires, brain-to-brain each time we bring her aboard, for she has no memory of the previous "abductions" in spite of our calibration of movements.

"You mean a treat?" she asks with her mouth, which can speak and smile simultaneously. Such a skill!!!

The bonbon is the size of a plum (pretty close) but leaden with sugar and other refined Earthly tongue stimulants blended. She mashes the WHOLE THING inside one cheek painfully (so it appears), straining out in a plum-sized bulge. She swings her left foot around over and over. With the tongue tucked and lopped over and stuff squeezing around in there, this creature muffingly speaks with a slight heave of the chest, "Thank you very much. You are so nice whoever you are." Crashing out through the pink parts of her eye coverings are thousands of minute newborn stars. This makes us even more still. More awed. How can this be?!!! This is it! Finally. Our aisles and aisles of compartments of Earth samples, vegetable, mineral, gasses, and these heads (ours) full of data. The billions of centuries of our labors here, to bring our hypothesis to its moment of truth, the great grunting lurid truth that this planet is the *only location* in the whole universe where exists both *torment and delight at the same time, in the same place.*

 ### Sleeping late on a Saturday morning in her city apartment, total submission for Ivy.

She is really dug in under the covers, eyelids fluttering. Her dreams are always in color and this one is no exception. YELLOW is prominent.

Yeah, in this dream, she's a heavy equipment operator.

The end.

P.S.

(see next page)

JANUARY

 Two ounces.

This place, this hour is just plain ol' Maine. Gordon feels today as though there is nothing left to know in life. Nothing that matters more than this bright white-gray day. He feels thin, and sad, and wise. Though he has had some days lately where his old silliness has visited him, that teasy twinkle in one eye. Yeah, outrageousness and goofballness are like weather. Somedays his weather is fair. The kids walk with him out to the edge of the woods. They say they have a surprise. They all wollumph along, the snow semideep. The surprise is behind the large solar cottage where Aurel and Josee and their kids and Jane live.

And Jane is along for the adventure. No secret agent heart-shaped glasses today. Just a new look in her eyes. A stirring.

The air is nice. The day is not cold, smells perfectly of the inscrutable, goodly-drear woods!

All over the snow are the heart-shaped tracks of gray squirrels who have been here earlier, hop-bounding from tree to tree. And now the marks of human feet and the round print of Gordon's cane.

So Jane and Carmel, Erin, Lindsay, and Dara have been sticking with him, but Ricardo has abandoned them, way off ahead there, pulling the baby fast on the toboggan. This is Natty's baby. Natty, one of Gordon's "wives." Baby not very old. And so someday the baby will not remember this, only in some whiffy, gray way.

This baby has no thumbs. Ten fingers instead. A birth defect. He's dressed in a way that makes him look like a troll, layers and layers of flannel and "fur" and wool. All in bright colors and embroidered in more colors. Purple and goldenrod gold, scarlet, blue, forest green. Pointed hood. Tassels sewn onto the point.

The baby has big eyes.

Gordon feels he has big eyes, too.

Out here is one birch tree and it is hung with brightly painted bird feeders.

The surprise is a trick where they lay a baby in the snow and cover him with sunflower seeds. Today, this baby will do. Then everybody leaves the baby alone, waving his arms, talking to himself.

In no time, the baby is covered with chickadees. Kind of creepy at first thought. But after you see the baby is talking louder and waving harder and singing "zzzzzzzzzzzzheeeeeeee!" you realize it's okay to the baby, awesome actually.

Gordon stands with both hands on the cane, smiling crookedly and all around him the girls and Ricardo are also smiling, glancing at each other to connect without words. And while the chickadees flit to and fro, removing all the seeds from the baby, the gray sky grows whiter and more fortified, readying itself for another big snow.

It is so soft, so quiet, so full. Sound could be something that is part of ancient history, this earth having evolved now to perfect *silence*.

Until Gordon huskily whispers in his new stammering way, "If I lie down . . . here, will . . . you cover . . . me with seeds? Got . . . enough seeds?"

"We got ten million seeds!" Lindsay assures him.

They watch while Gordon arranges himself in the snow, his legs out straight, arms spread eagle, his dark hair long enough again to open out halo-ish around his head. Then the seeds go on.

"I feel like a bagel," Gordon jokes.

Lindsay and Carmel pat him, pretend to press the seeds in. "Funny bagel," Carmel teases.

Gordon aches from the push of many palms, that bright ache of the Settlement's inexhaustible heart and mind, of its risks and of its careenings. He hears the boot-scrunches of them all standing back.

And almost instantly, he is blanketed with little feet and wings that go "*brrrt*" like soft breaths. The birds do not weigh anything, perhaps all together they weigh as much as the human soul, which is said to be two ounces. There are even seeds on his face, and in his dark and graying beard, so a chickadee walks on his forehead; its little toenails, he can feel them, but so lightly he wonders if he's mistaken. He feels the seeds lift away. Mostly, what he feels is the "*Brrrt! Brrrrt!*" of the wings, the little disturbance of air caused by the wings.

The end.

Please—
Stay tuned.

Author's Notes

Since the rude invasion of computers into our formerly gentler slower society, I would not be able to publish my work if not for my neighbor Sara DeRoche, her patience and her skill. I can't remember the number of drafts she's done of this book and often from handwriting that looks like razor wire and blobs of blood. Thank you's to Sara!

My old friend Jacquie Giasson Fuller made it possible for the Maine Acadian French ("Acadian patois" or, as some would say, "North American patois") to be spoken on these pages. She is translator of some, while of some she is their author, their grace. She told me to be sure to say that she couldn't have done it without her mother and sister-in-law, Lucienne Merservier Giasson and Lorraine Bissonette Giasson. Before approving these particular pages, they all got together and went over the nuts and bolts of this beautiful, mostly oral, language of love, work, and home, no better experts anywhere than they, and I am grateful. Also thank you Mary Bradeen for extra last minute checks, Mary of THE County!

Peter Holmes of Liberty Hall, Richard Grossman of POCLAD, CELDF and "FEAR ART!", Thomas Naylor of the Second Vermont Republic, and the Honorable Julian Holmes. All gone from us (in Heaven). But your places at our table are still reserved. Your voices of reason live on. The 2nd Maine Militia salutes you! (by shooting twenty-one TVs).

Official and Complete and Final ☺ List of Acknowledgments

While working on *Treat Us Like Dogs* over the last twenty years, so many friends, family, and other heroes would, in the nick of time, save the day for this author who was in need of moral support or inspiration or groceries or information or the opportunity to do research. Through the years I put their names in a hat, took a bunch out to thank in *The School on Heart's Content Road,* which was at one time all part of the same manuscript with *Treat Us Like Dogs* and *The Mother of Men,* the one I'm firming up now. So I include here some of those names remaining in the hat, drawing them with closed eyes. Next book I'll include the rest. No order, alphabetical or otherwise, only as I draw them, all equally important. *Huge* gratitude goes to:

Maureen DeKaser, Jenny Pap Hughes Yoxen, Ann Searcy (Little Falls, second grade, 1970s. My daughter's teacher but inspirational to me always), the Kukka-Roberts family (Chris, John, Jin, Molly, Lemony, and Daisy), Cecelia and Tabitha Waite (two sisters, curled up in chairs asleep while the grown-ups talked into the night), Sandy and Cyndy (my sisters), Dr. Arthur Chapman III (thank you for the typewriter!), Laurel MacDuffie, David Orser, Carolyn Eyler, Elizabeth Olbert (I wish *my* mother had been an anarchist!), Dana Hamlin (in Heaven), Stephen and Tabitha King (without you there'd be no security office, thus no solitude, thus no novel), Jim Page ♫, Jonah, Sara, Ceiba, Kana, David "Howlin' Wilkie" Wilkinson, Janet Beaulieu (in Heaven), Frank Collins (in Heaven), Balenda Ganem, John Sieswerda, Rick and Jeff Libby, Phil Worden, Reverend Ken Carstens, Reverend Billy of the Church of Stop Shopping, Michele Cheung, Ruth Webber, Russell Webber (in Heaven), Reverend Leaf Seligman, Dave Haag, Hal Miller (in Heaven), Patrick Quinlan, Andy Yale, Christina, Cullen and Sarah Stuart, George Garrett (in Heaven), Jean and Alfred Eastman, Sally and Mike Leahy, Eunice Buck Sargent, Nick Kingsbury, Morgan MacDuff (in Heaven) and Samantha, Bendella Sironen and David White and all, Tina Gilbert, Ellen Weeks and Rose Metcalf Postmistresses Extraordinaire!, Wayne Burns (in Heaven) and Stephanie Johnson (Dragon of the West) and Effi (in Heaven), Evelyn and Joe Butler, Yelena and Todd, Stasik and Charlie, Joy Scott, John Muldoon (without you and Henry and Douglas there'd have been no security office, thus no novel), Elisabeth Schmitz, best editor on planet Earth (Cork, you are the best editor in Heaven), Gwen North Reiss (one of the only publicity people I've known who didn't talk like a nurse in an old-age facility) and also you are my dear friend, Sheila Smith ♥, Secret Agent Jane Gelfman ♥♥, "Miss Cathy" Gleason, Cousin Katie Raissian (another world's best editor!), and Caroline Trefler World's Best Copy Editor (If Earthling is capitalized in this book, it's not because Caroline didn't try to make it right. Grays seem to have their own ideas). And thank you Robyn Rosser (sister), Michael Rothschild and all our friends on Tory Hill (especially Ana and James), Jamie Gleason, Bill K., Don Kerr, Tom and Alison Whitney, Sub Steve Kelley, the Parsonsfield Union Church Society (which has too much fun), Peggy and Ray Fisher (for our friendship, for a place to work, for *The Lovell News!*), Will Neils (thanks for all the memories!!), Jim Bancroft of New Jersey, Mark Hanley,

Lisa Gardner, Ed Gorham, Wendell Berry, Mike Ruppert (in Heaven), Anagreta and Glenn Swanson, Audrey Marra, everybody at BPCP in Brunswick, Fenderson cousins Jesse, Judy, Jake, and Cookie (deer meat, food pantry rides, dog searches, and good company), Joanna Morrisey, Katy and Chris Barnes, Victor Lister, sheriffs Scott and Tom for assistance in apprehension of three runaway Scottish terriers, also Marcie and Finley (you save lives!), Ken Rosen, Little Elise Rau, Peter Kellman and Rebekah Yonan, all at the Limerick Library, Linda DeArmott and Donna's church, University of Michigan's NELP and NELPers, Rob Waite, Hillary Lister, Isabelle Trodec, Madison Bell and Beth Spires, David Diamond, Cynthia Riley, Michele Cheung, Angelo Roy of "THE County," Marlene Livonia, the Federal Food Stamp Program for helping us (welfare encourages productivity!), Jeannie and John Matthew, Gloria Hermantz and Diane Morrill, W.D., Rita and Kathy, Lieutenant Colonel Bob Bowman, Ret., Alexander Cockburn (in Heaven, I think), Lance Tapley (who suggested the Anti-Rich Society), Helen Peppe, all at JED, Pal Tripp (storyteller-wiseman-friend, in Heaven), John Lesko, Guy Gosselin, Dan C., Roger Leisner, Steve Kelley, Bill Pagum, Charles Woods and Gretchen and their cover solutions extraordinaire, Lynn C., Laura Childs, Michael and Carol of the Victory Gardens, Edie and Harriet, all our family: Prindalls, Pennys, Chutes, Morrills, Bowies and Goodriches, insiders and X's. And *very* special thanks to my woofers who lived, died, and some still going strong throughout the long years of work on this book, your interruptions were inspiring.

Character List

The Prophet

Guillaume (**Ge-yome** *hard* **G like golly!**) **Gordon or Gordo or Gordie St. Onge, aka the Prophet.** Age thirty-nine until September. He is six-foot-four or -five, depending. In the winter gets a thick waist and an extra neck but in summer works it off. Work, work, work, work, though not without talk, talk, talk, talk, and preach, preach, preach, preach. Darkish hair. Darkish beard with a splutter of gray beginning on the chin. Dark brows and lashes with weird pale greenish eyes. Significant French-Italian nose. Add to that a Tourette's sort of flinch to one side of the face, especially the eye. Not a forgettable face. Drink is a problem for him at times, during spells of getting worked up over life's cruelties and injustices, bothered and stirred, moody and broody. He has been accused of loving everyone in the world equally; that his love is too easy, too diluted.

In an earlier time when Gordon was first married to Claire, married by the laws of the state of Maine, he got some cousins and friends together to start the Settlement on land his mother gave him, land and an old farmhouse where he had grown up. This wasn't just some ol' hippy commune but a statewide cooperative in furniture, alternative energies, farm produce, and trade. The Settlement is thought to be a school by some who live out in the world. Citizens of the Settlement see it as home.

The Fourth Estate

Ivy Morelli. A native Mainer, Ivy is a reporter and columnist for the *Record Sun,* the big daily. She is twenty-four, petite, with a big raspy *haw-haw* of a laugh. Her eyes are blue with black lashes. Her facial expressions at times would serve her well as a murderess or sorceress in an Elizabethan play (when evil truly reigned and the commons were being emptied). Her hair is bowl-style, very black, tinted violet. Wacky wardrobe. Wacky earrings. A tattoo of tropical fish circles her arm. Drives fast. Is rude to fellow motorists. Her editor is **Brian Fitch**, an ordinary-looking guy about forty, editorly pants and shirt and shoes. Twinkling gray eyes. Editorly hair trim. He is good-natured about all of Ivy's quirks.

Secret Agents

Jane Meserve (yes, a secret agent), age six (almost seven). Tall for her age, hushy velvety voice, tells us (very curious people that we are) much about what she observes. Our Jane is a gorgeous child with a head of dark ringlets, which she generally wears up in a queenly, countessy way, high on top with a glamorous spangled squeegie or flowery one. Jane is a fan of MTV, fast food, and great clothes. Some of these pleasures may have been developed through her mother, Lisa, but Granpa Pete blames it on Great Aunt Bette, long dead, a strong-willed lady who must have seen many personal demands fulfilled. Jane always walks in a graceful royal fashion, unless she's having a tantrum.

Her father, **Damon Gorely**, is handsome, she is told by her mum, and talented in rap. He is an African mix person, Lisa—Mum—is a European mix person. Yes, like most Americans, given time, the Heinz "57 Varieties" type.

Secret Agent Jane's spying career begins after a Settlement person gives her a pair of sunglasses that have pink heart-shaped lenses. Frames are white plastic. Jane's mother, Lisa, says those glasses will give Jane special viewing power. She suggests they are real secret agent glasses and that Jane can report to her all she sees. Lisa, is in jail, in deep trouble.

Jane's Family

Lisa Meserve. Dental assistant before her arrest. Hair a textured blonde from a product called Light 'n Streak. Less strong-willed than Jane. Before jail, wore lipstick. Noticeable blue eyes. Actually Lisa isn't guilty of crime, but with prohibitions you don't have to be guilty to be guilty, just poor.

    Cherish. Like Cannonball, Cherish is a Scottish terrier. Though this is not a common breed, there are, yes, two in this story, completely unrelated. Not *everybody* in America has a golden retriever. Cherish dies when cops leave her in a hot car. This happens before this story begins. So Cherish is a memory and a ghost.

    Peter Meserve, known as Pete or Granpa Pete. Owns a gas station. Old friend of Gordon St. Onge's. Father of Lisa.

Secret Agents Continued

Names sometimes mentioned, sometimes alias, sometimes real. Some of these are Special Agents (S.A.), others operatives. Agents appear in many scenes, scheming and plotting for "America." There are times when the Settlement is crawling with them.

More Spies

The grays. Sometimes you see them. Sometimes you don't.

Queen of the Settlement

Claire St. Onge. About age fifty. Once she and Gordon were legally married, but then divorced. She left. Now she's back. Claire is a short woman, short and fat. Graceful and seemingly light on her toes. Both of her parents are Passamaquoddy. She grew up in Princeton, upstate. Has many cousins, some who visit from the reservation, some who live at the Settlement. Claire's long black hair, beginning to gray, is often worn up in a bun for that teacherly effect when she has classes at USM (the University of Southern Maine), she being an adjunct history teacher. But often she wears it down and it is comely. While in the Settlement gardens, she wears jeans and long shirts but much of the time she wears homemade skirts with those frequent displays of embroidery many Settlement women also show off. One of Claire's most striking features are her old-timey spectacles: turn of the century, round steel frames. These give her a severe and grim sepia, quite managerial aspect. She is one of those who wears the red sash.

Some Others Who Wear the Red Sash

Bonnie Lucretia (Bonnie Loo). Her legal last name is Sanborn as she was married before to a young man by that name. He died in a tractor-trailer wreck. Bonnie Loo's maiden name is Bean. She is age twenty-six. A tall, rugged person, she wears her dark hair streaked orangey blonde from the bottle. She has a child, **Gabe,** from the trucker husband who died. Two additional youngsters by her present husband (wed by Settlement law). She wears regular glasses at times, rather bulky ones, but her contacts are her favorites. Her eyes are golden green-brown. Movie star eyebrows curved exquisitely, one of her best features but she is raw to look at sometimes, and snarly of manner. But also curious and smart and witty. Most people at the Settlement think of her as the head cook.

    Penny. One of the first Settlement citizens, one of the founders. She is a tall honey-haired woman, late thirties. She is the mother of the oldest Settlement-born child, fifteen-year-old **Whitney** (Whitney is Penny's legal *last* name by outside law). Penny is a pleasant, easygoing person who enjoys Settlement life. She loves books and quiet evenings alone but also she's there for the social stuff. She has a lot of overly full daytimes. She enjoys long walks in the fields. Many people swear that Penny is so classically lovely she is prettier than her daughter who, though a handsome and bright girl, has too many goofy expressions.

    Stephanie (Steph). In her early forties, she is a rosy-cheeked, brown-haired quiet type. Her daughters, Margo and Oceanna, (pronounced O-shi-ahna) are twins. Margo looks "just like" Steph and has her mother's wallflower ways. Oceanna looks more like a skinny feral cat, but wears a lot of purple.

Gail. About age forty-five, mother of **Michelle**. Gail is another early Settlementer. Michelle is fourteen, only a bit younger than Penny's Whitney. Meanwhile Gail, an ex-biker and recovering alcoholic, a semirecovered smoker, still has a biker-style of dress and her collarbone and entire neck have a ring of roses tattooed there forever. Her voice is husky. Eyes dark and close together. Nose a big puggy. Hard lines in the skin from hard livin'. Quiet. Reserved. Hair is straight, dark, shoulder-length and sometimes neglected, sometimes silky and fresh.

Lee Lynn St. Onge. Witchy. Looks witchy. Has witchy ways. Mid-thirties, has a year-old tyke named **Hazel**. Lee Lynn is busy collecting healing herbs, makes salves and tonics, herby teas. Very affectionate with everyone. She has wild hair, early gray. She is always braless and wears long flowing dresses, clanking bells (at the throat, for instance), and around one ankle a rusty leg iron (looks like the real thing) like a slave. Her high thin voice is cutting to some ears, and her roaring enthusiasm over everything goes against the grain of some of the more curmudgeonly personalities and maybe even some patient ones.

Beth. She is rough of speech. You might say "like a sailor." She has longish blonde curly ringlets. A short stocky shapely person. Two kids: **Montana**, age eight, and **Rhett**, five.

Glennice. A Christian woman. Late forties or fifty. She was married before to a man who left her with an envelope of money (his week's pay), their kids, and their home, taking only his beagle puppy and guns. Glennice grew up around tractors and trucks and farming. She's very good with vegetables and machines. She loves the Settlement life and is a wonderful teacher of all the Settlement youngsters. Glennice is a churchgoer and believes in a big biblical God. But she also sees Gordon as a supernatural godlike being, which is a bit of a joke for other Settlement people, who see Gordon as full of the weakness of mortals. Glennice has features too small for her large face. Big glasses. Light brown hair sometimes permed.

Brianna (Bree) Vandermast. She is only age fifteen. Her hair is thick, ripply orange; orange like a crayon. Honey-color eyes. She has always, and still does, work in the woods with her brothers and father on their logging crew. She is a strong, fit girl, sort of tomboyish.

She has zealous revolutionary intentions. Does lyrical writing in bold calligraphy and stunning drawings and paintings. Studies and reads and schemes all the time. Has a girlish giggle and romantic hungers. She was born with a deformed face, her honey eyes too far apart, the bridge of her nose stretched wide. She is the founder of the True Maine Militia.

Vancy. Also quite young. Pregnant. Not considered pretty but she is a skilled midwife and natural with elderly and the sick and therefore she is a precious jewel to Settlement life. She has a rather square boxy face, square boxy body (even before pregnant). Her hair is flat and rumply brown, never fussed over. She tends to wear big white blouses (even before pregnant). Her eyes are sort of lashless, bottom lip erect, jawline primitive.

Leona. One of Claire's cousins, also from the reservation. Leona was one of the first Settlementers, a founder. Leona has many kids, including **Cory,** who is younger than Whitney by only a few weeks. So Cory is also age fifteen but almost six-foot-two. **Katy** and **Karma** are two of the youngest of Leona's kids. **Andrea** a bit older. Many in-betweens such as **Oz, Shanna**, and **Draygon.** Leona has a great tail of black, black hair. Has a thing for peasant blouses.

Geraldine. Leona's sister. Short hair in various cuts. Very attractive gal. Not married. No kids of her own but does a lot of activities with Settlement kids. Enjoys horses and Settlement trips.

Natasha (Natty). Age eighteen (almost). She is sharp-featured, blonde. Until arriving at the Settlement she was a prostitute in Boston, a runaway girl from Ohio. She loves working in the orchards and leatherworking, cobbling, and sugaring. She's a storyteller, always draws a circle around her of listening ears. By late summer has a new baby who has a nice head of dark hair but no thumbs.

Misty. Short dark hair. Lovely neck. Graceful, almost tiptoey ways. No kids of her own. Lots of snobby cats live with her in her cottage. But she enjoys reading to kids in the library or hearing one read aloud, one at a time, yes, her and *one* tyke, *one-on-one*. She understands shyness. But also she thinks up a lot of artful projects such as the sign she and a couple of nine-year-olds made for the wall over the smallest library loveseat: LIE BERRY made entirely with acorns painted different colors and glued on. Most of the acorns have stuck to this day.

Mother

Marian Depaolo St. Onge. Actually, her name isn't Marian but Mary Grace but she is into name-changing for status purposes. Her husband (deceased), Guillaume, she called Gary. Guillaume, the son, is Gordon. She is tall (taller than her husband had been). She has light eyes. Her dark hair has a lot of attractive gray. Her glasses are of an attractive style. She has wonderful posture. Gordon is her only child. Her brothers and uncles are Depaolo Bros. Construction. They do huge projects around New England such as schools, banks, malls, big box stores, office complexes. They always have a family member or close buddy in the state senate. Marian lives in Wiscassett, a bit of a drive. Gordon visits her once a week. They argue.

Brother

Richard (Rex) York. Captain of the Border Mountain Militia and blood brother to Gordon St. Onge. Does not live at the Settlement. His age is about fifty. Keeps his thinning hair trimmed and tidy. Wears military boots, usually with pant legs over. His pale eyes have a way of gauging you totally. He is not shy but seems unable to verbalize information unimportant to meetings and maneuvers of the citizens' militia movement of America or the work he does as an electrician. He has a dark walrussy mustache. He doesn't eat desserts. He has an exceedingly fit appearance, possibly due to all the push-ups, deep-knee bends, and sit-ups he has done every day since Vietnam. Lives with his mother, **Ruth.** She is quiet. Bakes desserts for the American Legion, which she is involved in since her dead husband was alive and an active member. Also she makes desserts for home. Rex doesn't eat desserts but his militia does.

   Glory York. Almost twenty. Rex's only child. Her mother lives in Massachusetts, divorced from Rex and remarried. Glory is quite freckled, has long, thick, wow-type hair, dark auburn. She is beautiful in every way. But also she flaunts it and has a drinking problem and causes mess and havoc wherever she goes. She is not evil, just young and foolish.

Cousin Who Is Like a Brother

Aurel (pronounced Oh-RELL) Soucier. Still wears his bush hat from the Vietnam war. Speaks with oceanic rolling *R*s, the accent and sometimes grammar of "THE County," more specifically, *the Valley* of "THE County," where the Acadian patois is still spoken by his generation. He is one of the founders of the Settlement. Has intense glittering deep-set dark eyes, trim dark beard. A trim-in-all-ways gentlemanly fellow. Short. Wiry. Works caring for livestock. Also busy with the solar and wind projects. Like Gordon, he is a motormouth.

    Josee Soucier. Her identical twin is Jacquie. Her husband is Aurel. She wears large-frame glasses, fashionable through the 1990s. Hair blonde. From a bottle. Shoulders sloped and soft. She dresses youthfully. She is a lively person. Speaks English with the accent of the patois of "THE County."

    Kids of the Souciers. Included but not limited to **Lydia (Liddy), Rachel, Rusty, Tamya, Michel.**

    Jacquie and Paul Lessard. Yes, Jacquie Lessard is Josee Soucier's twin. She and Paul have a daughter **Alyson**, a pleasant gentle adolescent, loves animals, wears long skirts a lot. Paul's father is **Reggie Lessard** who speaks very little English. Loves music. All except Alyson started off life in "THE County."

Some Other Settlement People

Bev and Barbara. Actually they live in town but arrive every day to teach and tutor kids, or to be on various crews. They are always in the midst. Both are short, square, and ruddy, gray-haired, wear glasses. Bev has a Maine accent, Barbara a New York accent. They have a yellow house with a swimming pool, which probably explains their ruddiness.

    Stuart Congdon. Head sawyer of the sawmill crews and active in various committees. He is the image of the troll dolls of the 1970s, bit of a belly, bright blue eyes, stand-up red hair, a red beard in his case, and short, technically a midget, thick legs and arms. Sturdy. Likeable and gently supervisorly.

Nathan Knapp. Known to the young people as their "peace man," he lives with his wife in one of the cottages. You never see her. She works outside the Settlement and neither one comes for the big meals. But Nathan, spiritual and well-read, is the leader of Settlement salons and other discussiony get-togethers. He wears a lot of black. His hair is very black and combed wetly to submission. His eyes are black. His skin is sallow. He seems underwater and distant but always watching you.

John Lungren. A Settlement man about age sixty more or less. High hairline, gray, shaved. Light eyes. Wears jeans, work boots, T-shirts, plaid shirts, billed caps. Not a motormouth but not shy. One you can depend on, a rock.

Cindy Butler. Only been at the Settlement a couple years but her kids fit right in. **Chris** has a love of piano and group discussions and field trips but rests, too, due to a severe skin affliction he was born with. **Samantha (Sammy)** is quite the ticket, often wears an Apache rag around her straight white-blonde hair. She is flashy and mouthy. And central.

Eddie and Lorraine Martin. Lorraine, short hair, tidy, schoolteacher-looking. She's from THE County but Eddie is not. Eddie ordinary-looking in a crowd except when he wears his bejeweled studded belt. Also he wears a very nice smile. Their youngest son is twelve-year-old **Kirk (Kirky)** who loves flashy clothes and inventions. **Evan** is about fifteen, dark-haired, struggles with acne. **Butch (real name is Edward, Jr.)** about twenty, then probably twenty-one by fall, not awfully chatty but sometimes teases, always dependable for hard physical work and working with oxen and on cars, keeps a kazoo in his pocket. Muscular, dark-haired, light-brown eyes, *somewhat* handsome, maybe in part due to his silence. Later in the summer he grows a big dark "military" mustache. He's not tall, or short, but being older than his two brothers gives him stature.

Ray and Suzelle (Gordon's cousin) Pinette. Both from THE County. Their teenage daughter is **Erin**, homely by most standards but nobody notices due to her smiles and her always having been part of things.

Catherine Court Downey. Comes to live at the Settlement from Portland. USM art teacher. Rather beautiful, interesting eyebrows,

green-brown eyes, dark hair. Nervously assertive. Her son is **Robert,**
age five.

    Brady and Sadie. Brother and sister. Both blond and sort of elegant.
Reserved. Brady is dying.

    Michael (Mickey) Gammon. Fifteen years old. Not a big guy, a
bit scrawny and shrimpy, with a blond and brownish ponytail so thin
and insignificant it twists to one side and up. He does not bathe or
change routinely. He stays too busy going and coming back, walking for miles, smoking. His eyes are gray. He has a cold aspect. Not
a talker. Much of the time, his jeans and T-shirts are rags. Lives in a
treehouse on Settlement land since his older brother kicked him out.

Neighbors

William (Willie) Lancaster. A wild unpredictable thirty-nine-year-
old. In some ways he is predictable. Meanwhile, he is a member of
Rex York's militia. Willie is gray-eyed and somewhat bucktoothed.
Hair, brown. A brown beard, sort of pointed. And an insincere mus-
tache. He's medium height. Has the athletic qualities of a squirrel.
His work involves climbing trees with ropes and cleats. Tree expert.
Landscaper. He wears the single dog tag of his brother's dead body
returned from "the conflict."

    Delores (Dee Dee) Lancaster St. Onge. One of three daughters of
Willie and Judy Lancaster. She is age nineteen but looks eleven. A
small, smiley person. She spends a lot of time at the St. Onge Settle-
ment. Her cheery manner has no small effect on the atmosphere of
Settlement life. Brown hair, which has natural spurts and catlicks.
She is *very* pregnant.

    Lou-EE St. Onge (Dee Dee's young husband). Also about age
nineteen; (Louis is pronounced Lou-EE as they do up in the St. John,
Valley of Aroostook "THE County," whence he has come), is a cousin
to Gordon. Lou-EE had lived at the Settlement awhile before he married Dee Dee. Now they live in the dooryard of the Lancasters' mobile
home complex. The Lou-EE–Dee Dee residence is a weird five-stories
(each story only sixteen by sixteen feet), painted pink. Lou-EE is built
like a tapeworm, no shoulders, just arms, legs, long neck, little head.
On top a big brown mountain hat made of felt. Long black beard

protects his significant Adam's apple from view, though the beard is thin, just a scraggly, smoky swirl of a thing. While his father-in-law, Willie, is loud and full-throttle, Lou-EE is like a quaint stage prop but with wonderful eyes, the irises green and golden brown, ringed in black-brown.

Cannonball. A Scottish terrier, huge teeth, broad chest, short legs. She is black, though some Scotties are brindle. She is round and solid, like, yes, a cannonball, cast iron. She likes food and Lou-EE. Willie rescued her from a life tied to a doghouse. Yes, Willie stole her. But she loves Lou-EE. She is not fond of kids. *Hates* other dogs.

Other Lancaster dogs. A churning mass of homely squish-faced curl-tailed free-as-the-breeze short-haired small white smelling-of-the-swamp thieving piss-on-everything dogs.

Jaxon Cross. One of the central figures of a gang (or "collective" depending on your views) of anarchists called the Anti-Rich Society. Looks like a pirate. His smile seems more threat than friendship but his accent is not just a bit Southern but full-rolling, full-embrace, full-summer North Carolina. Intensely well-informed. Always pushing books and articles and essays on you. A philosopher. Has EMT training but no job, no car of his own. Eats only seeds and nuts and such but is not gaunt. His one dangling earring resembles a doubloon. Bad acne scarring. Short beard, brown shortish moody hair. Eyes gray like his father's, his father Lyman (Ly) Cross who he is at war with, it is said.

Vandermasts. These are Brianna Vandermast's father **John (Pitch)** Vandermast, her brothers **Dana** and **Mark (Poon)**, and a married brother **Ben** who lives elsewhere. Only Ben has kids.